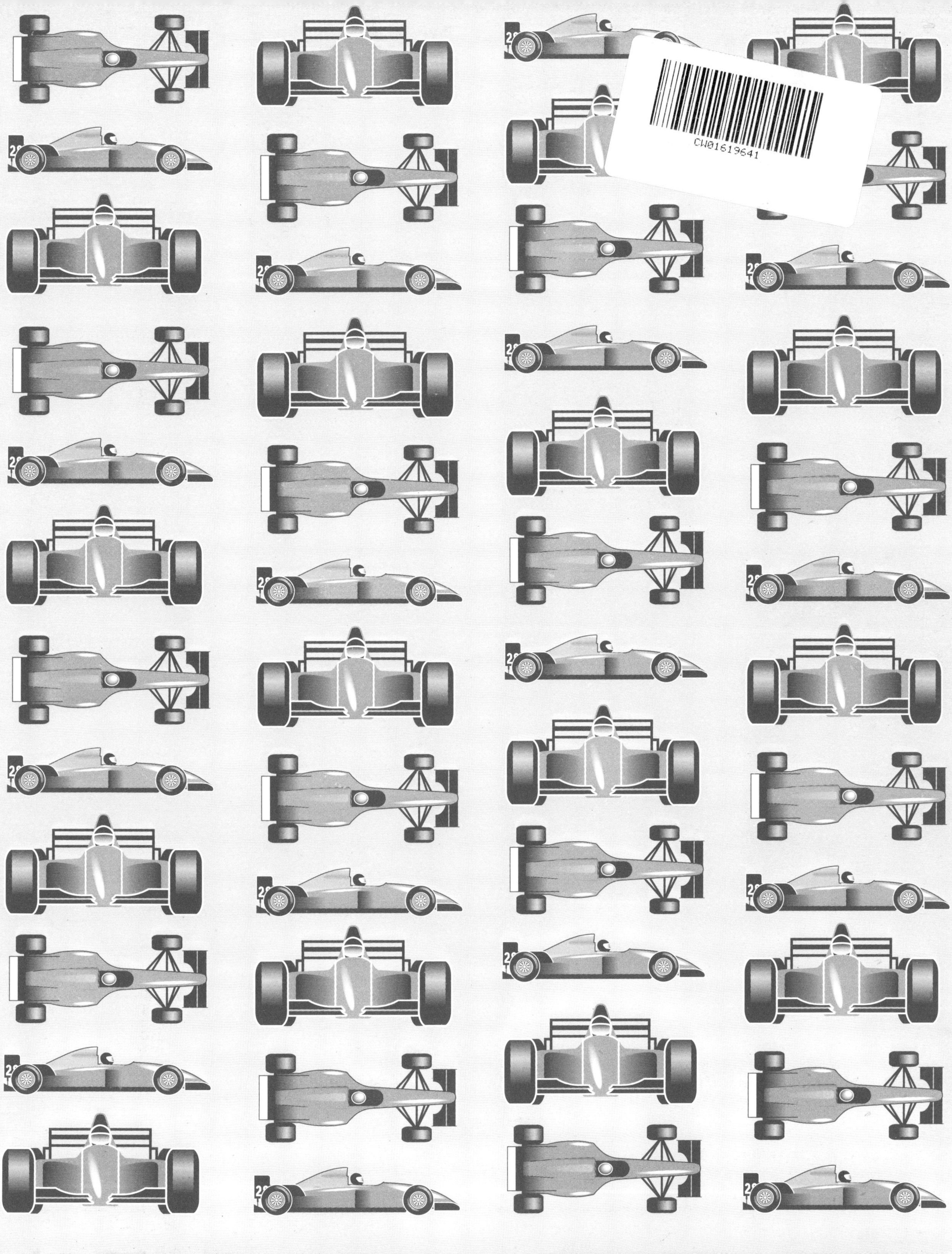

THE ULTIMATE ENCYCLOPEDIA OF

Formula One

TED SMART

GEMINI
CAR ALARMS
Nigel Mansell
elf
Mansell
RENAULT

THE ULTIMATE ENCYCLOPEDIA OF

Formula One

THE DEFINITIVE ILLUSTRATED GUIDE TO GRAND PRIX MOTOR RACING

General Editor: **Bruce Jones**
Editor of *Autosport*

Foreword by **Damon Hill**

THIS IS A CARLTON BOOK

Specially produced for The Book People in association with Carlton Books Limited, 20 St Anne's Court, Wardour Street, London W1V 3AW

ISBN 1 85613 208 8

Project Editor: Martin Corteel
Art Direction: Robert Fairclough
Picture Research: Sharon Hutton
Designers: Norma Martin,
Chris Aldridge & Peter Charles
Production: Garry Lewis

Printed and bound in Great Britain

(Previous page) **The view from the cockpit** *Nigel Mansell in practice at Estoril in 1991.*

General Editor

BRUCE JONES edits the weekly colour magazine *Autosport*, the acknowledged world authority on motor sport at all levels from the pinnacle of Formula One to the grass-roots formulae. He has been a contributor to many motor sport books and magazines world-wide, including biographies of Formula One team owners Frank Williams and Colin Chapman, plus a large number of motor sport annuals. He has also conducted video interviews for satellite sports channels and tried his hand at racing with limited success before leaving that game to those who *were* quick rather than simply thought they were ...

Other Contributors

ANDREW BENSON The news editor on the world's leading motor sport magazine, Benson has been with *Autosport* for three years since arriving from university with a wealth of knowledge of Formula One. He has a keen awareness of the political goings on that make the Grand Prix world more of a soap opera than "real life".

ADAM COOPER Living out of a suitcase, Cooper is a truly international go-anywhere and cover-anything reporter and feature writer. He has been involved as a motor racing journalist for 10 years, after cutting his teeth as a team "gopher" in the late 1970s. Following an unusual course, he based himself in Japan for two years in the early 1990s, before moving to Indianapolis for a year in order to gain a world-wide view of Formula One and its feeder formulae.

TONY DODGINS Winner of the prestigious William Lyons Award for motoring journalists in the early 1980s, Dodgins joined *Autosport* magazine in 1984, moving up through the ranks with many of today's Formula One stars. Having opted to go freelance in 1992, Tony has returned to *Autosport* as one of its two dedicated, globe-stomping Grand Prix reporters.

LAURENCE FOSTER A former aerospace engineer who burst into the ranks of motor sport journalists by winning a national talent search competition. This former kart racer possesses an incisive technical mind, bringing explanation of the many technical changes to a world-wide audience through the pages of *Autosport* magazine.

GENERAL EDITOR'S ACKNOWLEDGEMENTS

The General Editor and his fellow contributors found the following books and magazines very useful sources of information when researching this book:

Autocourse magazine
Autosport magazine
A–Z of Formula Cars by David Hodges
Chequered Flag – 100 Years of Motor Racing by Ivan Rendall
Formula 1 by Doug Nye, David Hodges and Nigel Roebuck
Formula 1 by Michael Turner and Nigel Roebuck
The Grand Prix Drivers by Alan Henry
The Guinness Complete Grand Prix Who's Who by Steve Small
Winners by Brian Laban

CONTENTS

7 **FOREWORD BY DAMON HILL**

8 **THE ORIGINS OF FORMULA ONE**
Looks at the 19th-century pioneers of motor racing, the reckless bravado of the early drivers and the impact of inter-war industrialization.

14 **THE WORLD CHAMPIONSHIP**
A season-by-season account of the world's premier motor racing competition, with statistics on the Drivers' Championship and Constructors' Cup.

74 **THE TEAMS**
Profiles of 30 of the most famous and successful motor racing marques and their celebrity owners, from Alfa Romeo to Wolf.

105 **LEGENDS OF THE TRACK**
Pays tribute to 10 of the greatest Grand Prix drivers of all time, including their principal career achievements and complete Grand Prix statistics.

126 **THE GREAT DRIVERS**
Profiles of the speed kings of Formula One, from Alboreto to Zanardi, with a verdict on what made them great.

180 **THE GREAT RACES**
Reports on 12 epic encounters to take the chequered flag – the occasions of motor racing mastery.

194 **THE FAMOUS CIRCUITS**
Descriptions of the world's most famous race tracks, from the high-speed banking of Monza to the picturesque streets of Monaco.

221 **THE BUSINESS OF FORMULA ONE**
Reviews the multi-million-pound marketing of Grand Prix racing and the escapades of the Formula One media circus.

227 **THE CARS, EQUIPMENT & THE RULES**
Showcases the hi-tech cars and driver's equipment that are an integral part of the motor racing scene, plus an explanation of the rules of Formula One.

234 **THE CULTURE OF FORMULA ONE**
Celebrates the fans who are the lifeblood of motor racing, from Italy's *tifosi* and Britain's "Mansell Maniacs" to Brazil's Ayrton Senna worshippers and Japan's fanatical followers of Formula One.

240 **CONTROVERSIES AND DISASTERS**
Describes the machinations and manoeuvrings that take place before the cars ever get to the starting grid, and pays tribute to the drivers who sadly lost their lives in pursuit of glory.

246 **CHAMPIONSHIP RECORDS**
Who won what, when, from whom, in what and by what margin.

250 **CHRONOLOGY OF FORMULA ONE**
The milestones of motor racing history from the first race in France in 1894 to the present day.

252 **INDEX**

The World Championship *Damon Hill,*

Legends of the Track *Juan Manuel Fangio.*

The Famous Circuits *Rio de Jainero.*

FOREWORD

Winning a race will give anyone a huge feeling of satisfaction, of a job well done. In the early part of my career, I enjoyed my share of winning on two wheels and on four. But there's nothing to touch the emotion of winning a Grand Prix.

Formula One is the pinnacle of motor sport and just being there is to be part of the greatest sporting show there is. Winning at this level is something else – perhaps my most important victory (so far, anyway!) was when I won the British Grand Prix at Silverstone in 1994. It was as if all my birthdays had come at once, a day made in heaven.

Inevitably it is the driver who gets the glory but, as this encyclopedia reveals, Formula One is as much about team work as it is about individuals. Sure, I won at Silverstone, but without the brilliance of Patrick Head and his design team; without the power and reliability of our Renault engine; and without the dedication and expertise of the Williams mechanics, I would have been nowhere.

As befits its name, *The Ultimate Encyclopedia of Formula One* goes underneath the carbon fibre skin of a Grand Prix car to explain the intricacies of its chassis and engine and how it is built around a complex set of rules and regulations. It lays bare the business of Formula One – I was particularly interested in the section on drivers' wages ... The encyclopedia has a good pedigree, too. General editor Bruce Jones edits *Autosport*, the weekly 'must-read' for everyone in the business, while writers like Tony Dodgins and Andrew Benson are known and respected throughout the sport.

Formula One is about the future. At every test and practice session, and even on race day, we are trying to extract more from the car. We are constantly developing new technologies, many of which have direct applications to future generations of road cars.

Yet Formula One is also about the past. Grand Prix racing has been my life, all my life. When I was born, in 1960, my father was already an established Grand Prix driver, going on to win two World Championships. I grew up surrounded by some of the true greats of the sport, people like Stirling Moss, Jackie Stewart, Jim Clark and John Surtees. And I've been privileged to be team-mate to three of the greatest drivers of them all, Alain Prost, Nigel Mansell and the incomparable Ayrton Senna. Reading about them here reminds me how fortunate I am to be a part of it all.

I guess, just like you, I'm a motor racing fan at heart.

DAMON HILL
London, March 1995

Boy racer *Young Damon prepares to burn rubber with his father.*

THE ORIGINS OF FORMULA ONE

The first ever motor race, in France in 1894, bemused onlookers, but road racing was soon all the rage, until ever-increasing speeds confined racing to specially built circuits. And the cars just went faster and faster…

THE PIONEERING RACERS

Motor racing has changed a great deal since the first competition took place in 1894, but its essential nature has not: brave and talented men (and occasionally women) do battle in the fastest and most sophisticated machinery of the day. Motor racing has always been dangerous and, although the attitude to safety has become less cavalier (especially in the last few years) and the likelihood of injury has become increasingly less common, danger still exists – and that is part of the sport's undying attraction for its ever-growing legion of fans. Grand Prix racing has been many things to many people over the years, but to those who take part in it and are involved in it, whether as drivers, team managers, owners or mechanics, it remains one of the last great challenges left on this earth.

Almost as soon as the car was invented, enthusiasts began to create competitions for it. It was less than ten years from the appearance of the first car to the organization of the first race, an exceedingly gentlemanly affair, far removed from the intense competition at the Grands Prix of today. It was arranged by Pierre Gifard of the the newspaper Le Petit Journal and the winner of the trip from Paris to Rouen – with a stop for lunch! – was to be the vehicle which covered the 80 miles "without danger, was easy to handle and cheap to run".

Although the internal-combustion engine had been invented in Germany and Britain had led the Industrial Revolution, both countries were initially hostile to the car. But the French immediately took to it and soon established the largest industry in the world, at a time when racing on public roads was banned in the other two leading European nations. This enthusiasm and technical prowess, combined with rivalry between manufacturers and the existence of many straight roads, produced the first age of motor racing. With cars like Peugeot and the Panhard, the French dominated racing until the end of the nineteenth century and, despite the gentle ethos behind the first race, it didn't take long for racing to distil to today's "fastest wins" philosophy.

While the idea behind racing may have been essentially similar to today, the cars were not. Early Panhards were steered by a lever, not unlike the tiller on a boat, and Peugeots had a handlebar. The steering wheel soon replaced them, although it took rather longer for pneumatic tyres to supersede the solid ones.

In the early years racing took the form of town-to-town events, organized in the same way as rallies are today – cars started individually, and the winner was decided on aggregate time. In 1896 the Automobile Club de France (ACF) organized a race from Paris to Marseilles and back, and by 1897 there was the first sign that racing cars were becoming different to road cars: the professionals stripped off non-essentials like mudguards and seat cushions, and manufacturers developed more powerful engines.

During these first forays into racing power outputs grew enormously, and there was growing unease about cars hurtling along public roads lined with crowds, most of whom had not the faintest idea of what a car was capable. This unease was heightened by racing's first fatality. Shortly after the start of the 1898 Paris–Nice race, Benz driver M de Montariol waved through his friend, the Marquis de Montaignac, who took his hands off the tiller to wave back. The car swerved, and took de Montariol's machine off the road. It shot up a bank and overturned. De Montariol was thrown clear, but his mechanic suffered fatal head injuries. De Montaignac turned to watch the accident, and overturned his own car. He survived long enough to accept the blame.

While the deaths could be put down to incompetence, that did little to mollify the Paris police chief who tried to stop the running of the

The first disaster *During the 1898 Paris to Nice road race the Marquis de Martaignac and the riding mechanic of his good friend M. de Montariol were killed.*

First race *The first motor car competition was a road test from Paris to Rouen.*

First winners *The winning cars in the Paris–Rouen three- and four-seater*

THE BIRTH OF THE PETROL ENGINE

Although the petrol engine was probably the single most influential invention of the twentieth century, the history of its evolution is not as clear as might be expected. The various features that are involved in its operation were created by a number of people, usually working alone in different countries. Their ideas were often picked up by someone else or stumbled upon independently.

The idea of firing an object down a barrel came from the cannon. Then the principle of turning the power into rotary motion was developed and perfected by steam engine designers such as James Watt as long ago as the 1770s.

From 1794 there is vague evidence of an early form of combustion engine made by a certain Robert Street who powered an engine with a mixture of turpentine, spirit and air, but there is no accurate account of how the machine worked.

In 1860 a Frenchman, Etienne Lenoir, patented "an engine dilated by the combustion of gas" which probably takes the prize for the first practical internal-combustion engine. The burning of coal gas was not very efficient, and his engine produced only half a horsepower.

The next major step was the invention in 1876 by Nikolaus Otto of the four stroke internal-combustion engine. Both Gottlieb Daimler and Karl Benz independently investigated coal-gas engines but dropped the idea in favour of benzene. Daimler started experimenting with "hot-tube" ignition which raised engine speeds to 1000rpm. After trying the engine in a boat, he mounted one in a second-hand horse carriage without shafts – and the car had arrived.

Paris–Amsterdam race later that year. He failed, outfoxed by the competitors who decided to take their cars on a train to a starting point outside his jurisdiction, and again at the end when he realized it was ill-advised to interfere with a huge crowd celebrating the triumph of the winner, Fernand Charron.

By the turn of the century, a British newspaper magnate, John Gordon Bennett, had decided that it was time the motor industry in Britain was given a kick-start, and he conceived the idea of organizing a race between teams representing countries rather than manufacturers.

The French were hostile, because entries were limited per country but, after a few years of being run alongside the great town-to-town races, in 1904 the Gordon Bennett race received a considerable boost when it was hosted by Germany for the first time. The event enjoyed a couple of years of glory before it was killed off by the French in 1906, when they refused to organize it alongside their new Grand Prix de l'ACF.

Meanwhile, the infant motor racing had ridden out a crisis – twice. In the 1901 Paris–Berlin event a boy had been killed as he stepped into the road to watch a passing car and was hit by the next one. The French government banned racing, but it eventually bowed to pressure from the influential motor industry and allowed it to start again.

A worse tragedy was to follow. In 1903 the ACF organized the Paris-Bordeaux–Madrid event, three million people lined the route. But cars crashed into trees, their drivers' views obscured by dust. Spectators, having difficulty in allowing for the speed of the cars (Louis Renault averaged 65mph on the first leg), were hit, and the event was cancelled when it reached Bordeaux after the Spanish and the French governments stepped in to ban it.

Again, though, the French government gave way to pressure and allowed racing, provided the roads were sealed by barriers and races were held in sparsely populated areas. This was the start of racing on closed roads, a form that was to develop into circuit racing as we know it.

THE FIRST GOLDEN AGE

Fiat's fliers *Pietro Bordino and Carlo Nazzaro were in a class of their own in 1923.*

Ironically, the first Grand Prix, organized by the Automobile Club de France, was to mark the end of the era of French domination of racing. The sport became more professional and, together with cars from Germany, Italy, Britain and America, came a new generation of professional drivers – men like Felice Nazzaro, Georges Boillot and Jules Goux.

Germany, Italy and Britain wanted races on their own soil but, when the first purpose-built track was opened at Brooklands in Surrey in 1907, racing was already heading towards a crisis. There was an economic recession, and conflicting interests over the regulations and the sites of races led to the French pulling out in 1909.

In America, however, racing was beginning to boom. During the first decade of the twentieth century the Americans were consistently humiliated by the successes of imported European cars, and often of European drivers, but the opening of the Indianapolis Motor Speedway in 1909 gave a glimpse of the future. Racing spread westwards, and more and more speedways – or tracks – were constructed. Most popular were the one- or two-mile ovals built quickly and relatively cheaply out of wood. The promoters loved them because it meant that the spectators were all in one place and could be charged admission, while the spectators also approved: they could see the entire track and, better still, the racing was close, fast and dangerous. And by 1917 the American Automobile Association's national championship was made up entirely of oval races, many on these wooden "roaring boards".

Popular they may have been, but these ovals were lethal. Yet the drama and danger merely added to the interest of watching heroes like Ralph de Palma and Dario Resta battle it out. Back in Europe, the recession lifted again in 1911 and, in the couple of years before the First World War, racing enjoyed a brief flowering, and car design underwent

Fabulous Alfa *Antonio Ascari wins at Spa in 1925 in his mighty P2.*

a revolution. Circuits were becoming more winding and twisting, whereas before most had been little more than triangles, and so emphasis switched from brute power to greater manoeuvrability, much better brakes and more flexible engines. By 1914 the racing car had arrived at a basic form it would keep more or less unchanged for the next 40 years.

The war, however, left racing in Europe in a parlous state, and it took some time to re-establish itself. The effects of the war can be judged by the 1921 ACF Grand Prix at Le Mans, in which the American visitors wiped the floor with the Europeans. Engineers, though, had learnt a great deal during the war and their knowledge was about to open the way to a period of technical advance. This was to have two results: the domination of European racing by Italy and a technological divorce between the Americans and Europeans.

In America, cars like the slim-line Miller 122 were being developed exclusively for use on speedways, while in Europe, Fiat worked on the high-revving overhead camshaft engine and mated it to the lightweight 805 chassis. The cars bettered 105mph, and Felice Nazzaro, driving one, dominated the 1922 French Grand Prix at Strasbourg, the scene of racing's first mass start.

The 1923 Fiat 805.405, the first Grand Prix car to have a supercharger, was developed in a wind-tunnel. It handed a first victory to a British car in the French Grand Prix, though, after its supercharger ingested dust, Henry Segrave won in a Sunbeam, which, ironically, had been copied off the previous year's Fiat. But after that the Fiats were in a class of their own, driven by Pietro Bordino and Nazzaro.

Alfa-Romeo, keen not to lose out to its rivals, designed for 1923 the P1, which was superseded in 1924 by the P2, a seminal Grand Prix car. It easily won the newly organized World Championship for Manufacturers in 1925, and was unbeaten until Ascari's all-out style caused him to clip the fencing at the French Grand Prix at Montlhery. The car rolled and Ascari was killed.

The Golden Age ended as abruptly as it had begun. Alfa pulled out, declaring that racing was too expensive, and in 1926 the world was heading towards one of its biggest economic slumps.

The Great Depression was to have a devastating effect on many aspects of European political, economic and social life, not least on motor racing.

End of an era *This is a 1926 V12 Sunbeam, capable of over 150 mph.*

THE TWIN-OVERHEAD-CAM ENGINE

From the moment that designers started coaxing more power out of petrol engines the rule was the bigger the better. The only technical constraint was the problem of holding these increasingly large and heavy units together.

By 1906 size versus power was such an accepted correlation that the internationally agreed racing formula was a maximum weight limit of 1000kg. At this time the average size of a racing engine was around 12 litres, with some as large as 19 litres.

Two years later a formula was introduced that limited the piston area, but the cars were still monsters by the standards of road cars. Peugeot, an old industrial company, started competing in smaller classes of racing with some success.

The French Grand Prix was revived in 1912 and it was natural that Peugeot should help defend French honour against the all-conquering Mercedes from Germany.

The works team of Georges Boillot, Jules Goux and Paul Zuccarelli persuaded Peugeot to finance a new car for the race. Working with the Swiss designer Ernest Henry, they came up with a revolutionary engine that had two camshafts mounted in the cylinder head.

These operated directly on four valves in each cylinder, inclined to give a near perfect hemispherical combustion chamber. The result was a unit that could create as great a flow of air as a much bigger engine and then burn it much more effectively. With a capacity of 7.6 litres it produced 130bhp, nearly as much power as engines of almost twice its capacity. Boillot won the race and the car set trends that were soon copied.

In the years that followed some stalwarts held out, notably Ettore Bugatti with his three-valve arrangement. Today, however, the concept is universal to all purpose-built race engines although many subtle refinements are incorporated.

DEPRESSION AND FASCISM, WAR AND PEACE

Alfa's dominator *Tazio Nuvolari swept all before him in his P2.*

As the Great Depression took effect, the sport's governing body tried to impose a formula for 1.5-litre cars. Following the death of Ascari and of those American heroes Resta, Jimmy Murphy and Joe Boyer, safety concerns assumed paramount importance. In the United States the American Automobile Club introduced a stock car formula for Indianapolis (quickly dubbed the "Junk Formula" by purists) in an attempt to attract manufacturers back. By 1930, with the Depression lifting, it was beginning to work.

In Europe there was a similar situation, with most promoters accepting come-as-you-are entries in an attempt to fill grids. Far from causing a period of stagnation in racing, the years of the Depression were a breeding ground for some of the greatest drivers ever as well as for one of the most fabulous cars. The Formula Libre races provided the ideal training opportunities for professional, independent drivers racing quasi-works cars.

This was the era of Achille Varzi, Louis Chiron, Rudolf Caracciola and, the greatest of the time, Tazio Nuvolari. These drivers plied their trade on classics like the daunting Targa Florio road race in Sicily and the Mille Miglia (literally "1,000 miles") which was an epic journey on public roads through the mountains from Brescia to Rome and back.

The 1930 Mille Miglia saw Nuvolari and Varzi pitched against each other in the same Alfa-Romeo team. At dawn on the second day Varzi, three minutes ahead of Nuvolari on the road, but behind on aggregate time, saw the pattern of Nuvolari's headlights on the road behind him. The race, he thought, was lost. But then the lights disappeared, and Varzi allowed himself to dream that Nuvolari had dropped out. He was startled, less than 30 miles from the finish, by a flash of lights and the blast of a horn. Nuvolari had been behind him, lights off, as they plunged through the mountain passes…

Nuvolari enjoyed heroic status in Italy. His driving was all flair and verve, which reflected his personality. Varzi, by contrast, was ice-cool of nerve, and smooth and clinical in the car. Enzo Ferrari said of the early 1930s: "The outstanding man was Nuvolari, but he found a worthy adversary in Varzi, who surpassed him in his cool, perfect style." These greats raced for manufacturers from their native countries. Nuvolari for Alfa, Caracciola for Mercedes and Chiron for Bugatti. Only Varzi would change from car to car, searching for the best drive, although Caracciola drove Alfas when Mercedes pulled out in 1932.

For five years, from the late 1920s to the early 1930s, these drivers dominated racing. And, in 1932, Nuvolari and Caracciola battled it out in one of the greatest racing cars ever, the Alfa-Romeo P3. It handled like a dream, and in the hands of Nuvolari, Caracciola and Baconin Borzacchini it won nearly every race it contested. But, almost as soon as it had begun, the era of P3 domination was over. The Alfa board pulled out, and left its team, Scuderia Ferrari, to carry on with older Monza cars.

The technological revolution

In January 1933 Adolf Hitler and the Nazi party were elected to power. The new German chancellor was a fast-car enthusiast, and wanted to use racing as a platform for Nazi propaganda. A new formula was announced, with a minimum weight of 750kg, and the German government's subsidy was split between Mercedes and Auto Union. The German public relations drive was to lead to a rapid evolution in the technology, power, speed and spectacle of racing.

It also led to a time of complete domination by the German teams, whose first cars, the Mercedes W25 and Auto Union Type A, were in a class of their own when they appeared at Avus in Berlin in mid-1934. Mechanical teething troubles caused them some problems, although Hans Stuck won at the Nurburgring for Auto Union, and Manfred von Brauchitsch at the Eifelrennen for Mercedes.

No one recognized the challenge more than Nuvolari who, since Mercedes had a full team (Caracciola, Luigi Faglioli and von Brauchitsch), asked Auto Union for a drive. Astonishingly, it turned him down. It had signed up Varzi who, despite his great respect for his rival – and probably because of it – had always said that he would never drive in the same team as Nuvolari. Since Stuck, too, was not very keen to have the greatest driver of the era signed up, Nuvolari had to return to Ferrari and Alfa. But he was to exact revenge at the race which mattered most to the Germans.

The Italian Job in Germany

The year was a Mercedes benefit, with Auto Union picking up some of the pieces along the way, and Caracciola won all the important races to take the first European Drivers' Championship. All except one, that is – at the classic and daunting Nurburgring in Germany, when 300,000 spectators witnessed a German victory. At the end of the first lap, though, Nuvolari's P3 was behind the leader Caracciola. By lap nine he had fallen behind new Auto Union recruit Bernd Rosemeyer, Faglioli and Chiron's Alfa as well, and had to stop for tyres.

There now began one of the greatest drives ever seen. From a seemingly impossible position, the little Italian clawed his way to second place, battling for four hours on the tortuous mountain circuit, with only his natural ability, aided by a fine drizzle, keeping him in touch. Nuvolari made up 45 seconds on the final lap, before a tyre blew on leader von Brauchitsch's Mercedes, handing Nuvolari a victory for genius over technology in front of a silent German crowd.

The following year it was Auto Union's turn to dominate, with the European Championship surrendering to Rosemeyer, a former motorcycle ace, in a revised, better-handling car, the Type B. Rosemeyer was the personification of Hitler's Aryan dream – blond, good-looking and heroic. "Bernd literally did not know fear," said Caracciola, "and sometimes that's not good. We actually feared for him in every race. Somehow I never thought a long life was on the cards for him."

Sadly, Caracciola was right. Rosemeyer was killed in a speed record attempt in 1938 and was replaced by Nuvolari. Caracciola won his third European title in four years.

Although Rosemeyer was a dream for a Hitler, he also was a reminder that, while the drivers of these teams were picked for propaganda purposes, they did not always fulfil them as readily as might have been hoped. In the 1937 German Grand Prix Rosemeyer had again been the star, finishing third, less than a minute behind winner Caracciola, despite losing more than three minutes in the pits over repairs and then a further minute in another off-road incident. On the rostrum, Caracciola was presented with an effigy of the goddess of speed by Adolf Huhnlein, a Brown Shirt appointed as Hitler's man in the field. When Huhnlein momentarily had his back turned, Rosemeyer stuck his cigarette between its lips and, as the crowd laughed, Huhnlein spun around again, only to see Rosemeyer with his cigarette back in his mouth and the picture of innocence.

The Aftermath of War

The era of German domination ended with the Second World War and, although motor racing started again soon after the bomb had been dropped on Hiroshima, it took some time to re-establish itself, since there was a shortage of oil.

By 1947 racing was again under a formula and by 1948 it was back on its feet. The year was a turning point. It was to see Nuvolari's last great drive (in the Mille Miglia) when, at 56, he showed that all his skill remained – leading, and carrying on despite spitting blood from his lungs, destroyed from years of breathing noxious car fumes, until his Alfa's brakes failed at Parma.

Later in the year Varzi was killed in a wet practice session at the Swiss Grand Prix at Berne. And 1948 was also the year in which a little-known driver from Argentina, Juan Manuel Fangio, scored his first win in Europe, in the Pau Grand Prix.

A World Drivers' Championship was just around the corner, andthe world of motor racing had a new sense of purpose.

DEVELOPMENTS IN CHASSIS DESIGN

The Mercedes and Auto Unions, which dominated racing throughout the 1930s, represented a revolution in chassis design, funded by Hitler. Both cars were more powerful by far and handled better than their rivals. Both used light alloys in their construction and independent suspension on all four wheels, but they differed in one fundamental way: the Mercedes W25, and subsequent W125 and W154 voiturette, had their engines in the conventional place, at the front. Auto Union put theirs behind the driver, which made it nervous to drive, but still extraordinarily fast in the hands of greats such as Varzi, Rosemeyer and, in 1938, Nuvolari.

The Mercedes W25 brought together for the first time in a front-engined Grand Prix car independent suspension, hydraulic brakes and a gearbox and differential attached to the frame and therefore the sprung weight of the car. The exceptional Mercedes of the era was the 1937 W125. It was longer and handled better than the W25, and its 5.6-litre supercharged engine produced 610 brake horsepower.

The Auto Union was even more novel. Apart from the rear-mounted engine, which was not to be seen on a Grand Prix car again until the late 1950s, the body was in light alloy, and the fuel was carried between the engine and the driver, as in modern cars, to ensure that the handling remained constant whatever the fuel load.

But this also provided its weak point. The suspension design exacerbated the nervous handling produced by having the driver so far forward. This meant that only when Rosemeyer drove did it have a real chance of consistently beating the Mercedes – until the Type D appeared in 1938.

It was more compact, with the cockpit further back in the chassis, and a new suspension made the car Nuvolari was to drive more controllable than the previous models. But it was kept from challenging the more conventional Mercedes by a power handicap, and Nuvolari's skill was depended upon rather more than the car to beat the Mercedes in 1938.

On the banking *Hermann Lang's Mercedes takes the high line in 1937.*

THE WORLD CHAMPIONSHIP

Think of Formula One and, according to your age, you will recall the great drivers such as Juan Manuel Fangio and Stirling Moss in the 1950s, Jim Clark and Jack Brabham in the 1960s, Jackie Stewart and Niki Lauda in the 1970s, Nelson Piquet and Alain Prost in the 1980s, and Ayrton Senna and Michael Schumacher in the 1990s. You will all have your favourites, since few sports arouse as much passion as motor racing. Formula One is truly the battle of man versus machine at its most extreme. Danger is always around the corner — and financial ruin more of a certainty for many teams than World Championship points.

Formula One – like the motor car that has been made faster, safer and more economical as a result of the technical spin-off – has moved ahead with gigantic strides since the World Championship began in 1950.

Not only have the cars changed out of all recognition, but the circuits, too, largely at the behest of Stewart in the 1970s, who had grown tired of seeing his contemporaries crashing with fatal consequences.

Senna's death in 1994 accelerated a second wave of driver-led safety consciousness.

Fiercest of competition

However, for all the changes, there is one thing that has not changed: the will to win and the fierce competition that surrounds this. The scoring system used in Formula One since 1950 has been 9–6–4–3–2–1 for the first six finishers. Until 1992, that is, when a win was boosted to ten points. From 1950 until 1960 inclusive, the Indianapolis 500 counted as a World Championship round, although it was contested by an almost entirely separate set of drivers in different cars. On several occasions, half points have been awarded if a race was shortened either because of a major accident – for instance the 1975 Spanish Grand Prix – or because track conditions had become unsafe – as with the 1991 Australian Grand Prix.

Sharing a drive was another reason for fractions of points to be scored, such as in the 1955 Ar0gentine Grand Prix when Farina, Maglioli and Trintignant shared a Ferrari and came home third, thus leaving them to split the points three ways (i.e. 1.33 each).

1950

The World Championship was held for the first time in 1950, linking the established Grands Prix of just six countries. Alfa-Romeo and its drivers Farina, Fangio and Fagiola dominated, but Ferrari was waiting to pounce.

In the years after the end of the Second World War it did not take long for motor racing to re-establish itself, and by 1950 the governing body had decided that the time was right to launch a World Championship. There was plenty of prewar equipment available and also no shortage of drivers who had raced in the 1930s. True, they had lost some of the best years of their careers but, despite the enforced break, were still at the top of their game.

Championship rivals *Fangio (sitting in his Alfa) and Farina at Silverstone.*

Alfa-Romeo out in front

Alfa-Romeo's superb squad comprised the legendary "three Fs": Dr Giuseppe "Nino" Farina (then aged 44), Juan Manuel Fangio (38) and Luigi Fagioli (53). Equipped with an update of the prewar Tipo 158, they steamrollered the opposition, which was led by Ferrari.

Ferrari had been disappointing in 1949 and the team was absent from the very first race of the new series, held at a bleak Silverstone on May 13 in the presence of the royal family. There were 21 cars in the field for this first race, and Farina had the honour of taking the first pole position. Old stager Fagioli led initially, but dropped to third behind Farina and Fangio. When the latter's engine failed, Fagioli took second, ahead of of local star Reg Parnell.

A week later at Monaco Farina's luck changed when he triggered a nine-car pile-up, which also took out Fagioli. Fangio was ahead of the carnage, and somehow survived when he came across it on the next lap. He went on to score a memorable win. Ferrari entered the championship for the first time, and 31-year-old Alberto Ascari was rewarded with second place, one lap down. Farina and Fagioli scored a one-two in the Swiss Grand Prix at the tricky Bremgarten road circuit, and once again Fangio suffered an engine failure – as did all three works Ferraris. At Spa Fangio fought back with his second win of the year, ahead of Fagioli. Variety was provided by Raymond Sommer, who led in his Talbot before blowing up.

Farina's laurels

The first championship, like so many to follow, came to a head in the final round at Monza. Fangio had 26 points to the 24 of the consistent Fagioli, and the 22 of Farina. Fangio and Farina had the new and more powerful 159 model, but the title was settled when Fangio retired with a seized gearbox. Farina won the race, and with it the championship. Ferrari had been working hard on a new unsupercharged engine during the season, showing well in non-championship races, and Ascari was on the pace with the latest model. When his car retired, he took over the machine of team-mate Dorino Serafini and finished second, ahead of Fagioli. The most talked about car never appeared at a Grand Prix race. The much-vaunted V16 BRM made an ignominious debut in the International Trophy at Silverstone in August, retiring on the line with driveshaft failure.

DRIVERS' WORLD CHAMPIONSHIP

Pos.	Driver	Nat.	Make	Pts
1	Giuseppe Farina	It	Alfa	30
2	Juan Manuel Fangio	Arg	Alfa	27
3	Luigi Fagioli	It	Alfa	24
4	Louis Rosier	Fr	Talbot	13
5	Alberto Ascari	It	Ferrari	11
6	Johnny Parsons*	USA	Wynn's Kurtis	8
7	Bill Holland*	USA	Blue Crown	6
8	Prince Bira	Thai	Maserati	5
9	Reg Parnell	GB	Alfa	4
	Louis Chiron	Mon	Maserati	4
	Peter Whitehead	GB	Ferrari	4
	Mauri Rose*	USA	Keck Offenhauser	4

Best four scores from seven races to count *denotes points scored in Indy 500

1951

Alfa-Romeo continued to set the pace, but Ferrari came close to toppling the champions. Mechanical problems had robbed him the previous year, but now Juan Manuel Fangio was dominant and claimed his first title.

For 1951 Alfa broke up the "three Fs" team, replacing Fagioli with 48-year-old Felice Bonetto. Froilan Gonzalez, who had previously driven a Maserati, joined Ascari and Luigi Villoresi at Ferrari. The stocky young Argentinian, known as the "Pampas Bull", was to become a major force during the season.

The championship was expanded to a total of seven races, with Monaco missing and events in Germany and Spain added. This time the series began in Switzerland, and in soaking conditions Fangio scored a fine win.

Moss makes his mark

Meanwhile, a promising young Englishman made his debut in a British HWM, qualifying 14th and finishing eighth. His name was Stirling Moss.

Pampas Bull *Froilan Gonzalez receiving a kiss from his wife after winning the British Grand Prix at Silverstone.*

Farina and Fangio dominated the Belgian Grand Prix at Spa, but when Fangio pitted, a rear wheel stuck on and his race was ruined. Farina won from the Ferraris of Ascari and Villoresi, while a fired-up Fangio set the fastest lap – but finished ninth and last.

Fagioli was back in an Alfa at Reims, and went on to score his first victory – but only after Fangio took over his car when his own mount had retired in a race of high attrition. Another shared car, the Ferrari of Gonzalez and Ascari, took second, ahead of Villoresi. After tyre troubles, Farina was a distant fifth.

A Ferrari win seemed on the cards, and the first finally came at Silverstone where Gonzalez put in a fine performance to take the lead from countryman Fangio when the Alfa driver pitted for fuel. The BRM made its first championship appearance, with Reg Parnell taking a promising fifth and Peter Walker seventh.

Success for Ferrari

Ferrari proved the dominant force at the Nurburgring, the first championship race held on the long, tortuous circuit. Ascari notched up his first win, despite a late stop for rear tyres. Fangio, who required an extra scheduled fuel stop, took second for Alfa. Third to sixth places were filled with Ferraris, while Farina retired with gearbox trouble.

Monza was the penultimate round this year, and Ascari and Gonzalez celebrated a fine one-two for Ferrari in front of the home crowd. Alfa had a much-modified car, the 159M, and Fangio was battling for the lead until a tyre failed. His storming recovery drive ended with engine failure. Farina retired early, but took over Bonetto's car and eventually earned third place.

The final race at Pedrables in Spain proved to be Alfa's swansong. Despite his Monza retirement, Fangio led Ascari by 28 points to 25 going into the race, and a dominant win secured Juan Manuel's first crown. The Ferraris suffered tyre troubles, with Gonzalez and pole man Ascari taking second and fourth, split by Farina's Alfa.

At the end of the year Alfa withdrew from Grand Prix racing, unable to finance a new car to challenge Ferrari in 1952.

Partly in response to Alfa's departure, the Fédération Internationale de l'Automobile announced that for 1952, the World Championship would run to less powerful Formula Two rules. It was hoped that this would encourage a wider variety of cars and avoid a Ferrari walkover.

DRIVERS' WORLD CHAMPIONSHIP

Pos.	Driver	Nat.	Make	Pts
1	Juan Manuel Fangio	Arg	Alfa	31
2	Alberto Ascari	It	Ferrari	25
3	Froilan Gonzalez	Arg	Ferrari	24
4	Giuseppe Farina	It	Alfa	19
5	Luigi Villoresi	It	Ferrari	15
6	Piero Taruffi	It	Ferrari	10
7	Lee Wallard*	USA	Belanger	8
8	Felice Bonetto	It	Alfa	7
9	Mike Nazaruk*	USA	Jim Robbins	6
10	Reg Parnell	GB	Ferrari/BRM	5

Best four scores from eight races to count ***denotes points scored in Indy 500**

1952

Ferrari responded to the Formula Two rules changes by dominating the season. Alberto Ascari won every race he entered to became world champion. An injured Fangio could only watch these events from the sidelines.

Despite the change of regulations, Ferrari entered 1952 as the major force. The marque had already been highly successful in Formula Two, and had a first-class driver squad. Ascari, Villoresi and Piero Taruffi were joined by Farina – on the market after Alfa's withdrawal. The main opposition should have come from reigning champion Fangio, who had switched from Alfa to Maserati to drive the new A6GCM. However, he was forced to miss the entire season after breaking his neck in a crash during a non-championship race at Monza.

New faces

The rule change achieved its aim of attracting a variety of cars to take on the red machines. From France came the Gordinis of Jean Behra and Robert Manzon, while in Britain there was a host of projects under way, including the Cooper-Bristol, Connaught, HWM, Alta, Frazer Nash and ERA.

The most successful of these would prove to be the Cooper-Bristol, an underpowered but superb-handling machine. Its brilliant young driver was the flamboyant Englishman, Mike Hawthorn, who was the find of the year.

The championship began with the Swiss Grand Prix, notable for the absence of Ascari, who was busy with Ferrari commitments at Indianapolis. Taruffi scored an easy win, well ahead of local Ferrari privateer Rudi Fischer. The Gordini showed promise, with Behra taking third. That place was held by Moss in the HWM, but his car was withdrawn after two of its sister entries suffered hub failures.

Ascari returned at Spa, and scored his first win of the new Formula Two era in soaking conditions, ahead of team-mate Farina. Manzon gave Gordini another third, but all eyes were on Hawthorn, making his championship debut. He ran third and, after a fuel leak delayed him, finished a fine fourth. It was the highest place to date for a British car, and the first sign of great things to come from John Cooper's small company.

Behra's Gordini beat the Ferraris at Reims but, unfortunately for him in this particular year, it was a non-championship race.

Ferrari triumphs again

The French Grand Prix moved to Rouen a week later, and Ascari, Farina and Taruffi finished one-two-three, with Manzon fourth. At Silverstone Ascari and Taruffi were one-two, but Hawthorn was the darling of the crowd, rising to the challenge and finishing third. Dennis Poore also impressed with his Connaught, leading Hawthorn until a long fuel stop, before coming fourth.

The German Grand Prix at the Nurburgring was a complete Ferrari whitewash, with Ascari heading Farina, Fischer and Taruffi. Ascari had to work hard for his win: a late pit stop for oil dropped him to second and forced him to catch and repass Farina. The new Dutch event at Zandvoort saw Ascari heading home Farina and Villoresi, with Hawthorn again leading the challenge in a gallant fourth with his Cooper-Bristol.

Ascari had clinched the title before the finale at Monza, where he scored his sixth win from six starts.

Picture perfect *Alberto Ascari in his Ferarri had a perfect year.*

DRIVERS' WORLD CHAMPIONSHIP

Pos.	Driver	Nat.	Make	Pts
1	Alberto Ascari	It	Ferrari	36
2	Giuseppe Farina	It	Ferrari	25
3	Piero Taruffi	It	Ferrari	22
4	Rudi Fischer	Swi	Ferrari	10
	Mike Hawthorn	GB	Cooper-Bristol	10
6	Robert Manzon	Fr	Gordini	9
7	Troy Ruttman*	USA	Agajanian	8
	Luigi Villoresi	It	Ferrari	8
9	Froilan Gonzalez	Arg	Maserati	6.5
10	Jim Rathmann*	USA	Grancor-Wynn	6
	Jean Behra	Fr	Gordini	6

Best four scores from eight races to count ***denotes points scored in Indy 500***

1953

Alberto Ascari claimed his second crown as Ferrari were again supreme in the second and final year of the Formula Two category. Fangio struck back for Maserati signalling the start of four years of domination by the maestro.

Fangio was fit and back at the start of 1953, and heading a Maserati outfit which looked as if it might upset the Ferrari bandwagon. Joining him in a strong Argentinian line-up were Gonzalez and Onofre Marimon. Meanwhile, Hawthorn's performances with the Cooper had not gone unnoticed, and he had earned a seat with Ferrari, alongside Ascari, Farina and Villoresi. With Hawthorn gone Cooper lacked a driver of substance, and Gordini provided the only real opposition to the Italian cars.

Tragedy at Buenos Aires

For the first time the World Championship tag was justified by a race outside Europe, with the series kicking off at Buenos Aires. Unfortunately the race was marred by undisciplined spectators, and Farina was involved in a tragic incident when he hit a boy who crossed the track. Nine people were killed in the mayhem that followed. It was the first fatality in a championship race.

Meanwhile, Ascari and Villoresi scored a Ferrari one-two, ahead of debutant Marimon. Hawthorn had a steady race to fourth, while local hero Fangio ran second, before retiring. Maserati's new car arrived for Zandvoort. It showed promise, but Ascari and Farina took the usual Ferrari one-two, with the best Maserati – shared by Bonetto and Gonzalez – in third. Fangio broke a rear axle. At Spa the Maseratis were the cars to beat. Gonzalez and Fangio led the field until retiring. Inevitably Ascari was there to pick up the pieces, scoring his ninth consecutive win.

The French race was back at Reims, and proved to be a classic encounter which saw Hawthorn come of age. After taking two fourths and a sixth in the opening races, he emerged as a front-runner, getting the better of a sensational duel with Fangio to score his first win – and the first for any British driver. Strangely, Hawthorn could not repeat his French form at Silverstone, where Ascari was utterly dominant. Fangio chased hard, and finished ahead of Farina, Gonzalez and Hawthorn.

At the Nurburgring Ascari won, again the man to beat, but he lost a front wheel early on. He made it back to the pits, and later took over Villoresi's fourth-placed car. Farina maintained Ferrari's record, winning ahead of Fangio and Hawthorn. In his new car Ascari was closing in on the British driver when the engine blew.

DRIVERS' WORLD CHAMPIONSHIP

Pos.	Driver	Nat.	Make	Pts
1	Alberto Ascari	It	Ferrari	34.5
2	Juan Manuel Fangio	Arg	Maserati	28
3	Giuseppe Farina	It	Ferrari	26
4	Mike Hawthorn	GB	Ferrari	19
5	Luigi Villoresi	It	Ferrari	17
6	Froilan Gonzalez	Arg	Maserati	13.5
7	Bill Vukovich*	USA	Fuel Injection Special	8
8	Emmanuel de Graffenried	Swi	Maserati	7
9	Felice Bonetto	It	Maserati	6.5
10	Art Cross*	USA	Springfield Welding	6

Best four scores from nine races to count ***denotes points scored in Indy 500**

Ascari's year

Ascari clinched his second title at the penultimate race in Switzerland, yet it was anything but easy. Fangio led Ascari initially until gearbox and engine troubles intervened, and then Ascari lost the lead with a plug change. He dropped to fourth, but worked his way back to the lead, heading home Farina and Hawthorn.

Maserati had threatened to win all year, and it eventually happened in the finale at Monza – in bizarre circumstances. After a great slipstreaming battle Ascari looked set to win, but on the last lap he spun and forced Farina wide. The lapped Marimon also got involved, and through the dust cloud emerged Fangio, to score his first win since 1951.

The double
Alberto Ascari kicked off with three wins on the trot.

1954

Mercedes finally returned to racing and the "blank cheque" operation immediately set new standards. Juan Fangio and his wonderful W196 Silver Arrow were unstoppable. But Britain found a new star in Stirling Moss.

After two years of Formula Two it was all change for 1954, with the introduction of new 2.5-litre regulations. The big story was the decision by Mercedes-Benz to return to Grand Prix racing for the first time since the Second World War. The legendary Alfred Neubauer was still at the helm, and he snapped up Fangio to join Hans Herrmann and Karl Kling. The new W196 was a technical marvel, but was not ready until the third race of the year.

Also on the way was Lancia's new D50. The marque hired Ascari and Villoresi to drive it, but it was ready even later than the Mercedes. After two consecutive titles, Ascari effectively wasted the season. Fangio was luckier, for he was allowed to start the year in the new Maserati, the 250F. An attractive and effective car, it would be one of the mainstays of Grand Prix racing for the next few seasons. Ferrari had lost Ascari and Villoresi, but Hawthorn, Farina, Gonzalez and Frenchman Maurice Trintignant were on hand to drive the latest model.

Blast off *No one could live with the full-bodied Mercedes W196 streamliners at Reims.*

Fangio leads the field

Fangio's decision to start the year in a Maserati was a wise one, for he duly won the opening events in Argentina and Belgium. The first race was a chaotic, rain-hit affair with the track changing several times. Quick in the wet, Fangio won through ahead of the Ferraris of Farina, Gonzalez and Trintignant. Farina led the early laps in Belgium, but when he hit trouble Fangio went by, and headed home Trintignant. Moss showed he would be a force to be reckoned with by taking third.

Mercedes finally appeared at Reims with three of the magnificent W196s in streamlined, full-bodied form. The cars were perfectly suited to the fast track, and Fangio and Kling finished one-two, with Hermann setting fastest lap. However, Mercedes came down to earth with a bang at Silverstone, for the streamlined bodies did not like the airfield circuit. Fangio finished fourth in his battered car, while Gonzalez scored his second British Grand Prix win.

Death at the Nurburgring

Tragedy struck at the Nurburgring when Marimon was killed in practice; he was the first driver to die at a World Championship event. Countrymen Fangio and Gonzalez were distraught but, to his credit, Fangio got on with the job and won the race, his Mercedes now using the new open wheel body.

In Switzerland Fangio led from start to finish. Moss pursued him until retiring, and then Gonzalez took up the challenge. Monza established Moss as a star of the future. His performances had earned him a works Maserati seat, and he led until nine laps from the end when the oil tank split. He would eventually push the car over the line in 11th. Meanwhile, Fangio swept by to win in the streamlined Mercedes from Hawthorn. The Lancia team was finally ready for the last race in Spain. The car showed promise, for Ascari led for ten laps before retiring, and set fastest lap. Hawthorn went on to score his second win, ahead of Maserati's young find, Luigi Musso. Mercedes had a bad day, and Fangio finished only third. But his second title was in the bag.

DRIVERS' WORLD CHAMPIONSHIP

Pos.	Driver	Nat.	Make	Pts
1	Juan Manuel Fangio	Arg	Maserati/Mercedes	42
2	Froilan Gonzalez	Arg	Ferrari	25
3	Mike Hawthorn	GB	Ferrari	24.5
4	Maurice Trintignant	Fr	Ferrari	17
5	Karl Kling	Ger	Mercedes	12
6	Bill Vukovich*	USA	Fuel Injection Special	8
	Hans Herrmann	Ger	Mercedes	8
8	Jimmy Bryan*	USA	Dean Van Lines	6
	Giuseppe Farina	It	Ferrari	6
	Luigi Musso	It	Maserati	6
	Robert Mieres	Arg	Maserati	6

Best five scores from nine races to count *denotes points scored in Indy 500

1955

Mercedes, Fangio and Moss dominated the season, but the appalling tragedy at Le Mans, which cost over 80 lives, overshadowed everything. Mercedes later announced that it was withdrawing from Grand Prix racing.

June 11, 1955, is perhaps the blackest day in motor racing history. More than 80 people were killed when Pierre Levegh's Mercedes crashed into the crowd during the early laps at Le Mans. Grand Prix stars Fangio and Hawthorn were both closely involved in the incident, which had major repercussions for the sport. The Grands Prix in France, Germany, Switzerland and Spain were all cancelled, and, in fact, motor racing would never return to Switzerland.

German confidence

The German team went into the season with morale high. Neubauer had signed up Moss to partner Fangio, and now had two race-winning drivers in his Silver Arrows. Maserati signed up Jean Behra to replace Moss, while Mike Hawthorn left Ferrari to drive the patriotic Vanwall. The season opener in Argentina was run in sweltering conditions which saw Fangio score a comfortable win. He was one of only two drivers able to go solo. The three pursuing cars were each shared by three drivers apiece as the heat took its toll. At Monaco Ascari was really in the headlines, for he managed to flip his car into the harbour. He escaped this alarming incident with minor injuries. At the time he was leading, for Fangio and Moss had both retired their Mercedes. Trintignant proved a popular and surprise winner, ahead of the Lancia of Eugenio Castellotti.

Four days later Ascari was killed in a bizarre accident at Monza, while testing a Ferrari sports car. Already struggling for finance, Lancia announced its withdrawal from the sport, regrettably before the D50 had been able to fulfil its initial promise. Mercedes bounced back at Spa, where Fangio and Moss ran one-two with ease. Castellotti was allowed a final fling in a Lancia – as a privateer – and ran third before retiring from racing.

The following weekend came the Le Mans tragedy and, despite the outcry, the Grand Prix circus reconvened at Zandvoort just a week later. Fangio and Moss scored another Mercedes one-two, chased by Musso's Maserati. By now Hawthorn had given up on the Vanwall project, and his return to Ferrari was rewarded with a creditable seventh place.

DRIVERS' WORLD CHAMPIONSHIP

Pos.	Driver	Nat.	Make	Pts
1	Juan Manuel Fangio	Arg	Mercedes	40
2	Stirling Moss	GB	Mercedes	23
3	Eugenio Castellotti	It	Lancia	12
4	Maurice Trintignant	Fr	Ferrari	11.33
5	Giuseppe Farina	It	Ferrari	10.33
6	Piero Taruffi	It	Mercedes	9
7	Bob Sweikert*	USA	John Zink Special	8
8	Robert Mieres	Arg	Maserati	7
9	Tony Bettenhausen*	USA	Chapman Special	6
	Jean Behra	Fr	Maserati	6
	Luigi Musso	It	Maserati	6

Best five scores from seven races to count ***denotes points scored in Indy 500**

Racing at Aintree

The British Grand Prix moved to Aintree for the first time, and Mercedes scored a crushing one-two-three-four. This time Moss headed home Fangio, with Kling and Taruffi following on. It was Stirling's first win, but for years people wondered if Fangio had allowed him to take the glory at home. At the back of the grid in a little Cooper was a rookie called Jack Brabham...

With all the cancellations, only the Monza race remained to be run, this time on the banked circuit. After Moss retired, Fangio headed Taruffi in another one-two, with Castellotti third in a Ferrari. Fangio's third title was already secure, with Moss a distant second. But both men would be hit hard when Mercedes announced its withdrawal.

A significant result came in a non-championship at the end of the season, when Tony Brooks took his Connaught to victory at Syracuse It was the first major British win of the World Championship era.

Peek-a-boo
Juan Manuel Fangio won four races from a possible six.

1956

Following the withdrawal of Mercedes, Fangio switched to Ferrari and won his fourth World Championship. But the Argentinian needed some luck – and the incredible generosity of his sensational new team-mate, Peter Collins.

The two Mercedes stars did not spend much time contemplating unemployment. Fangio joined Ferrari, where another fresh face was talented British youngster Collins, along with Musso and Castellotti. The promising Lancias had also found a new home at Ferrari. They had, in fact, been entered by the Scuderia at Monza the previous year, but had non-started owing to tyre troubles. Modified over the winter, they became Lancia-Ferraris.

Meanwhile, Moss returned to Maserati to race the still competitive 250F alongside Behra. Prospects looked good for the British teams. Hawthorn and Tony Brooks joined BRM, while Vanwall had modified cars for Trintignant and Harry Schell. Connaught hoped to build on the Syracuse success.

Moss wins with Maserati

Fangio won the opener in Argentina, but he had to take over Musso's car after his own retired. The Maseratis struggled, although Behra took second place. Maserati hit back at Monaco, where Moss scored a fine second Grand Prix victory. A seemingly very off-form Fangio damaged his own car and this time took over the sister machine of Collins, which he maintained in second place.

At Spa Fangio and Moss both hit trouble, and Collins scored a famous victory in his Lancia-Ferrari. He became the third British race winner in as many seasons. Local star Paul Frère earned a fine second place, while Moss took over another car and recovered third. Collins scored his second win at Reims a month later, heading home Castellotti, Behra and Fangio, the champion, delayed by a pit stop. Surprise of the race was Harry Schell, who flew in the Vanwall after an early delay.

Collins went into the British Grand Prix leading the championship from the consistent Behra and Fangio. His thunder was stolen by Hawthorn and Brooks, who led the field on the return of BRM. Both hit trouble early on, however. Moss and Roy Salvadori each led until retiring, which allowed Fangio to take the honours. Collins took over the car of Alfonso de Portago and was runner-up, ahead of Behra. Fangio was an easy winner at the Nurburgring, while Collins was out of luck. His own car retired, and when he took over de Portago's machine, he crashed out of the race.

Ferrari's finest *Fangio on his way to winning the British Grand Prix.*

Rapt onlookers *The Ferrari team looking down the track.*

The struggle for the title

For the first time in several seasons the title fight went down to the wire at Monza. Fangio was well placed on 30 points, but Collins and Behra were eight behind – and could take the title by winning the race and setting fastest lap. Schell again surprised everyone by running at the front in the Vanwall and, when he retired, Moss, Fangio and Collins were left to fight it out. Fangio's hopes faded with steering trouble, but he was saved when Collins – who could still have won the title – stopped and handed his car over. It was a remarkable gesture, which Fangio would never forget.

Despite a scare when he ran out of fuel, Moss just held on from Collins/Fangio in an exciting finish. With BRM and Vanwall having already shown well during the year, it was Connaught's turn to earn some success as Ron Flockhart took advantage of a high attrition rate to come in third. Further British success seemed just around the corner.

DRIVERS' WORLD CHAMPIONSHIP

Pos.	Driver	Nat.	Make	Pts
1	Juan Manuel Fangio	Arg	Ferrari	30
2	Stirling Moss	GB	Maserati	27
3	Peter Collins	GB	Ferrari	25
4	Jean Behra	Fr	Maserati	22
5	Pat Flaherty*	USA	Zink Special	8
6	Eugenio Castellotti	It	Ferrari	7.5
7	Sam Hanks*	USA	Maley Special	6
	Paul Frère	Bel	Ferrari	6
	Francesco Godia	Sp	Maserati	6
	Jack Fairman	GB	Connaught	6

Best five scores from eight races to count ***denotes points scored in Indy 500**

1957

Fangio acquired his fifth and last title for Maserati, but Stirling Moss and Vanwall were the true stars of a year in which the all-British team won a remarkable three races. Ferrari was struggling desperately to keep up.

Finding the gap *Juan Manuel Fangio slides inside Tony Brooks's Vanwall in the Italian Grand Prix at Monza.*

There was plenty of activity during the winter, the most notable news being Fangio's switch from Ferrari to Maserati. It was quite a coup for Maserati to entice the reigning champion back to drive its latest 250F, and it proved to be a wise choice for Juan Manuel.

Meanwhile, Moss, always keen to drive British wherever possible, headed to Vanwall. He had already won the previous year's International Trophy for Tony Vandervell's promising concern. Hawthorn continued to hop back and forth across the English Channel, rejoining Ferrari for a third spell after a bad time with BRM. He teamed up with his great buddy Collins, plus Musso and Castellotti.

Once again Fangio won his home race in Argentina, heading home a Maserati one-two-three-four as the Ferrari challenge fell apart. Vanwall did not enter the race, and Moss had trouble at the start in his borrowed Maserati. He set fastest lap as he recovered to seventh. After the Argentine race the talented Castellotti lost his life in a testing crash at Modena, and he was replaced by Trintignant. Then the enigmatic Alfonso de Portago was killed in the Mille Miglia. It was a bleak period indeed for Enzo Ferrari.

Monaco saw a spectacular pile-up at the start which eliminated Moss, Collins and Hawthorn. Fangio scored an easy win, while Brooks took his Vanwall to second after extricating it from the mess. Star of the race was Jack Brabham, who got his underpowered Cooper up to third before the fuel pump failed. The plucky Australian pushed it home sixth.

A British triumph

The French Grand Prix returned to Rouen and Fangio stormed to victory ahead of the Ferraris of Musso, Collins and Hawthorn. The next race was at Aintree and it proved to be a memorable day for Britain. After Moss retired his leading Vanwall, he took over the sixth-placed car of team-mate Brooks. The opposition wilted, and when Behra blew his engine – and Hawthorn punctured on the debris – Moss swept home to a wonderful victory.

Vanwall was out of luck at the Nurburgring, with both cars suffering suspension problems. But the race is remembered as one of the all-time classics, as Fangio came storming back to win after a fuel stop, leaving Collins and Hawthorn in his wake. Fangio would always regard the race in Germany as his greatest ever

Because Spa and Zandvoort had been cancelled, an extra Italian race, the tortuous Pescara Grand Prix, was added to the series. Enzo Ferrari, supposedly opposed to Italian road circuits, did not enter Hawthorn and Collins, but loaned a "private" car to Musso. He was in front for the first couple of laps before Moss took the lead and scored his second win of the year. Fangio finished second, and sealed his fifth and final title.

The Monza finale, no longer using the banking, saw a spectacular fight between Vanwall and Maserati. Moss headed Fangio home, with the promising German, Wolfgang von Trips, upholding Ferrari honour in third. It was a lame year for the Prancing Horse. Ferrari had not won a race all year, and clearly needed to resolve that situation in 1958. The job was made easier when Maserati withdrew its works team at the end of the season, owing to lack of funds.

DRIVERS' WORLD CHAMPIONSHIP

Pos.	Driver	Nat.	Make	Pts
1	Juan Manuel Fangio	Arg	Maserati	40
2	Stirling Moss	GB	Vanwall	25
3	Luigi Musso	It	Ferrari	16
4	Mike Hawthorn	GB	Ferrari	13
5	Tony Brooks	GB	Vanwall	11
6	Harry Schell	USA	Maserati	10
	Masten Gregory	USA	Maserati	10
8	Peter Collins	GB	Ferrari	8
	Sam Hanks*	USA	Belond Exhaust	8
10	Jean Behra	Fr	Maserati	6
	Jim Rathmann*	USA	Chiropratic	6

Best five scores from eight races to count ***denotes points scored in Indy 500***

1958

Mike Hawthorn pipped Stirling Moss to the title, but his success was overshadowed by the death of his team-mate and friend, Peter Collins. Mike retired at the top, only to lose his life in a road accident soon after.

Ferrari flier *Mike Hawthorn during practice for the British Grand Prix.*

The departure of Maserati was a major blow to the sport, although the cars survived in the hands of privateers. The marque's withdrawal coincided with that of Fangio. He would run just two races in 1958, before calling it a day.

Ferrari abandoned the old Lancia-based cars, and had a new model, the 246 Dino, with Hawthorn, Collins and Musso the star drivers. Moss, Brooks and Stuart Lewis-Evans stayed with Vanwall, while John Cooper mounted a serious effort with Brabham and Roy Salvadori. Rob Walker entered a private Cooper-Climax for Trintignant, and Behra and Schell headed a revived BRM effort.

British successes

The season started off with a surprise in Argentina. Most of the British teams were absent, including Vanwall, so Moss was free to replace Trintignant in Walker's Cooper. He duly won the race in a canny display, although his tyres were worn out by the end. At Monaco Trintignant was in Walker's car and, amazingly, he scored his second success in the street race. Once again, the faster cars hit trouble, including Moss's Vanwall.

The British success continued at Zandvoort, where Vanwall swept the front row. Moss won, while the BRMs of Schell and Behra finished second and third after the other Vanwalls retired. Salvadori's Cooper was fourth, and even the best Ferrari – that of fifth-placed Hawthorn – had a British driver...

Ferrari had been without a win since 1956, but the waiting ended at Reims where Hawthorn scored what would be his only victory of the season. However, there was no celebrating. Team-mate Musso, who had qualified second, was killed in the race. Fangio finished fourth in his last race.

Triumph and tragedy

At Silverstone it was the turn of Collins to win for Ferrari, with Hawthorn taking second. But a fortnight later tragedy struck again when Collins lost his life in the German Grand Prix. Brooks went on to score a hollow victory.

Moss had retired while leading in Germany, and he gained some revenge at the new event in Portugal, winning from pole position with Hawthorn second. In one of the closest points battles ever, Moss led all the way and set fastest lap. But, with Brooks blowing up, Hawthorn eased into second place, which was all he required to take the crown. It was a disappointing day for both Vanwall and Stirling, made worse when Lewis-Evans succumbed to his injuries after crashing on lap 42. The only consolation for Vanwall was the inaugural constructors' title.

Then, after quitting the sport while at his peak, Hawthorn was killed in a road accident in January. He was just 29 years old.

DRIVERS' WORLD CHAMPIONSHIP

Pos.	*Driver*	*Nat.*	*Make*	*Pts*
1	Mike Hawthorn	GB	Ferrari	42
2	Stirling Moss	GB	Cooper/Vanwall	41
3	Tony Brooks	GB	Vanwall	24
4	Roy Salvadori	GB	Cooper-Climax	15
5	Harry Schell	USA	BRM	14
	Peter Collins	GB	Ferrari	14
7	Luigi Musso	It	Ferrari	12
	Maurice Trintignant	Fr	Cooper-Climax	12
9	Stuart Lewis-Evans	GB	Vanwall	11
10	Phil Hill	USA	Ferrari	9
	Wolfgang von Trips	Ger	Ferrari	9
	Jean Behra	Fr	BRM	9

Best six scores from 11 races to count

CONSTRUCTORS' CUP

Pos.	*Make*	*Pts*
1	Vanwall	48
2	Ferrari	40
3	Cooper	31
4	BRM	18
5	Maserati	10
6	Lotus	3

Golden boy *Hawthorn wins the Goodwood International 100m race.*

1959

The old order changed for ever when Jack Brabham took his Cooper-Climax to the 1959 championship. It was the first title for a rear-engined car, marking a triumph of handling over power. The revolution started here.

Cooper climax *Jack Brabham taking the chequered flag as he wins the British Grand Prix at Aintree.*

The big news of the winter was the surprise withdrawal of the Vanwall team, just as it had reached full competitiveness. But Cooper, BRM and Lotus upheld British honour. After the previous year's tragedies there were big changes at Ferrari. Brooks joined from Vanwall and Behra from BRM, while Phil Hill – an occasional Ferrari driver in 1958 – went full time. Moss kept his options open, and would appear in both Walker's Cooper-Climax, and a BRM in the colours of the British Racing Partnership.

Success for Cooper-Climax

In previous years Climax had given away a few cc, but the latest engine was a full 2.5-litre unit. Although still a little down on power compared with its rivals, the Cooper's handling proved vastly superior.

With Argentina cancelled, the series opened at Monaco. Behra's Ferrari led until retiring, and then Moss's nimble Cooper expired, leaving Brabham to score his first win in the works Cooper. Zandvoort saw a major surprise, as Jo Bonnier notched up BRM's first victory, nine years after the marque made its first, stumbling steps. The bearded Swede had to work hard to hold off the Coopers, and was helped when Moss retired. Ferrari fought back with a fine win for Brooks at Reims, teammate Hill following him home. Moss was in the BRP BRM on this occasion, and was battling for second when he went off the road. Three marques had won the first three races, but Cooper was back in the frame at Aintree as Brabham scored his second win, ahead of Moss's BRM. Stirling just held off young Kiwi Bruce McLaren – the second works Cooper driver was starting to make a name for himself. Ferrari did not turn up, blaming Italian industrial action.

For the first and only time the German Grand Prix was held on the daunting, banked Avus circuit in Berlin and, uniquely, the result was an aggregate of two 30-lap heats. Missing Aintree had obviously done Ferrari some good, for Brooks dominated the event. But, as at Reims the year before, Ferrari's celebration was muted by tragedy. Veteran Behra, who had been a mainstay of the championship since its inception, died after a crash in the sports car support race.

Brabham in command

Moss had to wait until the Portuguese race to pick up his first win of the year in Walker's Cooper. Brabham crashed out, but still led the championship as the circus moved to the penultimate race at Monza. Moss won again, ahead of Hill, while third place for Brabham kept his title challenge alive.

It was a full three months before the final race, the first ever US Grand Prix, and the only one to be held on the Sebring airfield track in Florida, home of the famous 12 hours sports car race. Moss could still lift the crown and, after taking pole, he was leading comfortably when his gearbox failed.

Brabham ran out of fuel and had to push his car home in fourth place, but the title was his come what may. A surprise win went to his team-mate McLaren, who at 22 became the youngest Grand Prix winner – a record which still stands. Trintignant was second in another Cooper, ahead of Brooks.

DRIVERS' WORLD CHAMPIONSHIP

Pos.	Driver	Nat.	Make	Pts
1	Jack Brabham	Aus	Cooper-Climax	31
2	Tony Brooks	GB	Ferrari	27
3	Stirling Moss	GB	BRM/Cooper-Climax	25.5
4	Phil Hill	USA	Ferrari	20
5	Maurice Trintignant	Fr	Cooper-Climax	19
6	Bruce McLaren	NZ	Cooper-Climax	16.5
7	Dan Gurney	USA	Ferrari	13
8	Jo Bonnier	Swe	BRM	10
	Masten Gregory	USA	Cooper-Climax	10
10	Rodger Ward*	USA	Leader Cards	8

Best five scores from nine races to count **denotes points scored in Indy 500*

CONSTRUCTORS' CUP

Pos.	Make	Pts
1	Cooper	40
2	Ferrari	32
3	BRM	19
4	Lotus	5

1960

Jack Brabham scored his second consecutive title win for Cooper, with Lotus emerging as a major force. But for a mid-season accident putting him out for several races, Stirling Moss might have won that elusive title.

Cooper revolution *Bruce McLaren (right) and Stirling Moss in Argentina.*

By 1960 the rear-engined machines were completely dominant. For the time being Ferrari stuck with its old car and won at Monza – but only because the British teams boycotted the event. Colin Chapman's Lotus team had been in Grand Prix racing for two years with very little success, but all that was to change with the new 18, the first rear-engined model.

BRM also had a new rear-engined car, which had debuted at Monza the previous year. Bonnier stayed on, joined by Graham Hill from Lotus and American Dan Gurney from Ferrari. Phil Hill and von Trips stayed with the Italian team, while Brabham and McLaren maintained their successful partnership at Cooper.

McLaren won the opening race in Argentina and Cliff Allison did well to get his Ferrari home second. Bonnier and Moss (still in Walker's old Cooper) had both led before retiring. Allison was seriously injured in practice at Monaco. Meanwhile, Moss got his hands on the new Lotus, and won in fine style in the rain, ahead of McLaren and Phil Hill. Once again, Bonnier's BRM led before retiring, while a notable newcomer was motorbike star John Surtees in a works Lotus.

Brabham had failed to score in either race, but bounced back by winning at Zandvoort. Innes Ireland took his Lotus to second, ahead of Graham Hill. For the second consecutive race Chapman gave a first chance to a future world champion. At Monaco it was Surtees and in Holland it was a young Scot called Jim Clark. He was battling for fourth when the gearbox broke.

Tragedy at Spa

Spa was one of the blackest weekends in Grand Prix history. During practice Moss crashed heavily, breaking his legs. Then two young Britons, Chris Bristow and Alan Stacey, were killed in separate accidents. Brabham and McLaren went on to score a Cooper one-two, but only after Hill's BRM blew up while running second.

At Reims Brabham took a third consecutive win, and on this fast track the front-engined Ferraris of Phil Hill and von Trips gave him a hard time until they broke. Graham Hill was the star at Silverstone. He stalled on the line, and drove superbly through to the lead before spinning off. Brabham came through to score his fourth straight win, followed by the very impressive Surtees and Ireland.

Victory for Brabham

Brabham scored a fifth win in Portugal, and with it clinched the title with two races still to run. After missing two races Moss was back, and ran second before he had problems.

Monza was a disappointment. The race was on the banked track once again, and the British teams boycotted it on safety grounds. Ferrari turned up in force, and Phil Hill scored a hollow victory.

The US Grand Prix moved from Sebring to Riverside in California, and Moss won. The race marked the demise of the 2.5-litre formula which had seen the transition from domination by Mercedes to the success of the British rear-engined machines.

CONSTRUCTORS' CUP

Pos.	Make	Pts
1	Cooper	40
2	Lotus	32
3	Ferrari	24
4	BRM	8
5	Porsche	1

DRIVERS' WORLD CHAMPIONSHIP

Pos.	Driver	Nat.	Make	Pts
1	Jack Brabham	Aus	Cooper-Climax	43
2	Bruce McLaren	NZ	Cooper-Climax	34
3	Stirling Moss	GB	Cooper/Lotus-Climax	19
4	Innes Ireland	GB	Lotus-Climax	18
5	Phil Hill	USA	Ferrari	16
6	Wolfgang von Trips	Ger	Ferrari	10
	Olivier Gendebien	Bel	Cooper-Climax	10
8	Richie Ginther	USA	Ferrari	8
	Jim Clark	GB	Lotus-Climax	8
	Jim Rathmann*	USA	Ken-Paul	8

Best six scores from ten races to count **denotes points scored in Indy 500*

1961

Ferrari was better prepared than anybody else for the new formula, and dominated the season. Phil Hill took the title, but in the most tragic circumstances after his team-mate, Wolfgang von Trips, lost his life at Monza.

It was all change for 1961 with the introduction of a 1.5-litre formula. The British manufacturers had been slow to respond, but not so Ferrari. Effectively sacrificing the previous season, the Italian team developed a rear-engined car, dubbed the "sharknose" – and a new V6 engine. Climax and BRM lagged behind, so much so that the only engine available for the British teams was the four-year-old 1475cc Climax F2.

Sharknose attack *Phil Hill on the last lap of his victorious drive in the Belgian Grand Prix.*

Arrival of Porsche

Von Trips, Phil Hill and American Richie Ginther were in the lucky position of having works Ferrari seats. Welcome variety was provided by Porsche. Already successful in Formula Two, the German marque signed Gurney and Bonnier from BRM. Lotus had an excellent new chassis, the 21, and the promising Jim Clark and Ireland to drive it. BRM and Cooper used developments of their old cars. Graham Hill and Brooks led the BRM attack, while once again Brabham and McLaren teamed up at Cooper.

More than ever before, Moss had underdog status. Walker was not allowed to buy a new Lotus 21, and had to make do with the old 18 model. And yet in Monaco Moss turned in one of the drives of his career, to brilliantly beat the Ferraris of Ginther and Hill.

Ferrari took its revenge when von Trips scored his first win at Zandvoort, with Hill in second. The result was reversed at Spa, where Ferrari finished one-two-three-four and Hill took his first win against a representative field, following that boycotted Monza race the previous year. Reims was a sensational race. Hill, Ginther and von Trips retired, and Giancarlo Baghetti – making his first start in a private Ferrari – just pipped Gurney's Porsche to the line. Baghetti remains the only driver to have won on his Grand Prix debut.

It was back to normal at Aintree as von Trips, Hill and Ginther finished one-two-three in the rain. Moss had tried to mix it with the Italian cars before his brakes failed, but then struck back at the Nurburgring. As at Monaco, he overcame the power deficiency to beat Ferrari, heading home Hill and von Trips. The new Climax V8 engine was finally ready.

Ferrari's revenge

Nobody objected to the banks at Monza this time. Ironically the race, which should have seen the title fight between von Trips and Hill reach a crucial stage, turned to tragedy. Clark and von Trips tangled early on, and the German star was killed, along with 12 spectators. Phil Hill won the race, and with it the title.

The US Grand Prix moved to a third new venue in as many years in the form of Watkins Glen. With Ferrari not entering, Moss and Brabham battled for the lead. When they both retired, Ireland came through to score his first (and only) win, and the first for the works Lotus team. Gurney was again second, ahead of the BRM of Brooks. At the end of the year Brooks announced his retirement, after a distinguished career which was often overshadowed by the heroic exploits of Moss and Hawthorn.

CONSTRUCTORS' CUP

Pos.	Make	Pts
1	Ferrari	40
2	Lotus	32
3	Porsche	22
4	Cooper	14
5	BRM	7

DRIVERS' WORLD CHAMPIONSHIP

Pos.	Driver	Nat.	Make	Pts
1	Phil Hill	USA	Ferrari	34
2	Wolfgang von Trips	Ger	Ferrari	33
3	Stirling Moss	GB	Lotus	21
	Dan Gurney	USA	Porsche	21
5	Richie Ginther	USA	Ferrari	16
6	Innes Ireland	GB	Lotus-Climax	12
7	Jim Clark	GB	Lotus-Climax	11
	Bruce McLaren	NZ	Cooper-Climax	11
9	Giancarlo Baghetti	It	Ferrari	9
10	Tony Brooks	GB	BRM	6

Best five scores from eight races to count

1962

Ferrari's star faded in the most dramatic fashion, as BRM and Lotus battled it out for the championship. Graham Hill beat Jim Clark to score his first title win at the beginning of another golden era for the British teams.

The biggest story of the 1962 season occurred in a non-championship race at Goodwood on Easter Monday. Stirling Moss suffered multiple injuries when he crashed his Lotus, and he was never to race at the top level again. Moss had not won a title, and yet had been at the top of the sport for a decade. Ferrari self-destructed over the winter, as some of the top staff walked out. The team carried on with virtually unchanged cars and drivers Phil Hill and Baghetti. Promising new boys, Mexican Ricardo Rodriguez, and Lorenzo Bandini, were also in the squad.

Ferrari in trouble

BRM had a powerful new V8 engine, and Graham Hill was joined by Ginther, who had left Ferrari. Meanwhile, the Climax V8 looked good and was the choice of many top teams. Brabham quit Cooper to design his own car – although he would start the year with a Lotus – so McLaren became team leader.

Lotus had another new car, the 25, which featured a revolutionary monocoque chassis. Clark and Trevor Taylor were the works drivers. An interesting newcomer was the Lola, entered by the Bowmaker team for John Surtees and Roy Salvadori, while Porsche had a new flat-eight engine for Gurney and Bonnier.

Unusually, the season opened at Zandvoort in May. Graham Hill scored his first win, and the first for BRM since Bonnier's victory at the same track three years earlier. Taylor finished second in only his second Grand Prix, ahead of Phil Hill. McLaren won at Monaco, chased home by Phil Hill in the Ferrari driver's best race of the year.

Spa was a historic occasion, as it marked the first win for Jim Clark, the Lotus driver coming home ahead of Graham and Phil Hill. Three marques had won the first three races, and it became four when Gurney gave Porsche its maiden victory at Rouen – but only after three leaders, Clark, Surtees and Graham Hill, had all retired.

Clark became the first repeat winner, dominating the British Grand Prix at Aintree ahead of Surtees and McLaren. Surtees continued his good form at the Nurburgring, finishing in second place behind Graham Hill's BRM, and just ahead of Gurney's Porsche.

Porsche first *Dan Gurney took the French Grand Prix.*

Dutch delight *Graham Hill leading at Zandvoort. Behind is Masten Gregory.*

Triumph for Graham Hill

Monza was the turning point in the title battle, for Graham Hill and Ginther gave BRM a one-two after a thrilling race, and Clark failed to finish. Clark fought back at Watkins Glen, heading Hill home.

For the first time the finale was held at East London in South Africa, on the amazingly late date of December 29. Clark took pole position, and was leading the race until his engine failed.

Graham Hill took the win and the championship crown. It was to be BRM's only success. McLaren finished second, and took third in the points after a consistent season as Cooper's top man.

It had been a poor year for Ferrari, and the team did not even enter the two final races. To make matters worse, up-and-coming star driver Rodriguez, who had finished fourth at Spa, was killed in practice for the non-championship Mexican Grand Prix. He was just 20.

DRIVERS' WORLD CHAMPIONSHIP

Pos.	Driver	Nat.	Make	Pts
1	Graham Hill	GB	BRM	42
2	Jim Clark	GB	Lotus-Climax	30
3	Bruce McLaren	NZ	Cooper-Climax	27
4	John Surtees	GB	Lola-Climax	19
5	Dan Gurney	USA	Porsche	15
6	Phil Hill	USA	Ferrari	14
7	Tony Maggs	SAf	Cooper-Climax	13
8	Richie Ginther	USA	BRM	10
9	Jack Brabham	Aus	Lotus/Brabham-Climax	9
10	Trevor Taylor	GB	Lotus-Climax	6

Best five scores from nine races to count

CONSTRUCTORS' CUP

Pos.	Make	Pts
1	BRM	42
2	Lotus	36
3	Cooper	29
4	Lola	19
5	Porsche	18
	Ferrari	18
7	Brabham	6

1963

The year proved to be a memorable one for Jim Clark and Lotus. Clark won seven races in all. It was the most devastating display of craftmanship by a single driver since the great triumph of Alberto Ascari 11 years previously.

Absent from the tracks in 1963 was the Porsche team, which had withdrawn to concentrate on sports car racing. The German marque would be back as an engine supplier more than 20 years later. The Lotus, BRM and Cooper line-ups were unchanged but, as usual, the off-season had been busy. Having lost his Porsche ride, Gurney teamed up with Jack Brabham to drive the double champ's own cars. The promising Bowmaker/Lola team withdrew, and the cars were bought by Reg Parnell for young Kiwi, Chris Amon.

With Bowmaker out, Surtees moved to Ferrari. He joined Belgian Willy Mairesse, who had shown some promise in the past. The Ferrari breakaway had spawned a new team, ATS, and a pair of works Ferrari drivers, Phil Hill and Baghetti, both jumped ship. They would come to regret their decision.

Monaco magic *Richie Ginther taking a corner ahead of Surtees and McLaren.*

Clark's great year

Clark led the opener at Monaco, but retired when the gearbox broke. It was to be his only retirement in an exceptionally reliable year for Lotus. With Clark out, Graham Hill and Ginther scored a one-two; it was the first of five successes in the principality for Graham.

BRM power *Graham Hill on his way to victory at the Monaco GP.*

Clark's luck changed at Spa, and he took a memorable win in the rain, ahead of McLaren and Gurney (scoring the Brabham team's first top three finish).

It was the same story at Zandvoort, where Clark led all the way to win from Gurney and Surtees, and at Reims, where even a misfire could not stop him. Clark scored his fourth win in a row at Silverstone, while Surtees took second after Graham Hill ran out of fuel on the last lap. Another motorcycle star trying four wheels was Mike Hailwood, who finished eighth. Surtees had threatened to win for a couple of years, and he finally came good at the Nurburgring, scoring Ferrari's first success since Monza in 1961. Clark took second, ahead of BRM's Ginther.

At Monza Ferrari had a new chassis, which owed a lot to Lotus thinking and was designed to accept the forthcoming 1964 spec V8 engine. John duly battled with Clark for the lead until the overworked V6 gave up. Clark headed home Ginther and McLaren, and clinched the championship – even though there were still three races to run.

Hill's mixed fortunes

Graham Hill had suffered from unreliability and sheer bad luck all year, but struck back as he headed Ginther and Clark home at Watkins Glen. By this time BRM had reverted to using its 1962 model. Clark was stymied by a flat battery, and had to start from the back. Pedro Rodriguez, brother of the late Ricardo, made his debut in a Lotus.

The Mexican Grand Prix was in the championship for the first time, and Clark scored his sixth win of the year. He added a record seventh in South Africa in December to cap an amazing season. Before dropped scores were taken into account, he had amassed 73 points. Brabham finished second in Mexico and then team-mate Gurney repeated the feat in South Africa, showing that "Black Jack" had got his sums right, and would be a force to reckon with.

CONSTRUCTORS' CUP

Pos.	Make	Pts
1	Lotus	54
2	BRM	36
3	Brabham	28
4	Ferrari	26
5	Cooper	25
6	Porsche	4

DRIVERS' WORLD CHAMPIONSHIP

Pos.	Driver	Nat.	Make	Pts
1	Jim Clark	GB	Lotus-Climax	54
2	Graham Hill	GB	BRM	29
	Richie Ginther	USA	BRM	29
4	John Surtees	GB	Ferrari	22
5	Dan Gurney	USA	Brabham-Climax	19
6	Bruce McLaren	NZ	Cooper-Climax	17
7	Jack Brabham	Aus	Brabham-Climax	14
8	Tony Maggs	SAf	Cooper-Climax	9
9	Innes Ireland	GB	BRP-BRM	6
	Lorenzo Bandini	It	Ferrari	6
	Jo Bonnier	Swe	Cooper-Climax	6

Best six scores from ten races to count

1964

John Surtees made racing history when he became the first man to win a World Championship on both two wheels and four. In a thrilling finale, Surtees, in his Ferrari, just outscored Graham Hill and Jim Clark.

DRIVERS' WORLD CHAMPIONSHIP

Pos.	Driver	Nat.	Make	Pts
1	John Surtees	GB	Ferrari	40
2	Graham Hill	GB	BRM	39
3	Jim Clark	GB	Lotus-Climax	32
4	Lorenzo Bandini	It	Ferrari	23
	Richie Ginther	USA	BRM	23
6	Dan Gurney	USA	Brabham-Climax	19
7	Bruce McLaren	NZ	Cooper-Climax	13
8	Jack Brabham	Aus	Brabham-Climax	11
	Peter Arundell	GB	Lotus-Climax	11
10	Jo Siffert	Swi	Brabham-BRM	7

Best six scores from ten races to count

CONSTRUCTORS' CUP

Pos.	Make	Pts
1	Ferrari	45
2	BRM	42
3	Lotus	37
4	Brabham	33
5	Cooper	16

Ferrari hopes looked up for 1964 as the new V8 engine was mated to the chassis which had shown promise at Monza the previous year. Surtees stayed on to lead the team alongside Lorenzo Bandini. Lotus produced an updated car for Clark, the 33. Peter Arundell was the team's new number two. Hill and Ginther stayed at BRM, and had a revised car, while Cooper tried to keep up with the new monocoque technology, updating a Formula Three chassis by welding on panels.

Fluctuating fortunes for Clark

Clark started on a high by leading at Monaco, but he had to pit when his rear roll-bar broke. Hill and Ginther scored another one-two for BRM and a late engine failure for Clark handed third place to team-mate Arundell. Clark made amends with a demonstration run to victory at Zandvoort, while Surtees gave notice of Ferrari's championship intentions with second place, ahead of the newcomer Arundell.

The Brabham team did not fare well in the early races, but at Spa Gurney led comfortably – until running out of fuel with two laps to go. In a farcical turn of events, Hill took the lead and suffered fuel pump failure; then McLaren also ran out of gas. This allowed a surprised Clark – who had made an early stop – to take victory. At least McLaren was able to coast home in second.

Gurney made amends at Rouen, by scoring a fine first victory for the Brabham team. Graham Hill pipped Brabham for third, while once again Clark led the early stages, before his engine failed.

For the first time the British Grand Prix moved to Brands Hatch, and Clark kept up his tradition of winning at home.

Hill was second and Surtees was happy to get third after two consecutive retirements. Surtees then began his surge towards the title by winning ahead of Hill and Bandini at the Nurburgring.

Success for Surteės

The first Austrian Grand Prix was held at Zeltweg, and took a high toll on machinery. Hill, Surtees, Clark, McLaren and Gurney were among the retirements, leaving Bandini to score his first Grand Prix win, ahead of Ginther. Jochen Rindt made a quiet debut in a Brabham-BRM.

Ferrari's run of success continued at Monza, where Surtees scored his second win of the year. It was a typically exciting slipstreamer and, after Clark and Gurney fell out, McLaren and Bandini completed the top three. Hill broke his clutch on the line in Italy, but kept his title challenge afloat by winning at Watkins Glen after Clark suffered engine problems. Surtees was second, ahead of an impressive Jo Siffert.

Three drivers went to the finale in Mexico City with a crack at the title. Hill led on 39 points, Surtees had 34 and outsider Clark 30. Hill was soon out of contention for points, and Clark looked set for the title. But with just two laps to go, he struck engine trouble. Surtees had worked his way up, and was waved into second by team-mate Bandini – it was enough to take the title from Hill.

Lotus laurels
Jim Clark with Colin Chapman.

1965

After retirements had robbed him during 1964, Jim Clark bounced back to win the 1965 title – and the Indy 500 – for Lotus. Once again a change of engine regulations at the end of the year was the signal of the passing of an era.

New boy *Stewart shone in his debut season in Formula One.*

The British teams struck back against Ferrari in 1965, with Lotus and Brabham using a new, 32-valve version of the Climax V8. Clark was joined by another new team-mate in the form of Mike Spence, who had driven at Monza for the team the previous year. Brabham and Gurney were joined by a newcomer from New Zealand called Denny Hulme, while Rob Walker entered Brabhams for Bonnier and Siffert.

Ferrari continued with Surtees and Bandini, and there was new competition, too, from Honda, who launched a full effort with Ginther and the little-known Ronnie Bucknum. Ginther's departure from BRM left a seat open alongside Graham Hill, and it was very ably filled by a promising young Scot who had not even driven in a Grand Prix; his name was Jackie Stewart. Talented Austrian Jochen Rindt joined McLaren at Cooper.

South Africa became the first race of the season rather than last, and Clark, still using the older Climax engine, scored a runaway win. Surtees continued his championship form with second, ahead of Hill. Debutant Stewart finished sixth.

Lotus at Indianapolis

Lotus was missing from the second race at Monaco. The team was competing instead at Indianapolis, where Clark notched up a historic first win for a rear-engined car. In his absence Hill scored a wonderful victory in the street classic, recovering from an early incident to pass Surtees and Bandini. Clark came back with a win at Spa in the wet, ahead of Stewart and McLaren, while Ginther picked up a point in the improving Honda. Clark and Stewart then repeated their double act in the French Grand Prix, held this year on the mountainous Clermont-Ferrand track.

Clark won the British Grand Prix at Silverstone for the fourth consecutive time. Clark continued his winning ways at Zandvoort, and for the third time countryman Stewart followed him home. The big surprise was the performance of Ginther, who led for two laps in the Honda.

Clark triumphant

At the Nurburgring Clark scored his sixth win of the year and his first on the daunting German track. With only six scores counting, he had reached maximum points, and the championship was his. He was in the lead pack at Monza and, after he retired with fuel pump trouble, Stewart scored a marvellous maiden win, fractionally ahead of Hill and Gurney. However, with the title sewn up, Clark's luck seemed to have deserted him. At Watkins Glen he retired with engine problems, and Hill scored BRM's third win of the year.

The season had a twist in the tail. In Mexico City Ginther gave Honda (and tyre maker Goodyear) a first win, leading from start to finish. It was the Californian's only win. The race also marked the end of the 1.5–l formula after four diverting years.

DRIVERS' WORLD CHAMPIONSHIP

Pos.	*Driver*	*Nat.*	*Make*	*Pts*
1	Jim Clark	GB	Lotus-Climax	54
2	Graham Hill	GB	BRM	40
3	Jackie Stewart	GB	BRM	33
4	Dan Gurney	USA	Brabham-Climax	25
5	John Surtees	GB	Ferrari	17
6	Lorenzo Bandini	It	Ferrari	13
7	Richie Ginther	USA	Honda	11
8	Bruce McLaren	NZ	Cooper-Climax	10
	Mike Spence	GB	Lotus-Climax	10
10	Jack Brabham	Aus	Brabham-Climax	9

CONSTRUCTORS' CUP

Pos.	*Make*	*Pts*
1	Lotus	54
2	BRM	45
3	Brabham	27
4	Ferrari	26
5	Cooper	14
6	Honda	11

Perfect score *Clark took six wins and the title.*

1966

It was all change in 1966 as the 3-litre formula was introduced and there was a race to get new engines ready in time. Jack Brabham was better prepared than most and earned a deserved third Championship in his own car.

Teams and engine builders were busy through the winter as they prepared for the new formula. There was no pukka new engine from Climax, so existing customers had to find their own solutions.

Brabham's technical success

The man who did the best job was undoubtedly Jack Brabham. He announced that he was using a new V8 from the Australian Repco company. The engine was not the most powerful, but it was reliable, light and compact, and mated well with an updated version of Brabham's existing chassis. Jack had not won a race himself since 1960, and the package was to give his career a new lease of life. With Dan Gurney moving on, Denny Hulme became his number two. Cooper had a more exotic solution, mating a Maserati V12 to a new chassis. Richie Ginther and Jochen Rindt were the works drivers, and Rob Walker bought one for Siffert.

Ex-Cooper driver Bruce McLaren followed Brabham's example and set up his own team, initially using a Ford engine sourced from Indy Car racing. Another driver to copy the Brabham example was Gurney, whose All-American Racers concern built the neat Eagle.

It was no surprise to see Ferrari follow the V12 route, and the Scuderia produced a promising new car for John Surtees. Lorenzo Bandini stayed on as his team-mate. Both BRM and Lotus were forced to use uprated 2-litre versions of their V8 and Climax engines. BRM had an unusual H16 under development, but it did not race until late in the year. That said, it started very well at Monaco where less powerful cars proved a match for the new machinery. Clark took pole but had an unlucky race, while Stewart won for BRM after Surtees had led with the new Ferrari.

Absolute champion *Jack Brabham in victorious pose at Silverstone.*

Spa turned to chaos when eight cars retired on the wet first lap, among them Stewart, who had the worst crash of his Formula One career. Surtees won after overcoming a challenge from Rindt's Cooper-Maserati. But a few weeks later John fell out with the Italian team and left to join Cooper.

A good year for Brabham

The new Brabham-Repco came good at Reims, Jack winning after Bandini had retired. Parkes finished a promising second. Brabham won again at Brands Hatch, with team-mate Hulme second. Jack picked up a third win at Zandvoort.

Brabham's winning streak continued at the Nurburgring, where he held off the Coopers of Surtees and Rindt. His luck ran out at Monza, where he retired. So did nearly all the top runners. Ferrari newcomer Ludovico Scarfiotti won.

Despite retiring in Italy, Brabham had clinched his third title. He was on pole at Watkins Glen, but retired. Clark won. Cooper-Maseratis finished second, third and fourth, and their good form continued in the finale in Mexico, won by Surtees.

DRIVERS' WORLD CHAMPIONSHIP

Pos.	Driver	Nat.	Make	Pts
1	Jack Brabham	Aus	Brabham-Repco	42
2	John Surtees	GB	Ferrari/Cooper-Maserati	28
3	Jochen Rindt	A	Cooper-Maserati	22
4	Denny Hulme	NZ	Brabham-Repco	18
5	Graham HIll	GB	BRM	17
6	Jim Clark	GB	Lotus-Climax/BRM	16
7	Jackie Stewart	GB	BRM	14
8	Lorenzo Bandini	It	Ferrari	12
	Mike Parkes	GB	Ferrari	12
10	Ludovico Scarfiotti	It	Ferrari	9

Best five scores from nine races to count

CONSTRUCTORS' CUP

Pos.	Make	Pts
1	Brabham	42
2	Ferrari	31
3	Cooper	30
4	BRM	22
5	Lotus	18
6	Eagle	4
7	Honda	3
	McLaren	3

1967

Brabham and Repco scored a second win through the efforts of Denny Hulme, but the story of the year was the arrival of the new Cosworth DFV engine. Packaged with the Lotus 49, it marked the beginning of an era.

Steady does it *Denny Hulme won but twice* en route *to the title.*

Lotus had struggled through 1966, but in March that year Colin Chapman had persuaded Ford to invest in a new engine, to be built by Cosworth. The British firm embarked on an all-new V8 design for 1967, which would initially be for the exclusive use of Lotus. Chapman drew a simple but effective car, the 49, to exploit it. He further strengthened his package by bringing Graham Hill back to join Clark.

That elevated Stewart to team-leader status at BRM, where he was joined by Spence. Chris Amon joined Bandini at Ferrari. Ex-Ferrari star Surtees was signed to lead Honda's effort, while Pedro Rodriguez joined Rindt at Cooper.

The season opened at the new Kyalami track in South Africa, and the race nearly saw a sensational win for privateer John Love in an old Cooper-Climax. A late stop for fuel dropped him to second, behind the Cooper-Maserati of Rodriguez.

Fiery end *Lorenzo Bandini's Ferrari alight and out of control at Monaco.*

Tragedy at Monaco

Grand Prix racing had been through a safe – or lucky – couple of seasons, but Ferrari ace Lorenzo Bandini was to lose his life at Monaco. He was leading when he crashed, and the car caught fire. Hulme won for Brabham, ahead of Hill and Amon.

Zandvoort saw the long-awaited debut of the Ford Cosworth and the Lotus 49. It was a historic day, for Clark took the win after poleman Hill's engine failed. At Spa Hill retired; then leader Clark had to pit for a plug change. Gurney took the often unreliable Eagle-Weslake to a memorable first (and only) win.

For one time only the French Grand Prix was staged at the Bugatti circuit at Le Mans. Both Lotuses broke their transmissions. It was obvious that their reliability could not back up their pace. That left Brabham and Hulme to finish one-two, ahead of Stewart. Lotus fortunes looked up at Silverstone, where Clark won the British Grand Prix for the fifth time in six years. Hill led much of the race, but had suspension problems before his engine blew. Kiwis Hulme and Amon finished second and third.

Mixed fortunes for Lotus

Lotus gremlins struck again at the Nurburgring, where Clark and Hill were both sidelined by suspension failures. Gurney looked set to win, but when the Weslake blew Hulme and Brabham scored a one-two.

For the first time the circus moved to the scenic Mosport track in Canada. Ignition problems put Clark out and – surprise surprise – Brabham and Hulme were there to take another one-two, with Hill a distant fourth. Clark was the hero at Monza, coming back from early problems to lead until he ran out of fuel. In a typically exciting finish, Surtees pipped Brabham to give Honda its first win of the 3-litre age. Luck swung to Lotus once again in Watkins Glen, where Clark and Hill managed a one-two.

Hulme had been a steady performer all year, and he just pipped his boss to the title in Mexico. Clark won from Brabham, but third was enough to keep Denny ahead.

CONSTRUCTORS' CUP

Pos.	Make	Pts
1	Brabham	67
2	Lotus	50
3	Cooper	28
4	Ferrari	20
	Honda	20
6	BRM	17
7	Eagle	13
8	McLaren	1

DRIVERS' WORLD CHAMPIONSHIP

Pos.	Driver	Nat.	Make	Pts
1	Denny Hulme	NZ	Brabham-Repco	51
2	Jack Brabham	Aus	Brabham-Repco	46
3	Jim Clark	GB	Lotus-BRM/Climax/Ford	41
4	John Surtees	GB	Honda	20
	Chris Amon	NZ	Ferrari	20
6	Pedro Rodriguez	Mex	Cooper-Maserati	15
	Graham Hill	GB	Lotus-BRM/Ford	15
8	Dan Gurney	USA	Eagle-Weslake	13
9	Jackie Stewart	GB	BRM	10
10	Mike Spence	GB	BRM	9

Best nine scores from 11 races to count

1968

Sponsorship and wings arrived on the Formula One scene, but the new developments were overshadowed by the death of Jim Clark. In the sad aftermath, Graham Hill bravely won his second title for the grieving Lotus team.

Several things happened in 1968 which were to have long-term effects on Formula One, but nothing shook the racing world quite as much as Jim Clark's death in a Formula Two race at Hockenheim. The season was perhaps most notable for the introduction of overt commercial sponsorship. The previously green and yellow Lotuses were now red, white and gold, thanks to backing from Gold Leaf cigarettes.

Double top *Graham Hill became world champion for the second time.*

Arrival of the DFV

Early in the year Lotus, Brabham and Ferrari began to experiment with downforce-enhancing wings, which soon became standard equipment. The DFV was made available to all comers, and for the next 15 years the engine would be both an affordable and competitive choice for anyone who wanted it.

Other big news was the arrival of Ken Tyrrell to run Matra-Fords. He scooped up Stewart as his driver, and the partnership would blossom for the next six seasons. Meanwhile Matra's own team, with Henri Pescarolo and Jean-Pierre Beltoise, became a serious force. Talented Belgian youngster Jacky Ickx joined Amon at Ferrari, while Hulme moved to join Bruce McLaren.

Clark and Hill continued to lead the Lotus challenge, with Siffert in a private Rob Walker car. A sign of what might have been came at Kyalami, when Clark dominated the race, ahead of team-mate Hill. By the next race, at the new Jarama track in Spain, Clark was gone. Jackie Oliver replaced him, and Hill revived Lotus morale with his first win with the 49, ahead of Hulme's McLaren. Graham then scored another victory at Monaco, where Richard Attwood finished a fine second in a BRM.

At Spa McLaren gave his marque its first victory after Stewart ran out of fuel. It was also the first win for a DFV in something other than a Lotus 49. The next was not long in coming, for Stewart gave Tyrrell's Matra-Ford its first win at Zandvoort. There was yet another different winner at Rouen, where young Ickx gave Ferrari its only win of the year in pouring rain. Surtees was second for Honda, but veteran team-mate Jo Schlesser was killed .

At Brands Hatch the popular Siffert gave Walker his first win in seven years with the private 49, heading home the Ferraris of Amon and Ickx after early leaders Hill and Oliver retired.

Belgian big wheel *Ferrari's Jacky also starred for Ford in sports cars.*

Stewart in fine form

The Nurburgring saw one of the greatest drives of all time, Stewart winning with a virtuoso performance in atrocious conditions. Hulme showed that his 1967 crown was deserved by winning the next two events at Monza and the Mont Tremblant circuit in Canada. At Watkins Glen newcomer Mario Andretti earned a sensational pole for Lotus, but Stewart took his third win of the year. In the Mexico City finale Stewart and Hill battled for the lead until Stewart fell back with handling problems, leaving Graham to score his third win of the year.

If the losses of Clark and Schlesser were not enough, BRM's Mike Spence was killed in a Lotus during practice at Indianapolis, and former Italian Grand Prix winner Ludovico Scarfiotti died in a hillclimb.

DRIVERS' WORLD CHAMPIONSHIP

Pos.	Driver	Nat.	Make	Pts
1	Graham Hill	GB	Lotus-Ford	48
2	Jackie Stewart	GB	Matra-Ford	36
3	Denny Hulme	NZ	McLaren-Ford	33
4	Jacky Ickx	Bel	Ferrari	27
5	Bruce McLaren	NZ	McLaren-Ford	22
6	Pedro Rodriguez	Mex	BRM	18
7	Jo Siffert	Swi	Lotus-Ford	12
	John Surtees	GB	Honda	12
9	Jean-Pierre Beltoise	Fr	Matra	11
10	Chris Amon	NZ	Ferrari	10

All scores counted

CONSTRUCTORS' CUP

Pos.	Make	Pts
1	Lotus	62
2	McLaren	51
3	Matra	45
4	Ferrari	32
5	BRM	28
6	Cooper	14
	Honda	14
8	Brabham	10

1969

Jackie Stewart marched forward to take the title with Ken Tyrrell's Matra-Ford, since there was virtually no one else who could offer a consistent challenge. It looked certain that now Stewart would be the man to beat.

Jackie Stewart had come close to the title the previous year, and in 1969 everything went his way. With Matra withdrawing its own team, all efforts were concentrated on Tyrrell's outfit. Stewart and team-mate Johnny Servoz-Gavin – who had impressed in 1968 – were joined by Jean-Pierre Beltoise. Rindt took up a golden opportunity and joined Hill at Lotus, while Ickx left Ferrari to replace him at Brabham. Jack had finally given up on Repco and joined the DFV bandwagon. Surtees was available because Honda had withdrawn at the end of 1968. The DFV supremacy had taken its toll. Also gone from the scene were Eagle-Weslake and Cooper-Maserati.

Six shot *Jackie Stewart won six times as he landed his first title.*

Four-wheel drive fiasco

The big development of the year was four-wheel drive. Matra, McLaren and Lotus all tried it, but it was a white elephant and none of the cars really worked. Stewart started the season in fine form, dominating the opening race at Kyalami. Andretti, who would have occasional drives in a third Lotus, gave him a hard time early on. Stewart won again at Montjuich Park circuit near Barcelona, but this time he was helped by retirements ahead. Amon's Ferrari broke when leading, while Lotus had a bad break. First Hill and then Rindt had huge crashes after their wings failed.

Rindt would have to miss Monaco, where the FIA announced an immediate ban on the high-mounted aerofoils which had proliferated. They soon crept back in, but in a new and less outrageous form, attached to the bodywork. Stewart and Amon both led but retired, allowing Hill to score a historic fifth win. Piers Courage finished second in a Brabham entered by Frank Williams — the first significant result for the British team owner.

The race at Spa was cancelled, and Rindt was fit enough to return at Zandvoort. He took pole and led until retiring, so Stewart scored another win. Jackie's fourth victory came at Clermont-Ferrand in France, where team-mate Beltoise did a good job to finish second.

Jackie's winning streak

Stewart won once more at Silverstone, where he battled hard with Rindt until the Austrian had to pit with a loose wing. Ickx had a good run to second with the Brabham, and two weeks later he went one better at the Nurburgring, where he gave the team its first win since 1967.

The Scot clinched the title with a sixth win in an epic, slipstreaming battle at Monza, where he headed home Rindt, Beltoise and McLaren. But, after such a run of success, Stewart failed to win any of the last three races. Ickx triumphed in Canada, Rindt scored his first success at Watkins Glen and Hulme provided more variety with a win for McLaren in Mexico. Missing from the Mexican race was Graham Hill, who had broken his legs in a massive accident at Watkins Glen. He was fit for the following season, but would never again win a Grand Prix.

DRIVERS' WORLD CHAMPIONSHIP

Pos.	Driver	Nat.	Make	Pts
1	Jackie Stewart	GB	Matra-Ford	63
2	Jacky Ickx	Bel	Brabham-Ford	37
3	Bruce McLaren	NZ	McLaren-Ford	26
4	Jochen Rindt	A	Lotus-Ford	22
5	Jean-Pierre Beltoise	Fr	Matra-Ford	21
6	Denny Hulme	NZ	McLaren-Ford	20
7	Graham Hill	GB	Lotus-Ford	19
8	Piers Courage	GB	Brabham-Ford	16
9	Jo Siffert	Swi	Lotus-Ford	15
10	Jack Brabham	Aus	Brabham-Ford	14

All scores counted

CONSTRUCTORS' CUP

Pos	Make	Pts
1	Matra	66
2	Brabham	51
3	Lotus	47
4	McLaren	40
5	Ferrari	7
	BRM	7

1970

Jochen Rindt was leading the Championship for Lotus when he lost his life at Monza, but the popular Austrian became the sport's first posthumous champion. In a dark year, Bruce McLaren and Piers Courage were also killed.

The big story of the winter was the arrival of March Engineering. Seemingly out of nowhere, the British company appeared at the first race with no fewer than five DFV-powered cars. March scored a coup by getting Ken Tyrrell's nod after Matra decided to come back with its own team and V12-powered cars. The works March team had strong drivers in Amon and Siffert. Ferrari looked well placed with the all-new 312B, and Ickx returned to drive it. BRM attracted backing from Yardley, and produced the much-improved P153.

Brabham had not won since the 1967 Canadian Grand Prix, but he started the year with a fine win in South Africa with his new BT33. Stewart led before dropping to third behind Hulme's McLaren.

On the way *Jochen Rindt (3) scored a surprise win at Monaco, taking the lead at the last corner.*

Early success for March

At Jarama Stewart gave March a win in the marque's second ever race. He was hounded by the rejuvenated Brabham, until Jack's engine broke. Brabham was to the fore at Monaco, holding off Rindt in a fine battle for the lead. But the Aussie slid off at the last corner, allowing Rindt to win. Tragedy struck before the next race in Belgium when Bruce McLaren was killed while testing a CanAm car at Goodwood. He had been a mainstay of Formula One since 1959.

BRM had not won since Monaco in 1966, but at Spa Rodriguez gave the team a sensational victory after holding off Amon's March. Zandvoort saw the delayed appearance of Chapman's slick new Lotus 72, and it scored a debut win in the hands of Rindt. Alas, Piers Courage perished when the De Tomaso crashed and caught fire. Another new face was dashing young Frenchman François Cevert, who joined Tyrrell when Servoz-Gavin abruptly retired. Rindt and the 72 won at Clermont-Ferrand, and then again at Brands Hatch after Brabham ran out of fuel, while leading Rookie Brazilian Emerson Fittipaldi drove a works Lotus 49C to eighth.

Ickx was having a bad season, with just four points on the board. He fought back with second in the German Grand Prix, held at Hockenheim, while Rindt took his fifth win. In Austria Ickx gave Ferrari a much-needed victory, heading home new team-mate Clay Regazzoni.

Death at Monza

Tragedy struck again in practice at Monza when Rindt crashed fatally after a mechanical failure; he was just 28 years old. The race went ahead without Lotus, and Regazzoni scored a fine win in only his fifth start. Rindt had led the title race comfortably, and the only man who could usurp him was Ickx. He led Regazzoni in a Ferrari one-two in Canada, finished fourth in Watkins Glen and then won in Mexico. It was not enough, but even he really did not want to win by default.

Canada saw the first appearance of another new marque. Ken Tyrrell had built his own car to replace the March. It showed promise in Stewart's hands, but would have to wait until 1971 for its first success.

CONSTRUCTORS' CUP

Pos.	Make	Pts
1	Lotus	59
2	Ferrari	55
3	March	48
4	Brabham	35
	McLaren	35
6	BRM	23
	Matra	23
8	Surtees	3

DRIVERS' WORLD CHAMPIONSHIP

Pos.	Driver	Nat.	Make	Pts
1	Jochen Rindt	A	Lotus-Ford	45
2	Jacky Ickx	Bel	Ferrari	40
3	Clay Regazzoni	Swi	Ferrari	33
4	Denny Hulme	NZ	McLaren-Ford	27
5	Jack Brabham	Aus	Brabham-Ford	25
	Jackie Stewart	GB	March/Tyrrell-Ford	25
7	Chris Amon	NZ	March-Ford	23
	Pedro Rodriguez	Mex	BRM	23
9	Jean-Pierre Beltoise	Fr	Matra	16
10	Emerson Fittipaldi	Bra	Lotus-Ford	12

All scores counted

1971

Jackie Stewart earned his second title with a dominant performance for Tyrrell. But once again, the year was tinged with sadness as racing recorded the deaths of two of the fastest and most popular stars on the circuits.

Super Swede *Ronnie Peterson driving a March-Ford came second overall without even winning a race.*

Jack Brabham was missing from the grids, having retired at the end of the previous year after 126 starts and three championships. He settled into life as a team owner, and Graham Hill signed up to drive.

The works March team had had a poor first season, and the star drivers left. Siffert joined Porsche sports car colleague Rodriguez at BRM, while Amon went to the promising Matra-Simca outfit. The third STP March driver, Mario Andretti, joined Ickx and Regazzoni to become Ferrari's third driver. Early in the year the Italian team lost Ignazio Giunti in a terrible sports car crash in Argentina.

To lead its challenge March signed up Ronnie Peterson, who had done a solid job in a private car the year before. The Swede soon emerged as a leading contender, although he would never actually win a race. Ferrari drew first blood in South Africa when Andretti scored his maiden triumph, although Hulme had looked set to win for McLaren. Stewart finished second and followed it up with wins in Barcelona and Monte Carlo. Peterson scored a fine second in the latter event.

Stewart struggled at a wet Zandvoort, finishing a disappointing 11th while Ickx won for Ferrari. The French Grand Prix moved to the modern Paul Ricard facility, where Stewart and Cevert scored a fine one-two. Not long afterward BRM star Rodriguez, who had finished second in Holland, was killed in a minor sports car race at the Norisring.

Stewart won again at Silverstone, followed home by Peterson and then, at the Nurburgring, he and Cevert picked up their second one-two; it was a repeat of the Scot's 1969 form. BRM bounced back in fine style with a sensational win for Siffert in Austria and an even more spectacular one for Peter Gethin at Monza. In Austria few noticed the low-key debut of Niki Lauda in a rented March, while at Monza Amon looked set to finally score his first win in the Matra-Simca – until he accidentally ripped off his visor in the closing laps. He finished sixth.

A good year for Jackie

Stewart's engine had broken in Italy, but he bounced back with a win in Canada, Peterson coming again second. In the finale at Watkins Glen it was the turn of Cevert to score his maiden win, after Stewart slipped to fifth with tyre troubles. The title was long since his in his pocket. Peterson was the big find of the year, finishing second in the championship thanks to his consistent results. Cevert, another brilliant youngster, took third.

Lotus had a disappointing year, the marque failing to win a race for the first time since 1960. A lot of effort was wasted with an Indy-derived gas turbine car, which never lived up to expectations. In October tragedy struck again: Siffert was killed when his BRM crashed and caught fire in a non-championship race at Brands Hatch. It was a sad end to the season.

DRIVERS' WORLD CHAMPIONSHIP

Pos.	Driver	Nat.	Make	Pts
1	Jackie Stewart	GB	Tyrrell-Ford	62
2	Ronnie Peterson	Swe	March-Ford	33
3	François Cevert	Fr	Tyrrell-Ford	26
4	Jacky Ickx	Bel	Ferrari	19
	Jo Siffert	Swi	BRM	19
6	Emerson Fittipaldi	Bra	Lotus-Ford	16
7	Clay Regazzoni	Swi	Ferrari	13
8	Mario Andretti	It	Ferrari	12
9	Chris Amon	NZ	Matra-Simca	9
	Peter Gethin	GB	BRM	9
	Denny Hulme	NZ	BRM	9
	Pedro Rodriguez	Mex	BRM	9
	Reine Wisell	Swe	Lotus-Ford	9

All scores counted

CONSTRUCTORS' CUP

Pos.	Driver	Pts
1	Tyrrell	73
2	BRM	36
3	March	34
4	Ferrari	33
5	Lotus	21
6	McLaren	10
7	Matra	9
8	Surtees	8

1972

Lotus returned once again to the top of the podium. Its rising star, Emerson Fittipaldi, who had shown much promise the previous year, became the youngest champion. There was no one else able to offer a season-long challenge.

Lotus went into 1972 armed with an updated version of the rather appropriately named 72 chassis, plus a dramatic new colour scheme. Gold Leaf had been replaced by the black and gold hues of John Player Special. The cigarette brand would become completely synonymous with the car, which would soon be known purely as a JPS. Other sponsors had been in the news as well. Yardley left BRM to join a revitalized McLaren effort, in which Hulme was partnered by Peter Revson, returning some eight years after a shaky debut in the mid-1960s.

Meanwhile BRM found major backing from Marlboro and, in what proved to be an over-ambitious plan, ran up to five cars per race. There were some changes at Brabham, which was acquired by businessman Bernie Ecclestone. Hill was joined by Argentina's Carlos Reutemann, the first talent to emerge from that country since the 1950s.

Newcomer Reutemann stunned the field when he took pole for his debut race at Buenos Aires, but it was back to normal in the race when he had to pit for tyres and Stewart won from Hulme. The Kiwi went one better in South Africa, giving McLaren its first win since the 1969 Mexican Grand Prix.

Fittipaldi gave JPS its first win in the non-championship event at Brands Hatch, and then dominated the Spanish Grand Prix. Monaco brought a total surprise when, in wet conditions, Beltoise drove a fine race for BRM. It was to be the marque's last ever win.

Fittipaldi won at the new and boring Nivelles track in Belgium, and Stewart triumphed at Clermont-Ferrand after Amon again lost a race in the late stages – this time with a puncture. Ickx's Ferrari led the British Grand Prix until the Belgian was stricken with an oil leak, allowing Fittipaldi to win. Ickx fought back with victory at the Nurburgring, ahead of team-mate Regazzoni. Fittipaldi won the next race in Austria and then triumphed again at Monza to clinch the title.

Shock result *Jean-Pierre Beltoise popped up to win for BRM at Monaco.*

Mixed fortunes for Stewart

Stewart had not had much luck, but a new car, introduced in Austria, improved his form. He finished the season with wins at Mosport and Watkins Glen, heading home Revson in the first race and Cevert in the latter. It was enough for Jackie to make a late run to second place in the championship, ahead of Hulme. The previous year's runner-up, Peterson, had a poor season. March's new car failed and a slightly more successful replacement was hastily built. However, Peterson had impressed the right people: for 1973 he earned himself a Lotus ride, alongside champion Fittipaldi.

But there was sad news for Ronnie's country as well. In June veteran Jo Bonnier was killed when his Lola crashed at Le Mans. He raced from 1957 to 1971, but never matched the form which had given him BRM's first win in 1959.

CONSTRUCTORS' CUP

Pos.	Make	Pts
1	Lotus	61
2	Tyrrell	51
3	McLaren	47
4	Ferrari	33
5	Surtees	18
6	March	15
7	BRM	14
8	Matra	12
9	Brabham	7

DRIVERS' WORLD CHAMPIONSHIP

Pos.	Driver	Nat.	Make	Pts
1	Emerson Fittipaldi	Bra	Lotus-Ford	61
2	Jackie Stewart	GB	Tyrrell-Ford	45
3	Denny Hulme	NZ	McLaren-Ford	39
4	Jacky Ickx	Bel	Ferrari	27
5	Pete Revson	USA	McLaren-Ford	23
6	François Cevert	Fr	Tyrrell-Ford	15
	Clay Regazzoni	Swi	Ferrari	15
8	Mike Hailwood	GB	Surtees-Ford	13
9	Chris Amon	NZ	Matra	12
	Ronnie Peterson	Swe	March-Ford	12

All scores counted

Brazilian hero *Emerson Fittipaldi claimed the crown for Lotus.*

1973

Jackie Stewart acquired his third title after a hard battle with Lotus and decided to quit while he was at the top. Once again the season was blighted, with the deaths of François Cevert and newcomer Roger Williamson.

Colin Chapman's fortunes certainly looked good. Fittipaldi and Peterson represented a Lotus team of two top drivers, but some people remembered the previous time the team tried that with Rindt and Hill in 1969 – and Stewart won the championship.

Stewart and Cevert had developed into a fine partnership, and Hulme and Revson looked good at McLaren. Ickx was joined at Ferrari by little Arturo Merzario, who had run a few races in 1972, while Regazzoni left to join Marlboro BRM. An intriguing new marque was the American-financed Shadow. The sinister black cars were handled by Jackie Oliver and George Follmer, an American veteran with no Formula One experience. Graham Hill quit Brabham to set up his own team.

Tyrrell wins
Jackie Stewart and François Cevert finished one–two in Holland.

Fittipaldi begins well

Fittipaldi had a dream start to his title defence, winning in both Argentina and his native Brazil. The first was by no means easy, since Regazzoni and Cevert both led before having problems. In South Africa McLaren introduced the sleek and very modern-looking M23, which would ultimately have a lifetime of six seasons. Hulme put it on pole, but fell to fifth as Stewart scored a fine win after a heavy practice crash. Hailwood became a hero in the race as he rescued Regazzoni from his burning car.

Fittipaldi scored a third win in Spain, and then Stewart added a second in Belgium, where the track broke up and many cars skated off. Jackie won again in Monaco to make it three each for the main contenders. The race saw the debut of Briton James Hunt, in a March run by aristocrat Lord Hesketh.

For the first time Sweden hosted a race at the Anderstorp circuit and, although local hero Peterson was on pole, Hulme gave the M23 its maiden victory. Ronnie got his revenge in France, finally scoring his first win after suffering appalling luck in the early races. It did not help him much at Silverstone, where the race was stopped after a multi-car pile-up was triggered by Jody Scheckter. Revson won the restarted race after Stewart spun out.

Death at Zandvoort

Tragedy returned to Zandvoort, when Roger Williamson – in only his second race – was killed in a fiery crash. Stewart and Cevert scored a one-two, a feat they repeated in Germany. In Austria, Peterson waved Fittipaldi through, but won anyway when Emerson retired. At Monza Peterson and Fittipaldi finished one-two, but the title went to Stewart. After an early stop he charged through the field to an amazing fourth place.

Revson won the chaotic, rain-hit Canadian race, which saw the first use of a pace car in Formula One. The circus moved to Watkins Glen where Stewart planned to have his 100th and last Grand Prix. But Cevert was killed in practice, and Tyrrell withdrew. It was a bitter end to a fantastic farewell season for JYS. In the race Peterson picked up a fourth win, but he was pushed hard by the fast-improving Hunt.

CONSTRUCTORS' CUP

Pos.	Make	Pts
1	Lotus	92
2	Tyrrell	82
3	McLaren	58
4	Brabham	22
5	March	14
6	BRM	12
	Ferrari	12
8	Shadow	9
9	Surtees	7
10	Iso	2

DRIVERS' WORLD CHAMPIONSHIP

Pos.	Driver	Nat.	Make	Pts
1	Jackie Stewart	GB	Tyrrell-Ford	71
2	Emerson Fittipaldi	Bra	Lotus-Ford	55
3	Ronnie Peterson	Swe	Lotus-Ford	52
4	François Cevert	Fr	Tyrrell-Ford	47
5	Pete Revson	USA	McLaren-Ford	38
6	Denny Hulme	NZ	McLaren-Ford	26
7	Carlos Reutemann	Arg	Brabham-Ford	16
8	James Hunt	GB	March-Ford	14
9	Jacky Ickx	Bel	Ferrari	12
10	Jean-Pierre Beltoise	Fr	BRM	9

All scores counted

1974

This was one of the closest championships for years, in which Fittipaldi and Regazzoni battled for top position. In a dramatic finale Fittipaldi claimed his second title – a first for the McLaren marque. At the year's end Denny Hulme retired.

The winter of 1973–74 was one of the busiest in memory. The big news was that Fittipaldi quit Lotus to join McLaren, along with substantial new backing from Texaco and Marlboro. Hulme stayed on as his team-mate, while a third car – in Yardley colours – was entered for Hailwood.

Ickx left Ferrari to join Peterson at Lotus, while Tyrrell found himself needing two new drivers. He hired Scheckter from McLaren and French newcomer Patrick Depailler. Revson also left McLaren, joining French youngster Jean-Pierre Jarier at Shadow. Hill's team swapped from Shadow to Lola chassis, while Hesketh built its own car for Hunt. BRM had new French sponsors, and Beltoise led a squad of three French drivers. Amon's career took another dive as he tried to run his own team.

Shake-up at Ferrari

At Ferrari personnel changed and a completely new car was produced. Regazzoni rejoined after a year at BRM, and brought with him Lauda, who had shown some promise. From the start the revised Ferrari line-up was competitive. Hulme won the first race in Argentina, but Regazzoni qualified on the front row and Lauda took second in the race.

In Brazil Peterson and Fittipaldi duelled for the lead until the Swede punctured, leaving Emerson to score McLaren's second. Reutemann led that race, too, and finally came good by winning in Kyalami – Brabham's first success for exactly four years. Sadly, in pre-race testing Revson was killed when he crashed the Shadow.

At Jarama Ferrari's promise produced results when Lauda won. Fittipaldi scored a second win in Nivelles, and then Peterson triumphed at Monaco. Two weeks later Tyrrell new boys Scheckter and Depailler scored a brilliant one-two in Sweden.

Lauda and Regazzoni scored a Ferrari one-two in the French Grand Prix at the new Dijon track, and then Scheckter took his second at Brands Hatch. Lauda led until puncturing near the end, and his exit from the pit lane was controversially blocked by hangers-on and an official car. He was eventually awarded fifth. At the Nurburgring Lauda threw it away on the first lap, leaving Regazzoni to save face for Ferrari. Reutemann won in Austria, and then Peterson was on top at Monza when the Ferraris failed.

Fittipaldi stakes claim

Fittipaldi made his claim in the penultimate race at Mosport, winning ahead of Regazzoni. Incredibly, they went into the final race on equal points. In the end a fourth place was enough for Emmo, with neither of his rivals scoring. McLaren also beat Ferrari to the constructors' title. But the race was marred by the death of Austrian rookie Helmuth Koinigg. The North American events saw the debut of two intriguing new marques from the USA, which had long been without representation in Formula One. Penske and Parnelli had plans to compete in Europe.

DRIVERS' WORLD CHAMPIONSHIP

Pos.	Driver	Nat.	Make	Pts
1	Emerson Fittipaldi	Bra	McLaren-Ford	55
2	Clay Regazzoni	Swi	Ferrari	52
3	Jody Scheckter	SAf	Tyrrell-Ford	45
4	Niki Lauda	A	Ferrari	38
5	Ronnie Peterson	Swe	Lotus-Ford	35
6	Carlos Reutemann	Arg	Brabham-Ford	32
7	Denny Hulme	NZ	McLaren-Ford	20
8	James Hunt	GB	Hesketh-Ford	15
9	Patrick Depailler	Fr	Tyrrell-Ford	14
10	Mike Hailwood	GB	McLaren-Ford	12
	Jacky Ickx	Bel	Lotus-Ford	12

All scores counted

CONSTRUCTORS' CUP

Pos.	Make	Pts
1	McLaren	73
2	Ferrari	65
3	Tyrrell	52
4	Lotus	42
5	Brabham	35
6	Hesketh	15
7	BRM	10
8	Shadow	7
9	March	6
10	Iso	4

New hues *McLaren gained Texaco and Marlboro. And another title.*

1975

Niki Lauda dominated the season in brilliant style. Amazing to record, it was Ferrari's first championship since Surtees had triumphed 11 years earlier. Graham Hill's death in a plane crash brought a tragic end to the year.

The winter season saw few changes among the front-runners. Graham Hill planned a switch from Lola to his own Hill team. Following the first two races, he announced his retirement after an incredible 176 starts.

Jean-Pierre Jarier had shown flair on occasions, but no one expected him to start the new season in the way he did. He gave Shadow its first pole in Argentina, but non-started when the transmission broke on the warm-up lap. Fittipaldi won for McLaren, ahead of Hunt's Hesketh after the Englishman lost the lead with a mistake.

In Brazil Jarier again took pole, and led for 28 laps before retiring. Pace scored a popular first win in his home country, ahead of local hero Fittipaldi. Pace and Reutemann shared the front row in South Africa, but Scheckter scored a home win for Tyrrell.

Ferrari flier *Niki Lauda came on strong and claimed the crown.*

Disaster at Montjuich

At the Spanish race the Ferraris were the pacesetters, with Lauda and Regazzoni on the front row. But the event was beset by a dispute over safety standards at the Montjuich Park track. Eventually a boycott was avoided, but the race turned to chaos. Half the field crashed, including the Ferraris. Rolf Stommelen led in the Hill, but crashed when the rear wing broke, killing several onlookers. The race was stopped early with Mass leading.

In a soaking wet race at Monaco Lauda and the 312T came good, winning from Fittipaldi. Lauda followed that with wins at Zolder and Anderstorp. Zandvoort brought a popular first win for Hunt and the Hesketh team. Neither had been taken seriously when they started two years earlier, but James had developed into a top-rank driver, and in Holland beat Lauda in a dramatic wet/dry fight. The result was reversed when Lauda won at sunny Paul Ricard.

Golden boy *James Hunt scored his first win in Holland.*

Silverstone chaos

The rain returned at Silverstone – for another dramatic weekend which saw 15 cars crash. Pryce stunned everyone with pole and he, Pace, Regazzoni, Jarier and Hunt all took turns in the lead. When the crashes finally forced a red flag, Fittipaldi was ahead. Surprisingly, it was to prove his last ever Formula One victory.

In Germany, Reutemann survived as most of the front-runners had punctures, and then in Austria rain and confusion struck once more. The popular Brambilla was ahead when the race was curtailed to give the works March team its first win – and the first for any March since 1970. Tragically, however, American driver Mark Donohue crashed his Penske-entered March in the warm-up and subsequently succumbed to head injuries.

Lauda had been quietly racking up the points, and clinched his first title with a third at Monza, as team-mate Regazzoni won. Just Watkins Glen remained, and Lauda added yet another win. Lotus had its worst season to date, Peterson and Ickx wasting their time with the ancient 72.

November brought a tragedy which shocked the racing world. On the way back from a test session at Paul Ricard, Hill crashed his light plane. The double world champion and several of his team were killed.

CONSTRUCTORS' CUP

Pos.	Make	Pts
1	Ferrari	72.5
2	Brabham	54
3	McLaren	53
4	Hesketh	33
5	Tyrrell	25
6	Shadow	9.5
7	Lotus	9
8	March	6.5
9	Williams	6
10	Parnelli	5

DRIVERS' WORLD CHAMPIONSHIP

Pos.	Driver	Nat.	Make	Pts
1	Niki Lauda	A	Ferrari	64.5
2	Emerson Fittipaldi	Bra	McLaren-Ford	45
3	Carlos Reutemann	Arg	Brabham-Ford	37
4	James Hunt	GB	Hesketh-Ford	33
5	Clay Regazzoni	Swi	Ferrari	25
6	Carlos Pace	Bra	Brabham-Ford	24
7	Jochen Mass	Ger	McLaren-Ford	20
	Jody Scheckter	SAf	Tyrrell-Ford	20
9	Patrick Depailler	Fr	Tyrrell-Ford	12
10	Tom Pryce	GB	Shadow-Ford	8

All scores counted

1976

This season will go down as one of the most dramatic in the history of Formula One. Niki Lauda survived a terrible accident in Germany and was quickly back in harness, but James Hunt beat him to the title in the Japanese finale.

As in 1974, Emerson Fittipaldi was at the centre of the news. After two years he decided to quit McLaren and join his brother's team, Copersucar. McLaren was left stranded without a number one driver, but the timing was perfect.

Lord Hesketh had decided to pull the plug on his very competitive team, and Hunt was unemployed. It did not take long for him to find his way to McLaren. Ferrari, Shadow, Brabham and Tyrrell continued as before, but there were a couple of novelties on the car front.

Brabham secured Alfa engines, while Tyrrell stunned everyone by announcing a six-wheeled car, the P34. There was confusion at Lotus. Chapman designed a new car, the 77. Ickx left for Wolf-Williams, and Peterson was joined at the first race by Andretti, a Lotus driver back in 1968–69. Neither was certain to stay, and matters were not helped when they collided in the first race in Brazil.

Once again Jarier shone in Interlagos, while Hunt repaid McLaren's faith with pole. But Lauda started, as he had finished the previous season, with a win. Hunt was on pole in Kyalami, but again Lauda won. Peterson had quit Lotus to rejoin March. An exciting addition to the calendar was a street race at Long Beach in California, dubbed the US Grand Prix West. Regazzoni led the whole way.

The European season began at Jarama. All the cars were different since new rules banned tall air boxes, and the race saw the debut of the six-wheeler. Hunt beat Lauda, but was disqualified when the car was found to be fractionally too wide. Lauda won in Belgium and Monaco, and at neither race did Hunt score. Sweden saw a fabulous one-two for the six-wheelers, Scheckter heading home Depailler. Hunt's luck turned at Paul Ricard, when the Ferraris broke and he won easily. The same week he was reinstated as Spanish winner, but at Brands Hatch fortune did not favour him. Lauda and Regazzoni collided at the first corner, Hunt became involved and the race was stopped. He won the restart in brilliant style, but was disqualified because he had not been running at the time of the red flag. It gave Lauda another win.

In Germany disaster struck when Lauda crashed heavily and was badly burned. Hunt won the race, but the world waited for news on Lauda. Somehow he pulled through and began a remarkable recovery. Unbelievably, Lauda was back in Monza, where Peterson won for March and Niki finished fourth. Hunt scored nothing, but struck back with wins at Mosport and Watkins Glen. That put him to within three points of Lauda as the circus moved to Fuji for the first Japanese Grand Prix. The weather was atrocious, and Lauda immediately pulled out. In a thrilling chase, Hunt came storming back from a tyre stop to take the third place he required.

CONSTRUCTORS' CUP

Pos.	Make	Pts
1	Ferrari	83
2	McLaren	71
	Tyrell	71
4	Lotus	29
5	Ligier	20
	Penske	20
7	March	19
8	Shadow	10
9	Brabham	9
10	Surtees	7

DRIVERS' WORLD CHAMPIONSHIP

Pos.	Driver	Nat.	Make	Pts
1	James Hunt	GB	McLaren-Ford	69
2	Niki Lauda	A	Ferrari	68
3	Jody Scheckter	SAf	Tyrrell-Ford	49
4	Patrick Depailler	Fr	Tyrrell-Ford	39
5	Clay Regazzoni	Swi	Ferrari	31
6	Mario Andretti	USA	Parnelli/Lotus-Ford	22
7	Jacques Laffite	Fr	Ligier-Matra	20
	John Watson	GB	Penske-Ford	20
9	Jochen Mass	Ger	McLaren-Ford	19
10	Gunnar Nilsson	Swe	Lotus-Ford	11

All scores counted

British hero *James Hunt struggled at Monaco, but triumphed six times.*

Pit-lane glamour *James Hunt and his first wife Suzy.*

1977

Niki Lauda was most certainly not the fastest driver, but he was consistent and the Ferrari proved to be extremely reliable. He succeeded in beating off strong challenges from Andretti, Hunt and Scheckter to win his second title.

Masked man *Niki Lauda put the horrors of 1976 behind him to win again.*

After three seasons Scheckter quit Tyrrell to join an intriguing new team, Walter Wolf Racing. Hunt and Mass stayed at McLaren to drive the new M26, the replacement for the ageing M23 and, even before the end of 1976, Reutemann left Brabham to join Ferrari. Peterson replaced Scheckter at Tyrrell, and Watson left the now defunct Penske team to replace Reutemann at Brabham.

Debut of the 78

Chapman had pulled another surprise, providing Andretti and his new team-mate, Gunnar Nilsson, with the stunning 78, the first "ground-effects" car. It had prominent side pods with sliding skirts which produced masses of down force The latest Brabham-Alfa was quick, Watson leading the opening race in Argentina until it broke. Team-mate Pace and Hunt also led, but victory went to Scheckter and the new Wolf. Ferrari was also competitive. Reutemann won in Brazil, and then at Kyalami Lauda scored his first success since his accident. The race was marred by the death of Tom Pryce, the Welshman hitting a marshal who ran across the track. Before the next race Carlos Pace lost his life in a plane crash.

Scheckter led most of the way at Long Beach but, when he punctured, Andretti went ahead to give the Lotus 78 its first win. He quickly added a second in Spain.

Scheckter took his second of the season in Monaco, which marked the 100th win for the Cosworth DFV. In Belgium there was a typically confusing wet race and it resulted in a fine win for Nilsson in the second Lotus. Hunt had had no luck in his title defence, but at Silverstone he beat Watson in a splendid duel. The race saw the debut of Jean-Pierre Jabouille's Renault and its V6 turbocharged engine.

Success for Lauda

Lauda scored Goodyear's 100th win in Hockenheim, and once again Austria produced an unusual result, Aussie Jones giving Shadow its first win in another damp encounter.

The summer witnessed a spate of Cosworth engine failures. Andretti had four in a row, and Hunt and Scheckter also suffered. Meanwhile, Lauda quietly racked up the points, scoring another win in Holland. Mario's car held together long enough for him to win in Monza. At a wet Watkins Glen Hunt won after Stuck crashed, but Lauda's fourth place clinched the title. With that, he upped and left Ferrari.

There were still two races left. Scheckter won in Canada, after Mass tipped team-mate Hunt off. James ended on a high note with a win in Japan, where this time the sun shone. But the race was marred by the deaths of two spectators after Ferrari new boy Gilles Villeneuve tangled with Peterson and the car flipped over the barrier.

Fittipaldi had another bad season with his own car, although he occasionally broke into the top six, while Peterson and Depailler struggled all year with the latest six-wheeler. At the end of the year Tyrrell ditched the concept. In contrast, fellow veteran Regazzoni did great things with the little Ensign team, picking up a few points.

CONSTRUCTORS' CUP

Pos.	Make	Pts
1	Ferrari	95
2	Lotus	62
3	McLaren	60
4	Wolf	55
5	Brabham	27
	Tyrrell	27
7	Shadow	23
8	Ligier	18
9	Copersucar	11
10	Ensign	10

DRIVERS' WORLD CHAMPIONSHIP

Pos.	Driver	Nat.	Make	Pts
1	Niki Lauda	A	Ferrari	72
2	Jody Scheckter	SAf	Wolf-Ford	55
3	Mario Andretti	USA	Lotus-Ford	47
4	Carlos Reutemann	Arg	Ferrari	42
5	James Hunt	GB	McLaren-Ford	40
6	Jochen Mass	Ger	McLaren-Ford	25
7	Alan Jones	Aus	Shadow-Ford	22
8	Patrick Depailler	Fr	Tyrrell-Ford	20
	Gunnar Nilsson	Swe	Lotus-Ford	20
10	Jacques Laffite	Fr	Ligier-Matra	18

All scores counted

1978

Mario Andretti won the title after a brilliant run with Chapman's wonderful Lotus 79. But it was a year of mixed feelings for Mario, as team-mate Ronnie Peterson died from injuries received in a first-lap accident at Monza.

Nobody seemed to cotton on to the secrets of the Lotus 78, and rival teams were in for a shock when Colin Chapman introduced the beautiful 79. He had a new second driver, too: Peterson was back at Lotus, eager to restore his reputation. Meanwhile, Nilsson left to join Arrows, a team formed by a breakaway group from Shadow. Another former Shadow driver, Alan Jones, also linked up with what was effectively a new team.

Newcomer Didier Pironi joined Depailler in the four-wheel Tyrrell 008, while Patrick Tambay replaced Mass at McLaren. Villeneuve landed a full-time seat at Ferrari, alongside Reutemann. The new 312T3 was a superb machine, and the Italian team switched to Michelin, which had been introduced to Formula One by Renault.

Andretti's year

Starting the season with the old 78, Andretti won in Argentina, Lauda coming second. In Brazil Reutemann won for Ferrari, and Fittipaldi finally came good with second in the "family car". Kyalami was a classic. Patrese led in the new Arrows, and the race culminated in a fabulous duel between Peterson and Depailler, Ronnie just winning. Villeneuve starred at Long Beach, leading until he hit back marker Regazzoni and allowed Reutemann to score. Monaco saw Depailler finally earn his first win. In Belgium Mario debuted the 79, and gave notice of his intentions by disappearing into the distance, with Peterson taking second in the 78. They scored another one-two in Jarama.

By now the others were reacting. Scheckter had a proper ground-effect Wolf, and Brabham responded with the amazing "fan car". Lauda dominated in its only race at Anderstorp before it was abruptly banned. Mario and Ronnie scored a one-two in France. At Brands Hatch they both retired, and Reutemann passed Lauda to take his third win of the year.

Tragedy at Monza

Rain struck in Austria, and Peterson drove brilliantly to win the red-flagged race. At Monza, only Peterson could now beat Mario to the title, but he was happy to obey orders. He had to take the start in the old 78, and became entangled in a massive pile-up. After a long delay the race was restarted. Mario won from Villeneuve, but both were penalized for jumped starts. Lauda took the honours. Peterson died the following morning, and the racing world was stunned.

Jean-Pierre Jarier replaced him, and was the star of the last two races, although he and Mario retired in both events. Reutemann held off the improving Jones in Watkins Glen, while Villeneuve scored a popular win on a new track in Montreal.

There was more sadness when Nilsson succumbed to cancer 12 days after the Canadian race. He was just 29 years old.

Lotus domination *Andretti leads Peterson to another one–two in Holland.*

CONSTRUCTORS' CUP

Pos.	Make	Pts
1	Lotus	86
2	Ferrari	58
3	Brabham	53
4	Tyrrell	38
5	Wolf	24
6	Ligier	19
7	Copersucar	17
8	McLaren	15
9	Arrows	11
	Williams	11

DRIVERS' WORLD CHAMPIONSHIP

Pos.	Driver	Nat.	Make	Pts
1	Mario Andretti	USA	Lotus-Ford	64
2	Ronnie Peterson	Swe	Lotus-Ford	51
3	Carlos Reutemann	Arg	Ferrari	48
4	Niki Lauda	A	Brabham-Alfa Romeo	44
5	Patrick Depailler	Fr	Tyrrell-Ford	34
6	John Watson	GB	Brabham-Alfa Romeo	25
7	Jody Scheckter	SAf	Wolf-Ford	24
8	Jacques Laffite	Fr	Ligier-Matra	19
9	Emerson Fittipaldi	Bra	Copersucar-Ford	17
	Gilles Villeneuve	Can	Ferrari	17

All scores counted

1979

Ground-effect cars took over the Formula One scene, although some worked better than others. In a very competitive season the reliability of the Ferraris gave them top place and helped Jody Scheckter to scoop the title.

Canadian hero *Gilles Villeneuve won three times for Ferrari.*

World Champion *Jody Scheckter was a model of consistency.*

Things looked good at Lotus as Ferrari ace Reutemann joined Andretti, Martini replaced JPS as title sponsor and Chapman still had the inside line on new technology. Or did he? The wingless Lotus 80 was supposed to be a leap forward, but it did not work.

Problems with cars

Williams was also spot on with its new car, the FW07. It was not ready at the start of the season, so Jones and new team-mate Regazzoni started out in the old machine. Ferrari was also late with the 312T4. It did not prove to be as a good a ground-effect car as the aforementioned machines, but it was powerful and reliable. Scheckter quit Wolf to join Villeneuve. After 18 months in the background, Renault expanded to a second entry for René Arnoux and built the effective RS10.

Ligier started the season with a bang, and Laffite won the races in Argentina and Brazil. The new Ferrari arrived at Kyalami, and Villeneuve and Scheckter finished one-two. Significantly, Jabouille's Renault took its first pole. Villeneuve and Scheckter repeated the result at Long Beach, where they were chased by Jones in the old Williams. Ligier bounced back in Spain, sweeping the front row; Depailler led throughout. Lotus had a rare good day, Reutemann and Andretti taking second and third.

Zolder saw the debut of the Williams FW07, and the goalposts suddenly moved. Jones led easily until retiring, leaving victory to Scheckter. Jody won again in Monaco, chased home by Regazzoni's FW07. After retiring in this race, Hunt decided that he had had enough and hung up his helmet. Wolf signed fiery Finn Keke Rosberg to replace him.

Renault's achievement

In France, Renault's dreams came true when Jabouille gave the team its first win. In a thrilling finale, Villeneuve just edged Arnoux out of second after the pair banged wheels around the last lap. Then luck went the way of Williams. Regazzoni gave the team a fabulous first win at Silverstone, which was followed by successes for Jones at Hockenheim, the Osterreichring and Zandvoort. In Holland Villeneuve dragged his three-wheeled wreckage back to the pits after he had blown a tyre while leading.

Scheckter kept collecting points, and by winning at Monza he had amassed enough to claim the title with two races to go. Villeneuve, under orders, followed in his wheel tracks. By Montreal, Brabham had abandoned the awful BT48 and replaced it with the neat DFV-powered BT49. It did not interest Lauda, who announced that he was quitting.

The race saw a fine battle between Jones and Villeneuve, which went the way of the Williams driver as he took his fourth win of the year. The pair fought again at a wet Watkins Glen, but Jones lost a wheel after a pit stop, and the gutsy little Canadian won with another display of Ferrari reliability.

CONSTRUCTORS' CUP

Pos.	Make	Pts
1	Ferrari	113
2	Williams	75
3	Ligier	61
4	Lotus	39
5	Tyrrell	28
6	Renault	26
7	McLaren	15
8	Brabham	7
9	Arrows	5
10	Shadow	3

DRIVERS' WORLD CHAMPIONSHIP

Pos.	Driver	Nat.	Make	Pts
1	Jody Scheckter	SAf	Ferrari	51
2	Gilles Villeneuve	Can	Ferrari	47
3	Alan Jones	Aus	Williams-Ford	40
4	Jacques Laffite	Fr	Ligier-Ford	36
5	Clay Regazzoni	Swi	Williams-Ford	29
6	Carlos Reutemann	Arg	Lotus-Ford	20
	Patrick Depailler	Fr	Ligier-Ford	20
8	René Arnoux	Fr	Renault	17
9	John Watson	GB	McLaren-Ford	15
10	Mario Andretti	USA	Lotus-Ford	14
	Jean-Pierre Jarier	Fr	Tyrrell-Ford	14
	Didier Pironi	Fr	Tyrrell-Ford	14

Best eight scores from 15 races to count

1980

Alan Jones triumphed in the 1980 World Championship despite a strong challenge from Nelson Piquet. However, for the first time in its history, Formula One politics began to attract almost as much attention as the sport itself.

Just as Colin Chapman failed to follow up his 1978 success, so Enzo Ferrari's team lost its way in 1980. The new 312T5 was not a very efficient ground-effect car.

Another merger

The Wolf and Fittipaldi teams merged but retained their respective drivers. Rosberg and Emerson started the season in the rebadged 1979 Wolfs, while a new F8 came on stream later. Alfa-Romeo now returned with two Marlboro-backed machines for Bruno Giacomelli and Depailler. Jones began the season much as he finished 1979. He dominated in Argentina, despite spinning three times. Piquet scored his best result to date with second, while Rosberg gave some hint of his potential with third. Long Beach saw the end of Clay Regazzoni's career. He crashed and was paralysed.

Meanwhile, Piquet took pole and scored his first win, ahead of Patrese and Fittipaldi. Most of the big names retired, including Depailler, who held a fine second with the new Alfa. The FW07B made its bow at Zolder and, although it was quick, Jones and Reutemann were led home by Pironi, another first-time winner. Didier was on form again at Monaco but, after he hit the barrier, the steady Reutemann took victory.

At Jarama politics and racing collided head on, as FOCA was in dispute with FISA. A confusing weekend ended with a "Formula DFV" race going ahead without Ferrari, Alfa and Renault. The Renaults were quick but fragile in Germany and, when leader Jones had a puncture, Laffite took the victory. Sadly, in pre-race testing Depailler crashed fatally in the Alfa.

France took another win in Austria, Jabouille scoring his second success as he held off the determined Jones. Lotus test driver Nigel Mansell was finally given his chance in a third car, only to have to start the race in a fuel-soaked race suit. In Holland, Jones threw it away by damaging a skirt on a kerb. Piquet, who was developing into a deadly rival, took the win, ahead of Arnoux.

The Italian Grand Prix moved to Imola for the first time, and Piquet scored another win from a brake-troubled Jones.

Duel at the top

The situation was tense going to Montreal, and it blew up when Piquet and Jones tangled on the first lap and caused a huge pile-up. For the restart, Piquet had to ride in the spare, and his qualifying engine duly failed. Pironi led all the way, but was penalized for a jumped start. Jones sat in second and took maximum points, and the title.

Two big names drove their final races at the Glen. Having failed to qualify the dreadful Ferrari in Canada, Scheckter finished 11th and last. Meanwhile, Fittipaldi broke his suspension on lap 15, ending another trying season with his own team.

CONSTRUCTORS' CUP

Pos.	Make	Pts
1	Williams	120
2	Ligier	66
3	Brabham	56
4	Renault	38
5	Lotus	14
6	Tyrrell	12
7	Arrows	11
	Fittipaldi	11
	McLaren	11
10	Ferrari	8

DRIVERS' WORLD CHAMPIONSHIP

Pos.	Driver	Nat.	Make	Pts
1	Alan Jones	Aus	Williams-Ford	67
2	Nelson Piquet	Bra	Brabham-Ford	54
3	Carlos Reutemann	Arg	Williams-Ford	42
4	Jacques Laffite	Fr	Ligier-Ford	34
5	Didier Pironi	Fr	Ligier-Ford	32
6	René Arnoux	Fr	Renault	29
7	Elio de Angelis	It	Lotus-Ford	13
8	Jean-Pierre Jabouille	Fr	Renault	9
9	Riccardo Patrese	It	Arrows-Ford	7
10	Derek Daly	Ire	Tyrrell-Ford	6
	Jean-Pierre Jarier	Fr	Tyrrell-Ford	6
	Keke Rosberg	Fin	Fittipaldi-Ford	6
	Gilles Villeneuve	Can	Ferrari	6
	John Watson	GB	McLaren-Ford	6

Trophy man *Alan Jones claimed the title with five wins.*

Just Williams *Alan Jones motors his way to victory at Brands Hatch.*

1981

Nelson Piquet successfully turned the tables on Alan Jones in 1981, winning his first World Championship and the first for Brabham since Bernie Ecclestone took control. Unfortunately, off-track disputes dominated the headlines.

In a spin *Nelson Piquet rotates his Brabham in Spain. But he had the last laugh, and claimed the World Championship.*

After the disaster of 1980, Ferrari fought back. The biggest change was the switch to the new V6 turbo engine, the Italian team becoming the first to follow Renault's pioneering route. Unfortunately, the chassis was just about as bad as any the company had produced. The other big engine novelty was the return of the Matra V12. After two years with DFVs, Ligier went back to French power and had strong backing from Talbot. The recuperating Jabouille joined Laffite on the driving squad.

New-look McLaren team

The other big news of the winter was the takeover of McLaren by Ron Dennis and his Project Four organisation. The old management was swept away and John Barnard set to work on a revolutionary carbon fibre chassis. Prost had fallen out with the old regime, and his prayers were answered as he replaced Jabouille at Renault. Andretti ended his relationship with Chapman and joined Giacomelli at Alfa-Romeo. The Mexican Hector Rebaque replaced Zunino as Piquet's team-mate, while Mansell became de Angelis's full-time partner at Lotus, Eddie Cheever joined Tyrrell and Fittipaldi signed Chico Serra to replace himself alongside Rosberg.

The March name returned after a four-year hiatus, and the ambitious Toleman team also made its debut with the Hart turbo engine and Britons Derek Warwick and Brian Henton driving.

Fortunately, the political fighting, which had raged throughout the winter, did not result in there being two championships, but tensions still ran high. Indeed, the season started with a non-championship race, the South African Grand Prix being run devoid of the "manufacturer" teams. Reutemann won the wet event.

The championship proper began at Long Beach and with sliding skirts officially banned. Also missing was Goodyear, the American firm having announced its withdrawal as a protest. The entire field now ran on Michelin. Then there was the Lotus 88 affair – Chapman had come up with a revolutionary "twin chassis" concept and, after a lot of arguing, the car was not allowed to race.

The Californian event saw Patrese take a surprise pole with the Arrows, but victory went to champion Jones, ahead of Reutemann and Piquet. The Ferraris were quick, but fragile. In Brazil the new rules turned to farce. Brabham had a perfected a hydro-pneumatic suspension system – the car was legal in the pits, but on the track it sat down and the skirts touched the ground.

Piquet took pole, started the wet race on slicks and blew it. Reutemann led Jones home, which caused some controversy, since he was supposed to let Jones past. Alan was not a happy man. Patrese was

Lead battle *Prost holds off Jones and Piquet at Hockenheim.*

The runner-up *Carlos Reutemann was a frequent rostrum visitor for Williams. Here he heads for second at Long Beach.*

third, and Swiss Marc Surer took a sensational fourth in the Ensign.

In Argentina Piquet made no mistake, winning easily, while unrated team-mate Rebaque ran second until his car broke. Brabham had made a joke of the rules. Reutemann and Jones were second and third, and Williams and others were hard at work at their own, less subtle control system.

The European season started at Imola with the newly invented San Marino Grand Prix – an excuse to have two races in Italy. The disputes continued with a ban on flexible skirts. This was an attempt to handicap anyone using a system to lower the car – which by now, meant almost everyone.

Villeneuve and Pironi were the stars, both leading the wet race early on. Piquet came through to win from Patrese and Reutemann. By now Avon and Pirelli had joined as tyre suppliers, while Lotus stayed at home – working on a replacement for the now completely banned 88.

Disaster at Zolder

Zolder was another black weekend. A mechanic from the small Osella team died after being struck by a car in practice, and an Arrows mechanic suffered broken legs when he went to Patrese's stalled car on the grid – just as the race started. And the skirt business rumbled on. Pironi led until his brakes went, Jones crashed out after earlier knocking Piquet off and the win went to Reutemann, ahead of Laffite's Ligier and the impressive Mansell.

Nigel was in great form at Monaco, qualifying third behind Piquet and Villeneuve. Nelson led, but Jones put him under pressure and the Brazilian crashed out. Jones suffered a fuel pick-up problem and Villeneuve sped by to score a superb win in the unwieldy Ferrari. Amazingly, he repeated that success at Jarama. After Jones fell off, Gilles led a train comprising Laffite, Watson, Reutemann and de Angelis. No one could get past him. The Lotuses were sporting JPS backing for the first time since 1978, while Jabouille, off-form since coming back from injury, announced his retirement. Tambay replaced him.

Dijon was another odd race, which saw the return of Goodyear on the Williams and Brabham cars. Rain split the event into two parts, and Prost scored his first win in the Renault – there were many more to come. Watson and Piquet completed the top three.

Triumph for Watson

Wattie's big day came at Silverstone. Prost and Arnoux took turns in the lead, but when they failed John was in the right place. It was his first win since Austria in 1976, the first for Mclaren under Ron Dennis and the first for a carbon tub.

Reutemann took second, ahead of Daly. Jones was eliminated when Villeneuve spun on the third lap, while Piquet survived a heavy crash later on. In Germany Jones, Prost and Reutemann had engine problems of varying degrees, and Piquet took a canny win, with Prost second. Austria brought a popular win for Laffite and the Ligier-Matra. Villeneuve, Prost and Arnoux had all taken turns in the lead.

At Zandvoort Prost and Jones fought hard in the early stages, until Alan's tyres went off. Prost pulled away to win from Piquet, with Jones third. Reutemann tangled with Laffite, so Piquet took the title lead from the Argentinian.

Prost led all the way at Monza, winning from Jones and Reutemann. Piquet looked set for third until his engine went on the last lap. Carlos regained the points lead.

The Canadian Grand Prix was an exciting, wet event. Jones spun off while leading, Prost took over for a while, then Laffite got to the front and held on to score his second win of the year.

Watson was second, ahead of Villeneuve, who was in spectacular form. Piquet was fifth and Reutemann failed to score, so they headed for the finale with Carlos on 49, Piquet on 48, and Laffite with an outside chance on 43.

The next race was held in a car park in Las Vegas on a course winding between concrete blocks. Reutemann did the job in practice, taking a superb pole, but in the race he faded away. Jones won ahead of Prost and Giacomelli, while Piquet took fifth place – and won the championship by a point. It was an amazing end to a strange and somewhat unsatisfactory season.

DRIVERS' WORLD CHAMPIONSHIP

Pos.	Driver	Nat.	Make	Pts
1	Nelson Piquet	Bra	Brabham-Ford	50
2	Carlos Reutemann	Arg	Williams-Ford	49
3	Alan Jones	Aus	Williams-Ford	46
4	Jacques Laffite	Fr	Ligier-Matra	44
5	Alain Prost	Fr	Renault	43
6	John Watson	GB	McLaren-Ford	27
7	Gilles Villeneuve	Can	Ferrari	25
8	Elio de Angelis	It	Lotus-Ford	15
9	Rene Arnoux	Fr	Renault	11
	Hector Rebaque	Mex	Brabham-Ford	11

All scores counted

CONSTRUCTORS' CUP

Pos.	Make	Pts
1	Williams	95
2	Brabham	61
3	Renault	54
4	Ligier	44
5	Ferrari	34
6	McLaren	28
7	Lotus	22
8	Alfa-Romeo	10
	Arrows	10
	Tyrrell	10

1982

The 1982 season proved to be one of the most turbulent – and tragic – in the history of Formula One. Keke Rosberg became the first man since 1964 to secure the championship with just a single victory to his name.

Icy atmosphere *Didier Pironi is pleased with his win at Imola.*

Niki Lauda was back. Apparently bored with running his airline, the double world champion returned after two years away to join Watson at McLaren. Williams took a long time to decide upon a replacement for Jones, and settled on Keke Rosberg, who had struggled with the Fittipaldi for a couple of seasons. He and Reutemann started the year with the FW07C, but the new FW08 was on the way.

Brabham looked stronger than for several years, as the team had hired a decent team-mate for Piquet in Riccardo Patrese. Both men had the use of the turbo BMW-powered BT50. Andrea De Cesaris moved from McLaren to Alfa, while the American, Eddie Cheever, was a surprise choice to partner Jacques Laffite at Ligier.

Drivers on strike

Although the technical squabbles had died down, another blew up at Kyalami. The drivers were unhappy with the small print of the new FISA Super Licence and staged a strike. Eventually all was resolved and practice went ahead. Piquet crashed in the race, and the Renaults dominated until Prost had a puncture. But he charged from eighth to take the lead from Arnoux, who also had tyre trouble. Reutemann managed to split the Renaults by finishing in second place.

In the Brazilian Grand Prix, Villeneuve blasted into the lead, staying there until he crashed out. Piquet, who had switched back temporarily to the DFV-powered BT49, took over the lead and headed Rosberg home. Nelson collapsed on the rostrum, such was the heat, but both he and Rosberg were later disqualified. Their cars had large water tanks for "brake cooling", which were deemed to be for disposable ballast, allowing the cars to run underweight. Thus Prost was given the victory, from Watson and Mansell.

Reutemann had collided with Arnoux in Brazil and surprised Williams by announcing his retirement. Mario Andretti, who had returned to the Indycars scene, was a one-off replacement at Long Beach, where Lauda was the star. De Cesaris amazed everyone by putting the Alfa on pole, and surprised no one when he hit the wall in the race. Second on the grid, Lauda got into the lead and stayed there. Rosberg took second from Villeneuve, although the latter was disqualified for running with an illegal double rear wing.

San Marino was a half-hearted event with just 14 cars entered. The Brazilian disqualifications had led the FOCA teams to announce they were boycotting the race.

Tyrrell, bound by Italian sponsors, broke ranks to join the manufacturer outfits. Pironi and Villeneuve dominated the race, and traded places in what many thought was a show for the fans. Indeed, Gilles was expecting Didier to let him win and had plenty in reserve. The Frenchman chose to pass on the last lap, took the chequered flag and victory. And so, a deadly feud began.

Disaster at Zolder

The feud rumbled on to Zolder where, in final qualifying, desperate to outgun Pironi, tragedy struck. Villeneuve hit the back of Jochen Mass's March and was launched into a frightening roll. The most entertaining driver of the era was killed. The race went ahead without Ferrari. Arnoux led until the throttle linkage broke and Rosberg took over. He was chased by Watson, who took the lead with just two laps remaining.

Monaco was a hugely dramatic race. Arnoux led until spinning, then Prost took over until crashing heavily by the harbour with three laps to go as rain started to sprinkle. Patrese, switching once more to the DFV, took over the lead. He spun, and Pironi and de Cesaris went by. Then, with one lap to go, Pironi stopped with electrical problems, de Cesaris ran out of fuel and the Williams replacement driver, Derek Daly, retired after clouting the barrier. Patrese somehow recovered to score his first win.

The circus moved to the USA for a new race on a bumpy street track in downtown Detroit. Prost led but had engine problems, and Watson tigered through the field to win – from 17th on the grid. Cheever was a surprise second, ahead of Pironi.

Tragedy struck again in Montreal, now named the Circuit Gilles Villeneuve. Poleman Pironi stalled on the grid and was hit by Riccardo Paletti. The young Osella driver was killed. Brabham dominated the restart. Piquet, who failed to qualify with a BMW in Detroit, passed Arnoux for the lead and his BMW held together. Patrese, with a DFV, followed in second. Watson, again picking up points with third, now led the championship by ten points.

At Zandvoort Ferrari finally had some good news, Pironi winning in fine style as new second driver Patrick Tambay settled in well. The Renaults were quick, but Arnoux had an accident when his suspension failed. Brands Hatch saw Lauda take his second win of the year, ahead of Pironi and Tambay. Brabham had planned to make fuel stops and had new equipment ready, but neither driver made it that far, with Patrese crashing with Arnoux on the line and Piquet retiring while leading. The star of the race was Derek Warwick, who got the tank-like Toleman-Hart up to second place before being forced to retire.

Pironi went to Hockenheim leading by nine points. But in wet practice he struck the back of Prost's Renault and was launched into an accident eerily reminiscent of that suffered by Villeneuve. He survived, but his legs were broken and his Formula One career was over. And the title was now up for grabs.

The following day Tambay drove his heart out to score his first win in the second Ferrari, ahead of Arnoux and Rosberg. Piquet led, but tangled with back marker Eliseo Salazar at one of the chicanes. He made his feelings known to the Chilean with a couple of televised punches.

Side-by-side finish

Austria saw an excellent race. Patrese and Piquet led, and both finally got a chance to try out their scheduled stops. But both retired. Prost took the lead, but suffered mechanical gremlins with five laps to go. That left the Lotus 91 of de Angelis in a surprise lead, with Rosberg catching him. They crossed the line side by side, Elio getting the verdict in one of the biggest upsets for years.

For the first and only time a championship round Swiss Grand Prix was held at Dijon. Yes, Dijon in France, as a Swiss statute still existed that banned all racing on Swiss soil, this a legacy of the 1955 Le Mans tragedy. The Renaults led, but Rosberg came through to win from Prost. Keke had been piling up the points and, with Pironi out of action and Watson not scoring for six races, he had managed to take the lead. However, he failed to score at Monza when his wing broke, while Watson was fourth.

All attention was on Ferrari, however, as Andretti returned and took pole. Arnoux won the race from Tambay, with Mario third. Watson now had to win the final race, at Las Vegas, to deprive Rosberg of the title. Arnoux and Prost both led, but a shock victory went to Alboreto, who had been quietly learning his craft in the Tyrrell.

Watson was second, but it was not enough and fifth-placed Rosberg took the honours. Andretti, driving in what would be his last Grand Prix, retired with a broken suspension.

DRIVERS' WORLD CHAMPIONSHIP

Pos.	Driver	Nat.	Make	Pts
1	Keke Rosberg	Fin	Williams-Ford	44
2	Didier Pironi	Fr	Ferrari	39
	John Watson	GB	McLaren-Ford	39
4	Alain Prost	Fr	Renault	34
5	Niki Lauda	A	McLaren-Ford	30
6	Rene Arnoux	Fr	Renault	28
7	Michele Alboreto	It	Tyrrell-Ford	25
	Patrick Tambay	Fr	Ferrari	25
9	Elio de Angelis	It	Lotus-Ford	23
10	Riccardo Patrese	It	Brabham-Ford	21

All scores counted

CONSTRUCTORS' CUP

Pos.	Make	Pts
1	Ferrari	74
2	McLaren	69
3	Renault	62
4	Williams	58
5	Brabham	41
6	Lotus	30
7	Tyrrell	25
8	Ligier	20
9	Alfa-Romeo	7
10	Arrows	5

Flying Finn *Keke Rosberg went down to the wire in winning the World Championship.*

1983

Nelson Piquet notched up his second world title as Alain Prost and Renault threw away their chances during what was a safe season, without strikes or technical squabbles. The action on the track was all that mattered.

Thwarted ambition *Alain Prost went into the final race leading the World Championship, but it was not enough. His retirement allowed Piquet to snatch the title.*

After all the acrimony of previous years, the season was remarkably free of off-track dramas. New flat-bottom regulations cut down force and got rid of the side pods, while turbos (and planned pit stops) became absolutely essential. As in 1966 there was a mad scramble among the teams to find the best package. Some did better than others, and a few would have to wait another season.

That group included Williams, for whom Keke Rosberg stayed on and was joined by Jacques Laffite. The champions would have to spend another season with DFV power in the updated FW08C until its Honda-powered car was ready to race. The Japanese manufacturer was back in Formula One after a 15-year break, and it made a low-key start with the small Spirit team and Stefan Johansson. McLaren, too, had to be patient. It had arranged for sponsor TAG to pay for Porsche's new V6 and, until that was ready, Lauda and Watson would stick with the DFV.

Death of Colin Chapman

Colin Chapman had scored a coup by securing Renault engines, but the legendary Lotus boss died suddenly in December. The team carried on: de Angelis had the new car for the second race, while Mansell used DFV power until mid-season.

Of those with turbo experience, Piquet and Patrese had stuck with BMW power and had the superb new BT52 to play with, while Arnoux left Renault to join Tambay at Ferrari. The Toleman-Hart team had a much-improved car for Warwick and Giacomelli, who had quit Alfa. The other leading teams were stuck with DFV power, these including Ligier (veteran Jarier and Raul Boesel), Arrows (Marc Surer, Chico Serra and, later, newcomer Thierry Boutsen) and Tyrrell (Alboreto and American rookie Danny Sullivan).

Piquet begins well

Piquet won in impressive style in Rio, but Rosberg drew all the attention. He led, had a fire at his pit stop, recovered to second and was then excluded for a push start. Lauda and Laffite thus took the remaining rostrum places. Prost's Renault ran second but was slowed by a tyre vibration.

Long Beach was a rare opportunity for the DFV cars to shine. Watson and Lauda qualified 22nd and 23rd, but they got the race set-up right and came charging through to finish one-two, with Arnoux third. Rosberg had a wild race, spinning and tangling with Tambay.

Unusually, the European season kicked off at Paul Ricard. Renault continued its habit of winning at home, Prost coming in ahead of Piquet and Cheever.

San Marino was a memorable event. Tambay scored an emotional win for Ferrari, well aware that 12 months earlier his friend Villeneuve had been robbed by Pironi. Patrese led, lost the lead at a bungled pit stop and then claimed it back. A few seconds later he slid into the barrier and Tambay regained the lead. Prost took second, ahead of Arnoux.

Monaco was another chance for the DFVs to shine. Rosberg qualified sixth behind the turbos, but it rained before the start and he made a brave decision to start on slicks. He was in the lead by the second lap and pulled away as the others pitted. The other team which might have shone was McLaren, but Watson and Lauda failed to qualify after problems on Thursday and rain blitzed them on Saturday.

After a 13-year break, the Belgian Grand Prix returned to Spa. The track had been rebuilt and was much shorter than the original, but it was instantly regarded as the best on the schedule. De Cesaris charged into the lead, but succumbed to engine problems. Prost took over and held on to the flag, with Tambay and Cheever giving chase.

Detroit looked likely to give the "atmo" runners another chance and, sure enough, it did. Alboreto scored his second win for Tyrrell on a temporary track, taking the lead when Piquet had to pit with a puncture. Rosberg and Watson made it a Ford one-two-three. This was the 155th victory for the Ford Cosworth, and no one could guess that it would also be the last. In Canada Arnoux dominated and scored a great win for Ferrari, ahead of the consistent Cheever and Tambay. Prost, struggling with engine problems and a puncture, was fifth, while Piquet retired when third.

Prost scored a brilliant win at Silverstone. The Ferraris led, but Prost pushed them and they used up their tyres. Piquet came through to take second, with Tambay third. Mansell finally got into the cockpit of a Lotus-Renault after being stuck with a DFV, and finished a crowd-pleasing fourth, having started 18th on the grid. Honda made a quiet return with Spirit, six years to the weekend since Renault started the turbo revolution.

Arnoux scored another win at Hockenheim, although he defied team orders at the start when he was supposed to let Tambay stay ahead. Tambay retired, while Piquet lost second with a major fire. De Cesaris took a lucky second, ahead of Patrese and Prost, who had gearbox problems. Alain was now 11 points clear of Piquet in the title race.

Champion again *Nelson Piquet sits and waits in his Brabham.*

Prost leads Piquet

Prost had to work hard to win in Austria, passing Arnoux with six laps to go. Piquet kept his title hopes alive with third, despite engine problems. Prost's lead was now 14 points. He got it badly wrong in Holland, sliding into Piquet and putting them both out. Although Nelson did not score, after the incident the tide turned in his favour. Arnoux drove a good race to win from tenth, with Tambay second. Watson drove a brilliant race to finish third, while Warwick gave Toleman its first points with fourth. Lauda gave the McLaren-TAG turbo a strong debut.

Prost now led Arnoux by eight points and Piquet by 14. However, it was getting close, and for Prost Monza brought the worst possible result – Piquet won and Arnoux was second. When Alain's turbo failed, he was not even running in the points. Now it was Prost 51, Arnoux 49, Piquet 46.

Britain had a second race, the Grand Prix of Europe, at Brands Hatch. Piquet won again, but Prost kept his hopes alive with second. Arnoux spun out of fifth, while de Angelis and Patrese tangled early on when battling for the lead. So it was Prost 57, Piquet 55, Arnoux 49.

Just South Africa remained. Piquet was quick in the first half, while Arnoux stopped early and Prost became bogged down in a battle for third. But his turbo was failing, and he retired. Piquet subsequently dropped to third, but ensured that he scored the vital points needed for the title. Renault and Prost were devastated. Patrese won the race from de Cesaris, while Williams ran its Honda-powered cars for the first time, and Rosberg took fifth. There was plenty more to come.

CONSTRUCTORS' CUP

Pos.	Make	Pts
1	Ferrari	89
2	Renault	79
3	Brabham	72
4	Williams	38
5	McLaren	34
6	Alfa-Romeo	18
7	Lotus	12
	Tyrrell	12
9	Toleman	10
10	Arrows	4

DRIVERS' WORLD CHAMPIONSHIP

Pos.	Driver	Nat.	Make	Pts
1	Nelson Piquet	Bra	Brabham-BMW	59
2	Alain Prost	Fr	Renault	57
3	René Arnoux	Fr	Ferrari	49
4	Patrick Tambay	Fr	Ferrari	40
5	Keke Rosberg	Fin	Williams-Ford	27
6	Eddie Cheever	USA	Renault	22
	John Watson	GB	McLaren-Ford	22
8	Andrea de Cesaris	It	Alfa-Romeo	15
9	Riccardo Patrese	It	Brabham-BMW	13
10	Niki Lauda	A	McLaren-Ford	12

All scores counted

1984

Niki Lauda once again took advantage of the opportunity to display his judgement and guile when he beat his faster and younger team-mate, Alain Prost, to take the title. This was to be the first of many great years for McLaren.

Flying start *Derek Warwick led first time out for Renault, but he didn't win.*

Just like Emerson Fittipaldi ten years earlier, Alain Prost stunned the Formula One world when he upped and joined Marlboro McLaren. He had fallen out with the Renault management, and McLaren was the only logical home. With the TAG/Porsche engine up to speed, McLaren looked like being the team to beat, especially since there was a new 220-litre fuel limit, and Porsche had experience in endurance racing on which to draw. All year, the canny Lauda let Prost out-qualify him – and concentrated on the race.

There was a clean sweep at Renault. Cheever joined Prost in the queue at the exit, the pair being replaced by Tambay and Toleman's Derek Warwick. Cheever found a new home at Alfa, who had attracted support from the Benetton clothing company, and he was joined by Patrese, who left Brabham.

Turbo-less Tyrrell

Ligier had sourced Renault engines, and attracted de Cesaris from Alfa. He joined French newcomer François Hesnault. Arrows had a BMW deal, and two good drivers in Boutsen and Marc Surer, although they would start the year with Cosworth power. Everyone had a turbo – except Tyrrell. Having passed on Renault at the very dawn of the turbo era, Tyrrell was the last bastion of Cosworth power. The team produced a nimble car – the 012 – and were blessed with two great rookie drivers, Stefan Bellof and Martin Brundle.

Alboreto led away in Brazil, but spun out. Lauda and Warwick took turns in front, but Derek's suspension broke after an early clash with Lauda. Prost came neatly through to win his first race in a McLaren, while Rosberg demonstrated the potential of the Honda with second, ahead of de Angelis. Brundle showed promise with fifth, while Toleman's new signing, Ayrton Senna, qualified 16th.

McLaren was dominant in South Africa. Piquet led until encountering turbo problems, and Lauda sailed to an easy win. Prost had to start in the spare, and stormed through from the back to take second, with Warwick third. Senna scored his first point with sixth.

The European season kicked off in Belgium and a return to the unloved Zolder. Alboreto took pole and led all the way for his first win in a Ferrari. Warwick again scored well with second, ahead of Arnoux. Rosberg made a bad start but charged to third, only to lose a spot when he ran out of fuel.

McLaren was on form at Imola. Prost led all the way, despite a spin. Lauda was never in the lead battle, and retired with engine failure. Piquet held second until a turbo failure, so Arnoux inherited the place, ahead of an out-of-fuel de Angelis. Williams had its worst race in years, with Rosberg and Laffite retiring. Renault desperately wanted to win in France, and Tambay obliged with pole at Dijon. He led three-quarters of the race, but had brake and clutch problems. Lauda got ahead and motored to victory, the team having overcome engine dramas in practice. Mansell was third, while Prost, troubled by a loose wheel, was seventh.

Trouble at Monaco

Monaco brought heavy rain. Renault drivers Tambay and Warwick crashed on the first corner, while poleman Prost led Mansell. Mansell took the lead and pulled away in style, only to crash – and, infamously, blame a "white line". Prost regained the lead He was still in front when the race was finally red-flagged, and half points were

awarded. At Montreal Piquet and Brabham were back on form. The car had a new oil cooler in the front, intended to help with weight distribution, but the side effect was that Piquet burned his feet while leading from start to finish!

Detroit started with a controversial shunt between Piquet, Prost and Mansell, for which Nigel got the blame. All three were back for the restart, and Piquet showed that the BT53 could be effective on street circuits by leading all the way. Star of the race was Brundle, who did a magnificent job to climb to second in the Tyrrell. De Angelis took third, ahead of Teo Fabi and Prost. Lauda only just broke into the top six before retiring with electronic problems.

Disaster at Dallas

From Detroit it was straight to Dallas for yet another race on a temporary track. It was ragingly hot, the track broke up, many crashed and the circus never went back. Rosberg was the hero of the hour, winning in style with the difficult Williams-Honda. Arnoux and de Angelis survived the carnage to take second and third. Mansell led much of the way, but his gearbox eventually broke and he collapsed while trying to push the car over the line. Among those in the wall were Lauda, Prost, Piquet, Tambay and Alboreto.

Sanity returned when the circus came back to Europe for Brands Hatch, although the race would be stopped after Jonathan Palmer crashed his RAM. Prost led until his gearbox failed, leaving Lauda to win from Warwick and the improving Senna. Ayrton's team-mate Johnny Cecotto suffered badly broken legs in a practice shunt, ending his Formula One career. Most attention turned to a dispute between Tyrrell and FISA over water irregularities found in Detroit.

De Angelis and Piquet both retired while leading at Hockenheim, leaving Prost to win from Lauda and Warwick. In Austria Prost spun off when second, and a gearbox-troubled Lauda won from Piquet and Alboreto. Piquet led early on in Holland, until he suffered an oil leak. Prost and Lauda completed another demonstration run, ahead of Mansell. By now the McLaren stars had a lock on the title: Lauda 54, Prost 52.5.

Prost's engine went on the fourth lap in Monza, and once Piquet did his usual trick of retiring while leading, Lauda cantered to victory ahead of Alboreto and Patrese. By now the Tyrrell affair had blown up. The team was banned from the championship and lost all its results and points. Many saw sinister undertones in the way the sole Cosworth runner was hounded out.

Lauda 63, Prost 52.5. For the first time Formula One went to the new Nürburgring for the European Grand Prix. Prost led all the way, while Alboreto and Piquet – both out of fuel – were second and third. Niki finished fourth after a spin: Lauda 66, Prost 62.5. The finale was at, Estoril in Portugal. Prost won his seventh of the year, while Lauda did all he needed to do and secured the title with second place: 72 to 71.5, the closest winning margin ever. Senna confirmed his talent with third. Another reliable run to fifth helped secure third in the championship for de Angelis.

Comeback king *Niki Lauda lifted his third World Championship title, some seven years after he had claimed his second crown.*

CONSTRUCTORS' CUP

Pos.	Make	Pts
1	McLaren	143.5
2	Ferrari	57.5
3	Lotus	47
4	Brabham	38
5	Renault	34
6	Williams	25.5
7	Toleman	16
8	Alfa-Romeo	11
9	Arrows	6
10	Osella	4

DRIVERS' WORLD CHAMPIONSHIP

Pos.	Driver	Nat.	Make	Pts
1	Niki Lauda	A	McLaren-Porsche	72
2	Alain Prost	Fr	McLaren-Porsche	71.5
3	Elio de Angelis	It	Lotus-Renault	34
4	Michele Alboreto	It	Ferrari	30.5
5	Nelson Piquet	Bra	Brabham-BMW	29
6	René Arnoux	Fr	Ferrari	27
7	Derek Warwick	GB	Renault	23
8	Keke Rosberg	Fin	Williams-Honda	20.5
9	Nigel Mansell	GB	Lotus-Renault	13
	Ayrton Senna	Bra	Toleman-Hart	13

All scores counted

1985

Alain Prost finally made it to the top in 1985. After being squeezed out in the previous two years, the Frenchman secured his first title at the end of a highly competitive year in the McLaren-TAG. Nothing could stop him now.

Two future world champions made big career moves for 1985. Nigel Mansell, who had been at Lotus since his debut in 1980, moved to Williams-Honda. Team leader Keke Rosberg did not like the idea at first... Meanwhile, hot property Ayrton Senna wriggled out of a commitment to Toleman to join Lotus, alongside de Angelis.

After two unproductive years with Williams, Jacques Laffite headed back to Ligier, where de Cesaris was still incumbent. Arrows signed promising Austrian Gerhard Berger, who had gone well for ATS, while Teo Fabi led a reorganised Toleman from Monaco on. Tyrrell had finally joined the turbo club, landing a Renault deal for his young chargers, Brundle and Bellof.

Several new teams appeared on the scene. Inexperienced Italian Pierluigi Martini handled the Minardi, which was seen briefly with Cosworth power before the Motori Moderni turbo was introduced. From Germany came touring car specialist Zakspeed, with Jonathan Palmer driving. The ambitious team made its own turbo engine. But the most talked about project originated in America. Indycar entrant Carl Haas had massive backing from Beatrice Foods and enticed Alan Jones out of retirement to drive a new Lola.

Good start for Alboreto

Alboreto began the season in fine form, putting the Ferrari on pole in Rio. Rosberg was alongside, and both led the race, but victory went to Prost. The Frenchman started his title assault in style, while Alboreto took second, ahead of de Angelis. Arnoux finished fourth in the second Ferrari, but shortly afterwards fell out with Enzo. He was replaced by Stefan Johansson, who finally had the golden opportunity many felt he deserved.

Senna showed his true class by putting the Lotus on pole in Portugal. The race was soaking wet, but the weather only emphasised the Brazilian's skills as he stormed to his first victory. Alboreto was a minute behind in second place, with Tambay's Renault third. Ayrton was again on pole in San Marino, a race which was to turn to farce. Senna led for 56 laps until running out of fuel. Johansson looked set to win his second race for Ferrari, but he too ran dry. Prost took over and won – only to be disqualified for the car being underweight. Victory was awarded to de Angelis. Everyone else was a lap behind, including the new runner-up Boutsen, who did a good job with the Arrows-BMW.

Senna was on pole yet again in Monaco, with Mansell alongside. Ayrton and Alboreto both took turns in the lead, but Prost came through to achieve his second win of the year. Alboreto kept up his scoring rate with second, ahead of de Angelis, while Piquet and Lauda both crashed out. In Canada Lotus swept the front row, de Angelis ahead of Senna. Elio led for 15 laps before Alboreto took over for his first win of the year. Johansson made it a Ferrari one-two, with Prost third.

Senna was back on pole in Detroit, but he was one of many drivers to crash out, along with Mansell and Prost. Rosberg took the lead early on to give Williams-Honda its first win of the year. Ferrari was again on form, with Johansson and Alboreto filling the podium. History was made by the car in fourth place. Bellof's Tyrrell gave the Cosworth its last ever top six finish, 18 years to the month after its debut. Rosberg was on pole at Paul Ricard, but for the only time all year it was Brabham's day. Piquet won and gave Pirelli its first success since Monza 1957! Rosberg led for ten laps and took second, ahead of Prost.

Rosberg shines at Silverstone

Silverstone saw perhaps the most impressive qualifying performance of the year as Rosberg stormed to pole at nearly 161mph. He could not match that result in the race, and Senna led for 58 laps until he slowed and stopped, having run out of fuel.

Breakthrough *Michele Alboreto's win in Canada put him in the title race.*

Prost took over the lead and won by a lap, from Alboreto and Laffite. Piquet managed to wring another finish out of the Brabham, but it was only fourth place.

The new Nurburgring played host to the German Grand Prix for the first time. Teo Fabi took a surprise pole position in the Toleman-Hart, the team now showing some promise. Ferrari men Alboreto and Johansson tangled at the first corner, but Alboreto recovered to win after Rosberg and Senna both had spells in the lead. Prost continued to pile up points with second place. The Austrian Grand Prix was restarted after a first lap crash. Lauda led 14 laps – his first time in front this year – and, after he retired with turbo failure, Prost went on to win. Senna and Alboreto completed the top three. The race was noted for a spectacular roll by de Cesaris. Ligier had tired of his antics and, after one more race, replaced him with Philippe Streiff.

The historic Zandvoort track hosted a Formula One race for the last time. Piquet took pole, but Rosberg led early on. Prost took control when Rosberg retired yet again with a failed engine, but then Lauda came through to score his first win of the season – and what turned out to be the last of his career. Monza was a familiar story, with Senna taking pole and Rosberg starring in the early stages. But victory went to Prost, ahead of Piquet and Senna. Prost was on pole at Spa, but Senna scored his second win of the year, ahead of Mansell. Prost finished third, and put himself within reach of the title.

Mansell shows form

As in 1983, Brands Hatch hosted the European Grand Prix. Mansell had been overshadowed by Rosberg for much of the year, but in front of his home crowd he came good in fine style, scoring his first win ahead of Senna and Rosberg. Meanwhile, fourth place clinched the title for a cautious Prost. With Lauda injured, Watson made a one-off return to McLaren; it was his last Formula One drive.

Mansell was on top form now, and at Kyalami he took pole and led Rosberg home, with Prost a distant third. The season ended with a new Australian race on the streets of Adelaide. Senna took pole, but Prost won the high-attrition event. Ligier ended the season on a high note, with Laffite and Streiff taking second and third after an entertaining fight. Lauda led a couple of laps, but crashed. For the second time he retired from racing, but this time the decision was a permanent one. The works Renault team quit, too, at the end of an awful season.

Although Formula One had enjoyed a relatively safe season, two talented drivers lost their lives in sports cars: Manfred Winkelhock, of the ATS team, died at Mosport in August, while Tyrrell's Bellof, who had the potential to become one of the all-time greats, was killed at Spa in September.

McLaren again *Alain Prost was the clear winner of the Silverstone race when Ayrton Senna ran out of fuel.*

CONSTRUCTORS' CUP

Pos.	Make	Pts
1	McLaren	90
2	Ferrari	82
3	Lotus	71
	Williams	71
5	Brabham	26
6	Ligier	23
7	Renault	16
8	Arrows	14
9	Tyrrell	7

DRIVERS' WORLD CHAMPIONSHIP

Pos.	Driver	Nat.	Make	Pts
1	Alain Prost	Fr	McLaren-Porsche	73
2	Michele Alboreto	It	Ferrari	53
3	Keke Rosberg	Fin	Williams-Honda	40
4	Ayrton Senna	Bra	Lotus-Renault	38
5	Elio de Angelis	It	Lotus-Renault	33
6	Nigel Mansell	GB	Williams-Honda	31
7	Stefan Johansson	Swe	Ferrari	26
8	Nelson Piquet	Bra	Brabham-BMW	21
9	Jacques Laffite	Fr	Ligier-Renault	16
10	Niki Lauda	A	McLaren-Porsche	14

Best 11 scores from 16 races to count

1986

This saw one of the most dramatic conclusions of recent years. Mansell and Piquet had fought hard all year, but in the final race Nigel blew a tyre, Piquet made a precautionary stop, and a disbelieving Prost sped through to the title.

Last race star *Keke Rosberg dominated the Australian Grand Prix until he had a blow-out, as did Nigel Mansell soon afterwards.*

Having lost Lauda to retirement, Ron Dennis replaced him with another proven champion: Keke Rosberg. It was a great chance for the Finn to win in something other than a Williams, but for some reason the McLaren did not suit his style. Keke was himself replaced at Williams by a world champion. Piquet had been with Brabham since 1978, but relished the chance of driving the Williams-Honda. Another Brazilian was at the centre of the news, and he was not moving teams. Lotus wanted to hire Warwick, but Senna did not want a top name alongside him. The team settled for Johnny Dumfries, fresh from Formula Three.

The Lotus vacancy was created by the end of yet another long-term relationship. De Angelis, who had been with the Norfolk team since 1980, moved on to Brabham. Patrese, who had been away at Alfa for a couple of disastrous years, joined him. Over the winter Toleman turned into Benetton, and the talented Berger joined Fabi. BMW engines, perhaps the most powerful in the field, replaced the Harts. Among other changes, Tambay joined Jones at Beatrice/Haas – and had the use of the new Ford – while Arnoux reappeared at Ligier.

Piquet got off to the best possible start at Williams, winning his home Grand Prix at Rio. Senna took pole, and both he and Prost had spells in the lead before Piquet took control. Senna made it a good day for Brazil with second.

Grand Prix returns to Spain

After a break of several years Spain had a Grand Prix once more, on the new tight and twisty Jerez track. Unexpectedly, it produced a thrilling race, ending with Senna just holding off Mansell by 0.014 sec. Prost was third, with Rosberg a lapped fourth. Senna was on pole in Spain, and was quickest once more at Imola. However, an errant wheel bearing forced him into retirement, while Rosberg fell from second to a non-running fifth, his tank dry of fuel. Piquet and Rosberg both led, but the ever-reliable Prost was there to win from Piquet. Berger gave the new Benetton team its best result to date with third.

Prost broke Senna's string of poles at Monaco, and led home Rosberg in the race. Senna, who had led briefly, fell back and finished third, ahead of Mansell, who collected three points.

The new Brabham BT55 had been a major disappointment, and tragedy struck the team when the popular de Angelis was killed in a testing accident at Paul Ricard. Piquet took pole at Spa, while Berger made full use of BMW power to share the front row. After a disappointing spell, Mansell fought back with his first win of the year, ahead of Senna and Johansson, both of whom led at one stage.

Death and injury

In a black weekend in June, former Osella driver Jo Gartner was killed at Le Mans, while Arrows star Marc Surer was badly injured in a rally accident. He was replaced by Christian Danner.

In Canada Brabham was back up to strength, Warwick returning from his Jaguar sports car commitments to replace de Angelis. Mansell took pole and won from Prost, Piquet, Rosberg and Senna. Senna returned to form in Detroit, scoring his second win of the year from pole. But both Ligiers took a turn in the lead, with Laffite finishing a fine second, ahead of Prost. Mansell, who shared the front row, picked up a couple of points with fifth. He continued his charge with another win at Paul Ricard, finishing ahead of Prost, Piquet and Rosberg.

Nobody was going to stop Mansell at home, but rival Piquet pipped him for pole at Brands Hatch. Nigel had a

Williams war *Mansell leads Piquet at Brands Hatch.*

drive shaft break at the start, but his day was saved by a red flag. Johansson and Laffite collided and the Frenchman hit the barrier head on, breaking his legs. The track was blocked as most of the rear of the field became involved. The incident marked the end of Laffite's distinguished career, just as he reached Graham Hill's record of 176 starts. On the restart Mansell won after a fine tussle with Piquet, leading his rival home.

The German Grand Prix returned to Hockenheim. On this power track it was a surprise to see Rosberg and Prost take the front row ahead of the Hondas and BMWs. Keke led for a while, but Piquet won and kept his title challenge alive. Senna and Mansell completed the top three.

two-hour mark. Senna and Piquet shared the front row, but the race positions were reversed, with the Williams driver on top. Mansell took third, while Dumfries got the second Lotus into the points with fifth.

In Austria the BMWs came into their own. Fabi and Berger dominated the front row in their Benettons, although few expected them to last in the race. Berger led for 25 laps before his turbo blew, and in a race of high attrition it was inevitably Prost who kept in one piece to win. Ferrari had been out of it for a while, and Alboreto was happy to take second ahead of teammate Johansson.

Fabi was again the star of Monza qualifying, securing pole with what was possibly the most powerful car ever seen in Formula One. He shared the front row with Prost, but both had problems and did not take up their places. Prost started in the spare, but was disqualified for swapping cars too late. Meanwhile, Piquet led Mansell to a Williams one-two, with Johansson giving the locals something to cheer in third. Senna was on pole in Portugal, but Mansell continued his title charge by leading all the way to victory, ahead of Prost and Piquet. The third new track of

DRIVERS' WORLD CHAMPIONSHIP

Pos.	Driver	Nat.	Make	Pts
1	Alain Prost	Fr	McLaren-Porsche	72
2	Nigel Mansell	GB	Williams-Honda	70
3	Nelson Piquet	Bra	Williams-Honda	69
4	Ayrton Senna	Bra	Lotus-Renault	55
5	Stefan Johansson	Swe	Ferrari	23
6	Keke Rosberg	Fin	McLaren-Porsche	22
7	Gerhard Berger	A	Benetton-BMW	17
8	Michele Alboreto	It	Ferrari	14
	René Arnoux	Fr	Ligier-Renault	14
	Jacques Laffite	Fr	Ligier-Renault	14

Best 11 scores from 16 races to count

the year was in fact an old one – but the circus had not been to Mexico City since 1970. The Benetton finally held together and Berger took his first win, and only the second of the modern era for Pirelli. Prost, Senna and Piquet were next.

In a dramatic finale in Adelaide, with both Williams drivers and Prost up for the title, Mansell pipped Piquet to pole, and was perfectly placed to take the title when a rear tyre blew. Williams made Piquet stop for a precautionary change, and he fell to second behind Prost. Victory gave the Frenchman his second title. Rosberg was the star of the race. He led for 57 laps, but failed to finish. He was one of the few drivers to walk away from Formula One while at the top. It was also the last race for Jones – four years after his first retirement.

CONSTRUCTORS' CUP

Pos.	Make	Pts
1	McLaren	90
2	Ferrari	82
3	Lotus	71
	Williams	71
5	Brabham	26
6	Ligier	23
7	Renault	16
8	Arrows	14
9	Tyrrell	7

Formula One goes East

The second new circuit on the schedule was the Hungaroring, Formula One's first visit to the Eastern bloc. The circuit was tight and so slow that the race had to be stopped a lap early as it breached the

Great white hope *Nigel Mansell talks tactics.*

1987

Team-mates Nelson Piquet and Nigel Mansell fought for the title, and the Englishman was a strong contender until an accident sidelined him in Japan. Piquet accepted the laurels for the third time, even before the race started.

Championship charge *Nelson Piquet leads the field early in the Hungarian Grand Prix, a race he went on to win.*

The turbo era was, perhaps, getting just a bit out of hand. Cars were too powerful, engine development expensive and, according to FISA, turbos had not proliferated in the road car market place to the expected extent. Thus it was that a new formula was announced, the first big change since 1966. From 1989 onwards, Formula One would go back to the old atmospheric engines, but at the larger 3.5-litre capacity. There would be two interim years while the two types of car ran alongside each other, and to encourage teams to change, a separate classification was introduced for 1987 only. "Atmo" drivers battled for the Jim Clark Cup.

It was no surprise to see Cosworth rapidly produce the new DFZ, nor were people shocked when Ken Tyrrell was the first major team owner to build cars for the formula. He hired Palmer and Streiff, and they would dominate the new category. Their opponents were mostly French: AGS and a new team from former Renault Sport boss Gerard Larrousse.

There were plenty of changes on the engine front. After a year as just an engine supplier Renault had withdrawn, and Lotus landed on its feet by attracting Honda – leading Japanese driver Satoru Nakajima came as part of the package. And the JPS colour scheme had finally gone, replaced by Camel's yellow hues.

Two Japanese firsts

With Haas out, Ford found a new partner in Benetton. The V6 was still not a match for the opposition, but it was getting better. Boutsen joined Fabi in the team, as Berger had been attracted to Ferrari, where he partnered Alboreto. There was little new in the teams which fought out the 1986 title. Johansson left Ferrari to join Prost at McLaren, while Williams continued with Mansell and Piquet. Nigel was desperate to gain some revenge. Nigel and Nelson shared the front row in Rio and, although Piquet led early on, Prost won the race. Nelson finished second, while Johansson began his McLaren career with third.

In Imola luck went against Piquet when he had a serious accident in practice, and was not even able to start the race. Senna gave the Lotus-Honda its first pole, and led the first lap, but Mansell powered past to victory. In a distant sixth, Nakajima became the first Japanese driver to score a point.

Mansell and Piquet were on the front row at Spa. The race was stopped after Tyrrell twins Streiff and Palmer crashed on the second lap, but the big story of the day was a collision between Mansell and Senna which put them both out and led to a confrontation in the pits afterwards. Prost won the race after Piquet retired with turbo failure, with team-mate Johansson making it a McLaren one-two and de Cesaris taking a surprise third for Brabham.

Mansell was on pole at Monaco and led until his turbo broke. Senna took over and scored the first of his many victories in the principality, using an early form of active suspension on the Camel Lotus. Piquet was second, ahead of the Ferraris of Alboreto and Berger. The result was similar at Detroit. Mansell was on pole and led the first half of the race, but Senna took over as Mansell was hit by cramp and won in the "active" Lotus, ahead of Piquet and Prost. Mansell finished fifth. Things finally went his way at Paul Ricard, where he won from pole.

As usual, few would bet against Mansell winning in Britain. He did not disappoint, despite losing pole to Piquet. After a late tyre

Beaten again *Nigel Mansell missed the last two races.*

stop, he beat the Brazilian in an entertaining charge which culminated in a famous passing move at Stowe corner. It was a great day for Honda, and Senna and Nakajima followed the Williams pair home, albeit at a respectful distance.

Mansell was back on pole in Germany, but in the race his engine failed and Piquet won, while Johansson struggled home second with a flat front tyre. Just seven cars finished on a day when the turbo cars fell apart and three DFZs made the top six. Mansell's story was the same in Hungary – he took pole, failed to finish when he lost a wheel nut, and Piquet won, ahead of Senna and Prost in third.

The circus visited the magnificent Osterreichring for what turned out to be the last time since, like Zandvoort, the Austrian event could not survive financially in the commercialized Formula One world. The race was stopped twice by multiple crashes on the pit straight, but when it finally got under way safely, Mansell won easily from Piquet – and nearly knocked himself out on a low beam when he was being driven to the rostrum.

In both Austria and Italy Piquet pipped Mansell to pole, and in the Monza race Nelson took victory with Mansell third, the pair split by Senna, who led much of the race. Ferrari had a disappointing home race, Berger salvaging fourth. Portugal brought a welcome change when Berger took pole. In the race he led most of the way but Prost took the victory. Piquet took four vital points with third, while Mansell retired with engine failure.

Nigel was back on the title trail after a win at Jerez, ahead of Prost, Johansson and Piquet. Then he made up for the previous year's mistake by winning in Mexico, a race split neatly into two by a huge accident from which Warwick emerged unscathed. Piquet was second, ahead of Patrese.

Mansell out of contention

For the first time since 1976 Japan had its own Grand Prix, at the magnificent, Honda-owned Suzuka track. Piquet held the upper hand in the title race, but Mansell could still catch him. All was resolved when Nigel crashed in practice and hurt his back. Piquet celebrated, for Mansell was out for the weekend, and neither did he go to Adelaide. Ironically, Piquet did not score points in either race. Instead, victory in both went to Berger's Ferrari. Senna and Johansson followed him home in Japan, and in Australia, the Austrian led all the way to win from Senna. However, the Lotus was disqualified for having illegal brake ducts, and it cost Ayrton second place in the championship to Mansell. Gerhard's team-mate Alboreto took second from Boutsen's Benetton. Just nine cars made the flag, and both Prost and Johansson crashed. Patrese, who was due to drive for Williams in 1988, replaced the injured Mansell.

Jonathan Palmer was the leading light in the "atmo" category for most of the year, winning the Jim Clark Cup, while Tyrrell won the constructors' version. Not that many people really noticed or cared, although J.P. placed a respectable 11th in the overall scheme of things.

The Australian race marked the last appearance of the TAG/Porsche engine. It had won three titles, but clearly in this final year its best days were behind it. Johansson was also shown the door. McLaren had alternative plans for 1988.

DRIVERS' WORLD CHAMPIONSHIP

Pos.	Driver	Nat.	Make	Pts
1	Nelson Piquet	Bra	Williams-Honda	73
2	Nigel Mansell	GB	Williams-Honda	61
3	Ayrton Senna	Bra	Lotus-Honda	57
4	Alain Prost	Fr	McLaren-Porsche	46
5	Gerhard Berger	A	Ferrari	36
6	Stefan Johansson	Swe	McLaren-Porsche	30
7	Michele Alboreto	It	Ferrari	17
8	Thierry Boutsen	Bel	Benetton-Ford	16
9	Teo Fabi	It	Benetton-Ford	12
10	Eddie Cheever	USA	Arrows-Megatron	8

Best 11 scores from 16 races to count

CONSTRUCTORS' CUP

Pos.	Make	Pts
1	Williams	137
2	McLaren	76
3	Lotus	64
4	Ferrari	53
5	Benetton	28
6	Arrows	11
	Tyrrell	11
8	Brabham	10
9	Lola	3
10	Zakspeed	2

Ready to move *Ayrton Senna won twice for Lotus, then left the team.*

1988

Alain Prost scored more points than McLaren team-mate Ayrton Senna, but the Brazilian claimed the title because he could count his best 11 results from the 16 rounds and, moreover, had eight wins to Prost's seven.

Home win *Ferrari ace Gerhard Berger won where it counted, in Italy.*

Their battle began in Brazil, and Prost won. Senna qualified on pole from Williams team leader Nigel Mansell, with Prost third and Ferrari's Gerhard Berger fourth. However, Senna had to start from the pits in his spare car. Prost powered past Mansell. So did Berger. And no one headed Prost again. Senna drove the crowd wild as he powered from 21st at the end of lap one to second by lap 20, but he was disqualified for using the spare car. Thus, Berger finished second and Nelson Piquet third for Lotus. So, Senna had a point to prove at Imola. And this he did, leading all the way, helped by Prost being slow off the line.

Senna goes home

If you live in Monaco, as many drivers do, the race through the streets is your "home" Grand Prix. Senna lived there in 1988 and was thus able to make a bolt for his apartment when he threw away the lead. He was almost a minute up on Prost, with a dozen laps to go, when the front left wheel of his McLaren grazed the barriers just before the tunnel. Bang! That was it. It was several hours before he re-emerged from his apartment nearby, by which time Prost had cruised to victory, drunk the champagne and hosted the victory conference.

The race in Mexico was a McLaren one and Prost beat Senna by seven seconds with the rest nowhere. In fact, only Berger remained on the same lap. In Canada it was another McLaren one-two, although this time Senna won from Prost.

Detroit, home of the American automotive industry, was the venue for the US Grand Prix. A street circuit, it had a very different nature from the track used in Canada. However, it did nothing to the overall sequence, with Senna, Prost and Boutsen finishing in precisely the same order, albeit with the Belgian lapped this time. Mansell retired for the sixth race in a row. In France, anxious that Senna was eroding his points advantage, Prost won in unusually press-on style. Senna was a distant second, suffering from a gearbox problem.

A nasty Silverstone

As dry and sunny as it had been in France, it was wet and horrid when the circus moved to Silverstone. So difficult were the conditions that few will remember that Senna won. What people will recall is that Prost pulled off, saying the conditions were too dangerous. The Press had a field day. Senna's win did not come without a fight in the deluge as he was led away by Berger and Alboreto and took 14 laps to hit the front. The Ferraris were not to score, though, as Mansell came good for second and Nannini was third, for his first visit to the rostrum. This was the first of four consecutive wins for Senna.

The next victory came in Germany where he was able to gain yet more ground on Prost as the Frenchman finished second. Again it was wet and again Senna looked more at ease in the conditions, although Prost did make a fight of it. Senna led for the bulk of the race in Hungary, then came upon traffic on the main straight. Prost dived down the inside of Senna, but he was unable to take the corner as he would have wished. Senna let him slide by, then took a tighter line on the exit and regained the lead. They finished just half a second apart, the result putting them equal on points.

Sponsors' delight *Berger raises the trophy after winning at Monza.*

Senna's fourth win on the trot came in Belgium, where he overcame a poor getaway to trounce all challengers at Spa and move into the championship lead. Prost was second, while Boutsen and Nannini were third and fourth for Benetton.

Breakthrough for Ferrari

Just when people had become convinced it would never happen, it did: something other than a McLaren won a race. The car to break this run was a Ferrari, the driver Berger. To make matters better, it was a Ferrari one-two, with Alboreto finishing half a second behind. Better still, the race was in Italy, home of Ferrari...

But what of the McLaren men? Prost retired when in second place with engine failure, while Senna had a more dramatic departure. On the penultimate lap, he was leading, but was losing time to the Ferraris as he struggled with his car's thirst for fuel. He was still five seconds ahead of Berger, though, when he came across the Williams replacement driver, Jean-Louis Schlesser, driving in place of Mansell who had a viral infection. The pair met at one of Monza's many chicanes. The Frenchman appeared not to see the Brazilian and they touched, sending Senna into retirement. The crowd went wild. Team-founder Enzo Ferrari would have loved the result, but he had died earlier in the year. Eddie Cheever and Derek Warwick finished in third and fourth places for Arrows.

McLaren returned to winning ways in Portugal, as Prost took the spoils after a fraught battle at the start with Senna. The race had to be restarted and the Brazilian led the first lap and swerved at Prost when he tried to pull alongside as they passed the pits. Those hanging over the pit wall recoiled as the red and white blur flashed by. Prost kept his foot in and took the lead. Senna fell back with handling problems and Ivan Capelli became Prost's challenger. Driving his March like never before, the Italian was the star of the race. He eventually settled for second. Boutsen was third.

Prost won again in Spain and the points were worth double, for Senna struggled home fourth, troubled throughout by a computer that gave confusing readings about his critical rate of fuel consumption. Senna made a bad start from pole and fell behind Prost and Mansell.

After half distance he dropped behind Capelli, too. Capelli was not to finish, though, his engine blowing, and so Nannini came third.

Senna stalled on the grid in Japan and was in 14th going into the first corner. But he fought back as only he could. Prost thus found himself in the lead and must have felt confident of having a shot at the title. But first he had to contend with Capelli, who had the temerity to lead, briefly. A few laps after that, the March's electrics failed and Capelli was out. By this time Senna was up to second, with 31 laps to go. Senna did not need that many and overtook Prost eight laps later, then motoring on to score his eighth win of 1988, wrap up the title and go partying. Prost made it home second, with Boutsen third yet again.

Prost completed the season by winning in Australia from Senna and Piquet. And so the turbo era in Formula One came to an end. But Senna's mastery of Grand Prix racing was getting ever tighter.

DRIVERS' WORLD CHAMPIONSHIP

Pos.	Driver	Nat.	Make	Pts
1	Ayrton Senna	Bra	McLaren-Honda	90
2	Alain Prost	Fr	McLaren-Honda	87
3	Gerhard Berger	A	Ferrari	41
4	Thierry Boutsen	Bel	Benetton-Ford	27
5	Michele Alboreto	It	Ferrari	24
6	Nelson Piquet	Bra	Lotus-Honda	22
7	Ivan Capelli	It	March-Judd	17
	Derek Warwick	GB	Arrows-Megatron	17
9	Nigel Mansell	GB	Williams-Judd	12
	Alessandro Nannini	It	Benetton-Ford	12

Best 11 scores from 16 races to count

CONSTRUCTORS' CUP

Pos.	Make	Pts
1	McLaren	199
2	Ferrari	65
3	Benetton	39
4	Arrows	23
	Lotus	23
6	March	22
7	Williams	20
8	Tyrrell	5
9	Rial	3
10	Minardi	1

Promise fulfilled *Ayrton Senna won the world title with one race to go.*

1989

The McLaren steamroller rolled on inexorably. This time it was the turn of Alain Prost to take the world title, and join the serried ranks of three-time winners. The trouble was that he was no longer on speaking terms with Senna...

It could be said that Prost and Ayrton Senna were being childish. In their cars they would both push to the extremes. Away from them they would do the same, each trying to find that little advantage over the other. It was not a situation that could last, so Prost looked elsewhere, choosing Ferrari for 1990, much to the disappointment of the McLaren boss Ron Dennis.

In 1989 Nigel Mansell would be competing against the McLarens with a new weapon. He had left Williams for Ferrari to drive alongside Gerhard Berger. Williams had got rid of its Judd engines and signed with Renault, a deal that would do them proud for the years ahead.

And so to the first race, the Brazilian Grand Prix. Senna claimed pole from Patrese, but the Brazilian went off at the first corner with Berger, and Patrese got the early lead, although Mansell soon took over and was able to control the race as Prost struggled with a broken clutch. Ferrari fans the world over went crazy. The meeting was run under a shadow, with French driver Philippe Streiff having crashed his AGS and broken his neck in testing. He remains a paraplegic to this day.

Starting in style
Nigel Mansell won the opening race in Brazil for Ferrari.

Bad blood at San Marino

San Marino was next, and this time Senna made no mistake. However, this is where some of the antagonism with Prost was born. Senna led away, but the race had to be stopped when Berger had a fiery crash at Tamburello – the corner that was to claim Senna's life in 1994. The Austrian was luckier, escaping with a broken rib and minor burns. Prost made the better getaway at the restart but Senna overturned a pre-race deal and snatched the lead at Tosa, then motored clear to win by fully 40 seconds. Prost was livid at this betrayal.

And so to Monaco. Senna and Prost started from the front row, their McLarens streets clear of the opposition which was headed by Boutsen's Williams.

Senna led all the way to win by over 50 seconds from Prost, while Martin Brundle was denied third by an electrical problem, letting his Brabham team-mate Stefano Modena claim the position. Berger was back in time for Mexico, albeit driving with a heavily strapped hand. But he had to play a support role as Senna led all the way from pole. Prost chose the wrong tyres and struggled to fifth. Mansell ran second, but his gearbox failed, letting Patrese and Tyrrell's Michele Alboreto complete the rostrum.

Just when Prost became convinced that all the team's luck was with Senna, he won the US Grand Prix, a race of attrition on the streets of Phoenix. Senna led, but his electrics failed, leaving Prost free to win from Patrese. McLaren domination was interrupted in Canada when Boutsen scored his first ever win after both McLarens retired. Senna, cruelly, pulled out of the lead just three laps from the end with engine failure. Patrese – second again – made it a one-two for Williams.

Prost moves ahead

Having failed to qualify his Benetton in Phoenix, the heavy braking required being too much for his still injured feet, Herbert was fired by Benetton and his place taken at the French Grand Prix by Emanuele Pirro, who had scraped into the race. The day belonged to Prost, though, leading all the way as Senna retired on lap one. The first lap of the restart, that is to say, as Mauricio Gugelmin caused the race to be stopped when he flipped his Leyton House on the run to the first corner. Mansell was second, after a phenomenal charge, having started from the pit lane as his Ferrari had been damaged by Gugelmin's aerobatics. Patrese was third, just ahead of stunning Formula One debutant Jean Alesi who replaced Alboreto at Tyrrell.

Senna failed to score again at the British Grand Prix, spinning out of the lead to let Prost in for his second win in a row. Mansell delighted the partisan crowd with second, despite

Champion again *Alain Prost acknowledges his victory at Silverstone.*

delays with a puncture. Nannini was third. Senna struck back at the German Grand Prix. He led from Prost, but had a slower pitstop to change tyres and emerged in second. Prost was confident of holding on to win. But, three laps from home, his gearbox started balking and Senna shot past. Mansell was a distant third.

However, Mansell's form was to improve in Hungary when he tigered from 12th to win in an extraordinary drive on a circuit notorious for its lack of overtaking possibilities. He gained four places on the first lap and finally hit the front after 58 of the 77 laps, never to be dislodged. Senna was a way behind in second, Boutsen third and Prost fourth.

It was wet for the Belgian Grand Prix, and Senna led all the way. Prost resisted Mansell to be second. Darker even than the weather was the mood at Lotus, for neither car qualified. The sun was out again at the Italian Grand Prix – well, for Prost at least, as he won from Berger and Boutsen. Senna led until nine laps out when his engine blew.

In Portugal, Berger went one better and won from Prost and Stefan Johansson. There had been drama aplenty, though, for Mansell overshot his pit, reversed and was black flagged. This he ignored and then Senna closed the door on him and both spun off into retirement, helping Prost's cause no end. He now had a 24-point lead with three races to go.

Trouble for Mansell

Mansell left Estoril with a $50,000 fine for ignoring the black flags. He was subsequently given a one-race ban, so he took no part in the Spanish Grand Prix and threatened to quit Formula One. This left Senna to win as he pleased with Berger second and Prost a cautious third.

What happened in the Japanese Grand Prix was to set the tone for years to come as Prost and Senna clashed and settled the World Championship, this time in the Frenchman's favour. Their contact came with seven laps to go and saw Senna dive up the inside into the chicane. Prost refused to cede and they spun. Prost retired on the spot, but Senna was push-started to get his car out of a dangerous position, pitted for a new nose-cone and still was first to the chequered flag. But he was disqualified for receiving external assistance, giving Nannini his first win. Patrese and Boutsen were thus second and third.

Driving in the wet seemed to suit Boutsen, for he wrapped up the season with his second win, in the Australian Grand Prix. Senna had stormed clear, but was unsighted as he ploughed into Brundle's spray-hidden Brabham. Boutsen took over and won from Nannini and Patrese.

DRIVERS' WORLD CHAMPIONSHIP

Pos.	Driver	Nat.	Make	Pts
1	Alain Prost	Fr	McLaren-Honda	76
2	Ayrton Senna	Bra	McLaren-Honda	60
3	Riccardo Patrese	It	Williams-Renault	40
4	Nigel Mansell	GB	Ferrari	38
5	Thierry Boutsen	Bel	Williams-Renault	37
6	Alessandro Nannini	It	Benetton-Ford	32
7	Gerhard Berger	A	Ferrari	21
8	Nelson Piquet	Bra	Lotus-Judd	12
9	Jean Alesi	Fr	Tyrrell-Ford	8
10	Derek Warwick	GB	Arrows-Ford	7

Best 11 scores from 16 races to count

CONSTRUCTORS' CUP

Pos.	Make	Pts
1	McLaren	141
2	Williams	77
3	Ferrari	59
4	Benetton	39
5	Tyrrell	16
6	Lotus	15
7	Arrows	13
8	Brabham	8
	Dallara	8
10	Minardi	6
	Onyx	6

Forza Ferrari *The* tifosi *dubbed Nigel Mansell* Il Leone.

1990

It was Ayrton Senna versus Alain Prost for the third season in a row. As in 1988, the Brazilian took the spoils, with no-one else in sight. But at one time it looked as though he wasn't going to be allowed to start the championship at all.

Bird's eye view *Ayrton Senna encounters some heavy traffic around the streets of Phoenix.*

The trouble between Senna and the authorities stemmed from the way in which he and Prost had clashed in Japan in 1989, and the fact that the Brazilian had been disqualified after crossing the line first.

He then accused Jean-Marie Balestre, the FISA president, of manipulating the championship in Prost's favour and was subsequently refused entry for the 1990 championship. A winter of impasse followed and it was only with the first race approaching that Senna was finally readmitted.

Senna gets going

Oh, but how Senna started his campaign! Kicking off with the US Grand Prix around the streets of Phoenix, he tracked down surprise leader Jean Alesi's Tyrrell, took the lead, was cheekily re-passed by the Frenchman, then pulled in front for good. Thierry Boutsen was a distant third in his Williams. And Prost's Ferrari? Well, that started seventh, climbed to fourth and retired.

The win in Phoenix did plenty for Senna's attitude, but failing to score his first win on his home patch in Brazil brought the winter's frown back. Indeed, he had been set for victory when Japanese driver Satoru Nakajima collided with him and forced him to pit for a new nosecone. The delay cost him the race, confining him to third behind Berger and, worst of all, race winner Prost.

At the third round, the San Marino Grand Prix at Imola, neither Senna nor Prost took the spoils, these going to Riccardo Patrese, the Italian Williams driver ending a seven-year drought. Senna led from pole but a stone jammed in his brakes and he spun off, while Prost finished seven seconds behind Patrese, yet was classified fourth behind Berger and Benetton's Alessandro Nannini.

With the next stop being Monaco, there was only ever going to be one winner: Senna. Sure enough, he delivered, chased home by Alesi, who was proving a street circuit expert in his nimble, if somewhat under-powered, Tyrrell. Third place for Berger kept him in the title hunt. Prost ran second, but retired.

Canada provided a different pattern, but the same winner: Senna. Berger jumped the start at Montreal and was given a one-minute penalty. With rain falling, it became clear that grooved tyres would be required, so McLaren called Berger in and then Senna. With time to make up, Berger was driving faster than anyone else and Senna waved him past. Yet, charge as he did to cross the line 45 seconds clear of Senna, the Austrian could make up only enough time for

Job done *Senna takes the chequered flag at Phoenix.*

Pure concentration *Senna on the grid, preparing for the task ahead.*

fourth, behind Nelson Piquet's Benetton and Nigel Mansell's Ferrari, but ahead of Prost.

Prost forges ahead

The Mexican Grand Prix provided Prost's turn for glory. But it not seem a likely outcome after qualifying, with the Frenchman down in 13th. However, he drove a patient race on a track that ate tyres. Berger had to pit as early as lap 12 for fresh rubber. Senna was more careful and led the first 60 laps, but had a puncture and was stranded, handing the race to Prost. Mansell and Berger banged wheels around the mighty, banked Peralta corner, with Nigel on the outside, but the Englishman held on to complete a Ferrari one-two.

Back in Europe for the French Grand Prix, it was Prost who took the laurels, but there had nearly been a major shock: Ivan Capelli had led for 45 laps for Leyton House, a team that had hitherto scored not a point. It seemed that the smooth track at Paul Ricard suited the Leyton House cars. Indeed, Mauricio Gugelmin ran behind his team-mate Capelli until his engine tightened and went pop. It was not to be, and Prost stole into the lead three laps from home. However, Capelli was delighted with second all the same.

Mansell did not win the next race, the British Grand Prix, but he stole the headlines by announcing his retirement at the end of the season. Victory on the day went to Prost, once Mansell had pulled off with gearbox problems and Boutsen snatched second, with Senna coming back from a spin to take third. Germany was next up, and it was Senna's turn to win from Nannini after struggling to re-pass the Italian's Benetton which ran a non-stop strategy to Ayrton's one planned stop. Berger was third and Prost a distant fourth.

Senna was close to winning at the next race, the Hungarian Grand Prix, but missed out by a few feet to Boutsen, having taken off a charging Nannini shortly before the flag. It was only right that the two leading drivers should finish first and second in the Belgian Grand Prix.

The Italian Grand Prix was another event that would be recalled for an incident rather than the outcome of the race. This time it was Derek Warwick's Lotus that caught the attention, destroying itself against the barriers while coming on to the pit straight at the end of lap one. Amazingly, he ran back to the pits and climbed into the spare car for the restart. For the records, Senna won from Prost.

Mansell left his mark in Portugal, by not assisting Prost to close down on Senna's points lead. Mansell chopped across on his team-mate at the start, causing him to lift off the throttle. In an instant, Prost was back to fifth and the way was clear for Mansell to motor untroubled to victory, from Senna and Prost.

Lotus hit problems again at the Spanish Grand Prix at Jerez. This time it was not Warwick, but Martin Donnelly. And he was unbelievably lucky to survive an accident in qualifying that left him lying in the track, his car having disintegrated on impact with the barriers. This time Prost won, gaining doubly valuable points as Senna retired.

Prost and Senna in dispute

A year on from their clash in Japan, Senna and Prost did it again at Suzuka, this time on the opening lap. Both were out on the spot, giving Senna the title. Then the bitter quarrels began. Almost obscured by this drama, Piquet led home a Benetton one-two ahead of childhood friend Roberto Moreno who had replaced Nannini after the latter had severed one of his hands in a helicopter crash.

Benetton won again in Australia, through Piquet. Mansell and Prost were second and third respectively, Senna having crashed out of the lead at three-quarters distance after a fine scrap with Mansell. And that was that, with Senna champion from Prost. By dint of having scored two wins to Berger's none, Piquet claimed third in the final standings.

CONSTRUCTORS' CUP

Pos.	Make	Pts
1	McLaren	121
2	Ferrari	110
3	Benetton	71
4	Williams	57
5	Tyrrell	16
6	Lola	11
	Leyton House	11
8	Lotus	3
9	Arrows	2
	Brabham	2

DRIVERS' WORLD CHAMPIONSHIP

Pos.	Driver	Nat.	Make	Pts
1	Ayrton Senna	Bra	McLaren-Honda	78
2	Alain Prost	Fr	Ferrari	71
3	Nelson Piquet	Bra	Benetton-Ford	43
4	Gerhard Berger	A	McLaren-Honda	43
5	Nigel Mansell	GB	Ferrari	37
6	Thierry Boutsen	Bel	Williams-Renault	34
7	Riccardo Patrese	It	Williams-Renault	23
8	Alessandro Nannini	It	Benetton-Ford	21
9	Jean Alesi	Fr	Tyrrell-Ford	13
10	Ivan Capelli	It	Leyton House-Judd	6
	Roberto Moreno	Bra	Benetton-Ford	6
	Aguri Suzuki	Jap	Lola-Lamborghini	6

Best 11 scores from 16 races to count

1991

Ayrton Senna and McLaren made it two world championships in succession, while Nigel Mansell elected not to retire but to race for Williams, who were in strong form . He would challenge Senna, but would fall short.

Top dog *Ayrton Senna was first past the chequered flag seven times.*

Senna could not have kicked off in better fashion: he won the first four races from pole. The first was the US Grand Prix at Phoenix, when he blasted clear on the first lap and, even though he backed off, won by 16 seconds from Alain Prost's Ferrari and Nelson Piquet's Benetton. A notable drive came from Formula One debutant Finn, Mika Hakkinen, who shone despite having his steering wheel come off in his hands.

Senna wins at home

It was closer in the Brazilian Grand Prix, as Senna made it only three seconds clear of a fast-closing Riccardo Patrese's Williams, with McLaren team-mate Gerhard Berger just two seconds further back. But only one thing mattered to Senna: he had won his home race at his eighth attempt, when it was starting to look as though it would always elude him. Indeed, it nearly did this time. Pressed by Mansell early on, he was relieved when the Englishman's gearbox jammed. But then Senna's started to misbehave, and he ran the last lap with it stuck in sixth.

The San Marino Grand Prix was easier for Senna, only Berger finishing on the same lap as McLaren steamrollered the opposition. Patrese became the first driver to lead Senna, but his Williams slowed after ten laps with engine problems. Mansell went off on the first lap after colliding with Martin Brundle's Brabham. But this was further than Prost got, for he fell off a wet track on the parade lap.

So to Senna's stamping ground at Monaco. He duly won. The closest anyone got to him was Stefano Modena with his best ever drive in a Tyrrell. But his engine blew, also accounting for Patrese who went off on the resultant slick. Mansell claimed second. The Canadian Grand Prix will be remembered as the one in which Mansell failed within sight of the line. He was streets clear, waving to the crowds, delighted to have broken the McLaren stranglehold, but then his engine died and Piquet went by for victory. Modena finished second, to atone for his Monaco disappointment. Senna ran third, but retired.

Down Mexico way, Patrese hit the top after a late-race challenge from team-mate Mansell. Senna followed them home, but he had already had a topsy-turvy weekend, having flipped his McLaren in qualifying. He stepped away unscathed, then attacked Honda for not developing an engine capable of matching the Williams-Renaults.

Boost for Mansell

Mansell finally took his first win of the year in the French Grand Prix, this being held at Magny-Cours for the first time. He swapped the lead with Prost, but was in front when it counted. Senna resisted a late challenge from Alesi for third. A week later Mansell repeated his success in the British Grand Prix at Silverstone in front of wild scenes of Mansellmania. Starting on pole, leading every lap and setting fastest lap gave a clue to his dominance. Senna should have been second, but he ran out of fuel on the last lap, letting Berger and Prost past.

Senna's once huge points lead was reduced further in the German Grand Prix when Mansell made it three in a row. Amazingly, Senna ran out of fuel on the last lap again, los-

Wet then dry *Conditions at Imola caught out many, but not Senna ...*

ing fourth place and more valuable points. Patrese made it a Williams one-two ahead of Alesi. Prost fought with Senna until he fell off up an escape road, only stoking their fiery relationship.

With his points advantage over Mansell down to eight, Senna was delighted to win the Hungarian Grand Prix. Indeed, with the power circuits lying ahead, it was to be his last likely victory until a return to the twistier tracks later in the year. Mansell pushed Senna hard, but the Brazilian outqualified him on this narrow track that offers almost no overtaking points.

Spa is a circuit that favours those with power aplenty, such as the Renault in Mansell's Williams. So it was a surprise to see Senna win. A bit of a surprise to him, too, as his gearbox was playing up again. Also, he was outpaced first by Mansell and then by Alesi, but both retired. Andrea de Cesaris was heading for second for Jordan, but his engine gave up three laps from home, depriving him of his best ever result.

Schumacher makes debut

His team-mate that day was one Michael Schumacher, making his first appearance in Formula One. He outqualified de Cesaris, but was out on lap one. Before long, we would hear a great deal more from him. Indeed, at the very next race he was driving for Benetton in place of Roberto Moreno.

Mansell won the Italian Grand Prix to stay in the title chase. Senna led for many laps, but was eating his tyres in an attempt to stay ahead of first Patrese, then Mansell, so he had to settle for second place. Schumacher scored his first points, coming in fifth place. Clearly, the 22-year-old German was not going to wait to be shown the way by the establishment.

After a season of much promise but scratchy results, Patrese won again in Portugal, but this was handed to him when Mansell lost a wheel leaving a pit stop. The wheel was reapplied, but in an illegal place, so Mansell was disqualified. Second place for Senna put him 24 points clear with three races to go. Doing his best, as ever, Mansell won the Spanish Grand Prix from Prost and Patrese with a perhaps nervous Senna fifth. It was Berger's turn to win in Japan, albeit only after Senna slowed on the final lap to let him past. By then he no longer needed the extra four points as the title was already his, having seen Mansell spear off on lap ten. Sadly, Senna could not steer away from controversy and took the occasion of his third Formula One title to attack outgoing FISA president Jean-Marie Balestre, raking over old ground and accusing the Frenchman of preventing him from winning the 1989 title.

Luckily, the season was brought to a happier end at the Australian Grand Prix when Senna was best of the field in torrential conditions in a race that was halted after 14 of 81 scheduled laps. Only half points were awarded. There was some bad taste circulating, though, for Prost had been kicked out of Ferrari. He was going anyway, tired of the politics, but he had not expected not to be driving in Adelaide. In view of the conditions, however, he was probably not terribly disappointed.

On top of the world
Riccardo Patrese waves to the the crowd after his victory in the Mexican Grand Prix.

CONSTRUCTORS' CUP

Pos.	Make	Pts
1	McLaren	139
2	Williams	125
3	Ferrari	55.5
4	Benetton	38.5
5	Jordan	13
6	Tyrrell	12
7	Minardi	6
8	Dallara	5
9	Brabham	3
	Lotus	3

DRIVERS' WORLD CHAMPIONSHIP

Pos.	Driver	Nat.	Make	Pts
1	Ayrton Senna	Bra	McLaren-Honda	96
2	Nigel Mansell	GB	Williams-Renault	72
3	Riccardo Patrese	It	Williams-Renault	53
4	Gerhard Berger	A	McLaren-Honda	43
5	Alain Prost	Fr	Ferrari	34
6	Nelson Piquet	Bra	Benetton-Ford	26.5
7	Jean Alesi	Fr	Ferrari	21
8	Stefano Modena	It	Tyrrell-Honda	10
9	Andrea de Cesaris	It	Jordan-Ford	9
10	Roberto Moreno	Bra	Benetton-Ford	8

All scores counted

1992

This was the year when Nigel Mansell finally showed the racing world he could be a champion, not just a melodramatic bit-player. Seldom has any driver dominated the Formula One championship to such an extent as he did.

It was the sixth race before Mansell was actually beaten and his victory tally stood at eight after the first ten. At the very next race he wrapped up the world title he had been chasing for so long, and there were still five Grands Prix to run. By season's end, Nigel had almost double the score of the second man in the rankings, Williams team-mate Riccardo Patrese. While Nigel's driving was from the very top drawer throughout 1992, he was given a huge step up by the Williams team with its fabulous chassis and world-beating Renault engine. Sad thing was, Mansell did not have the good grace to acknowledge that he was playing with a hand blessed with four aces.

Mansell's run of victories

It started in South Africa for the first time since 1985 when victory had been taken by a Williams driver by the name of N. Mansell. Clearly he enjoyed his reacquaintance with Kyalami, for he planted his Williams on pole and led every lap of the race from Patrese, winning by 24 seconds. Mexico was the next stop. And it was the same story, with Mansell leading home a Williams one-two. Again, the third-placed finisher was ten seconds adrift of Patrese, although this time it was Schumacher making his first visit to the rostrum. Senna ran third but retired early on. Williams finishing first and second were clearly part of the year's plan, for they did so again in the Brazilian Grand Prix at Interlagos, with Mansell beating Patrese, this time by fully half a minute. Again Schumacher was a lapped third.

With Mansell dominating the Spanish Grand Prix at Barcelona, the major surprise was that it was Schumacher not Patrese who finished second. The reason for this? Patrese spun out of second place in the wet. Jean Alesi brought his Ferrari home third.

Imola, home of the San Marino Grand Prix, was the venue for the fifth of Mansell's wins, with Patrese keeping his nose clean for his fourth second place. Senna fought his way around to third, but his physical input had been so great that it was 20 minutes before he was able to climb out of his McLaren.

Senna's close win at Monaco

Mansell's record run had to come to an end some time. And so it did, in Monaco. But only just. Indeed, Mansell was only 0.2 seconds away from victory when he crossed the finish line. This was after a monumental struggle to re-pass Senna after the Brazilian had hit the front when Mansell felt one of his tyres start to deflate. He pitted and closed up on Senna when he rejoined. But Monaco is almost impossible for overtaking, and Senna hung on to win.

The Canadian Grand Prix provided a real surprise result: victory not to Mansell, Patrese or Senna. It went to Gerhard Berger instead, his McLaren crossing the line 12 seconds clear of Schumacher. Senna had led past half-distance, but his electrics failed, by which time Mansell had already spun out of second place. This elevated Patrese to second behind Berger, but his gearbox broke. The French Grand Prix was the one that should have heralded Patrese's first win of the year. But the race was halted by rain and he lost out on the restart as team orders forced him to wave Mansell past. Patrese was not happy about the situation. Mansell was, for it helped him equal Jackie Stewart's tally of 27 wins. Brundle made it to the rostrum in third.

There was only going to be one winner of the British Grand Prix: Nigel Mansell. In fact, he did not just beat the opposition at Silverstone, he

Seven up *And it was only July. Mansell celebrates at Silverstone.*

demoralized them. Pole, fastest lap and victory by 40 seconds was proof of that. Patrese was second again and Brundle third after passing Senna near the end as the Brazilian pulled off. A fortnight later Mansell won again, this time in Germany ahead of Senna, with Schumacher a distant third just ahead of Brundle.

The Hungarian Grand Prix was the one that finally determined that Mansell would be world champion. He hoped to wrap it up with another win, but had to play second fiddle to Senna. However, that was enough for him to claim the coveted crown. Even so, there was typical drama when Mansell had a puncture at

Untouchable *Six wins in the first seven races set Mansell on his way.*

three-quarters distance and had to fight his way past Berger.

Then Schumacher scored the first of what would be many victories by winning in Belgium with a lucky break. Everyone started on slicks despite light rain before the start. But the rain worsened and only Senna fought on with slicks, falling back as others pitted for treaded tyres. If the rain had stopped it would have been a masterstroke, but it did not and Senna would finish fifth. Schumacher was third for much of the race, but ran wide and dropped behind Brundle. In an instant he noticed that his team-mate's tyres were blistering. Reckoning that his would be doing likewise, he dived into the pits. It proved the optimum moment, for it put him in the lead ahead of Mansell and Patrese by the time they too had pitted.

Mansell bows out

The Italian Grand Prix was overshadowed by two major news stories. Firstly, Mansell announced, yet again, his retirement from Formula One. Secondly, Honda was pulling out, too, so McLaren would have to look elsewhere for its engines. Of the race, Mansell led, then ceded the lead so Patrese could win on his home patch, but both cars hit gearbox problems. Mansell retired, while Patrese limped home fifth as Senna came through to win from Brundle and Schumacher.

Next stop was Estoril and Mansell was back to winning form, breaking a record for the number of wins in a season. This was his ninth win of 1992. Cruising to victory he was nearly caught out by Patrese or, more to the point, by wreckage from Patrese's car that was spread across the track on the main straight after the Italian suffered a huge aerial accident when he clipped Berger's pitbound McLaren. Berger was able to continue and finished second, while Senna made it past Brundle to claim the third spot on the rostrum.

Japan was next and, for once, there was no acrimony at Suzuka. Mansell played the gallant hero and waved Patrese into the lead, but then his engine blew and so Berger and Brundle completed the top three.

Mansell mania *Silverstone exploded when 'Nige' won again.*

The season came to an end on the streets of Adelaide and saw Berger grab his second win of the year ahead of Schumacher and Brundle in a race that lost Mansell and Senna in a shunt when the Brazilian was attempting to take the lead, hitting the Williams up the rear. So, no happy story for either of the main men, and Senna fell from third to fourth in the final rankings.

CONSTRUCTORS' CUP

Pos.	Make	Pts
1	Williams	164
2	McLaren	99
3	Benetton	91
4	Ferrari	21
5	Lotus	13
6	Tyrrell	8
7	Footwork	6
	Ligier	6
9	March	3
10	Dallara	2

DRIVERS' WORLD CHAMPIONSHIP

Pos.	Driver	Nat.	Make	Pts
1	Nigel Mansell	GB	Williams-Renault	108
2	Riccardo Patrese	It	Williams-Renault	56
3	Michael Schumacher	Ger	Benetton-Ford	53
4	Ayrton Senna	Bra	McLaren-Honda	50
5	Gerhard Berger	A	McLaren-Honda	49
6	Martin Brundle	GB	Benetton-Ford	38
7	Jean Alesi	Fr	Ferrari	18
8	Mika Hakkinen	Fin	Lotus-Ford	11
9	Andrea de Cesaris	It	Tyrrell-Ilmor	8
10	Michele Alboreto	It	Footwork-Honda	6

All scores counted

1993

Domination by one driver was the name of the game. And again the driver was in a Williams, but this time it was Alain Prost, who had been helped by a year away from the cockpit to regain his composure and passion for racing.

Prost had not fallen out of touch with the sport, since he had spent 1992 commentating for French television. Indeed, it was known early in Mansell's championship year that team boss Frank Williams was anxious to have Prost for 1993. He wanted the Frenchman and Ayrton Senna, too, in place of Mansell, precipitating the Englishman's departure to Indycars.

Number four *Seven wins brought Prost his fourth World title.*

Good start for Prost

Thus, Williams began 1993 with Prost in the lead car and Damon Hill upgraded from the test team to drive the second. Prost got straight into the groove, winning the first round, the South African Grand Prix at Kyalami. Senna had made the early running for McLaren, but Prost hit the front at one-third distance and remained there to beat Senna by 20 seconds, with Mark Blundell a surprise third.

Having finally won in Brazil in 1992, Senna repeated the feat with an outstanding tactical victory at Interlagos. Prost was leading when rain started to fall and he hit a car that had spun. This put Hill in front, but he was to be Senna's prey. However, Hill was happy with a second place finish.

Rain was becoming the theme of the year when it struck the European Grand Prix at Donington Park, but Senna put on one of the greatest drives of all time as he forced his way from fourth on the grid into the lead by the end of a stunning first lap and roared away as his rivals tiptoed in his wake. The Williams drivers were simply not in the same class and Senna led Hill home by over a minute. Prost showed his dislike for the rain and was a lapped third.

Furious at the slating he received from the Press in France for his lack-lustre drive at Donington, Prost answered them with a controlled win at Imola, albeit only after fighting with a sticking throttle. Hill led the early laps but spun off. Senna was running second when his hydraulics failed, so he yielded his position to Schumacher.

Hill was clearly anxious to notch up his first win at Barcelona. He led from the start, dropped behind Prost but reapplied the pressure and was looking good until his engine blew, leaving Prost to win as he pleased from Senna and Schumacher. Of note was the fact that Senna's team-mate, Michael Andretti – son of 1978 world champion Mario Andretti – finally finished a race, scoring two points for fifth. His graduation from being the star of Indy Car racing was not proving altogether easy.

Senna fights for top place

Monaco, it has to be Senna. Well, it was, for the sixth time, but the race did not go his way as others had before it. Prost led early on, but was given a stop-and-go penalty and magnified the punishment by stalling in the pit lane. This put Schumacher in front, but his hydraulics failed and so Senna took the lead. Hill came second, hoping that Senna would retire so he could win the race that his father, Graham Hill, won five times. Jean Alesi was third for Ferrari. The Canadian Grand Prix marked the start of a four-race winning streak for Prost. No one else got a look-in, as Schumacher benefited from Senna's late race retirement to trail home second, with Hill third.

Considering the technical superiority of the Williams, it was

Great show *Senna's drive at Donington was one of the best.*

Blast off *Damon Hill leads away in Hungary. Schumacher, Berger (28), Senna (8) and Patrese give chase. This was Hill's first victory in Formula One.*

surprising that it took until the eighth round before they scored a one-two. Fittingly, it was on the home patch of their engine supplier, Renault. Hill led from pole, but was delayed in the pits and was bumped to second by Prost. That was how it stayed, this pair crossing the line nose-to-tail. Schumacher was third.

If Prost was able to win on home ground, so was Hill in the British Grand Prix. Or so Damon thought. Sadly, it did not work that way. In front from the start, he saw his efforts come to nought when his engine blew at two-thirds distance. Prost needed no second asking and motored on to victory, his 50th win. Benetton boys Schumacher and Riccardo Patrese finished second and third.

Hill's winning streak

It seemed fate was to stand between Hill and victory, for he appeared set for success in Germany until disaster struck two laps from the end. In front for 43 laps, he had a tyre blow. Prost, ten seconds behind after suffering another stop-and-go penalty, flew past as Hill tried in vain to struggle back to the pits, and so Schumacher and Blundell were second and third.

Finally, it happened: Hill won, at the Hungaroring where Mansell had clinched the 1992 title. Despite qualifying behind Prost, Hill led all the way when Prost was forced to start from the rear of the grid after stalling on the parade lap. Senna shadowed Hill in the early laps, but retired and left the way clear for Patrese and Berger to complete the rostrum.

The next two races had two things in common: both were won by Hill, and both witnessed accidents of shocking proportions. First off, Alessandro Zanardi had a big one while qualifying in Belgium, rattling his Lotus off the barriers at the fearsome Eau Rouge corner. Then, in Italy, Christian Fittipaldi clipped his team-mate's car on the sprint to the line and flipped his Minardi. It was something of a miracle that it landed the right way up.

Schumacher and Prost trailed Hill home at Spa, while Alesi and the maligned Andretti were second and third at Monza. Prost should have won in Italy and with it clinch his fourth world title, but his engine blew five laps from home.

Schumacher scores

Schumacher had promised so much all year, so it was not surprising when he scored the second win of his career, in Portugal. However, he really had to work for it, as Prost was in his wheel tracks and the German's tyres were almost finished. But he stayed out and won.

Prost, one second behind, claimed the world title and with it announced his retirement. Hill qualified on pole, stalled and tigered through to third from the rear of the grid. And so to Japan. Senna won in style, but he courted controversy by going to see debutant Eddie Irvine who, he felt, had blocked him.

A thrown punch got Senna into trouble once more. It also marked Irvine (who finished an astonishing sixth for Jordan) as a driver to watch for all the wrong reasons. Prost and Mika Hakkinen – in at McLaren in place of Andretti – ran second and third all race. The season ended in Adelaide, and victory for Senna helped McLaren pass Ferrari to become the most successful Formula One team of all time. Prost was second, Hill third, and the rest a lap adrift. That summed up the season.

DRIVERS' WORLD CHAMPIONSHIP

Pos.	Driver	Nat.	Make	Pts
1	Alain Prost	Fr	Williams-Renault	99
2	Ayrton Senna	Bra	McLaren-Ford	73
3	Damon Hill	GB	Williams-Renault	69
4	Michael Schumacher	Ger	Benetton-Ford	52
5	Riccardo Patrese	It	Benetton-Ford	20
6	Jean Alesi	Fr	Ferrari	16
7	Martin Brundle	GB	Ligier-Renault	13
8	Gerhard Berger	A	Ferrari	12
9	Johnny Herbert	GB	Lotus-Ford	11
10	Mark Blundell	GB	Ligier Renault	10

All scores counted

CONSTRUCTORS' CUP

Pos.	Make	Pts
1	Williams	168
2	McLaren	84
3	Benetton	72
4	Ferrari	28
5	Ligier	23
6	Lotus	12
	Sauber	12
8	Minardi	7
9	Footwork	4
10	Jordan	3
	Larrousse	3

1994

It was a memorably bad year, a championship marred by Senna's death and spoiled by controversy. It went down to the wire in Adelaide and then Michael Schumacher clinched the crown — in questionable fashion.

Wunderkind *Michael Schumacher was in a class of his own.*

Few people were interested in betting on the outcome of the championship. It was going to be Ayrton Senna for Williams, no question about it. But this is not how it worked out. At the time of his death in May, the great Brazilian had scored no points from the first two races, while Germany's Michael Schumacher had two wins to his credit in the lead Benetton. So, what was going on? Technology had changed from 1993, with driver aids – such as traction control – having been banned. Refuelling was a prerequisite for 1994, so tactics became more crucial than ever.

Senna led in Brazil. However, the first round of pit stops revealed something important: Benetton were the kings of the pit stop. They had Schumacher back out faster than Williams could return Senna to the fray. So, Schumacher found himself in front and there he stayed. Senna could not keep up and spun into retirement in his efforts to do so, thus letting teammate Damon Hill finish second, with Jean Alesi third for Ferrari. The race will be remembered for a huge accident that culminated in Jos Verstappen flipping the second Benetton and clouting Martin Brundle's McLaren as he landed. Amazingly, no one was injured.

The all-new TI Circuit in Japan was next, hosting a Grand Prix for the first time. Any thoughts of another contest between Senna and Schumacher were scuppered at the first corner of this narrow circuit when Senna was tipped into the gravel by McLaren's Mika Hakkinen. This left Schumacher clear to win as he pleased from Berger's Ferrari and an ecstatic Rubens Barrichello who scored the Jordan team's first podium placing.

Tragedy at San Marino

Then came the worst weekend in living memory: the San Marino Grand Prix. Friday qualifying nearly saw the demise of Barrichello with an accident at the final chicane. He was lucky, but the following day Austrian Roland Ratzenberger fatally hit a wall at nearly 200mph in his Simtek. Then, the cruellest and most unbelievable event befell them: Senna crashed out of the lead at the flat-out Tamburello kink. The man who seemed more than mortal had died.

Monaco was run in the shadow of this double fatality, so nothing could have been worse than what happened in qualifying, for Karl

Men of war *Winner Hill, flanked by Hakkinen (right) and Coulthard, in Portugal.*

Second generation *Damon Hill performed like his double world champion father, Graham. Here he wins at Estoril.*

Wendlinger had a minor crash in his Sauber, but received a blow to the head and went into a coma for a month. Schumacher made it four from four on race day. Martin Brundle was over 30 seconds behind him in second for McLaren, with Berger third.

By the time of the Spanish Grand Prix, the drivers had insisted on changes to the Barcelona circuit to make it safer. This meant the introduction of several temporary chicanes to slow the cars down where they felt the run-off was insufficient. The result of the race was what everyone wished for: a Williams win. Schumacher led but became stuck in fifth gear and Hill went by. Amazingly, Schumacher was able to finish second, with Mark Blundell third for Tyrrell. Schumacher returned to his winning ways in Canada. He won from Hill by 40 seconds, with Alesi and Berger next up. Coulthard scored his first points in fifth after earning the displeasure of Hill by leading his team-mate early on.

Worried by falling TV viewing figures, Nigel Mansell was brought back from Indy Cars for a one-off in the French Grand Prix. Renault paid for his return, hoping he would give them a win on home soil. Well, despite qualifying on the front row alongside Hill, neither Williams driver led into the first corner and neither won. Schumacher did both, blasting off at the start in an unbelievable manner. Hill finished second and Berger third.

The British Grand Prix was next. And it was at Silverstone that the "fun" began. Schumacher broke grid order, twice powering ahead of pole-man Hill on the parade lap. This is illegal and so he was shown the black flag during the race. Instead of pitting, he ignored the flag. This was to earn him a two-race suspension. Eventually he came in for a stop-and-go penalty, and so Hill won at home, with Schumacher second and Alesi third.

Comeback for Ferrari

Determined not to miss his home race, Schumacher's team arranged for the suspension to be deferred, but Schumacher was not to win at Hockenheim. Victory, instead, went to Berger, breaking a 58-race victory drought for Ferrari. However, the race will be recalled more for a pit fire that engulfed Verstappen's Benetton. Incredibly, Verstappen escaped with minor burns. The race also suffered a first corner shunt that took out 11 cars – for which Hakkinen was blamed and given a one-race ban.

Things could only get better in Hungary. And they did, especially for Benetton, with Schumacher and Verstappen sandwiching Hill in first and third. Controversy returned at Spa. Schumacher won from Hill and Hakkinen. But he had ground away too much of the underside of his "plank" (a strip on the underside of the car that is to stop the cars running too low), and was disqualified, elevating Verstappen to third.

Schumacher missed the next two races, in Italy and Portugal. It was essential that Hill win both. And he did. At Monza he worked his way past the Ferraris and was heading a Williams one-two when Coulthard's ran out of fuel on the last lap, letting Berger and Hakkinen claim second and third. Then, at Estoril, Hill overcame being flipped in qualifying to lead Coulthard home, with Hakkinen in third.

And so the stage was set for the last three races, with Hill just one point behind Schumacher. The German came back in the best possible fashion, beating Hill at Jerez when the Williams would not take on the right amount of fuel in a pit stop. Once again, Hakkinen was third.

Japan, the most thrilling race of the year, was run in heavy rain. Schumacher took the lead, but Hill stuck to his tail, able to see nothing in the spray. The race turned on the fact that Schumacher chose to make two pit stops, Hill just one. The final laps were desperate as Schumacher used his fresher tyres to close in on Hill. It was very close, but Hill held on. Alesi was third. It was a vital win, as Schumacher went to the last race with just a one-point advantage.

As in Japan, Schumacher and Hill were the class of the field in Adelaide. Just before mid-distance, Schumacher ran wide and grazed a wall. Hill dived for a gap at the next corner and the German, knowing his car was damaged, drove into Hill. Schumacher was tipped out of the race, but he had made himself the new champion, since Hill's car was too damaged to continue. Thus Mansell was left to win from Berger and Brundle.

CONSTRUCTORS' CUP

Pos.	Make	Pts
1	Williams	118
2	Benetton	103
3	Ferrari	71
4	McLaren	42
5	Jordan	28
6	Ligier	13
	Tyrrell	13
8	Sauber	12
9	Footwork	9
10	Minardi	5

DRIVERS' WORLD CHAMPIONSHIP

Pos.	Driver	Nat.	Make	Pts
1	Michael Schumacher	Ger	Benetton-Ford	92
2	Damon Hill	GB	Williams-Renault	91
3	Gerhard Berger	A	Ferrari	41
4	Mika Hakkinen	Fin	McLaren-Peugeot	26
5	Jean Alesi	Fr	Ferrari	24
6	Rubens Barrichello	Bra	Jordan-Hart	19
7	Martin Brundle	GB	McLaren-Peugeot	16
8	David Coulthard	GB	Williams-Renault	14
9	Nigel Mansell	GB	Williams-Renault	13
10	Jos Verstappen	Neth	Benetton-Ford	10

All scores counted

THE TEAMS

Although it is drivers who receive the laurels, they invariably pay tribute to the crew in the pits and the technical experts, without whom no team can succeed.

Team work *No driver can win without the best support.*

Grand Prix racing began with rich individuals only behind the wheel. Indeed, the very early road races often saw these gentlemen pedalled by their chauffeurs. But, inevitably, things changed as racing became more competitive and cars more hybrid.

The 1920s saw the manufacturers take over from the wealthy individuals. And so Alfa-Romeo won most of the early laurels, to be displaced by Auto Union and Mercedes-Benz.

By the late 1950s, with Ferrari, Maserati and Mercedes at the head of the game, the force of the owner/engineer was beginning to be felt, with British brains pushing Formula One technology on at a startling pace. And it was in the 1960s that individual teams truly formed their own identity. Later dubbed "the garagistes", these teams popped up, literally from lockups under the railway arches. And so teams such as Lotus, Brabham and McLaren came to the forefront.

Teams have come and gone ever since, often according to the prevalent economic climate, occasionally because the team owner has been disgraced. However, we have reached the mid-1990s with the British McLaren, Williams and Benetton teams joined in the big four only by Formula One stalwarts Ferrari, the world's most popular team. The rest, it has apparently been deemed, will fight over what is left.

ALFA ROMEO

COUNTRY OF ORIGIN:	ACTIVE YEARS IN FORMULA ONE:
Italy	**1950–85**
DATE OF FOUNDATION:	CONSTRUCTORS' CUP VICTORIES:
1909	**none**

Alfa-Romeo was an evocative motor sporting name of the 1920s and 1930s, also prominent immediately after the Second World War. The name is an emotive one, but the company last won a Grand Prix in 1951.

Alfa-Romeo entered the Grand Prix arena in 1924. One of the most brilliant designers of the age was Vittorio Jano. After 12 years with Fiat, one of the most successful makes from the sport's early days, Jano was lured to Alfa-Romeo in 1923 and his P2 became the standard setter for the next two years. Antonio Ascari won the car's first race, at Cremona and, so crushing was the Italian superiority in the 1925 Belgian Grand Prix at Spa, that Jano actually laid out a quality lunch in the pits and called his drivers in to partake while mechanics polished the cars. The team then continued with their display!

Their fortunes changed when Ascari was killed in the French Grand Prix at Montlhery, but Alfa still took the manufacturers' championship title and added a laurel wreath to its distinctive badge.

The Tipo B

Another Jano great was the Alfa Tipo B which was fielded in 1932. Between then and 1934, it won every Grand Prix for which it was entered, driven by the likes of Rudolf Caracciola and the great Tazio Nuvolari, whom many rate as the greatest driver ever. In 1933 Alfa-Romeo was nationalized and officially withdrew from the sport, although Ferrari continued to field the cars on a semi-works basis.

Even against the might of the emerging German marques like Mercedes and Auto Union, Nuvolari managed some great feats with the Tipo B, none better than his win in the 1935 German Grand Prix.

Alfa took full control of its racing programme again in 1938, but the war intervened. Put off by the German dominance of Grand Prix racing in the late 1930s, Gioacchino Columbo designed an Alfa-Romeo Tipo 158 for the smaller voiturette class in 1939. It was hidden in a cheese factory while the Germans occupied Italy but under the new, pragmatic postwar regulations it automatically became a Grand Prix car and dominated the scene for the remainder of the 1940s. Alfa-Romeo enjoyed a string of 26 unbroken wins.

By 1951, some 13 years after it was designed, the supercharged car, now in 159 guise, took Juan Manuel Fangio to his first world title in the final race of the season, the Spanish Grand Prix, in a shoot-out against the Ferraris of Alberto Ascari, Froilan Gonzalez and Piero Taruffi. It was the car's last race and Alfa-Romeo then concentrated on sports car racing.

The Brabham-Alfa

In the mid-1970s their flat-12 sports-car engine started to attract the interest of the Formula One brigade, who were watching Ferrari dominate the proceedings with an engine of similar configuration. Former Ferrari engineer Carlo Chiti was responsible for the engines and he did a deal with Bernie Ecclestone to supply them to the Brabham team.

Autodelta was Chiti's company and the organization which conducted Alfa's racing programme. The Brabham-Alfas started to show good form and, despite a strong union movement that was opposed to rich man's sport, Alfa-Romeo was not slow to recognize the possible benefits of its own programme. In 1979 Bruno Giacomelli debuted the ugly-looking Tipo 177 in the Belgian Grand Prix at Zolder.

As Brabham reverted to Ford power, the new Alfa V12 was put into a new Tipo 179 chassis and, with Giacomelli joined by Patrick Depailler for 1980, the outlook was healthier. Sadly, though, Depailler was killed in testing at Hockenheim and, although Giacomelli led the US Grand Prix at Watkins Glen before the car expired, Alfa-Romeo was not destined to enjoy the success of its heyday. Andrea de Cesaris led the Belgian Grand Prix at Spa in 1982, but the marque did not win another Grand Prix before quitting again.

First winner *Giuseppe Farina pushes his Alfa Tipo 158 to victory at Silverstone in the first World Championship Grand Prix, in 1950.*

ARROWS

COUNTRY OF ORIGIN:	ACTIVE YEARS IN FORMULA ONE:
Great Britain	**from 1978**
DATE OF FOUNDATION:	CONSTRUCTORS' CUP VICTORIES:
1977	**none**

Arrows was formed nearly 20 years ago, but has yet to score its first Grand Prix win. Ironically, its second race, the South African Grand Prix of 1978, is the nearest it has come. Emerging young Italian Riccardo Patrese led convincingly until his engine expired.

Arrows was established in controversial circumstances as key members of the Shadow team broke away. Shadow had been sponsored by the Italian, Franco Ambrosio, later imprisoned on charges of financial irregularity. Ambrosio became the "A R" of the Arrows name and the other initials belonged to current financial director Alan Rees, the former Grand Prix driver and now managing director Jackie Oliver, and designers Dave Wass and Tony Southgate.

Swede Gunnar Nilsson was to lead the team, but developed stomach cancer and died less than a year later. Arrows opted for Patrese who, in his early days, was quick but wild.

Legal problems

After preparing its car in just 60 days and having a good start to the season, Arrows hit trouble. Shadow was of the opinion that Arrow's car was a copy of the new Shadow design to which it owned the rights. The High Court ruled in favour of Shadow and told Arrows that it could not race its car.

Arrows then had to build a replacement, which it managed to do even more quickly than it had the original, and continued without missing a race. Then, in the Italian Grand Prix, Ronnie Peterson was killed after his Lotus was involved in a multiple starting-line accident. After a witch-hunt by some of the sport's top names, including Niki Lauda and James Hunt, Patrese was held responsible and banned from the US Grand Prix.

The early Arrows cars raced in the distinctive gold livery of the Warsteiner beer company, and the 1979 car, the futuristic-looking A2 "buzz bomb" was much discussed. But it was not successful and the team reverted to more conventional thinking.

As racing developed in the 1980s, it was no longer sufficient to bolt on a customer Ford Cosworth V8 and go racing. A manufacturer link became increasingly important to cope with turbocharged engines from BMW, Renault and Ferrari. When BMW pulled out officially, its powerful four-cylinder turbo engines were renamed Megatrons and were used to good effect by Arrows. But still the elusive first win did not come.

The deal with Footwork

As the 1980s drew to a close, the Japanese Footwork corporation was anxious to break into Formula One and they struck a deal with Jackie Oliver. The team was renamed Footwork and it seemed that the injection of Japanese funding could move the Milton Keynes team to the forefront, especially when a deal with Porsche was struck for engines.

Alan Jenkins was design chief by this stage and had enjoyed successful days at McLaren when the team swept the board with the Porsche-built TAG turbo engines. Any hopes of a repeat were quickly dispelled when the first 12-cylinder engine (effectively two sixes joined together) arrived. Whereas a typical unit might have weighed 145–150 kilos, the new Porsche weighed over 210! Jenkins remembers it as one of the most depressing days of his life.

Rapidly the Porsche association came to an end and Footwork soldiered on. They ran with Japanese Mugen engines and Aguri Suzuki alongside Michele Alboreto, then Derek Warwick. The Milton Keynes headquarters had its own two-fifths scale wind-tunnel built and, when electronic technology took over, Footwork made early moves to buy the technology from McLaren. Then the governing body banned the systems.

For 1994 Jenkins designed the neat FA15 chassis for a customer Ford, with some trick rear-end aerodynamics. But rapidly introduced new regulations after early-season fatalities spoiled the cars, which were driven by Christian Fittipaldi and Gianni Morbidelli. Footwork boss Wataru Ohashi reduced his involvement and the team reverted to being Arrows Grand Prix International.

Flying cigar tube *The Arrows AZ, raced by Riccardo Patrese in the 1979 British Grand Prix, was not the marque's best.*

BENETTON

COUNTRY OF ORIGIN:	ACTIVE YEARS IN FORMULA ONE:
Italy/Great Britain	**from 1986**
DATE OF FOUNDATION:	CONSTRUCTORS' CUP VICTORIES:
1986	**none**

With his base in Treviso, northern Italy, Luciano Benetton built a chain of shops selling colourful clothing with a young appeal. He saw Formula One as the ideal way of promoting them. In the early 1980s the company sponsored Tyrrell, Alfa-Romeo and the Toleman team, which Benetton bought in 1986 and fielded the cars as Benettons.

A name to be reckoned with

With turbocharged BMW engines, they were tremendously powerful and Gerhard Berger took their first victory in Mexico.

Benetton began to emerge in the late 1980s. In 1989 they had Italian Alessandro Nannini as lead driver and signed Johnny Herbert as his team-mate. English team boss Peter Collins had given Herbert the chance, but when Flavio Briatore took over as kingpin in the Benetton organization both Collins and Herbert were soon shown the door. Briatore replaced Herbert with Emanuele Pirro, not the most inspired of moves, but Nannini finished the year with a win in the controversial Japanese Grand Prix after Senna was disqualified.

In 1990 the team signed three times world champion Nelson Piquet, then in the twilight of his Formula One career. Piquet turned in some fine performances and, as before, Benetton picked up the pieces in Japan when Senna and Prost collided.

But Benetton's future was shaped by the events of 1991 when a youthful Michael Schumacher burst on to the scene. Already a German Formula Three Champion and Macau winner, Michael was also a member of the Mercedes sports car junior team when he made his Formula One debut in a Jordan at Spa. He stunned the regulars by qualifying seventh.

Benetton had seen enough. After some ugly scenes at Monza the team managed to prise Schumacher away from Jordan and sign him to a long-term contract. Benetton engineering director Tom Walkinshaw was responsible for running the Jaguar sports car programme and he had had first-hand experience of Schumacher's ability.

Schumacher's dazzling performance

The German was brilliant from the start. He immediately outpaced Piquet and regularly brought the car home in the points. Benetton realized that it had a future champion on its books and Briatore instigated a build programme for a new technical facility in Cotswold country, bringing the operation together under one roof. In 1992 Schumacher was unable to go for the championship because Williams had mastered active suspension first, allowing Nigel Mansell and Riccardo Patrese to finish one-two in the title race. Schumacher, though, scored a wonderfully judged first Grand Prix win at Spa.

In 1993 Benetton made great strides towards closing the gap to Williams with the introduction of a semi-automatic gearbox and active suspension. But, sadly for Schumacher, he did not have traction control until Monaco, where he led, but by this time it was too late to stop Prost and Williams.

However, 1994 was the year. The Benetton B194 was the first chassis to see daylight from the "big four" teams and Ford had done a tremendous job with the Zetec-R V8. Schumacher won the first two races of the year and, when Senna was killed in the Williams at Imola, he was left on his own as Formula One's front-runner.

Benetton then endured a bitter few months with suggestions of illegality clouding their achievements. Schumacher suffered a two-race ban for ignoring a black flag at Silverstone and was then disqualified on a technicality at Spa. By the end of the season he went to Adelaide with just a single point advantage over Damon Hill's Williams. The championship was decided when the pair collided on lap 36 after Schumacher had made a mistake moments earlier. It left a bitter taste in the mouth but there was no doubting the fact that Schumacher and Benetton were worthy champions.

Benetton's champion *Michael Schumacher was the dominant force in 1994 after Senna's death.*

BRABHAM

Country of origin:	Active years in Formula One:
Great Britain	**1962–92**
Date of foundation:	Constructors' Cup victories:
1963	**1966, 1967**

Jack Brabham is the only driver to win the world championship in a car bearing his own name.

Brabham won back-to-back titles for Cooper in 1959–60, but returned home to Australia and struck up a business partnership with Ron Tauranac, an aircraft engineer.

They came to England and set up Motor Racing Developments (MRD). The cars were known as MRDs until someone pointed out that, if said rapidly in French, it sounded like something dogs did on the pavement. So, Brabham, never a publicity-seeking man, allowed his own name to be used.

In 1963 the Brabham Racing Organization was formed, using cars built by MRD. It won its first Grands Prix in 1964, when Dan Gurney was first past the flag in the French and Mexican Grands Prix.

Years of triumph

Lotus dominated in 1965, but for the following year there was a new 3-litre formula in Formula One and Brabham had an engine built by the Australian Repco company. With it, Brabham became the first driver to score a win in a car bearing his own name, at the French Grand Prix, and went on to win his third World Championship.

The following season saw the introduction of the Cosworth DFV. The new engine won first time out in Jim Clark's Lotus, but consistency allowed Denny Hulme to win a second successive championship for Brabham.

Then the team missed out. Brabham managed to sign up-coming Austrian Jochen Rindt for 1968 and there is no doubt that, if the engines had been up to it, Rindt could have prolonged the success. But the new four-cam Repco was neither quick nor reliable. Rindt left for Lotus at the end of the season.

After Jackie Stewart and Matra dominated in 1969, Brabham, now 44, decided that 1970 would be his final year. Tauranac produced his first monocoque Brabham, the BT33, and Jack won the opening race in South Africa. He should also have won in Monaco but allowed himself to be pressured into a mistake at the last hairpin by a charging Rindt.

Then Lotus upped the ante with its new Type 72. After outdriving Rindt at Brands Hatch, Brabham ran out of fuel on the last lap and that was the end of his challenge that year. Rindt then became the sport's only posthumous champion after an accident at Monza, and Brabham returned to Australia.

After struggling on in 1971, with Graham Hill and Tim Schenken, Tauranac sold the company to Bernie Ecclestone. One of Tauranac's design assistants, South African Gordon Murray, then became responsible for the Brabhams which, instead of taking over an "EM" (Ecclestone/Murray) tag, continued as BTs. Murray's distinctive BT44 was one of the prettiest Formula One cars ever built and won three races in 1974 with Carlos Reutemann driving.

Fading glory

Ferrari domination with flat-12 engines caused Ecclestone to turn to Alfa-Romeo for a similar unit but, despite signing Niki Lauda from Ferrari, the team could not win another championship. Lotus was pioneering aerodynamic wing cars and ground effect and, to counter the suction effect, Murray built a BT46B with a huge fan on the back which sucked the car on to the track. Lauda immediately blew the Lotuses away in the Swedish Grand Prix. It was brilliant but was rapidly banned.

Nelson Piquet joined the team in 1978 and became a great Brabham favourite after Lauda retired the following year. Nelson won world championships for Brabham in 1981 and 1983. But the Brazilian left at the end of 1985 and Brabham rapidly declined. Elio de Angelis was killed testing the lay-down BT55 and at the end of 1987 Ecclestone withdrew Brabham from the championship.

The team returned in 1989 after being sold to a Swiss financier who ended up in jail for massive fraud. Its ownership then became even murkier and, although the team raced until 1992, it was an embarrassment to its former self before finally disappearing.

1978 frontrunner *The BT46, seen here with Niki Lauda aboard, won twice, once with a special fan fitted.*

BRM

COUNTRY OF ORIGIN:	ACTIVE YEARS IN FORMULA ONE:
Great Britain	**1951–77**
DATE OF FOUNDATION:	CONSTRUCTORS' CUP VICTORIES:
1949	**1962**

BRM roots go back to 1947 when the British Motor Racing Research Trust was formed with the idea of building a British challenger to break the Italian stranglehold.

The man behind it was Raymond Mays, who was the first to bring commercial support to motor racing when he persuaded companies to back his English Racing Automobiles (ERA) efforts in the 1920s and 1930s. BRM (British Racing Motors) was a similar idea.

The original BRM team was a co-operative and the plan was to build a two-stage supercharged engine producing 600 brake horsepower. Unfortunately, when the car made its debut in the non-championship International Trophy at Silverstone, it was a disaster. With Raymond Sommer driving, the car qualified on the back of the grid and broke a drive-shaft on the line. Spectators threw coins at it as it was pushed off.

The research trust lasted until 1952, when Sir Alfred Owen of the Owen Organization took over BRM. No great progress was made until the 1960s, as Cooper and Lotus overtook BRM in the effort to establish Britain at the forefront of the international racing scene.

Year of victory

BRM went into 1962 with just one Grand Prix victory to its name – the Dutch Grand Prix of 1959 with Jo Bonnier – and an ultimatum from Owen to win the championship or else. Peter Berthon, part of BRM since the start, was no longer on the scene and Tony Rudd, a former Rolls Royce apprentice who had worked for Merlin engines, took over as chief engineer and team manager, doing much work on the new BRM V8 engine.

Graham Hill showed the car's potential by winning the first heat of the Brussels Grand Prix in its debut race and then beat Jim Clark's Lotus by a nose length in the International Trophy at Silverstone. He went on to score his first Grand Prix win in the opening round of the championship.

Hill won again in the German Grand Prix and then finished one-two for BRM with Richie Ginther at Monza. He was now embroiled in a championship battle with Clark's Lotus which went right down to the wire in South Africa. Clark took off into the lead with Hill second, but an engine problem put him out and Hill won the world championship for BRM in the Type 578.

Clark dominated in 1963, but BRM came back with its first monocoque car, the P261, the following year. Hill won two Grands Prix and was only prevented from taking a second championship by John Surtees' Ferrari in the final race of the season, where Hill's BRM was clobbered by Surtees' young Ferrari team-mate Lorenzo Bandini. Hill reputedly sent Bandini a "Learn to Drive" manual for Christmas.

New technical developments

For the new 3-litre formula of 1966, Rudd developed the H16 engine, which was effectively two V8s mounted on top of each other with the cylinder banks opened out to lie horizontally. It was not a success despite best efforts over the next two years, and was replaced by a conventional V12 in 1968.

By this time the BRM chassis was a little long in the tooth. Talented young designer Tony Southgate now joined the organization and designed the P153 and P160 chassis, which put BRM back into the winner's circle when Pedro Rodriguez won a close battle with Chris Amon in the 1970 Belgian Grand Prix at Spa.

The emerging young Niki Lauda turned in some promising drives to launch his career with BRM in 1973, but at the end of the following year the Owen Organization withdrew its support. Louis Stanley tried to keep the team afloat but it all fell apart in 1977. The new P207 was late and, when it did arrive, neither Conny Andersson nor Teddy Pilette could qualify it and Rotary Watches withdrew their sponsorship. The last championship appearance was from Larry Perkins in the 1977 South African Grand Prix.

Mexican marauder *Pedro Rodriguez a much-loved driver at BRM, driving the P153 at the 1970 British Grand Prix.*

COOPER

COUNTRY OF ORIGIN:	ACTIVE YEARS IN FORMULA ONE:
Great Britain	**1950–69**
DATE OF FOUNDATION:	CONSTRUCTORS' CUP VICTORIES:
1946	**1959, 1960**

Cooper was responsible for the switch to rear-engined cars in Formula One, a move which won back-to-back world titles for Jack Brabham in 1959–60.

It all began when Charles Cooper, a racing mechanic before the war, built son John a 500cc motorcycle-engined racing car. Using a chain-driven JAP engine, the car had to have the power unit close to the driven rear axle, with the cockpit in front.

The cars were very successful and the Cooper Car Company was established to build more. Their 500cc Formula Three cars quickly began to dominate, but there were doubts about whether the same principles could be successfully applied with more potent machinery. People were mindful of the difficult rear-engined Auto Unions.

Mid-engined cars

Cooper concentrated on other projects before returning to the mid-engined concept. An experimental Cooper was run by Jack Brabham in the 1955 British Grand Prix, equipped with a 2-litre six-cylinder Bristol engine. A new 1500cc Formula Two class was due for introduction in 1957 and Cooper geared up for it by putting a Climax engine in the back of a developed version of its earlier chain-driven Formula Three cars. During 1957 enlarged versions of the cars made a few Grand Prix appearances and clearly outhandled the bigger front-engined machinery, but were too underpowered to do serious damage.

For 1958 Rob Walker, heir to the Johnny Walker whisky fortune, ordered a new engine from Coventry Climax for a Cooper and recruited Stirling Moss. Moss beat the Ferraris in Argentina in his blue Cooper T45, fooling the Ferraris into thinking he would need a tyre stop but driving cautiously so that he made the finish without one, although his rubber was worn through to the carcass. It was the first World Championship win by both a rear-engined and privately entered car.

Moss reverted to a Vanwall thereafter but Maurice Trintignant won in Monte Carlo aboard the Cooper. The cars were still underpowered but clearly the rear-engined concept had merit, although Vanwall recovered and won the constructors' championship.

The successful years

By 1959 Vanwall had withdrawn from Formula One and Jack Brabham, working closely with John Cooper, helped to develop the T51. Coventry-Climax produced a 2.5-litre engine, giving Cooper competitive engines for the first time. Brabham won the Monaco and British Grands Prix and his championship win was sealed when team-mate Bruce McLaren became the youngest winner of a Grand Prix, aged 22, at Sebring.

The US Grand Prix was new on the calendar that year and Moss had given himself a second successive shot at the title in the last race of the year by winning the previous two races in Rob Walker's private Cooper. He took off into the lead at Sebring but retired with a common gearbox failure, leaving the championship to either Brabham or Tony Brooks, who could win for Ferrari if he took the race with Brabham failing to score. Brabham led but ran out of petrol on the final lap, leaving McLaren to beat Trintignant, with Brooks third. New champion Brabham pushed his Cooper across the line in fourth place.

New Coopers were built for 1960 and, after McLaren won the opening race, Brabham scored five consecutive wins to make sure of back-to-back championship wins. Cooper's pioneering development was overtaken by more sophisticated designs from Ferrari, BRM and Lotus over the following seasons. Cooper came back with a monocoque chassis in 1966 but Maserati and then BRM engines were not competitive. Also, John Cooper had been seriously injured driving an experimental Mini Cooper. The marque disappeared from Formula One at the end of 1968.

Cooper's champion *Jack Brabham on the move at Silverstone in 1960 en-route to his second Formula One crown.*

FERRARI

COUNTRY OF ORIGIN: **Italy**	ACTIVE YEARS IN FORMULA ONE: **from 1950**
DATE OF FOUNDATION: **1939**	CONSTRUCTORS' CUP VICTORIES: **1961, 1964, 1975, 1976, 1977, 1979, 1982, 1983**

The most famous Grand Prix team of them all and, until its victory tally was caught by McLaren in the early 1990s, the most successful.

The Ferrari prancing horse logo came from an Italian World War I fighter pilot, Francesco Baracca, of Ravenna. At a race there in June 1923, Baracca's parents presented Enzo Ferrari with a shield, like the one their son had carried on his planes.

After fielding semi-works Alfa-Romeos before World War Two, Ferrari later emerged as a force in his own right, carrying the fight to the Alfa 159s with the Ferrari 375 in 1951. Ferrari lost narrowly to Alfa in the final race of the season.

The governing body then ran its championship races to 2-litre regulations, but Ferrari was prepared and Alberto Ascari dominated the championship in 1952–53. Ferrari then fell behind Maserati and Lancia as 2.5-litre regulations were introduced and, in 1957, failed to win a championship race for the first time.

Arrival of the Tipo 146

The Tipo 146 put Ferrari back on the map in 1958, the car being christened Dino, after Enzo Ferrari's son, who had worked with Vittorio on the new engine, and later died of muscular dystrophy. Although many believe that Stirling Moss was the rightful champion that year, the crown fell to Mike Hawthorn and Ferrari in the final race at Morocco.

After the little mid-engined Coopers had dominated in 1959–60, Ferrari was back in 1961, fully prepared for new 1.5-litre regulations with the Tipo 156 "shark-nose". The cars dominated but, as he stood on the brink of world championship success, German ace "Taffy" von Trips was killed in the Italian Grand Prix at Monza after a clash with Jim Clark. American Phil Hill went on to clinch the championship for Ferrari.

John Surtees took another title for Ferrari in 1964, becoming the only man to win world championships on both two wheels and four, but the new 3-litre regulations which came into effect in 1966 saw Ferrari struggling to match Cosworth's superb DFV, which was introduced at the Dutch Grand Prix in 1967.

The dominant years

Although Jackie Ickx enjoyed some success in 1970, it was not until 1974 that Ferrari looked like genuine championship contenders again. Niki Lauda was quick but inexperienced, losing out to McLaren and Emerson Fittipaldi. Lauda made amends by taking the flat-12 312T (transversal) to the championship the following year, and would have retained his title in 1976 had it not been for his near-fatal fiery accident at Nurburgring. As it was, he lost out to James Hunt and McLaren by a single point, but regained the crown with great consistency in 1977.

In 1979 Jody Scheckter beat spectacular young Ferrari team-mate Gilles Villeneuve to the championship with the ugly Ferrari 312T4, but the following season's T5 was a disaster as everybody began to master ground effect aerodynamics.

By now, 1.5-litre turbocharged engines were taking over from 3-litre normally aspirated ones and Ferrari produced the 126C. The car was agricultural to say the least, but Villeneuve scored remarkable wins with it at Monaco and Jarama.

Ferrari employed British designer Harvey Postlethwaite and the 1982 Ferrari 126C2 was the class of the field. But Villeneuve was killed in practice at Zolder and Didier Pironi smashed his legs in an accident at Hockenheim while leading the championship.

Not since 1983 has Ferrari looked like winning the crown again. But Michele Alboreto was competitive in 1985 and Alain Prost came close to breaking the McLaren stranglehold when he won five races in 1990, losing to Ayrton Senna in controversial circumstances in Japan.

Famous colours *Blood red with a yellow badge adorned with a black prancing horse means only one thing to race fans the world over – Ferrari.*

HESKETH

COUNTRY OF ORIGIN:	ACTIVE YEARS IN FORMULA ONE:
Great Britain	**1973–78**
DATE OF FOUNDATION:	CONSTRUCTORS' CUP VICTORIES:
1973	**none**

Lord Alexander Hesketh was a larger-than-life extrovert who enjoyed a considerable inheritance and had a good time spending it. Always a racing enthusiast, he was a friend of Anthony "Bubbles" Horsley, who was having little success in Formula Three in the 1970s.

At the same time, James Hunt was trying to make a name for himself. James was quick but down on his luck, having just been fired by the March works team after a disagreement with Max Mosley, when he met Horsley in a muddy field in Belgium. They came to an arrangement for James to drive a Formula Three car, with backing from the good Lord.

For 1973 Hesketh bought a Formula Two Surtees, but James shunted it in testing and the good Lord decided he might as well go the whole hog and rented a Formula One Surtees. Hunt was third in the Race of Champions at Brands Hatch and Hesketh decided it was time to forget about the junior ranks. He ordered a new March and managed to persuade one of March's young brains, Harvey Postlethwaite, to design a new car, working from Hesketh's Easton Neston estate.

Hunt immediately showed great promise: he scored his first point in the French Grand Prix; he was fourth after a stirring drive at Silverstone; and capped the year with a fabulous second behind Ronnie Peterson at Watkins Glen.

A touch of class

In that first year Hesketh Racing was looked on with something approaching scorn by the Establishment. They partied everywhere, taking butlers, champagne and Rolls Royces. But all this belied latent talent and their results showed that they had to be taken seriously.

Jackie Stewart's retirement meant the chance for a new order to establish itself and Hunt was one of those at the forefront. Postlethwaite's Hesketh 308 was ready for the International Trophy at Silverstone in 1974 and James scored a tremendously popular win. With their teddy bear mascot, Hesketh Racing was catching the public imagination.

The 1974 season continued Hesketh's promise but the Ferraris emerged as the cars to beat, even though the title eventually went to Fittipaldi's McLaren. Hunt again finished the year with a tremendous drive at Watkins Glen.

The speed was clearly there and at Zandvoort in 1975 the team achieved a fantastic first and only win. In a wet/dry race Hunt gambled on an early change to slicks and managed to hold off Lauda's Ferrari for the rest of the race, crossing the line with both fists punching the air.

Financial problems

Hesketh had always run its cars without commercial backing but even the Lord did not have bottomless pockets and 1976 was looking a bit dubious. Hunt was now in demand and, when Fittipaldi unexpectedly left McLaren to set up his own operation with backing from the Brazilian sugar corporation, Hunt was given his seat and went on to win the 1976 championship after an epic battle with Lauda.

Hesketh called a halt and the cars were sold off to Frank Williams, who had just gone into what was to prove an ill-advised partnership with Walter Wolf, a Canadian oil millionaire. Postlethwaite's 308C became the Wolf-Williams.

Horsley kept Hesketh Racing ticking over for a couple of seasons using updated versions of the old car, with paying drivers, and engineer Frank Dernie penned the 308E. Without a driver of Hunt's calibre on the books, however, the motivation of the early days was gone and Hesketh Racing wound down, concentrating on servicing customer Cosworth engines for a time. One of the great chapters of classic British racing romanticism was at an end.

Paddock chic *Lord Hesketh puts on the style in 1977.*

HONDA

COUNTRY OF ORIGIN:	ACTIVE YEARS IN FORMULA ONE:
Japan	**1964–68**
DATE OF FOUNDATION:	CONSTRUCTORS' CUP VICTORIES:
1962	**none**

Honda grew rapidly after World War Two, establishing itself in the motorcycle field before making the decision to enter Formula One in 1964. The man with the responsibility for this was development engineer Yoshio Nakamura.

The first Honda Formula One car, the RA 271, using a 60-degree transverse V12 1.5-litre engine, appeared in the German Grand Prix, driven by American Ronnie Bucknum. Bucknum had never driven a single-seater before and retired with four laps to go when the steering failed while he ran 11th. He then held down fifth at Monza before an overheating engine put him out.

Japanese success

Honda recruited Richie Ginther in 1965 to partner Bucknum and the RA272 chassis showed promise on the quicker circuits. Reliability, unfortunately, was poor but there was a sweetener at the end of the year. In the Mexican Grand Prix, held at altitude, Ginther led from start to finish for the first Japanese win in the history of Formula One.

Sadly for Honda, Formula One was to have new 3-litre engine regulations for 1966. Suspicions that the Japanese would pull out at the end of their second season proved unfounded. Spurred by the Mexican success, Soichiro Honda gave the go-ahead for a new car, equipped with a V12 engine. The unit was powerful but overweight and the Honda weighed in at more than 200 kilos over the limit.

For the following season Nakamura persuaded John Surtees, the only man to have won world championships on two wheels and four, to join the team. Surtees had seen what Honda could do in motorcycling and figured that it would only be a matter of time before they achieved a similar level of success in Formula One.

The RA273 was still badly overweight and Surtees's best result was third in South Africa. At Monza, though, a new chassis, the RA300, appeared. Lola had been involved in the construction of the car, which still used the V12 Honda engine. It was built at Surtees's factory in Slough and became known as "the Hondola".

That 1967 Italian Grand Prix has become one of the most talked about races. Dan Gurney led it before his clutch failed and then Jim Clark took over until he had a puncture which cost him a whole lap. He rejoined a lap down, but slipstreamed past the leaders and began the task of making up the lost ground. Incredibly, he managed it and went past Brabham and into the lead of the race with a few laps to go. Then he ran out of fuel on the last lap! Clark's drive somewhat overshadowed everything else, but Brabham was left to race wheel-to-wheel with Surtees, who went inside at the Parabolica on the final lap to score a debut win for the new Honda.

Weight problems

The 1968 season saw the emphasis on solving Honda's perennial weight problem. The new RA301 chassis was developed with the input of Lola's Eric Broadley and his team, but the car was not ready in time, a situation that was not eased by the need for Anglo-Japanese communication. Honda was also behind on its development of the V12 engine. The Japanese produced an entirely Honda-built RA302, with an air-cooled V8 engine, but Surtees did not like the way the car handled and refused to drive it.

Honda took on French driver Jo Schlesser, who lost control of the car early in his Formula One debut in the French Grand Prix at Rouen. The Honda speared off the road with a full fuel load and Schlesser died as the car, equipped with magnesium wheels, burned out. Surtees, in the RA301, was second in the same race to Jackie Ickx's Ferrari.

At the end of the season Honda pulled out of Formula One and did not return until the early 1980s, and then only as an engine supplier. Massive investment reaped reward and the company won successive world championships with McLaren between 1988 and 1991.

Stunning start *John Surtees took the new RA300 to a last-lap victory on its first outing at Monza in 1967.*

JORDAN

COUNTRY OF ORIGIN:	ACTIVE YEARS IN FORMULA ONE:
Great Britain	**from 1991**
DATE OF FOUNDATION:	CONSTRUCTORS' CUP VICTORIES:
1981	**none**

Irishman Eddie Jordan typifies the brand of wheeling and dealing livewire team owners who are almost as much a part of racing as the cars themselves.

A journalist countryman of Jordan's was responsible for the idea that Eddie had not so much kissed the blarney stone as swallowed it!

Jordan was a Formula Atlantic champion in Ireland and a promising Formula Three driver before he decided to set up Eddie Jordan Racing in 1981. With Martin Brundle in 1983, he came very close to taking the British Formula Three Championship after a season-long battle with Ayrton Senna.

Jordan finally claimed the Formula Three Championship in 1987 with Johnny Herbert driving. Moving up into Formula 3000 the partnership continued, but Herbert was seriously injured in a crash at Brands Hatch in 1988.

Jordan has always fancied himself as something of a talent spotter and, after Jean Alesi had been through a tough Formula 3000 year in 1988, Eddie offered the Frenchman a drive in his Camel-sponsored team in 1989. Alesi repaid him by winning the Formula 3000 championship in fine style, putting both his and Jordan's Grand Prix aspirations on a firmer footing.

Into Formula One

Jordan expanded from his Silverstone industrial unit to new premises across the road from Britain's Grand Prix circuit and formed Jordan Grand Prix. He took the plunge into Formula One in 1991, when Gary Anderson designed the attractive 191, which turned out to be one of the cars of the year.

In fact, some Jordan opportunism surrounds the car's designation. It was originally dubbed the Jordan 911, but Porsche objected to the use of a type number it owned the rights to. Jordan allegedly complained that Porsche was putting him to big expense in demanding he change to the 191 and reprint all his promotional material. In typical style he ended up with a Porsche 911 out of the deal.

Bertrand Gachot and Andrea de Cesaris were Jordan's drivers in 1991 but the season was disrupted when Gachot sprayed gas in a taxi driver's face after an altercation at Hyde Park Corner, ending up with a jail sentence.

At Spa, Jordan gave Michael Schumacher his first Grand Prix and unleashed on Formula One the greatest natural talent since Ayrton Senna. Sadly, Jordan could not hang on to Schumacher. Some Machiavellian manoeuvring saw the talented German spirited away to Benetton before the next race, leaving Jordan fuming.

Jordan had Ford HB engines in 1991 and the new team was regularly embarrassing Benetton, the Ford works team. With no guarantee of top specification engines in 1992, Jordan struck a deal with Yamaha for engines. After all the promise of Jordan's first season, the Yamaha V12 was a disaster and the two companies severed the agreement after the opening year.

Improving fortunes

In 1993 Jordan used Brian Hart's new V10 engine and signed Rubens Barrichello, the youngest driver in Formula One. The Brazilian showed himself to be at home in Formula One almost immediately, equalling Jordan's best fourth place result.

Ivan Capelli, Thierry Boutsen, Marco Apicella and Emanuele Naspetti all drove the second car before Eddie Irvine did a tremendous job to score a point on his Grand Prix debut with Jordan in the Japanese Grand Prix.

For 1994 Jordan kept his pairing of promising young drivers, although Irvine made something of a bad boy reputation for himself, earning a three-race ban for an incident he allegedly caused in the season-opening Brazilian Grand Prix.

Barrichello finished sixth in the championship, earning the team's first podium in the Pacific Grand Prix at Aida and finishing fourth four times. He also scored the team's first pole in wet/dry conditions at Spa.

Jordan stood out behind Formula One's "big four" – Williams, Benetton, McLaren and Ferrari – and his company earned itself a three-year works engine deal with Peugeot when McLaren had defected to Mercedes.

Debut dazzlers *Jordan's first year of Formula One was full of promise with drivers such a Bertrand Gachot, here at Monaco.*

LANCIA

COUNTRY OF ORIGIN:	ACTIVE YEARS IN FORMULA ONE:
Italy	**1954–55**
DATE OF FOUNDATION:	CONSTRUCTORS' CUP VICTORIES:
1906	**none**

Vincenzo Lancia was one of the charismatic early racing pioneers. Born in 1881, the son of a soup manufacturer, he was an apprentice to the Ceirano brothers, whose firm became Fiat. He was chosen as their test driver and then raced in some of the sport's earliest events. In one he was flying the Italian flag admirably when a holed radiator eliminated his Fiat. Lancia wept bitterly.

In 1906 he founded his own company to build touring cars and racing cars, although he continued to drive for Fiat. Gianni Lancia took over the company from his father and decided to return to motor racing in 1954. After two years racing to Formula Two rules, the World Championship was run to a new Formula One for 2.5-litre cars.

The great D50

Lancia recruited highly respected designer Vittorio Jano to build a car, which did not appear until late in the season. It also had the dominant Mercedes W196 to contend with. Although the W196 was renowned for its high-level technology, Jano's Lancia D50 was in fact more novel. The engine was positioned diagonally in the chassis, allowing the propshaft to pass through the cockpit without going under the driver's seat. This meant that the car could be built closer to the ground, which was better for the handling.

The D50 was Lancia's first Grand Prix car and it utilized an ultralight chassis of small diameter tubes, while the engine block and crankcase were stressed. Fuel and oil were carried in special side pontoons between the wheels on each side. The trend at the time was for rear tanks behind the axle line. As the fuel load changed on the Lancia, the variable weight was actually between the wheels and so did not have such a marked effect on the handling. Another positive spin-off was a cleaning up of the turbulent area between the wheels. Tipping the scales at just 620 kilos, the D50 was one of the lightest contenders.

The Lancia drivers were Alberto Ascari and Luigi Villoresi, who were loaned to Maserati while the D50 was finished. It finally made its debut in the Spanish Grand Prix of 1954, where Ascari was fastest in practice and showed everyone a clean pair of heels until he retired after nine laps with clutch failure.

Brief success

Things looked highly promising for 1955, although Mercedes had signed Moss to back up Fangio and the pair made for formidable opposition. Fangio won the opening Grand Prix amid tremendous heat in his native Argentina, but the D50s won minor races with Ascari in Naples and Turin.

Lancia ran Ascari, Villoresi, Castellotti and Louis Chiron – at the age of 56 – in the Monaco Grand Prix. Moss and Fangio took an early lead but had engine trouble and retired, leaving Ascari in front until he made a big error and landed himself in the harbour. He was rescued from drowning but, back on the track, Castellotti was beaten by Trintignant's Ferrari. Just four days later Ascari was killed testing a Ferrari at Monza. Like his father Antonio 30 years before him, Alberto was killed on the 26th of the month and was driving in a borrowed helmet.

Ascari's accident was inexplicable, some people feeling that he was still affected by his Monaco accident, but both Villoresi and Gianni Lancia were deeply upset. Lancia decided not to continue and the D50 raced as a Lancia just once more, when Castellotti entered one privately in the Belgian Grand Prix.

In addition to his feelings for Ascari, Lancia was also having to cope with the fact that his company was in financial trouble. He sold Lancia and handed over the D50s to Enzo Ferrari, complete with all his spares, designer Jano and Castellotti. There was also a five-year Fiat subsidy arranged. That was Lancia's last appearance in Formula One.

L is for Lancia *This is the D50, the ultra-light car that stood the team in good stead in its two-year existence in Formula One.*

LIGIER

COUNTRY OF ORIGIN:	ACTIVE YEARS IN FORMULA ONE:
France	**from 1976**
DATE OF FOUNDATION:	CONSTRUCTORS' CUP VICTORIES:
1971	**none**

Guy Ligier is a former butcher's assistant who played international rugby for France and made his fortune in the road construction industry, his company being responsible for the construction of many French autoroutes.

Always a motor-racing enthusiast, Ligier drove Cooper-Maserati and Brabham-Repco Formula One cars in the mid-1960s and then teamed up with his long-steading friend Jo Schlesser to drive a pair of Formula Two McLarens in 1968.

Ligier was appalled by Schlesser's death in a fiery accident aboard the new air-cooled Honda in the French Grand Prix at Rouen. He withdrew from driving and ran a GT programme with a car designed by Frenchman Michel Tetu. Ligier races his cars with the "JS" model designation in Schlesser's memory.

In 1975 Ligier achieved second place in the Le Mans 24 Hours, with backing from the Gitanes cigarette company, which was keen to move up to Formula One.

Ligier founds his company

France was lacking a national Formula One effort after the withdrawal of Matra Sports and talented French design engineer Gérard Ducarouge joined Ligier from Matra. The first Formula One Ligier, the JS5, arrived on the scene in 1976 and was a distinctive car. Ducarouge persuaded Matra to develop its V12 engine to give the Ligier project more of a Gallic flavour. Jacques Laffite, dominant in Formula Two, was taken on as driver.

The JS5 had a distinctive high airbox which earned the car its "teapot" nickname. Laffite qualified it on pole for the Italian Grand Prix.

In the new JS7 Laffite won the Swedish Grand Prix at Anderstorp the following year, the first win by a French driver in a French car with a French engine since the World Championship began.

The Swedish win was fortunate and it could never be said that the Ligiers looked set to dominate. But all that changed in 1979 when the team switched to Ford engines and built the ground effect JS11 with its distinctive aerodynamic kick-ups.

Lord of Ligier *No-one did better for the team than Jacques Laffite. Guy Ligier leans in for a chat with his star driver.*

Promising developments

Ground effect cars were something of a black art. The Lotus 79 had worked superbly in 1978, but the new Type 80 was a lemon, while Ligier's JS11 was suddenly the class of the field. Nobody at Ligier really knew why, but Laffite won the two opening races of the season, in Argentina and Brazil. He was now teamed with Patrick Depailler, who had left Tyrrell, and his new teammate took another win in Spain. Depailler then broke both his legs in a hang-gliding accident and was replaced by Belgian Jacky Ickx, then in the twilight of his career.

As 1979 progressed the new Williams FW07 proved a phenomenal car and Ligier could not maintain its early form. The Ferrari 312T4 was also a respectable car and the championship eventually fell to Jody Scheckter.

For 1980 Ligier secured the services of upcoming young Frenchman Didier Pironi, who won in Belgium and drove one of the races of the year at Brands Hatch. That, though, was the team's zenith. Never again has it enjoyed the pre-eminence of those early days.

At the beginning of 1992 there was talk of a tie-up between Ligier and Alain Prost but, although Prost tested the car, he decided on a sabbatical year. Ligier himself then moved more into the background and sold out to Cyril de Rouvre, who ended up in jail on financial charges.

Ligier looked shaky at the beginning of 1994, but Benetton boss Flavio Briatore bought the team and the reigning Formula 3000 champion, Olivier Panis, had a stunning debut Formula One season in which he finished 15 of the 16 races. Ligier never managed to capitalize on a three-year deal for Renault's powerful V10 engine, but the potential for a recovery is there, with Briatore landing technical backing from Benetton and a Mugen Honda engine contract in place for 1995.

LOTUS

COUNTRY OF ORIGIN:	ACTIVE YEARS IN FORMULA ONE:
Great Britain	**1959–94**
DATE OF FOUNDATION:	CONSTRUCTORS' CUP VICTORIES: **1963, 1965, 1968, 1970, 1972, 1973, 1978**
1952	

Lotus founder, the late Colin Chapman, has many times been dubbed a genius.

Chapman was an enthusiastic member of the 750 Motor Club who took to building his own cars, calling them Lotuses. He founded the Lotus Engineering Company in 1952 with some money borrowed from his wife to be, Hazel.

Chapman started by building lightweight sports cars before constructing his first single-seater, the Type 12, in 1957, aimed at the new Formula Two category. The more sophisticated Lotus 16 was run in Formula One in 1959, but proved fragile.

Chapman followed the mid-engined concept and built the brilliant Lotus 18 for 1960, Stirling Moss giving the marque its first Grand Prix win in a Rob Walker-entered car at Monaco.

Lotus triumphant

Lotus really made its name in the 1960s with legendary Scot Jim Clark. Ferrari had been ready for the new 1.5-litre Formula One regulations in 1961, but the British constructors were forced to use stopgap Formula Two Climax engines. Despite that, Stirling Moss scored that historic win at Monaco against Richie Ginther's "shark-nose" Ferrari.

In 1962, Chapman introduced the Lotus 25 monocoque chassis at the Dutch Grand Prix, following trends in aircraft design. Clark was unfortunate to lose the championship to Graham Hill's BRM, but he made amends the following year. With the car in updated Lotus 33 form, Clark won his second title for Chapman in 1965, also winning the Indianapolis 500 in the same year.

Jack Brabham's Repco-engined Brabhams were the class of the field in 1966 but, with exclusive use of the new Cosworth DFV in 1967, Lotus hit back hard with the 49. Tragically, Clark died in a Formula Two race at Hockenheim in April 1968, the first time that Lotus had run in Gold Leaf colours. Chapman was devastated, but Graham Hill provided a tonic by winning the next two Grands Prix and going on to take the championship.

Chapman managed to replace Clark with the fiery young Jochen Rindt, regarded as the quickest driver in Formula One. The Austrian dominated most of the 1970 season in the brilliant Lotus 72, but died in practice at Monza when a brake shaft broke. Rindt became the sport's first and only posthumous champion.

New technology

Emerson Fittipaldi took over and won another title with the 72 two years later, but Lotus then lost its way until 1977, when it reaped the reward of developing ground effect principles. Simply stated, Venturi tunnels on each side of a slim chassis created a vacuum and sucked the car on to the track.

Mario Andretti won four times with the Lotus 78 in 1977, but could not stop Lauda's consistent Ferrari taking the title. However, in 1978 the refined Lotus 78 was dominant in the hands of Andretti and Ronnie Peterson. Tragically, Andretti's moment of triumph was soured by Peterson's death as a result of injuries sustained in a multiple pile-up at the start of the Italian Grand Prix.

Continuing his reputation for innovative design, Chapman came out with the twin-chassis Lotus 88, but it was banned by the authorities, leaving a seething Chapman threatening to finish with the sport. It was he who gave Nigel Mansell his Grand Prix break, but in later years Chapman's name was to be tarnished by reports of the De Lorean fraud. Under pressure, in 1982 he succumbed to a heart attack.

Lotus has never been the same without him. The team enjoyed limited success in the mid-1980s, but even with turbo engines from Renault and Honda and Ayrton Senna in the cockpit, could do no more than win the occasional race.

Former manager Peter Collins bought his way into the team in 1990, but on September 11, 1994, he had to give up the unequal financial struggle and place the company in administration. It was acquired by David Hunt, brother of 1976 world champion James, but the future looks bleak.

Famous style *Colin Chapman made this cap his trademark.*

MARCH

COUNTRY OF ORIGIN:	ACTIVE YEARS IN FORMULA ONE:
Great Britain	**1970–77, 1981–83 then 1987–92**
DATE OF FOUNDATION:	CONSTRUCTORS' CUP VICTORIES:
1969	**none**

Works winner *Vittorio Brambilla (pictured in Germany) won in Austria in 1975.*

The idea of a group of enthusiasts banding together to set up a Formula One team at the same time as selling customer cars, employing the reigning world champion and taking pole position at their first race seems ludicrous. But that is exactly what March did.

The four founding members were current FIA president Max Mosley, Alan Rees, Graham Coaker and Robin Herd. Herd was a highly regarded young designer who had worked at McLaren and designed the stillborn Cosworth four-wheel drive car. They got together in 1969 and moved into a small factory in Bicester.

Jackie Stewart had just won the World Championship in a Matra. The French company was determined to use its own V12 engines in 1970 and neither Stewart nor Ken Tyrrell wanted that. Instead, they were faced with the prospect of finding an alternative chassis.

Opportunity knocks

Enter March. Jumping at the opportunity to grab the reigning champion after attempts to lure Jochen Rindt from Lotus had failed, they ended up fielding a works team as well as selling customer cars in Formula One. There were four March 701s on the grid in South Africa.

They also built customer cars for Formula Two, Formula Three and Formula 5000. The works drivers were Chris Amon and Jo Siffert, with backing coming from STP and a spare car provided for Mario Andretti in selected races.

The 701s were hurriedly built, but that did not stop Amon from winning first time out in the Silverstone International Trophy. Stewart then won the Race of Champions at Brands Hatch and started from pole at Kyalami, with Amon alongside. But in the race, Jack Brabham's BT33 won convincingly, while Amon retired and Stewart finished third.

Stewart won in Spain but soon the heavy 701 was struggling, especially against the new Lotus 72. At the end of the year Stewart left to drive the first Tyrrell.

March signed promising young Swede Ronnie Peterson and Herd came up with the distinctive 711, featuring the famous "dinner plate" front wing. Peterson was highly competitive with the car and, although Stewart was the dominant force for Tyrrell, Ronnie placed second no fewer than six times and ended the season championship runner-up.

Herd then embarked on the innovative 721X, which featured a gearbox mounted between the engine and the axle in the interests of improved handling. March took no notice when an inexperienced Niki Lauda told them the car was hopeless, and it required Peterson considerably longer to come to the same conclusion. March then scrabbled together a replacement 721G, based on its Formula Two car. The "G" designation was an in-house joke, standing for Guinness Book of Records, a reflection on how quickly it was thrown together!

Money problems

For 1973 March lost Peterson to Lotus and, always under both financial and customer time pressure, adopted the policy of fielding beefed-up Formula Two cars in Grands Prix, generally with pay drivers at the wheel. Although Stewart had won that second race in Spain in 1970, the first "works" victory did not come until 1975 in Austria, when Vittorio Brambilla, "The Monza Gorilla", won a rain-shortened race. He threw both arms into the air and shunted on the slowing down lap.

Peterson returned in 1976 and won the Italian Grand Prix in the 761 before leaving for Tyrrell. March disappeared from the Formula One scene at the end of the following season, returning a decade later with backing from the Japanese Leyton House concern of Akira Akagi, who was later prosecuted in Japan for massive fraud.

Ivan Capelli showed flashes of brilliance with Adrian Newey's 881 and CG901 designs, coming second in Portugal in 1988 and second again in France in 1990, this time having led until just before the end, but March disappeared again at the end of the 1992 season, in which it had struggled against a severe shortage of money.

MASERATI

COUNTRY OF ORIGIN:	ACTIVE YEARS IN FORMULA ONE:
Italy	**1950–60**
DATE OF FOUNDATION:	CONSTRUCTORS' CUP VICTORIES:
early 1920s	**none**

The Maserati brothers were involved in early Italian motor sport before setting up their first business, making sparking plugs, before the First World War.

When hostilities ended Alfieri Maserati raced his own special and then the brothers embarked on building a straight-eight engine for the Diatto Grand Prix car. They bought it to modify for the 1926 regulations, Alfieri taking a class win in that year's Targa Florio.

Rivalry with Alfa-Romeo

Maserati then did some twin-engined experimentation before building the 8C- 2500 and 2800 chassis. The 8CM was built to take the fight to rival Alfa-Romeo's P3 and was the start of a rivalry between the two marques that would continue until after the Second World War. Baconin Borzacchini was an early Maserati faithful, and was joined in an 8CM by Tazio Nuvolari in 1933.

One of Alfa-Romeo's greats was Giuseppe Campari, who had joined Alfa in his teens as a test driver. He was a great music and opera lover and was married to the singer Lina Cavalleri. At Monza Campari said that he would retire at the end of the meeting. Sadly, he was involved in a tussle with Borzacchini's Maserati, during which they both hit a patch of oil and crashed fatally. Bugatti driver Count Czaikowski hit the same spot and was also killed.

Maserati could not match the German challenge of the mid- and late 1930s and the company was taken over by Cavallieri Adolfo Orsi, with the Maserati brothers remaining as part of the firm. In the early 1940s Maserati moved from Bologna to Modena.

The Maserati 4CLT was a competitive proposition just after World War II, if a little underpowered. The brothers then began work on a sports car before leaving to found Osca. The engine from this car was the basis of a Formula Two car which became eligible for the World Championship when Formula One fell by the wayside in 1952–53. This was a time of Ferrari domination, but Fangio won for Maserati at the Italian Grand Prix.

A promising period

Maserati looked good for the newly introduced 2.5-litre formula of 1954, but once again Mercedes was to launch a major onslaught and spoil the Italian party. Fangio won the first two Grands Prix for Maserati in 1954, while he waited for the Mercedes programme to come on-stream. He was driving the 250F, which was destined to become the best-known Maserati ever.

The 250F proved a very popular car among privateers and was progressively improved, with various weight-saving exercises being carried out. With Mercedes withdrawing,, Stirling Moss won two races for Maserati in 1956, while Fangio took his fourth world title for Ferrari. The next year Fangio, disgruntled with the politicking at Ferrari, returned to Maserati. He won four races to collect his fifth title and seal the constructors' championship for Maserati. He did it with one of the most memorable drives in race history, at the Nurburgring. With one of the hub nuts lost during his pit stop, Fangio rejoined about 45 seconds behind the Ferraris of Mike Hawthorn and Peter Collins. On the last lap, he passed both to win by just over three seconds. Afterwards, he said: "I don't ever want to have to drive like that again."

Maserati also gave Fangio his last Grand Prix, at Reims in 1958, although by that time the factory team was no more. Despite a successful 1957, Maserati was in big financial trouble and the 250F continued to race only in private hands until outmoded by mid-engined development.

Moss is boss *Stirling Moss (right) had two spells at Maserati. Here he heads for victory in the 1956 Monaco Grand Prix.*

MATRA

Country of origin:	Active years in Formula One:
France	**1966–72**
Date of foundation:	Constructors' Cup victories:
1965	**1969**

It was the French Matra company that helped to take Jackie Stewart to his first World Championship success in 1969.

Matra was a big French aerospace concern, whose more lucrative products included guided missiles. They knew all about monocoque construction through involvement in the aircraft industry and they also had a plastics division.

Matra supplied car bodies to René Bonnet, who was running Formula Junior monocoque cars until he went bankrupt. At that point, Matra executive Jean-Luc Lagardère decided to form Matra Sports to take over where Bonnet had left off. The Matra Formula Three cars were renowned for quality workmanship and when Ken Tyrrell went looking for a chassis, he approached Matra.

Tyrrell had already secured the new Cosworth DFV for 1968 and he had Jackie Stewart signed up, with money and support fron Dunlop tyres. After two years of running Matra chassis in Formula Two, Tyrrell went Formula One with the MS10 in 1968, adding the Matra name to the world championship victory roll at the Dutch Grand Prix. Stewart remained in contention for the championship until the final round in Mexico, where he was pipped by Graham Hill's Lotus.

Outside assistance

Matra had funding from Elf and the French government voted an £800,000 grant to Matra to develop its own engine. The French built a V12, which was raced in an MS11 chassis by Jean-Pierre Beltoise. The V12 was not competitive against the Cosworth, however, and for 1969 Beltoise joined Stewart in Tyrrell's DFV-powered team. Matra, meanwhile, concentrated on sports car racing and on developing the V12.

The new Matra MS80 for 1969 was around 15 kilos lighter than the MS10 and it allowed Stewart to dominate the season. After winning in South Africa with the MS10, he gave the MS80 a successful debut in the non-championship Race of Champions at Brands Hatch. He then went to Barcelona, where the Matra team scored a fortunate win when both Lotus 49s suffered failures to the newly introduced high rear wings.

Unfortunately, the Matra broke while Stewart was leading convincingly from pole around the streets of Monaco, but team and driver were dominant thereafter. The British Grand Prix, one of the all-time great races, featured a tremendous duel between Stewart's Matra and Rindt's Lotus. Mechanical problems hampered Rindt and Stewart took another win.

Monza that year was another epic. The famous track was bereft of chicanes in those days and the Italian Grand Prix was usually a slipstreaming classic. Stewart had selected a top gear ratio ideal for the sprint to the line out of the last corner. Although Rindt passed him going in, Stewart led coming out and headed a four-car blanket finish to seal the championship.

Doomed to failure *Johnny Servoz-Gavin streaks clear at Monaco in 1968—but he later clipped a barrier and retired.*

A successful year

Although Matra could bathe in the glory of building the championship-winning chassis, it was very much a British success. Both the team and engine manufacturer were based in England and the driver was Scottish.

France had not been properly represented in Formula One since 1957 and for the 1970 season, Matra insisted on using its own V12 engine. Tyrrell and Stewart did not trust the unit and bought a March chassis instead.

Matra's small sports car company had been taken over by Simca and so a Matra Simca MS120 was raced by Beltoise and Henri Pescarolo in 1970, achieving three third places. Chris Amon replaced Beltoise for 1971 and won a non-championship race in Argentina. But over the next two seasons, despite sounding glorious, the cars never won a Grand Prix.

Matra then concentrated on winning the Le Mans 24 Hours and withdrew from Formula One. The V12 engines appeared in a Ligier chassis and Jacques Laffite won the 1977 Swedish Grand Prix with one, but the Matra team never returned.

McLAREN

COUNTRY OF ORIGIN:	ACTIVE YEARS IN FORMULA ONE:
Great Britain	**from 1964**
DATE OF FOUNDATION: **1963**	CONSTRUCTORS' CUP VICTORIES: **1974, 1984,1985,1988,1989,1990,1991**

Kiwi Bruce McLaren is the man behind the McLaren name. Born in Auckland, he won a New Zealand scholarship to race in Europe in 1958. His results in Formula Two Coopers earned him a place in the Grand Prix team in 1959, alongside Jack Brabham. At Hendrick Field near Sebring that year McLaren became the youngest ever Grand Prix winner, aged 22.

Inspired by Brabham, McLaren constructed his own cars and formed Bruce McLaren Motor Racing Ltd. His first Formula One chassis, the M2B, was designed by Robin Herd and built in 1966. It had a Mallite chassis, a sandwich of two layers of aluminium bonded to balsa wood. Unfortunately, the first year of the 3-litre engine formula found suitable power units hard to come by and McLaren had to turn to an under-powered Italian Serenissima engine. His first point was scored with this combination when he was sixth in the British Grand Prix.

The M7 in action

Before Herd left to join Cosworth, he penned the M7 McLaren, which became a potent weapon when fitted with a Ford Cosworth engine. Bruce gave the car a debut win in the Brands Hatch Race of Champions and the then reigning world champion, Denny Hulme, fought out the 1968 crown down to the final race before losing out to Graham Hill.

In CanAm the McLarens of Bruce and Denny swept all before them but, on June 2, 1970, Bruce was killed testing an M8 at Goodwood.

The McLaren M19 was a good, workmanlike chassis but the car that really put McLaren on the map was the M23, with which Hulme and Peter Revson won three races in 1973. In 1974 Emerson Fittipaldi joined from Lotus and won the World Championship after three wins and a number of consistent finishes in the first year of backing by Marlboro, a name that was to become synonymous with McLaren.

Fittipaldi lost out to Niki Lauda and Ferrari in 1975 and then left to set up his own Copersucar team. James Hunt replaced him and, after one of Formula One's most dramatic seasons, took the championship by a single point.

Hunt won three more races as Lauda claimed back the title in 1977, but McLaren seemed overtaken by the ground effect technology which took Formula One on to a new plane in the late 1970s.

The years of victory

The foundations of the McLaren steamroller of the 1980s were laid when principal Teddy Mayer sold out part of the company to Project Four Formula Two boss Ron Dennis. The latter brought meticulous attention to detail and designer John Barnard penned one of the Formula One classics, the carbon fibre MP4, originally manufactured by the Hercules Corporation.

Dennis, who ran a BMW Procar for Niki Lauda in 1979, persuaded the Austrian out of retirement and Niki won at Long Beach and Brands Hatch in 1982. The team struggled with normally aspirated engines against the emerging turbos in 1983, but the debut of a new TAG-badged Porsche V6 turbo was promising.

For 1984 Dennis swooped when Alain Prost suddenly became available. Lauda and Prost dominated the championship, with Alain winning seven races to Niki's five, although the Austrian took the title by half a point. Prost made amends in 1985 and then won another title in 1986 despite the Williams-Honda combination of Mansell and Piquet being clearly superior.

Williams delivered in 1987 but for the following year Dennis had the ultimate superteam: Prost, Ayrton Senna and Honda engines. Senna won the first of three titles in four years with McLaren, although Prost left for Ferrari as champion in 1989, a state of open warfare existing with his "team-mate".

The withdrawal of Honda in 1992 rendered McLaren comparatively impotent, but the brilliant Senna still managed five wins in 1993 before leaving for Williams. His presence had ensured that McLaren usurped Ferrari's position as the most successful team in racing history.

New for 1995 *The McLaren MP4/10 with its famous mid-wing.*

MERCEDES

COUNTRY OF ORIGIN:	ACTIVE YEARS IN FORMULA ONE:
Germany	**1954–55**
DATE OF FOUNDATION:	CONSTRUCTORS' CUP VICTORIES:
1906	**none**

Mercedes has played a significant part in Grand Prix history, although in spectacular bursts.

The name dates back to the first Grand Prix of 1906, in which three Mercedes competed. The three-pointed star badge signifies engines produced for land, sea and air.

Mercedes in the Nazi era

A great Mercedes onslaught came in the early 1930s shortly after Adolf Hitler had risen to power. Hitler wanted to use motor sport to prove the superiority of German engineering and had his transport minister grant a large fund for those building Grand Prix cars. It was shared between Mercedes and Auto Union.

The German development went hand in hand with a new 750-kg formula and there was progress made on the chassis side, with independent suspension on each wheel improving cornering power.

On the Mercedes driving strength for 1934 were Rudolf Caracciola, Manfred von Brauchitsch and Luigi Fagioli. Both Mercedes and Auto Union missed Monaco so that their cars could make a patriotic debut at Avus in front of over 200,000 people and the Führer himself. Mercedes had some engine problems and withdrew rather than risk losing to the Italians.

This disaster was overcome at Nurburgring a couple of weeks later. Von Brauchitsch and Fagioli led and the Italian was quicker. A German was supposed to win, however, and team manager Alfred Neubauer signalled Fagioli to slow down. This led to a huge row between the two at one of the pit stops, after which Fagioli hounded von Brauchitsch until he decided to park up and let Stuck finish second for Auto Union.

Duel with the Italians

The Germans then suffered an Alfa one-two-three in the French Grand Prix before starting a run of victories which convinced the top Italians that they had to drive for the German teams. Mercedes already had Fagioli, and Achille Varzi signed for Auto Union, where he refused to have Tazio Nuvolari, "the Flying Mantuan", who was acknowledged as the greatest driver of the age. Nuvolari therefore drove an Alfa for Enzo Ferrari.

The German motor sport governing body had suggested a European Drivers' Championship, which was won by Rudolf Caracciola in the Mercedes W25. The Germans were generally dominant but, ironically, the feature of 1935 that will always be remembered is Nuvolari's fantastic drive in the German Grand Prix at the Nurburgring with an outdated Alfa P3. After applying relentless pressure, Nuvolari won in front of over 300,000 silent Germans as von Brauchitsch's Mercedes blew a tyre on the last lap.

Caracciola and Mercedes suffered at the hands of Auto Union and Bernd Rosemeyer in 1936, but came back strongly the following year with a new racing department under Rudi Uhlenhaut and the superb new W125. Caracciola took his second European championship.

There was a new 3-litre formula for 1938 and Mercedes dominated until the outbreak of World War II, beaten only a couple of times by Auto Union's Type D, now finally in the hands of Nuvolari.

Postwar fortunes

Mercedes did not come back into Grand Prix racing until 1954, with its technically advanced W196, which could be run in either open-wheeler or streamlined format. Once more it was dominant, with Juan Manuel Fangio winning the French, German, Swiss and Italian Grands Prix.

The domination continued in 1955, when Fangio was joined by Stirling Moss, who usually ran shotgun to the great Argentine, now claiming his third world title. Moss, however, scored an emotional win in the British Grand Prix in front of 150,000 people, which second-placed Fangio insists was won on merit. The year also witnessed the Le Mans tragedy: 80 spectators and Pierre Levegh perished when the Frenchman's Mercedes went into the crowd. Mercedes withdrew at the end of the year. They have never returned as a constructor.

After supplying engines to Sauber in 1993 and 1994, Mercedes signed a five-year engine supply deal with McLaren, beginning in 1995.

Championship year *Fangio cleaned up in 1955 in this W196.*

MINARDI

COUNTRY OF ORIGIN:	ACTIVE YEARS IN FORMULA ONE:
Italy	**from 1985**
DATE OF FOUNDATION:	CONSTRUCTORS' CUP VICTORIES:
1980	**none**

The Minardi Grand Prix team is a modern-day David in among the Goliaths. Giancarlo Minardi knows he will perhaps never be an Enzo Ferrari, but his little team are true racers and have a special place in the hearts of most Grand Prix enthusiasts.

Minardi was born in 1947 and owned a Fiat dealership in Faenza. From 1974 he began running cars in Formula Two, with a Chevron chassis and a Ferrari V6 engine. He has close ties with Maranello and fielded an ex-works Formula One Ferrari in Scuderia Everest colours in 1976.

Minardi became a constructor in his own right in 1980, building attractive Formula Two chassis driven by Alessandro Nannini.

Pierluigi Martini was European Formula Three Champion in 1983 and made his Formula One debut with Toleman the following year. His first full-time ride, however, coincided with Minardi's move up to Formula One in 1985.

Minardi enters the field

Minardi entered just a single car for Martini in 1985, taking part in the first two races of the season with a Ford Cosworth engine. By this time, however, a turbo was a prerequisite in Formula One, with the TAG Porsche V6 doing all the winning in the hands of Alain Prost and Niki Lauda at McLaren.

At the San Marino Grand Prix Minardi started to use a Motori Moderni turbo engine, but found that it was woefully uncompetitive. The unfortunate Martini was roundly panned and said to be out of his depth because there was no second car to compare him with. In fact, the lack of competitiveness was the fault of the equipment.

For 1986 Martini lost his place and went to contest the Formula 3000 category, introduced in 1985. In his place came the two-car, all-Italian line-up of Andrea de Cesaris and old Minardi Formula Two driver Nannini. They fared little better.

Minardi plugged on with the Motori Moderni turbos in 1987, this time with Spanish journeyman Adrian Campos in place of de Cesaris. Again, there were no points and the cars were makeweights.

In 1988 Minardi reverted to Ford Cosworth power and took Martini back into the fold, alongside another, more promising Spaniard, Luis Sala. Martini scored the team's first point when he was sixth of the nine finishers after 63 laps of the streets of Detroit.

Some successes

In 1989 Minardi made it into the championship top ten, an important step for a small team because it confers long-distance freight benefits. Minardi was delighted when both Martini and Sala finished in the points at Silverstone: Then, at Estoril, Martini was fifth again and made a little piece of history for the Faenza team by leading the race for a lap... He was also sixth in Adelaide.

For 1990 Martini was partnered by Paolo Barilla and then Gianni Morbidelli but there were no more points, although the 1991 season looked positive when Minardi struck a deal with Ferrari for V12 engines. The results were not as spectacular as the team had hoped, but they did manage to finish seventh in the manufacturers' series. Portugal was the happy hunting ground for the team again when Martini achieved its best result with fourth place, just ten seconds behind Alesi's third placed Ferrari.

For 1992 the Ferrari engines were replaced by Lamborghini V12s and, with Martini entering the Dallara-Ferrari team, reigning Formula 3000 champion Christian Fittipaldi joined Gianni Morbidelli at Minardi and scored the only point of the season at Suzuka.

Customer Ford HB engines saw many steady if unspectacular performances from the team throughout 1993 and 1994, when Martini was back, partnered by Michele Alboreto. A big blow was the loss of an expected Mugen Honda engine deal to Ligier before the start of the 1995 season. The team, it seems, is destined to stay among the minnows, but there is no doubting the enthusiasm.

In the money *Christian Fittipaldi heads for fourth place in South Africa in 1993 to claim rare points for Minardi.*

PACIFIC

COUNTRY OF ORIGIN:	ACTIVE YEARS IN FORMULA ONE:
Great Britain	**from 1994**
DATE OF FOUNDATION:	CONSTRUCTORS' CUP VICTORIES:
1984	**none**

Keith Wiggins proved how difficult it is to break into Formula One in the 1990s when he tried to move up after running highly successful teams in the junior categories.

Pacific had an enviable pedigree. The team was started in late 1984 and in its first season, with Marlboro support, took Bertrand Gachot to the RAC British Formula Ford 1600 title, against the likes of Damon Hill, Johnny Herbert and Mark Blundell.

Moving up to Formula Ford 2000, Gachot won the British championship again the following year, with Finnish driver J.J. Lehto continuing the tradition in 1987. The team pursued its policy of moving up the ladder in 1988, when it attacked Formula Three, the domain of highly professional specialist teams such as West Surrey Racing. Again, Pacific rapidly got to grips with the task, Lehto winning the British Formula Three title at the first attempt.

In 1989 Pacific jumped straight into Formula 3000 for a third successive year with the Finn, this time partnered by Eddie Irvine. With the Mugen engine in Europe for the first time, it seemed as though success could almost be taken for granted, but Pacific came up against strong, highly organized opposition in the form of Eddie Jordan Racing, with Jean Alesi and Martin Donnelly driving.

Minor triumphs

Lehto then made the move to Formula One, while the Pacific Formula 3000 team did not make much progress with Stephane Proulx driving. In 1991, though, it all came right. Christian Fittipaldi fought out a season-long duel with fellow Reynard runner Alessandro Zanardi, taking the title in the final round at Nogaro. Pacific had now won the championship in every formula it had contested and Wiggins started to plan for the move up to Formula One.

Reynard had originally intended its own Formula One team, but when there was no works engine deal forthcoming, plans foundered. Key members of the Reynard design team, such as Rory Byrne, rejoined Benetton and Pacific took on the remnants of the Reynard project with former Zakspeed engineer Paul Brown in charge of development.

Lack of finance

Other aspects of the project such as the aerodynamic data had been sold off elsewhere, however, and then Wiggins had to shelve his plans for a 1993 appearance because lack of finance.

However, he committed himself to action in 1994, forming Pacific Grand Prix to run the PR01 and hiring Gachot again, alongside wealthy Frenchman Paul Belmondo, son of the film star, Jean-Paul. A deal was done to run Ilmor V10 engines.

The season was a disaster and the team never finished a race. The car proved to have no rigidity and, with a lack of initial data, the team had very little to work on. There were also a number of problems with the engines and after the Canadian Grand Prix at Montreal Pacific failed to make the grid again.

The team would have preferred to abandon 1994 and concentrate on the design of the new PR02 for 1995, but the championship regulations demand appearance at every race or substantial penalties, which could include the cancellation of the team's championship entry.

Gachot declared the Saturday morning of Adelaide "one of the happiest days of my life, because I will never have to drive that thing again..."

Behind the scenes, however, Pacific was working away at securing backing from a Japanese entrepreneur. They had also employed an experienced aerodynamicist and had Frank Coppuck and Geoff Aldridge working on the new car. A customer engine deal was agreed with Cosworth and there was even the suggestion that Lehto might renew his partnership with Wiggins after the disappointment of his injury-afflicted season with Benetton. The team can only go up.

Pacific heights *Bertrand Gachot gave it his best shot in 1994, here at Interlagos, but seldom qualified the recalcitrant Pacific PR01.*

PENSKE

COUNTRY OF ORIGIN:	ACTIVE YEARS IN FORMULA ONE:
USA	**1974–76**
DATE OF FOUNDATION:	CONSTRUCTORS' CUP VICTORIES:
1974	**none**

Roger Penske runs what many experts acknowledge as the best racing team in the world. Interestingly, however, his business interests in the USA have caused him to concentrate on domestic racing programmes since having a foray into the Formula One world in the mid-1970s.

Penske has won the Indianapolis 500 a record nine times. A measure of the dominance that he has achieved in America was graphically illustrated in 1994 when his Marlboro-backed cars finished one-two-three in the Indycar World Series. Al Unser Jr took the title, admirably backed up by twice-world champion Emerson Fittipaldi and young Canadian Paul Tracy, who took the opportunity to test a Benetton Formula One car at the end of the 1994 season.

A successful businessman

Penske is entirely self-made, starting off as a tin salesman and building the Penske Corporation into a huge conglomerate. He has a seat on the board of Philip Morris, whose Marlboro brand backs his Indycars, and he is now involved with the Mercedes motor sport programme. Mercedes is a major stakeholder in Penske's successful Detroit Diesel company and Roger himself owns 25 per cent of Ilmor Engineering, which will prepare the Mercedes engines for the three-pointed star's new five-year agreement with McLaren.

Penske was a promising driver in his own right but hung up his helmet at the age of 28 to concentrate on business. Starting his own team, he struck up a hugely successful partnership with experienced American ace Mark Donohue.

In 1971 Penske rented a McLaren M19 and Donohue drove it to third place in the wet Canadian Grand Prix. Penske then started to think about a full Grand Prix effort. He bought a factory at Poole, in Dorset, and recruited Geoff Ferris, who had learned his trade with Ron Tauranac at Brabham, to design him a car.

The first car appeared in late 1974, with the testing done by Donohue, who had retired. The project sparked his enthusiasm, however, and Mark agreed to commit to a full Grand Prix programme with Penske in 1975.

Entry into Formula One

With First National City Bank support and a Cosworth engine, Penske hardly set the world on fire and, midway through the season, replaced the PC1 with a March 751. In practice at the Osterreichring, Donohue suffered a deflating tyre and flew off the road, hitting television station scaffolding. Although at first he appeared to have escaped with a headache, Donohue fell into a coma and died from his injuries.

Penske signed John Watson and, with Ferris's elegant new PC4, the combination started to run at the front in 1976. By mid-season Watson was challenging for a win which, somewhat ironically, came at Osterreichring exactly a year after Donohue's death there.

Formula One was enjoying its epic Hunt versus Lauda season and Watson's sudden intrusion was something that Hunt could have done without, as Niki lay in a Mannheim hospital trying to recover from his Nurburgring accident. Watson also battled hard with Hunt's McLaren at Zandvoort before retiring.

At the end of 1976 First National City Bank defected to Tyrrell, attracted by the exposure potential to be generated by the Tyrrell six-wheeler. Penske decided to halt his Formula One campaign and concentrate on the Indycar scene.

Despite the occasional rumour, Penske has never returned to Formula One. In 1994, however, his closeness to Mercedes, through both business and personal friendships, convinced many that he would play an active role in the McLaren-Mercedes link. Only time will tell, though.

Into the lead *John Watson (28) outdrags James Hunt's McLaren in the 1976 Austrian Grand Prix, the team's only win.*

RENAULT

COUNTRY OF ORIGIN:	ACTIVE YEARS IN FORMULA ONE:
France	**1977–85**
DATE OF FOUNDATION:	CONSTRUCTORS' CUP VICTORIES:
1900	**none**

Marques such as Ferrari and Alfa-Romeo have long racing histories, constant in the case of Ferrari. But for Renault the decision to enter the world championship in 1977 was risky, especially with a 1.5-litre turbocharged engine against 3-litre normally aspirated opposition.

Formula One was the domain of British manufacturers which used customer engines and gearboxes. For a company the size of Renault to do less than win would be disastrous.

Since 3-litre engines were introduced in 1966, an equivalence formula existed which allowed a 1.5-litre turbo engine. It was never regarded as a feasible proposition, but Renault gained a lot of turbo experience in sports car racing.

The Renault RS01 appeared at the British Grand Prix in 1977, with Jean-Pierre Jabouille at the wheel. Initially, the Formula One project was hampered by split resources with the sports car programme and the preoccupation with winning the Le Mans 24 Hours. Once that was achieved in 1978, the Formula One project became much more serious.

Appearance of the RS10

In 1979 Renault introduced the RS10 ground effect cars at Monte Carlo and Jabouille scored a popular first win in the French Grand Prix at Dijon, a race that was also memorable for a crazy last-lap tussle between Villeneuve's Ferrari and Arnoux in the second Renault.

The Renault turbos were devastatingly effective in the high altitude of Kyalami, where the normally aspirated cars were left gasping for breath. Arnoux won in South Africa and Brazil in 1980 and it was soon obvious that turbocharging was the way to go.

But Renault had a head start and for 1981 it signed the brilliant young Alain Prost. Immediately the Frenchman was competitive and won three races, including his home Grand Prix, but lost out to Nelson Piquet's Cosworth-powered Brabham in the championship.

By 1982 BMW and Ferrari had turbo engines up and running and were rapidly closing the gap with Renault. The Ferraris looked probable champions but Villeneuve was killed in a qualifying accident at Zolder and team-mate Didier Pironi ended his career when he smashed his legs after colliding with Prost's Renault in poor visibility at Hockenheim. Keke Rosberg wound up champion with a single victory. This was the last time that a normally aspirated car would get the better of the turbos.

Up to speed *After a slow start, Renault started winning in 1979. This is Rene Arnoux at Silverstone.*

An unlucky year

The 1983 season looked to be Renault's year. Prost had three wins and a 14-point lead in the championship when the circus got to Austria, but he warned that Piquet and the Brabham-BMW had overtaken the Renault team's level of development.

The championship went right down to the wire at Kyalami, with Renault sending many staff and journalists along in anticipation of Prost's crowning glory. But Prost was out early on and Piquet's Brabham stroked home to the championship, team-mate Riccardo Patrese finishing second to rub salt into the wound.

Prost spoke out and said what he thought, promptly getting his marching orders as a result. Ironically, he went to McLaren and enjoyed the best years of his career.

Renault took on Derek Warwick and Patrick Tambay for 1984. Warwick led in Brazil, but he tangled with Lauda and retired with suspension problems. With rival engines now just as good, Renault was facing a tough time and there were no more wins as McLaren's MP4 dominated the scene, ironically with Prost aboard.

After another struggling season when its drivers dubbed their chassis "tow-car of the year", Renault quit Formula One.

The company continued as an engine supplier from 1986 and began its association with Williams in 1989. Nigel Mansell and Alain Prost took consecutive drivers' titles in 1992–93, while Williams-Renault won the constructors' title three years in a row.

SAUBER

Country of origin: **Switzerland**	Active years in Formula One: **from 1993**
Date of foundation: **1970**	Constructors' Cup victories: **none**

Peter Sauber was born in 1953 in Zurich. His first racing experience was aboard a VW Beetle, but he started building his own cars in 1970. Although Sauber finished second in the 2-litre class at Le Mans in 1978 with Marc Surer, he became better known when he built the Sauber C6 and entered the new Group C sports car category.

Sauber entered his first Mercedes-powered car in 1985 and his team, based at Hinwil near Zurich, went on to set new standards in sports car racing. At first the team entered Sauber chassis with Mader engines, but as the cars became the class of the field, so Mercedes invested more money and technical support and became an official entrant. In 1989 the Sauber-Mercedes won Le Mans and the World Sports Car series.

Going Formula One

Formula One was the next logical step. But in November 1991 Mercedes announced that it would not be making the move into Grand Prix racing. It did, however, promise financial and technical support for Sauber. Designer Harvey Postlethwaite had already left Tyrrell to draw the new Sauber C12, but when he heard that Mercedes was not coming in behind it, he quit. Sports car designer Leo Ress and former McLaren and Ferrari man Steve Nichols were then responsible for development.

Sauber himself designed the company's state-of-the-art factory. The building is four stories high with a showpiece elevator capable of lifting a 40-ft truck to any part of the factory.

Much wind tunnel work was done before the car's introduction in 1993, using both a university tunnel and the full-scale Mercedes facility in Stuttgart. The car showed immediate pace, but lacked much of the electronic technology, such as active ride, which was starting to become a prerequisite in Formula One.

Sauber chose J.J. Lehto and Karl Wendlinger as his first-year drivers. Lehto arrived on the recommendation of Nichols, who had worked with the Finn at Ferrari, and Wendlinger had been part of the Mercedes Junior Team in sports cars, with Schumacher and Heinz-Harald Frentzen.

Early success

The team made a stunning debut in the 1993 South African Grand Prix when Lehto qualified sixth and finished fifth, the first time that a new team had scored points in its first Grand Prix since Jody Scheckter won the 1977 Argentine Grand Prix for Wolf. But it had come into the season with a lot of testing under its belt and was thus well prepared. As other teams came on strong with their new machinery, Sauber struggled to maintain that kind of performance level.

There were slightly strained relations between the drivers after they collided at Monaco, for which Lehto was blamed, but there were some solid performances. Lehto was fourth at San Marino, with Wendlinger getting a similar result at Monza. They finished the year 12th (Wendlinger) and 14th (Lehto) in the championship standings.

For 1994 Lehto lost his seat to Frentzen, who immediately proved one of the revelations of the season. Frentzen qualified fifth on his Formula One debut in Brazil and then finished fifth in the Pacific Grand Prix at the new TI circuit in Japan.

But then things started to go wrong for Sauber. The team suffered a big blow when Wendlinger crashed in practice at Monaco: he lost the car under braking for the harbour front chicane. He went into a coma and his life hung in the balance for some time. Happily, he made a complete recovery and was testing again before the end of the year, after Andrea de Cesaris had deputised.

There were also sponsorship problems and then Mercedes announced its move to a new five-year deal with McLaren, and the end of its association with Sauber. However, Ford, having lost Benetton to Renault, then agreed a works deal for 1995.

Strong debut *Karl Wendlinger propelled the team into the points in its first year. Here he heads for his best result of 1993, fourth place at Monza.*

SHADOW

COUNTRY OF ORIGIN:	ACTIVE YEARS IN FORMULA ONE:
USA	**1973–80**
DATE OF FOUNDATION:	CONSTRUCTORS' CUP VICTORIES:
1968	**none**

Shadow boss Don Nichols was first active on the sports car scene in America. Jackie Oliver drove a Shadow CanAm car in 1971 and Nichols persuaded Universal Oil Products (UOP) to back the team.

Oliver regularly ran at the front with the black-painted cars in 1972, when Shadow announced its plan to go Formula One the following year.

Nichols recruited former BRM designer Tony Southgate, with Oliver and veteran American sports car ace George Follmer to drive. Kit cars were supplied to Graham Hill's newly established team.

Nichols set up a British base for his team in Northampton after Southgate had built the first car in the garage of his Lincolnshire home. The Cosworth-powered DN1 was not spectacular but ran in the top half of the field regularly.

Success and tragedy

Oliver drove only the CanAm cars in 1974, winning the championship against thin opposition, while rapid Frenchman Jean-Pierre Jarier and American Peter Revson were drafted into the Formula One team. Things looked promising until Revson was killed in a pre-season testing accident at Kyalami. Brian Redman raced briefly before handing over to Welsh hot-shoe Tom Pryce.

As young drivers fought to establish themselves in the post-Stewart era, it was evident that Shadow had two of the quickest, even if reliability was not all that it might have been.

Pryce won the Race of Champions for Shadow at the beginning of 1975 and Jarier sometimes got very close to the qualifying pace of Niki Lauda's dominant Ferrari. Still, solid results did not come and the team struggled when UOP withdrew its support at the end of the year.

Oliver had now hung up his helmet and was the team's main sponsorship sourcer. The DN5 had become a little long in the tooth, but Southgate's new DN8 looked highly promising. The only problem was that Southgate himself had been lured to Lotus temporarily before returning to Shadow.

Main backing was now coming from Tabatip cigarillos, but Italian financier Franco Ambrosio also became involved until he was jailed on charges of financial irregularity.

A poor year

Shadow started 1977 with Pryce and Italian Renzo Zorzi, who had sprung a surprise in the previous year's Monaco Formula Three race. But at Kyalami tragedy struck. Zorzi stopped on the far side of the main straight, just after a hump in the track. There was no problem and he was getting himself out and trying to extricate his helmet oxygen supply when a young marshal ran across the track to stand by in case of fire. Pryce crested the brow, killed the marshal instantly and died when he was hit by the fire extinguisher.

Alan Jones replaced Pryce and brought a partial sweetener to a sad year with the team's one and only win. Niki Lauda was on the way to taking his title back after his Nurburgring accident of the year before, when the circus arrived at his home Osterreichring track. In a wet/dry race, Jones outdrove the Austrian and beat the Ferrari into second place.

Financial problems led to a team split in 1977, with Oliver, Alan Rees and Southgate heading off to form their own Arrows set-up. The Arrows A1, unsurprisingly, looked very similar to Southgate's unfinished drawings for the Shadow DN9. Nichols got a decision in his favour from the High Court which led to Arrows having to build a new car. Meanwhile, John Baldwin finished the DN9 and Shadow continued with Hans Stuck and Clay Regazzoni.

The team went into 1979 with the young Elio de Angelis/Jan Lammers pairing and then in 1980 with Geoff Lees and David Kennedy. It finally collapsed after failing to qualify for the French Grand Prix in 1980.

The Greatest day *Alan Jones holds off Niki Lauda's Ferrari and Jochen Mass's McLaren in the team's first win, in 1977.*

SIMTEK

COUNTRY OF ORIGIN:	ACTIVE YEARS IN FORMULA ONE:
Great Britain	**from 1994**
DATE OF FOUNDATION:	CONSTRUCTORS' CUP VICTORIES:
1994	**none**

Simtek Grand Prix was one of two teams new to the Grand Prix scene in 1994. Team boss Nick Wirth, at 28, was the youngest team owner in Formula One and very much the design and engineering force behind Simtek.

The name is short for "simulated technology", which reflects work carried out by Wirth's already established sister company. Clients included some of the motor industry's major manufacturers and, before Wirth's direct involvement as a team owner, the FIA itself.

No longer is Grand Prix racing possible with an off-the-shelf customer chassis, engine and gearbox. Teams have to build their own cars, even if the work is contracted out. And, in the 1990s, so sophisticated and expensive are the materials that it is not so much a case of entering a sport as beginning a manufacturing industry.

Whereas a budget for a leading Grand Prix team will be well over £20 million, not including free works engines, a new team like Simtek will operate on something much closer to £5 million. There will be no specialized test team, no 200-plus employees and no fancy hotels.

David Brabham joins

Wirth went into the challenge with his eyes open and recruited David Brabham, youngest son of triple-world champion Sir Jack, to do the driving. Brabham Sr had shares in Simtek and, despite the 30 years that had gone by since he was a constructor/driver, valuable experience.

Sadly, the fledgling team suffered Grand Prix racing's first fatality at an event for 12 years when Roland Ratzenberger crashed on the flat-out approach to Imola's Tosa corner. The likeable Austrian had done a deal for five races with Simtek, achieving his lifetime ambition of making it to Formula One.

The team's telemetry showed that Ratzenberger had left the circuit on the lap before his fatal crash, probably weakening the front wing assembly in the process. The nose section flew off the car as it reached maximum speed and thus maximum down load on the straight, causing the Simtek to spear straight on.

In the past it was customary for a team to withdraw its other entry in the event of a fatality to one of its drivers. But Brabham, looking around and seeing the desperation, particularly among the older members of the team, decided that in order to lift spirits and keep the team together, he should carry on.

Italian Andrea Montermini drove for Simtek at the Spanish Grand Prix in Barcelona and was also involved in a sickening crash in practice. Happily, he escaped with a slight ankle injury but, with another damaged monocoque, the team was under enormous pressure.

Seeing the year out

Frenchman Jean-Marc Gounon was then signed as partner to Brabham and actually achieved the S941's best finish of the season when he was ninth in his home Grand Prix at Magny-Cours. Brabham, meanwhile, was tenth in Barcelona and brought the car to the finish six times. He was also involved in a couple of controversial incidents with Jean Alesi's Ferrari when the Frenchman was lapping him.

Gounon's Simtek deal took him as far as Portugal and then the team ran Italian Domenico Schiattarella at Jerez and Adelaide, with Japanese driver Taki Inoue in the car at Suzuka.

With the 1995 season fast approaching, the team suffered a blow when Brabham decided to accept a BMW ride in the British Touring Car Championship. Wirth faced the perennial problem of finding the funding necessary to get the car to the grid, while running a driver quick enough to achieve results that would attract additional backing. The team ran in its first year with support from Russell Athletic, MTV and Barbara MC, a Monaco-based sports agency.

New for 1994 *Simtek had the most torrid of debut seasons, with David Brabham (in car) fighting like a Trojan.*

SURTEES

COUNTRY OF ORIGIN:	ACTIVE YEARS IN FORMULA ONE:
Great Britain	**1970–78**
DATE OF FOUNDATION:	CONSTRUCTORS' CUP VICTORIES:
1969	**none**

John Surtees is the only man to have won world championships on two wheels and four.

Surtees had his first experience of four wheels in one of Ken Tyrrell's Formula Two Coopers before joining Ferrari in 1963. He took a close World Championship for the Scuderia in 1964, but left suddenly in the middle of 1966.

Wide-ranging interests

Surtees did not restrict his racing to Formula One and was an active sports car driver for Ferrari as well, setting up his own small team in association with Lola's Eric Broadley.

Surtees had a huge accident in a Lola CanAm car at Mosport in 1965 when suspension failure pitched him off the track. He was seriously injured but fought back to fitness and broke the lap record at the Ferrari test track when he returned to the team.

Ferrari team boss Eugenio Dragoni was not convinced about his recovery, however, and was also a mentor of Ferrari's second driver, Lorenzo Bandini, whom Surtees usually shaded without much ado. Despite being favourite to take the championship and winning at Spa in the teeming rain, Surtees and Dragoni had one run-in too many and John left immediately to join the Cooper-Maserati team.

For the following two seasons he drove for Honda and then had a year with BRM before deciding to build his own car.

The first Surtees Grand Prix car made its debut in the British Grand Prix at Brands Hatch, where Surtees ran seventh before retiring. He scored his first points as a Formula One constructor with the TS7 when he finished fifth in the Canadian Grand Prix. His first win came in the non-championship Oulton Park Gold Cup.

The next TS9 followed for 1971, with Rolf Stommelen joining Surtees in his last full season as a driver. For 1972 Surtees concentrated on running his team for motorcycle-racing buddy Mike Hailwood and Tim Schenken. Hailwood had made a promising debut for the team the previous year, when he had come second in the Italian Grand Prix.

Fade-out at Monza

Surtees's last Grand Prix was at Monza in 1972 when he debuted the new TS14. Hailwood led the Race of Champions at Brands Hatch with the car in 1973 until he crashed heavily after a mechanical failure. He was joined thereafter by promising Brazilian Carlos Pace, who finished on the podium in Austria.

The 1974 season was grim. Jochen Mass and Pace started the year, but Carlos soon left and later in the year Derek Bell and Jean-Pierre Jabouille drove. The team was operating on a shoestring and both cars failed to qualify at Monza. Austrian Helmut Koinigg drove a TS16 in the Canadian Grand Prix, finishing ninth, but was killed in a slow-speed accident next time out at Watkins Glen.

John Watson drove for Team Surtees in 1975 before joining Penske. Surtees then did a deal leading to what his cars were probably most famous for: racing in Durex livery. Alan Jones was the first driver and, ironically, the TS19 proved much more competitive than most of the chassis that had gone before. It led to a very public withdrawal of the BBC TV's cameras from the pre-season non-championship British races.

The TS19s did not actually achieve much in the form of hard results and Vittorio Brambilla was driving one when he was injured in the multiple accident at the start of the 1978 Italian Grand Prix.

René Arnoux looked the most promising driver to try the new TS20 and, with ground effects technology taking over, Surtees planned the TS21 with that in mind for 1979. Unfortunately, however, sponsors would not commit to the team and so Surtees decided to bring down the curtain on his team's Formula One participation.

Fellow biker *Surtees ran a car for Mike Hailwood in the early 1970s. Here his TS14A is unloaded at Silverstone in 1973.*

TYRRELL

COUNTRY OF ORIGIN:	ACTIVE YEARS IN FORMULA ONE:
Great Britain	**from 1970**
DATE OF FOUNDATION:	CONSTRUCTORS' CUP VICTORIES:
1960	**1971**

Ken Tyrrell is a Surrey timber merchant who became captivated by motor racing in the 1950s. Tyrrell drove until 1958, then concentrated on team management.

He founded the Tyrrell Racing Team in 1960 and was responsible for giving John Surtees his first race on four wheels. He managed the Cooper Formula One team when John Cooper was injured in a road accident, but his path to the top was linked to his discovery of the young Jackie Stewart.

Timmy Mayer, brother of early McLaren boss Teddy, was one of Tyrrell's drivers until he was killed in an accident in Tasmania. Tyrrell was advised to give Stewart a test in his new Formula Three car at Goodwood and, when the brilliant Scotsman quickly proved faster than Bruce McLaren, Ken signed him immediately.

Stewart joins the team

Stewart drove for Tyrrell in Formula Two while driving for the BRM Grand Prix team, their Formula One partnership only beginning in 1968. Ken had secured one of the new Cosworth DFV engines and a chassis from Matra. Stewart fought out the championship and lost only in the final round. But in 1969 the Stewart/Matra combination was unbeatable, winning six races and the championship.

In 1970 Matra would not build a car to accept the Ford V8 rather than its own V12, which Stewart and Tyrrell did not want to use. The old car did not satisfy new regulations and so the reigning champion had to drive a customer car from the brand-new March factory.

In one of Formula One's best kept secrets, Tyrrell had also recruited Derek Gardner to pen the first Tyrrell Grand Prix car and, when the March proved uncompetitive later in the season, Stewart switched to the new Tyrrell 001, and led both North American races before retiring.

In 1971 Stewart and Tyrrell were the dominant forces in Formula One, Jackie clinching his second title with six wins, while Frenchman François Cevert showed great promise in the second car.

Stewart's 1972 season was disrupted by one of the most publicized ulcers of all time, but he returned in 1973 to clinch his third championship, taking his victory tally to a record 27 in the process.

As early as April that year, Jackie had told Tyrrell of his intention to retire after the last Grand Prix at Watkins Glen, his 100th. But as things turned out, the championship was won with the best drive of his career at Monza, a fourth place after an early puncture, and he never did drive at The Glen. While in practice Cevert was killed in an horrendous accident and Stewart's entry was withdrawn.

While it is true that Tyrrell has never again achieved anything like that early success, there have been other high points in a quarter of a century of racing history.

A six-wheeler

In the immediate post-Stewart era, Jody Scheckter and Patrick Depailler both won races for Tyrrell and the team developed the Project 34 six-wheeler. The theory was that four small wheels would put more rubber on the road for greater purchase and produce a cleaner front end in terms of aerodynamics. Initial tests were good, and at Anderstorp in 1976 Scheckter and Depailler finished in first and second places. Ronnie Peterson replaced Scheckter the following season. But by then the cars were uncompetitive.

After finishing second in no fewer than eight races, Depailler finally brought home a Grand Prix victory for the Tyrrell team at Monaco in 1978. In those ground effect days Tyrrell produced copies of the leading Lotus and Williams designs but did not win another race until Michele Alboreto joined the team.

Throughout the 1980s and early 1990s the team was a shadow of its formerself, the high spot being Jean Alesi's stunning drives with Harvey Postlethwaite's 018/019 designs in 1989–90.

The 1994 season, with the addition of works Yamaha engines and driving skills of Ukyo Katayama, was the team's most promising for a long while.

Big Ken *Racer turned champion team owner Ken Tyrrell.*

VANWALL

COUNTRY OF ORIGIN:	ACTIVE YEARS IN FORMULA ONE:
Great Britain	**1954–60**
DATE OF FOUNDATION:	CONSTRUCTORS' CUP VICTORIES:
1954	**1958**

Tony Vandervell was an industrialist, racing fan and patriot. One of the original backers of the BRM project, he became frustrated at the lack of progress and went his own way.

Vandervell bought a Ferrari 125 in 1949 with the intention of testing it and helping the BRM learning process. The car ran as a Thinwall, a Vandervell trade name.

After a couple of years of Formula Two rules, the World Championship conformed to a new 2.5-litre formula in 1954. Vandervell commissioned John Cooper to construct a new chassis for a 2-litre, four-cylinder engine built by Vandervell and based on four Norton motorcycle engines. This was developed into a full 2.5-litre unit by 1955.

The car became known as a Vanwall for the first time, a combination of Vandervell's name and his Thinwall bearing business. But racing then was dominated by the Mercedes-Benz team and the lone Vanwall was raced by Peter Collins. Harry Schell and Ken Wharton drove in 1955 but there was little to write home about.

Chapman's chassis

In 1956 Vandervell commissioned a new chassis from Colin Chapman. The bodywork was styled by aerodynamicist Frank Costin and the engine produced a respectable 285 brake horsepower. Schell, Maurice Trintignant and Mike Hawthorn were the drivers, but before the Grand Prix season started, Stirling Moss gave the car a winning debut in the International Trophy race at Silverstone.

In the French Grand Prix at Reims Chapman himself was entered by Vanwall but his brakes locked up in practice and he rammed Hawthorn! The brakes could not be repaired and he did not start the race.

Schell gave the Ferraris a shock in the race, passing Collins and Castellotti, and getting up alongside race leader Fangio on two occasions.

The 1957 season saw Vanwall emerge as a force to be reckoned with. The team could boast Stirling Moss, along with Tony Brooks and newcomer Stuart Lewis-Evans.

The British Grand Prix at Aintree brought the day Vandervell had been waiting for. Moss qualified on pole, with Jean Behra's Maserati between him and Brooks. Moss took the lead but Behra hauled him in when the Vanwall started to misfire and Stirling had to pit for attention to an earth lead. Still there was a problem and so Brooks was called in to hand over his car to Moss, who resumed ninth. He was soon up to fourth, behind Lewis-Evans, Hawthorn and Behra. But the gods were looking after him. Behra's flywheel shattered and Hawthorn punctured a tyre on the debris, allowing Moss to win. It was the first time that a British car had won a major Grand Prix since 1923 and the first victory by a British car and driver in the British Grand Prix.

The little mid-engined Coopers made a sensational start to the 1958 season, with Vanwall not ready for the hastily arranged Argentine Grand Prix. But then Moss won in Holland and Brooks in Belgium. Brooks won again in Germany, a win spoiled by Peter Collins' death in a Ferrari. Moss won in Portugal before Brooks was successful again at Monza.

Constructors' crown

The championship went to the wire in Morocco and was between Moss with three wins and Hawthorn's Ferrari with one, but five second places. Moss won superbly but teammate Lewis-Evans died from burns in an accident. Hawthorn was second, enough to clinch the title. On the way, however, he had gone off, stalled and push-started his car against the flow of traffic. He was disqualified but Moss said he had seen him pushing the car only on the pavement, which was permitted. Hawthorn was reinstated, costing Moss the title. Sportsmanship was different then. But at least Vanwall won the manufacturers' crown.

Vandervell was shaken by the accident to Lewis-Evans and, in poor health, gave up his involvement in 1959. With the rear-engined revolution on the way, a chapter of British racing history was over.

Teething troubles *Peter Collins struggled with the team in 1954.*

WILLIAMS

COUNTRY OF ORIGIN: **Great Britain**	ACTIVE YEARS IN FORMULA ONE: **from 1973**
DATE OF FOUNDATION: **1968**	CONSTRUCTORS' CUP VICTORIES: **1980, 1981, 1986, 1987, 1992, 1993, 1994**

Frank Williams is proof positive that determination will triumph over adversity.

An amateur driver of talent, he gave up racing and started buying and selling racing cars. He struck up a great friendship with Piers Courage and ran a Formula One Brabham BT26 for Piers in 1969. A fine second place behind Graham Hill in Monaco attracted the attention of De Tomaso. Williams ran their car in 1970, but he was devastated when Courage was killed at Zandvoort.

Williams struggled financially in the early 1970s, running a selection of paying no-hopers. A liaison with Walter Wolf in 1976 turned sour but led to the turning point for Williams, the decision to found Williams Grand Prix Engineering with Patrick Head.

Williams invested a lot of time and effort into attracting Saudi Arabian backing and Head's functional FW06 allowed Australian Alan Jones to turn in some fine performances in 1978.

Arrival of the FW07

The following year Head came up with the superb ground effects FW07. Clay Regazzoni scored the team's first Grand Prix win at Silverstone and Jones went on to dominate the second half of the year. In 1980 Jones was teamed with Carlos Reutemann and the duo proved formidable. Jones won five times and Reutemann triumphed in Monte Carlo. The Australian won the drivers' championship and Williams took the constructors' crown.

Jones narrowly lost out to Nelson Piquet in 1981 and announced his retirement, whereupon Williams signed Keke Rosberg.

By 1982 turbocharged engines were proving too strong for normally aspirated opposition but Rosberg managed to win the last championship for the Ford Cosworth engine, despite taking just one victory.

Williams then forged an alliance with Honda. The V6 turbo was brutal and heavy in its early days, but constant development meant that by the end of 1985, by which time Nigel Mansell was on board, the Williams-Honda combination was the one to beat.

Rosberg left for McLaren at the wrong time and, although Nelson Piquet and Mansell were the class of the field in 1986, Prost's McLaren stole the title in Adelaide when Mansell suffered an exploding tyre with just 18 laps to go.

Williams suffered an even bigger blow in March of that year, however, when Frank himself was paralysed in a car accident on the way back from a test at Paul Ricard.

In 1987 Piquet was generally outpaced by team-mate Mansell but used consistency to take his third world title in FW11. Piquet then left for Lotus and Williams lost its Honda engines.

The 1988 season was a watershed year with normally aspirated Judds, but a deal with Renault brought Williams back as a major strength although, with Riccardo Patrese and Thierry Boutsen on the books, the team lacked a recognized top-line driver until Mansell returned for 1991 after a two-year spell at Ferrari.

Victory for Williams

Patrick Head's FW14 was a superb car and Mansell lost out to Senna's McLaren in 1991 only because of reliability problems with the semi-automatic gearbox in the early races. By 1992 Williams had mastered active suspension and, with FW14B, Mansell was unbeatable. He won a record nine races en route to the championship.

After a contractual dispute with the team, Mansell left to try his hand on the Indycar circuit. Alain Prost took up where he left off and won the second consecutive drivers' and constructors' double for the Williams FW15 in 1993.

Frank Williams was the man who first gave Ayrton Senna a Formula One test. He had wanted the Brazilian ever since and, in 1994, he got him. Tragically, the great Brazilian died in an FW16 at Imola. Damon Hill then rose in stature and saved a desperately sad year by challenging Michael Schumacher for the drivers' title, losing out after a controversial clash in the final round at Adelaide. Williams, though, won the constructors' crown again.

Poised for glory *Alan Jones was not the first Williams winner – Clay Regazzoni was – but he lifted the 1980 world title.*

WOLF

Country of origin:	Active years in Formula One:
Great Britain	**1977–79**
Date of foundation:	Constructors' Cup victories:
1977	**none**

Walter Wolf was an Austrian who made his fortune in the oil business in Canada. A lifelong racing enthusiast, he used his new-found wealth to forge an involvement in the sport.

Wolf first appeared on the Formula One scene in 1975 and was courted by Frank Williams who, at that time, was still struggling to make an impression on the sport.

Wolf and Williams struck a deal for 1976, but it soon became apparent that Wolf was an autocrat who did not wish to adopt a mere supporting role. The Hesketh team was winding down, so Wolf took on Harvey Postlethwaite's promising 308C design and the man himself.

An unpromising start

The 1976 season was disastrous. Jackie Ickx was the driver, but he was not impressed with the car and did not gel with Postlethwaite. Williams did not like working for anyone else and decided to cut his links and go his own way with designer Patrick Head.

Wolf had a major reorganization for 1977. He recruited former Lotus team manager Peter Warr to run his team and he signed Jody Scheckter from Tyrrell. Postlethwaite's neat Wolf WR1 chassis looked promising and Scheckter took advantage of some good fortune to win on the car's debut in Argentina.

Good luck he may have had, but the WR1 was a good car and the team was well drilled. Scheckter led a great tussle involving Niki Lauda's Ferrari and Mario Andretti's Lotus in Long Beach, only losing out in the closing stages when a tyre went down.

Lauda had won for the previous two seasons in Monte Carlo, but Scheckter went to the Principality, where he lived, and outdrove the Ferrari to claim his second win.

Scheckter remained in contention for the championship throughout the year but the crown eventually went to a consistent Lauda. Andretti's Lotus was the class of the field, but the American did not have the best of reliability. One of the places where Scheckter gained by that was Mosport. There he scored an emotional "home" triumph for his team boss.

Triumph of ground effects

The form shown by Andretti and Lotus had served a warning that a ground effects car would be a pre-requisite for success in 1978, and so it proved. The Lotus 79s of Andretti and Ronnie Peterson proved unbeatable. At Wolf, Postlethwaite came up with the WR5, but the team could not add to its victory tally, a pair of seconds in Germany and Canada being their best results.

Scheckter was becoming disgruntled and an offer to join Ferrari was quickly accepted, the South African going on to win the championship the following season. Wolf took on James Hunt who was also disgruntled at McLaren's inability to crack the ground effect concept.

On paper this looked good. Hunt and Postlethwaite, of course, went back to Hesketh's glory days and the new WR7 looked as if it should work. Like the successful Ligier JS11, it had distinctive aerodynamic kick-ups ahead of the rear wheels and a futuristic shape.

It was a rush to get the car ready in time, however, and the results did not come. Hunt was always aware of his profession's inherent dangers and, with just one finish behind him, he did not want to put his life on the line for a sixth or seventh place. He had the trappings of wealth and announced his sudden retirement mid-season. Wolf then took on the aggressive young Keke Rosberg, but even the exuberant Finn could do little with the Wolf.

A man used to success, Walter Wolf did not take kindly to being an also-ran and folded his team at the end of its fourth season.

Flying start *Jody Scheckter gave the Wolf team the best start possible by winning in Argentina on its debut.*

LEGENDS OF THE TRACK

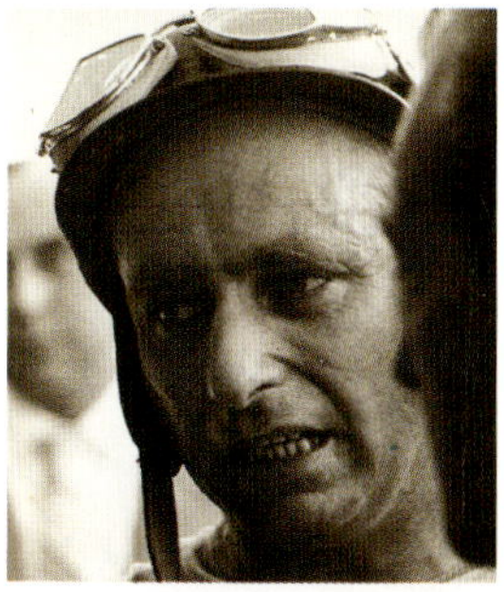

All drivers who reach Formula One are something a little bit special, however much we like to think we could do the same from the comfort and safety of our armchairs. Nevertheless, certain drivers stand out as being just that little bit more special than the others.

Comparing drivers of different generations is a difficult and, perhaps, pointless task. The machinery used was different, the level of competition was different. And, let's face it, the weather conditions were probably different, too. Many say that the battle for the mantle of the greatest driver of all time is between Fangio and Senna. It is forever a subject of bar-room debate. That said, the ten drivers we have chosen here stand out as being the top ten since the Formula One World Championship began in 1950. Some, such as Mike Hawthorn, Jochen Rindt, Ronnie Peterson, Mario Andretti and Gilles Villeneuve have shone, but only briefly. Others have never even won races, but had the talent to do so if had they been given the right equipment, such as Chris Amon and Jean Alesi. Formula One is a fickle beast. However, the ten drivers chosen rose to the top and stayed there. They are legends whose talent endured.

BRABHAM

"Jack's final year showed that he hasn't changed very much since he first came over. He's always been a top-flight driver, exceedingly competent and as cunning as a fox."

AUTOSPORT MAGAZINE, ON BRABHAM'S RETIREMENT

GRAND PRIX STATISTICS

1955	1 Grand Prix, 0 points
1956	1 Grand Prix, 0 points
1957	5 Grands Prix, 0 points
1958	9 Grands Prix, 3 points, 17th overall
1959	8 Grands Prix, 1 pole, 1 fastest lap, 2 wins, 31 points, 1st overall
1960	8 Grands Prix, 3 poles, 3 fastest laps, 5 wins, 43 points, 1st overall
1961	8 Grands Prix, 1 pole, 4 points, 11th overall
1962	8 Grands Prix, 9 points, 9th overall
1963	10 Grands Prix, 14 points, 7th overall
1964	10 Grands Prix, 1 fastest lap, 11 points, 8th overall
1965	6 Grands Prix, 9 points, 10th overall
1966	9 Grands Prix, 3 poles, 1 fastest lap, 4 wins, 42 points, 1st overall
1967	11 Grands Prix, 2 poles, 2 wins, 46 points, 2nd overall
1968	11 Grands Prix, 2 points, 23rd overall
1969	8 Grands Prix, 2 poles, 14 points, 10th overall
1970	13 Grands Prix, 1 pole, 4 fastest laps, 1 win, 25 points, 5th overall
Career tally	126 Grands Prix, 13 poles, 10 fastest laps, 14 wins, 253 points

AN UNCOMPROMISING MAN

Although he was known as "Black Jack", Brabham's nickname did not reflect an affinity with the gaming tables but his demeanour. As uncompromising as they come, he was a driver who combined dedication and determination with a shrewd nature and the mechanical know-how to forge a remarkable career.

Living in the relaxed Australian environment where space was not a problem, Jack was behind the wheel of a family car by the age of 12 and always showed interest in and aptitude for things mechanical. He started a motor repair business at the age of 20 and involved himself in midget racing.

A commercial allegiance

New South Wales champion in his first season, Brabham also forged an early alliance with Ron Tauranac, with whom he would later form Brabham, the "BT" designation of the cars standing for Brabham Tauranac. Tauranac was active in hill climbing and, after winding up the establishment with his Midget car, Brabham turned to more conventional machinery, eventually procuring a Cooper-Bristol with the support of Redex additives. When the Australian sporting body objected to advertising on the car, Brabham turned his attention to the Kiwi scene and impressed in the 1954 New Zealand Grand Prix.

He was soon persuaded to make the trip to Europe. He became associated with John Cooper and made his World Championship debut in the 1955 British Grand Prix aboard a Cooper-Bristol. Jack joined Cooper as a works Formula Two driver, also taking part in World Championship races which had a Formula Two class. By 1959 the Coopers, with 2.5-litre Climax engines, were a force in Formula One, driven by Brabham, Stirling Moss, Maurice Trintignant, Bruce McLaren and Masten Gregory. Although Moss took pole and led for much of the season-opener at Monte Carlo, it was Brabham who was there at the end.

Jack may not have been the quickest, but he was consistent. He won again at Aintree, was second to Jo Bonnier's BRM at Zandvoort and third at Monza and Reims. He sealed his championship in dramatic style at Sebring by pushing his car to the finish in fourth place after running out of fuel on the last lap. If anybody felt that Brabham's title had been a touch fortunate, their doubts were quashed in 1960 when he won back-to-back titles for Cooper-Climax. His season included five straight wins – at Zandvoort, Spa, Reims, Silverstone and Oporto. Cooper had pioneered the rear-engined designs in Formula One and Brabham had reaped the reward, but for 1961 there was a new 1.5-litre engine formula and Ferrari leapt to the fore with Wolfgang von Trips and Phil Hill. The German was killed at Monza and Hill took the championship.

Ever shrewd, Brabham saw the potential for a production racing car concern and, with Tauranac, formed Motor Racing Developments. The first Brabham made its debut in 1962, and a fourth place by Brabham at Watkins Glen brought the first points ever scored by a driver in a car of his own manufacture.

Dan Gurney joined Jack on the driving strength and, although they won non- championship races at Solitude and Zeltweg, they did not win a pukka Grand Prix until Rouen in 1964. A popular misconception of racing history is that Brabham won the first Grand Prix for the cars and team which bore his own name, but in fact it was Gurney. It was not until Reims, two years later, that Jack finally won in a Brabham.

Back—with Hulme

The demands of the business sent Brabham into semi-retirement in 1965. He then decided to come back full time alongside Hulme for 1966, when he clinched his third championship. That Reims win was followed up by successive victories at Silverstone, Zandvoort and the Nurburgring.

The following season Hulme kept the momentum going with a consistent year which brought another championship for Brabham – Repco, beating the boss into second place. Hulme then moved to McLaren and Jack signed up the rapid young Austrian Jochen Rindt. All but unbeatable in Formula Two, Rindt had problems with the unreliable new Repco engine.

Rindt left for Lotus and Brabham was joined by the young Belgian driver Jacky Ickx. While Brabham's season was hampered by a broken ankle sustained in a testing accident, Ickx finished second overall to Jackie Stewart's dominant Matra-Ford and was snapped up by Ferrari. Having his young hot shoes poached was becoming tedious for Brabham, who had retirement in mind.

He was approaching 44 and determined that 1970 would be his final year. It was, after all, his 23rd season in a sport not renowned for its forgiveness. It started well, with Jack overhauling reigning world champion Stewart in the new March and winning at Kyalami. In the final analysis, the pair would finish the year joint fifth, as Rindt became the sport's only posthumous world champion.

What sticks in the memory from 1970 are two incredible races in which Brabham lost out to Rindt on the very last lap. At Monaco he was pursued relentlessly by the flying Austrian and went straight on at the final hairpin. He reversed out and finished second, but never had Black Jack's face been blacker.

He hung up his hat after the Mexican Grand Prix that year, some 16 seasons after his Aintree debut, with 14 wins from his 126 outings.

CAREER MILESTONES

1926	Born in Hurstville, New South Wales, Australia
1948	Midget racing
1952	Switched to hill climbs
1953	Australian hill climb champion
1954	Started circuit racing in a Redex
1955	Made Formula One debut for Cooper
1956	Raced in sports cars for Cooper
1958	Won London Trophy and Gold Cup for Cooper
1959	Won Formula One World Championship for Cooper
1960	Repeated the feat
1961	Had a shot at the Indy 500
1962	Drove a Lotus while building first Brabham chassis
1966	Won World Championship in own car
1967	Second in World Championship to team-mate Hulme
1970	Fifth in final season of Formula One

CLARK

"If it could happen to him, what chance did the rest of us have? I think we all felt that. It seemed like we'd lost our leader."

Chris Amon, ON HEARING OF CLARK'S DEATH IN A CRASH AT HOCKENHEIM IN 1968

GRAND PRIX STATISTICS

1960	6 Grands Prix, 8 points, 8th overall
1961	8 Grands Prix, 1 fastest lap, 11 points, 7th overall
1962	9 Grands Prix, 6 poles, 5 fastest laps, 3 wins, 30 points, 2nd overall
1963	10 Grands Prix, 7 poles, 6 fastest laps, 7 wins, 54 points, 1st overall
1964	10 Grands Prix, 5 poles, 4 fastest laps, 3 wins, 32 points, 3rd overall
1965	9 Grands Prix, 6 poles, 6 fastest laps, 6 wins, 54 points, 1st overall
1966	8 Grands Prix, 2 poles, 1 win, 16 points, 6th overall
1967	11 Grands Prix, 6 poles, 5 fastest laps, 4 wins, 41 points, 3rd overall
1968	1 Grand Prix, 1 pole, 1 fastest lap, 1 win, 9 points, 11th overall

Career tally – 72 Grands Prix, 33 poles, 28 fastest laps, 25 wins, 255 points

A SMOOTH OPERATOR

An unassuming man out of a cockpit, Jim Clark was a genius in one. When motor racing enthusiasts get together to debate who was the greatest driver ever, Clark invariably enters into the discussion alongside Juan Manuel Fangio and Ayrton Senna.

Born the son of a Scottish farmer, Clark had his first contact with racing when his eldest sister married a local racer who took him to Charterhall, and it left an impression. It still seemed certain that farming would be his career but, shortly after his 17th birthday, local garage owner Jock McBain, advised him to enter an auto test. He did and won it.

After a number of local rallies, a close friend, Ian Scott-Watson, lent Clark a DKW in which to have his first race. For the following year, Scott-Watson bought a Porsche and Clark became serious. Interestingly, at this stage Scott-Watson seemed more ambitious for Clark than he himself was, acutely aware of his responsibilities on the farm. In 1958 McBain re-formed the Border Reivers team and bought an ex-Archie Scott-Brown D-type Jaguar. The car was more powerful than anything Clark had driven and he admitted to being scared of it. But that did not stop him scoring 12 wins from 20 starts.

If this was the season in which the wider racing world started to see Clark's ability, it was also one in which he had a chastening experience at Spa. He was entered in the D-type for a top-class sports car race. Warned of Spa's unforgiving nature, he treated it with respect, later vividly remembering being lapped by Masten Gregory in great style. Later in the race Scott-Brown was killed when he was caught out by Spa's frequently changing conditions. It sowed the seeds of a career-long dislike which Clark had for the majestic Ardennes track. But it was not so strong that it would stop him winning four consecutive Belgian Grands Prix there during 1962–65.

A break with Lotus

Fate took a hand when Scott-Watson bought a Lotus Elite and Clark had a superb scrap with Colin Chapman on his first visit to Brands Hatch. Chapman's new Lotus company was in the embryonic stages and, when a Formula One deal that Clark had been promised with Aston Martin failed to materialize, he joined Lotus to drive in Formula Two and Formula Junior.

He started winning immediately and Chapman was so convinced of his potential that he entered him in the Dutch Grand Prix, where he ran as high as fifth before retiring. Then it was Spa, and the jinx struck again. Team-mate Stirling Moss had a bad accident in practice and broke both his legs. Then, in the race, Clark was first on the scene at Chris Bristow's crash. He later wrote of seeing a marshal run on to the road while another flagged him down:

"He bent and grabbed this thing by the side of the road. It looked like a rag doll. I'll never forget the sight of his mangled body being dragged to the side. I remember at the end of the race finding that my car was spattered with blood. This put me off completely. Toward the end of the race, my team-mate, Alan Stacey, was also killed. A bird flew into his face and his car went off the road. Thankfully, I didn't see the accident or the car. Had I done so, I'm convinced I would have given up motor racing for good."

But Clark overcame the experience and by 1961 was a full-time Grand Prix driver. That year, however, there was more upset when he was involved in the accident which resulted in the death of German driver Wolfgang von Trips and 13 spectators at Monza and the authorities sought to blame Clark for the tragedy.

Chapman designed the monocoque Lotus 25 for the following year and Clark scored his first Grand Prix win with it. He battled down to the wire with Hill for the championship before losing out at the final round when the car broke while he was leading. Clark was untouchable in 1963 and set a record for the number of victories in one season, when he took seven wins from ten starts. He also finished second in the Indy 500 with the rear-engined Lotus, to the astonishment of the American establishment.

Victory in the Indy

In 1965, victories in the South African, Belgian, French, British, Dutch and German Grands Prix gave him a second championship and he also won the Indy 500.

With the new 3-litre Formula introduced for 1966, Lotus did not have the engines to mount a serious challenge and it was not until the Cosworth DFV was introduced in 1967 that Clark was back as the man to beat. He gave the engine a debut win at Zandvoort and pushed Denny Hulme hard for the title.

Clark started 1968 by winning in South Africa to break Fangio's record of 24 Grand Prix victories. Then, driving in a Formula Two race at Hockenheim, his car flew off the road, hit a tree and he was killed instantly. He need not have been racing, but he loved racing anything, any time, anywhere. The racing world was stunned.

Natural combination *Lotus was the only Formula One team Clark drove for.*

CAREER MILESTONES

- **1936** Born in Kilmany, Scotland
- **1954** Took part in local rallies
- **1956** First race, at Charterhall
- **1958** Drove for Border Reivers sports car team
- **1959** First single-seater race, in Formula Junior
- **1960** Formula One debut for Lotus. Third at Le Mans for Aston Martin
- **1962** First Grand Prix win, at Spa for Lotus. Second overall
- **1963** Won World Championship for Lotus. Second in Indy 500
- **1965** Won World Championship again, plus Indy 500 for Lotus
- **1967** Gave Ford Cosworth DFV a winning debut in Dutch Grand Prix
- **1968** Killed in Formula Two race at Hockenheim

FANGIO

"In my day it was 75 per cent car and mechanic, 25 per cent driver and luck. Today it's 95 per cent car."

JUAN MANUEL FANGIO

GRAND PRIX STATISTICS

1950	6 Grands Prix, 4 poles, 3 fastest laps, 3 wins, 27 points, 2nd overall
1951	7 Grands Prix, 4 poles, 5 fastest laps, 3 wins, 31 points, 1st overall
1953	8 Grands Prix, 2 poles, 2 fastest laps, 1 win, 28 points, 2nd overall
1954	8 Grands Prix, 5 poles, 3 fastest laps, 6 wins, 42 points, 1st overall
1955	6 Grands Prix, 3 poles, 3 fastest laps, 4 wins, 40 points, 1st overall
1956	7 Grands Prix, 5 poles, 4 fastest laps, 3 wins, 30 points, 1st overall
1957	7 Grands Prix, 4 poles, 2 fastest laps, 4 wins, 40 points, 1st overall
1958	2 Grands Prix, 1 pole, 1 fastest lap, 7 points, 14th overall

Career tally – 51 Grands Prix, 28 poles, 23 fastest laps, 24 wins, 245 points

FIVE TIMES CHAMPION

Juan Manuel Fangio came to be known universally and simply as "the maestro". For many, the greatest racing driver there has ever been, he won five World Championships, in 1951 and from 1954 to 1957. He won 24 races from 51 starts, a record at the time.

Born in Balcarce, Argentina, Fangio was the son of an Italian immigrant. During his childhood he had a passion for football and his nickname of El Chueco ("Bandy Legs") reputedly came from his playing style. He had his first taste of motor racing came while riding as a mechanic in a Chevrolet driven by a customer of the garage in which he worked. After military service Fangio opened his own garage and started to drive in long, arduous and hazardous South American road races. He was beginning to enjoy great success until wartime restrictions intervened. For a while there was no racing, but Fangio practised by taking time out to drive great distances at racing speed.

Racing returned in 1947 and Fangio was intrigued by the visiting Italian drivers, Achille Varzi and Luigi Villoresi. The Argentine Automobile Club had bought two Maseratis to be driven against them and one was entrusted to Fangio.

During some brief racing in Europe, Fangio also came across leading racing driver Jean-Pierre Wimille and was highly impressed by the European scene, but he came close to stopping racing before achieving any of his great fame. On his return home to Argentina, he crashed in a road race and his co-driver and close friend was killed. And, shortly afterwards, Wimille was killed in Argentina.

Leaving Argentina behind

With the backing of the Perón regime and a Maserati, Fangio was sent to Europe and started to win regularly in 1949. The loss of Wimille and, by now, Varzi, had left Alfa-Romeo without drivers as they prepared for the first World Championship in 1950, and Fangio was given a drive. He lost out by the narrowest of margins to team-mate Nino Farina, but gained the first of his titles the following season.

The Tipo 159 Alfa-Romeo was by now past its sell-by date and Fangio moved to Ferrari, but broke his neck in an accident at Monza, which kept him out of the cockpit until the following season. He returned with Maserati, for whom he won the Italian Grand Prix, but the scene was dominated by his old Ferrari team.

Fangio won the first couple of races in 1954 with Maserati, but Mercedes-Benz then poached him to head their team. Fangio won another four races in Mercedes' silver cars that year before taking a second title in 1955 with four victories, in Argentina, Belgium, Holland and Italy.

At the end of that season Mercedes-Benz withdrew in the wake of the Le Mans disaster and Fangio rejoined Ferrari. The championship that year became a race between Fangio, his team-mate, Peter Collins, and Stirling Moss in the Maserati. At Monza Collins handed over his own car to Fangio after Juan's had failed, guaranteeing the great man a fourth title.

For 1957 Fangio returned to Maserati and won the championship for the last time. The race that clinched it for him will be remembered as his greatest – the German Grand Prix at the Nurburgring. Ferrari had Peter Collins and Mike Hawthorn ranged against him and Maserati tried starting Fangio with a light fuel load in the hope that he could build up a lead and then refuel and still get out in front. But a slow stop meant that Fangio was three-quarters of a minute behind when he rejoined the track and he was forced to drive like a man possessed to catch the British pair. And now, of course, Fangio was carrying a heavier fuel load than his adversaries.

He started to take six seconds per lap out of the Ferraris at first, then even more. He blasted past Collins and with a lap and a half to go and forced his way past Hawthorn. It was a breathtaking performance.

In 1958 Fangio was fourth in his home Grand Prix and then drove his last race in the French Grand Prix at Reims, where he also finished fourth. His Maserati was in trouble near the finish when race leader Hawthorn caught him just as Fangio was about to cross the line. Hawthorn braked and allowed Fangio to cross the line ahead of him as a mark of respect for the man whom his contemporaries regarded as the master.

Winning at the slowest speed

Fangio was noted for being able to win a race at the slowest possible speed, to judge things to perfection. Although he was older than many of his rivals, he had enormous staying power. Stirling Moss was the only driver who was really capable of giving him a hard time. Moss beat Fangio on the last lap of a superb 1955 British Grand Prix, and there has always been the question as to whether the great man let him.

Fangio retired as the reigning champion, a title which Hawthorn took over at the end of that season and enjoyed for all too short a time.

Fangio then concentrated on business in his native Buenos Aires. He was always regarded as a great sportsman and carried a dignified air, something some of the stars of today would do well to imitate.

The Maestro *Fangio driving at Silverstone in the 1950 British Grand Prix.*

CAREER MILESTONES

1911	Born Balcarce, Argentina
1938	Road racing in Argentina
1948	Turned to single-seaters Made first foray to Europe
1949	Won many Libre races in Europe
1950	Second in Formula One for Alfa Romeo
1951	Won World Championship for Alfa Romeo
1952	Broke his neck and missed season
1953	Second for Maserati
1954	Moved to Mercedes and won World Championship
1955	Won World Championship again
1956	And again, this time for Ferrari
1957	Another World crown, this time for Maserati
1958	Retired after a handful of races

HILL

"... he did not suffer fools gladly and was not afraid to show it. He did not change over the years, but he mellowed. He was a great ambassador for our sport."

Jackie Stewart
ON GRAHAM HILL

GRAND PRIX STATISTICS

1958	9 Grands Prix, 0 points
1959	7 Grands Prix, 0 points
1960	8 Grands Prix, 1 fastest lap, 4 points, 15th overall
1961	8 Grands Prix, 3 points, 13th overall
1962	9 Grands Prix, 1 pole, 3 fastest laps, 4 wins, 42 points, 1st overall
1963	10 Grands Prix, 2 poles, 2 wins, 29 points, 2nd overall
1964	10 Grands Prix, 1 pole, 1 fastest lap, 2 wins, 39 points, 2nd overall
1965	10 Grands Prix, 4 poles, 3 fastest laps, 2 wins, 40 points, 2nd overall
1966	9 Grands Prix, 17 points, 5th overall
1967	11 Grands Prix, 3 poles, 2 fastest laps, 15 points, 6th overall
1968	12 Grands Prix, 2 poles, 3 wins, 48 points, 1st overall
1969	10 Grands Prix, 1 win, 19 points, 7th overall
1970	11 Grands Prix, 7 points, 13th overall
1971	11 Grands Prix, 2 points, 21st overall
1972	12 Grands Prix, 4 points, 12th overall
1973	12 Grands Prix, 0 points
1974	15 Grands Prix, 1 point, 18th overall
1975	2 Grands Prix, 0 points

Career tally – 176 Grands Prix, 13 poles, 10 fastest laps, 14 wins, 270 points

MR DETERMINATION

Determined, intense, record-breaking, humorous, the perfect ambassador of the sport of motor racing. All this and much more has been said of Graham Hill, the only man to have won the triple crown of World Championship, Indy 500 and the Le Mans 24 Hours.

It has become something of a cliché to say that Hill was a man who worked at his driving rather than being imbued with natural ability. One of the reasons is that he was such a latecomer to the sport. Born in Hampstead, London, Hill did not pass his driving test until he was 24 years old. The same year in which he passed his test, Graham paid the princely sum of £1 for four laps at a racing school at Brands Hatch. He was hooked.

Working as an apprentice with Smiths Instruments at the time, Hill gave it up and started to work as a mechanic at the racing school. Money was short and he soon agreed to take a race in one of the school cars in lieu of payment. His race debut was in a Cooper-JAP at Brands Hatch in 1954.

Hill then met Colin Chapman and went to work for him as Colin strove to build up his Lotus company. Chapman helped him and Hill built his own Lotus 11 for 1956, when he almost won the Autosport club racing championship, but unfortunately suffered a mechanical failure in the final round. He drove a variety of machinery in 1957 but then went back to Chapman as a works Lotus driver in 1958.

Hill made his Grand Prix debut in a Lotus at Monaco and ran as high as fourth before a rear wheel parted company with the car. Monaco was, however, to become synonymous with Graham. Throughout a career which spanned 176 Grands Prix, a record at the time, he would win five times around the streets of the Principality, earning himself the "Mr Monaco" title.

It was one of those records that everyone thought would remain in motor racing folklore forever, but, amazingly, it was bettered. It needed a driver of Ayrton Senna's prowess to do so, however, the Brazilian winning for the sixth time at Monte Carlo in 1993.

Hill became disenchanted with the fragility of Chapman's Lotuses, and left the team for BRM at the end of 1959. As well as following his Formula One career, he also drove sports and saloon cars and became a feared competitor in whatever category he was contesting. In 1961 Hill achieved nothing memorable, but the following year, equipped with a new V8, he was a potent force. He won the Dutch, German and Italian Grands Prix to set up a South African finale to his season-long battle with Jim Clark. Clark led but when the Lotus broke, Hill snatched victory and the championship.

He was runner-up to Clark, John Surtees and Clark again in 1963, 1964 and 1965. His defeat by Surtees was particularly galling as he had scored more points than the former motorcyclist, but lost out by one point when dropped scores were taken into consideration.

In 1966 Graham won the Indianapolis 500, the year after Jim Clark had ruffled the establishment with a British success. There was a good slice of fortune involved, however, as Jackie Stewart led convincingly until robbed by a technical problem. There then came one of the famous Hill stories. It surrounds the drinking of the traditional milk after the 500. Hill did not care for the stuff and, when confronted with the suggestion that he had not actually won the race, Graham replied: "No way, mate. I drank the milk."

After a troubled 1966 season, the first year of the new 3-litre Formula, Hill was tempted back to Lotus as team-mate to Jim Clark. The Scot narrowly missed out on the 1967 championship to Denny Hulme, but the Lotus 49 with the new Cosworth engine looked promising.

The fastest milkman

Clark started well enough, winning the South African Grand Prix, but was killed in a Formula Two race at Hockenheim in April. The Scot's death devastated Chapman, but Hill put the team back on course by winning the Spanish Grand Prix at Barcelona. He fought a three-way tussle for the championship with Jackie Stewart's Matra and Hulme's McLaren, winning his second title with victory in the Mexican Grand Prix season finale.

In 1969 Hill was outpaced by his new team-mate, Jochen Rindt. Then, at Watkins Glen, he spun and popped his seatbelt. Unable to fasten it again, he resumed but suffered a nasty accident as a result of a deflating tyre. He was thrown out and broke both his legs. It looked to be the end of the road for Britain's best loved racer, but he was determined to return. In truth, he was never the same driver again.

A sadly short retirement

Finally Graham vacated the cockpit in favour of up-and-coming Briton Tony Brise. He had won the Le Mans 24 Hours in 1972 for Matra, ensuring himself a place in the record books and now he intended to concentrate on team management. Tragically, it was not to be. Piloting his own plane on his return from a test at Paul Ricard, he hit a tree on the approach to Elstree. Hill and Brise died in the crash, along with the team manager, designer and two mechanics. In one stroke the British racing fraternity had lost its best loved racing ambassador and its most promising talent.

CAREER MILESTONES

1939	Born Hampstead, London
1954	Contested school races at Brands Hatch
1956	Raced in Autosport sports car series
1957	Formula Two and sports cars for Lotus
1958	Made Formula One debut for Lotus
1960	Joined BRM
1962	Won World Championship for BRM
1963	Runner-up for BRM
1964	Runner-up for BRM
1965	Runner-up for BRM
1966	Won Indy 500 for Lola
1968	Won World Championship for Lotus
1969	Broke legs at Watkins Glen
1971	Moved to Brabham
1972	Won Le Mans 24 Hours for Matra
1973	Formed own team, using Shadow chassis
1974	Ran Lola chassis
1975	Raced own chassis, then retired from racing. Killed in aircraft crash

LAUDA

"You appreciate that it is very easy to die and you have to arrange your life to cope with the reality."

NIKI LAUDA

GRAND PRIX STATISTICS

1971	1 Grand Prix, 0 points
1972	12 Grands Prix, 0 points
1973	14 Grands Prix, 2 points, 17th overall
1974	15 Grands Prix, 9 poles, 4 fastest laps, 2 wins, 38 points, 4th overall
1975	14 Grands Prix, 9 poles, 2 fastest laps, 5 wins, 64.5 points, 1st overall
1976	14 Grands Prix, 3 poles, 4 fastest laps, 5 wins, 68 points, 2nd overall
1977	14 Grands Prix, 2 poles, 3 fastest laps, 3 wins, 72 points, 1st overall
1978	16 Grands Prix, 1 pole, 4 fastest laps, 2 wins, 44 points, 4th overall
1979	13 Grands Prix, 4 points, 14th overall
1982	14 Grands Prix, 1 fastest lap, 2 wins, 30 points, 5th overall
1983	14 Grands Prix, 1 fastest lap, 12 points, 10th overall
1984	16 Grands Prix, 5 fastest laps, 5 wins, 72 points, 1st overall
1985	14 Grands Prix, 1 fastest lap, 1 win, 14 points, 10th overall

Career tally – 171 Grands Prix, 24 poles, 25 fastest laps, 25 wins, 420.5 points

COMEBACK HERO

By the end of 1976 Niki Lauda was possibly the world's best-known sportsman. He had missed out on the World Championship following a horrific accident in which he nearly died, but this gritty hero had become one of the sport's great survivors.

He cut his teeth on hill climbs, first with a Mini Cooper and then with a Porsche 911, which he bought with money borrowed from his grandmother. With a bank loan Niki bought himself a place in the March Formula Two team in 1971. At Rouen he had needed to be given the "slow" signal to prevent him beating team-mate Ronnie Peterson.

He made an inauspicious Grand Prix debut at the Osterreichring and, getting further into hock with the bank, arranged to buy himself into the March Formula One team for 1972. It looked hopeless and his family had his loan stopped. Niki went out and persuaded the bank to soak up the money over five years in return for him wearing their decals on his helmet.

The March was a lemon and Niki had nothing to show for his gamble. However, for 1973 he was offered a lifeline: the third BRM alongside Jean-Pierre Beltoise and Clay Regazzoni. Both were Grand Prix winners and things looked up when he started to outpace them. He was fifth in the Belgian Grand Prix and led the restarted race at Silverstone after Jody Scheckter's infamous first lap accident. Now, however, BRM's Louis Stanley started to pay him and Niki could maintain his bank payments. In Canada he led in the rain and attracted the attention of Ferrari. By 1974 Niki was with Ferrari and did much to restore the team to the head of the pack.

He scored his first win at Jarama, then backed it up with another at Zandvoort. Nine times he started from pole and he looked favourite to win the title until he made a couple of errors. He dominated at Brands Hatch until a puncture caused him to pit. Because of poor organization he was stranded in the pit lane as Scheckter swept to victory. Anxious to make amends at Nurburgring, he made a mistake on the opening lap and crashed. Then he ran off the road on a patch of oil when leading in Canada and critics started to question his temperament.

In 1975, after a winter of testing, a more reliable Niki dominated with the 312T, putting Ferrari back on top. His year included a hat-trick of wins in Monaco, Belgium and Sweden. Nothing looked more certain than that Lauda would win back-to-back world titles in 1976. He won five of the first six races, despite driving in Spain with broken ribs after overturning a tractor on top of himself.

The day it all went wrong

But at Nurburgring he crashed inexplicably on the first lap, his car bursting into flames. Niki was pulled from the car by three fellow drivers, but was badly burnt and had inhaled poisonous fumes. His life hung in the balance and he was shocked to find himself being administered the last rights. Incredibly, he was back, badly scarred, at Monza, where he turned in a heroic drive to fourth.

A tremendous late season run by James Hunt threatened his lead and, in the last race at Fuji, Niki pulled out after a single lap in appalling conditions. Hunt went on to finish third, taking Niki's title by a single point. It was the most incredible tale. In fact, Niki needed an operation on his eyelids, which were not allowing him to blink. Water welling up in his eyes was making it difficult for him to see. Lady Luck had dealt him the cruellest of hands.

Ferrari had signed Carlos Reutemann to lead the team, convinced that Niki would not be the driver he had been. With feisty determination, though, Niki tested furiously and won the third race of the year at Kyalami. He was fortunate to finish, having run over the roll hoop of Tom Pryce's shattered Shadow after the Welshman's fatal accident. Further wins in Holland and Germany, and a string of point-scoring finishes gave him his title back. Angered at Ferrari politics, however, Niki left for Brabham, where he did not enjoy similar success. But in 1978 he did win in Sweden, beating the all-conquering Lotus 79s with the distinctive BT46B "fan car".

By the end of 1979 Lauda had retired. He felt it had been too soon, though, and in 1982 he was back, winning two Grands Prix with a Marlboro McLaren. It was the beginning of the turbo era, however, and not until McLaren got hold of its TAG-Porsche turbos was it a front-runner. In 1984 Niki used his craft to overcome the speed of his emerging team-mate Alain Prost. Although Niki finished the year with five wins to Prost's seven, he was a vital half-point ahead after battling his way through to second in the last race.

His final year was 1985, and he knew he would not be able to hold Prost again. He did win a superb battle with the Frenchman at Zandvoort to score his last triumph. He led his last race confidently in Adelaide, too, before retiring to bring down the curtain on a remarkable career.

Airborne *Lauda gets some air in qualifying on the track that almost killed him.*

CAREER MILESTONES

1949	Born Vienna, Austria
1968	Hill-climbed a Mini Cooper
1969	Formula Vee
1970	Formula Three
1971	Formula Two, then Formula One debut for March
1973	Joined BRM and scored first points
1974	Joined Ferrari and scored first win
1975	World champion for Ferrari
1976	Runner-up for Ferrari. Badly burned in German Grand Prix
1977	World champion for Ferrari
1978	Joined Brabham
1979	Quit Formula One
1982	Returned with McLaren
1984	Won third World title for McLaren
1985	Retired from racing to concentrate on his airline

MANSELL

"I represented England at the age of nine on karts and here I am, thirty years later, world champion. When you've got as close as I've been and you don't crack it, you begin to think you never will."

ON WINNING THE 1992 WORLD CHAMPIONSHIP

GRAND PRIX STATISTICS

1980	2 Grands Prix, 0 points
1981	13 Grands Prix, 8 points, 14th overall
1982	13 Grands Prix, 7 points, 14th overall
1983	15 Grands Prix, 1 fastest lap, 10 points, 12th overall
1984	16 Grands Prix, 1 pole, 1 fastest lap, 13 points, 9th overall
1985	15 Grands Prix, 1 pole, 1 fastest lap, 2 wins, 31 points, 6th overall
1986	16 Grands Prix, 2 poles, 4 fastest laps, 5 wins, 70 points, 2nd overall
1987	14 Grands Prix, 8 poles, 3 fastest laps, 6 wins, 61 points, 2nd overall
1988	14 Grands Prix, 1 fastest lap, 12 points, 9th overall
1989	15 Grands Prix, 3 fastest laps, 2 wins, 38 points, 4th overall
1990	16 Grands Prix, 3 poles, 3 fastest laps, 1 win, 37 points, 5th overall
1991	16 Grands Prix, 2 poles, 6 fastest laps, 5 wins, 72 points, 2nd overall
1992	16 Grands Prix, 14 poles, 8 fastest laps, 9 wins, 108 pts, 1st overall
1994	4 Grands Prix, 1 pole, 1 win, 13 pts, 9th overall

Career tally – 185 Grands Prix, 32 poles, 30 fastest laps, 31 wins, 480 points

THE DRAMA KING

The world's most dramatic driver, the most courageous, too. And, rather late in his career, one of the very fastest. He moans, he groans, he's monotone. But the public loves him, as there is never a half-way house with Nigel Mansell.

Neither rich nor poor, neither quick nor slow – this was Mansell in his early racing days. The only thing that Nigel was, without question, was unpopular. He thought he was the best and could not understand why others refused to see this. Even when he had been given a shot at Formula One back in 1980 few took him seriously. He was competent, but nothing special. What they should have heeded that weekend in Austria was that he was courageous, for he drove most of the distance with leaking fuel burning his skin.

On the brink of the big time

The 1986 season was truly a low for Mansell. Despite five Grand Prix victories, the year ended in disappointment. Few who watched the Australian Grand Prix will forget the image of his left rear tyre exploding as he arrived at the end of the main straight. How he kept his snaking car away from the walls is not known, for this was not a puncture, but a blowout. A similar thing happened at the end of 1987. This time he was in a straight fight for the title with Williams team-mate Nelson Piquet, a driver for whom he had little time or respect. Heading for the penultimate race in Japan, Mansell had just beaten Piquet to victory in Mexico – his sixth win of the year – yet was lying 12 points behind the Brazilian. But he came to grief in qualifying, his Williams arcing into the air before landing with a jolting crash that injured his back and finished his season. The following season was a disaster, Mansell finishing only ninth overall, and without a win.

He made a bold career move in 1989, joining Ferrari. This most English of men was not expected to blend into the wholly Italian outfit, but he did, earning the instant adoration of the Italian fans by winning first time out, in Brazil. From then on, he was dubbed *Il Leone* ("The Lion"). Fired by this appreciation, he was happy and drove very well to finish the year fourth.

Prost joined Mansell at Ferrari in 1990 and this soon fazed Mansell. He was convinced that Prost was getting better equipment and the moaning returned. He won only once, that year, chopping across the bows of his team-mate on the run to the first corner at Estoril. This forced Prost to slow and he fell to fifth in an instant, losing the world title to Senna. So it was back to Williams for 1991 and back to winning ways. Indeed, Mansell won five races, yet still had to play second fiddle to Senna's McLaren.

Success at last

Then, finally, Mansell got it all right in 1992. Not only did he win a record nine times, but he stormed to the World Championship, completing the season with almost double the points tally of the driver who came second, Williams team-mate Riccardo Patrese.

There is no doubt that he drove magnificently, but his Williams-Renault was the class of the field, often leaving the best of the rest several second per lap slower in qualifying. This sort of domination occurs from time to time in Formula One, but sadly Mansell did little for his reputation by refusing to have the grace to acknowledge his team's technical superiority.

Amazingly, by the time Mansell settled the outcome of the championship with five races still to go, it was clear that Williams did not want to retain his services. Prost was going to be at Williams in 1993 and now Senna had offered his services for nothing, Not wishing to be a team-mate of either, Mansell decided it was time to quit.

A whole new beginning

However, all was not lost, for Mansell decided to take his talents across the Atlantic for a shot at Indy Car racing in the USA. And what a first season he had with the Newman/Haas team, of which actor Paul Newman is a part-owner.

He won the first race, then crashed heavily when he tried a banked oval for the first time, yet was back up to speed for the biggest race of the year: the Indianapolis 500. He nearly won that, too, only dropping to third in the closing laps.

Mansell learned from his mistakes, though, and won next time out. Two more wins followed on the ovals before August was over, putting him into a points lead he was never to lose. It had been an outstandingly successful visit.

Sadly, success one year does not guarantee it the next, and so it proved in 1994 when his Lola chassis was no longer the one to have. The rival Penske team cleaned up, its three cars often filling all three rostrum places. No wins came Mansell's way, so it made him restless again. He returned to Formula One in mid-season driving for Williams for four races, winning the Australian Grand Prix. In 1995 he joined McLaren, but never settled down, and announced his retirement after just two races.

Tough lesson *Mansell learns that (oval) walls bite, in 1993.*

CAREER MILESTONES

1953	Born at Upton-upon-Severn, Worcestershire
1969	Third in World Karting Championship
1977	BRDC Formula Ford champion
1979	British Formula Three
1980	Formula One debut with Lotus
1985	First Grand Prix win, at Brands Hatch for Williams
1986	Second in World Championship, winning five times for Williams
1987	Second again, this time with six wins
1989	Moved to Ferrari. Fourth with two wins
1991	Moved back to Williams. Second with five wins
1992	World Champion for Williams, with nine wins
1993	Won Indy Car title for Newman/Haas. First person to hold back-to-back F1 and Indy Car titles
1994	Eighth in Indy Cars, also four Grands Prix for Williams
1995	Joined McLaren. Retired.

MOSS

"If Stirling had put reason before passion, he would have been world champion. He was more deserving of it."

Enzo Ferrari
DESCRIBING MOSS AFTER HE HAD BEEN PIPPED AT THE POST IN THE WORLD TITLE RACE BY FERRARI'S MIKE HAWTHORN IN 1958

GRAND PRIX STATISTICS

1951	1 Grand Prix
1952	5 Grands Prix
1953	4 Grands Prix 1 point, 18th overall
1954	6 Grands Prix, 1 fastest lap, 0 wins, 4 points, 12th overall
1955	6 Grands Prix, 1 pole, 2 fastest laps, 1 win, 23 points, 2nd overall
1956	7 Grands Prix, 1 pole, 3 fastest laps, 2 wins, 27 points, 2nd overall
1957	6 Grands Prix, 2 poles, 3 fastest laps, 3 wins, 25 points, 2nd overall
1958	10 Grands Prix, 3 poles, 3 fastest laps, 4 wins, 41 points, 2nd overall
1959	8 Grands Prix, 4 fastest laps, 2 wins, 25.5 points, 3rd overall
1960	5 Grands Prix, 4 poles, 2 fastest laps, 2 wins, 19 points, 3rd overall
1961	8 Grands Prix, 1 pole, 2 fastest laps, 2 wins, 21 points, 3rd overall

Career tally – 66 Grands Prix, 16 poles, 20 fastest laps, 16 wins, 185.5 points

THE BEST OF BRITISH

Mention Stirling Moss and people will describe him as the best driver never to win a World Championship. Stirling looked a sure bet to be Britain's first world champion, yet he was runner-up four years in a row in the late 1950s, three of these to Juan Manuel Fangio. And on the last of these occasions, in 1958, he was pipped at the post by Mike Hawthorn who thus became the first British World Champion, in spite of winning just one Grand Prix that year to Stirling's four.

Born into a family steeped in motor sport, Stirling soon showed an interest and, at the age of 18 in 1948, cut his teeth on local hill-climb events. That was fun, and he was successful, but he turned his hand to circuit racing in 1949 and there was no looking back as he racked up Formula Three wins.

Stirling was already attracting the attention of talent spotters, and he was signed to drive the HWM Formula Two car in 1950, as well as taking part in every sports car race he was offered a ride in, usually with great success. Even rallying was considered in a quest to further his career, and Stirling finished second on his first attempt at the Monte Carlo Rally in 1952.

His Grand Prix outings stood little chance of success between 1951 and 1953, since he was behind the wheel of British cars that had no answer to the superior performance of the Italian Alfa-Romeos and Maseratis. He even turned down an offer from Ferrari. For 1954, however, Stirling decided that he would widen the net in his quest for a competitive ride. Neubauer, boss of the Mercedes team was approached, but he suggested Stirling should spend the season showing what he could do in a competitive car, so a Maserati 250F was purchased. Taking third place first time out in the Belgian Grand Prix confirmed that he had done the right thing.

Joining the master

Stirling's form during 1954 convinced Neubauer to sign him up for Mercedes in 1955 to drive alongside Juan Manuel Fangio. And so began one of the best driver pairings ever, a teacher-pupil relationship that really worked. It even yielded his first World Championship win, when Fangio let him by in the British Grand Prix at Aintree.

They ended the season with Fangio claiming the World title for the third time and with Stirling runner-up. The other drivers were only bit players that year. Thoughts of this dream pairing continuing in 1956 were thwarted by Mercedes' decision to withdraw from racing in response to the disaster as Le Mans in which more than 80 spectators were killed. So Stirling went to Maserati while Fangio joined Ferrari. Stirling won twice, one less then Fangio, and again wound up second overall to the great Argentinian.

Back to British

Stirling returned to racing in British machinery in 1957 with the Vanwall team. Three wins came his way, but still he ended the year in the wake of Fangio. Staying with Vanwall in 1958, he raised his total of victories another peg to four. But, you guessed it, he ended up as runner-up for the fourth year in succession. He lost out at the final hurdle when rival Mike Hawthorn scrabbled his way past Ferrari team-mate Phil Hill in the Moroccan Grand Prix to claim the extra point he needed to pip Stirling, the race winner that day.

For 1959 and 1960 Stirling drove assorted cars, but was predominantly seen in a Cooper, winning twice in 1959. However, he also raced a Lotus and gave the marque its first ever win at Monaco in 1960. He won again later in the year after recovering from leg and back injuries inflicted when he was thrown out of his car while qualifying for the Belgian Grand Prix.

The world of Formula One changed radically in 1961 with the traditional 2.5-litre engines being outlawed. Henceforth, said the rule-makers, 1.5-litre engines would be used. Ferrari was well prepared and its new engine was the class of the field, yielding the World title to team leader Phil Hill after its other challenger, Wolfgang von Trips, had been killed in the Italian Grand Prix.

Stirling went racing with the less powerful Coventry Climax engine in his Lotus and still managed to win on two occasions, on circuits where there were corners aplenty on which he could make time through his peerless driving skills.

All this skill was brought to a close in the Easter non-championship meeting at Goodwood in 1962. Stirling crashed head-on into an earth bank, incurring head injuries. The bloody images of Stirling being cut out of the wreck shocked the nation but, mercifully, he recovered his faculties. Stirling took the decision not to return to the cockpit, though, feeling that little something he once had was gone.

Mercedes man *Moss's breakthrough was his win in 1955's British Grand Prix.*

CAREER MILESTONES

1929	Born in Middlesex
1948	Hill-climbed a Cooper
1949	Started circuit racing
1950	Raced in Formula Two. Won Tourist Trophy sports car race
1951	Made Grand Prix debut for HWM
1952	Drove for HWM, ERA and Connaught
1953	Drove for Connaught and Cooper
1954	Drove for Maserati
1955	Joined Mercedes, scored first Grand Prix win. Second overall. Won Mille Miglia
1956	Returned to Maserati. Second again
1957	Drove for Vanwall. Second again
1958	Drove for Vanwall. Second again
1959	Drove a Cooper for Rob Walker and, occasionally, a BRM
1960	Drove a Cooper and Lotus for Rob Walker
1961	Drove a Lotus for Rob Walker
1962	Crashed at Goodwood, ending driving career

PROST

"Apart from being one of the real greats as a driver, the guy's a gentleman, a joy to work with … "

Frank Williams,
AFTER PROST HAD WON THE 1993 WORLD CHAMPIONSHIP

GRANDS PRIX STATISTICS

1980	11 Grands Prix, 5 points, 15th overall
1981	16 Grands Prix, 2 poles, 1 fastest lap, 3 wins, 43 points, 5th overall
1982	16 Grands Prix, 5 poles, 4 fastest laps, 2 wins, 34 points, 4th overall
1983	15 Grands Prix, 3 poles, 3 fastest laps, 4 wins, 57 points, 2nd overall
1984	16 Grands Prix, 3 poles, 3 fastest laps, 7 wins, 71.5 points, 2nd overall
1985	16 Grands Prix, 2 poles, 5 fastest laps, 5 wins, 73 points, 1st overall
1986	16 Grands Prix, 1 pole, 2 fastest laps, 4 wins, 72 points, 1st overall
1987	16 Grands Prix, 2 fastest laps, 3 wins, 46 points, 4th overall
1988	16 Grands Prix, 2 poles, 7 fastest laps, 7 wins, 87 points, 2nd overall
1989	16 Grands Prix, 2 poles, 5 fastest laps, 4 wins, 76 points, 1st overall
1990	16 Grands Prix, 2 fastest laps, 5 wins, 71 points, 2nd overall
1991	15 Grands Prix, 1 fastest lap, 34 points, 5th overall
1993	16 Grands Prix, 12 pole positions, 6 fastest laps, 7 wins, 99 points, 1st overall
Career tally	201 Grands Prix, 32 poles, 41 fastest laps, 51 wins, 768.5 points

THE PROFESSOR

Hailed as the ultimate professional and supreme race tactician by some observers and as a scheming political animal by others, Alain Prost has won more Formula One Grands Prix than anyone in history and, together with them, four World titles.

Unusually for someone who was dubbed "the Professor" throughout his Formula One career, Alain Prost could have been a professional footballer. Yet a dalliance with karts led to him winning the 1973 World title before he turned to cars. The rest, as they say, is history.

Indeed, as success followed success and title followed title, this bent-nosed little Frenchman racked up the world-beating tally of 51 wins at an average of almost four points per race in the 199 Grands Prix he started. That is equivalent to third place every time he raced. Apart from Juan Manuel Fangio and Alberto Ascari in the less competitive 1950s, no one else has matched that average.

To many, Alain's lack of flamboyance is something that is cited against him. But he did not need to hang the car's tail out to go fast. He was too good for that: no fuss, no bother, just blindingly quick. More often than not, he was undramatic in a race, biding his time and waiting to make his move rather than rushing in as though every lap was the last.

Victor or villain?

He was not afraid to pull off if he thought conditions were too dangerous, as he did in the 1988 British Grand Prix. His detractors would claim that he was the sort of driver who always worked the team around to his way of thinking at the expense of the other driver. But if he was given the latest equipment ahead of his team-mate it was because he would make better use of it. And thus Prost was cast as the villain in many a partnership. Yet, through all the carping, Alain kept on winning. Four world titles came his way – in 1985, 1986, 1989 and 1993. And that says all that needs to be said.

After his ultra-successful career in the junior formulae, Alain leapt past Formula Two to make his Formula One debut in Argentina in 1980. His car, a McLaren, was not one of the quick ones of the time, but he outpaced his much more experienced team-mate, John Watson, and hauled it into the points in sixth. Fifth place followed in Brazil, but then he broke his wrist in South Africa, forcing him to miss that and the fourth round.

At season's end, Alain was ranked just outside the top ten drivers in the authoritative annual *Autocourse*. "Had the list been prepared after South America," wrote Maurice Hamilton, "the pressure to place Prost in the top five would have been overwhelming."

With fortunes improving in the Renault team, it was anxious to sign the best French talent to lead its patriotic attack, so Alain was at the wheel of one of its yellow cars in 1981. And so he started his winning ways, fittingly taking the chequered flag at the French Grand Prix. Two more wins followed, in Holland and Italy, to leave Alain fifth overall. In 1982 he went one place better. Then, in 1983, was runner-up by just two points to Nelson Piquet.

Fed up with being blamed by the French Press for losing out to Piquet, he returned to McLaren for 1984. Runner-up to team-mate Niki Lauda by half a point at his first attempt, Alain finally, in 1985, gained the World title that he had been threatening for so long to win. And he did the same again in 1986, clinching the crown in the famous three-way shoot-out in Adelaide in which Nigel Mansell lost with a huge blow-out. Worried the same would happen to him, Nelson Piquet pitted for fresh tyres, allowing Alain through to win the race and, with it, the crown. Amid all this drama for the Williams drivers, Prost completed the race with a fuel gauge long since reading empty. Three more seasons with McLaren resulted in fourth overall, second to team-mate Senna in 1988 and then first again in 1989,after a fractious time with Senna in Japan.

Mutual antipathy

Their mutual antipathy was to rear its head again in 1990, when Alain had moved on to Ferrari. Leading into the first corner at Suzuka, Senna kept on coming up the inside. They clashed and Senna was the champion, Prost the runner–up. The following year was the first in which he failed to win a race since his debut season. Disillusioned with his car and with Ferrari politics, he spoke out once too often and was fired, going off to spend a season as a commentator for French TV.

However, the lure of racing was too much and he returned for a swansong season with Williams in 1993. An incredible year yielded seven wins and his fourth title. However, news that Senna was to join him in 1994 saw Alain tender his resignation: he just could not face the prospect of rejoining battle with his number one enemy.

Renault's rocket *Prost hit the big time during his time with Renault.*

CAREER MILESTONES

1955	Born in St Chamond, France
1973	Won World Karting title
1975	Won Pilote Elf prize at Winfield Racing School
1976	Won French Formule Renault title
1977	Won French Formule Super Renault title
1979	Won European Formula Three title
1980	Made Formula One debut with McLaren
1981	Moved on to Renault. Scored first win
1984	Returned to McLaren
1985	Won World title for McLaren
1986	Won World title again for McLaren
1989	Won third World title for McLaren
1990	Moved to Ferrari
1992	Took sabbatical. Did French TV commentary
1993	Returned to Formula One to win World title for Williams

SENNA

"In modern times, Ayrton was in a class of his own. I put him among the greatest: Nuvolari, Fangio, Jimmy Clark and him. The irony of the whole thing is that, apart from Clark, he is the only really great driver to have been killed in a race."

Stirling Moss

GRANDS PRIX STATISTICS

1984	14 Grands Prix, 1 fastest lap, 13 points, 9th overall
1985	16 Grands Prix, 7 poles, 3 fastest laps, 2 wins, 38 points, 4th overall
1986	16 Grands Prix, 8 poles, 2 wins, 55 points, 4th overall
1987	16 Grands Prix, 1 pole, 3 fastest laps, 2 wins, 57 points, 3rd overall
1988	16 Grands Prix, 13 poles, 3 fastest laps, 8 wins, 90 points, 1st overall
1989	16 Grands Prix, 13 poles, 3 fastest laps, 6 wins, 60 points, 2nd overall
1990	16 Grands Prix, 10 poles, 2 fastest laps, 6 wins, 78 points, 1st overall
1991	16 Grands Prix, 8 poles, 2 fastest laps, 7 wins, 96 points, 1st overall
1992	16 Grands Prix, 1 pole, 1 fastest lap, 3 wins, 50 points, 4th overall
1993	16 Grands Prix, 1 pole, 1 fastest lap, 5 wins, 73 points, 2nd overall
1994	3 Grands Prix, 2 poles, 0 points

Career tally – 161 Grands Prix, 64 poles, 19 fastest laps, 41 wins, 610 points

THE FASTEST EVER

Ayrton Senna was a genius, a tyrant, a benevolent and humble person, an arrogant son of a gun, a man who divided opinion like no other. But there was one thing that no one could deny. He was the fastest driver the Formula One world has ever seen.

Ayrton was a natural talent who won kart races from the moment he started competing at the age of 13. He was Brazilian champion as soon as he was old enough to race in the senior category, lifting the South American titles in 1977 and 1978. And, when he came to Britain to race in Formula Ford 1600 in 1981, it took him only until his third race to notch up his first win.

Big decision time

Ayrton could not adapt to being away from Brazil. Besides, he had decided to marry his childhood sweetheart and, on top of this, there was the sponsorship that he neded for his graduation to the next formula. So he went back to São Paulo. However, he neither stayed nor married, but instead returned to Britain, this time to take his racing seriously. He was shy by nature and his fierce concentration made many consider him aloof. But his intensity paid off, for he won the British and European Formula Ford 2000 titles.

It was up to Formula Three for 1983, the last stop for the quick before Formula One. And so it proved. Ayrton won the final round against Martin Brundle to claim the title and the Formula One tests with McLaren and Williams that came with it. They were impressed, but neither signed Ayrton, leaving him to settle for a ride with the lesser Toleman team for 1984.

Moving up to Formula One is a daunting task, since nothing prepares a driver for the gigantic changes in performance, financial stakes and professionalism. But Ayrton's innate skills took care of the first hurdle, his faithful Brazilian backers insured the second and his already honed approach sorted the third. In an instant he was going faster than people had expected in the little-fancied Toleman.

A move to Lotus for 1985 brought his first win, in treacherously wet conditions, at Estoril. Another win followed in Belgium and Ayrton ended the year fourth overall. Moves were made to introduce Derek Warwick as his team-mate for 1986, but Ayrton balked at this, earning a great deal of flak from sections of the Press.

His decision may have been vindicated, as he finished fourth overall again, two wins being scored. Then, at Monaco in 1987, he scored his fifth win, one that was special, as it started his love affair with the famous street circuit. He was to win there on five more occasions before his death. A further win that year helped him to third place overall, but his rate of progress was insufficient, so he joined McLaren in 1988.

At last Ayrton had a team that could meet his needs. Eight wins were his reward in 1988 and a highly emotional championship title.

The next few years were to prove his purple patch, with second place overall in 1989 being followed by his second and third World Championship crowns in 1990 and 1991. Indeed, during these glory years, only Alain Prost and Nigel Mansell shared the top step of the rostrum with him on a more than an occasional basis.

Ayrton may have been handicapped by his equipment in these years, but he never let it stop him from giving his all. No one who was present at Donington Park for the 1993 Grand Prix of Europe will forget Ayrton's lap charge in the mighty rain. As ever, the tricky conditions had allowed him to display his otherworldly car control in an age in which in-cockpit technology conceals the inadequacies of many lesser drivers.

The final chapter

For 1994, with Mansell racing in the USA and Prost having hung up his helmet, the way was clear for what many saw as the creation of the ultimate partnership in modern-day Formula One: Senna, Williams and Renault engines.

The season kicked off in Brazil with pole position, but Senna was overtaken by Benetton driver Michael Schumacher when they made their first fuel stops and Senna spun off trying to make up lost ground. Ayrton's engine would not restart, and that was that. Round two at Aida in Japan saw Ayrton on pole again, but he was hit from behind by erstwhile McLaren team-mate Mika Hakkinen at the first corner and forced into retirement. Schumacher won both races. And then came Imola.

Ayrton was in front after a restart caused by Pedro Lamy hitting J.J. Lehto on the starting grid and he was being pressured by Schumacher. But then, starting the second lap after the cars were sent on their way again, Ayrton's Williams speared right at Tamburello, hit the wall and came to rest on the side of the track. For an instant Ayrton moved. Then he became still as if he appeared to lose consciousness.

His death was more than the loss of the greatest driver ever to grace a racing circuit, it was the extinction of perhaps the ultimate sportsman, the man who came as close to perfection in his chosen pursuit as any driver in history.

Mr Monaco *Six wins around the street circuit made it Senna's patch.*

CAREER MILESTONES

1960	Born in São Paulo, Brazil
1964	Given his first kart
1973	Started kart racing
1977	Won first South American Karting Championship
1978	Won first Brazilian Karting Championship
1981	Won Brazilian Karting Champion for the third year running and British FF1600 Championship
1982	Won the British and European FF2000 Championship
1983	Won the British Formula Three Championship
1984	Made Formula One debut with Toleman
1985	Moved to Lotus and scored first Grands Prix wins
1988	Moved to McLaren and won first World Championship
1990	Won World Championship for the second time with McLaren
1991	Back-to-back World Championship victory with McLaren
1994	Died in high speed accident at San Marino Grand Prix

STEWART

"Jackie was the first of the modern-style drivers, a man who drove fast enough to win, but at the slowest possible speed."

Stirling Moss

GRANDS PRIX STATISTICS

1965	10 Grands Prix, 1 win, 33 points, 3rd overall
1966	8 Grands Prix, 1 win, 14 points, 7th overall
1967	11 Grands Prix, 10 points, 9th overall
1968	10 Grands Prix, 2 fastest laps, 3 wins, 36 points, 2nd overall
1969	11 Grands Prix, 2 poles, 5 fastest laps, 6 wins, 63 points, 1st overall
1970	13 Grands Prix, 4 poles, 1 win, 25 points, 5th overall
1971	11 Grands Prix, 6 poles, 3 fastest laps, 6 wins, 62 points, 1st overall
1972	11 Grands Prix, 2 poles, 4 fastest laps, 4 wins, 45 points, 2nd overall
1973	14 Grands Prix, 3 poles, 1 fastest lap, 5 wins, 71 points, 1st overall

Career tally – 99 Grands Prix, 17 poles, 15 fastest laps, 27 wins, 359 points

A SPONSOR'S DREAM

Think of Jackie Stewart and you think of a blue Tyrrell notching up yet another win, you think of his sunglasses and sideburns. But you also think of a champion with an alert business brain and possibly the shrewdest driver ever to compete in Formula One.

World champion in 1969, 1971 and 1973, Jackie was also possessed of great commercial acumen, pushing back the barriers so that the drivers of today can earn such large retainers. Having seen too many of his friends and contemporaries die, he also wanted Formula One to be made safer and for drivers to be remunerated for the risks they took. While others were unwilling to rock the boat, this little Scotsman stood his ground.

Adjusting his aim

He had found himself trapped in his inverted car at Belgian Grand Prix in 1966, with petrol pouring over him. Thankful that no spark ignited and that he was rescued to fight another day, he did not want to find himself in a situation like that again. Thus, he began a safety crusade that undoubtedly saved many lives. Today, Jackie heads a body that provides assistance to mechanics should they be injured. Few others would bother, but he is a man not only of principle, but of action.

While Prost wanted to be a footballer, Jackie was a long way toward becoming a top-line marksman when he failed to qualify to represent Britain in the 1960 Olympic Games. Perhaps it was the disappointment of this that spurred him to follow his older brother, Jimmy, into racing as an outlet for his competitive nature. Whatever the reason, his early races with the Ecurie Ecosse team demonstrated that Jackie was more than a little special behind the wheel of a car.

Sports and GT cars were not to contain him for long and Ken Tyrrell spotted him and placed him in his Formula Three car. Victories were soon the order of the day and he was pressed hard to sign for Lotus for 1965 but, although he drove for Lotus in Formula Two later that year, he turned them down and joined BRM instead.

There are very few drivers who win races in their first season of Formula One, but Jackie was one such, triumphing in only his eighth outing – the Italian Grand Prix. That he ended his first year third overall behind Jimmy Clark and BRM team-mate Graham Hill was proof that he was a man on the move.

Still with BRM, Jackie kicked off his 1966 campaign with BRM in the best possible style, winning on the streets of Monaco. But that was to be a freak result, for the BRM was not to prove as competitive again when the Brabham team took control. Jackie did not win another race until the Dutch Grand Prix in 1968, by which time he was reunited with earlier patron, Ken Tyrrell.

The Tyrrell years

Six years out of Jackie's nine year spell in Formula One were spent driving for Ken Tyrrell. At first this was in a Ford-powered Matra entered for the French marque by the British team owner, with three wins coming his way in 1968. The combination's second year was even more successful, with Jackie winning six races and the title.

In a purple patch for British drivers, his World Championship crown was the sixth for a Briton since Graham Hill won it seven years earlier. Then, in 1970, the Matra was replaced by the British-built March. But Jackie could not live with Jochen Rindt's Lotus or the Ferraris. Finally, in 1971, the team sent Jackie and team-mate François Cevert out to do battle in self-built Tyrrells at a time when few could cope with the speed and consistency of the blue, Elf-sponsored cars. Perfecting his art of driving a storming opening lap that would see him drop all his rivals and then control the race at his own pace, Jackie went on to triumph six times in 1971.

The following year yielded four more wins, but he was beaten to the title by Lotus driver Emerson Fittipaldi. Then, in 1973, he had five wins in the bag when he reached Watkins Glen, home of the American Grand Prix.

It was at this tricky circuit in upstate New York that Jackie elected to hang up his helmet, with immediate effect. Not because it was the end of the season and he had had enough of the travelling, but because of the death of team-mate Cevert in an accident in qualifying. This was too much for Jackie to bear. Ken Tyrrell withdrew his entry and Jackie was never to race again. His record tally of 27 Grand Prix wins (from 99 starts) was to stand until overhauled by Prost in the 1987 Portuguese Grand Prix (his 118th Grand Prix).

No peace in retirement

Unlike many drivers, Jackie has seemingly increased his input into the sport since his retirement. As a consultant and ambassador to many blue-chip companies, he continues to be a dynamo. Today, he is Formula One's most respected elder statesmen as well as its busiest. With son Paul running a highly successful racing team in Formula 3000, Formula Three and Formula Vauxhall, and eyeing Formula One, Jackie may yet be involved in Formula One again.

Life before Tyrrell *Stewart drove for BRM for this first three seasons.*

CAREER MILESTONES

1939 Born in Dumbarton, Scotland
1961 Made racing debut in a Marcos
1963 Joined Ecurie Ecosse sports car team
1964 Drove for Ken Tyrrell in Formula Three. Made Formula Two debut for Lotus
1965 Made Formula One debut with BRM. Won Italian Grand Prix
1968 Moved to Tyrrell's Matra team
1969 Claimed first World Championship title, for Matra
1970 Drove a March, changing mid-season back to Tyrrell
1971 World champion again, for Tyrrell
1973 Won third World title, for Tyrrell. Retired from racing

THE GREAT DRIVERS

Motor racing fans have thrilled to the exploits of the speed kings of Formula One down the years. Here is a selection of 200 of the fastest of them all .

Apart from the legends listed in the previous chapter there are a myriad drivers who have run races, lost races, starred and disappointed in Formula One since its inception in 1950. Here is a selection of 200, ranging from world champions such as Mike Hawthorn, Denny Hulme and James Hunt to those who shone but failed in their quest to hit the top and to those with interesting stories to tell. After all, Eddie Irvine will be recalled more in years to come for the fact that he was bopped on the chin by Ayrton Senna on his Grand Prix debut rather than for scoring a championship point. Every man and woman in this list had a dream. Some achieved it, others did not. Indeed, it is immensely sad to note how many of these were killed in their bid for glory. Thankfully, racing is a far safer game today than when drivers used to go forth in short-sleeved shirts and, perhaps, a flat cap.

A

Michele Alboreto

Nationality: Italian
Born: 1956

This dignified Italian had a long and frustrating Formula One career that petered out in 1994 and he followed a phalanx of his former rivals into the world of touring car racing. Second in the 1979 Italian Formula Three series, Michele won the European crown in 1980. Formula Two beckoned for 1981, but Michele so impressed Tyrrell with a one-off at the San Marino Grand Prix that they gave him a contract until the end of 1983. During the next three years he won twice, both times on North American soil. His second win – at Detroit in 1983 – was a landmark as the last win for a normally aspirated engine before the turbocharged cars completed their stranglehold. Ferrari followed from 1984 to 1988, and he won on his third outing, at Zolder, helping him to fourth place overall. Two wins assisted Michele to second overall in 1985, but thereafter his career tailed off. He returned to Tyrrell in 1989, then crossed to Larrousse in mid-season. Three years with Footwork with little or no reward followed before his worst year: 1993, with the new Scuderia Italia team. The car was a beast, and Michele failed to qualify five times. A year with Minardi restored his pride, but he now accepted that his best days were over and headed off to join the German Touring Car Championship at the controls of a works Alfa-Romeo.

CAREER RECORD

** 194 Grand Prix: 5 wins (Caesars Palace GP 1982, US GP 1983, Belgian GP 1984, Canadian GP 1985, German GP 1985):*
** No championship title (best result – 2nd overall 1985)*

Jean Alesi

Nationality: French
Born: 1964

Born in France of Sicilian parents, Jean was viewed as an outsider until he started to shine in the junior formula, and only then was he considered a Frenchman. Running with next to no sponsorship, he starred in the 1986 French Formula Three Championship, finishing second to Yannick Dalmas. He went one better in 1987 before moving up to Formula 3000 in 1988. Halfway through his second year in this cate-

Mr Superstition *Alberto Ascari lived and died by his beliefs.*

Ever the bridesmaid *Jean Alesi has done everything except win.*

gory, a vacancy came up at Tyrrell for the French Grand Prix and his team boss Eddie Jordan propelled Jean into the seat. Jean responded in style, taking fourth place. And there has been no looking back since. Promising form in the remainder of 1989 was soon put into the shade by his first race of 1990, as Jean swapped the lead with Ayrton Senna's McLaren at the first race, crossing the line second. Another second followed at Monaco. But, somehow, even after moving to Ferrari for whom he has raced since 1991, that first-ever Grand Prix win still eludes him. If and when he wins, there will be no more popular winner in the world.

CAREER RECORD

** 85 Grands Prix, no wins (best result – 2nd US GP 1990, Monaco GP 1990, Italian GP 1993, British GP 1994)* No championship title (best result – 5th overall 1994)*

Philippe Alliot

Nationality: French

Born: 1954

Philippe began his career racing with three years in the French Formule Renault series, claiming the title in 1978. Formula Three proved an even harder nut to crack, for it took him four years before he moved on to Formula Two for 1983. There followed two years with the unsuccessful RAM team in Formula One. He then moved to Ligier for the second half of 1986, before joining the Larrousse Lola team, for whom he raced for three seasons, scoring points on four occasions. A return to Ligier was fruitless in 1990 and curtailed his Formula One career. However, he bounced back with Larrousse in 1993 and scored his only fifth place, at the San Marino Grand Prix. Hopes of a Grand Prix swansong with McLaren in 1994 thanks to French engine supplier Peugeot were disappointed when team boss Ron Dennis chose Martin Brundle instead, even though Philippe had a run-out in place of the suspended Mika Hakkinen in Hungary. Accepting that his day had passed, Philippe quit dyeing his grey hairs and turned to touring-car racing.

CAREER RECORD

** 109 Grands Prix, no wins (best result – 5th San Marino GP 1993)* No championship title (best result – 16th overall 1987)*

Chris Amon

Nationality: New Zealander

Born: 1932

This affable Kiwi did everything in Formula One except win a race, or a World Championship one at least. Chris was spotted by team owner Reg Parnell and invited to contest the 1963 Formula One season, arriving in Europe while still a baby-faced 19-year-old and claiming his first points before his 21st birthday. Parnell's death left Chris in limbo in 1965 and 1966, but Ferrari signed him for 1967 and he went straight in with third place at Monaco. A win would surely follow. Wrong. Second at Brands Hatch in 1968 was the best he could do. A move to the fledgling March team for 1970 enabled Chris to win a Formula One race – the International Trophy at Silverstone – but, sadly, this was a non-championship affair. His championship season saw him twice second and seventh overall. A two-year spell at Matra was next and produced victory first time out, in the Argentinian Grand Prix. But this was another non-championship affair. It almost went right at Clermont-Ferrand in 1972. The race was his for the taking when he suffered a puncture. A season with Tecno in 1973 produced nothing. His move to run his own car in 1974 was even less successful. A few races for the under-financed Ensign team in 1975–76 reminded people of his undoubted speed, but despite flashes of genius came to little. Truly this was a talent wasted.

CAREER RECORD

** 96 Grands Prix, no wins (best result – 2nd British GP 1968, Belgian GP 1970, French GP 1970)* No championship title (best result – 4th overall 1967)*

Mario Andretti

Nationality: American

Born: 1940

Here is a man who wanted to race more than almost any man before him – or since. And this will to race stayed with Mario until his retirement at the end of 1994, helping him to achieve one of the most comprehensive career tallies of all time. Starting in sprint cars on the local dirt ovals. "Super Wop", as he was known, graduated to Indy Car racing in 1964 and amazed the establishment by winning the title in 1965. Another title followed in 1966 and a third in 1969. But, by the time of the third crown, he had already achieved an ambition by making his Formula One debut (for Lotus) at the end of 1968. Again Mario upset the establishment, for he qualified on pole first time out at Watkins Glen. A mixed Formula One programme followed from 1969 to 1974 with Lotus, March, Ferrari – including victory in the 1971 South African Grand Prix – and Parnelli, as he split his time with Indy Car and sports car racing before he joined the Grand Prix circus full-time with Parnelli in 1975. Parnelli folded and Mario joined the team that gave him his Formula One break: Lotus. It was in a poor state, but he and boss Colin Chapman rebuilt it, winning the 1976 Japanese Grand Prix. More progress was made in 1977 and Mario was crowned world champion in 1978 after winning six races. Two more years followed with Lotus before he raced for Alfa-Romeo in 1981. Then it was back to Indy Cars and a full-time diet of American racing from 1982. He won the Indy Car title for the fourth time in 1984 and was on the pace right until his final few years.

"Super Wop" *Mario Andretti was a champion on both sides of the Atlantic.*

CAREER RECORD

** 128 Grands Prix, 12 wins (South African GP 1971, Japanese GP 1976, US GP 1977, Spanish GP 1977, French GP 1977, Italian GP 1977, Argentine GP 1978, Belgian GP 1978, Spanish GP 1978, French GP 1978, German GP 1978, Dutch GP 1978)* World Champion 1978*

Michael Andretti

Nationality: American
Born: 1962

Michael, son of Mario, ripped through the junior ranks of American racing, winning the Formula Super Vee and Formula Atlantic titles en route to graduating to the Indy Car scene in 1984. He was second in 1986, 1987 and 1990, before he claimed the Indy Car title in 1991. Egged on by his father, Michael tried Formula One with McLaren in 1993. What a disaster! It seemed that if there was an accident, he was in it. But this is unfair, for he had the mighty Ayrton Senna as a team-mate and a McLaren chassis that did not want to play the game. Perhaps one of his biggest mistakes was attempting to commute from the USA, since the team never really felt he was part of the outfit and he was replaced after peaking with a third in the Italian Grand Prix. Winning ways soon came back on his return to Indy Cars, giving Reynard victory on the marque's first ever race in the formula.

A family affair *Michael Andretti failed to emulate father Mario.*

CAREER RECORD

** 13 Grands Prix, no wins (best result – 3rd Italian GP 1993)* No championship title (best result – 11th overall 1993)*

René Arnoux

Nationality: French
Born: 1948

One of the fruits of a government-backed scheme to unearth French talent in the 1970s, René did all the right things as he rocketed to Formula One. It was only when he reached the highest echelon that he started to run off the rails. His speed was never in question, simply his application. He beat future Formula One rival Patrick Tambay to take the French Formule Renault title in 1973. An abortive move to the European Formula 5000 Championship in 1974 was followed by a return to the French ladder to stardom in Formule Super Renault in 1975. He duly won the title and progressed to Formula Two in 1976, being pipped to the title in the final round by Jean-Pierre Jabouille. He went one better in 1977. Then came Formula One, albeit with a slow start in 1978 with the fledgling Martini team. It folded mid-season and René had a couple of runs for Surtees. However, for 1979 it all came right and he joined Jabouille in the Renault works team. A brace of wins at the start of 1980 pushed him into the limelight, but his form faded until he won the 1982 French Grand Prix against team orders ahead of team favourite Alain Prost. For 1983 René moved to Ferrari, winning three times as he was placed third overall behind Nelson Piquet and Prost. These were to be his last wins, though, and he was shown the door after the first race of 1985. In 1986 he was back, this time with Ligier, with whom he raced for four seasons, but produced next to no results after the first of these. Since retiring from Formula One, René has been involved with the DAMS (Driot Arnoux Motor Sport) Formula 3000 team, the most successful in the history of the formula.

Loose cannon *Rene Arnoux was always fast, but seldom disciplined.*

CAREER RECORD

** 149 Grands Prix, 7 wins (Brazilian GP 1980, South African GP 1980, French GP 1982, Italian GP 1982, Canadian GP 1983, German GP 1983, Dutch GP 1983)*
** No championship title (best result – 3rd overall 1983)*

Peter Arundell

Nationality: British
Born: 1933

Peter Arundell shone like a star, but his career became unstuck when he had a major accident in a Formula Two race at Reims and he was never as quick again. Strong form in the junior categories earned Peter the attention of Lotus boss Colin Chapman, who snapped him up for Formula Junior and he won the 1962 British title. Although anxious to move into Formula One, he waited to make his break with Lotus, and thus had to spend 1963 contesting non-championship Formula One races in addition to Formula Junior. For 1964, though, Peter was in Formula One with Lotus. Third in his first two races, at Monaco and then Zandvoort, he had driven in only four races when he spun in his concurrent Formula Two race at Reims and was T-boned by Richie Ginther. Thrown from the cockpit, he suffered numerous broken bones and it was two years before he was fit enough to race in Formula One again. However, his return season with Lotus yielded just one sixth place and his career fizzled out.

CAREER RECORD

** 11 Grands Prix, no wins (best result – 3rd Monaco GP 1964, Dutch GP 1964)*
** No championship title (best result – 8th overall 1964)*

Alberto Ascari

Nationality: Italian
Born: 1918
Died: 1955

He was Mr Superstition– a great racing driver , a double world champion, but also a man ruled by lucky charms and coincidence. Born into a motor racing family – his Grand Prix racer father Antonio died in an accident at the Montlhery track near Paris when Alberto was seven – he soon turned to motorized competition, starting with motorcycles. He progressed to cars in 1940, competing in the mighty Mille Miglia road race for Ferrari. His deal was clinched as team patron Enzo Ferrari was a former team-mate of Alberto's father. Alberto had his first taste of Grand Prix racing in 1947. Between then and the start of modern-day Formula One in 1950, he won several Grands Prix and was thus an obvious choice to lead the Ferrari team in the 1950 Formula One World Championship, in which he placed fifth. His form was better in 1951 and he won twice to finish the year runner-up to Juan Manuel Fangio. A change in the rules meant that Formula One was run to 2-litre regulations in 1952 and this played into Alberto's hands, for Ferrari had a good engine ready. He missed the first race, in which team-mate Piero Taruffi was victorious, but duly won six races and the title. Indeed, he kept this winning streak going into 1953, taking the first three races as he motored to his second consecutive title. A change to Maserati in 1954 while waiting for the Ferrari-run Lancias to be ready proved little. Indeed, it was not until the start of 1955 that the Lancias were up to speed. However, Alberto was soon to perish in a freak accident when testing a sports car at Monza for protégé Eugenio Castelotti. Acknowledging Alberto's attention to numbers and dates, it is uncanny to note that, like his father, he had died on the 26th of a month, at the age of 36, at the exit of a fast left-hander, four days after walking away from another accident...

CAREER RECORD

** 31 Grands Prix, 13 wins (German GP 1951, Italian GP 1951, Belgian GP 1952, French GP 1952, British GP 1952, German GP 1952, Dutch GP 1952, Italian GP 1952, Argentine GP 1953, Dutch GP 1953, Belgian GP 1953, British GP 1953, Swiss GP 1953) * World Champion 1952 and 1953*

Richard Attwood

Nationality: British
Born: 1940

After an apprenticeship in Formula Junior, during which he won the Monaco support race in 1963, followed by an unhappy period with a limited Formula One programme with BRM in 1964, Dickie went on to enjoy a shot at the big time with a Reg Parnell Racing Lotus-BRM in 1965, collecting a couple of sixth places. However, he stepped back and raced sports cars for the next two seasons before joining BRM as a replacement for Mike Spence who was killed in a crash at Indianapolis. His achievement of second place first time out at Monaco amazed all and sundry. Sadly, this form was never repeated and he was to race sports cars from then on, winning the Le Mans 24 Hours for Porsche in 1970. Despite retiring at the end of 1971, Dickie now features on the historic racing scene.

CAREER RECORD

** 17 Grands Prix, no wins (best result – 2nd Monaco 1968)* No championship title (best result – 13th overall 1968, 1969)*

B

Giancarlo Baghetti

Nationality: Italian
Born: 1934

It is unlikely that anyone will ever match his feat of winning his first-ever Grand Prix. Yet this is what happened when Giancarlo joined Ferrari for the 1961 French Grand Prix at Reims. Like many Italians of his age group, he raced sports cars in the late 1950s, competing on the Mille Miglia. Formula Junior attracted Giancarlo to try single-seaters in 1958. Success in this propelled him to Ferrari in 1961 when he won the non-championship Syracuse and Naples Grands Prix. Then came his big day at Reims and Giancarlo resisted everything that Porsche driver Dan Gurney could throw at his shark-nose Ferrari on this slipstreaming circuit. A limited programme with Ferrari in 1962 was followed by a spell with the Italian ATS team in 1963 and another racing a Scuderia Centro Sud BRM in 1964. But Giancarlo was never to step on to a Formula One rostrum again.

CAREER RECORD

** 21 Grands Prix, 1 win (French GP 1961)*
** No championship title (best result – 9th overall 1961)*

Julian Bailey

Nationality: British
Born: 1961

One of the quickest of the quick in British club racing in the early 1980s, Julian overcame a huge shunt to win the Formula Ford Festival in 1982. A lack of cash restricted his subsequent movement up the hierarchy, but he made it to Formula Three by 1985 and on to Formula 3000 by 1987. He won once, at Brands Hatch. Finally,

So near yet ... *Julian Bailey was thwarted in Formula One.*

he made it to Formula One by 1988, racing for Tyrrell. Unfortunately, he chose a year when Tyrrell was not very competitive, frequently failed to qualify and collected no points. It looked as though he had had his shot and missed, as he disappeared into the ranks of sports car racers. However, ever resourceful, Julian raised the money to buy a seat at Lotus in 1991 and scored his best finish, a sixth place at the San Marino Grand Prix before his money ran out after four races. Since then he has raced both sports cars and touring cars for the Toyota works team.

CAREER RECORD

** 7 Grands Prix, no wins (best result – 6th San Marino GP 1991)* No championship title (best result – 18th overall 1991)*

Maura Baldi

Nationality: Italian
Born: 1954

Several seasons at the front end of the grid in the European Formula Three Championship in the late 1970s saw Mauro come on strong to win the prestigious Monaco Formula Three race in 1980. Electing to stay on for a fourth year of Formula Three in 1981, he won the European title and then bypassed Formula Two to join the Arrows Formula One team for 1982. His first point came at the Dutch Grand Prix. A move to the works Alfa-Romeo team for 1983 was not a success, although it yielded a few points. However, Mauro was not invited to stay for the following season and so found himself with the new Spirit team in 1984. This was floundering by early 1985 and since then Mauro has raced with great success in sports cars, winning the 1990 world title.

CAREER RECORD

** 36 Grands Prix, no wins (best result – 5th Dutch GP 1983)* No championship title (best result – 16th overall 1983)*

Lozenzo Bandini

Nationality: Italian
Born: 1935
Died: 1967

Lorenzo's racing career started in saloon cars loaned to him by the owner of the garage at which he was a mechanic. By 1959 he was on the grid for the new Formula Junior category, and his form over the next two seasons was enough to attract the attention of Ferrari. He was pipped for a vacant seat at the team early in 1961 by Giancarlo Baghetti who went on to win at his first attempt, thus forcing Lorenzo to look elsewhere. Scuderia Centro Sud gave him his Formula One debut in a Cooper-Maserati and he drove well enough to join Ferrari for 1962. Lorenzo was third at his first attempt, at Monaco. Despite being selected only occasionally by the team, he also won the non-championship Mediterranean Grand Prix. Dropped in 1963, he was soon back at Ferrari after Willy Mairesse was injured. He even won the Le Mans 24 Hours for the marque. Lorenzo's only Grand Prix triumph came in 1964 when he won the Austrian Grand Prix at Zeltweg, becoming fourth overall at the end of the season, three places behind team-mate John Surtees. Monaco was to prove his happiest hunting ground in 1965 and 1966, with second place each time. And it was in the second half of 1966 that he finally became Ferrari's number one driver on the departure of Surtees. However, it was Monaco that was to prove his undoing. Running second behind Denny Hulme's Brabham in 1967, Lorenzo's Ferrari clipped the barriers at the chicane and flipped. Instantly it caught fire and Lorenzo was terribly burned while an inadequately equipped crew of marshals extricated him. He died of his burns before the week was out.

CAREER RECORD

** 42 Grands Prix, 1 win (Austrian GP 1964)* No championship title (best result – 4th overall 1964)*

Rubens Barrichello

Nationality: Brazilian
Born: 1972

Seen by many as the next Brazilian hot-shot after Ayrton Senna, Rubens had one of the fastest climbs ever from karting to Formula One. The key to this speedy progress, his fantastic speed apart, was the long-term backing of a Brazilian sponsor, Arisco. Like Senna, Rubens came from São Paulo, his home overlooking the Interlagos circuit. After collecting five national karting titles, Rubens arrived in Europe at the age of 17 and won the GM Euroseries. Formula Three followed in 1991 and he pipped David Coulthard to the British title for the famous West Surrey Racing team, an outfit that helped Senna to the same title in 1983. Formula 3000 was not so successful with the financially overstretched Il Barone Rampante team in 1992, but he was still third overall and thus ready for Formula One before his 21st birthday. Eddie Jordan snapped him up and they have been together ever since. Rubens nearly landed second place on only his third outing, the European Grand Prix, but fuel feed problems pulled him up short. However, 1994 was kinder and Rubens was third at the second round, at the TI Circuit, claimed pole in the wet at Spa and finished fourth on no fewer than five occasions to become sixth overall.

CAREER RECORD

** 31 Grands Prix, no wins (best result – 3rd Pacific GP 1994)* No championship title (best result – 6th overall 1994)*

The next Senna *Rubens Barrichello carried the hopes of an expectant nation.*

Jean Behra

Nationality: French
Born: 1921
Died: 1959

After a career racing motorcycles "Jeannot" switched to four-wheeled competition in 1949 and was elevated to Formula One with Gordini in 1952, a year in which, amazingly, he won the well-supported Reims Grand Prix ahead of the best of the Ferraris. Sadly for Jean it was a non-championship event. But it earned him the undying devotion of his home fans. Tenth overall in his first season, he stayed on with Gordini for two more years but became frustrated by numerous mechanical breakages and so moved on to the works Maserati team for 1955. He kicked off with non-championship wins at Pau and Bordeaux supported by many sports car victories, but success eluded him when it counted, i.e. in the World Championship. Fourth overall in 1956, a year during which he crashed in the Tourist Trophy and sliced off one of his ears, Jean scored his best-ever Grand Prix result in the 1957 Argentinian Grand Prix when he finished second to team-mate Juan Manuel Fangio. Heading for victory in that year's British Grand Prix, he was thwarted by clutch failure and his career was on a downer from then on. A drive for BRM in 1958 yielded nothing special and so the offer to join Ferrari for 1959 was eagerly accepted. Sadly, he failed to last the season, being killed in a sports car race in Germany when he flew off the top of the banking at Avus and was hurled into a flagpole.

CAREER RECORD

** 52 Grands Prix, no wins (best result – 2nd Argentine GP 1956, Argentine GP 1957) * No championship title (best result – 4th overall 1956)*

Le Mans hero *Derek Bell made more out of sportscars than Formula One.*

Derek Bell

Nationality: British
Born: 1941

Very few British drivers have driven in Formula One for Ferrari. However, of those who have, few have failed to make their mark in the sport's top category. Derek was, however, one of the unlucky ones. Propelled through the junior formulae first by his charismatic stepfather and then by Peter Westbury, Derek starred in Formula Two, catching the eye of Enzo Ferrari who signed him up for the last few Grands Prix of 1968. However, no regular drives followed, and the next three years saw him turn out for three different teams in only four Grands Prix, peaking with sixth at the 1970 US Grand Prix for Surtees. Things looked better for 1972 when he managed five races for the Martini team. But there was no joy, so he rejoined Surtees for 1974, but qualified only once in five attempts. He now looked to sports cars for his glory and has won the Le Mans 24 Hours five times.

CAREER RECORD

** 9 Grands Prix, no wins (best result – 6th US GP 1970) * No championship title (best result – 22nd overall 1970)*

Stefan Bellof

Nationality: German
Born: 1957
Died: 1985

Germany had long been aware of its failure to win the World Championship and, if Stefan Bellof had not been killed in a sports car race in 1985, it could all have been very different. Exciting is a description that does not really do justice to Stefan's driving: it was electrifying. He was, in short, a joy to watch – on the ragged edge of control where others would long previously have lost it. Fresh out of karting, he won the German Formula Ford Championship, vaulted to Formula Three for 1981 and was third overall. In Formula Two in 1982 he drove with great success for the Maurer team, winning the first two races. However, results tailed off, with retirements blunting his achievement. So a second Formula Two season became essential, dovetailed with sports car races for the works Porsche team. He made it to Formula One in 1984 with Tyrrell and was challenging for victory at Monaco but heavy rain stopped play when he was third, thwarting both he and Ayrton Senna as they closed on Alain Prost. However, the Tyrrell team was found to have committed a technical irregularity and all his points were removed for the 1984 season. At least Stefan was able to enjoy winning six times for Porsche en route to claiming the World title. For 1985 he found the Tyrrell to be less competitive, and had only a fourth and a sixth to his name when he overstepped the mark in a sports car race at Spa, failing in a crazy attempt to overtake in the daunting Eau Rouge corner. He died instantly.

CAREER RECORD

** 20 Grands Prix, no wins (best result – 4th US East GP 1985)* No championship title (best result – 15th overall 1985)*

Jean-Pierre Beltoise

Nationality: French

Born: 1937

Hugely successful as a motorcycle racer, Jean-Pierre first raced a car in 1963, and indeed his early sports car races nearly cost him movement in one of his arms after a crash at Reims in 1964. However, he fought back to win the French Formula Three title in 1965 for Matra, embellishing this with victory in the Monaco Formula Three race in 1966, and several months later made his Grand Prix debut, winning the Formula Two class in the German Grand Prix. It was not until 1968 that he was given his first run in a Grand Prix in a Formula One car, still with Matra. However, this produced fifth place and he was allowed to continue, soon exceeding this result with second at the Dutch Grand Prix. His progress continued into 1969 and a further second place helped him to fifth overall. He stayed on with Matra for 1970 and 1971, but things turned sour when he was threatened with the suspension of his licence following the death of Ignazio Giunti after an incident involving Jean-Pierre in a sports car race in Argentina. Then, in 1972, it all came right – at Monaco at least, when he won in torrential conditions for BRM. That was his only ever win, however, and he faded from Formula One after two further seasons with BRM.

CAREER RECORD

** 86 Grands Prix, 1 win (Monaco GP 1972)*

** No championship title (best result – 5th overall 1969)*

Gerhard Berger

Nationality: Austrian

Born: 1959

Gerhard has never become world champion, but has been twice third overall and always been competitive. While Mauro Baldi started racing in Renault 5s, for Gerhard it was Alfasuds. But Formula Three soon followed and at this he was very successful, chasing Ivan Capelli for the European title in 1984. At the end of that year, he had a shot at Formula One with ATS, finishing sixth on his second outing, even though he was not eligible for points. Things looked good for 1985, but Gerhard broke his neck in a road accident. Defying doctors' orders, he was up and about far ahead of their predictions and joined Arrows for 1985, scoring points in the final two races. A move to the new Benetton team in 1986 produced his first win, in Mexico, and helped Gerhard land a ride with Ferrari for 1987. Again he peaked at the end of the year, this time with two wins. Another win and more consistent scoring permitted him to finish third overall in 1988, his final season with Ferrari seeing him fail to finish a race until September. Angered by this lack of mechanical fortitude, Gerhard moved to McLaren for 1990 to drive alongside Ayrton Senna. Seldom as quick as Senna, at least he taught the Brazilian to smile and Gerhard was a regular front-runner until the end of 1992 when he returned to Ferrari. The pressures of leading Ferrari fell on to his shoulders as its longest winning streak kept on stretching. Eventually, at the 1994 German Grand Prix, he brought this to a close. Then he should have added to this in the Australian Grand Prix, but he ran wide and let Nigel Mansell through, thus coming home second there to ensure he ended up third overall. For many, the fact that Gerhard was still racing at the end of 1994 was remarkable, for the sport had claimed the lives of his best friend (Senna), his compatriot (Roland Ratzenberger) – and nearly that of his protégé, Karl Wendlinger.

Mountain man *Gerhard Berger has kept Austria's great history on the boil.*

CAREER RECORD

** 163 Grands Prix, 9 wins (Mexican GP 1986, Japanese GP 1987, Australian GP 1987, Italian GP 1988, Portuguese GP 1989, Japanese GP 1991, Canadian GP 1992, Australian GP 1992, German GP 1994)*

** No championship title (best result – 3rd overall 1988, 1994)*

Eric Bernard

Nationality: French

Born: 1964

After victory in the national kart series, Eric beat Jean Alesi to win the prestigious Winfield school scholarship in 1983, launching him into Formule Renault. A strong run in this was followed by title success in 1985 that boosted him into Formula Three, in which he finished second to Alesi in 1987. Formula 3000 was another category that took two bites, with Eric finishing third overall for DAMS in 1989. His two Formula One outings that year for Larrousse were backed up with a full-time ride for 1990, with Eric claiming fourth at the British Grand Prix. A weak 1991 season followed, and it was curtailed when he broke a leg in Japan. To many this would have been the end, but Eric fought back and returned to the Ligier team in 1994, peaking with third place at the extraordinary German Grand Prix, his only scoring drive of the year. However, as rookie team-mate Olivier Panis outpaced him more often than not, it spelt the end of Eric's Formula One career.

CAREER RECORD

** 45 Grands Prix, no wins (best result – 3rd German GP 1994)* No championship title (best result – 13th overall 1990)*

Lucien Bianchi

Nationality: Belgian
Born: 1934
Died: 1969

Born into an Italian family that was tempted to Belgium to work for racing driver Johnny Claes, Lucien cut his teeth in sports cars and rallying before moving on to racing single-seaters for 1959. The first Grand Prix for which he qualified was, fittingly, the Belgian in 1960 and he drove his Cooper into the points there, finishing sixth. However, he dropped back to sports cars, and it was not until 1968 that Lucien had a decent crack at Formula One, albeit with the little fancied BRM-powered Cooper. That year, though, his highlight was winning the Le Mans 24 Hours. And it was to sports cars that he turned in 1969, but they claimed his life at Le Mans in practice when he lost control of his Alfa-Romeo.

CAREER RECORD

** 17 Grands Prix, no wins (best result – 3rd Monaco GP 1968) * No championship title (best result – 17th overall 1968)*

"B Bira"

Nationality: Thai
Born: 1914
Died: 1985

Prince Birabongse Bhanuban, a colourful figure on the European social scene in the mid-1930s, was also a car fanatic from an early age and, when at school in England, made it his ambition to become a racing driver. He eventually graduated to a mighty ERA, but his career was interrupted by the Second World War, after which he won various Formula Two races before making his Formula One debut in 1950 for Maserati, for whom he finished fifth at Monaco and then fourth in the Swiss Grand Prix. Running in Maserati, then Gordini, then Connaught, then Maserati again, "B Bira" raced on until the start of 1955 when he decided to retire.

CAREER RECORD

** 19 Grands Prix, no wins (best result – 4th Swiss GP 1950, French GP 1954)* No championship title (best result – 8th overall 1950)*

Broken promises *A broken leg hindered Eric Bernard.*

Mark Blundell

Nationality: British
Born: 1966

Mark arrived in Formula Ford at the age of 17 as a seasoned competitor after years of racing in motocross. Armed with family wealth and the "will to win", he contested some 70 races that year. This propelled him into Formula Ford 2000 for the next couple of years, racing with and often beating his rivals Damon Hill, Johnny Herbert and Bertrand Gachot. Most people would then have gone to Formula Three in 1987, but not Mark who leapt directly to Formula 3000. A chance to drive for the works Lola team came his way in 1988, but this bombed after he had achieved second place in the first round. Staying on for 1989, he had an even worse season. But sports cars came to his rescue and he drove with great speed for the works Nissan team. A test-driving contract for Williams followed in 1990, and Mark made his Formula One racing debut with Brabham in 1991. Dropped to sports cars again in 1992, he was back in Formula One with Ligier in 1993 and scored third place first time out, ending up tenth overall. A move to Tyrrell in 1994 saw him suffer at the hands of Japanese team-mate Ukyo Katayama, raising cries of unfair treatment but, either way, it cost Mark the chance to stay on for 1995.

CAREER RECORD

** 46 Grands Prix, no wins (best result – 3rd South African GP 1993, German GP 1993, Spanish GP 1994) * No championship title (best result – 10th overall 1993)*

Raul Boesel

Nationality: Brazilian
Born: 1957

Having decided that making it to Formula One was his aim, Raul travelled to Britain and showed an ability to learn quickly when he came second in the British Formula Ford series in 1980. Using his head to make sure that he scored points rather than threw them away in a win-or-bust approach, Raul finished third in the British Formula Three championship and leapt into Formula One for 1982. But the March team was not the one to be with that year and his best result was eighth at the Belgian Grand Prix. Frustrated, he moved to Ligier for 1983 and went one better with seventh place in the US Grand Prix West. However, no points came his way and Raul headed to the USA and Indy Cars. A period racing for the Jaguar sports car team netted Raul the 1987 World title, but he returned to Indy Cars to become a front-runner in the mid-1990s.

Foiled ambition *Raul Boesel had to go Stateside to find success.*

CAREER RECORD

** 23 Grands Prix, no wins (best result – 7th US West GP 1983)* No championship title*

Felice Bonetto

Nationality: Italian
Born: 1903
Died: 1953

The average age of drivers in the first-ever Formula One World Championship race in 1950 was almost double the age of today's grid and, when Felice made his debut in the Swiss Grand Prix that year, he was five days short of his 47th birthday. A star in the great Italian road races of the 1930s, his move to Formula One came with Ferrari for whom he shone in several non-championship races. He entered his own Maserati in several Grands Prix in 1950 and was signed to drive a works Alfa in 1951, finishing third in the Italian Grand Prix. A move to sports cars followed, but he returned to Formula One at the end of 1952 and was going well in the works Maserati in 1953 before being killed on the Carrera Panamericana road race through Mexico.

CAREER RECORD

** 15 Grands Prix, no wins (best result – 3rd Italian GP 1951, Dutch GP 1953) * No championship title (best result – 8th overall 1951)*

Joakim Bonnier

Nationality: Swedish
Born: 1930
Died: 1972

Having begun his career in rallying and then honed his skills in ice races, Jo was awarded the Swedish

BRM breakthrough *Sweden's Joakim Bonnier was the first driver to win for BRM.*

Alfa-Romeo franchise and used its Disco Volante in sports car races. An affair with Maseratis followed and he bought a 250F with which to race in Formula One, starting at the 1956 Italian Grand Prix. Jo's first full season was 1958 and his results improved when he moved to BRM, taking fourth in the Moroccan Grand Prix. However, just two races into 1959, he took the chequered flag at Zandvoort and marked the end of BRM's long wait for a Grand Prix win. That was his golden moment, and for the following year and a half he produced only a trio of fifth places. Jo raced a Porsche in 1961–62, but he was overshadowed by team-mate Dan Gurney and his success was restricted to sports car races. Jo was held in high esteem by the drivers, since it was he who founded the Grand Prix Drivers' Association which fought to make circuits safer. Three years with Rob Walker's team, driving Coopers and Brabhams saw many fifth and sixth places and, though Jo chipped away with his own privately entered Coopers and McLarens until 1971, that was to prove his lot. He was killed in the 1972 Le Mans 24 Hours.

CAREER RECORD

** 102 Grands Prix, 1 win (Dutch GP 1959) * No championship title (best result – 8th overall 1959)*

Slim Borgudd

Nationality: Swedish
Born: 1946

Slim used the money gained from his musical exploits as Abba's drummer to go racing. It was not until 1978 that he broke out of the Swedish racing scene, contesting the European Formula Three series. In his second season he finished third in the European championship, which was won that year by a certain Alain Prost. The whole of 1980 was spent trying to raise the cash to race in Formula One, and so he made his debut in 1981 with ATS, scoring his solitary point for sixth place in the British Grand Prix. His money ran out after only three races with Tyrrell in 1982 and Slim's greatest success since has been in truck racing, although a move to touring cars clinched him the poorly supported Nordic Touring Car title in 1994.

CAREER RECORD]

** 10 Grands Prix, no wins (best result – 6th British GP 1981) * No championship title (best result – 18th overall 1981)*

Thierry Boutsen

Nationality: Belgian
Born: 1957

Very quick in everything he drove, Thierry rocketed through Formula Ford. His maiden year in Formula Three in 1979 was not quite so sweet, but he came good at the end and landed a works ride for 1980, eventually finishing second overall to Michele Alboreto. Formula Two followed and he was second again, this time to Geoff Lees. Staying on to claim the title did not work, but he had done enough to impress the right people. And so Thierry made it to Formula One for 1983 with Arrows, with whom he stayed until 1986, peaking with second place at Monaco in 1985. A move to Benetton in 1987 saw him finish eighth overall. Five third places in 1988 helped Thierry to fourth overall. A move to Williams in 1989 yielded two wins, both in the wet. Although he won again in 1990, holding off massive pressure from Ayrton Senna in Hungary, his contract with Williams was not to be renewed. Quite simply his face did not fit, and so Thierry moved to Ligier for 1991 and 1992. This proved to be a mistake, the team being uncompetitive even when it ran with Renault engines. When Ivan Capelli was sacked by Jordan in 1993, Thierry moved in there, but he did not last the season, retiring for good at his own Grand Prix at Spa. Thierry now races in touring cars, like so many of his generation.

CAREER RECORD

** 163 Grands Prix, 3 wins (Canadian GP 1989, Australian GP 1989, Hungarian GP 1990) * No championship title (best result – 4th overall 1988)*

Famous son *David Brabham's father was a triple world champion.*

David Brabham

Nationality: Australian
Born: 1965

Youngest of Sir Jack Brabham's three sons, David considered racing only after spending a summer watching brother Geoff race in the USA. As soon as he returned to Australia he started in single-seaters, then joined his parents in England and was an instant hit in Formula Three. He won a long, hard fight with Allan McNish for the 1989 title and backed this up by winning the Macau Grand Prix, the unofficial world final for Formula Three. David made his Formula One debut in 1990 when Middlebridge, the team that was set to run him in Formula 3000, bought the Brabham Grand Prix team, an outfit that had been sold off by his father when he retired from racing in 1970. However, the car was not a gem and David was dropped at the end of the year, turning successfully to sports cars. After a spell with Jaguar and then Toyota, he made it back to Formula One with the formation of the Simtek team in 1994. It was a ghastly year, for team-mate Roland Ratzenberger was killed at Imola and the taciturn David showed great inner strength to remotivate the team. Fighting from the back of the grid, he gave it his all, with a best finish of tenth place, but he could not find the money to continue and became a works BMW touring car driver.

CAREER RECORD

** 24 Grands Prix, no wins (best result – 10th Spanish GP 1994) * No championship title*

Jack Brabham

Nationality: Australian
Born: 1926

see Legends of the Track pp 106–07

Vittorio Brambilla

Nationality: Italian
Born: 1937

Born at Monza, he raced motorcycles, then karts, before joining his brother Tino in Formula Three in 1968. Despite not doing all the rounds, Vittorio finished second overall. He went one better in 1969. The brothers teamed up in Formula Two in 1970, but Vittorio spent much of the year blowing engines in his efforts to keep up with drivers in newer machinery. Occasional quick drives were not enough, especially with Vittorio junking several chassis, and money was too tight for success to follow. Only when Beta Tools agreed to finance him in 1973 did he make progress. He took Beta Tools to Formula One in 1974 with March and he scored his first point before the year was out. His second season promised so much, with pole in Sweden, but offered frequent retirements until he held it all together to win the Austrian Grand Prix after a downpour. Seconds after crossing the finish line, Vittorio punched the air with delight and crashed. He moved to Surtees in 1977 and did poorly, with the exception of a fourth place in Belgium. Then came disaster in the 1978 Italian Grand Prix when he was struck on the head in the accident that was to inflict fatal injuries on Ronnie Peterson. It was not until a year later that Vittorio was back in the cockpit, returning at Monza for Alfa-Romeo. However, the old speed was not there and he retired from Formula One after a handful more Grands Prix.

CAREER RECORD

** 74 Grands Prix, 1 win (Austrian GP 1975)*
** No championship title (best result – 11th overall 1975)*

Monza Gorilla *Vittorio Brambilla was known for his uncompromising style.*

Tony Brise

Nationality: British
Born: 1952
Died: 1975

Tony could have been a British world champion, but he died in the same light aircraft accident that claimed the life of Graham Hill. Encouraged into the sport by his father, a former racer, Tony started in karts at the age of ten and shone in Formula Ford, finishing second in the 1971 British series. Moving up to Formula Three in 1972 was not a great success, since he had the wrong car. However, he picked up a drive with the GRD team for 1973 and won the British title ahead of Alan Jones and Jacques Laffite. For 1974 Tony tried Formula Atlantic with a works Modus and finished third overall. Hill signed him up for F1 for 1975, and Tony did great things with what was clearly not a very quick car, getting it into the points in Sweden, but that plane crash denied us the knowledge of just how far he would have gone.

CAREER RECORD

** Ten Grands Prix, no wins (best result – 6th Swedish GP 1975) * No championship title (best result – 19th overall 1975)*

Chris Bristow

Nationality: British
Born: 1937
Died: 1960

After starting in an MG special, Chris was helped into more competitive equipment by his father in 1957, and his form in 1958 led him to be signed up by the British Racing Partnership for 1959. This offered him the chance to race single-seaters as well as sports cars, and he made his Grand Prix debut in the British Grand Prix, albeit in Formula Two equipment. The death of team-mate Harry Schell pitched Chris into the role of team leader shortly after the BRP put him into Formula One with a Yeoman Credit Racing Cooper. Sadly, he suffered a fatal accident in the Belgian Grand Prix on a dark day at Spa that also claimed the life of compatriot Alan Stacey.

CAREER RECORD

** 4 Grands Prix, no wins (best result – 10th British GP 1959) * No championship title*

Tony Brooks

Nationality: British
Born: 1932

Tony Brooks was a driver of consummate skill. If he had not been bitten by the racing bug he would have gone on to become a dentist, dabbling in sports cars as a pleasant distraction from his studies. However, in 1955 he went abroad and raced a Connaught. In only his second race, the non-championship but nevertheless well-attended Syracuse Grand Prix, he thrashed all comers. It was the first win by a British driver in a British car since 1924... World Championship Formula One followed in 1956 with BRM, but his season was foreshortened when he was thrown from his car at Silverstone and broke his jaw. Vanwall signed him up for 1957. Second place first time out, at Monaco, was followed by victory at the British Grand Prix, an event in which he started but handed over his car in mid-race to Stirling Moss as he himself was suffering from leg injuries inflicted during the Le Mans 24 Hours. Staying with Vanwall for 1958, he was tipped by the retiring Juan Manuel Fangio as the likely world champion, but though Tony won three times – each time on the real drivers' circuits – he wound up third overall. Ferrari signed him for 1959 and Tony won twice more, ending the year second to Jack Brabham. The following two seasons saw him drive a Cooper for Yeoman Credit Racing and then a works BRM, but he was no longer prepared to take what he now considered to be unnecessary risks. Thus he retired at the end of 1961 to run a motor business.

CAREER RECORD

** 38 Grands Prix, 6 wins (British GP 1957, Belgian GP 1958, German GP 1958, Italian GP 1958, French GP 1959, German GP 1959) * No championship title (best result – 2nd overall 1959)*

Martin Brundle

Nationality: British
Born: 1959

How a driver who made Ayrton Senna work so hard for the British Formula Three title could race in Formula One for a decade and not score a win is a mystery. Senna had whipped all comers in the first half of 1983, but Martin became the quicker of the two in his Eddie Jordan Racing Ralt and took the title down to the wire. Ken Tyrrell was not slow to identify this talent and signed Martin for 1984. He was fifth in his first Grand Prix, in Brazil. Coming second in Detroit behind Nelson Piquet propelled Martin to the

McLaren men *Martin Brundle (right) chats to Mika Hakkinen.*

Marlboro
McLAREN INTERNATIONAL
Marlboro
BOSS
TAG HEUER
OMP
Brundle

brink. But a race later he broke his ankles at Dallas. To add insult to injury, Tyrrell was adjudged to be running illegal cars, and all the team's results were cancelled. In 1986 he had four points-scoring drives, but his career took a dive when he chose to join the German Zakspeed team in 1987. It was hopeless and Martin found himself without a drive in 1988. Fortunately, he raced for Jaguar and won the World Sports Car Championship, also having a one-off drive for Williams at Spa. For 1989 he drove for Brabham, but this was not the team it had been and he went back to sports car racing for 1990, winning the Le Mans 24 Hours. A return to Brabham for 1991 was not a success since the Yamaha engines were no match for the opposition. Then came his big break, a ride at Benetton. The trouble was that he was alongside Michael Schumacher who soon proved himself team leader as Martin struggled to finish races in the first half of the year. From San Marino on, though, he scored points in all but one race to claim sixth overall, usually racing better than Schumacher. But what hurt Martin was his inability to put in a flier in qualifying, and thus he was always starting further back on the grid than necessary, making progress harder. A move to Ligier in 1993 produced more regular points scores and seventh overall. Then it looked as though he was out of a top ride for 1994, but he hung in there for a McLaren seat and claimed it at the last minute. Again no wins, but Martin was twice on the rostrum and placed seventh overall.

CAREER RECORD

** 131 Grands Prix, no wins (best result – 2nd Italian GP 1992, Monaco GP 1994)*
** No championship title (best result – 6th overall 1992)*

Ronnie Bucknum

Nationality: American
Born: 1936
Died: 1992

An American in Formula One in the 1960s was something of a rarity and when Ronnie arrived to lead the new Honda works team towards the end of 1964, no one really knew very much about him. Nursing a broken leg, he was in trouble at the start of 1965 and was soon very much number two to team-mate Richie Ginther. Indeed, when Ronnie finally scored his first points, for fifth in Mexico, he was again overshadowed, for Ginther chose that day to mark up Honda's first win... Ronnie drifted away from Formula One, but shone in all areas of American racing for many years before hanging up his helmet. He died of diabetes in 1992.

CAREER RECORD

** 11 Grands Prix, no wins (best result – 5th Mexican GP 1965)* No championship title (best result – 14th overall 1965)*

C

Alex Caffi

Nationality: Italian
Born: 1964

A hot-shot on the Italian racing scene, Alex looked to be ever the bridesmaid. He was second in the Italian Formula Three series in 1984 and 1985, then third in 1986. His Formula One break came in 1987 when he drove the unwieldy Osella. His fortune was better in 1988 with a Scuderia Italia Dallara. Staying on for 1989, he took fourth place at Monaco and was then running fifth at Phoenix (having been second earlier on) when team-mate Andrea de Cesaris tipped him into the wall... A change of scene in 1990 saw Alex move to Arrows. It was not a success. Staying with the team, now renamed Footwork, he found his chances were hampered by heavy and uncompetitive Porsche engines and then by a jaw-breaking road accident. He qualified only twice. Just when he thought it could get no worse, it did: he joined the new Andrea Moda team for 1992. Realizing that this was leading nowhere, he quit after two races and moved to compete in the Italian Touring Car Championship.

Nearing the end *Ivan Capelli's stay at Jordan was a short one.*

CAREER RECORD

** 56 Grands Prix, no wins (best result – 4th Monaco GP 1989)* No championship title (best result – 16th overall 1989 and 1990)*

Ivan Capelli

Nationality: Italian
Born: 1963

Hot from karting, Ivan went direct to Formula Three and dominated the Italian series at his second attempt, in 1983. Staying with Enzo Coloni's team for 1984, he won the Monaco race and later the European Championship ahead of Gerhard Berger and Johnny Dumfries. A limited Formula 3000 campaign in 1985 produced a win at the Osterreichring and promoted Ivan to the Tyrrell Formula One team for a couple of races. Amazingly, he was fourth on his second outing, in Australia, yet no offer for 1986 was forthcoming. So Ivan returned to Formula 3000, winning the title for Genoa Racing. He joined March for 1987 and claimed a point at Monaco. But 1988 was better, as he was in the points six times, chasing Alain Prost's McLaren in Portugal before settling for second. The 1989 season was an unmitigated disaster, the March chassis handling like a pig. But 1990 was much better and Ivan led the French Grand Prix for 46 laps before Alain Prost pushed his Ferrari ahead with just three laps to go. Third place at the following race looked to be his reward, but a fuel pipe frayed and he was out. After a troubled season in 1991 he was signed for Ferrari for 1992. But points were few and far between, and after just two races for Jordan in 1993, he was fired.

CAREER RECORD

** 92 Grands Prix, no wins (best result – 2nd Portuguese GP 1988, French GP 1990)*
** No championship title (best result – 7th overall 1988)*

Eugenio Castellotti

Nationality: Italian
Born: 1930
Born: 1957

Eugenio cut a swathe through European sports car racing in the early 1950s. He made his Formula One debut at the 1955 Argentinian Grand Prix with Lancia and swept to second place on his second outing, at Monaco. On the death of team-mate Alberto Ascari, he became team leader and scored three more times to be third overall. Continuing with the Lancia-Ferrari set-up in 1956, Eugenio was second in the French Grand Prix and finished sixth overall in the championship. He won the legendary Mille Miglia road race to make up for his disappointment with his Formula One results. Eugenio was only to race in one more Grand Prix, however, being killed when testing for Ferrari at its Modena testing circuit in early 1957.

CAREER RECORD

**14 Grands Prix, no wins (best result – 2nd Monaco GP 1955, French GP 1956)*

** No championship title (best result – 3rd overall 1955)*

Johnny Cecotto

Nationality: Venezuelan
Born: 1956

After becoming the youngest ever 350cc motorcycle world champion, Johnny swapped across to four wheels with a drive in Formula Two in 1980. By 1982 he was a front-runner, only losing out on the title to works March team-mate Corrado Fabi when dropped scores were taken into consideration. His Formula One debut came in 1983 when he joined the little Theodore team, amazingly finishing in sixth place in his second race, at Long Beach. No more points followed, and he moved to Toleman for 1984, but his single-seater career was cut short with a leg-breaking shunt at Brands Hatch. Subsequently, Johnny has won numerous titles in touring car racing in Italy and Germany.

CAREER RECORD

** 18 Grands Prix, no wins (best result – 6th US West GP 1983) * No championship title (best result – 19th overall 1983)*

François Cevert

Nationality: French
Born: 1944
Died: 1973

Fate struck a cruel blow when it claimed the life of this talented Frenchman at the 1973 US Grand Prix, for he was poised to assume Jackie Stewart's role as Tyrrell team leader and thus make a bid to become the first French world champion. French Formula Three champion in 1968, François was promoted by Tecno to its Formula Two squad and finished third overall in 1969. Tyrrell snapped him up for 1970 and put him under the tutelage of Stewart. François was twice second in 1971 before winning the final race of the season, at Watkins Glen, the track that would later claim his life. This helped him to third overall behind Stewart and Ferrari's Jacky Ickx. The 1972 season was not such a success, with two more second places, yet François made up for this by finishing second in the Le Mans 24 Hours. In 1973 he was second six times, three times behind Stewart. Then then came that fateful day in upper New York State...

CAREER RECORD

** 47 Grands Prix, 1 win (US GP 1971)*

** No championship title (best result – 3rd overall 1971)*

Eddie Cheever

Nationality: American
Born: 1958

Eddie shone in Formula Three and then in Formula Two and was looking to jump into Formula One at the end of 1977 at the age of 19. A seat at Ferrari seemed a possibility, but Gilles Villeneuve got there first. Eddie rolled out for Theodore and had a one-off for Hesketh in 1978, but elected to return to Formula Two, and it was not until 1980 that he graduated full-time, with the new Osella team. Sadly, the Italian team was out of its depth and he was able to show his hand only when he moved to Tyrrell in 1981, putting in five points-scoring drives. He hit the rostrum in 1982 with Ligier, peaking with second at Detroit. And this helped him land a ride for 1983, but this was alongside Alain Prost at Renault and Eddie could not live with the comparison, even though his eventual sixth overall marked his best-ever year in Formula One. Two years with the Benetton-Alfa team and three with Arrows, followed but the star was fading and Eddie headed to Indy Cars.

CAREER RECORD

** 132 Grands Prix, no wins (best result – 2nd US GP 1982, Canadian GP 1983)*

** No championship title (best result – 6th overall 1983)*

Louis Chiron

Nationality: Monegasque
Born: 1899
Died: 1979

Louis scored more than a dozen Grands Prix wins before the Second World War and several more after it. Nicknamed "the old fox" in deference to his advanced age and wily tactics, he was on the grid for the first World Championship race in 1950, driving a works Maserati. Third place at his native Monte Carlo was his best result that year. The unreliability of the Lago-Talbot he raced in 1951 wasted that year, and it signalled the end of his serious bid for Formula One glory, although he turned out for assorted Grands Prix until 1956.

CAREER RECORD

** 15 Grands Prix, no wins (best result – 3rd Monaco GP 1950)* No championship title (best result – 9th overall 1950)*

Teenage prodigy *Eddie Cheever never lived up to his initial promise.*

Jim Clark

Nationality: British
Born: 1936
see Legends of the Track pp 108–09

Peter Collins

Nationality: British
Born: 1931
Died: 1958

The tricks learned in three years of Formula 500 racing were to stand Peter in good stead throughout his career, and he made a big impression when he moved up to Formula Two with HWM in 1952 at the age of 20. Sadly, the cars were not very reliable, but Aston Martin was sufficiently impressed to sign him for its sports car team. The next few seasons were a bit of a mish-mash, with a ride with BRM in 1955 limited by the late arrival of its new car. However, Ferrari signed Peter for 1956 and it was with this team that he was to race for the rest of his career. Two wins, in Belgium and France, followed, helping Peter finish third overall behind Juan Manuel Fangio and Stirling Moss. The following year was not so good, and he failed to win as his Lancia-Ferrari was outclassed by the rival Maseratis and Vanwalls. Peter was back on form with the advent of Ferrari's classic Dino 246 Grand Prix car in 1958. Cruelly, just a fortnight after he stormed home ahead of Hawthorn in the British Grand Prix, he was killed at the Nurburgring when chasing Tony Brooks's Vanwall for the lead in the German Grand Prix.

CAREER RECORD

** 32 Grands Prix, 3 wins (Belgian GP 1956, French GP 1956, British GP 1958)*
** No championship title (best result – 3rd overall 1956)*

Erik Comas

Nationality: French
Born: 1963

Too many talented drivers from one country arriving at the top will spoil one another's chances. Thus Erik found himself competing with Jean Alesi and Eric Bernard. Erik won the French Formule Renault title in 1986 and then suffered from being number two to Bernard when he graduated to Formula Three. Thus, it was not until his second year in Formula Three, in 1988, that he won the French crown. Formula 3000 saw Erik partner Bernard again, but he scored more points this time, although he lost the title to Alesi by the smallest of margins. Yet again he stayed on for a repeat, winning the 1990 Formula 3000 crown. Two years in Formula One with Ligier were his reward, but no points were forthcoming as the team struggled with Lamborghini engines in 1991. The second year was better, with Renault engines, with points-scoring drives in Canada, France and Germany. Then Erik had a huge shunt at Spa from which he was lucky to escape. Larrousse was his home for the next two years, but a trio of sixth places was his paltry recompense.

CAREER RECORD

** 59 Grands Prix, no wins (best result – 5th French GP 1982) * No championship title (best result – 11th 1992)*

Flying Scot *David Coulthard has been a F1 frontrunner from the outset.*

David Coulthard

Nationality: British
Born: 1971

After a hugely successful career in karts, David graduated to Formula Ford in 1989 and drove so well that he became the first winner of the McLaren/Autosport Young Driver of the Year award, being given a run in a Formula One car as a prize. Spurred on by this, he made short work of the junior categories, although he was beaten by Rubens Barrichello in both the GM Euroseries and then in the 1991 British Formula Three series. Formula 3000 is a very expensive place to trip up, but it appeared that this had happened to David when he placed only ninth in 1992 for Paul Stewart Racing. However, he was on the rostrum at the last two races and carried this form into 1993, when he won at Enna and finished up third. A greater success that year, though, was his role as Williams test driver. No Formula One ride was forthcoming for 1994, so it was back to Formula 3000 and more test driving. Second place in the season opener was followed by Senna's death in the San Marino Grand Prix and thus David moved up to Formula One. The rest, as they say, is history, as he soon got on to Hill's pace and peaked with second place in Portugal, before he had to make way for Nigel Mansell in the final three races. He had done enough, however, to keep the ride alongside Hill for 1995, making Mansell look elsewhere.

CAREER RECORD

** 8 Grands Prix, no wins (best result – 2nd Portugal 1994)* No championship title (best result – 8th 1994)*

Helmeting up *Peter Collins prepares for the 1956 British Grand Prix at Silverstone.*

Piers Courage

Nationality: British
Born: 1942
Died: 1970

Born the heir to the Courage brewing fortunes, Piers cared little for brewing and chose to race cars instead. Since his father refused to give him financial support he had to make his own way in racing. With Jonathan Williams he formed Anglo-Swiss Racing and went after Formula Three glory across Europe. It was a hand-to-mouth existence, with both men looking to survive on their prize money. A more professional approach was employed in 1965 and Piers started to win races. However, he had a tendency to spin away good positions, and it was not until 1968 that he was given a proper crack at Formula One after shining in the Tasman series in New Zealand. Piers was given his break by Tim Parnell who asked him to drive a BRM, and was in the points before the year was out. For 1969 he teamed up with Frank Williams and was promptly second at Monaco, matching this with second in the US Grand Prix. For the following season Williams ran him in a de Tomaso, but it was not a patch on the Brabham he used in 1969. But then Piers was killed in a fiery accident in the Dutch Grand Prix.

CAREER RECORD

* 28 Grands Prix, no wins (best result – 2nd Monaco GP 1969, US GP 1969)
* No championship title (best result – 8th overall 1969)

Smiling through *Yannick Dalmas bounced back from Legionnaires' Disease.*

D

Yannick Dalmas

Nationality: French
Born: 1961

Yannick was French Formule Renault champion in 1984 and landed a top drive in Formula Three for 1985 with the crack ORECA team, finishing second overall. In time-honoured fashion, he stayed on to become team leader and win the title in 1986. Formula 3000 was next and Yannick won twice, but poor results elsewere left him fifth. Before the year was out, however, he had his first taste of Formula One with the Larrousse Calmels team, scoring fifth place at his third attempt. However, he was adjudged not to have competed in enough Grands Prix to be eligible for points. Staying on with the team in 1988, he was not at his best, which he put down to ill health. Back with Larrousse in 1989, things were even worse and Yannick was forced out of the team to make way for Michele Alboreto. He picked up a ride with the tiny AGS team, but often failed to make it through pre-qualifying. The 1990 season was only slightly better. Career salvation came with a drive in the Peugeot sports car team, and Yannick won the Le Mans 24 Hours in 1992. Since 1993 it has been mainly a diet of touring cars for Yannick.

CAREER RECORD

* 23 Grands Prix, no wins (best result – 7th Monaco GP 1988, US GP 1988)
* No championship title

Derek Daly

Nationality: Irish
Born: 1953

He was Irish Formula Ford champion in 1975, Formula Ford Festival winner in 1976 and won the BP British Formula Three crown in 1977. Derek kicked off his Formula One career with the Hesketh team in 1978 by leading until spinning off in a very wet International Trophy at Silverstone. His form in the World Championship was not so good, as he failed to qualify on all three outings. Crossing to Ensign was an improvement, and he scored a point before the year was out. A move to Tyrrell halfway through 1979 preceded a full season with Tyrrell in 1980 and his most spectacular shunt of all on the opening lap of the Monaco Grand Prix when he became airborne and landed right on his team-mate, Jean-Pierre Jarier. His ride with March yielded not a point in 1981. A ride with Theodore in 1982 looked equally dire, but Carlos Reutemann quit suddenly, and Derek was asked to take his place at Williams alongside Keke Rosberg. The Finn went on to win the title, while the Irishman never made it to the rostrum and quit for Indy Cars. Despite a leg-smashing shunt in 1984, Derek went on racing in Indy Cars and then sports cars until 1992, and has since been a commentator.

CAREER RECORD

* 49 Grands Prix, no wins (best result – 4th Argentinian GP 1980, British GP 1980
* No championship title (best result – 10th overall 1980)

Christian Danner

Nationality: German
Born:.1958

Christian first came to prominence when he raced a BMW M1 in 1980. BMW signed him on a three-year contract and placed him in the works March Formula Two team for 1981,

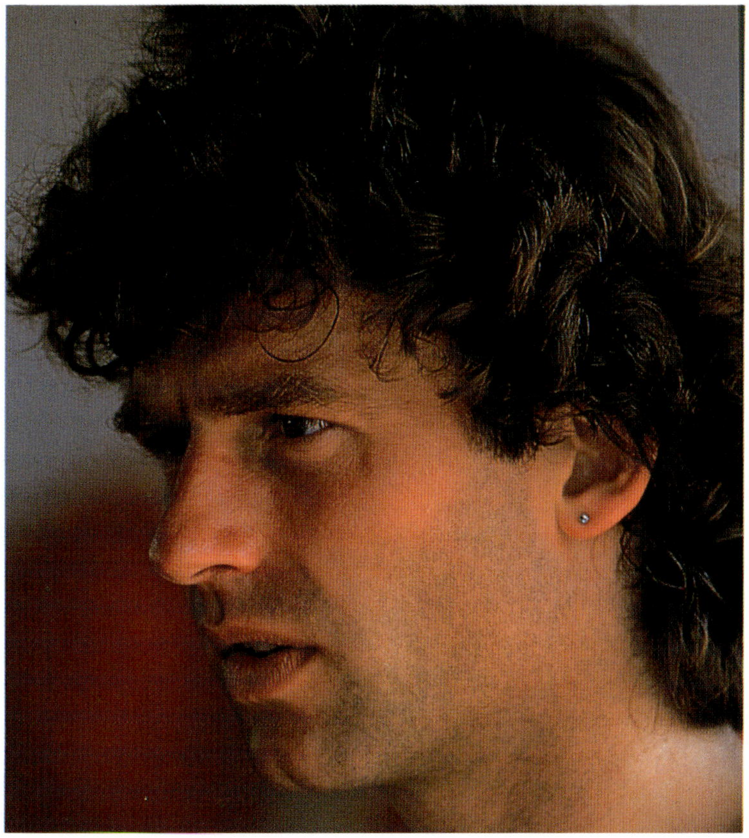

First F3000 champion *Christian Danner never shone as well in Formula One.*

RollyGo
TISSOT F1
Elio
Simpson
ESSEX
RollyGo

Italian great *Elio de Angelis had it all … then lost it all.*

despite his having no single-seater experience. It took him until the end of 1983 to get on to the pace. Driving for Bob Sparshott, he was the inaugural Formula 3000 champion in 1985 and was given two Formula One outings by Zakspeed. A move to Osella for 1986 produced little and Christian joined Arrows in mid-season, hitting the points in Austria. Back to Zakspeed in 1987, he had little to cheer about. Christian's final shot at Formula One was with the new Rial team in 1989 and he scored fourth place in Phoenix, but only qualified once thereafter, and with that he quit Formula One for touring cars.

CAREER RECORD

** 36 Grands Prix, no wins (best result – 4th US GP 1989)* No championship title (best result – 18th 1986)*

Elio de Angelis

Nationality: Italian
Born: 1958
Died: 1986

Very few drivers have reached Formula One as early in life as Elio did, for he had a full-time ride when 20. Coming from a wealthy family, he cut his teeth on karts, then blasted into Formula Three, pipping Piercarlo Ghinzani to the 1977 Italian crown. The following year produced victory in the Monaco Formula Three race but little to shout about in Formula Two. Family backing propelled him into Formula One for 1979 with Shadow. The car was not the most competitive, but Elio picked up a fourth place at Watkins Glen. He was signed for Lotus for 1980 and made the most of the superior equipment to finish second in his second outing, in Brazil. The following year showed consistent points scoring, then in Austria in 1982 he had his first win, by a nose, from Keke Rosberg's Williams. A change to Renault engines scuppered 1983, but 1984 was much better and Elio ended up third overall. A second win was picked up in San Marino in 1985, and he led the title race awhile before falling back to fifth at season's end. Elio moved to Brabham for 1986 and it was while testing at Paul Ricard that he crashed and died.

CAREER RECORD

** 108 Grands Prix, 2 wins (Austrian GP 1982, San Marino GP 1985) * No championship title (best result – 3rd 1984)*

Andrea de Cesaris

Nationality: Italian
Born: 1959

Andrea's passage to Formula One was eased by strong Marlboro connections. However, along the way, he was world karting champion, finished second to Chico Serra in the 1979 British Formula Three series and placed fifth for Ron Dennis's Project Four Formula Two team. Before 1980 was out Andrea made his Formula One debut with Alfa-Romeo. But it was with McLaren that Andrea raced in 1981. And was he wild! Indeed, by season's end, he had scored but one point and junked numerous chassis. If it had not been for his powerful backers, his Formula One career would have ended there, particularly if the other drivers had been given a say. He simply scared them all with unpredictable driving. However, Andrea stayed on, spending 1982 and 1983 with Alfa-Romeo. Amazingly, he came third at Monaco in 1982 but he could have won. Lying second going on to the final lap behind Didier Pironi, he was made a gift of the lead when the Ferrari's electrics failed but, cruelly, Andrea had run out of fuel. Thus Derek Daly was expected to win, but his gearbox packed up and through it all came Riccardo Patrese's Brabham. Andrea led again, at Spa in 1983, but his engine blew, and even though he scored two second places, he was on to pastures new – Ligier – for 1984. Two seasons with the French team produced little, so then Andrea went to Minardi, then Brabham, then Rial, then Dallara, then Jordan, then Tyrrell, Jordan again and finally to Sauber before his Formula One days ended in 1994 with Andrea, the second-most experienced Formula One driver ever, behind Riccardo Patrese. But still with no win …

Fast, but flawed *Andrea de Cesaris arrived in Formula One with a bang!*

CAREER RECORD

** 208 Grands Prix, no wins (best result – 2nd German GP 1983, South African GP 1983) * No championship title (best result – 8th overall 1983)*

Emmanuel de Graffenried

Nationality: Swiss
Born: 1914

"Toulo", as he was known, or Baron de Graffenried to be correct, was one of the main stars in the immediate post-war years, winning the British Grand Prix in 1949 in a Maserati. When the World Championship began in 1950, he was at the wheel of the same car and struggled against the newer equipment of his rivals. However, Alfa-Romeo gave him a run in one of its cars at the non-championship Geneva Grand Prix and "Toulo" came second. Alfa signed him up for 1951. In 1952 and 1953, he raced with a Maserati, coming fourth in the 1953 Belgian Grand Prix – his best-ever result. He also triumphed in the non–championship Syracuse Grand Prix that year.

CAREER RECORD

** 22 Grands Prix, no wins (best result – 4th Belgian GP 1953)* No championship title (best result – 8th overall 1953)*

Alfonso de Portago

Nationality: Spanish
Born: 1928
Died: 1957

Of aristocratic Spanish lineage, "Fon" was larger than life in all he did. A champion jockey (he raced twice in the Grand National), swimmer and bobsleigher, he took to racing in 1954 in sports cars. By 1955 he was a member of the works Ferrari team and for 1956 he was entered in several World Championship races and shared a car with Peter Collins in the British Grand Prix, coming second. He also

Mr Second Place *Patrick Depailler looked ever to be the bridesmaid, until …*

won the Tour de France sports car race that year. In 1957 he again ran a mixed programme of Formula One and sports car races. Sadly, one of these sports car events was the Mille Miglia road race, and he crashed into a crowd, killing himself, his co-driver and ten spectators.

CAREER RECORD

** 5 Grands Prix, no wins (best result – 2nd British GP 1956) * No championship title (best result – 15th overall 1956)*

Patrick Depailler

Nationality: French
Born: 1944
Died: 1980

For years it looked as though this little Frenchman would always be a bridesmaid in Formula One. Then, at the Monaco Grand Prix in 1980, after collecting eight second frustrating places, he finally came good to climb the top step on the rostrum. Patrick had a lengthy but muddled schooling in Formula Three and Formula Two that saw him step back down to Formula Three in 1971 and claim the French title. Armed with this, he won the Monaco Formula Three race and was rewarded with two Formula One outings by Tyrrell, finishing seventh at Watkins Glen. However, he spent the rest of the year in Formula Two, and 1973 and 1974, when he won the European title. But 1974 was also his first full season of Formula One. Patrick did well, with second place in Sweden. The next four years were spent with Tyrrell, with points scores aplenty, but only that one win at Monaco to his name. A move to Ligier in 1979 brought another win, in Spain, but then Patrick smashed up his legs in a hang-gliding accident. Joining Alfa-Romeo for 1980 did not go according to plan, for the car was hugely unreliable. Then, when testing before the German Grand Prix, Patrick crashed fatally at very high speed.

CAREER RECORD

** 95 Grands Prix, 2 wins (Monaco GP 1978, Spanish GP 1979) * No championship title (best result – 4th overall 1976)*

Martin Donnelly

Nationality: British
Born: 1964

One of the bright lights of the British scene in the mid-1980s, this Ulsterman was quick both in Formula Ford 2000 and then in Formula Three. Halfway through 1988, he jumped up to Formula 3000, scoring two wins and two second places from four outings for Eddie Jordan Racing to place third overall. Staying on in Formula 3000 in 1989 was not proving so successful, but Martin took the opportunity to make his Formula One debut in France for Arrows. A full-time ride with Lotus was his reward for 1990 and Martin was doing increasingly well, matching the pace of experienced team-mate Derek Warwick, when he had a monster shunt in qualifying for the Spanish Grand Prix. His car disintegrated and Martin was left in the middle of the track strapped only to his seat. His injuries were horrific but, bit by bit, he fought back to health. To see if he could still do it, he subsequently had a test run in a Formula 3000 car but has since concentrated on managing a team in Formula Vauxhall.

CAREER RECORD

** 13 Grands Prix, no wins (best result – 7th Hungarian GP 1990) * No championship title*

Mark Donohue

Nationality: American
Born: 1937
Died: 1975

Truly Mr Successful in American racing, Mark never made the grade in Formula One. His early career was financed by sports car driver Walt Hangsen, but then Roger Penske signed Mark up. This pair won the TransAm title and the Daytona 24 Hours in both 1968 and 1969, then took second place in the 1970 Indy 500, won the TransAm series again, led the Indy 500 and won an Indy Car race. Mark made his Formula One debut in a Penske-entered McLaren in the Canadian Grand Prix, finishing third. He won the Indy 500 in 1972, but spoiled his season by injuring himself after crashing his CanAm Porsche. Using the same turbocharged Porsche 917/30, Mark stormed the 1973 CanAm series. He announced his retirement, but returned to the fold when Penske decided to go Formula One at the end of 1974. The Penske chassis was not a success and it was replaced with a March after Mark had scored one fifth place. He was fifth first time out in the March, but a crash in practice for the Austrian Grand Prix left him unconscious. He appeared to recover, but suffered a brain haemorrhage and died two days later.

CAREER RECORD

** 14 Grands Prix, no wins (best result – 3rd Canadian GP 1971) * No championship title (best result – 15th overall 1975)*

Johnny Dumfries

Nationality: British
Born: 1958

Johnny tried to pass himself off as a South London painter and decorator when he started racing in Formula Ford, certain that if people discovered he was the Marquis of Bute (aka Earl of Dumfries), they would make life hard for him. He need not have worried. He had a spectacular second season in Formula Three, winning the 1984 British championship and coming third in a close-fought European series. His crack at Formula 3000 with the Onyx team was not so successful and he quit mid-season. However, help was at hand, since Ayrton Senna did not want Derek Warwick to join him at Lotus in 1986, convinced that the team could not run cars for two topline drivers. So, amid a furore, Warwick was turned away and Dumfries found himself in Formula One. However, he was very much the team's number two, and he lost his drive at the end of the year when Lotus signed to use Honda engines in 1987 and a Japanese driver came as part of the deal. Exit Johnny. A spell in sports cars followed, and he won the 1988 Le Mans 24 Hours for Jaguar.

CAREER RECORD

** 15 Grands Prix, no wins (best result – 5th Hungarian GP 1986) * No championship title (best result – 13th overall 1986)*

E

Guy Edwards

Nationality: British
Born: 1942

Guy gained a reputation more as a sponsorship-chaser than for his driving. He scored his best results in the European 2-litre sports car series and in Formula 5000. In 1974 he got his break in Formula One with the Embassy Hill team, but it was not a front-runner. In 1976 he came back with a Penthouse-sponsored Hesketh, but found this even further off the pace and retired to the Aurora British Formula One series in which he had far more success. Since hanging up his helmet, he has worked as a sponsorship consultant, linking Silk Cut to the Jaguar sports car team before taking his portfolio to Lotus. However, this was not a success and the team folded at the end of 1994 with massive debts.

CAREER RECORD

** 11 Grands Prix, no wins (best result – 7th Swedish GP 1974) * No championship title*

Vic Elford

Nationality: British
Born: 1935

A winner in rallies, rallycross and sports cars, Vic was no slouch in Formula One machinery. He had a very good year in 1968, for he won the Monte Carlo Rally, the Daytona 24 Hours, the Targa Florio and the Nurburgring 1000 kms, and he made his Formula One debut, albeit in a Cooper when Coopers were no longer the cars to have. Somehow, he carried one around to a fourth and a fifth place finish. A privately entered McLaren followed for 1969, but Vic hit some debris in the German Grand Prix, crashed and broke his arm, putting his career into a downward spiral. Since 1974 he has run a racing school in the USA.

CAREER RECORD

** 13 Grands Prix, no wins (best result – 4th French GP 1968) * No championship title (best result – 13th 1969)*

Harald Ertl

Nationality: Austrian
Born: 1948
Died: 1982

This bearded Austrian journalist worked his way through the German Formula Vee, Super Vee and then Formula Three series before turning to touring cars, winning the Tourist Trophy for BMW at Silverstone in 1973. His Formula One break did not come until 1975 when he landed a ride in a privately entered Hesketh. Harald plugged away for the next two seasons with Hesketh and also raced concurrently in Formula Two. Then, in 1978, he changed across to an Ensign, but had little success and elected to race in the radical Group 5 series in Germany. Sadly, Harald lost his life in a light aircraft crash in 1982.

CAREER RECORD

** 18 Grands Prix, no wins (best result – 7th British GP 1976)* No championship title*

Philippe Etancelin

Nationality: French
Born: 1896
Died: 1981

"Phi Phi" was another of the over-50s gang who lined up on the grid at Silverstone in 1950 for the first-ever World Championship round. Famed for his back-to-front cloth cap, he had starred for Bugatti in the 1930s and had won the Le Mans 24 Hours for Alfa-Romeo in 1934. He raced an aged Lago-Talbot in 1950, yet still scored two fifth place finishes, before retiring from the World Championship in 1952.

CAREER RECORD

** 12 Grands Prix, no wins (best result – 5th French GP 1950, Italian GP 1950) * No championship title (best result – 13th overall 1950)*

Transatlantic flier *Teo Fabi has shone both in Formula One and Indy Cars.*

F

Teo Fabi

Nationality: Italian
Born: 1955

European karting champion in 1975, he duly graduated through Formula Three to land a ride in Formula Two for 1979. Despite a mixed season, he was signed to lead the works March squad in 1980, finishing third behind the dominant Tolemans. Set for a move with March to Formula One for 1981, he lost the drive to Derek Daly and so went to the USA and shone in the CanAm sports car series. Teo got his Formula One break in 1982, though, with Toleman. It was a wretched year and he was glad when long-time backer Robin Herd helped him land an Indy Car ride for 1983. Teo claimed pole for the Indy 500 and notched up four wins. Back in Formula One in 1984, with Brabham, he scored his first points with third place around ths streets of Detroit. His first pole came with Toleman in 1985, at the Nurburgring, but he retired with clutch failure. Indeed, Teo retired most races. Toleman metamorphosed into the Benetton team in 1986, and Teo took two more poles near the end of the year, again without results to match this expertise in qualifying in the wild days of turbocharged engines that would hold together only for a few pumped-up laps. The 1987 season was more successful in terms of gathering points, but it was to be Teo's last in Formula One, as he moved back to Indy Cars. He chose to drive the Porsche project car. It did not work, so he went sports car racing and won the 1991 world title for Jaguar. Since then he has drifted back to Indy Cars.

CAREER RECORD

** 64 Grands Prix, no wins (best result – 3rd US GP East 1984, Austrian GP 1987) * No championship title (best result – 9th overall 1987)*

Luigi Fagioli

Nationality: Italian
Born: 1898
Died: 1952

One of the top names in Italian racing in the 1930s, Luigi was a race winner for Maserati, Alfa Romeo and then Auto Union. He was almost 52 when the World Championship began in 1950. His maturity helped him collect points aplenty, with four second places, to finish third overall. Being asked in 1951 to hand his car over to Fangio during the French Grand Prix was too much for Luigi and, even though Fangio went on to win the race, he quit Formula One that very instant. A brief career in sports cars came to an end in 1952 when he crashed at Monaco and died of his injuries.

Straight-arm tactics *Guiseppe Farina has a distinctive driving style that took him to the 1950 world title.*

CAREER RECORD

** 7 Grands Prix, 1 win (French GP 1951, shared with Fangio) * No championship title (best result – 3rd overall 1950)*

Juan Manuel Fangio

Nationality: Argentinian
Born: 1911
see Legends of the Track pp 110–11

Jack Fairman

Nationality: British
Born: 1913

Jack shone in sports cars in the 1950s and progressed to Formula One when the chance arose. In Jack's case this was in the 1953 British Grand Prix with an HWM. Until 1961 he raced in the British Grand Prix and selected overseas Grands Prix principally for Connaught and Cooper, scoring twice for Connaught in 1956. He would drive anything, anywhere, any time.

CAREER RECORD

** 13 Grands Prix, no wins (best result – 4th British GP 1955) * No championship title (best result – 10th overall 1956)*

Giuseppe Farina

*Nationality:*Italian
Born: 1906
Died: 1966

"Nino" was the first world champion, cleaning up for Alfa-Romeo in 1950 by winning half the six races. He started in hill climbs in the early 1930s, but progressed to circuit racing with Maserati and learned from the tutelage of the legendary Tazio Nuvolari. He won the Italian drivers' title in 1937, 1938 and 1939, putting himself into a strong position when the war ended, and was duly rewarded in 1950. A model to other colleagues with his straight-arm driving style, "Nino" could not match team-mate Juan Manuel Fangio's pace in 1951. For 1952 he joined Ferrari, but this was not to produce a race win until the 1953 German Grand Prix as he was overshadowed by Alberto Ascari. Engulfed in flames in a sports car race at the start of 1954, "Nino" was not back in the cockpit until 1955, but he retired mid-season, unable to live with the pain of racing, even though he dosed himself with painkillers. He later dabbled with the Indy 500 but then retired, only to be killed in a road accident.

CAREER RECORD

** 33 Grands Prix, 5 wins (British GP 1950, Swiss GP 1950, Italian GP 1950, Belgian GP 1951, German GP 1953) * World champion 1950*

Christian Fittipaldi

Nationality: Brazilian
Born: 1971

As the son of Wilson Fittipaldi and nephew of double world champion Emerson, it was perhaps inevitable that Christian would go racing. He worked his way up the Brazilian rankings in short order, then turned to Europe and raced in the British Formula Three Championship for West Surrey Racing in 1990. Learning circuits as he went, he peaked with a fine victory in the final round, ahead of his team-mate, the 1990 champion Mika Hakkinen. Moving up to Formula 3000 with Pacific, Christian became one of those rare phenomena: a first-year Formula 3000 champion thanks to his consistency. And so he found himself in Formula One in 1992, joining Minardi ahead of his 21st birthday. He kicked off 1993 with fourth place in Brazil but this form was not to be repeated and his most famed manoeuvre all year was his attempt to pass team-mate Pierluigi Martini as they crossed the finish line at Monza in the Italian Grand Prix, with Christian clipping Pierluigi and somersaulting through the air, somehow landing on his three remaining wheels. His mother fainted on the pitwall. Two more fourth places followed for Footwork in 1994, but Christian became disaffected and moved to Indy Cars for 1995, much to the disappointment of the females of the paddock.

CAREER RECORD

** 40 Grands Prix, no wins (best result – 4th South African GP 1993, Pacific GP, 1994, German GP 1994) * No championship title (best result – 13th overall 1993)*

Family business *Christian Fittipaldi followed his father and uncle into F1.*

Emerson Fittipaldi

Nationality: Brazilian
Born: 1946

Few people have ever achieved as much as fast in motor racing as Emerson. Starting on 50cc motorbikes, he followed older brother Wilson into karts and both progressed to cars, racing, of all things, a Renault Gordini. Having trounced the opposition in Brazil, Emerson moved to Europe in 1969. He bought a Formula Ford car and could not stop winning. Racing school proprietor Jim Russell spotted this talent and signed Emerson to race his Formula Three Lotus. He won the Lombank Formula Three title that year and Lotus signed him for its Formula Two team for 1970 and, in mid-season, team boss Colin Chapman hurried Emerson into Formula One, partly to forestall rival team managers from signing him. Emerson won fifth time out, at Watkins Glen, giving Lotus a boost after the death of lead driver Jochen Rindt at the previous race. No wins followed in 1971, but Emerson claimed the 1972 title, in so doing becoming the youngest champion ever. Second to Jackie Stewart in 1973, he moved to McLaren and won the 1974 World title, following this with being runner-up to Niki Lauda in 1975. In 1976 he left McLaren to join brother Wilson's team, Copersucar. Emerson's brilliance coaxed the car into a top three position twice in the next five years but his talents were wasted in generally inferior equipment and then he called it a day and moved to Indy Cars, becoming the champion in 1989 for Patrick Racing, having won the Indianapolis 500. Emerson won the big race again in 1993 for Penske and remains one of the big names Stateside, continuing to outpace drivers half his age, including his nephew Christian.

CAREER RECORD

** 144 Grands Prix, 14 wins (US GP 1970, Spanish GP 1972, Belgian GP 1972, British GP 1972, Austrian GP 1972, Italian GP 1972, Argentinian GP 1973, Brazilian GP 1973, Spanish GP 1973, Brazilian GP 1974, Belgian GP 1974, Canadian GP 1974, Argentinian GP 1975, British GP 1975)*
** World Champion 1972, 1974*

Brazilian star *Emerson Fittipaldi salutes the crowd* en route *to the 1972 title.*

Wilson Fittipaldi

Nationality: Brazilian
Born: 1943

He may have started racing first, but he was almost immediately overshadowed by younger brother Emerson. He headed Emerson to Europe, but his foray was not so successful and he did not return there until 1970 to race in Formula Three. Formula Two followed in 1971 and Wilson was into Formula One in 1972 with Brabham. Two seasons yielded two points-scoring drives, and he lost third place in the 1973 Monaco Grand Prix when his car failed to pick up its fuel. And so Wilson quit Formula One in 1974. He was back a year later, though, with his own Brazilian-built car. It was not a success and he retired to run Emerson in the team for the next five years.

CAREER RECORD

** 36 Grands Prix, no wins (best result – 5th German GP 1973) * No championship title (best result – 15th overall 1973)*

Ron Flockhart

Nationality: British
Born: 1923
Died: 1962

Ron came to prominence on the British scene when he started racing an ERA in the early 1950s. He made his Grand Prix debut at Silverstone in 1954, then came home third in a Connaught in the 1956 Italian Grand Prix. He also won the Le Mans 24 Hours that year, and the next, before landing a full-time ride with BRM in 1959. The results he desired did not follow and Ron went off to become a pilot. He was to die in 1962, crashing in Australia while practising for a record attempt on the London to Sydney route.

CAREER RECORD

** 13 Grands Prix, no wins (best result – 3rd French GP 1956) * No championship title (best result – 11th overall 1956)*

George Follmer

Nationality: American
Born: 1934

Formula One seemed a long way from George's ambitions during his lengthy spell racing sports cars in the USA. However, at the age of 39, he found himself making his Grand Prix debut, for Shadow. This came in 1973 and he ran the whole season, peaking with third place second time out, at the Spanish Grand Prix. At the end of the year he returned to the US scene, racing again in the CanAm sportscar series and then winning the 1976 TransAm title.

CAREER RECORD

** 12 Grands Prix, no wins (best result – 3rd Spanish GP 1973) * No championship title (best result – 13th overall 1973)*

Heinz-Harald Frentzen

Nationality: German
Born: 1967

Born of a German father and a Spanish mother, Heinz-Harald graduated from karting to Formula Ford. Showing natural speed, he was pro-

Merc hope *Heinz-Harald Frentzen was groomed for stardom by Mercedes.*

moted in 1988 to the GM Euroseries, giving Mika Hakkinen and Allan McNish a hard time in the two season-closing races on the Iberian peninsula. He was second in the 1989 German Formula Three series, behind Karl Wendlinger but ahead of Michael Schumacher. A move into sports cars with the Mercedes junior team followed, easing Heinz-Harald into the limelight and helping him to become accustomed to having power under his right foot. Many thought at this stage that he was faster than Schumacher. He also raced for two seasons in Formula 3000 at the same time, but it did not propel him to Formula One, so he went to Japan to race in that country's Formula 3000 series. Good form out east saw him land a Formula One ride with Sauber for 1994 and he came home fourth in the French Grand Prix.

CAREER RECORD

** 15 Grands Prix, no wins (best result – 4th French GP 1994) * No championship title (best result – 13th overall 1994)*

Troubled progress *Gachot had a tricky climb to F1 … and to jail.*

Paul Frère

Nationality: Belgian
Born: 1917

A motoring journalist who came good, Paul was always eager to retain his training and race for fun. With remarkably little experience beyond racing an MG, he found himself driving an HWM in the 1952 Belgian Grand Prix. And he came fifth... Paul was in and out of drives in the latter half of the 1950s and thus his second-place finish for Ferrari at Spa in 1956 was the utmost surprise. He also managed to win the Le Mans 24 Hours in 1960.

CAREER RECORD

** 11 Grands Prix, no wins (best result – 2nd Belgian GP 1956) * No championship title (best result – 7th overall 1956)*

G

Bertrand Gachot

Nationality: Belgian
Born: 1962

A truly cosmopolitan mixture of Belgian, French and Luxembourgeois, Bertrand was the first driver to race under the flag of the European Community. Trained when in karting never to cede a corner to another driver, even if it meant crashing himself, Bertrand gained the reputation of being uncompromising. He was a contemporary of Damon Hill, Johnny Herbert and Mark Blundell in British Formula Ford in the mid-1980s, then finished up as runner–up to Herbert in the 1987 British Formula Three Championship, before graduating to Formula 3000 and then straight on to Formula One in 1989. Unfortunately, Bernard joined the Moneytron Onyx team and seldom qualified. An even worse year followed in 1990 when he attempted to qualify the overweight Subaru-powered Coloni. Salvation came in 1991, from Jordan. And all was going well, including fifth place in Canada, when Bertrand was jailed for spraying CS gas in the face of a London cabbie... Back with Larrousse in 1992, he struggled through 1994 with Pacific, and is now a shareholder of the team.

CAREER RECORD

** 36 Grands Prix, no wins (best result – 5th Canadian GP 1991) * No championship title (best result – 12th overall 1991)*

Howden Ganley

Nationality: New Zealander
Born: 1941

Lacking racing opportunities in his home country of New Zealand, Howden came to England at the age of 19 and found employment as a mechanic. That was in 1961, and it was not until 1967 that he had earned enough for a real crack at Formula Three. Success was slow in coming, and only in 1970 did he enter the limelight by finishing second to Peter Gethin in the Formula 5000 Championship. This helped him land a Formula One ride with BRM for 1971. Points were scored before the end of the year, and Howden stayed with BRM for 1972, albeit with little improvement in form, although he did finish second in the Le Mans 24 Hours. Changing to Frank Williams's young team in 1973 failed to help since the Iso chassis was no world beater, and he quit the sport's top category after two races with March and two non-qualifiying runs with the Japanese Maki chassis in 1974, the second of which left him with leg injuries. He joined forces with fellow Formula One racer Tim Schenken to form the Tiga (Tim/Ganley) race car manufacturing company.

CAREER RECORD

** 35 Grands Prix, no wins (best result – 4th US GP 1971, German GP 1972)*
** No championship title (best result – 12th overall 1972)*

Olivier Gendebien

Nationality: Belgian
Born: 1924

Olivier met up with a rally driver while he was working in the Belgian Congo and agreed to try his luck as a co-driver on his return to Europe in the mid-1950s. Their performances led to the offer of a works Ferrari sports car drive, backed up with selected Formula One outings. Amazingly, Olivier placed fifth on his debut, the 1956 Argentinian Grand Prix. By and large, though, such Formula One outings were limited and his success was restricted to sports cars: indeed, he won the Le Mans 24 Hours an incredible four times between 1958 and 1962. It was not until 1960 that he got a fair run, with a Yeoman Credit Cooper. Immediately the results came, with third place in Belgium followed by second in the French Grand Prix. However, after driving for a mixture of teams in 1961, he quit for sports cars.

CAREER RECORD

** 14 Grands Prix, no wins (best result – 2nd French GP 1960) * No championship title (best result – 6th overall 1960)*

Peter Gethin

Nationality: British
Born: 1940

A hundredth of a second was the advantage Peter had over Ronnie Peterson when he scored his one and only Grand Prix win, at Monza in 1971. It was the blink of an eye, but the moment of a lifetime. Having chosen not to follow his father and become a jockey, Peter served his apprenticeship in club racing instead, starting in 1962 in a Lotus 7. In Formula Three by 1965, he raced in Europe and graduation did not come until 1968. Minor success was achieved, but the formation of Formula 5000 in 1969 gave him the boost he needed in a semi-works McLaren. He won the title, and repeated the feat in 1970. By the time of the second title, though, he had a handful of Grands Prix under his belt, having been seconded into the McLaren line-up after Bruce McLaren's death, scoring once. He failed to score for McLaren in

1971, but changed to BRM and scored his famous win in Italy. He was only to score once more. Peter won the Pau Grand Prix for Formula Two cars and raced on in Formula 5000 until 1977.

CAREER RECORD

** 30 Grands Prix, 1 win (Italian GP 1971)*
** No championship title (best result – 9th overall 1971)*

Piercarlo Ghinzani

Nationality: Italian
Born: 1952

It was through the clinching of deals that Piercarlo extended his Formula One career from 1981 to 1989 with a points tally of just two... Considering he started in motor racing in 1970, his rise to Formula One was very slow. It took him until 1973 to reach Formula Three. He won the European title in 1977 and moved on to Formula Two. A Formula One ride was clinched in 1981 when he joined Osella, and he stayed with the team until mid-1985 when he crossed over to Toleman, scoring his only points at Dallas in 1984. He was back with Osella in 1986; then Ligier, Zakspeed and Osella for a third time followed before he called it a day.

CAREER RECORD

** 76 Grands Prix, no wins (best result – 5th US GP 1984) * No championship title (best result – 19th overall 1984)*

Money broker *Piercarlo Ghinzani landed more big deals than points*

Prince charming *Bruno Giacomelli had the speed to win Grands Prix, but never the equipment.*

Bruno Giacomelli

Nationality: Italian
Born: 1952

There was something about Bruno that appealed to both team managers (his speed), the press (his approachability) and fans (he looked so cuddly). He was first seen in Britain in 1976 when he did all he could to stop Rupert Keegan from winning the Formula Three title. March showed faith in him and Bruno raced for Robin Herd's team in 1977 in Formula Two, also making his Formula One debut for McLaren at Monza. McLaren ran Bruno again in 1978, briefly, and then Bruno joined Alfa, for whom he raced until the end of 1982, never landing the results to match the speed. A year with Toleman followed, before a six-year lay-off that was interspersed with sports car and Indy Car races and then a fruitless bid to qualify the hopeless Life chassis in 1990.

CAREER RECORD

** 69 Grands Prix, no wins (best result – 3rd Caesar's Palace GP 1981) * No championship title (best result – 15th overall 1981)*

Richie Ginther

Nationality: American
Born: 1930
Died: 1989

With the exception of Dan Gurney and Phil Hill, Richie was the only American Formula One driver to succeed in the 1960s. He made his name racing a Porsche in the late 1950s. This earned him a works Ferrari sports car contract and brought him to Europe for 1960. He drove in only three Grands Prix that year, scoring each time, peaking with second at Monza. Another second place followed in 1961, at Monaco, and another at the same venue in 1962 when he had joined BRM. Over the next two years he was second five more times, but that win finally came, for Honda, in Mexico in 1965. He quit racing in 1967.

CAREER RECORD

** 52 Grands Prix, 1 win (Mexican GP 1965)*
** No championship title (best result – 2nd overall 1963)*

Ignazio Giunti

Nationality: Italian
Born: 1941
Died: 1971

Ignazio gained his competitive instinct in hill climbs in the mid-1960s and was soon elevated to racing sports cars. He joined the Ferrari Formula One line-up for 1970 alongside Jacky Ickx and Clay Regazzoni. He did enough to stay on for 1971, by finishing fourth at Spa, but he was killed in a freak accident in a sports car race at Buenos Aires when he hit Jean-Pierre Beltoise's stranded Matra.

CAREER RECORD

** 4 Grands Prix, no wins (best result – 4th Belgian GP 1970) * No championship title (best result – 17th overall 1970)*

Solid performer *Froilan Gonzalez wouldn't fit in today's cars.*

Froilan Gonzalez

Nationality: Argentinian
Born: 1922

The "Pampas Bull", as Froilan was known, was a real character, built more like an all-in wrestler than a jockey. He made his Formula One debut in the Monaco Grand Prix, racing a Maserati for the Scuderia Argentina team in place of compatriot Juan Manuel Fangio who had crossed over to Alfa-Romeo. No results came his way in 1950, but 1951 was better, for he joined Ferrari and his exuberant, sideways-is-best style saw him on the rostrum for each of the five races he drove for the team, winning the British Grand Prix. Indeed, this was Ferrari's first victory in a World Championship Grand Prix. He backed this up by winning the non-championship Pescara Grand Prix, but signed for Maserati for 1952. No wins followed, so he went back to Ferrari in 1954 and again won the British Grand

Prix, also winning three non-championship races, the Le Mans 24 Hours and several other sports car races. Indeed, had it not been for Fangio, he would have been world champion. Thereafter he raced mainly at home and retired to run a garage business.

CAREER RECORD

** 26 Grands Prix, 2 wins (British GP 1951, British GP 1954) * No championship title (best result – 2nd overall 1954)*

Masten Gregory

Nationality: American
Born: 1932
Died: 1985

Family wealth made Masten's progress easy. If he wanted to race a car, he bought it. Having raced sports cars in the mid-1950s with growing confidence, he took the plunge and went Formula One in 1957 with a Scuderia Centro Sud Maserati, coming third on his debut at Monaco. Finishing in the points each time out, he placed sixth overall. And this was to prove his best year. Racing for Cooper in 1959 as number three to Jack Brabham and Bruce McLaren, Masten came second in the Portuguese Grand Prix. But then he crashed in a sports car race and was injured. Indeed, when Masten came to look for a Formula One ride for 1960, his reputation as a crasher went against him, and this led to him racing Cooper and then Lotus cars for four seasons with little success. He signed off with four races in a privately entered BRM in 1965, but it was in sports cars that he earned his glory, winning the Le Mans 24 Hours in 1965 with Jochen Rindt. Many other wins followed before he retired from racing in 1971.

CAREER RECORD

** 38 Grands Prix, no wins (best result – 2nd Portuguese GP 1959) * No championship title (best result – 6th overall 1957)*

Wide load *Olivier Grouillard became known for blocking in Formula One.*

Olivier Grouillard

Nationality: French
Born: 1958

After winning the French Formula Three title in 1984 at his second attempt, with the topline ORECA team, Olivier progressed with the team to Formula 3000 and showed well, but it was to be four years before he scored two wins for the GDBA team and ended up second overall to Roberto Moreno. He thus graduated from motor racing's second division, landing a ride with Ligier for 1989. Fittingly, Olivier scored his first points on home soil, but the next three seasons – spent with Osella, Fondmetal and then Tyrrell – produced nothing. Nothing except regular fist shaking from other drivers as he wandered into their path when they were on a flier in qualifying, or obstructed the leaders as they came up to lap him. No one was sad to see Olivier go and try his luck in Indy Cars.

CAREER RECORD

** 41 Grands Prix, no wins (best result – 6th French GP 1989) * No championship title (best result – 26th overall 1989)*

Roberto Guerrero

Nationality: Colombian
Born: 1958

Roberto's arrival in Britain was an immediate hit in Formula Ford in 1978 and he came joint second overall in the 1980 Formula Three series behind Stefan Johansson. Formula Two was not such a hit and, despite winning at Thruxton, Roberto ended up seventh overall in a year dominated by Geoff Lees. However, he had done enough to land a Formula One ride with Ensign for 1982. This was a foot in the door, but a move to the Theodore team for 1983 proved no more successful and so Roberto headed west for Indy Cars, anxious simply to have a car that stood a chance of winning. Second in the 1984 Indy 500 behind Rick Mears, he won twice in 1987 but then crashed and went into a coma. Although he fought his way back to fitness, his form was never the same. But then, to everyone's delight, this charming individual stuck his car on pole for the Indy 500 in 1992, only to crash on the parade lap ...

CAREER RECORD

** 21 Grands Prix, no wins (best result – 8th German GP 1982)* No championship title*

Mauricio Gugelmin

Nationality: Brazilian
Born: 1963

A friend of Ayrton Senna, Mauricio followed him to Britain. Echoing Ayrton's moves, he drove for West Surrey Racing in Formula Three and won the 1985 title plus the Macau Grand Prix. West Surrey decided to move up to Formula 3000 with Mauricio in 1986, but this proved a disaster. So Mauricio transferred to the works Ralt team in 1987 and won first time out, but dropped to fourth overall by year's end. However, this was enough to earn him a Formula One drive for 1988 with the Leyton House March team. For the next four years Mauricio was synonymous with the team's aquamarine colours. Results were mixed, but highlights included third place in Brazil in 1989 and running second in France behind team-mate Ivan Capelli in 1990 before retiring. Then Capelli fell back to second right at the end. The team folded and so Mauricio moved to the new Jordan team for 1992, but the Yamaha engine was gutless and this sounded the death knell of Mauricio's Formula One career. He is now an Indy Car regular.

CAREER RECORD

** 74 Grands Prix, no wins (best result – 3rd Brazilian GP 1989) * No championship title (best result – 13th overall 1988)*

Dan Gurney

Nationality: American
Born: 1931

To many fans, Dan is the greatest American ever in Formula One, even though statistics tell a different story. What made Dan stand out was that he built his own car – the Eagle – and won in that. A spell in the army in Korea intervened before he bought himself a Triumph TR2 and raced it. Over the next few years the cars became more exotic and Dan more successful, earning an invitation to race in Europe for Ferrari in 1958. He landed a contract to race Formula One for the team in 1959, with Enzo no doubt aware of the sales value of having American attention focused on Ferrari. And so began a long Formula One career, and he kicked off with second place behind team-mate Peter Collins in the German Grand Prix. However, he moved to BRM for 1960 and then on to Porsche for 1961. With reliability he had only dreamt of at BRM, he finished third overall despite not winning a race. Staying on for 1962, though, he did get to the top step of the rostrum, at the French Grand Prix. Indeed, Rouen was a happy stamping ground for Dan, for his next win came there in 1964, his second year with Brabham. And he rounded out that season with another win, in Mexico. Ironically, both 1963 and 1965 saw him in the points more often, frequently challenging the supreme Jim Clark. Then Dan bit the bullet and built his own cars for 1966. The Eagle came good in 1967 with Weslake power in place of Climax, and Dan brought this beautiful car home first in Belgium, but all too often it broke down. He won the Le Mans 24 Hours for Ford with A.J. Foyt. Success for Dan, it seemed, was henceforth to come from outside Formula One, with second place in the Indy 500 in 1968 and 1969 reminding Americans of his skills. However, on the death of Bruce McLaren, he went back to Formula One for one last go with McLaren's team. After that he concentrated on turning his Indy Cars into race winners. They picked up many honours Stateside, including the Indy 500, twice. Then, in the 1980s, Dan moved across to sports cars, successfully running Toyotas.

CAREER RECORD

** 86 Grands Prix, 4 wins (French GP 1962, French GP 1964, Mexican GP 1964, Belgian GP 1967)* No championship title (best result – 3rd overall in 1961)*

H

Mike Hailwood

Nationality: British
Born: 1941
Died: 1981

Best known as a nine-time motorcycle world champion, and 12-time winner of the Isle of Man's Tourist Trophy, Mike moved to four-wheeled sport in 1963 in Formula Junior, finishing fifth in his first race. He was invited to move to Formula One in 1964, driving an elderly Lotus for Reg Parnell. At the end of 1967 he decided to give up motorcycle racing and concentrate on motor racing, taking part in many sports car events, then winning in Formula 5000 in a car entered by another motorcycling world champion, John Surtees. Returned to Formula One in 1971, finishing fourth in the Italian Grand Prix after leading several times. He stayed on with Surtees in 1972 and 1973, with second place in the 1972 Italian Grand Prix proving his best result. Mike's Formula One career was brought to an end when he crashed his McLaren in the 1974 German Grand Prix, breaking a leg. He dabbled with motorcycles until 1979, then retired. Tragically, he and his two children were killed in a road accident two years later.

CAREER RECORD

** 50 Grands Prix, no wins (best result – 2nd Italian GP 1972)* No championship title (best result – 8th overall 1972)*

Mika Hakkinen

Nationality: Finnish
Born: 1968

Mika is one of the few of the new generation of stars with the natural speed to try to fill the gap left by the death of Ayrton Senna. He started in karting at an age when many would have been riding a bicycle with stabilizers. He followed in the tracks of compatriot JJ Lehto, buying JJ's Formula Ford and breaking most of his lap records en route to the 1987 European title. He won the GM Euroseries for Dragon Racing in 1988, then graduated with the team to British Formula Three. He joined West Surrey in 1990 and cleaned up, beating another Finn, Mika Salo. Much of this success was due to team boss Dick Bennetts. Mika should have won in Macau, but crashed on the last lap, handing Michael Schumacher his first big result. He made the unusual jump direct to Formula One, with Lotus. He often impressed, running with the big names until mechanical gremlins struck. Mika did better in 1992 to finish eighth overall, peaking with fourth in Hungary. Managed by 1982 world champion Keke Rosberg, he was sold a dummy and signed for McLaren. But then Ayrton Senna decided to race after all and Mika was left as test driver. However, he got to drive at the end of the year and outqualified Senna... Backed up with third place in Japan, he landed a full-time ride for 1994. This resulted in second place in Belgium and five third places, good for fourth overall.

Finnish flier *Mika Hakkinen has always been ultra-quick.*

Blonde bomber *Mike Hawthorn was the first British world champion.*

CAREER RECORD

** 48 Grands Prix, no wins (best result – 2nd Belgian GP 1994) * No championship title (best result – 4th overall 1994)*

Mike Hawthorn

Nationality: British
Born: 1929
Died: 1959

Tall, blond, bullish and never without a cap and bow-tie, this son of a Surrey garage owner gave the British public the international success it craved in the 1950s. Being brought up on the spectator banks at Brooklands circuit fired his enthusiasm for racing and so, with his father's assistance, Mike entered the world of competition at the 1950 Brighton speed trials. By 1952 he had graduated to single-seaters and had won his first race in a Formula Two Cooper, even beating a similarly mounted Juan Manuel Fangio later in the day. This was to be the making of Mike, and his Grand Prix debut followed, with fourth place at Spa behind the mighty Ferraris. Then he was third in the British Grand Prix and fourth overall at the year's end. Impressed by this newcomer, Enzo Ferrari offered Mike a works drive for 1953, something Mike accepted, winning the French Grand Prix as he worked his way to fourth overall again. Third overall was his reward for his performances in 1954, with victory in the Spanish Grand Prix. Mike's racing was then limited by the death of his father, but he bounced back in 1957, again proving a front-runner. However, 1958 was the year in which it all came right. He won only once, but consistent scoring gave him the title, making him Britain's first Formula One world champion. He then retired, only to be killed in a car crash in 1959.

CAREER RECORD

** 45 Grands Prix, 3 wins (French GP 1953, Spanish GP 1954, French GP 1958)*
** World Champion 1958*

Brian Henton

Nationality: British
Born: 1946

He rose to Formula Three after three years in the junior formulae and won the British title at his second attempt in 1974. Formula Two followed, with three unsuccessful outings for struggling Lotus. But then it was back to Formula Two and Brian found himself out of a ride after one race. He returned to Formula One in 1977 with a privately entered March. But he qualified just once. So it was back to Formula Two again in 1978, this time with a three-year spell that culminated in Brian beating Toleman team-mate Derek Warwick to the title in 1980. Both moved up to Formula One with Toleman, but that first season was a tough one and Brian qualified the heavy "General Belgrano" just once. Finally, he got a better shot, racing for Arrows in 1982 in place of the injured Marc Surer, then moved across to Tyrrell. He never quite scored and by the middle of 1983 had retired.

CAREER RECORD

** 19 Grands Prix, no wins (best result – 7th German GP 1982) * No championship title*

Back to Benetton *Johnny Herbert was with Benetton in 1989 and then in 1995.*

Johnny Herbert

Nationality: British
Born: 1964

Small, blond and chirpy, Johnny has spent all of his career as someone's protégé. Paul Newman (no, not the actor) helped him through his highly successful karting days, before former racer Mike Thompson guided Johnny into car racing, with a famous win-from-the-back coming in the 1985 Formula Ford Festival. The people on the inside of the sport recognized Johnny's talent and he was signed up by Eddie Jordan, winning the 1987 British Formula Three title. He was looking set for the 1988 Formula 3000 title when he suffered horrendous leg injuries in a multi-car pile-up at Brands Hatch on the very day he had signed a Formula One contract with Benetton. He fought back to fitness and finished an amazing fourth on his Formula One debut in Brazil, right behind Alain Prost. However, his shattered heels could not cope with the constant braking on the tighter tracks and he was dropped by the team. His fourth mentor was Peter Collins, who signed him for Lotus for 1990, and there Johnny stayed until 1994. However, the team became less competitive every year, so it pleased everyone when he was snapped up for 1995 to race alongside Michael Schumacher at Benetton.

CAREER RECORD

** 63 Grands Prix, no wins (best result – 4th Brazilian GP 1989, Brazilian GP 1993, European GP 1993, British GP 1993) * No championship title (best result – 9th overall 1993)*

Hans Herrmann

Nationality: German
Born: 1928

A sports car racer of some repute, Hans was elevated to the mighty Mercedes Formula One team in 1954. He was in the points before the year was out, but his 1955 season was interrupted by injuries collected in an accident at Monaco. When he was fit to return, Mercedes had quit racing in the wake of the Le Mans disaster and so Hans had to look elsewhere for a ride, driving cars from Maserati, Cooper, BRM, Porsche, Brabham and Lotus in the remainder of his career spread thinly between 1957 and 1969. It was in

A thinking man *Damon Hill is unusually intelligent in Formula One circles. And fast …*

sports cars that he shone in this period, signing off with victory in the 1970 Le Mans 24 Hours in a Porsche he shared with Richard Attwood.

CAREER RECORD

** 18 Grands Prix, no wins (best result – 3rd Swiss GP 1954) * No championship title (best result – 6th overall 1954)*

Damon Hill

Nationality: British
Born: 1960

Damon became the first "second generation" driver to score a modern-day Grand Prix victory when he won the 1993 Hungarian Grand Prix. Damon, 15 at the time of father Graham's death in a light aircraft crash, did not take to car racing until 1984 when he tried Formula Ford. Slow at first, he soon developed a turn of speed and three years in the competitive cauldron of British Formula Three peaked with third place in 1988 behind JJ Lehto and Gary Brabham. Three seasons of Formula 3000 followed, with the second seeing Damon lead race after race yet failing to win even once as mechanical gremlins struck. He made his Formula One debut in 1992, but he qualified just twice. Useful mileage was gained as test driver for Williams and the team signed him for 1993 to drive alongside three-time world champion Alain Prost. A spin at the first corner on his debut did not augur well, but he was soon leading races from the wily Prost. He was robbed of victory in Britain and in Germany, but it came good in Hungary and Damon followed this with wins in Belgium and Italy to claim third place overall. Staying on at Williams for 1994, this time with Ayrton Senna as team-mate, Damon was thrust into the role of team leader on the Brazilian's death and achieved a morale-boosting win in Spain. The year then became fraught with Michael Schumacher's disqualifications and Damon calmly closed the gap by winning four times more. Victory in the wet at Japan set the stage for a finale in the Australian Grand Prix, and Schumacher's chopping move that took Damon out was seen the world over. If only he had known that the German was effectively out of the race with a damaged car at the time he would not have tried the passing move. Like his father before him, Damon is not a natural, but a very good learner.

No nonsense racer *Denny Hulme was truly a drivers' racer.*

CAREER RECORD

** 34 Grands Prix, 9 wins (Hungarian GP 1993, Belgian GP 1993, Italian GP 1993, Spanish GP 1994, British GP 1994, Belgian GP 1994, Italian GP 1994, Portuguese GP 1994, Japanese GP 1994) * No championship title (best result – 2nd overall 1994)*

Graham Hill

Nationality: British
Born: 1939

see Legends of the Track pp 112–13

Phil Hill

Nationality: American
Born: 1927

Phil was the first American to make much of an impact in the European-centred Formula One of the late 1950s. After earning his spurs in sports car races he came to Europe in 1954 to race at Le Mans. Driving a privately entered Ferrari back in the USA in 1955, he went well enough to attract the attention of Enzo Ferrari and was signed up for a programme of European races in 1956. He moved to Ferrari's Formula One squad in 1958, being given his first full season in 1959, struggling with one of the old front-engined Ferraris. The first of his three Grand Prix wins came in 1960 at Monza, but 1961 was to be his best year as he took his "Sharknose" Ferrari to two wins which was enough to give him the title after the death of team-mate Wolfgang von Trips in the penultimate race. His Grand Prix career saw him run with Ferrari again in 1962, but then move on to less successful times at ATS and Cooper before he returned to sports cars. However, ill health forced Phil to retire in 1967.

CAREER RECORD ** 48 Grands Prix, 3 wins (Italian GP 1960, Belgian GP 1961, Italian GP 1961) * World Champion 1961*

Denny Hulme

Nationality: New Zealander
Born: 1936
Died: 1992

Known as "The Bear" for his taciturn manner and fast temper, Denny was revered by those close to him. He started racing at the age of 20 in 1956, hill climbing an MG TF. Success followed and he quit New Zealand for Europe in 1960 to race in Formula Junior. He went to work at Jack Brabham's garage in 1961, and so started a long relationship with his fellow Antipodean. Denny finished second to Brabham in the 1964 Formula Two series, and he joined his boss's Formula One team for 1965. Two solid seasons were followed by his best-ever year – 1967 – in which he won twice and claimed the World Championship. He joined compatriot Bruce McLaren's team for 1968 and stayed there until he retired from Formula One seven years later, scoring six more wins. During this time Denny also raced with huge success in CanAm sports cars. He returned to racing, only for fun, in the 1990s and died of a heart attack while competing in Australia's famous Bathurst touring car race.

CAREER RECORD

** 112 Grands Prix, 8 wins (Monaco GP 1967, German GP 1967, Italian GP 1968, Canadian GP 1968, Mexican GP 1969, South African GP 1972, Swedish GP 1973, Argentinian GP 1974) * World Champion 1967*

James Hunt

Nationality: British
Born: 1947
Died: 1993

James was tempestuous in his early years, leaving a trail of crashed cars behind him when he raced Minis and then in Formula Three. However, his talent was spotted and the wealthy Lord Hesketh helped "Hunt the Shunt" into Formula Two and then into Formula One with an off-the-peg March in 1973. James soon rattled the regulars by chasing Ronnie Peterson home for second place in the US Grand Prix. That vital first win came in Holland in 1975 and James resembled a latter-day Mike Hawthorn, with the

Marlboro
TEXACO
James Hunt

British hero *James Hunt made Formula One popular in the 1970s*

newspapers following his every move both on and off the track, his wooing of beautiful women and his anti-establishment antics. While this irked James, it helped Formula One gain a popular image in Britain. This was rewarded in 1976 when he moved to McLaren, scored six wins and claimed the title in dramatic fashion amid a downpour in the final race, in Japan. Friend and rival Niki Lauda pulled into the pits and said it was too dangerous to race. James stayed out and clinched the third place he needed to overhaul the Austrian's points tally. He won three more times, then drove for Wolf in 1979 and became disenchanted, retiring mid-season. He then moved into the commentary box as a perfect foil for the effervescent Murray Walker. His death, less than a year after Denny Hulme, also of a heart attack, sent a shock wave through the racing world.

CAREER RECORD

** 92 Grands Prix, 10 wins (Dutch GP 1975, Spanish GP 1976, French GP 1976, German GP 1976, Dutch GP 1976, Canadian GP 1976, US GP 1976, British GP 1977, US GP 1977, Japanese GP 1976) * World Champion 1976*

Belgian artist *Jacky Ickx never achieved the ultimate accolade.*

Jacky Ickx

Nationality: Belgian
Born: 1945

Jacky made his competition debut on motorcycles, much success coming when he was a teenager. National Service delayed his four-wheeled debut until 1965 when he started in saloons, twice winning the Spa 24 Hours. But he caught the eye of Formula One team boss Ken Tyrrell who put him into his Formula Three team. Jacky was fast straight away, but his Matra lacked reliability. Tyrrell promoted him to Formula Two for 1966, with some success. He won three races in 1967, even having the audacity to qualify third for the German Grand Prix when pitched in against the more powerful Formula One cars. Fourth place in this race ensured that he was promoted to Formula One for 1968, with Ferrari. Showing his skill, he was fourth overall in his first season, winning the French Grand Prix for good measure. In 1969 he moved to Brabham and won twice more, also winning the Le Mans 24 Hours, yet there was nothing he could do to keep the title from Jackie Stewart. Back with Ferrari in 1970, he won three times, but was runner-up again. Three more years with Ferrari became ever more frustrating as the Italian cars were clearly no match for the cars from Tyrrell and Lotus. So he joined for 1974, just as the team's fortunes started to slide, and those of Ferrari to improve. The twilight of his Formula One career was spent with Williams, Ensign and Ligier, and all were disappointing, so perhaps this is why Jacky draws so much satisfaction from his record tally of six wins in the Le Mans 24 Hours. He has since been involved with the modernization of Spa to a now permanent racing facility that is the jewel in Formula One's crown.

CAREER RECORD

** 116 Grands Prix, 8 wins (French GP 1968, German GP 1969, Canadian GP 1969, Austrian GP 1970, Canadian GP 1970, Mexican GP 1970, Dutch GP 1971, German GP 1972) * No championship title (best result – 2nd overall 1969 and 1970)*

Innes Ireland

Nationality: British
Born: 1930
Died: 1993

One of the true characters of British motor racing, Innes was a great party-goer and raconteur, and the strictures of contemporary Formula One were anathema to him. He did not start racing until he was 26 when he bought a Lotus XI sports car with which to participate. Strong form through 1957 and 1958 led to Lotus boss Colin Chapman signing Innes for his 1959 Formula One line-up. Although Innes showed good speed, the Lotus 16 was frequently breaking down. In 1960, with the arrival of the Lotus 18, all looked to be going Innes's way in the Argentinian season-opener and he was leading comfortably, but then the gear linkage broke. Two second places were the best he could manage. Despite breaking a leg at Monaco in 1961, it all came good in the last race of the year when Innes won at Watkins Glen. But then came the blow: Chapman dropped him from the team to make way for young hotshot Jim Clark. Innes was furious. He raced a privately entered Lotus in 1962 without much in the way of results. Driving for the British Racing Partnership in 1963 and 1964, he had little chance of success in the team's own BRP chassis. His final shot was with a Reg Parnell Racing Lotus in 1965, but this came to nought and Innes drifted away to race sports cars. He died of cancer shortly after taking over the helm of the British Racing Drivers' Club.

CAREER RECORD

** 50 Grands Prix, 1 win (US GP 1961) * No championship title (best result – 4th overall 1960)*

Eddie Irvine

Nationality: British
Born: 1965

It is incredible how many like-minded drivers are paired together in this chapter by alphabetical order. Like Innes, Eddie has always been a character since the day he first raced in Formula Ford. And one Ayrton Senna took exception to this cocky Ulsterman on his Grand Prix debut, in Japan in 1993. Senna felt that Eddie was a danger to all, for when he lapped Eddie, Eddie immediately took him back. A famous argument and a punch from Senna followed. However, there can be no denying that Eddie is quick. British Formula Ford champion in the mid-1980s, Eddie shone in Formula Three in 1988 and then moved up to Formula 3000 with Pacific Racing in 1989. Picked up by Eddie Jordan for 1990, he won at Hockenheim and ended up third overall. With no Formula One drive in the offing, Eddie raced sports cars and Formula 3000 in Japan for the next three seasons, before Jordan invited him to make that Formula One debut at Suzuka, where he claimed sixth place. In 1994 he was teamed with Rubens Barrichello at Jordan, but he suffered in the title race by being involved in a huge accident in the opening round that saw him banned for a race. His attitude at the hearing led to this ban being extended to three races. However, once back aboard, he ran strongly, often outpacing his Brazilian team-mate.

CAREER RECORD

** 15 Grands Prix, no wins (best result – 4th European GP 1994) * No championship title (best result – 14th overall 1994)*

Turbo pioneer *Jean-Pierre Jabouille was the first man to race a turbo.*

J

Jean-Pierre Jabouille

Nationality: French
Born: 1942

Jean-Pierre earned himself a permanent place in Formula One history when he scored the first victory for a turbocharged car, and the fact that it was at the wheel of a Renault in the French Grand Prix, in 1979, also guaranteed that the occasion was one of nationalistic fervour. That the popular Frenchman should have the honour of taking the first turbo victory was appropriate, for it was he who had had to pilot the hopelessly unreliable Renault turbo in its first steps in Formula One in 1977. After a successful career in Formula Two, he had made his Formula One debut in a one-off drive for Tyrrell in the 1975 French Grand Prix. However, he would only taste success at Renault, for whom he began his full-time Grand Prix career in 1977, after being involved in the turbo car's development from the very beginning. He won one further Grand Prix, in Austria in 1980, before breaking a leg in that year's Canadian race. He returned with Ligier in 1981 but, still not fully fit, he retired after just a few races. Jean-Pierre raced in Peugeot's sports car team in the early 1990s, before being placed in charge of the French manufacturer's motor sport programme.

CAREER RECORD

** 49 Grands Prix, 2 wins (French GP 1979, Austrian GP 1980) * No championship title (best result – 8th overall 1980)*

Jean-Pierre Jarier

Nationality: French
Born: 1946

Jean-Pierre raced in 134 Grands Prix during 1973–83 but, despite being both fast and brave, he never won one. He was at his best for the Shadow team in the mid-1970s, and lost the 1975 Brazilian Grand Prix only when a fuel-metering unit forced him to retire. Similarly, when a chance to revive his career came with Lotus in 1978, he was dominating the Canadian Grand Prix before brake problems intervened. Early in his career he had a reputation for wildness, but he brought himself under control and won the Formula Two title for the works March-BMW team in 1973, the year when he made his Formula One debut, also for March, before moving to Shadow. After 1978 his career began slowly to go downhill. Two years with Tyrrell provided him no breakthrough and, after a disastrous time with Osella and then Ligier in the early 1980s, Formula One left him behind at the end of 1983. He revived his fortunes in the mid-1990s, racing sports cars.

CAREER RECORD

** 134 Grands Prix. No wins (best result – 3rd Monaco GP 1974, South African GP 1979, British GP 1979)* No championship title (best result – 10th overall 1979 and 1980)*

Stefan Johansson

Nationality: Swedish
Born: 1956

After winning the British Formula Three Championship in 1979 and being a leading figure in Formula Two in the early 1980s, the genial and popular Swede clearly had Formula One potential, but it was not until mid-1983 that he made his debut, with the fledgling Spirit-Honda team. Honda switched its engine to Williams in 1984, and Stefan had to put up with a few guest drives for Tyrrell and Toleman, for whom he looked set to be the number one driver in 1985 before a dispute over tyres left him without a drive. Ferrari provided him with a lifeline, hiring Stefan to replace René Arnoux. The Swede earned two second places in 1985, and impressed enough to be

Chance missed *Stefan Johansson had the breaks, but not the wins.*

All or nothing *Jean-Pierre Janier didn't realize his Formual One potential.*

kept on for 1986, when a succession of mechanical problems and bad luck led to him being replaced by Gerhard Berger for 1987. Johansson went to McLaren, but not only was he outpaced by Alain Prost, he was only a stopgap before Ayrton Senna joined the team in 1988. Stefan left Formula One at the end of 1991 and now races in Indy Cars.

CAREER RECORD

** 79 Grands Prix, no wins (best result – 2nd Canadian GP 1985, US GP 1985, Belgian GP 1987)* No championship title (best result – 5th overall 1986)*

Alan Jones

Nationality: Australian
Born: 1946

Alan was the driver with whom the Williams team first made its breakthrough into the Formula One front line and the man who won the team its first World Championship. Ever since his father, Stan, raced in Australia in the 1950s, young Alan had decided he wanted to be world champion. But it was a tough road to Formula One success. He finally made his Grand Prix debut in 1975, at the wheel of a private Hesketh, and soon earned himself a reputation as a hard-trying charger – but certainly no natural, although he did score a fine victory in the 1977 Austrian Grand Prix for Shadow. But it was at Williams where his career really took off. Some excellent showings in 1978 were the precursor to true success in 1979, when he won four Grands Prix in Patrick Head's superb ground-effect FW07, and only early-season unreliability prevented an assault on the World Championship. No such mistakes were made in 1980, when six wins helped him storm to a title that he might well have retained in 1981 had it not been for more unreliability. He retired at the end of 1981, made a brief return for Arrows in 1983, and a full-time one with the Haas Lola team in late 1985 and 1986. But the car was a disappointment, and Alan and retired from Formula One at the end of the year.

CAREER RECORD

** 116 Grands Prix, 12 wins (Austrian GP 1977, German GP 1979, Austrian GP 1979, Dutch GP 1979, Canadian GP 1979, Argentinian GP 1980, French GP 1980, British GP 1980, Canadian GP 1980, US East GP 1980, US West GP 1981, Las Vegas GP 1981)* World Champion 1980*

Second bite *Alan Jones returned unsuccessfully to Formula One in 1985–86.*

K

Ukyo Katayama

Nationality: Japanese
Born: 1963

The best Grand Prix driver yet to come out of Japan, Katayama for some time looked out of his depth in Formula One, but some stirring performances in 1994 with Tyrrell, when he usually had the measure of his highly rated team-mate Mark Blundell, gave the lie to that. Ukyo won junior single-seater titles in Japan in 1983–84 and then came to Europe to race in Formula Renault and Formula Three in 1986 and 1987. From 1988 he went back to Japan to race in Formula 3000, and won the title in 1991, and the following year made his Formula One debut with Larrousse, where he showed well against Bertrand Gachot. A terrible 1993 followed and many thought his diminutive physique meant he would never be strong enough to drive a modern Formula One car. But in 1994 it became clear that a strong talent and natural speed were allied to what was now his famously sunny personality and sense of humour.

Japan's best *Ukyo Katayama has surprised many Europeans.*

CAREER RECORD

** 46 Grands Prix, no wins (best result – 5th Brazilian GP 1994, San Marino GP 1994) * No championship title (best result – 17th overall 1994)*

Rupert Keegan

Nationality: British
Born: 1955

Rupert was a fun-loving playboy who also possessed a fair amount of talent. He won the British Formula Three Championship in 1976 and graduated to Formula One the following year. The Hesketh he drove was one of the worst cars of the year, but to his credit Rupert managed to qualify for every race he entered. A season with the ailing Surtees team in 1978 was less successful, and he had to step back to win the British Formula One series in 1979. His return to Formula One in 1980 with a RAM Williams and briefly in 1982 with March brought little reward.

CAREER RECORD

** 25 Grands Prix, no wins (best result – 7th Austrian GP 1977)* No championship title*

Karl Kling

Nationality: German
Born: 1910

Karl Kling drove as an amateur before the Second World War and then raced sports cars until the start of the 1950s when success in Formula Two led to him being invited into the Mercedes sports car and Formula One teams. He won the Carrera PanAmericana sports car race in

RICARD

1952, and briefly drove for Alfa-Romeo in 1953, before rejoining Mercedes when it re-entered Formula One in 1954. Kling was overshadowed by Juan Manuel Fangio and slipped further behind in 1955, when Stirling Moss joined the team. He took up a management position with Mercedes in 1955.

CAREER RECORD

** 11 Grands Prix, no wins (best result – 2nd French GP 1954) * No championship title (best result – 5th overall 1954)*

Forced to touring cars *Nicola Larini is a driver whose talent deserves a full-time ride in Formula One.*

L

Jacques Laffite

Nationality: French
Born: 1943

Jacques' impish sense of humour and irreverence, allied to a considerable talent behind the wheel of a Formula One car, brightened the Grand Prix scene for over ten years during the 1970s and 1980s. Having won the French Formula Three title and the European Formula Two Championship in the early 1970s, Jacques made his Grand Prix debut for the Williams team in 1974. He and team boss Frank Williams got on well, and Jacques helped keep the team afloat by taking a timely second place in the German Grand Prix in 1975. The following year he joined the new Ligier team and they developed well together, until finally tasting victory in 1979 when the team switched from Matra V12 power to a Cosworth V8. Jacques and the new JS11 won the first two races of the season, but he did not win again until mid-1980. A return to Matra power in 1981 saw Jacques take two wins and make a late-season challenge for the World Championship, but after a dreadful 1982 he left to drive for Williams in 1983–84. Generally, though, he was overshadowed in the uncompetitive cars by team-mate Keke Rosberg, and he returned to Ligier in 1985 (pictured on left). The cars were quick, and Jacques went with them all the way, scoring a number of podium finishes and briefly leading the Detroit Grand Prix in 1986. However, an accident at the British Grand Prix the same year broke his legs and ended his Formula One career.

CAREER RECORD

** 176 Grands Prix, 6 wins (Swedish GP 1977, Argentinian GP 1979, Brazilian GP 1979, German GP 1980, Austrian GP 1981, Canadian GP 1981) * No championship title (best result – 4th overall 1979, 1980 and 1981)*

Jan Lammers

Nationality: Dutch
Born: 1956

The diminutive Dutchman progressed through the single-seater ranks in the 1970s, after winning the Dutch Touring Car Championship in 1973, his first year in racing. He won the 1978 European Formula Three Championship, and moved into Formula One in 1979 with the Shadow team, as team-mate to Elio de Angelis. But the cars were uncompetitive, and later spells with ATS, Ensign and Theodore did little to establish him in Formula One. Through the 1980s Jan established himself as a sports car ace. He returned briefly to Grand Prix racing in a March at the end of 1992, but plans for 1993 were thwarted when the financially troubled team was forced to close its doors.

CAREER RECORD

** 23 Grands Prix, no wins (best result – 9th Canadian GP 1979)* No championship title*

Pedro Lamy

Nationality: Portuguese
Born: 1972

Pedro is feted in his home country as a superstar, but it is not clear whether he will be a central feature in Formula One in the coming years after a terrible accident at Silverstone in 1994 broke both his knees. He swept the board in the junior formulae, winning the Vauxhall Euroseries in 1991, the German Formula Three title in 1992 before coming a close second in International Formula 3000 in 1993. Substantial backing from Portugal led to a few outings in an uncompetitive Lotus at the end of 1993, when he ran impressively close to team-mate Johnny Herbert. A full season would have followed in 1994 were it not for the Silverstone incident, when his Lotus flew into a spectator area during testing having lost its rear wing.

CAREER RECORD

** 8 Grands Prix, no wins (best result – 8th Pacific GP 1994) * No championship title*

Nicola Larini

Nationality: Italian
Born: 1964

Nicola dominated the Italian junior formulae in the mid-1980s, taking the Italian Formula Three title with Coloni in 1986, before moving up to Formula One with the team at the end of 1987. He switched to Osella in 1988–89, when some brilliant drives in uncompetitive machinery earned him a seat at Ligier for 1990. Unfortunately, neither this car nor the Lamborghini he drove in 1991 were competitive, and he left Formula One for touring cars in 1992. Nicola proved he was a top-class driver by winning the Italian title with Alfa-Romeo in 1992, and then going on to dominate the highly competitive German Championship for the marque in 1993. As the Ferrari Formula One team's test driver he stepped in to replace an injured Jean Alesi in early 1994, when he finished second in the ill-fated San Marino Grand Prix, but Alesi's return saw Nicola go back to touring cars.

CAREER RECORD

** 44 Grands Prix, no wins (best result – 2nd San Marino GP 1994) * No championship title (best result– 14th overall 1994)*

Niki Lauda

Nationality: Austrian
Born: 1949

see Legends of the Track pp 114–15

JJ Lehto

Nationality: Finnish
Born: 1966

Great success was forecast for JJ (real name Jyrki Jarvilehto) who had won the European, Scandinavian and Finnish Formula Ford 1600 titles by 1986. When he came to Britain in 1987 he dominated the national and European Formula Ford 2000 scene before winning the very closely fought British Formula Three Championship in 1988. Formula 3000 was a less fruitful hunting ground, but he established a respected and worthwhile Formula One reputation with drives at Onyx, Dallara and Sauber between 1989 and 1993 before being given the big chance with a seat at Benetton in 1994. Sadly, JJ broke his neck in a pre-season testing accident and, although he was close to the pace of team-mate and eventual world champion, Michael Schumacher, on his first race back, the deaths of Ayrton Senna and Roland Ratzenberger affected him deeply, and when it was clear that his neck was still not completely healed Benetton dropped him. With a drive in the German Touring Car Championship in 1995, it now seems as if Formula One has passed him by.

Points scorer *Lella Lombardi is the only female driver ever to finish in the top six.*

CAREER RECORD

** 60 Grands Prix, no wins (best result – 3rd San Marino GP 1991) * No championship title (12th overall 1991)*

Stewart Lewis-Evans

Nationality: British
Born: 1930
Died: 1958

The statistics of Lewis-Evans's career do not add up to much, but that belies a rare and delicate talent. This small, frail man was a leading exponent of Formula Three for five seasons before being given his Formula One chance by Connaught at the end of 1956. After showing well in the Connaught early in 1957, he was signed by Vanwall to partner its two stars, Stirling Moss and Tony Brooks. He put in some brilliant performances, but in World Championship races, although his flair and finesse were evident, he had only a fifth place at Pescara by the end of the year. Nevertheless, he won huge admiration from his team-mates, and played a crucial role in helping Vanwall win the first Constructors' title, in 1958. He appeared on the threshold of a splendid career, but he crashed heavily in the final, Moroccan, Grand Prix of 1958, and suffered severe burns in the ensuing fire. He died six days after the accident.

CAREER RECORD

** 14 Grands Prix, no wins (best result – 3rd Belgian GP 1958, Portuguese GP 1958) * No championship title (best result – 9th overall 1958)*

Guy Ligier

Nationality: French
Born: 1930

Guy did not start motor racing until he was in his 30s, having previously had a distinguished career in rugby. He had some top-six finishes in Formula Two in 1964 and moved into Formula One in 1966. Having broken his kneecap in mid-season, he returned in 1967, when he replaced his Cooper-Maserati with a more competitive Brabham, and scored his only point at the Nurburgring. Guy went back to Formula Two in 1968, but after the death of close friend Jo Schlesser he quit, only to return the following year. He started building sports cars in 1970, and that led to a Formula One team being set up in 1976. There have been brief periods when Ligiers have been competitive, but they generally failed to make the most of their resources. Ligier sold most of his shareholding in the team in 1992–93.

CAREER RECORD

** 12 Grands Prix, no wins (best result – 6th German GP 1967) * No championship title (best result – 19th overall 1967)*

Lella Lombardi

Nationality: Italian
Born: 1943
Died: 1992

The only woman to date to finish in the top six in a Grand Prix, in Spain in 1975. Spells in Formula Monza and Formula Three in Italy led to a Formula 5000 programme in 1974, in which she poked her critics in the eye by finishing fourth in the championship, and that earned her a full season in Formula One in a March in 1975, when she also finished seventh in the German Grand Prix. Lella then dropped out of Formula One, but continued her career in sports cars. She died of cancer in 1992.

CAREER RECORD

** 12 Grands Prix, no wins (best result – 6th Spanish GP 1975) * No championship title (best result – 21st overall 1975)*

John Love

Nationality: Rhodesian
Born: 1924

He never made it in Formula One in Europe. In 1964 however, he won the first of his six South African Formula One titles, and although he regularly raced in the country's World Championship Grand Prix, success eluded him. He came closest in 1967, when only a precautionary late pit stop for fuel lost him the race.

CAREER RECORD

** 9 Grands Prix, no wins (best result – 2nd South African GP 1967) * No championship title (best result – 11th overall 1967)*

Brett Lunger

Nationality: American
Born: 1945

The heir to the wealthy DuPont family, Brett's early racing career was interrupted by a spell in Vietnam. He resumed in Formula 5000 in 1971, where he raced until 1975, when he became James Hunt's team-mate at Hesketh. He switched to Surtees in 1976, and drove a private McLaren in 1977–78, with minimal impact.

CAREER RECORD

** 34 Grands Prix, no wins (best result – 7th Belgian GP 1977) * No championship title*

M

Bruce McLaren

Nationality: New Zealander
Born: 1937
Died: 1970

A talented driver and the man who established what is now the most successful Grand Prix team of all time, Bruce arrived on the Formula One scene in 1959 with a bang, putting in a series of assured performances with Cooper before winning the final Grand Prix of the year, the race in which his team-mate Jack Brabham clinched his first world title. After winning the opening race of 1960, McLaren slipped into a supporting role to Brabham, before becoming team leader in 1961 when Brabham left. But after several frustrating seasons, which had been briefly enlivened by victory in the Monaco Grand Prix of 1962, Bruce went off to form his own team in 1964, a move which inevitably led to a split with Cooper, at the end of 1965. In partnership with abrasive American Teddy Mayer, tolerant, popular McLaren built his company up into a successful, professional outfit with a reputation for technical excellence. In 1968 he enticed his friend Denny Hulme, the reigning world champion, to join the team and, while Hulme set the pace in Formula One, McLaren-Chevrolet cars dominated the American CanAm sports car series for the rest of the decade. Bruce continued to race in Formula One, and occasionally put in a performance of controlled brilliance, winning the 1968 Belgian Grand Prix, and dominating the Race of Champions the same year. But more than anything he had a reputation for consistency and safety, which made it tragically ironic that he should die in an accident while testing one of his CanAm cars at Goodwood in 1970. His name, though, would live on in the team which was to take an indelible place in Grand Prix history.

Founding father *Bruce McLaren gave his name to the team.*

CAREER RECORD

** 103 Grands Prix, 4 wins (US GP, 1959, Argentinian GP 1960, Monaco GP 1962, Belgian GP 1968) * No championship title (best result – 2nd overall 1960)*

Tony Maggs

Nationality: South African
Born: 1937

Tony came to the notice of the racing world in 1961 when, driving Ken Tyrrell's Cooper-Austin, he shared the European Formula Junior Championship with Jo Schlesser. He was snapped up by the Cooper Grand Prix team for 1962–63 and, although he finished second in the French Grand Prix both years, he was replaced by Phil Hill for 1964, and switched to BRM. He drove his last Grand Prix in South Africa in 1965, and raced in sports cars for the rest of the year until he killed a boy in a crash and was so upset that he quit.

CAREER RECORD

** 25 Grands Prix, no wins (best result – 2nd French GP 1962, French GP 1963) * No championship title (best result – 7th overall 1962)*

Umberto Maglioli

Nationality: Italian
Born: 1928

An accomplished sports car driver for nearly 20 years, Umberto only occasionally drove in Grands Prix as a junior driver for Ferrari in the mid-1950s, followed by three brief appearances for Maserati in 1956. Leg injuries interrupted his career after a crash at the Salzburgring, but he recovered and won the 1959 Sebring 12 Hours, a race he managed to win again in 1964. His final moment of glory was winning the 1968 Targa Florio driving a Porsche.

CAREER RECORD

** 10 Grands Prix, no wins (best result – 3rd Italian GP 1954, Argentinian GP 1955) * No championship title (best result – 19th overall 1954)*

Nigel Mansell

Nationality: British
Born: 1953

see Legends of the Track pp 116–17

Willy Mairesse

Nationality: Belgian
Born: 1928
Died: 1969

Willy was famous for his determination, but also for lurid accidents. Ferrari signed him in 1960 after he had some sports car success in 1959, and he flitted in and out of Formula One for the next two years, and was then signed up as number two to John Surtees in 1963. Burned badly at Le Mans when fuel ignited in the car, he ended his Grand Prix career after crashing heavily out of the German Grand Prix. Willy raced in sports cars until 1968, when he crashed in a Ford GT40 at Le Mans after a door flew open, and he suffered severe head injuries. He was ill for a year and, as he realized there was no place for him in racing any more, he committed suicide in 1968.

CAREER RECORD

** 12 Grands Prix, no wins (best result – 4th Italian GP 1962) * No championship title (best result – 14th overall 1962)*

Robert Manzon

Nationality: French
Born: 1917

He was a mainstay of the Gordini team in the early 1950s, but real success deserted him in an era dominated by Maserati, Ferrari and then Mercedes. However, there were excellent performances, including third places in the 1953 Belgian Grand Prix and at Reims in 1954. Robert took a couple of non-championship wins, but retired at the end of 1956.

CAREER RECORD

** 28 Grands Prix, no wins (best result – 3rd Belgian GP 1952, French GP 1954) * No championship title (best result – 6th overall 1952)*

Onofre Marimon

Nationality: Argentinian
Born: 1932
Died: 1954

A protégé of Fangio, Onofre joined the works Maserati team in 1954 after showing great promise in 1953. He stood in for Fangio in some early-season non-championship races, and when Fangio left to join Mercedes he found himself effectively leading the team. He finished an excellent third in the British Grand Prix, ahead of Fangio, and seemed destined for great things, but he was killed instantly in a crash at the Nurburgring during practice for the German Grand Prix.

CAREER RECORD

** 11 Grands Prix, no wins (best result – 3rd Belgian GP 1953, British GP 1954)*
** No championship title (best result – 11th overall 1953)*

Pierluigi Martini

Nationality: Italian
Born: 1961

Perennially underrated, Pierluigi has become a respected member of the Grand Prix fraternity. After winning the European Formula Three title in 1983 and failing to qualify a Toleman at the 1984 Italian Grand Prix, the inexperienced Martini suffered an appalling debut season in Formula One with the uncompetitive Minardi-Motori Moderni team. But a return to Formula 3000 saw him come back in 1988 a changed man, and in 1989 Formula One he was at his best, briefly leading the Portuguese Grand Prix and qualifying an amazing third in Australia. Since then he has been consigned to the midfield, alternating between Minardi and Scuderia Italia. He missed the first half of 1993, when dropped by Scuderia Italia, but returned with Minardi, for which he has driven consistently and well ever since.

CAREER RECORD

* 110 Grands Prix, no wins (best result – 5th British GP 1989, Portuguese GP 1989, Spanish GP 1994, French GP 1994)
* No championship title (best result – 11th overall 1991)

Mr Consistency *Pierluigi Martini has become a Formula One fixture.*

Jochen Mass

Nationality: German
Born: 1946

Jochen graduated to Formula One after some strong showings in Formula Two, but was struck by bad luck in 1974 when he drove for Surtees, which he eventually quit to join McLaren. He was an excellent number two to Emerson Fittipaldi, winning the Spanish Grand Prix in 1975, but dropped into a subordinate role, especially after James Hunt's arrival in 1976, when Mass could not match the Englishman's pace on the track. He moved to ATS in 1978, but broke a leg in a test at Silverstone. He drove for Arrows in 1979–80, had a year off in 1981 and returned for an uncompetitive season with March in 1982, after which he concentrated on sports cars, winning Le Mans for Mercedes in 1989. The following year he acted as tutor to the company's young stars before retiring at the end of 1991.

CAREER RECORD

** 105 Grands Prix, 1 win (Spanish GP 1975)*
** No championship title (best result –7th overall 1975)*

Arturo Merzario

Nationality: Italian
Born: 1943

Arturo made his name in small sports cars, and then joined the Ferrari team in 1970. By 1972 he had put in enough promising performances to be promoted to the Grand Prix team mid-season. His feistiness served him well through Ferrari's nadir in 1973. It also appealed to Frank Williams, who signed Arturo in 1974. He took a couple of good points finishes in 1975, but things did not go well the following year, and he quit mid-season. He drove a works March in 1976, and ran his own private March in 1977 before setting up his own team in 1978. The car, however, was a disaster, which struggled to qualify, and wound up his Formula One career and most of his money.

CAREER RECORD

** 57 Grands Prix, no wins (best result – 4th Brazilian GP 1973, South African GP 1973, Italian GP 1974) * No championship title (best result – 12th overall 1973)*

Roberto Mieres

Nationality: Argentinian
Born: 1924

Roberto won the Argentine sports car championship in 1950, which led to him being invited to join Juan Manuel Fangio and Froilan Gonzalez on a trip to Europe, where he took fourth place in the Geneva Grand Prix. His career took off with three drives for the Gordini factory team in 1953, and he impressed the Maserati factory team so much with his performances in a private 250F in 1954 that they drafted him into the factory team for 1955, when he finished forth in the Swiss and Spanish Grands Prix. He returned home to Argentina at the end of the year prompted by a desire to look afterhis business interests.

CAREER RECORD

** 17 Grands Prix, no wins (best result – 4th Swiss GP 1954, Spanish GP 1954, Dutch GP 1955) * No championship title (best result – 8th overall 1954 and 1955)*

John Miles

Nationality: British
Born: 1943

The son of actor Lord Miles, John began his motor racing career with an extremely successful period in Lotus sports cars during 1966–68. After a brief fling with Formula Two in 1969, he was entrusted by Lotus boss Colin Chapman with the development of the four-wheel drive Lotus 63. He became Jochen Rindt's number two in 1970 after Graham Hill broke both his legs in an accident, but as an engineer was nervous of the fragility of the Lotus 72, and was dropped after Rindt's death in the Italian Grand Prix, signalling the end of his Formula One career.

CAREER RECORD

** 12 Grands Prix, no wins (best result – 5th South African GP 1970) * No championship title (best result – 19th overall 1970)*

Stefano Modena

Nationality: Italian
Born: 1963

A splendid year in Formula Three, when he impressed the Grand Prix community in the support race to the Monaco Grand Prix in 1986, marked him as a man to watch, and as he assuredly went about winning the Formula 3000 title at his first attempt in 1987, he seemed set for stardom.

Shooting star *Stefano Modena shone bright then faded from Formula One.*

But his first three years in Formula One were with back-of-the-grid teams, and it was not until he joined Tyrrell-Honda in 1991 that his ability occasionally showed. However the car was not as good as expected and, after a splendid performance at Monaco when he qualified second to Ayrton Senna, and a superb second in the next race, at Montreal, Stefano became dispirited by the car's problems and faded badly. He was signed to drive for Jordan in 1992, but the project dramatically failed to gel, and Stefano's Formula One career came to an end. He has raced in touring cars since and his talent is blossoming again.

CAREER RECORD

** 70 Grands Prix, no wins (best result – 2nd Canadian GP 1991) * No championship title (best result – 8th overall 1991)*

Gianni Morbidelli

Nationality: Italian
Born: 1968

Gianni raced in karts for five years before moving up to Italian Formula Three in 1987. A propensity for accidents thwarted him until 1989, when he claimed the crown and that earned him a testing contract with Ferrari. He made a brief Grand Prix debut in Brazil in 1990 as a stand-in for Emanuele Pirro in a Dallara, and then replaced Paolo Barilla at Minardi for the final two races of the year after a year in Formula 3000. He stayed on at Minardi with Ferrari power in 1991 and, although the car failed to live up to expectations, he impressed enough to be drafted in to replace the fired Alain Prost at the Australian Grand Prix, where he scored a half-point for sixth place. An unsuccessful year with Minardi followed, after which Formula One left him behind for a year, and he raced in Italian touring cars before returning to put in some impressive performances with Arrows in 1994.

Mr Keen *Gianni Morbidelli has used his dogged determination to get ahead*

CAREER RECORD

** 50 Grands Prix, no wins (best result – 5th German GP 1994) * No championship title (best result – 22nd overall 1994)*

Roberto Moreno

Nationality: Brazilian
Born: 1959

Roberto's Formula One career was almost over before it started when he failed to qualify a Lotus at the 1982 Dutch Grand Prix. He was to get another chance, but that race handicapped him for a number of years. After finishing second to team-mate Mike Thackwell in the 1984 European Formula Two Championship, Roberto moved to Indy Cars. A return to Europe in 1987 saw him race in Formula 3000 and do a handful of Grands Prix for the fledgling AGS team. He stayed in Formula 3000 the following year and won the title impressively. Ferrari awarded him a testing contract and he joined Coloni, and then Eurobrun, before being given his big break at the end of 1990 at Benetton alongside Nelson Piquet and replacing the injured Alessandro Nannini. A second place behind Piquet at the Japanese Grand Prix ensured he was kept on for the following year, but he was kicked out of the team (ironically, after scoring his best result of the year, a fourth at the Belgian Grand Prix), as Benetton distastefully grabbed Michael Schumacher. A season with the hapless Andrea Moda outfit in 1992 was far less than his talents deserved.

CAREER RECORD

** 25 Grands Prix, no wins (best result – 2nd Japanese GP 1990) * No championship title (best result – 10th overall 1990 and 1991)*

Honda's man *Satoru Nakajima arrived in Formula One with Honda's engines.*

Stirling Moss

Nationality: British
Born: 1929
see Legends of the Track pp 118–19

CAREER RECORD

** 24 Grands Prix, 1 win (Argentinian GP 1956) * No championship title (best result – 3rd overall 1957)*

Luigi Musso

Nationality: Italian
Born: 1924
Died: 1958

Luigi dominated sports car racing in Italy in the early 1950s before buying a Maserati 250F, winning the non-championship Pescara Grand Prix and finishing second in the Spanish Grand Prix in 1954. A string of good results in 1955 saw him join Ferrari for 1956, and he won his first race, the Argentinian Grand Prix, sharing his Lancia-Ferrari with Juan Manuel Fangio. In 1957 he won the non-championship Marne Grand Prix, but was by now struggling to keep pace with team-mate Mike Hawthorn and Peter Collins. Chasing them at Reims, he ran wide on a long, fast corner, and the car flipped in a ditch. The unfortunate Luigi was killed on the spot.

N

Satoru Nakajima

Nationality: Japanese
Born: 1953

Japan's first regular Grand Prix driver, Satoru was Honda's representative on the grid in the late 1980s. After a glittering career in Japan, he moved up to Formula One and was made Ayrton Senna's team-mate at Lotus in 1987, when the team first ran Honda engines. Miles off Senna's pace, Satoru ran much closer to Nelson Piquet in the team in 1988, and in 1989 scored his best Formula

OMP

One result to take fourth in the torrential rains of Adelaide. He switched to Tyrrell for the next two seasons, before finally bowing out at the end of 1991. Since then, he has run a team in both Japanese Formula 3000 and Formula Three, concentrating on raising the next generation of Japanese drivers.

CAREER RECORD

** 74 Grands Prix, no wins (best result – 4th British GP 1987, Australian GP 1989) * No championship title (best result – 11th overall 1987)*

Alessandro Nannini

Nationality: Italian
Born: 1959

His Formula One career was cut short when his arm was severed in a helicopter accident. Micro-surgery reattached the limb, and Alessandro is now a race-winner in the German Touring Car Championship. Given his chance in Formula One with Minardi, he soon proved more than a match for his nominal team leader, Andrea de Cesaris, before receiving long-overdue reward by promotion to the Benetton-Ford team in 1988 (pictured on left), where he generally outpaced Thierry Boutsen. The genial Italian won the 1989 Japanese Grand Prix when Ayrton Senna was disqualified and, after being initially outpaced by Nelson Piquet in 1990, really came of age in the second part of the season. He was narrowly beaten by Senna in Germany, after a brilliant tactical drive, and lost the Hungarian Grand Prix only after being elbowed out of the way by Senna in the closing stages. But then, after he finished third in the Spanish race, came the helicopter accident. It is to the delight of the motor racing world that he has been able to continue in touring cars.

CAREER RECORD

** 77 Grands Prix, 1 win (Japanese GP 1989) * No championship title (best result – 6th overall 1989)*

Gunnar Nilsson

Nationality: Swedish
Born: 1948
Died: 1978

After winning the British Formula Three title in 1975, Gunnar was drafted into the Team Lotus Grand Prix outfit for the following year. He gelled well with Mario Andretti, his team-mate throughout his two years at Lotus. Gunnar won the wet 1977 Belgian Grand Prix in the ground-effect Lotus 78, picking his way through the field in calmly impressive style, but in the second half of the year he became increasingly inconsistent. No one knew it, but he was suffering from terminal cancer and, although he signed for the fledgling Arrows team in 1978, he was never well enough to drive the car. He set up the Gunnar Nilsson Cancer Treatment Campaign before dying in the autumn.

CAREER RECORD

** 31 Grands Prix, 1 win (Belgian GP 1977) * No championship title (best result – 8th overall 1977)*

A gentle man *Gunar Nilsson lost his tragic race with cancer.*

O

Jackie Oliver

Nationality: British
Born: 1942

Best known now as the boss of the Arrows team, Jackie had a distinguished driving career. Success with Lotus in Formula Two ensured that he was in the right place to be drafted into the Grand Prix team when Jim Clark was killed in 1968. Jackie crashed in his first two races, but led the British Grand Prix before his transmission failure and, although he rounded off the season with third in Mexico, he was dropped in favour of Jochen Rindt for 1970. He joined BRM for a couple of years, scoring two top-six finishes. Jackie returned to Formula One with the new Shadow team in 1973 and finished third in the Canadian Grand Prix at Mosport Park, although many people think he won on a day when lap charts were thrown into confusion by a wet/dry race and the use of a pace car. He drove for Shadow in 1977, but by then was heavily involved in the management of the team, which he quit to set up Arrows in 1978.

CAREER RECORD

** 50 Grands Prix, no wins (best result – 3rd Mexican GP 1968) * No championship title (best result – 13th overall 1968)*

P

Carlos Pace

Nationality: Brazilian
Born: 1944
Died: 1977

Having raced for most of the 1960s in Brazil, where his long-time friends and rivals were the Fittipaldi brothers, Carlos came to Britain in 1970. Success in Formula Three and Formula Two led to a drive with Frank Williams's Formula One team in 1972, for whom he showed well against team leader Henri Pescarolo. He left Williams at the end of the year to join Surtees, where some excellent performances were ruined by poor reliability and in mid-1974 he quit. Soon though, he was snapped up by Bernie Ecclestone's Brabham team, and in 1975 he took a fine victory in the Brazilian Grand Prix. Second place in the 1977 Argentinian Grand Prix boded well, but after three races he was killed in a light aircraft accident.

CAREER RECORD

** 72 Grands Prix, 1 win (Brazilian GP 1975) * No championship title (best result – 6th overall 1975)*

Man with the mike *Jonathan Palmer is now a TV commentator.*

Jonathan Palmer

Nationality: British
Born: 1956

After dominating the British Formula Three Championship in 1981 and then Formula Two in 1984, Jonathan drove first for RAM and then Zakspeed in Formula One, although he had shown well in a one-off drive with Williams in the 1983 European Grand Prix. There then started a three-year liaison with Tyrrell. In his first season, 1987, he won the Jim Clark Cup as best non-turbo driver, but 1988 was a disaster with an uncompetitive car. At the start of 1989, his career was briefly revitalized by the 018 chassis, only for him to be overshadowed by Jean Alesi in the latter half of the season. After that, Palmer, with some realistic self-appraisal, decided that his Grand Prix career was over. He is now a commentator for the BBC.

CAREER RECORD

** 82 Grands Prix, no wins (best result – 5th Monaco GP 1987, San Marino GP 1989) * No championship title (best result – 11th overall 1987)*

Olivier Panis

Nationality: French
Born: 1966

Olivier was runner-up in the French Formula Three Championship in 1991, before moving up to Formula 3000. His talent was strait-jacketed by the Lola chassis in 1992, but in 1993 he was a deserving and impressive champion for DAMS. His debut Grand Prix season, with Ligier, in 1994, demonstrated admirable pace and incredible consistency, Olivier finishing 15 of the 16 races. His best result was a somewhat fortuitous second in the German Grand Prix, when half the field was wiped out by accidents on the opening lap.

CAREER RECORD

** 16 Grands Prix, no wins (best result – 2nd German GP 1994) * No championship title (best result – 11th overall 1994)*

Mike Parkes

Nationality: British
Born: 1931
Died: 1977

Mike was elevated to the Ferrari Grand Prix team in 1966 after establishing himself as one of the world's leading sports car drivers. A brief, successful Formula One career followed, in which his best results were second place to Ludovico Scarfiotti in the 1966 Italian Grand Prix, and victory in the following year's International Trophy race at Silverstone. But a huge accident on the opening lap of the 1967 Belgian Grand Prix left Mike lying beside his upturned Ferrari with a broken leg and severe head injuries. The crash virtually ended his career. He managed teams for Fiat and Lancia in touring cars, and was then involved in the Lancia rally team, for which he was working when killed in a road crash near Turin in 1977.

Mr Consistency *Olivier Panis finished 15 out of 16 races in 1994.*

In for life *Riccardo Patrese is the longest serving Grand Prix driver of all time.*

CAREER RECORD

** 6 Grands Prix, no wins (best result – 2nd French GP 1966, Italian GP 1966) * No championship title (best result – 8th overall 1966)*

Reg Parnell

Nationality: British
Born: 1911
Died: 1964

Although what would have been the best years of his career were taken away by the Second World War, Reg was one of Britain's most respected professionals. Success in a Maserati in domestic events in the late 1940s meant he was invited to drive for the Maserati works team in 1950. He finished an excellent third in the first World Championship Grand Prix, at Silverstone. He drove Tony Vandervell's "Thinwall Special" Ferrari to a points finish in 1951, after which he raced twice more in British Grands Prix, but concentrated on national events around the world. He died of peritonitis after a routine appendix operation.

CAREER RECORD

** 6 Grands Prix, no wins (best result – 3rd British GP 1950) * No championship title (best result – 9th overall 1950)*

Riccardo Patrese

Nationality: Italian
Born: 1954

Although in the later stages of his career, Riccardo was one of the most popular personalities in Formula One, in his youth he was very much Grand Prix racing's "enfant terrible". The personality transformation took place over a decade at the beginning of what turned into Formula One's longest career – 256 Grand Prix starts. At the beginning he was quick but unruly and, although he led the South African Grand Prix in 1978 in the new Arrows team's second race, success eluded him until he joined Brabham in 1982. He won the Monaco Grand Prix, but he made too many mistakes and in 1983 threw away the San Marino Grand Prix, but put in a flawless performance to win in South Africa. In the mid-1980s his career went into a downward spiral, with Alfa-Romeo and then Brabham, only for him to be given a chance to revitalize it with Williams in 1988. He forged an excellent working relationship with technical director Patrick Head, and also returned to winning ways, finding a new serenity in simply being lucky enough, as he saw it, to be employed by a top team in a sport he loved. This rejuvenation was never more evident than when Nigel Mansell returned to the team in 1991, and had to play second fiddle to Riccardo through the first half of the season. In 1992, though, Riccardo was pushed into shadows by Mansell and, after a season at Benetton when he could not match Michael Schumacher's pace, Formula One left him behind. Despite offers to return in 1994, he preferred to concentrate on touring cars.

CAREER RECORD

** 256 Grands Prix, 6 wins (Monaco GP 1982, South African GP 1983, San Marino GP 1990, Mexican GP 1991, Portuguese GP 1991, Japanese GP 1992) * No championship title (best result – 2nd overall 1992)*

Henri Pescarolo

Nationality: French
Born: 1942

Henri was carried into Formula One by Matra on the strength of strong Formula Three, Formula Two and sports car performances, but not before his career had suffered a major setback when a crash at Le Mans in 1969 left him with severe burns. Nevertheless, fully recovered Henri was drafted into the Matra Formula One team in 1970, and took an excellent third place at Monaco, followed by a fourth place at Silverstone in Frank Williams's March in 1971. Henri dropped out of Formula One and only returned occasionally, before committing to sports car racing full-time at the end of 1976, notching up four wins in the Le Mans 24 Hours.

CAREER RECORD

** 57 Grands Prix, no wins (best result – 3rd Monaco GP 1970) * No championship title (best result – 12th overall 1970)*

Ronnie Peterson

Nationality: Swedish
Born: 1944
Died: 1978

Widely regarded as the fastest driver in the world in the mid-1970s, Ronnie's seat-of-the-pants driving style and astonishing car control won him an army of fans. This gentle man made his Grand Prix debut with the March team in 1970, having scored many successes in Formula Three for the outfit. The following year it became clear that Peterson was a world-class talent when he took five second places, and was runner-up to Jackie Stewart in the World Championship. He would not win a Grand Prix, however, until he left March to join Lotus in 1973, winning the French, Austrian, Italian and US East Grands Prix in the Lotus 72, and finishing third in the World Championship. He dragged the now aging car to three more victories in 1974, but a dreadful 1975 with Lotus prompted a switch back to March for the following year, when he took one win, before a lucrative offer to drive Ken Tyrrell's six-wheel P34 in 1977 turned into a disaster. Questions were asked about Peterson's ability, but he emphatically answered them after returning to Lotus in 1978 as number two to Mario Andretti. Together they dominated the season in the Lotus 79 and, as well as scoring two more superb wins, Ronnie often sat just feet from Andretti's exhausts, his integrity refusing to allow him to break his contract and pass the American. The season was enough to win him an offer to be McLaren's number one driver in 1979, but after an accident at the start of the Italian Grand Prix left him with serious leg injuries, a bone marrow embolism entered his bloodstream, and the Swede died the following morning, depriving Formula One of one of its most electrifying talents.

CAREER RECORD

** 124 Grands Prix, 10 wins (French GP 1973, Austrian GP 1973, Italian GP 1973, US East GP 1973, Monaco GP 1974, French GP 1974, Italian GP 1974, Italian GP 1976, South African GP 1978, Austrian GP 1978) * No championship title (best result – 2nd overall 1971 and 1978)*

An honourable man *Ronnie Peterson had an electric talent.*

Nelson Piquet

Nationality: Brazilian
Born: 1952

When Nelson joined Williams in 1986 it became clear that although he was one of Formula One's very top performers, his reputation had to some extent been founded on superior equipment at Brabham. Nelson shot to prominence winning the British Formula Three title in 1978 and, after a couple of races for McLaren and Ensign that year, the irreverent Brazilian was signed full-time by Brabham for 1979. He was immediately quick, pushing team leader Niki Lauda hard all the time, and when Lauda retired suddenly towards the end of 1979, Nelson became team leader. The following year saw him win three Grands Prix and push Alan Jones for the World Championship, which he clinched the following year, overhauling Carlos Reutemann in the final race, at Las Vegas. A switch to BMW turbos by Brabham in 1982 led to a season of unreliability and only one win, but in 1983 he took a second title, this time snatching it from Alain Prost at the final race, after a late-season push from BMW. In the

The joker *Nelson Piquet won three World Championships despite his levity.*

following years Brabham slowly drifted away from competitiveness, Nelson only taking three wins in two years, and he left at the end of 1985 to earn what he saw as his due at Williams. But a rude shock awaited him there in the form of Nigel Mansell, whom most Formula One observers had expected Piquet to outpace easily. Both Nelson and Mansell lost out on the 1986 World title to Prost, and Nelson was not amused by Williams's refusal to ask Mansell to give way to him, which in his view had allowed Prost to snatch the title. Still, he took a third title in 1987, relying on consistency and reliability after a heavy accident early in the season. There followed a disastrous two seasons with Lotus, which further damaged Nelson's reputation, although he went some way to repairing it at Benetton in 1990–91, when he won a further three races. Upon Michael Schumacher's arrival in 1991, however, Nelson became surplus to Benetton's requirements and, with no leading Formula One drives available, retired from Grand Prix racing. He entered the Indianapolis 500, but crashed heavily in qualifying, badly damaging his feet. Many thought the accident would end his career, but he returned to Indy in 1993.

CAREER RECORD

** 204 Grands Prix, 23 wins (US West GP 1980, Dutch GP 1980, Italian GP 1980, Argentinian GP 1981, San Marino GP 1981, German GP 1981, Canadian GP 1982, Brazilian GP 1983, Italian GP 1983, European GP 1983, Canadian GP 1984, Detroit GP 1984, French GP 1985, Brazilian GP 1986, German GP 1986, Hungarian GP 1986, Italian GP 1986, German GP 1987, Hungarian GP 1987, Italian GP 1987, Japanese GP 1990, Australian GP 1990, Canadian GP 1991) * World Champion 1981, 1983 and 1987*

Didier Pironi

Nationality: French
Born: 1952
Died: 1987

Motivated by a burning desire to be France's first world champion, Didier's cold, calculating, approach was disrupted for ever in August 1982 when he crashed with extreme violence in practice for the German Grand Prix, badly breaking both his legs and ending his motor racing career. An impressive debut year with Tyrrell in 1978, when his reputation was bolstered by a win at Le Mans in an Alpine-Renault, followed by marking time the following year, led him to a drive with Ligier in 1980, where he comfortably outpaced team leader Jacques Laffite. Didier scored his first Grand Prix win in Belgium that year and was extremely unlucky not to win in Britain, too, following a superb charge through the field. For 1981 he joined Gilles Villeneuve at Ferrari, and for the first time in his career was unable to get on terms with a teammate. A sole fourth place was all he could achieve in a year when the brilliant French-Canadian took two wins. Didier was determined that the same fate should not befall him in 1982, when he was at the centre of a tragic sequence of events. He snatched victory against team orders as Villeneuve was cruising to the flag at Imola. Villeneuve was killed at the following race, and now Didier looked set on a course for the world title. He won the Dutch Grand Prix in masterful style, and comfortably led the Championship when he arrived in Hockenheim. After the crash came dozens of operations, and although he vowed to return one day, it looked increasingly unlikely. For thrills Didier turned to powerboat racing. The Frenchman's approach had always been uncompromising and when he hit the wake of an oil tanker without easing off the throttle, his boat flipped, and Didier and his two crew members were killed instantly.

French flier *Pironi was cold-blooded in pursuit of glory.*

CAREER RECORD

** 70 Grands Prix, 3 wins (Belgian GP 1980, San Marino GP 1982, Dutch GP 1982) * No championship title (best result – 2nd overall 1982)*

Emanuele Pirro

Nationality: Italian
Born: 1962

A brilliant touring car driver, Emanuele never quite made the grade in Formula One. After a long apprenticeship in Formulae Three and Two, and then 3000, in all of which he took several victories, he became McLaren's test driver in 1988, before replacing Johnny Herbert at Benetton halfway through 1989. He was dropped at year's end, and drove for Dallara for the next two seasons, before returning to touring cars for good.

Touring car ace *Emanuelle Pirro was a Formula One also-ran.*

CAREER RECORD

** 37 Grands Prix, no wins (best result – 6th Monaco GP 1991) * No championship title (best result – 18th overall 1991)*

Alain Prost

Nationality: French
Born: 1955
see Legends of the Track pp 120–1

Tom Pryce

Nationality: British
Born: 1949
Died: 1977

Tom moved into Formula One in 1974 with the Shadow team after an excellent Formula Three career, and from the beginning showed himself to have great natural pace, putting the car on the second row of the grid in only his second race. He won the non-championship Race of Champions at Brands Hatch at the start of 1975, but it was an up-and-down year, highlighted by pole at the British Grand Prix and great drives in the German and Austrian races. Financial troubles blighted 1976, but a new sponsor provided fresh hope for 1977. Then, in a bizarre accident, Tom hit a marshal who was crossing the straight just over a blind brow in the middle of the South African Grand Prix. Tom was dead before the car had come to rest.

CAREER RECORD

** 42 Grands Prix, no wins (best result – 3rd Austrian GP 1975, Brazilian GP 1976) * No championship title (best result – 10th overall 1975)*

David Purley

Nationality: British
*Born:*1945
Died: 1985

"Purls" will forever be remembered for his efforts to save the life of Roger Williamson trapped in his burning vehicle in the Dutch Grand Prix of 1973, for which he was awarded the George Medal for his bravery. He had a brief Grand Prix career, starting in 1973, when he hired a private March with little success in terms of results. He then dropped back to a successful Formula Two season in 1974, and then an excellent two years of Formula 5000 before returning to Formula One in 1977, racing his own Lec chassis. He led the Belgian Grand Prix briefly during a sequence of pit stops, but then his front-line racing career ended with a horrific head-on crash into a wall in practice for the British Grand Prix, which he was lucky to survive. Having proved that he was well enough recovered to drive a Formula One car again, he turned to aerobatics to seek his dangerous thrills, and was killed when his Pitts Special crashed off the Sussex coast in 1985.

CAREER RECORD

** 7 Grands Prix, no wins (best result – 9th Italian GP 1973) * No championship title*

R

Hector Rebaque

Nationality: Mexican
Born: 1956

Hector entered Formula One with a Hesketh in 1977, before fielding Lotus 78s in 1978, with little success. A run of poor results in a Lotus 79 in 1979 led him to commission his own chassis, which appeared only at the last three events of the year. Hector joined Brabham alongside Nelson Piquet in place of Ricardo Zunino for the second half of the season, and benefited from the team's excellent car with a few top-six places in 1981. He raced briefly in Indy Cars in 1982 before retiring.

CAREER RECORD

** 41 Grands Prix, no wins (best result – 4th San Marino GP 1981, German GP 1981, Dutch GP 1981) * No championship title (best result – 9th overall 1981)*

Cruel conclusion *Clay Regazzoni was crippled by the sport he loved.*

Brian Redman

Nationality: British
Born: 1937

A top-line sports car driver, Brian had a low-key Grand Prix career, which he ended prematurely because he did not like the high-pressure atmosphere in Formula One. Making his debut with a Cooper in 1968, he had to withdraw after three races when he broke his arm in a crash at Spa, but he returned sporadically until 1974, in between a succession of superb performances for Ferrari and Porsche in sports car events, which he continued to compete in until the early 1990s.

CAREER RECORD

** 12 Grands Prix, no wins (best result – 3rd Spanish GP 1968) * No championship title (best result – 12th overall 1972)*

Clay Regazzoni

Nationality: Swiss
Born: 1939

Gianclaudio, also known as Clay, became one of Formula One's most respected performers – and also one of its saddest stories. He made his Grand Prix debut for Ferrari midway through a successful Formula Two season in 1970, and straightaway proved himself to be an accomplished driver. Not only did he take an excellent fourth place on his debut, in Britain, and follow it with a second place in Austria, but he assured himself of a place forever in the hearts of Ferrari fans when he won the Italian Grand Prix. Clay stayed with the Italian team for another two season, before being dropped for 1973, only to return in 1974 alongside Niki Lauda. He proved the perfect foil for the Austrian, coming close to winning the World Championship in 1974, and supporting Lauda ably for another two years, before he was replaced by Carlos Reutemann for 1977. Two years in the comparative wilderness with Ensign and Shadow were followed by a splendid return to the limelight in 1979 with Williams – indeed he gave the team its first Grand Prix win, at Silverstone, before again being replaced by Reutemann and returning to Ensign. However, in his fourth race of 1980, the car's throttle jammed open along the flat-out Shoreline Drive at Long Beach, and he careered down an escape road and into a concrete wall at unabated speed. He suffered severe spinal injuries which have kept him partially confined to a wheelchair ever since. His love of the sport, though, remains, and he is a commentator on Swiss television.

CAREER RECORD

** 132 Grands Prix, 5 wins (Italian GP 1971, German GP 1974, Italian GP 1975, US West GP 1976, British GP 1979) * No championship title (best result – 2nd overall 1974)*

Carlos Reutemann

Nationality: Argentinian
Born: 1942

Carlos was a supremely talented racing driver, who at his best was untouchable, but he could just as easily turn in a performance of overwhelming mediocrity as he could reduce a field of the best drivers in the world to bit players. Never was this more apparent than at the end of 1981 when, poised on the brink of the World Championship and after clinching pole position in brilliant style, he faded badly to eighth place in a race in which he only had to place ahead of Nelson Piquet – who finished the race semi-conscious in fifth place – to take the title. Carlos made a sensational Formula One debut in 1972, after placing second to Ronnie Peterson

An enigma *Carlos Reuteman was a great talent, but never a champion.*

Ford
SHELL

in the European Formula Two Trophy in 1971, putting his Brabham on pole position before finishing seventh. The following season saw him establish himself as a consistent topliner, and he started 1974 in brilliant style, leading the first two races until problems intervened, and winning the third, before his form tailed off until August, when he recovered to win the Austrian Grand Prix in brilliant style. Two more up-and-down seasons followed before he joined Ferrari for 1977, where he was overshadowed by Niki Lauda, and 1978, when he was back to his best alongside Gilles Villeneuve. Reutemann took four wins that year, only two less than world champion Mario Andretti in the dominant Lotus 79. A switch to Lotus for 1979 proved ill-judged, but the move to Williams in 1980 was not. He ably backed up Alan Jones to the title that first year, before mounting his own challenge in 1981. For most of the year it looked a certainty that he would tie up the championship well before the end of the season, but then came the almost inevitable slump. He returned in 1982, took an excellent second place in the first race, in South Africa, and then quit after the second. He is now a leading figure in Argentinian politics, and since 1991 has been the governor of the country's largest province, Santa Fé.

CAREER RECORD

** 146 Grands Prix, 12 wins (South African GP 1974, Austrian GP 1974, US GP 1974, German GP 1975, Brazilian GP 1977, Brazilian GP 1978, US West GP 1978, British GP 1978, US East GP 1978, Monaco GP 1980, Brazilian GP 1981, Belgian GP 1981) * No championship title (best result – 2nd overall 1981)*

Peter Revson

Nationality: American
Born: 1939
Died: 1974

After a brief fling with Formula One in 1964, Revson returned to race in sports cars in the USA until good performances in Indy Cars attracted the attention of the Formula One fraternity. He guested in a Tyrrell at the US Grand Prix in 1971 before signing up for Yardley McLaren for the following two years. He soon proved to be a reliable points scorer with a pace that surprised many. When the McLaren M23 came on stream in 1973, he took an excellent first victory in the British Grand Prix, grabbing the initiative in the wet early stages and heading an intense four-car battle towards the end. Another win followed in the confused and wet Canadian race. He left McLaren after he was offered only a third car in 1974 and switched to Shadow. But he was killed in testing for the South African Grand Prix at Kyalami when the front suspension failed and the car hit the barriers.

Austrian ace *Jochen Rindt became the only posthumous world champion.*

CAREER RECORD

** 30 Grands Prix, 2 wins (British GP 1973, Canadian GP 1973) * No championship title (best result – 5th overall 1972 & 1973)*

Jochen Rindt

Nationality: Austrian
Born: 1941
Died: 1970

Jochen's incredible car control enabled him to dominate Formula Two throughout the 1960s, but the Austrian found success in Formula One much harder to come by. He made a brief Grand Prix debut in 1964, before returning full-time in 1965 with Cooper, where he performed with enthusiasm but little success until 1967. A move to Brabham looked a shrewd one, given that the team had won the last two World Championships, but its new Repco engine was a failure, and he had only two third places to show for two years in the team when he joined Lotus in 1969. After feeling secure with the engineering standards at Brabham, Jochen did not trust Lotus boss Colin Chapman to anything like the same extent, and a broken rear wing, when he was heading for his first victory, at Silverstone, did little to bolster his confidence. Nevertheless, the Rindt/Chapman relationship did eventually gel, and he took his first win in the US Grand Prix at the end of 1969 (pictured on left). Another win followed in the venerable Lotus 49 at Monaco in 1970, before Chapman unveiled the sleek Lotus 72. The car took Jochen to four consecutive victories in the summer of 1970 but, although he was clearly on course for the World Championship, he felt increasingly unsafe after the deaths of his friends Piers Courage and Bruce McLaren. Sadly, in practice for the Italian Grand Prix, his fears were realized, and he was killed after crashing under braking for the Parabolica, thus becoming motor racing's only posthumous world champion.

Magical Mexican *Ricardo Rodriguez could have been one of the greats.*

CAREER RECORD

** 60 Grands Prix, 6 wins (US GP 1969, Monaco GP 1970, Dutch GP 1970, French GP 1970, British GP 1970, German GP 1970) * World Champion 1970*

Pedro Rodriguez

Nationality: Mexican
Born: 1940
Died: 1971

Pedro and his younger brother Ricardo were indulged with high-performance cars from an early age by their wealthy father, and first came to the notice of the European racing fraternity in a Ferrari at Le Mans in 1960, where they almost won. But while Ricardo shot straight into the works Ferrari Formula One team, Pedro's career needed a long time to take off, before he finally got a full-time drive with Cooper in 1967. Thanks to his car's reliability and to heavy attrition he won his first race for the team, switching to BRM in 1968, where his spirited driving lifted the team's morale after the death of Mike Spence at Indianapolis. He had a part-time role in Formula One in 1969, before returning to BRM in 1970, where he took one of the all-time classic victories, beating off race-long pressure from Chris Amon's March. This eccentric, who went everywhere with his famous deerstalker hat and bottle of Tabasco sauce for use at the world's finest restaurants, was now at the top of his game. He was acknowledged as a wet weather ace, and had also established himself as the world's leading sports car driver. Halfway through 1971, which looked set to offer Pedro even more success, he accepted an offer to drive in an insignificant Interserie race in Germany. While he was dicing for the lead, a slower car edged him into the wall and his Ferrari burst into flames. The Mexican died shortly after he was extricated from the wreck.

CAREER RECORD

** 55 Grands Prix, 2 wins (South African GP 1967, Belgian GP 1970) * No championship title (best result – 6th overall 1967 and 1968)*

Ricardo Rodriguez

Nationality: Mexican
Born: 1942
Died: 1962

Thought by many to have even more talent than his brother Pedro, Ricardo qualified an astonishing second on the grid at his first Grand

Prix, at Monza, when he was just 19 years old. Ferrari, unsurprisingly, signed him for the following year but, still a little raw and wild, he did not drive in every race. Annoyed that Ferrari did not send any cars to the non-championship Mexican Grand Prix – his home race – at the end of the season, Ricardo drove Rob Walker's Lotus 24 instead and, trying to snatch back pole position, he went into the daunting Peraltada corner too fast, and ran out of road on the exit. He suffered severe injuries and died soon afterwards.

CAREER RECORD

** 5 Grands Prix, no wins (best result – 4th Belgian GP 1962) * No championship title (best result – 12th overall 1962)*

Keke Rosberg

Nationality: Finnish
Born: 1948

Success in Formula One was a long time coming for this outspoken Finn, and the majority of his wins came in conditions where reflexes and stamina were all-important. He graduated to Formula One in 1978 after being a front-runner in Formula Atlantic and Formula Two, and set out an interesting pointer to future form by taking a win in the streaming conditions of the International Trophy race at Silverstone in 1978. Until 1982, however, when Williams signed him as a replacement for Alan Jones, he was never given equipment worthy of his talent. Keke made the most of his chance, scoring his first Grand Prix win en route to the World Championship title. The following season, however, the Williams team found itself lagging behind the turbo cars. Keke took an inspired win at Monaco, gambling correctly that the wet track surface would dry out, and left the rest of the field trailing. But the remainder of the year was a frustrating battle to keep up with the turbos. Although Williams had the Honda turbo in 1984, its car, the FW09, could not match the all-conquering McLarens, and Keke had to make do again with a single, inspired victory. At scorching Dallas, while most of his rivals either collapsed with heat exhaustion or crashed on the crumbling track surface, Keke took a brilliant victory. By the end of the year he had decided he would retire after a further two seasons. Two victories followed in 1985 for Williams, and then he switched to McLaren for his final year, where he was surprised by the pace of team-mate Alain Prost. "I thought I was the fastest driver in the world," he said, "until I came here." There were no wins in that final season, but he retired while leading his last race, the Australian Grand Prix, in typically exuberant style. Keke did return to the sport, however, first with Peugeot in the sports car World Championship in 1990–91, and then with Mercedes and subsequently Opel in the German Touring Car Championship.

CAREER RECORD

** 114 Grands Prix, 5 wins (Swiss GP 1982, Monaco GP 1983, Dallas GP 1984, US GP 1985, Australian GP 1985) * World Champion 1981*

Louis Rosier

Nationality: French
Born: 1905
Died: 1956

Louis's early career was disrupted by the Second World War, but he won several non-championship Grands Prix in the late 1940s as a member of the Talbot team. When the World Championship was established in 1950, his Talbot was always going to play second fiddle to Alfa-Romeo, but Louis picked up a number of points-scoring places, as well as winning the Le Mans 24 Hours, and in 1951 he won the non-championship Dutch and Bordeaux Grands Prix. He continued in Formula One, now past his best, in Ferraris and then Maserati 250Fs, in steady and reliable fashion, until he was killed when he crashed in the wet Paris 1000 km race at Montlhery in 1956.

CAREER RECORD

** 38 Grands Prix, no wins (best result – 3rd Swiss GP 1950, Belgian GP 1950) * No championship title (best result – 4th overall 1950)*

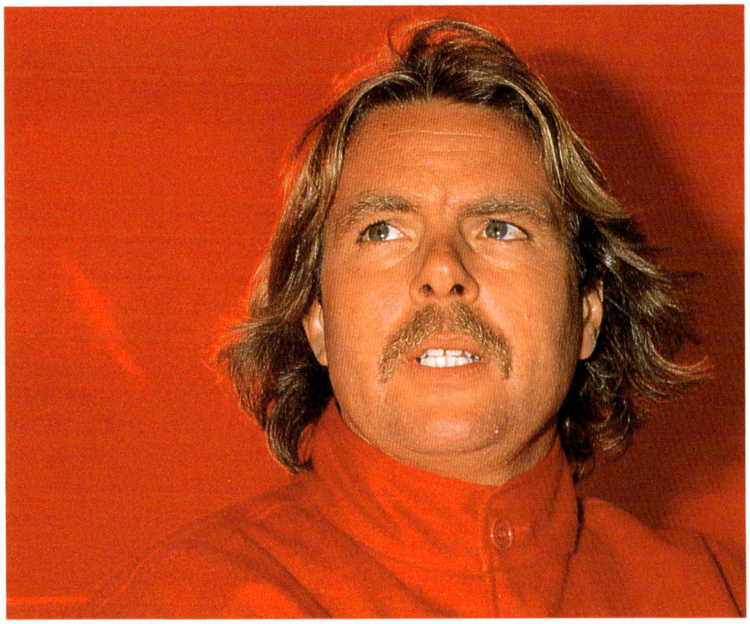

Flying Finn *Keke Rosberg was one of the most flamboyant drivers ever.*

S

Luís Pérez Sala

Nationality: Spanish
Born: 1959

Success in Formula 3000 was never matched by his form in Formula One. Luís took two wins in F3000 in each of 1986 and 1987, was second to Stefano Modena in the championship in the latter year, and looked quite promising when he stepped up to Formula One with Minardi in 1988. But when Pierluigi Martini joined the team he was overshadowed. He now races in the Spanish Touring Car Championship.

CAREER RECORD

** 26 Grands Prix, no wins (best result – 6th British GP 1989) * No championship title (best result – 26th overall 1989)*

Eliseo Salazar

Nationality: Chilean
Born: 1954

Most famous for being kicked and punched live on television by Nelson Piquet after the two had collided in the 1982 German Grand Prix, Eliseo showed well in Formula Three and the British Formula One series before joining struggling March and then Ensign in 1981. Success did not come any easier with ATS in 1982 when he was overshadowed by team-mate Manfred Winkelhock and, after a few brief appearances with the RAM team in 1983, he was out of a drive. Eliseo moved to race in Indy Cars in the 1990s.

CAREER RECORD

** 24 Grands Prix, no wins (best result – 5th San Marino GP 1982) * No championship title (best result – 18th overall 1981)*

Roy Salvadori

Nationality British
Born: 1922

In a Formula One career spanning ten years, Roy was perpetually overshadowed by his fellow-countrymen. But he was a splendid driver, especially in sports cars, and his finest hour came with a victory in the 1959 Le Mans 24 Hours for Aston Martin. Concentrating on sports cars in the mid-1950s, when he was a member of the factory Aston Martin team, Roy hit the Grand Prix front line with Cooper in 1958. He then switched to Aston Martin's unsuccessful Grand Prix assault just as Cooper became the team to beat in Formula One. Roy later drove a privately entered Cooper, almost winning the 1961 US Grand Prix, before retiring from Formula One in 1962 and from sports car racing a couple of years later.

Sports car hero *Ray Salvadori never got the breaks in Formula One.*

CAREER RECORD

** 47 Grands Prix, no wins (best result – 2nd German GP 1958) * No championship title (best result – 4th overall 1958)*

Consalvo Sanesi

Nationality: Italian
Born: 1911

Largely employed by Alfa-Romeo as a test driver, Consalvo scored some worthwhile results in the late 1940s, including finishing second to Achille Varzi at Bari in 1947, and raced spasmodically in 1950 and 1951, before concentrating on sports cars, most notably winning the Carrera PanAmericana in 1954.

CAREER RECORD

** 5 Grands Prix, no wins (best result – 4th Swiss GP 1951) * No championship title (best result – 13th overall 1951)*

Ludovico Scarfiotti

Nationality: Italian
Born: 1933
Died: 1968

Ludovico, the nephew of Fiat boss Gianni Agnelli, assured himself immortality in the annals of Italian motor racing when he won the 1966 Italian Grand Prix for Ferrari. A master at hill climbing, Scarfiotti made his Grand Prix debut in the 1963 Dutch Grand Prix a fortnight after winning Le Mans with Lorenzo Bandini. After sporadic appearances for Ferrari in the next couple of years, he was expected to appear full-time in 1967 following the Monza win, but was dropped in favour of newcomer Chris Amon. And when Bandini was killed and then fellow Ferrari driver Mike Parkes badly injured, Ludovico almost gave up. He returned to Formula One in 1968 with Cooper, but was killed when he crashed in a hill climb event in Germany.

CAREER RECORD

** 10 Grands Prix, 1 win (Italian GP 1966)*
** No championship title (best result – 10th overall 1966)*

Ian Scheckter

Nationality: South African
Born: 1947

The elder brother of Jody, Ian Scheckter made his Grand Prix debut in the South African Grand Prix of 1974, and competed sporadically until landing a full season with a works Rothmans March in 1977. But it was an unmitigated disaster and Ian quit Formula One at the end of the year. On his return to South Africa he won the Formula Atlantic title two years running.

CAREER RECORD

** 18 Grands Prix, no wins (best result – 10th Dutch GP 1977) * No championship title*

Jody Scheckter

Nationality: South African
Born: 1950

Jody burst on to the Formula One scene amid recriminations and controversy, but retired eight years later a respected elder statesman. In 1971 he raced in Formula Ford in Britain for the first time, and cut such a swathe through it and Formula Three that he was racing in the US Grand Prix car by the end of 1972. But, despite his dazzling progress – he was in the works McLaren team in 1973, and led the French race, only his third Grand Prix – there were demands that he be banned after he had caused a multiple pile-up that stopped the British Grand Prix two weeks later. Jody moved to Tyrrell for 1974, replacing the retired Jackie Stewart, and began to lose his wildness and his rough edge, taking two wins and third place in the World Championship. The following year was not so successful, but he made the six-wheel P34 a serious proposition in 1976, and again finished third in the title race. He risked switching to the new Wolf team in 1977, but it paid off with three victories and a runner-up spot in the World Championship. However, after a poor year in 1978, he moved to Ferrari with the express intention of becoming World Champion. He shrugged off the shock of being beaten by team-mate Gilles Villeneuve in the new 312T4's first two races, and knuckled down to a season of consistency and reliability – and three victories. And, although Villeneuve was often quicker than Jody, it was Jody's regular point scoring that ensured a narrow victory in the World Championship, secured by a triumph in the Italian Grand Prix with Villeneuve dutifully trailing him. With the title under his belt, 1980 was a disaster. The new Ferrari 312T5 was hopelessly off the pace and Jody was bemused and demoralized, and decided to retire, safe, at the end of the season.

Wild youth *Jody Scheckter had to control his ways to win in Formula One.*

CAREER RECORD

** 112 Grands Prix, 10 wins (Swedish GP 1974, British GP 1974, South African GP 1975, Swedish GP 1976, Argentinian GP 1977, Monaco GP 1977, Canadian GP 1977, Belgian GP 1979, Monaco GP 1979, Italian GP 1979) * World Champion 1979*

Harry Schell

Nationality: American
Born: 1921
Died: 1960

Harry began to make his mark in Formula One in 1953 when he joined the Gordini team, and was even more impressive in 1954 when he drove for Maserati. He was employed by both Vanwall and Maserati in 1955, and then gave the first showing of Vanwall's potential in 1956 when he snapped at the heels of the works Ferraris in the French Grand Prix. Harry was employed as support for Juan Manuel Fangio at Maserati in 1957, before moving to BRM in 1958, taking a career-best second place in the Dutch Grand Prix. He was driving a private Cooper when he crashed and died in the wet in practice for the Silverstone International Trophy in 1960.

CAREER RECORD

** 56 Grands Prix, no wins (best result – 2nd Dutch GP 1958) * No championship title (best result – 5th overall 1958)*

Tim Schenken

Nationality: Australian
Born: 1942

After a successful career in the junior categories, Tim was signed to partner Graham Hill at Brabham in 1971, and overshadowed the former World Champion for most of the year. A move to Surtees in 1972 proved to be a mistake and ended his chances of landing a competitive Formula One drive. He drove the uncompetitive Trojan in 1974 before concentrating on sports car events and retiring in 1977. He formed a company for building racing cars with fellow racer Howden Ganley.

CAREER RECORD

** 34 Grands Prix, no wins (best result – 3rd Austrian GP 1971) * No championship title (14th overall 1971)*

Mr Happy *Michael Schumacher never hides his emotions on the rostrum.*

Michael Schumacher

Nationality: German
Born: 1969

Despite clinching his first World Championship at the end of 1994, Michael is clearly still at the beginning of what will be a sparkling Grand Prix career. He exploded into Formula One at the 1991 Belgian Grand Prix, after serving a brilliant apprenticeship in Formula Three and qualified his Jordan seventh, way ahead of team leader Andrea de Cesaris, on a circuit he had never seen before. Following a bitter legal battle, he then switched to the Benetton team for the following race, and has been its lynchpin ever since. In his first full season, 1992, Michael's Benetton was outclassed by the dominant Williams-Renaults but he proved that not only was he incredibly quick – with some scintillating and assured performances, such as taking second place to Nigel Mansell in the soaking Spanish Grand Prix – he was remarkably consistent as well. He visited the rostrum no fewer than eight times, including an excellent, win in the wet/dry Belgian Grand Prix. He continued in the same vein in 1993. Although Williams, this time with Alain Prost, was once again the class of the field, Prost was occasionally overshadowed by Ayrton Senna in a McLaren, which had the same Ford engine as Michael's Benetton. The German did, though, take a superb victory in the Portuguese Grand Prix. At the beginning of 1994 Michael and Benetton surprised the entire Grand Prix world by proving a more competitive proposition than Senna and his Williams and, after Senna's death, Michael looked to be in an unassailable position as he headed to his first World Championship. But he and Benetton were almost swamped by allegations of cheating, disqualifications and bans, and in the end beat Damon Hill only narrowly to the World Championship after a controversial collision in the final race of the year in Australia.

CAREER RECORD

** 52 Grands Prix, 10 wins (Belgian GP 1992, Portuguese GP 1993, Brazilian GP 1994, Pacific GP 1994, San Marino GP 1994, Monaco GP 1994, Canadian GP 1994, French GP 1994, Hungarian GP 1994, European GP 1994) * World Champion 1994*

Ayrton Senna

Nationality: Brazilian
Born: 1960

see Legends of the Track pp 122–3

Chico Serra

Nationality: Brazilian
Born: 1957

A rival of fellow countryman Nelson Piquet in their early years in Brazilian racing, Chico was impressive in the junior formulae in Britain in the late 1970s, winning the Formula Ford title in 1977, placing third behind Piquet and Derek Warwick in Formula Three in 1978, and winning it in 1979. After a year in Formula Two, he moved into Formula One with Fittipaldi and, unsurprisingly, struggled with a team on its last legs. After four appearances with Arrows in 1983, he lost out to Thierry Boutsen, returning to Brazil to race saloon cars.

CAREER RECORD

** 18 Grands Prix, no wins (best result – 6th Belgian GP 1981) * No championship title (best result – 26th overall 1982)*

Johnny Servoz-Gavin

Nationality: French
Born: 1942

A handsome blond playboy, Georges-Francis ("Johnny") also possessed a significant talent. After proving quick but a little wild in Formulae Three and Two, he was given the opportunity to demonstrate his prowess in Formula One in 1968 when an accident to Jackie Stewart saw him drafted into Ken Tyrrell's Matra team at Monaco. He qualified a brilliant second, and shot off into the lead before clouting a barrier on the first lap. Returning for the Italian Grand Prix later in the year, he was an excellent second, and was kept on by Matra in 1969, when he not only won the European Formula Two title, but scored the only World Championship point ever won by a four-wheel-drive car, in the Canadian Grand Prix. He was signed as Stewart's team-mate in the Tyrrell/March team in 1970 but, after failing to qualify at Monaco, he announced his retirement, saying that, while driving an off-road vehicle, he had been struck in the eye by a branch, which had affected his vision.

CAREER RECORD

** 12 Grands Prix, no wins (best result – 2nd Italian GP 1968) * No championship title (best result – 13th overall 1968)*

Jo Siffert

Nationality: Swiss
Born: 1936
Died: 1971

Brave, versatile and underrated, Jo was a very talented driver, which was well demonstrated when he beat Jim Clark in the Mediterranean Grand Prix at Enna-Pergusa in 1964–65. Jo began his Formula One career in 1962, but despite a few top-six finishes, success eluded him until 1968, when, in his second year with Rob Walker's team, he had front-line equipment in the form of a Lotus 49 and took a fantastic victory in the 1968 British Grand Prix. Another season with Walker in 1969 led to an offer from Ferrari, but Porsche, for whom Jo raced in sports cars, was determined to hang on to him and they paid for a season at the wheel of a works March. The season turned into a disaster, however, and he was delighted to join BRM alongside Pedro Rodriguez in 1971. This was a volatile partnership and, although not close personally, they had great respect for each other's abilities. It was, however, to be a tragic year for BRM. After Rodriguez was killed in midsummer, Jo buoyed spirits with a superb victory in the Austrian Grand Prix, only to be killed himself in an accident in the non-championship Victory Race at Brands Hatch. His BRM plunged off the track at the fastest part of the circuit and burst into flames. Although Jo suffered only a broken leg in the impact, he died of asphyxia.

CAREER RECORD

** 96 Grands Prix, 2 wins (British GP 1968, Austrian GP 1971) * No championship title (best result – 4th overall 1971)*

Raymond Sommer

Nationality: French
Born: 1906
Died: 1950

Raymond was a key figure of the inter-war period of racing especially in sports cars, winning Le Mans in 1931–32, first with Luigi Chinetti and then with the legendary Tazio Nuvolari. Eschewing driving for teams in Formula One because of the constraints they put on him, Raymond delighted in taking on the mighty Ferrari and Mercedes teams and beating them as often as possible. After the war he consolidated his reputation for no-holds-barred racing with an excellent fourth place at Monaco in 1950 in a Formula Two Ferrari, before being killed in a non-championship race at Cadours towards the end of the year.

CAREER RECORD

** Five Grands Prix, no wins (best result – 4th Monaco GP 1950) * No championship title (best result – 13th overall 1950)*

Mike Spence

*Nationality:*British
Born: 1936
Died: 1968

Mike began his Formula One career as Jim Clark's team-mate at Lotus and, although he was overshadowed by the great Scot, often ran competitively in his two years at Lotus peaking with third place in Mexico in 1965. Mike switched to a semi-works BRM drive in 1966, before being promoted to the full works team in 1967, under the shadow of another great Scot, Jackie Stewart. That year he also raced the radical Chaparral sports car with some success. After competitive showings in non-championship races early in 1968, he seemed on the threshold of Grand Prix success, but died of head injuries following a crash at Indianapolis where, ironically, he was replacing Clark, who had been killed the previous month in a Formula Two race at Hockenheim.

CAREER RECORD

** 36 Grands Prix, no wins (best result – 3rd Mexican GP 1965) * No championship title (best result – 8th overall 1965)*

Jackie Stewart

Nationality: British
Born: 1939
see Legends of the Track pp 124–5

Rolf Stommelen

Nationality: German
Born: 1943
Died: 1983

After making his name taming the Porsche 917 sports car, Rolf entered Formula One with the Brabham team in 1970. He showed great promise with four top-six finishes, but seasons with Surtees and then the ugly Eifelland March all but destroyed his Formula One career. An occasional drive with Brabham in 1974 provided a lifeline, and he was offered a drive with the Hill team for 1975, only to be injured in a crash at the Spanish Grand Prix, when his car flew into the crowd and killed four spectators. When Rolf returned later in the year, he was off-form and was mainly away from Formula One until spending a season as an also-ran with Arrows in 1978, after which he returned to sports cars. He was killed in a crash at Riverside in California in 1983.

CAREER RECORD

** 54 Grands Prix, no wins (best result – 3rd Austrian GP 1970) * No championship title (best result – 11th overall 1970)*

Philippe Streiff

Nationality: French
Born: 1955

This tall, serious-minded Frenchman made his debut with a Renault in the 1984 Portuguese Grand Prix. Halfway through 1985, he replaced the accident-prone Andrea de Cesaris at Ligier, where he scored an excellent third place at the end-of-year Australian Grand Prix. Philippe's first full year came with Tyrrell in 1986, and he spent two seasons with the British team, where he was generally outpaced by his team-mates. A move to the tiny AGS team in 1988 revitalized him, and he impressed with a number of excellent performances, including a superb showing in qualifying at the San Marino Grand Prix. Streiff was to stay with AGS in 1989, but a heavy crash in testing for the Brazilian Grand Prix left him in a wheelchair.

Steady talent *Phillipe Streiff joined the AGS team in 1988.*

CAREER RECORD

** 54 Grands Prix, no wins (best result – 3rd Australian GP 1985) * No championship title (best result – 13th overall 1986)*

Hans-Joachim Stuck

Nationality: German
Born: 1951

The son of pre-war ace Hans Stuck, Hans Jr's natural talent rarely seemed to find full expression in Formula One. Already a touring car ace when he made his Grand Prix debut in 1974 with March, he proved somewhat inconsistent in the following three years. When Carlos Pace was killed early in 1977, Hans replaced him in the Brabham line-up, and scored superb third places at the German and Austrian Grands Prix. He proceeded to lead the end-of-season US Grand Prix only to slide off in the soaking conditions. He drove for Shadow in 1978 and ATS in 1979, but rarely featured prominently, before moving to a successful career in sports cars and touring cars.

CAREER RECORD

** 74 Grands Prix, no wins (best result – 3rd German GP 1977, Austrian GP 1977) * No championship title (best result – 11th overall 1977)*

Marc Surer

Nationality: Swiss
Born: 1952

Promoted to Formula One after winning the 1979 European Formula Two title Marc raced three times with Ensign in 1980, before moving to ATS in 1981 and badly damaging his ankles in a crash at the South African Grand Prix. In 1982, when he was driving for Arrows, he crashed in testing again but, once fit, he drove for Arrows until the end of 1984, earning admiration for his often skilled performances. Marc was finally given the chance to show his ability when he replaced François Hesnault in a Braham-BMW alongside Nelson Piquet in 1985, before moving back to Arrows in 1986. His career ended when he crashed a Ford RS200 rally car heavily. His co-driver was killed and Surer himself was badly burned. He is now manager of BMW's touring car programme.

CAREER RECORD

** 82 Grands Prix, no wins (best result – 4th Brazilian GP 1981, Italian GP 1985) * No championship title (best result – 13th overall 1985)*

John Surtees

Nationality: British
Born: 1934

The only man to have won the World Championship in both motorcyles and cars, John was one of four drivers who dominated Formula One in the mid-1960s. Having won seven World Motorcycle Championships, John showed such talent when he tried his hand at Formula Junior in 1960 that Lotus boss Colin Chapman invited him to drive for his Grand Prix team when the races did not clash with his motorcycle commitments. John did not disappoint, finishing second in the British Grand Prix and taking pole in Portugal, where he dominated until damaging a radiator against straw bales. A move to Ferrari for 1963 was the kick-start for success, and he took his first win at the Nurburgring. In 1964 he secured two more wins and snatched the world title at a nail-biting last race, in which the destiny of the championship first slipped from Clark's hands, then from Hill's before finally falling into John's grasp. The year 1965 was disrupted when he had a heavy crash in a Lola CanAm car,

Unique talent *Surtees won World Championships on two and four wheels.*

but his doggedness and determination pulled him through and he returned to Ferrari for 1966. He always excelled on the classic road circuits, and Spa 1966 was no exception, John taking a superb victory in the Belgian Grand Prix after an intense battle with Jochen Rindt. But that was followed by a falling-out with team manager Eugenio Dragoni, which caused a split with Ferrari. John drove for Cooper until the end of the season, winning the final race, before spending a difficult couple of years developing Honda's challenge, which included a victory in the 1967 Italian Grand Prix. He signed for BRM for 1969, but it was a trying year, made worse by medical complications which were a long-term effect of the CanAm crash. By now he had made up his mind to start his own team, where he would not need to compromise his ideas on the technical approach to racing. But the team was not a success. After a promising couple of years with John driving, he retired in 1972. The outfit struggled on until the end of 1978 when it ceased competing, a decision hastened by the onset of more medical problems for John.

CAREER RECORD

** 111 Grands Prix, 6 wins (German GP 1963, German GP 1964, Italian GP 1964, Belgian GP 1966, Mexican GP 1966, Italian GP 1967) * World Champion 1964*

Aguri Suzuki

Nationality: Japanese
Born: 1960

Aguri is Japan's most successful Grand Prix driver to date. After winning the Japanese Formula 3000 title in 1988, a dreadful first season in Formula One in 1989, in which he failed to qualify the Zakspeed-Yamaha, was erased from the memory by some superb performances for Larrousse in 1990, including a finish that brought him to the rostrum at his home Grand Prix. But a financially strapped season with Larrousse did nothing to help Aguri's reputation, which was further damaged by two seasons with Footwork, when he was overshadowed by Michele Alboreto and Derek Warwick. After that, it looked as if he had slipped away from Formula One for good, but he signed a contract to race with Ligier in 1995, and thus gave himself a chance to resurrect his career.

CAREER RECORD

** 58 Grands Prix, no wins (best result – 3rd Japanese GP 1990) * No championship title (best result – 10th overall 1990)*

T

Patrick Tambay

Nationality: French
Born: 1949

Patrick was for years underrated but, even when he was finally given the chance in a top team, he never quite achieved the results his talents promised. After success in Formule Renault and Formula Two, Patrick made his Grand Prix debut, for Ensign, at the same time as Gilles Villeneuve did for McLaren. Villeneuve was to become a close friend, but in fact McLaren preferred to employ Patrick for 1978, while Villeneuve went to Ferrari. The Frenchman came off worse, as McLaren was slumping into a period of uncompetitiveness. He was replaced by Alain Prost after two lean seasons, but went to the USA and won the CanAm title. He then returned to Formula One in 1981 to drive for Ligier, which also dropped him at the end of the season. At the beginning of the following year he announced his retirement from Formula One, but was recalled by Ferrari to be Didier Pironi's team-mate after Villeneuve's death. He was immediately impressive, winning the German Grand Prix before taking an emotional triumph at the San Marino Grand Prix in 1983. He challenged for the World Championship that year, but was dropped by Ferrari at the end of it, and in subsequent spells with Renault and the Haas-Lola teams this gentle and immensely popular man never had equipment worthy of a considerable talent.

CAREER RECORD

** 114 Grands Prix, 2 wins (German GP 1982, San Marino GP 1983) * No championship title (best result – 4th overall 1983)*

Gabriele Tarquini

Nationality: Italian
Born: 1962

Hugely underrated, Tarquini never had a Formula One car which was anywhere near justifying his ability. He caused a sensation in 1985 when, as reigning World Karting champion, he stepped straight into Formula 3000 and became an instant front-runner. However, two subsequent seasons left him short of ultimate success, before he graduated to Formula One with Coloni in 1988. Drafted in at AGS to replace the injured Philippe Streiff in 1989, Gabriele scored a priceless point at Mexico, earning the admiration of Ayrton Senna, but AGS slipped further and further down the grid over the next two years. He signed for Fondmetal in 1992, but success was

Prince Charming *Patrick Tambay's career never realized the man's potential.*

thwarted by huge financial problems, and the team dropped out of Formula One before the end of the season, taking Tarquini with it. He has since made a considerable reputation for himself in touring cars, winning the British title in 1994.

CAREER RECORD

** 37 Grands Prix, no wins (best result – 6th Mexican GP 1989) * No championship title (best result – 26th overall 1989)*

Piero Taruffi

Nationality: Italian
Born: 1906
Died: 1989

Piero was into his forties when the World Championship started in 1950. He only raced in the Italian Grand Prix that year, for Alfa-Romeo, but joined Ferrari in 1951, finishing fifth overall. The following year this all-round sportsman, who was also a doctor of industrial engineering, scored his only Grand Prix win, the Swiss, and that season was also his final full year in Formula One. Piero then concentrated on sports cars, although he did score a fourth and a second place in the British and Italian Grands Prix of 1954.

CAREER RECORD

** 18 Grands Prix, 1 win (Swiss GP 1952) * No championship title (best result – 3rd overall 1952)*

Trevor Taylor

Nationality: British
Born: 1936

Drafted into the Lotus Formula One team after winning two Formula Junior Championships on the trot in 1960–61, Trevor spent much of his career being compared to team-mate Jim Clark – and like every other driver of the era he was found wanting. After a single Grand Prix in 1961, Taylor was given a full season in 1962, when his best result was a second place in the Dutch Grand Prix. A succession of huge accidents, the vast majority of which he could not be blamed for, took away his competitive edge. A disappointing season with the BRP team was effectively the death knell for his career in Formula One, although he raced on in Formula 5000 until 1972.

CAREER RECORD

** 27 Grands Prix, no wins (best result – 2nd Dutch GP 1962) * No championship title (best result – 10th overall 1962)*

Mike Thackwell

Nationality: New Zealander
Born: 1961

The prickly Thackwell has the distinction of being the youngest ever Grand Prix driver, when he started the 1980 Canadian Grand Prix aged only 19, but his Formula One career never really got off the ground. A bad Formula Two accident the following year stalled his progress, but he bounced back to win the 1984 European Formula Two Championship, when he was given a chance to qualify a Tyrrell at the German Grand Prix, but because of its lack of power against the turbos he never really had a chance. His speed was proved in Formula 3000, Indy Cars and sports cars until he retired, disillusioned, in 1988.

CAREER RECORD

** 2 Grands Prix, no wins (best result – retired both races) * No championship title*

Maurice Trintignant

Nationality: French
Born: 1917

Maurice's career lasted on and off for 26 years. Having made a brief racing debut before the Second World War, he was a successful Grand Prix driver when the sport resumed. He cheated death in 1948 after a terrible accident in the Swiss Grand Prix which left him in a coma for eight days, to become a World Championship regular from 1950 to 1964. With two wins in World Championship events, he was always a factor to be reckoned with and occasionally could put in an excellent performance. When he briefly replaced Stirling Moss in 1962, he was still sprightly enough to show Jim Clark the way at Pau. But 1962 proved to be his last competitive year and he eventually retired in 1964.

CAREER RECORD

** 82 Grands Prix, 2 wins (Monaco GP 1955, Monaco GP 1958) * No championship title (best result –4th overall 1954 and 1955)*

V

Jos Verstappen

Nationality: Dutch
Born: 1972

Jos found himself a little out of his depth in Formula One in 1994 after possibly the fastest-ever rise to motor racing's highest echelon. After a successful career in karting, Jos displayed enormous flair in the GM Euroseries in 1992 before winning the prestigious German Formula Three Championship in 1993. Snapped up by Benetton for 1994, he found himself thrown in at the deep end when regular driver JJ Lehto broke his neck in pre-season testing and then failed to recover his form. But, after being involved in a frightening accident at the first race, Jos knuckled down to learning the ropes alongside Michael Schumacher and finished an impressive third in the Hungarian Grand Prix.

CAREER RECORD

** 12 Grands Prix, no wins (best result – 3rd Hungarian GP 1994) * No championship title (best result – 10th overall 1994)*

Gilles Villeneuve

Nationality: Canadian
Born: 1950
Died: 1982

Some thought Gilles personified everything good about motor racing, his astonishing natural speed and spectacular style complemented by an open, humorous, irreverent character. Others said his flamboyance bordered on the reckless. He shot to prominence by dominating his national Formula Atlantic scene in the mid-1970s, and wiped the floor at an international invitation race, which included world champion James Hunt, at the end of 1976. That performance led to a drive with McLaren in the 1977 British Grand Prix, where he stunned Formula One by running on the pace of the leaders in a two-year old car. Unfathomably, McLaren did not take up an option on his services, but Ferrari had more foresight and signed him to replace Lauda at the end of 1977. Gilles, revered to this day by the Italian fans, stayed with Ferrari until the end of his career. He scored his first win, at home in Canada, at the end of 1978, and would have gained the World Championship in 1979, when he won three Grands Prix, had he not honourably stood by team orders at the Italian Grand Prix and sat behind team-mate Jody Scheckter, who took the title instead. There followed two years in hugely inferior cars (although he took two brilliantly opportunistic wins in 1981) until in 1982 he finally had the equipment to win consistently. But, after having victory stolen from under his nose by team-mate Didier Pironi as he was cruising to the flag in the San Marino Grand Prix, Gilles was plunged into turmoil. He pledged never speak to Pironi again, and two weeks later, still furious with him, he crashed to his death in practice for the Belgian Grand Prix. The sport's loss was summed up by Scheckter who said: "Gilles was the fastest driver the world has ever seen."

CAREER RECORD

** 67 Grands Prix, 6 wins (Canadian GP 1978, South African GP 1979, US West GP 1979, US East GP 1979, Monaco GP 1981, Spanish GP 1981) * No championship title (best result – 2nd overall 1979)*

"The fastest ever" *Gilles Villeneuve has become a legend since his death.*

Luigi Villoresi

Nationality: Italian
Born: 1909

A successful Grand Prix driver before the Second World War, Luigi was marginally past his peak by the time the World Championship was founded, although he was still quick enough to win the 1949 Dutch Grand Prix. After years with Maserati and Alfa-Romeo, Luigi had moved to Ferrari in 1949 to encourage the career of his young friend Alberto Ascari, whom he recognized as having a far greater talent than his own. Luigi pulled out of Formula One temporarily after Ascari's death in 1955, returning in 1956 for Maserati, only to crash badly at the non-championship Rome Grand Prix and retire.

CAREER RECORD

** 31 Grands Prix, no wins (best result – 2nd Argentinian GP 1953, Belgian GP 1953) * No championship title (best result – 5th overall 1951 and 1953)*

Wolfgang von Trips

Nationality: German
Born: 1928
Died: 1961

Until Michael Schumacher won the World Championship in 1994, von Trips was Germany's most successful Grand Prix driver. Always quick, he shrugged off the reputation as a crasher he had garnered in his early career, when he rejoined Ferrari in 1960. A number of top-six placings that year were followed by a determined assault on the World Championship in 1961. Two wins and two second places from six races had him bang on target as he arrived at Monza for the Italian Grand Prix. But after taking pole, he made a poor start and, trying to protect his position on the first lap, collided with Jim Clark. His car crashed into the crowd, killing 14 spectators, and von Trips also died, leaving team-mate Phil Hill to clinch a bitter World title.

CAREER RECORD

** 27 Grands Prix, 2 wins (Dutch GP 1961, British GP 1961) * No championship title (best result – 2nd overall 1961)*

W

Derek Warwick

Nationality: British
Born: 1954

It seems inconceivable that the talented Derekcould spend ten years in Formula One and still not win a Grand Prix. Regarded as a better British prospect than Nigel Mansell in the early stages of his career, he appeared to have success in his grasp when he signed to replace Alain Prost at Renault in 1984. But the French team was into a terminal decline and, when he was blocked from joining Lotus in 1986 by Ayrton Senna, he temporarily left Formula One, only to return, for Brabham, after the death of Elio de Angelis. After three promising but fruitless years with Arrows, then an even worse one at Lotus, Derek quit Formula One for success in sports cars – in which he was World Champion in 1991 – before returning for another fruitless year with Footwork in 1993. But still the cards did not fall for him, and in 1994 Formula One passed him by. He has now turned to the British Touring Car Championship to seek success.

CAREER RECORD

** 147 Grands Prix, no wins (best result – 2nd Belgian GP 1984, British GP 1984) * No championship title (best result – 7th overall 1984 and 1988)*

Smooth operator *John Watson was a sensitive performer who could shine.*

Formula One frustration *Warwick – enormously popular, ever unlucky.*

John Watson

Nationality: British
Born: 1946

On his day, John could drive quite superbly, but those days did not come as often as he would have liked. After a slow rise through the single-seater echelons, he broke into Formula One in 1973, and drove for a number of middle-ranking teams until getting his break with Penske in mid-1975. He took a splendid victory for the team in the 1976 Austrian Grand Prix, and was signed to Brabham for the 1977–78 seasons, when a number of good results failed to translate into wins. He then spent a frustrating couple of seasons with McLaren before being the first beneficiary of the arrival of John Barnard and Ron Dennis in 1981. He was a World Championship contender when Niki Lauda returned from retirement in 1982 and, although somewhat overshadowed by the Austrian in 1983, John still managed a brilliant victory in that year's Long Beach Grand Prix. But the sacking of Prost by Renault at the end of 1983 was the death knell for Watson's career. The Frenchman took John's drive, and he was unable to find a seat for 1984. A brief return in 1985 was disappointing, and he enjoyed success in sports cars before setting up his own racing school.

CAREER RECORD

** 152 Grands Prix, 5 wins (Austrian GP 1976, British GP 1981, Belgian GP 1982, Detroit GP 1982, Long Beach GP 1983) * No championship title (best result – 2nd overall 1982)*

Karl Wendlinger

Nationality: Austrian
Born: 1968

Karl is a contemporary of Michael Schumacher and winner of the German Formula Three title in 1989, a year before Schumacher, both men being signed up for the Mercedes sports car junior team in 1990. Missing out on the opportunity to make the sort of electrifying Grand Prix debut Schumacher managed, Karl impressed enormously for the massively under-financed March team in 1992, before joining Sauber for 1993. He was involved in a number of accidents, but the team kept him on for 1994. A crash at the Monaco Grand Prix left him in a coma for 19 days, and took Formula One to the political brink after the deaths of Ayrton Senna and Roland Ratzenberger two weeks before, but he recovered well and was driving again before the end of the year, leaving Sauber to take up its option on him for 1995. Although he believes he will be as quick as ever, only time will show if the accident has left any permanent scars.

CAREER RECORD

** 35 Grands Prix, no wins (best result – 4th Canadian GP 1992, Italian GP 1993, San Marino GP 1994) * No championship title (best result – 11th overall 1993)*

Ken Wharton

Nationality: British
Born: 1916
Died: 1957

After cutting his teeth before the war in an Austin Seven, Ken made his Grand Prix debut in an old-fashioned Frazer-Nash at the 1952 Swiss Grand Prix and finished fourth. But that was to be his best result. A reliable and consistent finisher through 1953 and 1954, he called it a day in Formula One after an unproductive year for Vanwall in 1956, in which he received burns in an accident in the International Trophy at Silverstone. Wharton was killed in a crash in a Ferrari sports car in New Zealand in 1957.

CAREER RECORD

** 15 Grands Prix, no wins (best result – 4th Swiss GP 1952) * No championship title (best result – 13th overall 1952)*

On the brink *Karl Wendlinger's early promise has yet to be fulfilled.*

Peter Whitehead

Nationality: British
Born: 1914
Died: 1958

Peter was a wealthy businessman who raced for the love of it. He was robbed of victory in the 1949 French Grand Prix before problems with the gearbox dropped him to third, and raced on in Formula One, netting a couple of top-ten places in Ferraris, until the end of 1952, by which time he was finding success in sports car events. After 1952 he raced in Formula One only in the British Grand Prix, and pulled out altogether in 1954. He was killed when his half-brother Graham crashed the car in which both were racing in the 1958 Tour de France.

CAREER RECORD

** 10 Grands Prix, no wins (best result – 3rd French GP 1950) * No championship title (best result – 9th overall 1950)*

Roger Williamson

Nationality: British
Born: 1948
Died: 1973

A protégé of successful Midlands businessman and racing enthusiast Tom Wheatcroft, who is now the owner of the Donington Park racing circuit, Williamson was an impressive and spectacular race-winner in Formula Three and Formula Two. Wheatcroft wanted to fund him in a full season of Formula One in 1974, and to this end, they dipped their toes in the water in 1973 with a private March. But Roger was taken out of the British Grand Prix in the infamous Scheckter crash on the first lap. And then at Zandvoort a suspension failure caused him to crash. The car came to rest upside down and on fire and, apart from the brave David Purley, no one tried to rescue him. As the marshals stood by without fireproof clothing, Roger burned to death in front of millions of television viewers.

CAREER RECORD

** 2 Grands Prix, no wins (best result – retired from both races) * No championship title*

Manfred Winkelhock

Nationality: German
Born: 1952
Died: 1985

Manfred progressed quickly through the ranks with support from BMW, although he never won a race in Formula Two. Spending most of his career with ATS and RAM, he was rarely afforded the opportunity to shine, but his reflexes and bravery were used to good effect at the Detroit Grand Prix in 1982, when he qualified fifth. A good drive in a Porsche sports car provided him some welcome success, but he was killed in an accident at the Mosport Park 1000 km race in 1985.

CAREER RECORD

** 47 Grands Prix, no wins (best result – 5th Brazilian GP 1982) * No championship title (best result – 22nd overall 1982)*

Reine Wisell

Nationality: Swedish
Born: 1941

Reine was an arch-rival of fellow Swede Ronnie Peterson but had nothing like the talent of his compatriot and did not quite make the grade in Formula One. His performances in Formula 5000 in 1970 won him a Formula One drive with Lotus, and he finished third on his debut in the US Grand Prix that year. But as 1971 progressed he was increasingly eclipsed by team-mate Emerson Fittipaldi and, after a fruitless 1972 with BRM, he drifted out of Formula One into sports cars, finally leaving the sport for good in 1975.

CAREER RECORD

** 22 Grands Prix, no wins (best result – 3rd US GP 1970) * No championship title (best result – 9th overall 1971)*

Z

Alessandro Zanardi

Nationality: Italian
Born: 1966

Alessandro rocketed to the motor racing world's attention in 1991 when he was a surprise championship contender in Formula 3000. Although he eventually lost the title to the more consistent Christian Fittipaldi, Alessandro had made his Formula One debut by the end of the season, filling the seat vacated at Jordan by Michael Schumacher. An excellent drive in the wet in the Spanish Grand Prix showed that he had a talent worth following, and he landed a role as Benetton's test driver in 1992. The following year he signed for Lotus, when he was lucky to survive a huge accident at Eau Rouge in the Belgian Grand Prix, after which he was replaced by Pedro Lamy. He won his seat back in 1994 but the team was very short of money and, although he was loved by his team for his sunny personality as well as his tenacity, nothing worthwhile came of it, and he was without a drive in 1995.

CAREER RECORD

** 25 Grands Prix, no wins (best result – 6th Brazilian GP 1993) * No championship title (best result – 20th overall 1993)*

THE GREAT RACES

Do you remember when Damon Hill conquered the conditions in Japan and pipped Michael Schumacher to set up the 1994 world title for a grand finale? It was a superb race, yet others before have been even better. Some have been great for their sheer spectacle and the thrill of the chase. Others have had the added intrigue of a world championship hanging in the balance. But the best of all have been the races in which only a no-quarter-asked-or-given fight mattered.

Ask any group of motor racing fans which was the greatest Grand Prix of all time and you won't be able to get a unanimous verdict. However, there are a handful of races that would crop up in most people's top ten. Who could forget Senna and Bellof hauling in Prost in the rain at Monaco in 1984? Or Hunt's title-clinching race through the rain in Japan in 1976? Or Gethin getting his nose in front at Monza in 1971, when the first five cars home were covered by just a second? Or Fangio chasing and catching the Ferraris in Germany in 1957? Wicked races, vivid memories.

Zero visibility *Damon Hill puts Michael Schumacher under pressure in Japan 1994.*

Rothmans
MILD SEVEN
RENAULT
elf
MILD SEVEN
5
MILD SEVEN
SANYO

Blond bomber *Mike Hawthorn shot to stardom at Reims breaking the big-race domination of Alberto Ascari (right).*

FRENCH GRAND PRIX 1953

REIMS, JULY 5

Pos.	*Driver*	*Nat.*	*Make*
1	Mike Hawthorn	GB	Ferrari (113.65 mph)
2	Juan Manuel Fangio	Arg	Maserati
3	Froilan Gonzalez	Arg	Maserati
4	Alberto Ascari	It	Ferrari
5	Giuseppe Farina	It	Ferrari
6	Luigi Villoresi	It	Ferrari
Pole:	Ascari		

The years 1952 and 1953 were all about Alberto Ascari and Ferrari. The Italian, who many of his day thought better than Juan Manuel Fangio, won the World Championship in consecutive years, taking victory in 11 of the 15 Grands Prix. But this race at the Reims triangle was not one of them. Ascari was always a factor in a slipstreaming battle for the lead between the Ferrari and Maserati factory teams, but he was beaten into fourth for once, and everyone else was left in the shadows by a duel between Fangio and a young Briton called Mike Hawthorn, a battle of such intensity over the closing laps that the two of them passed the pits dead level on no fewer than ten occasions.

Hawthorn – rising star

Hawthorn loved parties and womanizing, and his performances in the car were necessarily dependent on the form the previous night's entertainment had taken. But that gorgeous summer day in northern France was one of his great days.

"The Farnham Flier" was the junior member of the Ferrari team, but he had already proved himself very fast indeed and was in among the leading group from the first lap.

Argentinian Froilan Gonzalez's Maserati took the lead, pulling out a second a lap, as he alone was to be stopping for fuel and tyres, but behind him a battle was raging between the Ferraris of Ascari, Luigi Villoresi, Hawthorn and Farina, and the Maseratis of Fangio and his protégé Onofre Marimon.

For lap after lap they swapped places back and forth, the Reims track, effectively three long straights, two fast corners and a hairpin, providing its usual great race. At the halfway point, the order was Fangio, Hawthorn, Ascari, Farina, Marimon and Gonzalez. But within seven laps, Gonzalez had moved up to fourth.

The great duel

By half-distance, Hawthorn and Fangio had moved away into a race of their own – but what a race! The Argentinian was bringing all his experience to the forefront, but Hawthorn, a veteran of only a couple of years of club racing, was proving a match. Fangio, though, had a problem which weighed the odds against him. "Soon after halfway," he recalled, "I found that I could not get first gear, which I needed for the hairpin at the beginning of the pit straight. It was not easy to disguise the fact." Indeed not, but the maestro did everything he could to minimize the problem.

With five laps to go, Fangio was a wheel-width ahead of Hawthorn as they came past the pits, but they headed off around that lap chopping and changing the lead innumerable times. With four laps to go, Hawthorn took to the grass as Fangio weaved to stop him passing, but was still alongside as they disappeared under the Dunlop Bridge.

They went into the last lap blasting past the pits in a dead heat and, as they disappeared from sight, binoculars were trained on the hairpin, and bets were being taken as to who would come out on top. In the end, however, the loss of first gear was too much for Fangio. Although he passed Hawthorn, the Englishman dived past under braking and, as he slammed the lever into first Fangio had no response and could only wait as the revs built up in second gear. So slow out of the hairpin was he that Gonzalez almost caught him on the line. Fangio was 40 yards behind Hawthorn, who had taken the first win by a British driver in a Grand Prix.

GERMAN GRAND PRIX 1957

NURBURGRING, AUGUST 4

Pos.	Driver	Nat.	Make
1	Juan Manuel Fangio	Arg	Maserati (88.70 mph)
2	Mike Hawthorn	GB	Ferrari
3	Peter Collins	GB	Ferrari
4	Luigi Musso	It	Ferrari
5	Stirling Moss	GB	Vanwall
6	Jean Behra	Fr	Maserati
Pole:	Fangio		

Ayrton Senna thought Juan Manuel Fangio the best driver that ever lived and, nearly 40 years after Fangio's retirement, that is perhaps the highest praise the great Argentinian can have, coming as it does from a man who was considered by so many to be the greatest of all time. Although Fangio was doubtless honoured when he first heard Senna's views, in fact his talent was so great, his record so peerless, that his career has no need of such recognition to stand proud.

Fangio won 24 of his 51 Grands Prix, started from pole in 27 and won a record five World Championships. Statistics such as these put Fangio alone, but not even they can do justice to the genius he displayed so often at the wheel, and which never shone as brightly as in the German Grand Prix at Nurburgring in 1957.

Fangio breaks lap record

Fangio made a poor start from pole, and dropped behind Hawthorn and his Ferrari team-mate Peter Collins. But, on his first flying lap, Fangio had lowered his own lap record – which he had left at 9min. 41.6sec. when he won for Ferrari in 1956 – by seven seconds, and he took the lead from the two Ferraris on lap three.

Fangio was planning to make a stop for fuel and tyres, while the Ferraris were not, so he would have to catch and pass Hawthorn and Collins a second time if he was to win. By the time of his stop, on lap 11 of 22, Fangio was 27.8sec in front, and everything appeared to be on schedule. The stop, though, went badly. By the time he rejoined he was over a minute adrift. Surely his chance had gone.

He took a couple of laps to settle, but then began lapping at unbelievable speeds, gaining eight or nine seconds per lap on the two Englishmen, who were desperately trying to pull out enough of a lead to protect themselves.

On lap 18 he dipped below his pole time for the first time, a 9min 25.3 sec lap, bringing him to within 20 seconds of the Ferraris. By now the crowd was on the edge of its seats, and the tension rose further with another lap record for Fangio on the 19th tour, a 9min 23.4sec lap closing the gap to Hawthorn and Collins to just 13 seconds.

Those watching realized they were seeing history in the making, and a huge roar went up from the grandstands as the Ferraris loomed into view, with Fangio less than a hundred yards behind them, having just lapped in an incredible 9min 17.4sec – six seconds faster than his own lap record, and eight faster than he had managed in qualifying.

A genius at the wheel

As the cars thundered past the pits and into the South Curve, Fangio closed right up to Collins's gearbox, and swept by with a wheel on the grass, peppering Collins with stones, one of which shattered his goggles.

Hawthorn understood that he had fought a losing battle, and Fangio sliced past before the two were halfway around that penultimate lap, then eased off to take the flag three seconds ahead.

It was Fangio's greatest, and last, victory – and it clinched him his fifth World title in seven years. "Even now," he says to this day, "I can feel fear when I think of that race. I knew what I had done, the chances I had taken. Without any doubt, the Nurburgring was my favourite circuit. I loved it, all of it, and I think that day I conquered it. On another day, it might have conquered me, who knows? I'd driven my car to the limit, and perhaps a little bit more. I'd never driven like that before, and I knew I never would again."

The best ever? *Juan Manuel Fangio drove his greatest race at the Nurburgring in 1957, catching the Ferraris to win from behind in his gorgeous Maserati 250F.*

Debut winner *Giancarlo Baghetti (50) won first time out for Ferrari as the opposition expired in the searing heat at Reims. He was never to win again.*

FRENCH GRAND PRIX 1961

REIMS, JULY 2

Pos.	*Driver*	*Nat.*	*Make*
1	Giancarlo Baghetti	It	Ferrari (119.85 mph)
2	Dan Gurney	USA	Porsche
3	Jim Clark	GB	Lotus-Climax
4	Innes Ireland	GB	Lotus-Climax
5	Bruce McLaren	NZ	Cooper-Climax
6	Graham Hill	GB	BRM
Pole:	Phil Hill	USA	Ferrari

A new formula was introduced into Grand Prix racing in 1961 and, as so often was the case in the past, Ferrari was ready for it before everybody else. Its beautiful Tipo 156 "shark-nose" was more powerful and generally faster than any of its rivals, and it was only beaten three times all year.

Ferrari in front

For the rest, it dominated, and the Scuderia's drivers Wolfgang von Trips and Phil Hill were soon in a battle of their own. Of the races Ferrari won that year, though, the French Grand Prix was the one it came closest to losing. Von Trips, Hill and Richie Ginther retired, and the race could so easily have slipped from Ferrari's grasp. That it didn't was all due to Grand Prix debutant Giancarlo Baghetti, a young Italian who was employed by Ferrari to race only in Italy and was entered in the French race unofficially.

Until after half-distance there seemed little to distinguish this Grand Prix from any other Ferrari victory. In searing heat – 95°F (35°C) in the shade and over 126°F (52.2°C) on the track – Hill, von Trips and Ginther dominated qualifying, and Hill and von Trips set a comfortable pace at the head of the field once the race was under way. Ginther was forced to fend off Stirling Moss – as usual the best of the rest in his Lotus – but gradually seemed to be establishing himself in third place.

Attention was focused on the battle for fifth, comprising Jim Clark, Innes Ireland, Graham Hill, Baghetti, Jo Bonnier, Bruce McLaren and Dan Gurney, who were engaging in a breathless slipstreaming battle on the ultra-fast Reims triangle. Slowly, Baghetti used the superiority of his equipment to haul himself to the front. And this is when it all began to go wrong for the main Ferrari team.

First von Trips coasted into the pits, after a stone had pierced his radiator. A few laps later Hill spun at the Thillois hairpin and was hit by Moss. He rejoined in tenth. Ginther was now in the lead, but his engine died, having used up all its oil.

Baghetti's triumph

So now it rested with Baghetti to uphold Ferrari honour. Ironically, he was the driver who had first given notice of the 156's potential, winning a non-championship race at Syracuse, and now he had to protect its reputation against two vastly more experienced drivers – Gurney and Bonnier in their Porsches.

Gregor Grant, in *Autosport* magazine, summed up those frenetic last few laps thus: "For lap after lap the trio swapped places, often travelling abreast. Gurney and Bonnier really went to work, but nothing seemed to shake the cool-headed Italian.

"Three laps from the end, Bonnier's engine went sick, and Gurney was left to deal with Baghetti. At Thillois on the last lap, Gurney had the lead, but about 300 yards from the finish, Baghetti pulled out of the Porsche's slipstream and darted in front, to the cheers of the excited crowd."

It was a season of highs and lows for Ferrari. Hill won the World Championship, but only after von Trips had been killed when he crashed into the crowd at the Italian Grand Prix; 14 spectators died as well. As for Baghetti, he drove in a further 20 Grands Prix, but was thwarted when Ferrari was left behind by the V8-engined opposition in 1962, and he struggled to land a regular drive, retiring in 1967. However, that first-time victory has guaranteed him a place in Grand Prix history that he will probably never lose.

GERMAN GRAND PRIX 1968

The daunting Nurburgring was at its most capricious this particular weekend in 1968. Rain and mist rendered the track treacherous and visibility virtually non-existent. And in these conditions the world's best drivers had to tackle the most challenging racing circuit in the world – all 14 miles and 187 corners of it – almost blind. In this soaking version of hell Jackie Stewart produced what many people believe was the greatest drive of one of the great careers.

What gave the Nurburgring its reputation was not just that it was difficult, but that it necessarily brought out the best in the greatest racers.

Juan Manuel Fangio's drive in 1957 was one illustration of this, Stewart's 11 years later was another. The fact that he drove with a broken wrist made his achievement all the more remarkable. Stewart was not on pole, that honour going to Jacky Ickx's Ferrari. But it was obvious within seconds of the start that Stewart – who lined up sixth – was fastest on race day. He was up to fourth as the field piled into the North Curve. By Adenau Crossing he was on the tail of Chris Amon's Ferrari, and just a little further on he was in a lead which he extended to eight seconds by the end of the first lap. After another 14-mile tour he was a further 25 seconds in front. After five of the 14 laps that gap had increased to over a minute.

Graham Hill, who would soon be crowned world champion, was second for Lotus, holding off a determined Amon and, although the dreadful weather conditions would punish any mistake, things looked set to stay that way until, with three laps to go, a differential problem caused Amon to spin, ending up on top of an earth bank.

That should have left Hill unchallenged in second, but since he could see only spray in his mirrors, he did not realize that Amon was out and continued to press on – until he spun. The car would not restart and he had to climb out and bump-start it. With Amon gone, he retained second, with Jochen Rindt closing quickly.

NURBURGRING, AUGUST 4

Pos.	Driver	Nat.	Make
1	Jackie Stewart	GB	Matra-Ford (86.86 mph)
2	Graham Hill	GB	Lotus-Ford
3	Jochen Rindt	A	Brabham-Repco
4	Jacky Ickx	Bel	Ferrari
5	Jack Brabham	Aus	Brabham-Repco
6	Pedro Rodriguez	Mex	BRM
Pole:	Ickx		

Final triumph

Stewart had been over three minutes in front before Hill's spin, and he crossed the line almost four minutes up, giving him time to climb out and accept congratulations before the others came in sight.

Nothing sums up Jackie's achievement better than this: "Had I not won a Grand Prix at the Nurburgring, there would have been something missing from my career – but wasn't it a ridiculous place? Leaping from one bump to another, 187 corners or whatever it was! The number of times I thanked God when I finished a lap. I can't remember doing one more balls-out lap of the 'Ring than I needed to. It gave you amazing satisfaction, but anyone who says he loved it is either a liar or wasn't going fast enough. I like that place best when I'm sitting by a log fire on a winter's night. Clear in my mind are all the braking distances and gear changes, and that's surely the only way I've ever lapped it without a mistake!"

The post-race photographs showing an exhausted Stewart clasping his injured arm are confirmation that there can have been few times in his career when Jackie wanted to be by that fireplace more. It was not, Stewart says, his greatest drive. That was the 1973 Italian Grand Prix, when he unlapped himself on an entire field. But this takes nothing away from our appreciation of one of the sport's greatest drives ever.

Atrocious conditions *Jackie Stewart called on all his skills and concentration to win at a frighteningly wet Nurburgring.*

ITALIAN GRAND PRIX 1971

MONZA, SEPTEMBER 5

Pos.	Driver	Nat.	Make
1	Peter Gethin	GB	BRM (150.75 mph)
2	Ronnie Peterson	Swe	March-Ford
3	François Cevert	Fr	Tyrrell-Ford
4	Mike Hailwood	GB	Surtees-Ford
5	Howden Ganley	NZ	BRM
6	Chris Amon	NZ	Matra-Simca
Pole:	Amon		

Before chicanes blighted its superfast layout, the autodrome at historic Monza could be relied upon to provide the best race of the year. It was effectively five corners joined by straights, and that rendered it almost impossible for a driver to make a break.

Gethin's instant of glory

It was not rare to see ten cars battling for the lead. But of all the slipstreaming battles, the one that has passed into history as the most thrilling was that won by Peter Gethin in 1971. It was to be his only Grand Prix win.

He had qualified 11th, the sort of grid position from which it is all but impossible to win a race these days. But the field at Monza was so close: he was just over a second from pole, which was occupied by Chris Amon's Matra.

Clay Regazzoni's Ferrari blasted through from the fourth row to lead at the end of the first lap. But there were no fewer than 15 cars nose-to-tail at the head of the field. Lap four saw the race gain its second leader, Ronnie Peterson's March drafting past the Ferrari around the back of the circuit. By the end of that lap Regazzoni was fourth, as Jackie Stewart's Tyrrell and Jo Siffert's BRM followed Peterson through.

Ronnie held the lead for four laps, but Stewart's team-mate François Cevert had moved from tenth to fifth, helped by a multi-car tow. He headed Jacky Ickx's Ferrari, the BRMs of Howden Ganley and Gethin, and Amon, now back in ninth with tyre trouble and rising engine temperatures.

Still the lead continued to change. Peterson took it back from Stewart, who had been displaced from second, first by Regazzoni, then by Cevert. There was nothing to chose between the first dozen, and whoever led at the back of the circuit never seemed to be in front when the cars reached the pits.

Within two laps at quarter-distance, the race lost both Ferraris and Stewart's Tyrrell, all with engine problems. This caused the race to split up. Peterson, Cevert, and Mike Hailwood – up from 17th! – led, eight seconds ahead of Ganley, Siffert and Amon, who were a small distance ahead of Jack Oliver and Gethin. Before long the pack began to close up. Hailwood led, then Siffert at half-distance. Then Amon decided to make his move. After sitting behind the first three – Peterson, Cevert and Hailwood – he suddenly flew past them all into the lead on lap 27, with 18 to go. With the Matra clearly fastest in a straight line, this looked as if it could be the race in which the famously unlucky New Zealander finally broke his duck.

He still led with just seven laps to go, but it then fate thwarted him again. Trying to remove one of his tear-off visors, the whole visor came away. With his eyes unprotected, he had to drop back.

Amazing final lap

Gethin had closed on to the tail of the leading pack. The crowd was on its feet as Peterson led Cevert, Hailwood and Gethin into the last lap. Cevert took the lead at Lesmo, Gethin moved into third and then, approaching the looping Parabolica, made his final do-or-die attempt, passing Peterson on the grass and arriving at the corner too fast, with wheels locked up and smoking between an alarmed Peterson and Cevert, who moved over fearing contact. As they crossed the line, Gethin led Peterson, Cevert, Hailwood and Ganley, with all five covered by 0.61sec, with Gethin winning by just 0.01sec. It was the fastest Grand Prix and the closest finish in Formula One history.

So close *Gethin (arm aloft), winner of the closest finish in Grand Prix history.*

BRITISH GRAND PRIX 1973

SILVERSTONE, JULY 14

Pos.	*Driver*	*Nat.*	*Make*
1	Peter Revson	USA	McLaren-Ford (131.75 mph)
2	Ronnie Peterson	Swe	Lotus-Ford
3	Denny Hulme	NZ	McLaren-Ford
4	James Hunt	GB	March-Ford
5	François Cevert	Fr	Tyrrell-Ford
6	Carlos Reutemann	Arg	Brabham-Ford
Pole:	Peterson		

The pre-race betting was on Jackie Stewart – but not as far as Peter Revson was concerned. The American had placed a wager of £100 on himself for victory.

The race could have been tinged with tragedy, for at the end of the first lap McLaren's young charger Jody Scheckter triggered an accident which took out nine cars and blocked the track.

A disastrous start

The South African newcomer had moved up into third, ahead of team-leader Denny Hulme, when the accident happened. He had moved by the New Zealander into the ultra-fast Woodcote corner, but was off-line and drifted wide, looping into a spin. He came back across the track, narrowly missing the front-runners, one of whom was Revson, his other McLaren team-mate, before colliding with the pit wall and collecting the midfield runners.

Although the accident halted the race and led to a chicane being built at Woodcote, it did nothing to stop a fantastic Grand Prix.

At the restart Ronnie Peterson's Lotus led from Niki Lauda's BRM, Jackie Stewart's Tyrrell, Emerson Fittipaldi's Lotus, Hulme and Revson. Stewart dropped back after gearbox troubles forced a spin at Stowe, and Lauda, who had jumped the start, was beginning to feel the pace and slip down the order.

Revson moved up to third behind Peterson and Fittipaldi, and began to sense he was going to win. He was relaxed, the car was handling superbly and he had chosen the right tyres. Revson closed up to Fittipaldi. But the Brazilian reigning world champion found there was nothing he could do to keep him from closing on Peterson, whose handling was deteriorating. He and Revson edged ever closer to Ronnie until, with 30 laps to go, Fittipaldi dropped out with transmission failure.

Then a light rain began to fall, making Peterson's difficult task impossible. Within two laps Revson was past. But while he might have been expected to pull away, he didn't and, although he was in control, he found himself only a second or two ahead of a titanic scrap between Peterson, Hulme and James Hunt, who was for the first time bringing himself to the notice of the fans with a stirring drive in a private March.

Revson under pressure

By Hulme's admission, Hunt, known better for his nickname "Hunt the Shunt" than for his driving, "was driving well, giving us a hard time".

Hulme, troubled by a too-soft front tyre, had let Hunt by into third, but into the last 12 laps, he closed up again and pushed Hunt on to Peterson's tail. Ronnie, in turn, was scarcely more than two seconds from Revson in the lead. Hulme sliced by Hunt with just over ten laps to go, but an oil slick prevented him pushing Peterson aside and making it a McLaren one-two.

But it was not for want of trying. Into the last corner, the trio looked almost like one machine. Peterson went wide and came frighteningly close to duplicating Scheckter's accident. Hulme dipped for the inside, hoping to take advantage of the mistake, and Hunt was trying for a way past both. But Peterson-Hulme-Hunt was how they finished, with 0.4sec between Hunt and Hulme, and 0.2sec separating him from Peterson. Revson, in the lead, was only 2.8 sec ahead.

"That really was an incredible race," Hunt would say later. "It was the first Grand Prix in which I was competitive. I was happy to be fourth, but I probably could have been second, had not my left front tyre blistered towards the end. I kept close to Ronnie and Denny, hoping they might take each other off. But the nearest they came to a mistake was when Ronnie got sideways on the grass – after the flag!"

Peter Perfect *Revson leads François Cevert's Tyrrell on the way to winnning his first Grand Prix at Silverstone, and his bet.*

JAPANESE GRAND PRIX 1976

FUJI, OCTOBER 24

Pos.	Driver	Nat.	Make
1	Mario Andretti	USA	Lotus-Ford (114.093 mph)
2	Patrick Depailler	Fr	Tyrrell-Ford
3	James Hunt	GB	McLaren-Ford
4	Alan Jones	Aus	Surtees-Ford
5	Clay Regazzoni	Swi	Ferrari
6	Gunnar Nilsson	Swe	Lotus-Ford
Pole:	Andretti		

At the end of a season full of drama and near tragedy, James Hunt needed to finish four points ahead of Niki Lauda to win the World Championship. The Englishman dominated the race, first in the most dreadful weather conditions and then just as effectively when the torrential rain stopped and the track began to dry.

Hunt's task was made easier when Lauda pulled out after one lap, having decided that the terrible conditions, the impossible visibility, were too much of a risk. He had nearly lost his life at the German Grand Prix, when his Ferrari was consumed by flames and clearly, important as the World Championship was, it was not important enough to risk losing his life.

Hunt's great getaway

Hunt had also not wanted to race on the sodden track, on which even the course car aquaplaned when it went out to inspect it. But once the race was under way, Hunt was in a better position than Lauda. A fantastic start had seen him leap into the lead, and that meant he was the only driver who could see where he was going.

Hunt was driving beautifully, holding off a brief challenge from the March of Vittorio Brambilla, which must have scared Hunt silly when "the Monza Gorilla" spun off while alongside him.

Hunt, though, was safe and, as the rain stopped, the track began to dry and Mount Fuji's snowy slopes appeared from behind the clouds, he seemed set to take the title in the most glorious way possible – with victory in the final race.

But Hunt was having problems. His wet tyres began to break up, and he was hauled in by Patrick Depailler's Tyrrell and Mario Andretti's Lotus. They swept by him soon enough, but Hunt's third place would be enough to clinch the title by one point, and when one of Depailler's tyres blew, second place was even better.

However, it was not going to be easy. His tyres were now in a parlous state, and he was looking to his pit for guidance as to when he should come in to change them. But they did not want to make the decision either, and James was growing increasingly frustrated and furious in the cockpit.

In the end the tyres made the decision for him. His front left shredded, and Hunt headed to the pits. When he rejoined he was back in fifth, with five laps to go. The Ferrari crew was jumping up and down in jubilation thinking that Lauda's title was secure, but that was counting without an inspired Hunt.

Missing the signals

Quickly he moved past Alan Jones and Clay Regazzoni to take third, but the communication breakdown with the pits meant that he did not know what position he was in and he carried on pushing for his life to catch Depailler.

A lap in front of them all, in the lead but just ahead on the road, was Andretti, who had driven at his own pace to keep his tyres in good shape and was reaping the benefits – and his presence must have confused James even further.

Andretti had been reading the illuminated lap board in the pits to gauge the situation, but Hunt, in a red mist, had not thought of doing that. At the end of the race, as he crossed the line in that championship-clinching third place, he still did not know that he had won.

As Hunt climbed out of his car, he set to berating team manager Teddy Mayer, livid about what he said had been atrocious pit signals. Indeed, he was oblivious to the grinning face in front of him, and it was only when a well-wisher got through to him that Hunt realized the magnitude of his achievement. He had won the World Championship. And, on that treacherous day at the foot of Mount Fuji, he truly deserved it.

Treading gingerly *James Hunt heads McLaren team mate Jochen Mass en-route to third place and the 1976 title.*

Super Swede *Ronnie Peterson marked his return to the sharp end of Formula One in 1978 with a thrilling last-lap victory for Lotus at Kyalami.*

SOUTH AFRICAN GRAND PRIX 1978

KYALAMI, MARCH 4,1978

Pos.	Driver	Nat.	Make
1	Ronnie Peterson	Swe	Lotus-Ford (116.698 mph)
2	Patrick Depailler	Fr	Tyrrell-Ford
3	John Watson	GB	Brabham-Alfa Romeo
4	Alan Jones	Aus	Williams-Ford
5	Jacques Laffite	Fr	Ligier-Matra
6	Didier Pironi	Fr	Tyrrell-Ford
Pole:	Niki Lauda	A	Brabham-Alfa Romeo

Ronnie Peterson had not won for over a year, and only six months previously the critics had said that the man who had been known as "The Fastest Man in the World" might never win again. But if you have as much ability as Peterson, then you do not lose it. It merely gets frustrated by years of inferior equipment.

But a switch to the resurgent Lotus team for 1978 gave him back all his enthusiasm. In truth, however, this was not a race which Peterson looked likely to win. It was a race which should have produced a victory for team-mate Mario Andretti, for a young Riccardo Patrese or for Patrick Depailler and the Tyrrell team.

Andretti begins well

Andretti started from the front row and streaked away into the distance. Indeed, it looked to be an Andretti and Lotus benefit, the second in three races, in what was to become Mario's World Championship year.

But at quarter-distance Andretti hit tyre trouble. If he carried on pushing at this speed, he would lose the race. But if he backed off to conserve it, then the chances were he would be able to pick up the pace again.

So he let past Jody Scheckter's Wolf, which was being pursued by Patrese's Arrows in only its second race. Patrese pushed Scheckter so hard that the Wolf's rear tyres went off and, after a spirited wheel-to-wheel battle, Patrese forged ahead.

The Italian, driving with a composure that was not always seen in his career, looked certain to win for the fledgling Arrows team. Then, with just 15 laps to go, the engine blew. It was not until 1982 that Patrese would score his first Grand Prix win.

That left Depailler in the lead, but with Andretti, John Watson and Peterson not far behind. This, in fact, had been a remarkable drive by Peterson, for he had been relegated to the sixth row of the grid by gearbox problems. But, once into the race, he picked his way through to the top six with aplomb.

Watson was next to go when he spun on oil, and that left Andretti, his car working perfectly again, catching Depailler for the lead, with Peterson closing up to both. Then Andretti's engine started to stutter. He was out of fuel, and livid because, to keep the weight of the car down, the Lotus team manager, Colin Chapman, had taken out some fuel on the grid.

Peterson hauls in Depailler

The day was not lost for Lotus, however, for Depailler's car was now trailing smoke. But Ronnie made no real inroads into the Tyrrell's lead until, with just five laps to go, the fates decided that the next dollop of bad luck was to go to the Frenchman, and the Tyrrell began to stutter – it too was having trouble picking up the last drops of fuel.

Peterson was gaining all the time. But, would it be enough? Would Depailler finally score his first Grand Prix win after five years, or would Peterson provide the best answer he could give to those who had said he was past it?

Into the last lap they went, with Peterson right on Depailler's tail. Side-by-side they ran, each driver's desperation to win plain to see as twice they banged wheels. But at the Esses, the last but one corner on the last lap, the blue and white Tyrrell slid sideways and the gleaming black Lotus slipped by to take the flag with just a three-length lead. Phew!

Back to front *John Watson made an art of winning races from the back of the grid – this was his most outstanding.*

UNITED STATES GRAND PRIX WEST 1983

LONG BEACH, MARCH 27

Pos.	*Driver*	*Nat.*	*Make*
1	John Watson	GB	McLaren-Ford (80.625 mph)
2	Niki Lauda	A	McLaren-Ford
3	René Arnoux	Fr	Ferrari
4	Jacques Laffite	Fr	Williams-Ford
5	Marc Surer	Swe	Arrows-Ford
6	Johnny Cecotto	Ven	Theodore-Ford
Pole:	Patrick Tambay	Fr	Ferrari

"Don't ask me to explain it," said John Watson, "because I can't." The Ulsterman, who had made it something of a speciality to win races from poor grid positions, had done it again. This one was the most extreme example of his art.

Watson started 22nd but, by the end of lap 26, when three of the four men who had set the pace eliminated themselves, he was up to sixth behind team-mate Niki Lauda, who had lined up a place behind him on the grid. With almost 50 laps to go, it began to dawn on some people that one of the McLarens would win. And the reason was tyres.

Tyre problems

McLaren were on Michelins, and the French company's tyres had failed to work in qualifying. While the Goodyear runners found up to three seconds a lap when they bolted on their super-soft "quallies", Michelin's soft compound was no quicker than its race tyre.

But although McLaren had been slow in qualifying before and had come through in the race, the pre-race warm-up, when they might have been expected to show their true form, gave them no solace this time; they were still off the pace.

In the pre-race build-up Watson made a decision that was to win him the event. While Lauda plumped for the tyre compound he had used in qualifying, Watson went for one which he had used to win with on the Detroit street circuit in 1982.

Watson and Lauda sliced through the back markers, as they might have been expected to do, but at one-third distance a win still looked unlikely. However, in the course of that lap, Keke Rosberg, whose Williams had been trapped behind Patrick Tambay's pole-sitting Ferrari, ran out of patience. He dived for the inside at one of the Long Beach street track's hairpins. But he was too far back and collided with the red car, which reared upon to two wheels. Tambay retired, but while Rosberg kept going, he collided with Jean-Pierre Jarier's Ligier at the following corner, putting both out.

Watson catches up

In a flash Watson was promoted into the top six. Ahead of him were Jacques Laffite's Williams with Riccardo Patrese's Brabham right behind him, the Arrows and Tyrrell of Marc Surer and Danny Sullivan, and Lauda, who, with Watson shadowing his every move, was 20 seconds behind the leading pair.

Laffite, on Goodyears, was losing grip and he began to come under heavy pressure from Patrese, on Michelins. By lap 42 the Italian was challenging for the lead, but now the McLarens, with Watson having passed Lauda, were only five seconds behind. A lap later Patrese missed his braking point at the end of Shoreline Drive. By the time he had rejoined, the McLarens were past. Within two more laps, they were running one-two.

From there, Watson had an easy run to the finish. Laffite was in increasing trouble with a lack of grip and was lapped only 24 laps after Watson had passed him for the lead, while Lauda was slowed by cramp.

"We still had too much understeer," said Watson, "but the grip was good all the way through. This wasn't like Detroit, though. There I felt from the beginning that I was going to win, even though I started way back. I'm delighted of course, but I'm also baffled."

It was all down to four round bits of black rubber and a healthy dose of luck. Yet it remained one of the most remarkable recovery drives ever.

MONACO GRAND PRIX 1984

MONTE CARLO, JUNE 3

Pos.	Driver	Nat.	Make
1	Alain Prost	Fr	McLaren-Porsche (62.619 mph)
2	Ayrton Senna	Bra	Toleman-Hart
3	Stefan Bellof	Ger	Tyrrell-Ford
4	René Arnoux	Fr	Ferrari
5	Keke Rosberg	Fin	Williams-Honda
6	Elio de Angelis	It	Lotus-Renault
Pole:	Prost		

Nigel Mansell could have won it, Ayrton Senna, in only his seventh Grand Prix, probably would have, but when the race was stopped after just 31 laps, Alain Prost had hung on to victory in one of the wettest-ever races in the principality.

Wet it might have been, but dull it was not. Prost put not a wheel wrong to continue what had been almost total domination of the season by McLaren, but had the chequered flag been shown one, perhaps two laps, later, then the race could have fallen to Senna, who first came to the world's attention on that soaking afternoon. And catching both of them was the German, Stefan Bellof, who put in the greatest drive of a tragically short career.

Mansell throws it away

Prost had started from pole, and led around the first lap – at the end of which, incredibly, Senna and Bellof were up to 9th and 11th places from 13th and 20th on the grid. Briefly, Prost extended his lead over Mansell, who, excellent as ever at Monaco, had lined up beside the Frenchman on the front row.

But by lap ten the Englishman's Lotus was right up with the McLaren, and quickly passed it for the lead. He pulled away until lap 16 when, going up the hill to Casino Square, with the power hard on, he hit the painted white line in the road with one of his rear wheels.

The car flicked right, then left, before clouting the barrier on both sides of the track. Mansell, his rear wing askew and suspension broken, tried to limp back to the pits but spun into retirement at Mirabeau a couple of corners later.

"The winner today," Prost had said before the race, "will not be the fastest man, but the one who makes the fewest mistakes." How Mansell must have been ruing those words as he sat, head in hands, on the barrier.

The race, though, was far from over. Within two laps of Mansell's retirement, Senna moved past Prost's team-mate Niki Lauda into second, and Bellof moved up into third not long afterwards. By lap 28, ten laps after he had passed Lauda, Senna had reduced the distance between himself and a Prost now in trouble with his brakes by ten seconds, and by lap 31 was just seven adrift, with Bellof's Tyrrell inching ever closer to the Brazilian's Toleman. But the world was denied the spectacle of one of these two young geniuses clinching his first victory in only his sixth Grand Prix, when red flags were suddenly produced, stopping the race.

Slippery slope *Nigel Mansell (left) challenges Alain Prost as they slither into Mirabeau in the wet at Monaco in 1984.*

A controversial finish

Race director Jacky Ickx, a renowned wet-weather expert in his days in Formula One, found himself in the midst of a political storm as he was accused of deliberately stopping the race to ensure Prost won. Ickx drove for Porsche in sports car racing, the conspiracy theory went, and so of course he wanted Prost, who was powered by a Porsche-built engine, to win. Many people pointed out that the rain was as hard when the race was stopped as at any time in the afternoon.

But much later Senna, despite this huge disappointment immediately after the race, indirectly shrugged his approval.

"I would certainly have overtaken Prost," he said, "but what would have happened then one can't say. Perhaps I would have won, perhaps I would have dropped out. I was on the limit as well. There were quite a few moments when it was very tight, when I was afraid I would fly off," he added.

Prost and Senna went on to dominate a decade of Formula One. But Bellof, who could have been up there with them, was killed in a sports car race at Spa a little over a year later.

PORTUGUESE GRAND PRIX 1985

PORTGUESE GP - ESTORIL, APRIL 21

Pos.	Driver	Nat.	Make
1	Ayrton Senna	Bra	Lotus-Renault (90.202 mph)
2	Michele Alboreto	It	Ferrari
3	Patrick Tambay	Fr	Renault
4	Elio de Angelis	It	Lotus-Renault
5	Nigel Mansell	GB	Williams-Honda
6	Stefan Bellof	Ger	Tyrrell-Ford
Pole:	Senna		

It was the first time that Formula One saw an already promising young driver blossom with the true signs of greatness. Ayrton Senna scored his maiden Grand Prix victory in the most dominant of styles in weather so bad that it caused a driver of Alain Prost's sublime ability to crash – but weather in which, throughout his career, Senna was time and again to put the crowning glory on his stature as the greatest driver of his age.

Senna's debut win

The 1985 Portuguese Grand Prix earned him the nickname "Magic" for his seemingly effortless progress through the unceasing torrential rains which hit Estoril that April afternoon. As Senna's rivals slithered and crashed somewhere in the dead reckoning behind him, his gleaming black Lotus – with that soon-to-be-famous fluorescent yellow helmet so clearly visible even through the clouds of spray thrown up by his tyres – seemed guided around the tricky Portuguese track by some invisible hand.

After the emotion of his first victory, Senna was feted by the entire Grand Prix fraternity, but he quickly came back down to earth again. "They all said that I made no mistakes," he said, "but that's not true. On one occasion I had all four wheels on the grass, totally out of control ... but the car came back on to the circuit. 'Fantastic car control,' everybody said. No way! It was just luck that I got back on the tarmac."

But Senna was selling himself short. He was on a separate plane from his rivals for the entire afternoon. He was already on pole position after one example of what was to become his trademark – a blinding qualifying lap, all drama and breathtaking beauty. And, after going into first place at the start, he quickly began pulling out a lead that very soon was clearly impregnable.

Effortless speed

But the astonishing thing was not that he was going so quickly, but that he was doing so in such an effortless way. Apart from the one instant he pointed out later, Ayrton never looked close to making a mistake.

Behind him the race was close, with Senna's Lotus team-mate Elio de Angelis fending off the advances of Prost's McLaren and the Ferrari of Michele Alboreto. And this intense battle was to provide a true indication of just how terrible the conditions were, as well as the sheer quality of Senna's driving.

Around mid-distance Prost was becoming increasingly frustrated by de Angelis and hit a puddle on the pit straight. The car aquaplaned instantly, and the great Frenchman, then a renowned wet weather expert, spun helplessly into the barriers.

"The past is just numbers to me," Senna was to say later in his career. "I only see the future."

And after the race Senna was to give an indication of this philosophy, while in the process providing one of the first insights into the methodical, disciplined approach with which he and Prost were to change the tempo of Formula One.

"The moments of joy in our sport are very intense," he said, "but very short. And they have to be overlaid very quickly by normal work if you want to continue to be successful."

The season was to provide a perfect illustration of what Senna meant. He led more laps than anyone else during 1985, but he only won once more, as time and again the Lotus-Renault let him down. It was not to be his season. Other years, of course, would be different.

Water wings *Ayrton Senna puts the first stamp of genius on a great career with this victory at a soaking Estoril.*

Blast off *Williams to the fore as Mansell slices ahead of team mate Patrese at the start of a race the Englishman was to lose at the final hurdle.*

CANADIAN GRAND PRIX 1991

CIRCUIT GILLES VILLENEUVE, JUNE 2

Pos.	Driver	Nat.	Make
1	Nelson Piquet	Bra	Benetton-Ford (115.276 mph)
2	Stefano Modena	It	Tyrrell-Honda
3	Riccardo Patrese	It	Williams-Renault
4	Andrea de Cesaris	It	Jordan-Ford
5	Bertrand Gachot	Bel	Jordan-Ford
6	Nigel Mansell	GB	Williams-Renault
Pole:	Patrese		

Nigel Mansell waved to the crowd as he started the last lap, but no driver who watched the race would do the same again.

It was set to be the first victory for Mansell and the Williams-Renault team in a year that had promised so much but had delivered so little. Yet as Mansell cruised to the flag, basking in the glory of what he thought was to be the justification of his comeback, something was about to go wrong.

Day of promise for Williams

At the beginning of 1991, Mansell had predicted that there would be days when the Renault-powered Williams FW14 would disappear into the distance. It was a sophisticated car with fantastic aerodynamics and it was extremely quick. However, its semi-automatic gearbox had proved to be fragile, and Ayrton Senna's McLaren-Honda had won the first four races.

Montreal – round five on the calendar – appeared to be Williams's chance to begin to close the already frighteningly large gap. Team mate Riccardo Patrese had been the quicker of the Williams drivers in the early part of the season, but in Canada, although the Italian claimed pole, a shunt in qualifying was to take the edge off his performance and it was left to Mansell to dominate. He grabbed the lead and led by two seconds at the end of the first lap, then stroked away into the distance.

Patrese was equally secure in second, albeit nursing the aches which remained from his shunt. Mechanical carnage accounted for Senna, his team-mate Gerhard Berger and Alain Prost's Ferrari.

This left Nelson Piquet's Benetton in third. And that was how it looked likely to finish. But no. Williams's day began to go wrong at two-thirds distance, when a puncture sent Patrese to the pits, dropping him to fifth, a lap down. Although he climbed to third, he fell behind Stefano Modena's Tyrrell again when his gearbox began to misbehave.

Tough luck for Mansell

This, however, was nothing compared to what was about to happen to Mansell. Round the last lap he went, almost a minute up on Piquet. Nothing, surely, could get in his way now. But it did. As he approached the hairpin, less than a mile from the finish, he had trouble selecting a gear and, with the revs plummeting, the engine died. The car ground to a halt. Benetton were on the radio to Piquet immediately.

"I'd slowed right down," Mansell's bitterest rival said. "There was no way to get near Mansell, and Modena was a long way behind. I wanted to be sure of second place. Then, suddenly, there was a scream on the radio: 'Push, push, push! Mansell is stopping!' I couldn't believe it."

He duly won, leaving a disconsolate Mansell to rue yet another gearbox failure. So what had gone wrong? Some suggested that Mansell, more concerned about waving to the crowd than the health of his car, had let the engine die. But his race engineer denied this. David Brown explained:

"In our gear-change strategy of the time, when the driver made a down change it would set a rev limit for the engine that was related to the road speed of the car and the gear you were trying to go into. Nigel was experiencing a balky down change, and was having to re-pull the lever to select a gear.

"Each time he did this, the revs were dropping, because, as he braked, the car's speed was going down. It got to a stage where the engine speed demanded was so slow that it stalled. It was a problem we'd never experienced before, and it took only five minutes to write a piece of software that prevented it happening again. But by then, we'd lost the race."

On such fine threads can hang a Grand Prix driver's fate.

THE FAMOUS CIRCUITS

If a driver can have talent, a car mechanical superiority and a team great organization, can a circuit have class? You bet ...Formula One Grands Prix have been held the world over, moving from circuit to circuit, yet some stand out as the greats. Try Spa, the Nurburgring, Monza and Silverstone for starters. Then there is that perennial classic, Monaco, with its narrow streets and beautiful people. These circuits stand out from the pack of increasingly bland newcomers.

Everyone has their favourite driver and some have their favourite team. However, almost to a person, Formula One fans have a favourite circuit. The mighty Spa is considered the ultimate by many; others opt for the Silverstone layout of the early 1970s; while some swear by the Osterreichring or Monaco. So, what is the difference? A very great deal.

When anyone builds a circuit from scratch in the 1990s, you will most likely be able to predict how the corners will be laid out and where the main straight will be located. In this age of circuit safety, with the latest round of changes made following the death in 1994 of Ayrton Senna, circuits are now designed to be able to contain the cars and their drivers, whatever happens.

It was not always so. When racing began a century ago, public roads were used. Permanent circuits did not come into existence until public pressure forced racing off the open road. Perhaps the greatest of the purpose-built tracks was that instigated by Hitler just before the Second World War: the Nurburgring. Over 17 miles long, it dipped and twisted through the Eifel forest. However, it was thought too dangerous by the mid-1970s and came close to claiming the life of Niki Lauda. And this was when the emasculation process began, and now, only the Monaco street race remains of the old tracks.

Brazilian backdrop *Alboreto leads Boutsen, Nannini et al in 1988*

USTOP
Shell
benetton
benetton

ARGENTINIAN GRAND PRIX

The worldwide success of Juan Manuel Fangio encouraged the popularity of motor racing in Argentina, and the country hosted the first World Championship Grands Prix to be held outside Europe – six years before the first US Grand Prix.

The Buenos Aires track was built with the support of President Juan Perón, who was keen to use Fangio and the sport in general as publicity tools. Opened in March 1952, the Autódromo Municipal de la Ciudad de Buenos Aires was located on the southern outskirts of the Argentinian capital in Parque Almirante Brown and featured more than a dozen track configurations, with some long straights linked by twists and turns around the pit and paddock area. The earlier races were run without the twists and turns, and lap speeds were correspondingly high. Whatever the layout, the first corner, an "S" after the main straight, has always been a fearsome stretch of track.

It was flat, but challenging. And the view from any of the grandstands was far-reaching, the best vantage point being the one on the old back straight, which also allowed the spectator to see across to the start/finish straight and down to the famous arch at the circuit entrance.

The main hazard in the early days was the crowd, who seemed to have little respect for fast-moving racing cars. As in all South American sporting events, the crowd was always massive and extremely voluble.

The first Argentinian Grand Prix was held in 1953, the fourth year of the championship. Back from plying his trade in Europe, Fangio received a hero's welcome. He had already won the title once, in 1951, and so his popularity at home was enormous. However, he failed to finish, and reigning champion Ascari took the laurels. The race was overshadowed by a terrible accident involving Farina. The Italian star survived, but nine spectators were killed.

Fangio made amends by winning in 1954 and, indeed, he won three more times in the following three years. It seemed nobody could beat him at home until, in 1958, Moss triumphed in his Cooper, with Fangio fourth. After one more start at the French Grand Prix, Fangio confirmed his retirement. It was no coincidence that there was no race in Argentina the following year, but it was revived in 1960, when Bruce McLaren gave Cooper another win.

Reutemann – rising star

There were no Grands Prix from 1961 to 1970, and it took the discovery of a new local hero to encourage its return. The old Autódromo was pressed back into service for a non-championship race in 1971, won by Amon. But all eyes were on newcomer Carlos Reutemann, who finished third. For 1972 the race was given world championship status. Reutemann joined Mario Andretti in the history books by taking pole for his first championship Grand Prix, although Stewart won.

Throughout the 1970s Argentina was established as the venue for the season-opening race, apart from 1976, when political unrest contributed to its cancellation.

In 1981 there was controversy as Piquet and his "hydraulic suspension" Brabham overcame the new ride-height rules. Reutemann was second: but he was never to win his home race.

The 1982 event was cancelled and Reutemann, having started the year with Williams, unexpectedly quit racing. Within weeks, Argentina and Britain had gone to war over the Falkland Islands and sport took a back seat.

Argentina was mooted as a possible Grand Prix venue once again in the 1990s and, with Reutemann now a politician, anything seemed possible. The race returned in 1995 and saw a fine win for Damon Hill.

BUENOS AIRES

Circuit distance: 2.647 miles (4.26 km)
Race distance: 190.571 miles (306.71 km)
No of laps: 72

Off the Grand Prix calendar for years, this famous track was eventually given the all-clear for a race in 1995 after its ancient pits were replaced. Sadly, the high-speed lay-out was eschewed and a tight, twisty circuit (derivative number six) used instead.

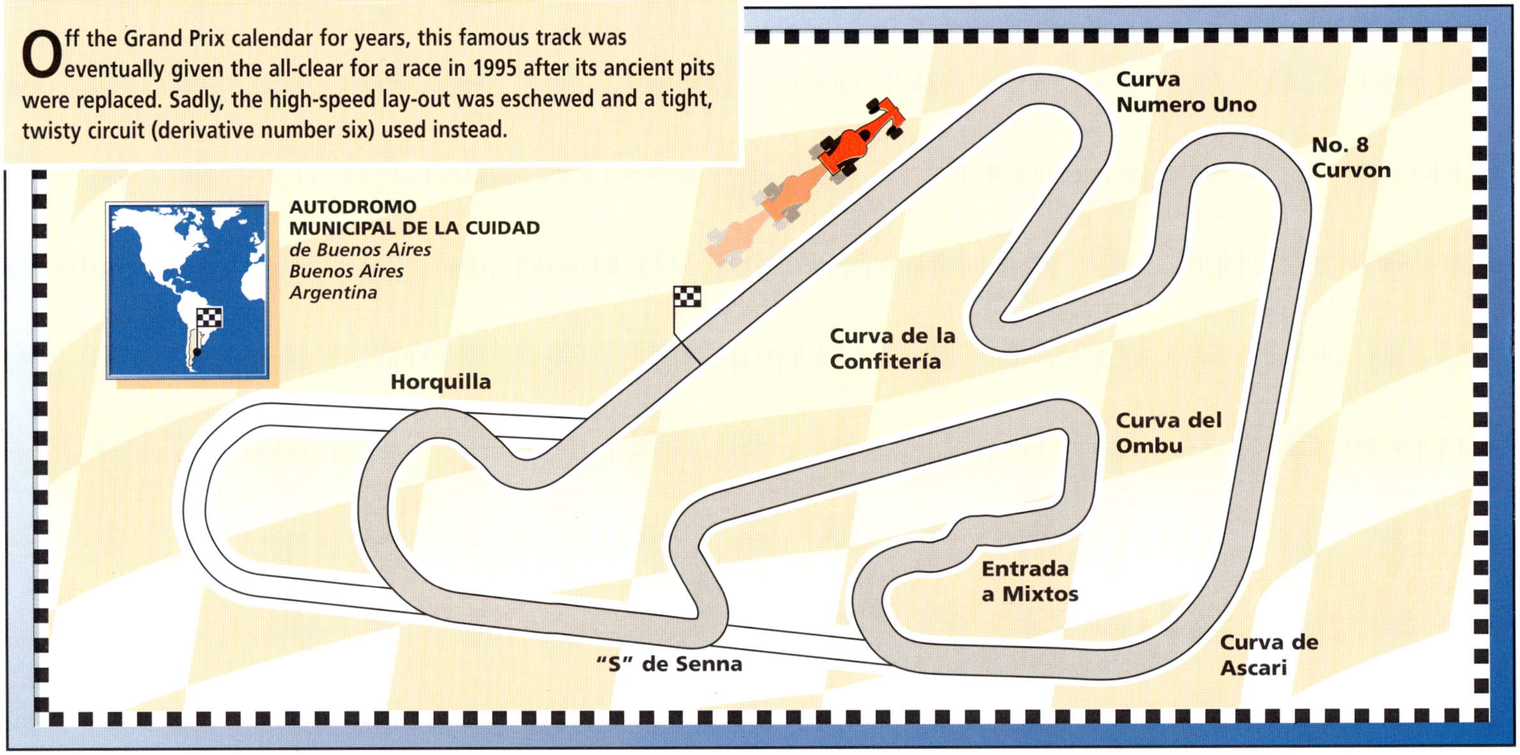

BRAZILIAN GRAND PRIX

Just as Juan Manuel Fangio encouraged the popularity of racing in Argentina, the success of Emerson Fittipaldi led to the inauguration of the Brazilian Grand Prix – in São Paulo, Emerson's home town.

In fact, the Interlagos track was around even before Fittipaldi was born. Set in the suburbs of São Paulo, running partly around a lake, the circuit had an unusual layout, with a sweeping "outer" section followed by a tight and twisty trail through the infield. That added up to an interesting track of 4.946 miles – one of the longest used in any era. The proximity to the big city meant that it always attracted huge crowds, which had eyes only for Fittipaldi and compatriots like Carlos Pace. Spectators had a great view, since the track was set in a natural amphitheatre.

Like all circuits located in the tropics, Interlagos is bumpy, upsetting the cars in the fast corners. This is no longer such a problem at the first corner, as a chicane has been inserted there to slow the cars down. The difficulty is that this funnels the cars into a tight "S", which has led to trouble on the opening lap, as shown by the acrobatics of Michael Andretti and Gerhard Berger there in 1993.

The track then feeds through a long right-hander on to the back straight before a left-hander that takes the track over a lake and on to another straight. At the end of this there is Curva do Laranja, which takes the track into an uphill section that twists along the top of the hill before feeding into a long, long left-hander on to the pit straight. Combine these twists with Brazilian heat and it's a car breaker.

Brazil held a poorly supported non-championship race in 1972. Fittipaldi led but retired, allowing Reutemann to win. In 1973 the race had World Championship status and for the rest of the decade would traditionally follow on from Argentina in a South American double-header.

Fittipaldi pleased his fans by winning in 1973 and 1974. Then Pace scored his one and only victory for Brabham in 1975. Ferrari won through Lauda in 1976, and Reutemann in 1977.

In 1978 the circus moved off to a new track at Jacarapagua, near Rio de Janeiro. A typical modern track of two straights (with the back straight the longer) and a mixture of slow- and medium-speed constant radius corners, it was well constructed and has a scenic mountainous backdrop, but lacks the character of Interlagos. Reutemann won again, while Fittipaldi took second, the best result of his five-year spell with the Fittipaldi team.

Rapid change of venue

The race returned to Interlagos in 1979–80 but, from 1981 onwards, it was back at Rio, amid some heavyweight politicking.

For some reason luck always shone on Prost in Brazil, and he won five times in the 1980s, while new local hero Piquet triumphed twice. Mansell won his first race for Ferrari in 1989, then cut his hands on the trophy...

That proved to be the last race at Jacarapagua. With domestic politics again clouding the issue, the race moved back to Interlagos in 1990, after a nine-year absence. But the track was very different, modernized, cut back to 2.687 miles and with the fast, challenging "outer" section all but gone. Fittingly, Prost won the first race, and then in 1991 Senna achieved his dream by becoming the fourth local star to win the Brazilian Grand Prix, a feat he repeated in a dramatic wet/dry affair in 1993. Mansell won in 1992.

The 1994 race marked Senna's first start for Williams. Great things were expected, but it didn't work out, and Schumacher scored the first success of his championship season. It was to be Senna's last Brazilian Grand Prix, and the mammoth turnout at his funeral showed the depths of emotion that he had stirred in the public. It is left to Barrichello to carry on Brazil's great racing tradition.

INTERLAGOS

Circuit distance: 2.687 miles (4.32 km)
Race distance: 190.77 miles (307 km)
No of laps: 71

Fast, bumpy and a shadow of its former self, this circuit nestles in the heart of Sao Paulo: the home of the late Ayrton Senna. The fervent atmosphere will never be the same there again. The super-fast first corner has been slowed by a chicane. Watch out for overtaking manoeuvres going into Curva 3 at the end of the back straight.

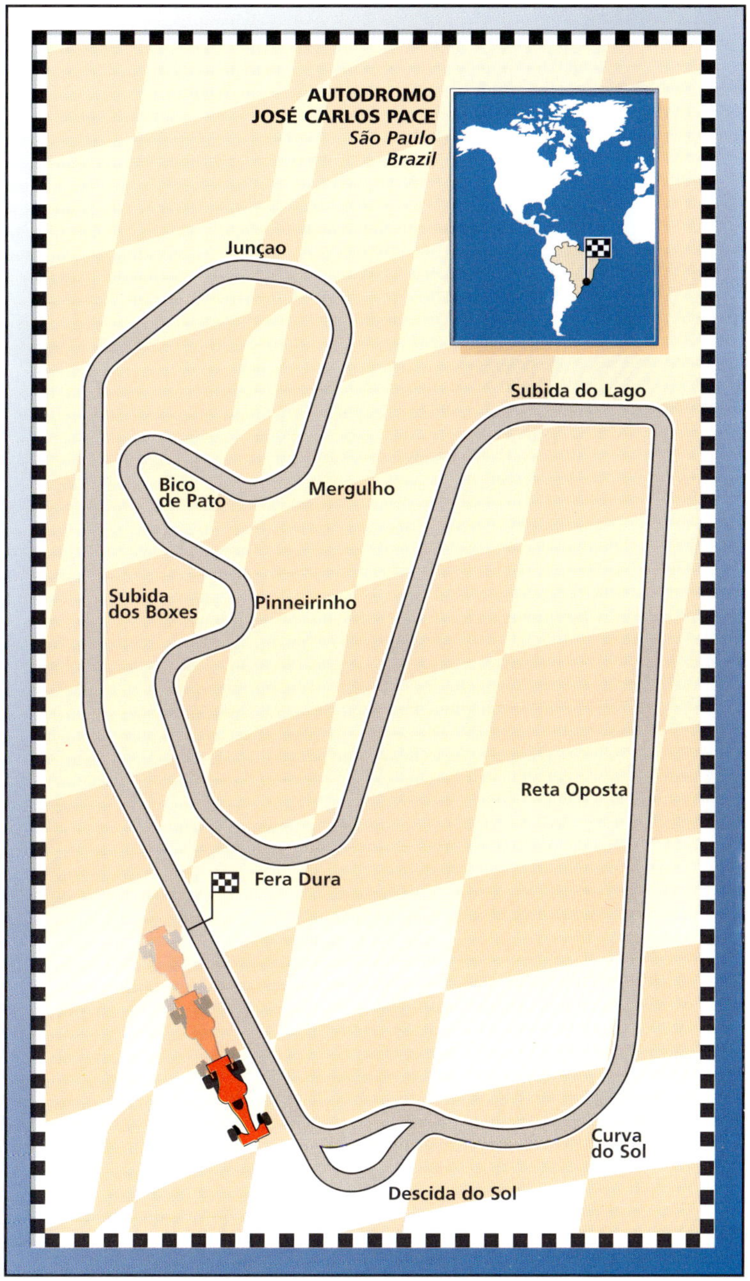

UNITED STATES GRAND PRIX

The United States can lay claim to more Grand Prix venues than any other country. No fewer than eight circuits have held World Championship races. One year there were three events in the United States – plus a fourth in Canada! That was in 1982, and yet Formula One has not visited the country at all since 1991.

The first US Grand Prix was held in 1959 at Sebring, the airfield circuit in Florida famous for its bumpy runways and its sports car race. Bruce McLaren won, and Cooper teammate Brabham took the title. Next year the event moved across the country to Riverside, the dusty Californian road course. This time Moss won, but once again the race was a one-off.

Finally, in 1961, the race found its true home. Watkins Glen, an undulating road course in upstate New York, was the host of the US Grand Prix until 1980. The event was popular with the teams, not least because in pre-FOCA days it paid the most prize money... The most famous section of the track was the dramatic uphill "S" soon after the start. The inaugural event in 1961 was won by Innes Ireland, and for the next six years Clark and Hill shared the victories.

The track was extended for 1971, when Cevert scored his first and only win. Two years later the Frenchman was killed in qualifying at the Glen, and a year after that Austrian rookie Helmuth Koinigg lost his life.

Despite the tragedies the race went on. But by 1980, with the turbo era dawning and the cars developing at an astonishing pace, it was clear that the Glen could not keep up. After that year's race, won by Alan Jones, the circus never went back.

Popularity of street racing

By now street racing had taken a grip. Back in 1976 British promoter Chris Pook introduced the US Grand Prix (West), taking advantage of a dispensation which allowed the States to have two events. The race was held over a challenging round-the-houses course at Long Beach in California (passing the permanently moored Queen Mary cruise liner), noted for a long, curving pit straight, followed by a tight hairpin. Clay Regazzoni was the inaugural winner and the race became a classic, but after 1983 Pook switched to Indy Cars – he was no longer willing to pay the fees Formula One demanded.

Others decided they could do a similar job to Long Beach, and in 1981 the Glen was replaced by an event at Las Vegas – held quite literally in the car park of the Caesar's Palace hotel. Jones won, but nobody liked the place and it lasted just two years.

In 1982 Long Beach and Vegas were joined by another street race, in Detroit, home of the US motor industry. That was rather more successful than Vegas, and produced some entertaining races and three wins for Ayrton Senna. It ran until 1988, when it too joined the Indy Car trail.

In 1984 Dallas became an Formula One venue – but it was a disaster, the track falling apart in the heat. The race turned into a one-off...

After the loss of Long Beach, Vegas, Dallas and Detroit, Phoenix stepped forward with yet another downtown event in 1989, despite the presence of a successful Indy Car oval just outside town. The race is best remembered for a wonderful fight between Senna and Jean Alesi, who in 1990 produced one of the best televised dices in years.

The US Grand Prix ran three times at Phoenix but, despite a long-term contract, the race disappeared from the calendar after 1991.

Since then there have been many rumours connecting both proposed road courses and street circuits with Formula One, but none has come to fruition. The domestic Indy Car series is getting ever stronger, and it is hard to find a promoter willing to put up the huge funding necessary.

Walled in *The concrete barriers surrounding the streets of Long Beach meant that there was no room for error*

SOUTH AFRICAN GRAND PRIX

A Grand Prix was first held in South Africa in the 1930s, but it was not until 1962 that the country hosted its first World Championship race.

The original venue was the 2.44-mile seaside track at East London. It was the closing race of a competitive season, and in fact practice started on December 26. The race was won by Hill and, with Jim Clark retiring, the moustachioed Englishman and BRM secured the drivers' and constructors' titles.

The race remained at East London for two more years, but in 1967 had a new home at Kyalami, near Johannesburg, and a new role as the season opener. Like so many classic circuits, Kyalami had a long pit straight, preceded by a fast final corner. The undulating 2.54-mile layout included a spectacular downhill run to the tricky first corner, Crowthorne. That led into the Barbecue/Jukskei Kink section, regarded as one of the most dramatic of any Grand Prix venue.

Pedro Rodriguez won in 1967, but privateer John Love nearly caused the biggest upset of all time by leading – until he had to make a late stop for fuel. In 1970 Jack Brabham scored his last Grand Prix victory, while the following year Andretti took his first.

Chopped and changed *Kyalami reappeared in 1992 with its previously fast sweeps tightened, but the atmosphere was lost*

Tragedy struck twice in the 1970s and both times the Shadow team was involved. American star Peter Revson was killed in testing in 1974, and three years later Welshman Tom Pryce lost his life when he struck a marshal who crossed the pit straight during the race. Lauda won that event – his first victory since his horrific Nurburgring crash.

One of the most exciting Kyalami races came in 1978, when Peterson and Depailler battled for the lead over the last few laps, Ronnie eventually winning and reaffirming that he could still do the job.

The 1979 event saw more excitement as Villeneuve put in a fine wet weather drive, beating team-mate Scheckter (who had won his home race in 1975). Rain struck again in 1981, when the race took place without the "grandee" FISA-aligned teams, and was outside the championship. That did not detract from a fine drive by Reutemann.

A controversial pre-practice drivers' strike is what the 1982 event is best remembered for. The race was eventually won by Prost, who recovered in great style after a puncture. For 1983 the race moved to the end of the season, and Prost lost a last-round title showdown to Piquet, although the Brazilian finished only third.

Prost in top form

Prost was the star in 1984, starting from the back in the spare car and charging through to second, behind team-mate Lauda. The following year Mansell backed up his maiden win at Brands Hatch with a second straight success.

Motor racing had retained links with South Africa far longer than most other international sports, but after the 1985 race the political pressure became so great – particularly in France – that Kyalami was dropped from the calendar.

However the political climate changed, and in 1992 the race was back, but on a substantially revised Kyalami track. This included sections of the old track, but not the long straight. Indeed, it was barely recognizable to the Formula One teams. Something of a bland, modern autodrome, it was slow and lacked the character of the original.

The first "new" race was won by Mansell, and it was as boring as the revised venue suggested. Fortunately, the 1993 event was rather more exciting, as Prost and Senna put on a spectacular show in the early laps. Prost, in his first race for Williams, came out on top.

That event was a much better advertisement for Kyalami than the previous race, but after a domestic financial wrangle the South African Grand Prix disappeared from the 1994 calendar. If the problems can be overcome, it may return in the future.

SAN MARINO GRAND PRIX

For many years Grand Prix racing stuck to the rule which stated that each country was entitled to only one race, although there was a rare exception in 1957, when Italy had events at both Pescara and Monza.

In 1976 it was decided that the United States was large enough to deserve East and West coast races, and in 1984 America actually had three events. In 1982 there was a one-off Swiss Grand Prix at Dijon, and since then Brands Hatch, the Nurburgring, Donington and Jerez have hosted extra races under the "European Grand Prix" title. Those were usually one-offs, but since 1981 Italy has run two Grands Prix on a regular basis, the second borrowing its title from the little-known principality of San Marino.

The first San Marino Grand Prix was held as a non-championship race in 1979, just a week after the Italian Grand Prix at Monza. The venue was Imola, a magnificent, 3.1-mile road course. It was built in the 1950s, but had rarely hosted major events and, like other established circuits emerging suddenly on to the Formula One scene, it had to be substantially rebuilt.

Popular with the drivers, the track was set in attractive wooded countryside and featured wonderful up and down sweeps, linked by unloved but necessary chicanes. Tamburello, the high-speed left-hander shortly after the pits, was a real test. Following this there was a blast down to Tosa, an uphill right-hander that leads on to the "back" section of the track that dives up and down – albeit with great corners like Acque Minerale chopped by the addition of a chicane – before doubling back with the double-apex left-hander at Rivazza and returning to the pit straight via a double chicane, where Barrichello crashed so dramatically in 1994. The Italian fans loved the place too, and the support of Enzo Ferrari – the track was renamed after his late son Dino – ensured that the race was a success.

IMOLA

Circuit distance: 3.042 miles (4.896 km)
Race distance: 191.630 miles (308.40 km)
No of laps: 63

A fabulous place to watch a Grand Prix, every grandstand bedecked in banners of Ferrari red, but its memory will always be tainted by the double fatality of Ayrton Senna and Roland Ratzenberger in 1994. Located in beautiful parkland, it has been modified greatly since the accidents, but now has the downhill Acque Minerale restored to its former glory.

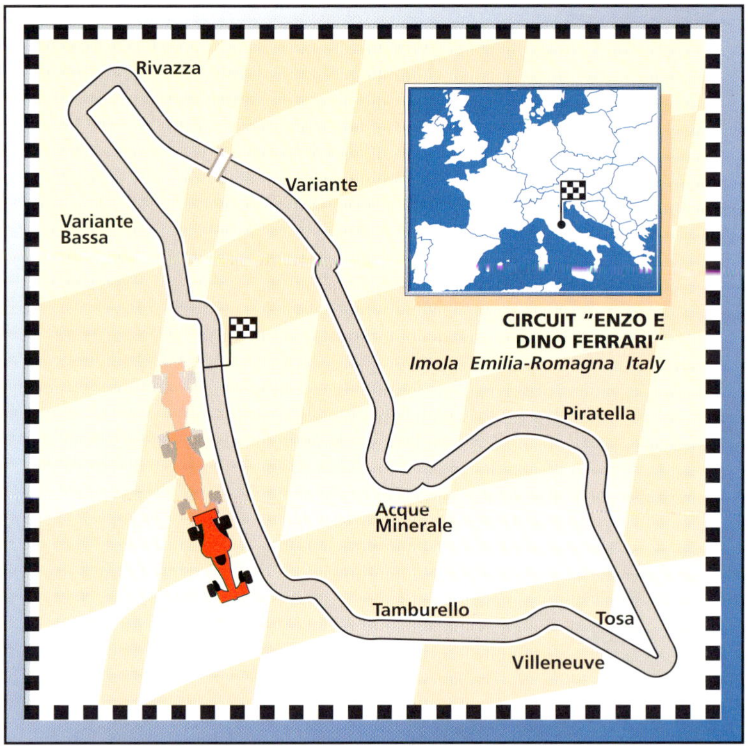

Ferrari country *The San Marino race is held outside the principality in Imola, Italy*

Lauda won that first event for Brabham and, after some political manoeuvring, Imola ousted Monza as host of the 1980 Italian Grand Prix. For the following season a suitable compromise was reached, and since then both circuits have held a race each year. San Marino has usually opened the European season.

Piquet won the one-off Italian Grand Prix and triumphed again in the first and very wet pukka San Marino event held the following April.

An eventful era

Imola soon developed a reputation for providing drama. The 1982 event was notable for a boycott by the British-based FOCA teams, and for the start of a feud between winner Pironi and Ferrari team-mate Villeneuve; the Canadian was killed at Zolder a fortnight later. Exactly a year after the feud started, Villeneuve's replacement, Tambay, scored an emotional win at Imola.

Imola is tough on fuel mileage, which was particularly important in the turbo era. In 1985 Prost ran out on the slowing-down lap – and was disqualified for being underweight. A year later he just stuttered across the line in front.

Mansell won in 1987 after team-mate Piquet survived a massive qualifying accident at Tamburello. In 1989 Berger crashed at the same place and it was a miracle that he escaped with his life.

Ferrari had some disappointing days at Imola, and none was worse than 1991. Prost spun off on the warm-up lap, and team-mate Alesi went off the road three laps later.

In 1992, Mansell set a record with his fifth straight win since the start of the season, and in 1993 Prost scored another Williams victory.

Unfortunately, Imola will always be known for the terrible 1994 event. Roland Ratzenberger died in qualifying, and then in the race Senna crashed to his death – at Tamburello – while leading. For many people Imola will never be the same again.

SPANISH GRAND PRIX

First sweeper *Jean Alesi rounds the first corner at the Circuit de Catalunya*

Like Portugal, Spain has never had a great Grand Prix driver, although Alfonso de Portago showed some promise before his death in 1957. However, the Spanish Grand Prix has a distinguished history, shared between five different circuits.

In its first incarnation the race was run twice – in 1951 and 1954 – at Pedralbes, a street circuit in the suburbs of Barcelona..

It was 14 years before Spain was back on the calendar. The race was alternated between two rival venues: Jarama and Montjuich Park. On the outskirts of Madrid, Jarama was one of the first purpose-built autodromes, designed by the man responsible for Zandvoort and Suzuka.

The 2.11-mile track consisted almost entirely of tight, slow corners and, as such, was perhaps 20 years ahead of its time! In total contrast Montjuich was a thrilling road circuit, winding up and down through a Barcelona park.

Hill won the first Jarama race in 1968. In the first Montjuich race, both he and team-mate Rindt suffered wing failures and had huge crashes.

Seven years later an uncannily similar fate befell Stommelen who, by coincidence, was driving a Hill-entered car. After crashes had wiped out much of the field, the German was in the lead when the wing failed. The car cleared a barrier, killing five onlookers. Jochen Mass was declared winner of the curtailed event, and from then on the race stayed at Jarama.

There was more controversy in 1976, when Hunt was initially disqualified for being too wide, and in 1980 when, at the heart of the FISA/FOCA dispute, the race went ahead without the FISA "grandee" teams, and was kicked out of the championship. Jarama rarely produced great racing, overtaking being difficult, but that very factor allowed Villeneuve to score a memorable win in 1981, with four cars on his tail!

Jarama was dropped, and it was five years before the Spanish Grand Prix re-emerged at a new track, Jerez, in the far south. The regional government supported the construction of the 2.62-mile track, which was composed of hairpins with a couple of blindingly quick turns behind the pits.

Drama at Jerez

The first Jerez race produced a thrilling finish as Senna held off Mansell by the slenderest of margins. However, subsequent events tended to be boring processions, with comfortable wins for Mansell (1987), Prost (1988 and 1990) and Senna (1989). In 1990 Martin Donnelly was hurt in a horrific crash in qualifying at one of the fast kinks.

That did not help to promote Jerez's case, and by 1991 the race had found yet another new venue, the Circuit de Catalunya, near Barcelona. The 2.94-mile track was adjudged better than most new facilities, with a long straight followed by hard braking.

The first two races were hit by rain, and both won by Mansell. In 1991 Nigel and Senna staged a fabulous if brief battle for second, running side by side down the straight. The following year Nigel was in a class of his own, and Senna was one of many to spin in his wake. In 1993 Prost proved a dominant winner.

Hill got his revenge, winning in 1994 after Schumacher hit trouble. At the end of that year Jerez made a reappearance as host of the European Grand Prix; Schumacher won on his return from suspension.

CATALUNYA

Circuit distance: 2.949 miles (4.746 km)
Race distance: 191.685 miles (308.49 km)
No of laps: 65

One of the modern circuits, albeit one with a little more to it than most. Mainly g-forces, actually, and an undulating crown to the track that keeps the cars unsettled. Watch for the chicane that acts as the first corner. Almost every race sees someone beached in the gravel trap there on the opening lap.

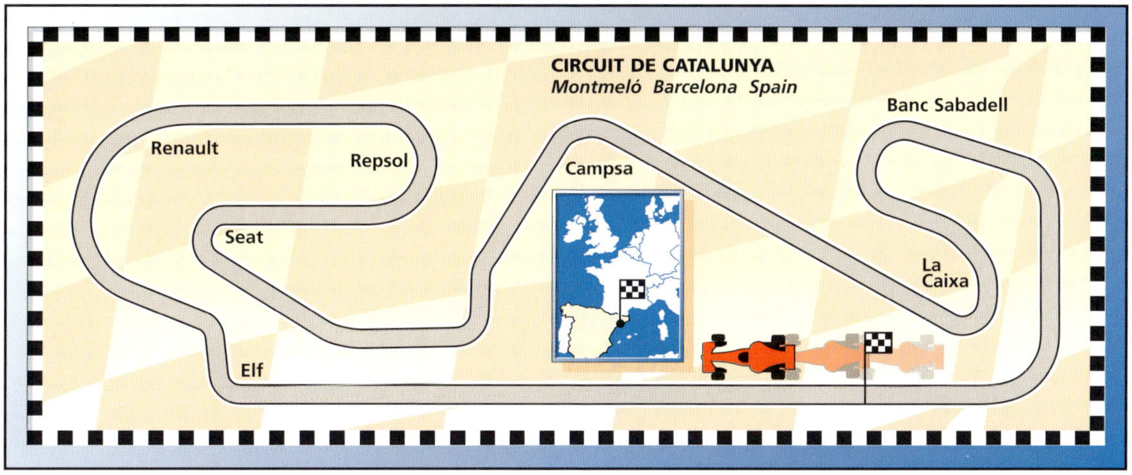

MONACO GRAND PRIX

The Monaco Grand Prix has a unique place in motor racing history, and is generally regarded as the most prestigious event in the Formula One calendar.

With its legendary casino and rows of millionaires' yachts bobbing up and down in the harbour, Monaco is still a glamorous locale for the rich and famous, for whom the race is of secondary importance to the socializing.

Winding its way around the streets of the tiny principality, the track has remained basically unchanged for decades, and much (but not all) of it would be familiar to drivers who raced in the 1950s. The same can not be said for the surroundings, since the skyline of Monaco has been changed by apartment blocks and huge hotels.

From the first corner at Ste Dévote the track blasts up the hill to Casino Square. From there its plunges down to the right-hander at Mirabeau, and then to the tight Loews (formerly Station) hairpin. Portier leads on to the seafront, and the charge through the tunnel to the harbour-side chicane. After that comes the left-hander at Tabac, the Swimming Pool section (which was substantially modified in the early 1970s), then finally the tight right at Rascasse and the pit straight.

Overtaking was never easy at Monaco, but in recent decades it has become virtually impossible. More than anywhere else, it is vital to qualify at the front. However, the attrition rate is often high, and careful driving can earn a midfielder valuable points.

Monaco's racing history

The Grand Prix was first held in 1929, and the pre-war races saw some great battles, with the legendary Nuvolari among the winners. Monaco hosted the second-ever round of the World Championship in 1950 – just a week after the opening race at Silverstone. Ten cars were eliminated in a first-lap crash and Fangio scored a famous win.

There was no race at all in 1951, 1953 and 1954, and the 1952 event was held for sports cars. Grand Prix star Luigi Fagioli was fatally injured.

The World Championship returned in 1955, and Monaco has had a race every year since – no other circuit can match that record (Monza lost the 1980 Italian race to Imola). In that 1955 race the Mercedes effort collapsed, and Trintignant scored a surprise win. But it is best remem-

Ever tight *Monaco offers little in the way of overtaking chances and the action is always most spectacular on the opening lap, as shown here in the 1990 race.*

bered for Ascari's flight into the harbour. Four days later the double champion died in a testing accident.

Moss won in 1956, when the chicane was tightened, but the following year Stirling and fellow Brits Hawthorn and Collins crashed at the chicane. Fangio won again.

Trintignant scored a second win in 1958 as the opposition faded away, and the victory was the first for a rear-engined car.

Moss often set the pace in Monaco, and in 1959 he lost out to Brabham through axle failure. Moss won in 1960, but his victory the following year was the one he is remembered for. In the first race of the 1.5-litre formula his underpowered Lotus held off the Ferraris of Ginther and Phil Hill.

For most of the 1960s Graham Hill was the undisputed king of Monaco. He won five times in all while, curiously, the great Clark – who scored five British Grand Prix wins and four at Spa – never won at the street circuit.

Hill first shone at Monaco in 1962, leading until his engine failed with just eight laps to go, allowing McLaren to win. Hill soon made amends, winning in 1963, 1964 and 1965. On the first two occasions he was certainly helped by problems for Clark, but Clark missed the third race to attend the Indy 500. However, that was perhaps Hill's greatest victory, for he had to recover from a trip up the chicane escape road when caught out by a slower car. Hill added further wins in 1968 and 1969.

Stewart scored his first Monaco victory in 1966 (he added two more, in 1971 and 1973), while Hulme scored his first ever Grand Prix win there in 1967. But that race was overshadowed by the death of Lorenzo Bandini, who crashed in flames at the chicane while pressing on in second place.

An exciting decade

The start of the 1970s saw two particularly memorable races. In 1970 Brabham slid into the barrier at the final corner, handing victory to the pursuing Rindt. Two years later the race was run in torrential rain and, against all odds, plucky Frenchman Beltoise beat the stars to give BRM its last-ever Grand Prix win.

The 1974 race saw a massive pile-up on the run from Ste Dévote to Casino Square, and in its aftermath Peterson scored a fine win in the old Lotus 72, even overcoming a spin.

Lauda was the master of Monaco in the mid-1970s, winning in 1975 (in the wet) and 1976. In 1977 he lost out to Scheckter's Wolf by less than a second, and in 1978 he set a new lap record as he chased Depailler, the Frenchman scoring his first Grand Prix win.

Another thrilling finish took place in 1979, veteran Regazzoni confirming his return to form as he pursued Scheckter's Ferrari. The 1980 race is remembered more for the start. Daly eliminated three other cars as he bounced high over the pack at Ste Dévote. Reutemann scored a canny win as others hit trouble.

Villeneuve added to his growing reputation by winning the 1981 event in the unloved Ferrari 126CK, while the next year brought one of the most memorable races of recent years. In the closing laps Prost and Daly both crashed, Pironi and de Cesaris ran out of fuel, and Patrese spun – but resumed to score an amazing success.

A virtuoso performance on a damp track earned a great win for Keke Rosberg in 1983, and in 1984 the rain returned in style. Much of the field fell off the road, including Mansell (who blamed a slippery road markings!). Amid much controversy the race was stopped prematurely with leader Prost being caught by newcomer Senna, who was in turn being reeled in by fellow rookie Bellof. Senna would get another chance! Prost won again in 1985 after a battle with Alboreto.

In the biggest change since the introduction of the Swimming Pool corners in the early 1970s, the chicane was completely rebuilt for the 1986 race. It was turned from a high-speed flick into a slow left, right, left. The result was the same, as Prost scored his third consecutive win. Each Monaco race seemed to produce a spectacular crash, and the victim this time was Tambay, who rolled his Haas Lola.

Prost's reign as Monaco's man to beat was almost over. The 1987 race saw Senna pick up his first win with the "active" Lotus, but only after Mansell's Williams-Honda retired.

The following year Senna was in a class of his own but, with a handful of laps to go, he made one of the most publicized mistakes of his career, hitting the barrier just before the tunnel. Prost nipped through to score his fourth (and last) triumph.

For the next five years Senna reigned supreme, winning each year from 1989 to 1993. More often than not, Mansell was his closest challenger, and Senna won the 1992 race after Nigel made a late stop with a loose wheel. And he won in 1993 only after Prost and Schumacher had encountered problems.

The 1994 Monaco race was the first Grand Prix after Senna's death, and he was much missed. This time Schumacher had no dramas, and he became the first winner other than Prost and Senna since 1983.

MONACO

Circuit distance: 2.068 miles (3.33 km)
Race distance: 160.68 miles (258.59 km)
No of laps: 78

Ever an anachronism in modern day Formula One. Yet this harbourside track nestling in the principality of Monte Carlo corners more glamour than the rest of the Grands Prix put together. It is incredibly bumpy and narrow, but the cars still hit a heck of a speed as they power out of the tunnel onto the waterfront And the sight of Formula One cars being flung between the barriers in Casino Square never fails to excite.

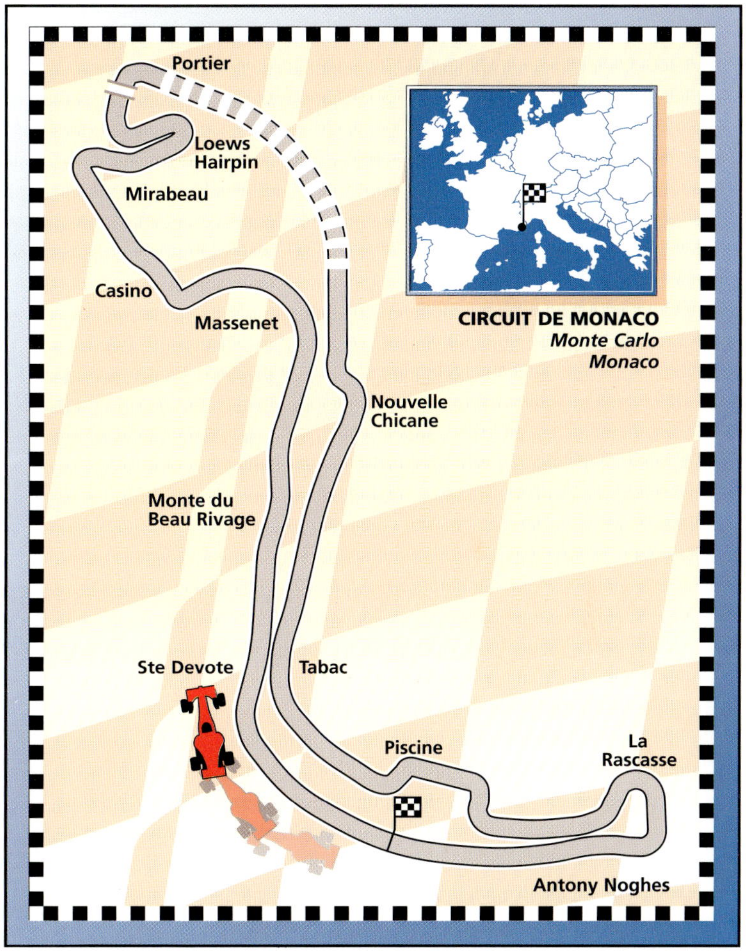

CANADIAN GRAND PRIX

Canada joined the Grand Prix calendar in 1967 and, apart from absences in 1975 and 1987, has been a regular fixture ever since. During that whole period the country has had only one regular Formula One driver – the great Gilles Villeneuve, whose talent shone so brightly from 1977 to 1982.

The original home of the Canadian Grand Prix was Mosport Park, in eastern Ontario. A magnificent road course, it ran up and down through wooded countryside and had some great corners, including the tricky Turn Two, a long left-hander. Moss won the first big event back in 1961, while the first World Championship race, in 1967, was won by Brabham.

Like Britain Canada planned to alternate the Grand Prix between its two major circuits. In 1968 and again in 1970 the race was run at Mont Tremblant at Ste Jovite in Quebec. It too was a challenging, tree-lined track, but was deemed dangerous even by the lax standards of the time. From 1971 Mosport became the race's permanent home.

Usually run as the penultimate event of the season, just before the US Grand Prix, Mosport saw some memorable races. One of the most unusual was in 1973, when rain caused chaos and a pace car was introduced for the first time. Revson was declared the winner. Three years later Hunt scored a superb win as his successful championship challenge built up momentum. The following year Scheckter gave the Canadian-owned Wolf team its third (and last) victory.

Mosport was always regarded as a dangerous and outdated venue, and for 1978 the race moved to a brand-new home in Montreal. Built on the Ile Notre Dame around the site of Expo 67, it was an unusual track. A cross between a street circuit and a permanent road course, it had lots of fiddly slow corners and some fast, barrier-lined sections as it ran around the Olympic rowing basin, surrounded by the water of the St Lawrence River on both sides. It was just minutes from downtown Montreal, and could even be reached by subway. The event proved a hit with the visiting teams.

From the start there is a chicane that catches many out on the opening lap. There is then a kink going into a hairpin that feeds on to a curving section punctuated by a left-right "S" and then a tight left before a more open right that leads the cars on to the back straight. Another chicane follows before a hairpin. Yet another chicane interrupts the flow on the way back to the start. No wonder the track breaks so many cars.

Downtown Montreal *This circuit is sited on an island in the St Lawrence River.*

MONTREAL

Circuit distance: 2.765 miles (4.45 km)
Race distance: 190.79 miles (307.05 km)
No of laps: 69

Surrounded by water, this track is built on the site of the EXPO pavilions and it's famed for being a car breaker. The track combines high-speed sections with some slow, blind corners and puts stress on the brakes and transmission like no other. Mansell fans will remember the Pits Hairpin for it was exiting here in 1991 that he waved on the final lap and lost all drive, and with it the race...

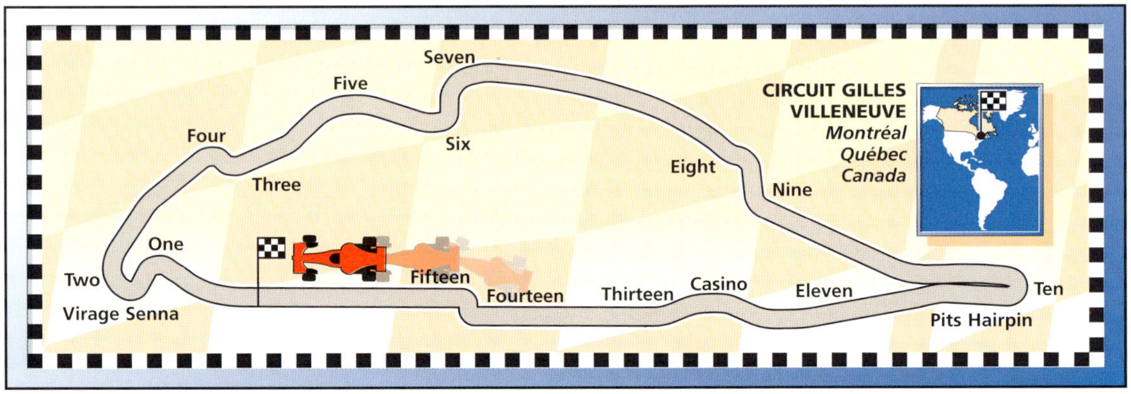

Brief triumph for Villeneuve

The first race produced the dream result: a maiden win for local hero Villeneuve. In 1981 the race was hit by rain. Villeneuve starred, but Jacques Laffite won for Ligier.

The 1982 race was run without Villeneuve, who had been killed at Zolder. The track was renamed in his honour, but saw another tragedy when Riccardo Paletti died in a starting line crash.

Oddly, Montreal has rarely provided a truly memorable lead battle. But the race has the distinction of twice having a "winner" docked a minute for jumping the start. In 1980 Pironi was the culprit, while Berger did the same in 1990. The beneficiaries on each occasion were Jones and Senna.

In 1989 Boutsen won a rain-soaked event; it was his first victory. The 1991 event saw one of the strangest finishes ever, when leader Mansell began celebrating a little too early and coasted to a halt when the Williams stalled. A surprised Piquet swept through to score his last (and luckiest?) victory.

The following year Mansell was again in the news, crashing over the final chicane. Berger got revenge for 1990 by winning after several front-runners retired. Prost scored his first and only Canadian success in 1993, while Schumacher triumphed in 1994, when a temporary tyre chicane was introduced in the aftermath of the Imola tragedies.

MEXICAN GRAND PRIX

The Mexican Grand Prix is unique in that it has twice been a regular Grand Prix fixture and twice been dumped from the calendar and quickly forgotten.

The race ran in its first form from 1963 to 1970, and had a second lease of life from 1986 to 1992. All events were held on the Hermanos Rodriguez Circuit in the suburbs of Mexico City. The track shared two characteristics with Italy's Monza. Firstly, it was located in a public park. Secondly, it had a fearsomely fast final corner, leading on to a long pit straight. But, unlike Monza's Parabolica, Mexico's Peralta was slightly banked, which made it even quicker – and even more apt to catch out the unwary. The first corner now has a chicane to slow it before turning right and going into a left-right flick, a hairpin, then a series of "S" bends on to the back straight and that final corner...

Mexico City is regularly shaken by earthquakes, and the tremors contributed to a notoriously bumpy surface which was often criticized. The other unusual factor was its high altitude, 7400 ft, to which both men and machines had to adapt.

Much of the inspiration for the Grand Prix was provided by brothers Ricardo and Pedro Rodriguez. Ricardo lost his life practising for the inaugural non- championship race in 1962, and the track was subsequently named after him. His brother was in the field for the first official Grand Prix a year later, and soon matured into one of the top stars of the decade.

Clark won the first championship race in 1963, and a year later Mexico was the scene of a dramatic title showdown involving Clark, Surtees and Hill. Gurney won the race, but Surtees took the title. In 1965 Ginther gave Honda its first-ever win, while to the end of the 1960s Surtees, Clark, Hill and Hulme each took turns on top of the rostrum.

Until 1970 the race was firmly established as the season-closer, but that year's race, won by Ickx, was notorious for the lack of crowd control. Drivers raced between human barriers, and it was a miracle that there were no incidents.

The race was dropped from the schedule for 1971. Pedro Rodriguez was killed in June, and with him went any chance that the Mexican authorities might push for the race to be back on the calendar. Pedro's name was later added to that of his brother in the official title of the circuit.

Grand Prix returns to Mexico

However, 16 years later the financial circumstances were right for FOCA and the race was indeed restored, with the track cut from 3.1 to 2.7 miles and suitably uprated with new (but outdated) pits. The Peralta turn was a wonderful challenge for the modern breed of Formula One cars, but over the years it would be the scene of several huge accidents, many of them on the exit.

Berger earned maiden wins for himself and the Benetton team in the 1986 event, while Mansell, Prost and Senna won over the next three seasons. The chicane at the end of the pit straight proved a popular passing place.

Prost won again in 1990, but the race is best remembered for a daring move by Mansell on Berger – on the outside at Peralta, ensuring a Ferrari one-two. Mansell was again second in 1991, this time behind Patrese.

The last Mexican Grand Prix was held in 1992. Not surprisingly, the Williams-Renault of Mansell – the best "active" car – rode the bumps to perfection and led all the way. Teammate Patrese finished second.

The race disappeared from the calendar in 1993, mainly due to finances.

Power down *The main straight at the Hermanos Rodriguez circuit is arrived at through the fearsome top gear Peralta turn.*

FRENCH GRAND PRIX

The French Grand Prix undoubtedly has the finest pedigree of any current motor race. The sport originated in France with the inter-city marathons such as the Paris-Bordeaux-Paris of 1895, and the very first French Grand Prix was run at Le Mans in 1906.

Le Mans was one of 11 venues used up until the outbreak of the Second World War, by which time the Grand Prix had found two regular homes in Reims and Montlhery, the banked track outside Paris.

Since the Grand Prix joined the World Championship trail in 1950, no fewer than seven tracks have played host to the race which, perhaps more than any other, has been subject to political manoeuvring at both the sporting and national level.

The only circuit used both before and after the war was Reims, which hosted the inaugural championship event in 1950. Dating back to 1925, Reims was a five-mile blast along public roads, although its shape was altered somewhat in 1953. Reims was best known for its long main straight – the Thillois straight – which made every race into a dramatic slip-streamer. Along with Spa, it was one of the fastest of the era. Fangio won the first races in 1950–51, taking over the car of Fagioli on the latter occasion.

Reims saw some great battles, and one of the best was in 1961, when young Baghetti overcame strong pressure to win his first championship race. It was also the scene of tragedy: Italian star Luigi Musso lost his life there in 1958.

New venues

Reims held the Grand Prix on 11 occasions: from 1950 to 1954, in 1956, from 1958 to 1961, in 1963, and finally in 1966, by which time it had come under severe pressure from alternative sites.

Indeed, as early as 1952 the French authorities were indulging in their habit of moving the Grand Prix about. In the early years the only alternative was Rouen-Les-Essarts, which held the race in 1952, 1957, 1962, 1964 and 1968.

Extended to 4.06 miles for the second event, Rouen was another fabulous circuit based on public roads, famous for its high-speed downhill plunge after the start, which led to the picturesque cobbled Nouveau Monde hairpin, before climbing up through the woods again, with several blind corners to keep the drivers on their toes. Fangio's win in 1957 is regarded as one of his best, while Jacky Ickx put in a fine performance to win in the rain in 1968. But that race is best remembered for the death of local veteran Jo Schlesser, who was making his Formula One debut for Honda. As with many other tracks, a serious accident heralded the end of Rouen as a Grand Prix circuit, although other forms of racing continued.

The mid-1960s was a confusing time for French fans, with four different tracks hosting the race from 1965 to 1968. In 1967 the race was held, for one time only, on the 2.74-mile Le Mans Bugatti circuit, which used the pits and starting line of the 24 hours track, linked by a purpose-built twisty section. The race was boring. Competitors did not like it and neither did the public. Formula One never went back.

With Reims pensioned off, Clermont-Ferrand emerged briefly as its natural heir. The race was first held there in 1965, and returned in 1969, 1970 and, lastly, in 1972. Opened in 1958, Clermont-Ferrand was a magnificent five-mile road course, set in the mountains of the Auvergne. Something of a mini-Nurburgring with twists and turns aplenty, it had a curious habit of inducing car sickness and of tiring even the best drivers. It was also known for the loose stones alongside the track, which often led to punctures and, in 1972, cost Austrian Helmut Marko the sight of one eye. That year's race was perhaps the most dramatic held at Clermont-Ferrand, as initial leader Amon fought back from a puncture to claim third behind winner Stewart.

After the challenges of Reims, Rouen and Clermont-Ferrand, the French Grand Prix moved to a very different home in 1971. Those dramatic road courses were replaced by a brand-new track at Le Castellet, north of Marseilles. Named after Paul Ricard, the aperitif manufacturer who built it, the track was perhaps the first of the bland, modern autodromes which would proliferate over the next two decades.

Teams liked Ricard because the weather and facilities were good, but the drivers were less impressed, although they appreciated the run-off areas and barriers. In contrast to its predecessors the 3.6-mile track was flat and dull, but it did have one

MAGNY-COURS

Circuit distance: 2.654 miles (4.27 km)
Race distance: 191.088 miles (307.53 km)
No of laps: 72

Little-loved venue for one of the traditional Grands Prix. Uprated from a club circuit at the behest of President Mitterand, it brought income to a rural region, but little in the way of excitement to Formula One fans. The Adelaide hairpin at the end of the back straight is the place to watch. The daft chicane just before the pit entrance is not...

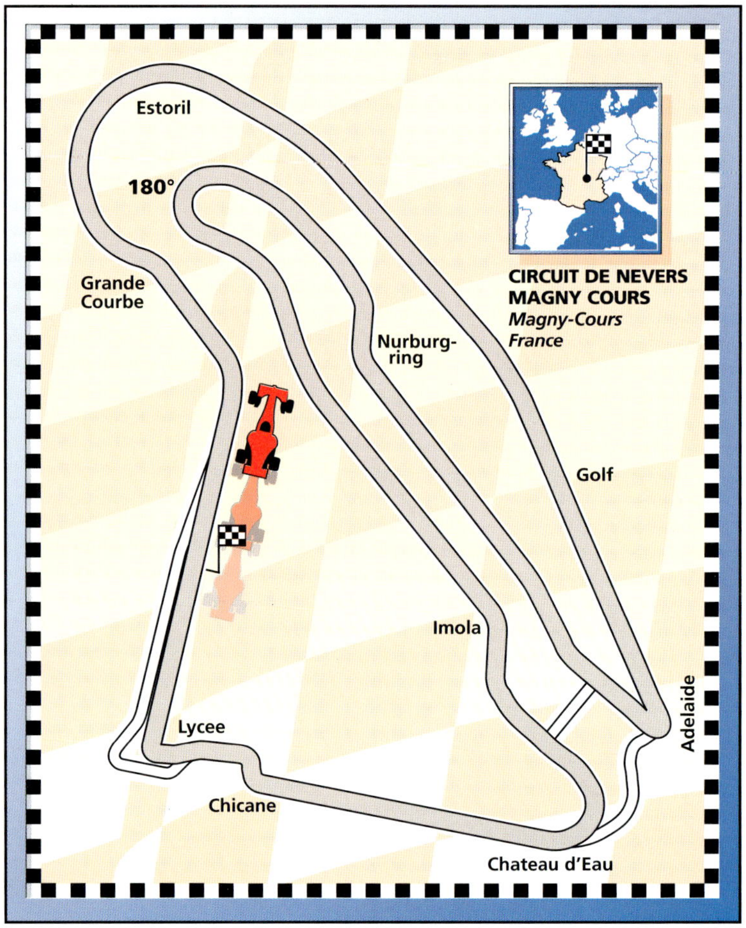

Deceptive Bends *The new-look Magny-Cours circuit claimed the French Grand Prix in the 1990s, but it has never interested the drivers, or the fans.*

sting in the tail – Signes, a fast right-hand kink near the end of the long back straight. That and the fast section beyond the pits were real tests.

A wide choice

Paul Ricard would become the main home for the Grand Prix for the next 20 years, hosting the race 14 times. However, for much of that period the alternating continued. The new second choice, introduced in 1974, was Dijon-Prenois. Initially, the fast, undulating track ran only 2.044 miles, producing a ridiculous lap time of less than a minute, and consequently a great deal of traffic problems. By the time the race returned in 1977, an extension had been added which brought it up to a more respectable 2.361 miles and, thanks to this sequence of slower corners, the lap time was increased by around 13 seconds.

Dijon hosted the Grand Prix five times, in 1974, 1977, 1979, 1981 and 1984, and had a bonus "Swiss Grand Prix" in 1982. Some memorable races took place, notably in 1979 when Jabouille gave Renault its first win, and Arnoux and Villeneuve battled hard for second. In 1981 a young Prost scored his maiden win in a race split into two parts by rain.

By the mid-1980s FISA was demanding that Grands Prix find long-term homes and, with Dijon dropped, Paul Ricard was sole host between 1985 and 1990. Once regarded as the state of the art in safety, Ricard saw tragedy when Elio de Angelis was killed in testing in 1986, after his wing failed approaching the fast sequence after the pits.

For that year's race the track was cut back to 2.369 miles, removing the section where de Angelis crashed, halving the back straight and slowing the approach to Signes. In its last years as a Formula One venue Prost was the king of Ricard, winning during 1988–90. The 1989 race is best remembered for a first corner crash which saw Gugelmin somersault over the pack, while in the following year Gugelmin and Leyton House team-mate Capelli stunned everyone with their pace. The Italian led for 45 laps and eventually finished second.

For 1991 the track was dropped and replaced by the Grand Prix's seventh home since 1950. With support from President François Mitterand, the club circuit of Magny-Cours was transformed, re-emerging as the Circuit de Nevers. It was a typical modern autodrome, full of slow turns and hairpins but boasting top-class pit and paddock facilities. The 2.654-mile facility did not offer much of a challenge, apart from the relatively fast left/right sequence after the start. The rest of it was very slow, and there was even an unnecessary chicane – right after a hairpin! That was later removed.

The first race turned out to be quite a good one, victory going to Mansell after a long battle with Prost's Ferrari. Mansell won again in 1992, a race split by rain. Then Prost added a third for Williams in 1993, pipping Hill. Schumacher won in 1994, but most eyes were on Mansell, making his comeback after a season and a half in Indycars. However, he failed to last the distance.

Magny-Cours is by no means secure as the long-term home of the French Grand Prix, and it may be ousted by the Le Mans Bugatti track, host of the unsuccessful 1967 race and not far from the road course which held the first Grand Prix back in 1906. As usual politics will determine which venue is used.

Paul Ricard *This was the home of the French Grand Prix until 1990.*

BRITISH GRAND PRIX

While France has had a Grand Prix since 1906, Britain's event was a late starter. Despite the fact that the wonderful, banked Brooklands course – a sort of odd-shaped oval – opened for business in 1909, it was not until 1926 that it first hosted a British Grand Prix. However, the two races held there were not great successes, and the idea was dropped.

In 1937 and 1938 Donington Park hosted two races which were British Grands Prix in all but name, attracting the might of Mercedes and Auto Union to its parkland setting south of Derby. However, the races are mentioned in the history books merely as Donington Grands Prix. Those who attended still remember the spectacle of powerful German cars surging out of the hairpin and flying over the brows.

The British Grand Prix proper started in 1948 at Silverstone , and in 1995 the former airfield in Northamptonshire is still the home of the country's premier race, and its fastest. The track has changed substantially during that time and on 17 occasions since it started the Grand Prix has taken place somewhere other than Silverstone.

The track used in 1948 was a one-off. While using some of the perimeter roads which would become so familiar, it also had two forays up the wide runways and into what is now the infield. But legendary corners such as Copse, Maggots, Becketts, Chapel, Stowe, Club, Abbey and Woodcote already had their names.

By the time of the first World Championship race in May 1950, only the perimeter roads were in use, and the track had assumed the 2.926-mile shape which would remain until 1975 and, in subtly modified form, until 1990. It was very, very fast, and no corner was more testing or more dramatic than Woodcote, the sweeping right-hander which led on to the what eventually became the pit straight.

Natural amphitheatre *Brands Hatch was a fabulous venue for spectators*

That first race was in fact the first-ever round of the World Championship, and was held with King George VI and Queen Elizabeth in attendance. Alfa-Romeo dominated and Farina, who would take the inaugural title, won the race. It was not until 1955 – and a change of venue was made – that the British Grand Prix had a home winner.

The move to Aintree

The driver was Moss, and the new track Aintree. The RAC had decided, somewhat controversially, that it should share the Grand Prix between Silverstone and the brand-new three-mile circuit built around the Grand National horse racing course in Liverpool. Aintree had some quick corners, but was a lot slower than Silverstone. Its great advantage was the facilities – the car and four-legged crowds shared the same grandstands.

As in the rest of the 1955 events, Mercedes proved dominant at Aintree, and Moss added to his growing status by leading team-mate Fangio home.

Aintree was to host the Grand Prix five times, alternating with Silverstone in 1955, 1957, 1959 and 1961, and then hanging on to the event for a second consecutive year

Former airfield *Silverstone's aviation background is obvious in this aerial shot taken at the 1993 British Grand Prix.*

in 1962. That upset much of the motor sporting establishment, who supported Silverstone's case.

Instead, Silverstone had a new rival in Brands Hatch. From 1964 to 1986 the two circuits would swap, Silverstone taking the race in the odd-numbered years.

Undulating its way through the Kentish countryside, the 2.65-mile track was specially extended for the 1964 British Grand Prix, with a loop into the woods added to the short circuit "bowl", at that time used only for national racing.

Brands was very different from the flat and fast Silverstone. It had some superb and challenging corners, none more popular with fans (and worrying to drivers) than Paddock Bend, the plunging right-hander after the start. In the vicinity of the original, short circuit it was possible to see much of the track, and that was where most of the fans tended to congregate, leaving the goings-on at tricky (and less accessible) places like Hawthorns and Westfield to their imaginations.

The venue may have been different, but the result was the same. Clark won at Aintree in 1962, Silverstone in 1963 and again at Brands Hatch in 1964. He would win the British Grand Prix twice more before his death.

The Silverstone/Brands Hatch mix was a good compromise, and both circuits proved popular with fans and competitors alike. And both had a tendency to produce memorable races, especially in the mid-1970s.

The action started at Silverstone in 1973, when Scheckter spun his McLaren at Woodcote and triggered a multiple pile-up at the start of the second lap.

The following year at Brands Lauda led until pitting with a late puncture, only to find the pit exit blocked by people and an official car. He was later awarded a token fifth place.

Changes at the major circuits

For 1975 Silverstone made its first important change for 25 years with the addition of a chicane at Woodcote, albeit quite a fast one. That did not prevent drivers taking to the fences at nearly every other corner in a dramatic, rain-hit race, which was forced to a stop, andeventually won by Fittipaldi.

Brands also made modifications for 1976, changing the line at Paddock Bend and modifying the straight behind an expanded pit complex for a new lap of 2.61 miles. The race went down in history thanks to a first-corner accident triggered by the Ferraris of Lauda and Regazzoni, and also involving Hunt. The Briton won the restart but was later disqualified.

There are other great memories: Hunt battling with Watson in 1977, Reutemann nipping past Lauda in 1978, Regazzoni giving Williams its first win in 1979, Jones beating the flying Ligiers in 1980, Watson avoiding a first-lap skirmish to win for McLaren in 1981 and Warwick hauling his "half-tank" Toleman up to a brief second place in 1982.

Brands Hatch boss John Webb managed to secure extra "European Grands Prix" in 1983 and 1985, the second of these giving Mansell his first-ever victory. But the 1986 British Grand Prix proved to be the last at the Kent track. Silverstone secured a long-term deal and, although the final Brands race saw Mansell score another fine win, a serious accident for Laffite underlined the fact that current cars had outgrown the tight confines of Brands.

Silverstone was not immune to safety concerns. For the 1987 race the 1975 chicane was replaced by a new, much tighter complex well before Woodcote. That year produced one of the best-ever races, as Mansell defeated team-mate Piquet. Mansell was always news, finishing second in the wet in 1988 and again after a puncture in 1989. In 1990 he announced an emotional retirement after his Ferrari's gearbox failed.

For 1991 the track was substantially rebuilt, re-emerging with a new 3.247-mile layout. The original Becketts was replaced by a new (and fast) complex, while the old Stowe was slowed to a much harder right, followed by a new left-hander called Vale, and a much slower Club. After Abbey there was a completely new section: a fast right-hander at Bridge, followed by double lefts of Priory, and double rights of Luffield.

Mansell won the first race on the new track, followed it up in 1992, and on both occasions the crowd went berserk. With Nigel gone to America the audience shrank in 1993, and those who turned up went home disappointed after Damon Hill's engine blew and Prost won.

Another major rebuild followed in 1994. Copse was reprofiled, and there were further modifications at Stowe. A new and slow complex was introduced at Abbey and the Priory corners were also changed. This time the fans got the result they wanted, Hill winning after Michael Schumacher was penalized.

Silverstone is likely to remain the venue of the British Grand Prix for the foreseeable future, despite the best efforts of Tom Wheatcroft, owner of Donington Park. He hosted a one-off European Grand Prix in 1993, a dramatic, wet race which produced one of Senna's greatest wins.

SILVERSTONE

Circuit distance: 3.142 miles (5.32 km)
Race distance: 191.662 miles (308.45 km)
No of laps: 61

The home of British motor racing. Once an airfield, it hosted the first ever modern-day Grand Prix and has frequently been transformed since then, largely to slow the cars down. The latest change has emasculated the once mighty Stowe corner, but the new-look Becketts esses is the most exciting squiggle in racing.

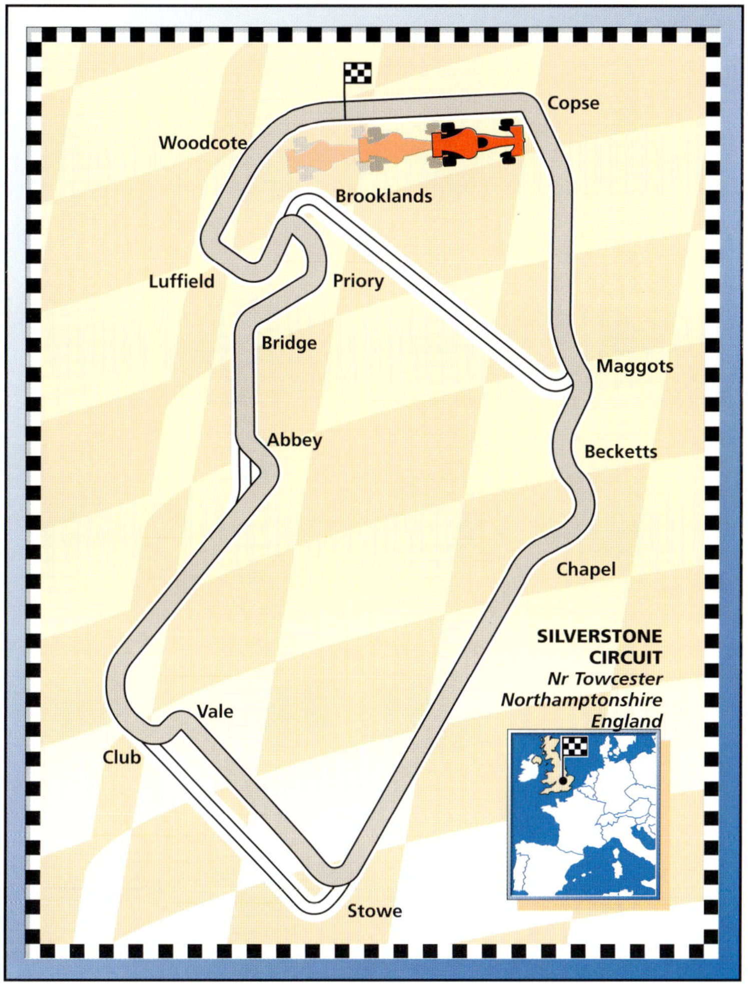

GERMAN GRAND PRIX

Into the forest *The cars head out of Hockenheim's Stadium section and into the forest during the 1987 German Grand Prix.*

Until 1976 the German Grand Prix was held on the most remarkable circuit of them all – the old Nurburgring. Since then it has found a second home at bland Hockenheim.

The very first German Grand Prix was held at Berlin's Avus in 1926, and the wet event was blighted by horrific accidents – including one which killed three officials in a timekeepers' box. Safety concerns precipitated a move to the Nurburgring – somewhat ironic, considering the reputation that the circuit was to acquire.

Primarily designed as a means to alleviate local unemployment, work on the 'Ring began in 1925 with full government backing. In its full glory it ran to 17.58 miles, including the Southern circuit "extension". In latter years this was excluded and races were held on the 14.17-mile Nordschliefe.

The 'Ring was a remarkable circuit, a seemingly endless chain of ups and downs, and twisting left and right curves between the pine trees. Corner names became part of motor racing folklore: Flugplatz, Bergwerk, the Karussel, Pflanzgarten. Much more than Spa-Francorchamps, the 'Ring separated the great from the average, but even the very best drivers took several years to feel fully at home with the demanding and hard-to-learn course.

What made the place yet more daunting was the weather. Even in the summer rain and fog were common, and conditions could change suddenly in the course of the lap.

The German Grand Prix was held at the 'Ring regularly until 1939, when war intervened. Racing resumed in 1949, and Germany joined the World Championship two years later when an estimated 180,000 fans turned up to see Alberto Ascari win for Ferrari.

A venue with a reputation

The early Grands Prix confirmed the 'Ring's dual distinction as both a creator and killer – of racing heroes. Ascari had one of his best races in 1952, recovering from a late pit stop to regain the lead from Farina. In 1957 Fangio drove what he regards as his best race, coming back from a fuel stop to pass Hawthorn and Collins. But a year later Collins crashed to his death, as had Fangio's protégé, Marimon, in 1954.

In 1959 the 'Ring was temporarily overlooked in favour of Avus, because crowds at the former had fallen. As in 1926, the track was basically a run up and down two sides of

Emasculated glory *The revised and shortened Nurburgring hosted Grands Prix in 1984 and 1985, the latter shown here.*

a dual carriageway, but since that first race it had been shortened and acquired banking at its north end. Uniquely, the race was run over two heats, Brooks winning, but Grand Prix great Jean Behra lost his life in a supporting sports car race and Formula One never went back.

The 1960 race was held on the 'Ring's short South circuit – and only for Formula Two cars – but for 1961 it was both back in the championship and on the familiar, long track. Moss scored his last (and one of his best) wins.

World champions Hill, Surtees, Clark, Brabham and Hulme won in the 1960s, but none more comprehensively than Stewart, who mastered dreadful conditions to win the 1968 race by over four minutes.

By the end of the decade pressure from Stewart and his colleagues had encouraged an increased emphasis on safety. In 1970, the year of the last race on the original Spa track, the Nurburgring underwent major modifications. Barriers were installed, the road was widened and reprofiled in places, and run-off areas were created.

While this was going on, the Grand Prix moved to a new venue at Hockenheim, near Heidelberg, built originally as a test track for Mercedes. Sadly, best known as the place where Clark lost his life in a Formula Two race in 1968, the 4.218 miles of Hockenheim consisted of two long blasts into and out of the forest, followed by a twisty section through a stadium, in front of huge grandstands. Since Clark's death, new barriers had improved matters somewhat, and the race was an exciting slipstreamer, won by Ickx.

For 1971 the Grand Prix moved back to the modified 'Ring, its essential spirit unchanged. Ickx, who had won the last race in 1969 in fine style, was again the pacesetter – but he crashed on the second lap, handing the win to Stewart. The Belgian made amends in 1972.

Despite the modifications the 'Ring remained an anachronism as the cars became quicker, and it was fortunate that no one was hurt in 1975 when much of the field suffered punctures. But the following year the track's tenure as the Grand Prix venue came to an end. Reigning world champion Lauda suffered horrific burns when he crashed on the second lap of the race and, while Lauda staged a recovery, the 'Ring did not.

Return to Hockenheim

For 1977 the race moved back to Hockenheim, itself now modernized by chicanes on the two straights. Appropriately, the first race was won by Lauda. The track was notable for a high attrition rate, the long flat-out blasts proving hard on engines. In addition, the start and chicanes tended to produce a lot of carnage.

In 1980 Hockenheim was once again the scene of tragedy, veteran Depailler losing his life in a testing crash at the fast Ostkurve, the link between the two long straights.

One of the most memorable races came in 1982, by which time a third chicane had been added at the Ostkurve. Pironi was injured in wet practice and in the race itself Piquet hit the headlines by trying to punch Salazar after they collided while Piquet was lapping the Chilean. Pironi's Ferrari team-mate, Tambay, scored an emotional win.

In 1984 the Grand Prix circus returned to the Nurburgring, for the European Grand Prix. But this was a very different 'Ring. Built alongside the original, it was a clinical 2.822-mile track. It had a few interesting corners, but the unnecessarily massive run-off areas – built in the name of safety, of course – made it somewhat soulless.

Prost won in 1984 and in 1985 when, for one time only, the new 'Ring hosted the German Grand Prix. Like nearly every race ever held at the place, there was a shunt at the first corner chicane, but Alboreto survived it to win.

Since 1986 the Grand Prix has been back at Hockenheim, which continues to extract a heavy toll on machinery. In 1987 Prost led until a failure with four laps to go, allowing Piquet to win. In 1989 Prost lost sixth gear with two laps to go, letting Senna through.

Senna won in 1988 and 1990, and Mansell in 1991 and 1992 before Prost finally scored his first Hockenheim win in 1993. This time he was lucky; he was given a controversial stop-go penalty, but took the lead when team-mate Hill had a late puncture.

The 1994 race was one of the craziest, with almost half the field disappearing in a series of first-lap incidents. After local hero Schumacher retired, Berger gave Ferrari its first win in four years.

Hockenheim has never been very popular with competitors but, as other less interesting venues have come on stream in the intervening years, the German track has acquired a certain charisma. After a ten-year absence from the schedule, the new 'Ring was hosted the European Grand Prix in October 1995.

HOCKENHEIM

Circuit distance: 4.234 miles (6.81 km)
Race distance: 190.53 miles (306.63 km)
No of laps: 45

No one has ever been fond of this place since it claimed the life of Jim Clark. It's largely characterless, with a high-speed blast through the forest interrupted by three chicanes. But the 'Autodrom' section is impressive, if only for the huge grandstands packed with flag-waving Schumacher fans.

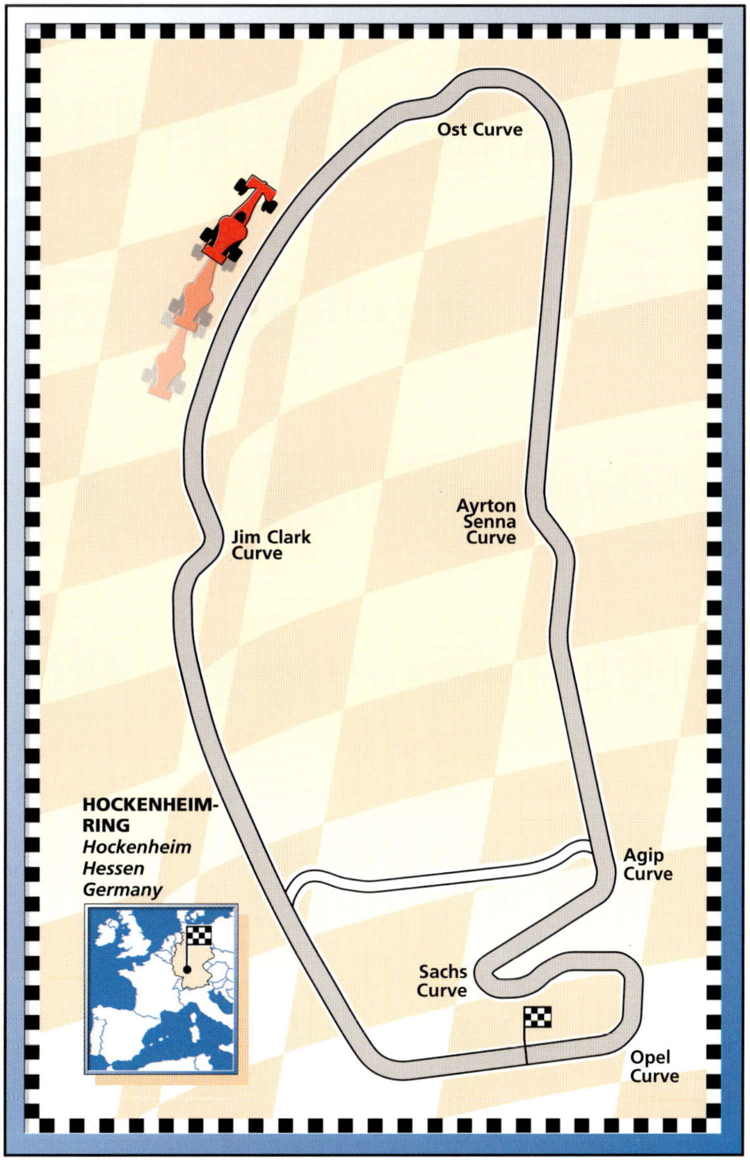

AUSTRIAN GRAND PRIX

First corner *Teo Fabi driving a Benetton leads the pack through the Hella Licht Esses in the 1987 Austrian Grand Prix.*

Despite its relatively small population, Austria has produced two great world champions in Jochen Rindt and Niki Lauda, plus Gerhard Berger, one of the most enduring stars of the past decade.

The country also has one of the fastest and most spectacular circuits, and it played host to the Austrian Grand Prix from 1970 to 1987 before the race was dropped from the schedule.

The very first Austrian Grand Prix was held at the Zeltweg airfield in 1964. Noted for its bumpy surface, the track proved to be a car breaker. Lorenzo Bandini's Ferrari survived the mechanical carnage to win. Being flat and uninteresting, Zeltweg was not a popular venue.

After a six-year break the Formula One circus returned to the Styrian area to find a brand-new venue: the Osterreichring. This new track was set in magnificent, mountainous countryside. It consisted almost entirely of high-speed sweeps and majestic corners, and was one of the fastest on the schedule. It was also the most scenic. Indeed, as a spectator venue, it was unrivalled, with those in the know hanging out at the first corner: the mighty Hella Licht Kurve. The cars would approach this up a steep hill, with the right-hand bend at the brow.

Traversing the hillside, the track rounds a right-hander, then climbs and kinks its way to its trickiest corner: the wonderful Bosch Kurve, a never-ending right-hander that tips the track downhill again.

A long left-hander brings the track back up to the Rindt Kurve, a double-apex right-hander that leads back on to the pit straight. In some places the barrier was alarmingly close to the trackside, while in others drivers had the luxury of hundreds of yards of grass before they came upon anything solid.

A brief but spectacular history

Rindt was the darling of the crowd at that first event in 1970, but the race was won by Ickx's Ferrari; Jochen would die a few weeks later at Monza. A tradition that the event would produce an unusual winner began in 1971 when Siffert won for BRM.

Perhaps the strangest race was in 1975, when heavy rain turned the event into a lottery. Italian veteran Brambilla was in front when the race was curtailed, and he marked his only Grand Prix victory by crashing on the slowing-down lap. Sadly, American driver Mark Donohue succumbed to injuries sustained when he crashed his Penske March that morning, and a chicane was subsequently built at the Hella Licht Kurve to slow the cars down.

Penske gained revenge in 1976 year when Watson scored his first (and Penske's only) win, while in 1977 Jones scored his maiden win – and the only success for Shadow. The 1978 race was again hit by rain, and Peterson survived the carnage to score his final win. Like Rindt, he was to die at Monza.

For the next few years Austria did not produce any truly unusual results, but in 1982 the race saw one of the closest finishes ever when de Angelis just held off Rosberg.

Lauda tried for many years to win at home and he finally managed it in 1984 during his successful campaign for his third title. Prost won in 1983, 1985 and 1986, while the 1987 event fell to Mansell, who banged his head on a girder when being driven to the podium. That race was started three times after two huge pile-ups on the narrow grid, and safety concerns contributed to the demise of the event.

Finances were also part of the equation, and the fact that the track was so far removed from major towns did not help in an era when corporate entertainment had become so important. Austrian fans had instead to travel to Italy, Germany or Hungary, but their superb circuit is fondly remembered.

HUNGARIAN GRAND PRIX

HUNGARORING

Circuit distance: 2.465 miles (3.97 km)
Race distance: 189.805 miles (305.46 km)
No of laps: 77

A wasted chance to make motorsport catch on as the Iron Curtain was lifted. It has a beautiful setting in a natural amphitheatre, with spectators able to see much of the track. But the track is too narrow and twisty for anything other than follow-my-leader processions. Watch for drivers going for a tow down the main straight on the run to the only overtaking place: the first comer.

Twists and turns *The Hungaroring offers plenty of turns, but little racing.*

In 1986 Formula One impresario Bernie Ecclestone achieved the impossible by taking Grand Prix racing into the Eastern bloc – well before the thawing of the Cold War. For some time there had been talk of a street race in Moscow, but nothing came of this. However, it did not take long for Ecclestone to persuade the Hungarian authorities to fill the gap.

Built in rolling countryside 12 miles north-east of Budapest, the 2.465-mile Hungaroring is a typical modern autodrome, somewhat lacking in character. Its corners are mostly slow and the track is narrow, limiting overtaking opportunities, which has led to frustration for quicker drivers and sometimes collisions. The first corner – a tight right-hander that drops away on its exit – sees quite a bit of action, but the preceding straight is too short for drivers to be able to get a good run on cars of similar speed.

The track drops down into a valley through a left-hander followed by a right. From the bottom the track climbs up towards a massive bank of spectators, darting right to traverse the face of the hill, then right again, followed by a sequence of twists before climbing up to the level of the pits once more. The last corner is a long right-hander, through which drivers must get close to the car ahead if they hope to slipstream past them on the straight.

For the first three years, the circuit was even slower than it was planned to be, for an extra kink had to be built to avoid an underground spring, discovered during construction. For the 1990 race the problem was solved and the section of track straightened.

A popular venue

The teams enjoy the trip to Hungary – the fine August weather certainly helps – and the local fans are wildly enthusiastic. A claimed 200,000 turned out for the first race, but since then estimates have dropped to a quarter of this figure.

There have been some entertaining and close races in Hungary, but thanks to the nature of the track, they have rarely featured much actual overtaking at the front; several years have seen flag-to-flag wins.

That said, the inaugural race saw Piquet beat arch-rival Senna after they swapped places during a close fight. The following year Piquet won again – but only after team-mate Mansell lost certain victory when a wheel nut worked loose with just six laps to go.

Senna was embroiled in another tight battle in 1988, this time with charging McLaren team-mate Prost, but the Frenchman dropped out with wheel bearing failure just as Senna began to feel the pressure.

The 1989 event was one of the more memorable races. Patrese led until his Williams sprang a water leak, leaving Senna in the lead. Mansell rose from 12th on the grid and ducked past the Brazilian in an opportunistic move in traffic.

Senna and Mansell were in the news again in 1990. Boutsen took pole and, against the run of form, led all the way. He came under strong pressure from Nannini, but there was no way past. The following Senna punted Nannini off, but he could not find a way past Boutsen in the closing laps. Meanwhile, Berger had pushed Mansell out of the way. The lack of passing places certainly irritated the drivers.

Senna won in 1991 after Mansell and Patrese used up the brakes on their Williams-Renaults, and Ayrton triumphed yet again in 1992. Despite a puncture Mansell finished second and clinched the world title.

Prost was destined never to win in Hungary, and he blew his last attempt in 1993 by stalling on the warm-up lap. Hill stormed to a magnificent first Grand Prix victory. The following year Schumacher earned Benetton its first Hungarian win, as Hill gave chase in second.

Rumours have suggested that Hungary might be dropped from the calendar, but so far it has survived.

BELGIAN GRAND PRIX

The Belgian Grand Prix has had three homes, but for most people only one matters: Spa-Francorchamps. The charismatic track has had two lives: the first until 1970 and the second in rebuilt and truncated form after 1983. It has always been regarded as the greatest challenge of the day.

Spa was first used in 1924 and joined the World Championship trail at the start, in 1950. Set in attractive wooded countryside in the Ardennes hills, it made use of public roads and ran for an incredible 8.76-miles, consisting almost entirely of long straights, punctuated by tricky kinks and, occasionally, a proper corner. Without doubt, the most famous section came at the start of the lap just after the pits – a terrifying downhill plunge followed by Eau Rouge and Raidillon, a left-right-left flick up and over a hill. This really sorted the greats from the ordinary.

The track then climbed to the top of the hill at Les Combes and plunged into the valley beyond, with a frighteningly adverse camber as it poured into a long right-hander. The driver had to be flat-out here, or he would be nowhere. Basically triangular in shape, the circuit then turned sharp right and climbed all the way back through the woods to the hairpin at the top, La Source, before dropping steeply back past the pits for another lap.

Because the track used virtually unprotected public roads, trees, lampposts, road signs and houses were among the "natural" hazards. And perhaps the most terrifying aspect of Spa was the weather. The sun could be shining in the pits while rain poured on one of the far-flung sections. Spa was, in a word, dangerous.

La Source *Treacherous conditions at the hairpin in 1989.*

Spa's perilous history

The Belgian Grand Prix ran at Spa from 1950 to 1970, with the exception of three years, and the list of winners shows its propensity for surrendering to the very best. Champions Farina, Ascari and Fangio won there, as did Brabham, Graham Hill and Surtees. The man who really made Spa his second home, though, was Clark who won four times from 1962 to 1965, although he hated the place.

The danger was ever present, and in 1960 British youngsters Alan Stacey and Chris Bristow were killed in separate accidents. By 1970 it was clear that speeds were getting out of hand: Pedro Rodriguez averaged a shade under 150 mph.

A new home was sought, and two were found. Nivelles, a bland new autodrome near Brussels, ran the race in 1972 and 1974 before being quietly forgotten. In the intervening year the race was run at Zolder, in the Flemish-speaking part of Belgium northwest of Liège. This was no Spa, but far preferable to Nivelles. In 1973 the track broke up badly, but Zolder became home to the Grand Prix from 1975 to 1982, often providing great races. Unfortunately, it is best remembered for the accident which claimed Villeneuve's life in 1982.

In 1983 the race returned to Spa after a 13-year break. The track had been shortened to 4.328 miles, cutting out most of the really dangerous road section with a purpose-built link road sporting some challenging new corners. Some of the old track remained, including the famous La Source hairpin and the Eau Rouge/Raidillon complex. From the start everybody loved the place, and most drivers regarded it as their favourite track.

Like the original track, the new Spa rewarded only the most talented. Senna won five times – including four consecutive victories from 1988 to 1991 – while Prost and Mansell also scored successes. Schumacher took his very first win in 1992, and Hill triumphed in 1993–94, but only after Schumacher was disqualified in 1994.

Eau Rouge remained the most exciting corner, but it was the scene of major accidents. In 1993 Zanardi was lucky to escape from a massive practice crash in his Lotus, and in the light of the Imola tragedies, a universally unpopular chicane was added in 1994. However, when new run-off were built in 1995, it allowed the old corner to be re-introduced.

SPA-FRANCORCHAMPS

Circuit distance: 4.350 miles (7.00 km)
Race distance: 191.400 miles (308.00 km)
No of laps: 44

The best of today's Grand Prix circuits by a country mile. This is the one the drivers like to get their teeth into as it climbs and falls, twists and turns through the Ardennes forests. The vicious, uphill Eau Rouge bend temporarily had its bite taken out of it by a chicane, but there's still the Blanchimont sweeper to test them.

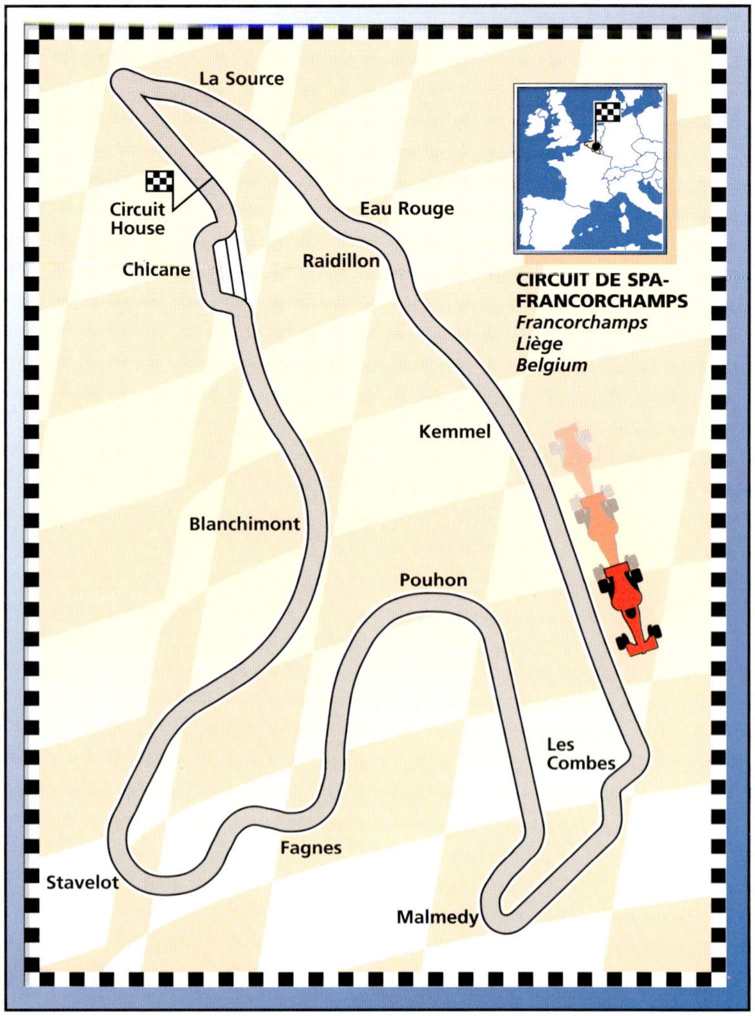

DUTCH GRAND PRIX

Together with the US, Austrian and South African events, the Dutch Grand Prix is one of several classic races which, sad to say, no longer has a place on the calendar.

The event was run 30 times between 1952 and 1985, initially in June and latterly in August, and every race took place at the same circuit – Zandvoort. Set in sand dunes just a few hundred yards inland of the North Sea, the resort town of Zandvoort was for decades one of the most popular stops on the schedule. The track itself, opened in 1948, was a clever design which encouraged entertaining racing.

A fast and difficult corner on to the long pit straight was followed by the slow right-hander at Tarzan, where heavy braking was required and overtaking opportunities were frequent. One of the most famous corners in racing, it was for years the scene of some exciting action, and occasionally, spectacular accidents. The rest of the track was basically a square, with one side interrupted by a chicane and another by an "S" which fed into the fast right-hander on to the long straight down to Tarzan. This loop was later chopped and altered in the name of safety. Sand blowing across the track was a constant hazard.

Backmarkers *Thierry Boutsen (ahead) and Huub Rothengatter round Hugenholtz and head for the country in the 1985 race.*

Triumph and tragedy

The list of Dutch Grand Prix winners reads like a Who's Who of motor racing's greats. Ascari won the first two races in 1952–53, while the 1955 event saw a victory for Fangio and the mighty Mercedes team. Moss won for Vanwall in 1958 and Jo Bonnier gave BRM its first victory a year later. All the big names triumphed in the 1960s: Brabham, von Trips, Hill, Clark (four times) and Stewart.

Everyone loved Zandvoort and its holiday atmosphere, but in the early 1970s the track hit the headlines for the wrong reasons. In 1970 Piers Courage died in a fiery accident with the Williams-entered de Tomaso, and then three years later the same fate befell fellow Englishman Roger Williamson, in only his second race with a privately-entered March.

But while concerns about safety were voiced, the race went on. Lauda registered one of his first triumphs in 1974, and in 1975 Hunt memorably scored his first win for Hesketh. He won again the following year for McLaren after a great battle with Watson. In 1977 Hunt tangled with Andretti, allowing Lauda to win. The 1978 race saw an Andretti/Peterson steamroller performance for Lotus.

The 1979 event is remembered not so much for Jones's victory, but more for the efforts of Villeneuve to drag his three-wheeled Ferrari back to the pits. A year later Daly flipped his Tyrrell at Tarzan, but escaped injury.

The 1983 event was notable for a collision between title contenders Piquet and Prost. Both men were out of the race, and victory went to Arnoux, who had survived a huge first-corner crash in 1982. Prost gained revenge by winning in 1984.

The Formula One circus visited Zandvoort for the last time in 1985, and the race was a classic, Lauda just holding off Prost as he scored his final victory. The track was coming under threat from developers, and suddenly Holland did not seem like a fashionable place to hold a Grand Prix. Indeed, the country had never produced a truly competitive driver, which made it hard to justify keeping the race when other venues were applying for dates.

Shortened and rebuilt, Zandvoort survives as a venue for mainly domestic racing, with the famous Tarzan corner thankfully still intact.

ITALIAN GRAND PRIX

The name Monza is one of the most evocative in motor sport and it reflects a remarkable heritage. Since 1950 the circuit has hosted the Italian Grand Prix every season except one – 1980, when the race was run at Imola.

In fact the history of the famous Autodromo goes right back to 1922, when it was first built. An Italian Grand Prix had been run for the first time at Brescia the year before, but Monza, set in an attractive park near Milan, soon became its rightful home.

A variety of configurations was available in the early days, but much of the track still used today was in place from the start. Monza has always been one of the fastest tracks on the schedule, even after the addition of chicanes in the early 1970s.

The Grand Prix has a wonderful atmosphere and always attracts a massive crowd of loyal Ferrari fans – known as the "tifosi". If their team is not winning, they soon make their feelings known...

The present track is 3.604 miles long. The wide pit straight, which passes the charismatic old grandstands, is curtailed by an absurdly tight double chicane, the Rettifilio, which nearly always produces first-lap drama. The sweeping Curva Grande right-hander is followed by a second chicane, Curva della Roggia, which leads to the legendary double Lesmo right-handers. Two of the most famous corners in motor racing, they were slightly realigned in 1994 as a result of a safety campaign.

The track then rushes under the old banked circuit (more of that later) to the relatively fast Vialone chicane. Then comes the much-photographed blast down the back straight, followed by the fast Parabolica corner, scene of many dramas over the years. That catapults the cars back on to the main straight.

Before the chicanes were built, the track was virtually a flat-out blast. More than any other, it saw wonderful slipstreaming battles, especially when cars became more "slippery" in the 1960s. However, it was also one of the toughest on machinery, and very often races were decided more by engine longevity than driver skill. It is still a circuit where power and straight-line speed are all-important.

MONZA

Circuit distance: 3.604 miles (5.80 km)
Race distance: 191.012 miles (307.40 km)
No of laps: 53

To many, this is the spiritual home of motor racing, its abandoned banked track a reminder of bygone days. Is blessed with long straights and fast comers that make for the best slipstreaming battles. The Lesmo bends are the biggest test, followed by a straight then one of the best chicanes in Formula One.

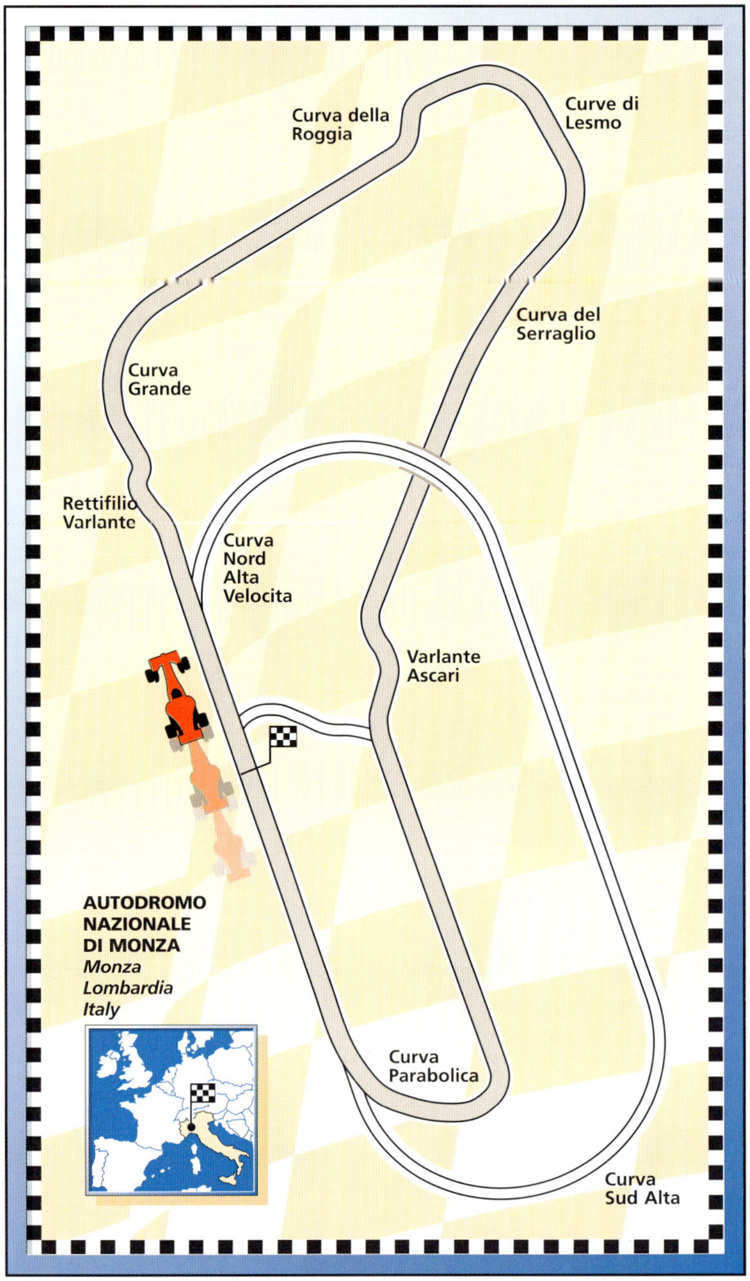

A remarkable history

Monza has seen some memorable races, but has also had more than its fair share of tragedy. Indeed, in the pre-war races several of the great stars of the day lost their lives. Three top drivers were killed in one event in 1933 alone.

Monza had a place in the very first World Championship calendar in 1950. Like most of the early races, it saw a battle between Alfa-Romeo and Ferrari; Farina won for the former.

The first of many dramatic finishes occurred in 1953. It was one of the rare occasions when the lead battle continued to the last lap, and was not compromised by mechanical failure. At the last corner Ascari spun, Farina took to the grass and Marimon hit Ascari. Fangio motored through the mayhem to win.

Ascari was killed testing a sports car at Monza in May 1955, and that year's Grand Prix saw a major change. A banked circuit had been added to the layout, and a long, 6.2-mile course was devised, incorporating both the original track and the two banked corners. The banking was bumpy and unpopular with the drivers, and proved particularly hard on tyres. Fangio won in 1955 (the last Grand Prix for Mercedes) and Moss triumphed in 1956 before the layout was temporarily abandoned. In the latter race Collins handed his car to Fangio and in doing so sacrificed his World Championship hopes to the Argentinian maestro.

Moss's 1956 win started a remarkable run of success for English-speaking drivers, who would win every Italian Grand Prix bar one until 1969. Perhaps the most galling loss for the local fans came in 1957 when Moss won for Vanwall, beating the beloved red cars.

In 1960 the race was, controversially, restored to the combined road/banked course, and the British teams boycotted the event. Finally, a Ferrari won again. It was the last victory by any rear-engined car, and driver Phil Hill was the first American to win a Grand Prix.

The following year Hill clinched the World title at Monza, but in tragic circumstances after team-mate Wolfgang von Trips and 12 spectators were killed. The race was back on the road course in 1962, and in 1963 an attempt to return to the banked course was abandoned after first practice. The banking was quietly forgotten.

The1960s races saw some wonderful dicing, but time and again it would be spoiled by leading cars dropping out. In 1965 Jackie Stewart scored his first-ever win, and in 1966 Scarfiotti beat the English-speakers as he led a Ferrari one-two.

In 1969 the race finally delivered the photo finish that had been promised since 1953. In the closing yards Stewart just pulled clear of Rindt, Beltoise and McLaren in a thriller.

Tragedy returned in 1970 when Rindt lost his life in qualifying. The race again saw a wonderful lead battle, from which Regazzoni emerged to score his first win. The following year brought the most sensational finish of any Grand Prix, as the unrated Gethin led a pack of five cars across the line.

McLaren muscle at Monza *Senna and Prost lead the field around on the parade lap before the 1988 Italian Grand Prix.*

Sweeping changes

In 1972 the face of Monza was changed forever with the introduction of a chicane beyond the pits, and another at Vialone. The days of wild, slipstreaming fights were over, and the first "new" race was won by Fittipaldi, who also clinched the title for Lotus.

In the early 1970s Peterson emerged as a Monza specialist, winning in 1973, 1974 and 1976. But the track was also to claim his life. A multiple pile-up at the start of the 1978 race saw him hospitalized with broken legs, and he died from complications the next day. It was a sad way for team-mate Andretti to win the title.

In 1980 the race moved – for one time only – to Imola (see San Marino story). The political problems were solved when Imola earned its own San Marino Grand Prix, and the Italian race returned to its original home in 1981.

Monza was a circuit where the turbo cars could really stretch their legs. In 1986, at the peak of the turbo era, Fabi's BMW-powered Benetton blasted to pole. But remarkably, neither he nor fellow front-row man Prost took up their grid positions after last-minute problems – a unique occurrence in Formula One history.

Three times in the late 1980s Senna lost Monza victories when he seemed to have the race won. In 1987 he went across the grass at the Parabolica, handing Piquet the lead. In 1988 he was leading comfortably when he tangled with back marker Schlesser, allowing Berger to score the last triumph of Enzo Ferrari's lifetime. Then in 1989 Senna's engine blew with nine laps to go, allowing Prost to win. The Frenchman gave his trophy to the fans in a calculated insult to team boss Ron Dennis.

Senna's luck finally changed when he won in 1990, but the luckiest man that day was Warwick, who survived a massive first-lap crash at the Parabolica, and even took the restart.

The 1991 event was one of the best of recent years, as Senna fought with the Williams-Renault pair of Mansell and Patrese. The Italian retired, Senna was forced to take new tyres and Mansell scored a memorable win. But Senna got his own back the following year when the Williams duo suffered unusual hydraulic pump belt failures, and the Brazilian took advantage.

As in the 1950s Monza continued to exert a mechanical toll. Prost was leading in 1993 when engine failure handed the win to team-mate Hill. The Englishman scored a second success in 1994. The track was modified to mollify safety concerns, but its essential spirit is unchanged.

PORTUGUESE GRAND PRIX

ESTORIL

Circuit distance: 2.709 miles (4.36 km)
Race distance: 192.339 miles (309.54 km)
No of laps: 71

Now one of the old-guard of Grand Prix circuits. And it still retains some character despite changes made in 1994 on safety grounds. Drivers love the challenge and know the track well from winter testing there. The key corner is the long, long last one leading onto the main straight. It's essential to get this right so you can slipstream down the straight to the first corner.

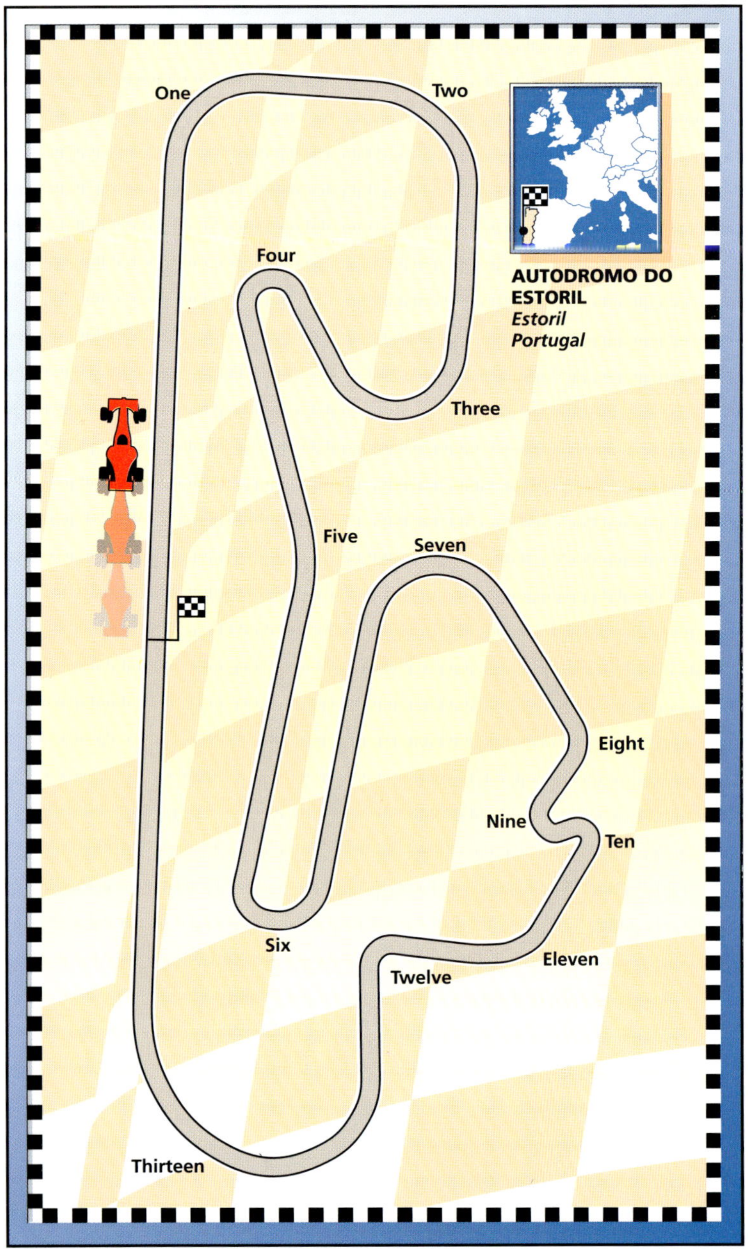

Portugal is a small country which has never had a great Formula One driver, and yet its Grand Prix is a well-supported event, often producing high drama.

The Portuguese Grand Prix had a brief flourish during 1958–60. In the even years it was held on the 4.65-mile Oporto street track – where tramlines and cobblestones were among the hazards – and in 1959 it was run at Monsanto, near Lisbon, an equally tricky 3.38-mile parkland venue.

The starting line at Oporto was situated near the harbour front and, like the modern Macau track, it combined long straights with twisty bits between buildings. Moss won the inaugural race, while Hawthorn very nearly threw away his World Championship after driving the wrong way after a spin. He escaped disqualification.

Moss was again class of the field in 1959, dominating proceedings in his Cooper. The race was started late to avoid the afternoon heat, and finished after 7pm! Moss, returning from injury, was never really in the hunt in the 1960 Oporto event, which was won by Brabham.

There followed a long interval before Formula One returned to the country – 24 years in fact. This time the venue was the permanent road course near the resort of Estoril. Built in 1972, the 2.70-mile Autodromo do Estoril hosted European Formula Two in the mid-1970s, but had largely been forgotten when it was resurrected and tidied up in 1984. Thanks to the year-round good weather, it soon became a popular testing venue.

A demanding circuit

Featuring up and down sweeps through barren, rocky terrain, the lap starts with a flowing right-hander that leads almost immediately into a wicked downhill right-hander and a hairpin. Then it's uphill to another hairpin and down the kinked back straight. A long left-hander, a short straight, then an uphill right-hander lead the track into a series of twists before a long, long right-hander on to the pit straight. It is tough on the drivers, but has more overtaking opportunities than most tracks built in recent years.

The 1984 event was held in October and proved to be the championship decider. Prost won the race, but Lauda did just enough to win the title – by half a point! The 1985 race was held just seven months later, in April, and Prost was one of several drivers to crash out in torrential conditions. The master on that memorable day was Senna, who collected his first win for Lotus.

After that experiment the race moved to September. Mansell won in 1986, while Prost triumphed again in 1987 (pressuring Berger into a spin) and again in 1988. One of the most controversial races came in 1989, when Mansell was black-flagged after reversing in the pits. He did not respond, and three laps later crashed out of the race with Senna. Berger made amends by winning.

Nigel was banned from the next event, but the following year he came back and beat Senna at Estoril – a rare good result during his miser able second season with Ferrari. But at the start he had lunged at team-mate Prost, costing them both positions.

Patrese won in 1991, after Mansell lost a wheel leaving the pits! Nigel was later black-flagged, and his title hopes took a major knock. He scored his third success in 1992. That race was notable for a spectacular accident involving Patrese, who nearly hit the pit straight bridge after striking a slowing Berger.

The 1993 race saw Schumacher score his second-ever win for Benetton after the team's superior pit strategy overcame that of Prost and Williams. This time Berger had a massive accident on the main straight, albeit at the other end – when leaving the pits!

In 1994 Hill took full advantage of the absence of a suspended Schumacher by winning. The track now has an absurdly slow chicane, introduced after the Imola tragedies.

JAPANESE GRAND PRIX

SUZUKA

Circuit distance: 3.644 miles (5.864 km)
Race distance: 182.150 miles (293.14 km)
No of laps: 50

A really tough and technical circuit, unusual for the fact that it crosses over itself. The crowds are always enormous and chase everything that looks looks like a driver with an autograph book. Toughest corner is 130R at the end of the back straight: it's very fast and narrow.

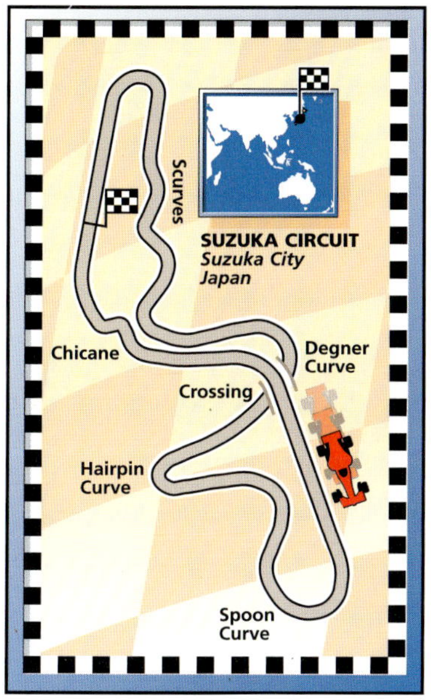

It has taken a relatively short time for the Japanese Grand Prix to become established as one of the great events on the calendar, but has done so for a variety of reasons. It is held on one of the best circuits, it usually plays a key role in the outcome of the World Championship and the inc-redible enthusiasm of the local fans ensures that the atmosphere is electric.

Japan's first involvement in Grand Prix racing was through Honda, which competed with limited success from 1964 to 1968. It was not until 1976 that the country hosted its first Grand Prix – indeed, it was the first to be held anywhere in the vast Asia-Pacific region.

The original venue was Fuji Speedway, a wonderfully charismatic circuit set on the slopes of Mount Fuji. It was notable for having one of the longest straights ever seen in Formula One, linked by a succession of fast, sweeping (and dangerous) corners.

The first, rain-soaked race went down in the history books as the one which gave James Hunt his World Championship after Niki Lauda pulled out. Few remember that Andretti gave the Lotus team its first win for more than two years. The sun shone in 1977 and Hunt scored his last-ever win, although it was overshadowed by the death of several onlookers after rookie Gilles Villeneuve vaulted over the back of Peterson's Tyrrell. The accident did Fuji's hopes no good at all and, with the Japanese motor industry at that time showing little or no interest in the sport, the Japanese Grand Prix disappeared for a decade.

It came back in 1987 at Suzuka, as a direct result of Honda's successful return to Formula One, this time as an engine supplier. Honda had owned the Suzuka track since it was openedin 1963, and made a considerable effort to bring the circuit up to scratch. Featuring a unique – for Formula One – "figure of eight" layout, the track had a variety of fast and slow corners, including 130R, the heart-in-mouth, flat-out left-hander before the pits.

A popular circuit

From the start the Suzuka was loved by the drivers. However, overtaking was not easy and it was made even more difficult when the chicane before the pits was tightened in 1991, spoiling the main passing opportunity that had been at the end of the main straight.

The first event in 1987 is remembered best for a practice accident which ended Mansell's title hopes, handing the honours to team-mate Piquet. The race itself was won by Berger's McLaren.

In 1988 Senna's growing status in Japan was confirmed when he won after recovering from a bad start. The following year he and McLaren team-mate Prost famously collided at the chicane when battling for the lead. Senna eventually crossed the line first, but his disqualification handed the win to Nannini.

In 1990 Prost (now with Ferrari) and Senna tangled again, going off into the gravel trap at the first corner. Senna claimed the crown and a year later admitted that it had been a premeditated move.

Senna was again at the forefront in 1991, when he led but moved over and allowed team-mate Berger to win at the last corner. In 1992 Patrese took advantage of the retirement of Mansell to score his last-ever Grand Prix victory.

Senna and Irvine clash

Senna bounced back to score a magnificent win in the McLaren-Ford in 1993, dominating a tricky wet/dry race. Afterwards he made the headlines by punching newcomer Irvine.

The 1994 race was one of the best to date. Once again rain struck, and a string of early accidents caused a pace car period and then a stoppage. After the restart Hill overcame Schumacher's first-part advantage to score perhaps the hardest-earned win of his career to date.

That season Japan earned a second race for the first time. Dubbed the Pacific Grand Prix, it was held at the narrow and tight TI Circuit in Aida, south of Suzuka. Against expectations the race, won by Schumacher, proved to be an organizational success. However, overtaking was an impossibility.

TI CIRCUIT

Circuit distance: 3.643 miles (5.863 km)
Race distance: 193.100 miles (310.76 km)
No of laps: 53

Stuck away in the middle of nowhere on Japan's southern island, TI Circuit is run as a private club for very wealthy individuals, as somewhere where they can store their supercars and take them out for an occasional blast. Far too narrow to permit any overtaking, so not for Formula One.

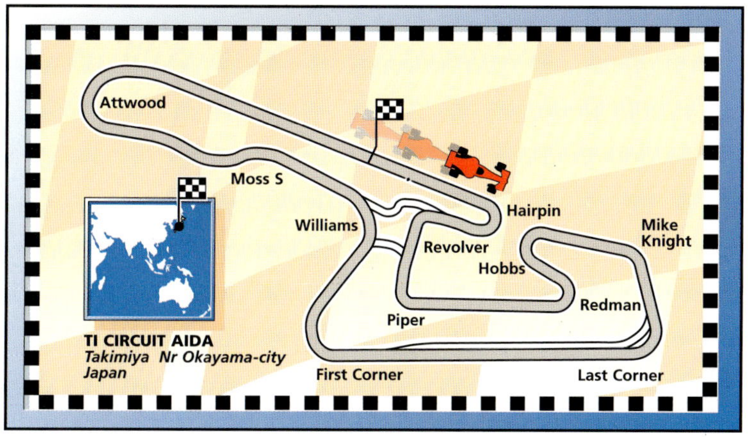

AUSTRALIAN GRAND PRIX

ADELAIDE

Circuit distance: 2.350 miles (3.78 km)
Race distance: 190.35 miles (306.18 km)
No of laps: 81

Popular as a great venue for an end-of-term race. Track is a real challenge and the concrete walls that line its length offer no mercy. Drivers like the kink that links the Jones Straight to the Brabham Straight. The hairpin that follows is the best overtaking point.

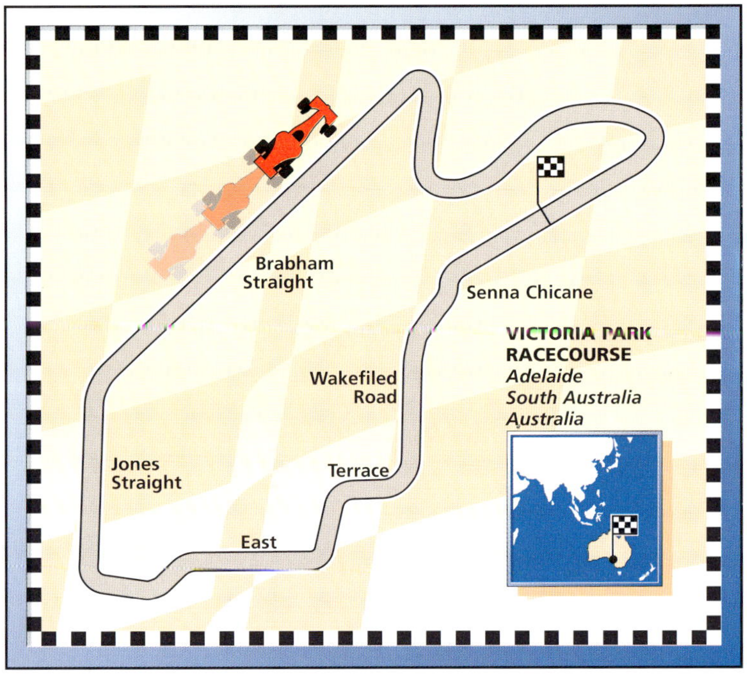

Despite the international successes of Jack Brabham and Alan Jones, it was not until 1985 that Australia first played host to a round of the World Championship. The venue was Adelaide, and it quickly became established as one of the most popular events on the calendar.

The race was introduced as part of a campaign to promote the South Australian city, which had always been in the shadow of Sydney and Melbourne. With the full support of the local government, nothing was left to chance in the planning stages, and over the years the Australian race has often been cited as the best-organized event of the year. It was also popular with teams because it came at the end of a long, hard season, and because the weather was usually splendid – unless it was raining...

The track itself is a temporary one, running partly on public roads in and around the Victoria Park horse racing facility. It is not a typical street circuit, in that it is very fast, with long, straight sections punctuated by slow, right-angle turns and some fast kinks – notably the tricky chicane at the first turn, where Michael Schumacher came to grief in qualifying in 1994. The tight hairpin at the end of Brabham Straight is a notable overtaking place, and has been the scene of much action over the years. Like most street circuits, though, there is no run-off area at all, just unyielding concrete walls.

Spectating is best from the temporary grandstands set up in the park, although hundreds of faces can be spied peering from the surrounding buildings where the track passes the city's fruit and vegetable market.

A memorable start

Rosberg won the inaugural race, which happened to be Lauda's last Grand Prix, but it was the 1986 event which stands out. Mansell was on course for the World title when his rear tyre blew, and millions of television viewers watched as his Williams skated down the escape road in a shower of sparks. Prost won the race, and with it his second title.

After a win for Berger in 1987 and a second for Prost in 1988, the 1989 race proved a memorable event. Rain had affected qualifying in the past, and for the first time it struck on race day. The Grand Prix was stopped after two laps, and Prost declined to take the restart. With many top drivers crashing, including Senna, Boutsen scored a hard-earned win in his Williams.

The following year Adelaide had the honour of hosting the 500th Grand Prix, and triple world champion Piquet won for Benetton after a strong challenge from Mansell. The rain came again in 1991, and the event lasted just 14 laps before being red-flagged, with Senna adjudged the winner. It was the shortest-ever World Championship event.

Senna was in the news the following year, too, when he and new champion Mansell collided, and Berger scored his second win. Ayrton gained revenge with a dominant victory in 1993. It was his last race for McLaren and his final Grand Prix win.

The 1994 event was a classic, the first final-round title showdown since 1986. The contest ended when Schumacher and Damon Hill collided in controversial circumstances while fighting for the lead, securing the title for the German. Having started from pole, returnee Mansell scored a surprise win after Berger made a mistake.

Adelaide is scheduled to hold the Grand Prix for the last time in 1995, the organizers having been outflanked and outbid by another venue. Ironically, the South Australian capital is due to be replaced by Melbourne, one of the cities which Adelaide had attempted to outshine by bringing the World Championship to Australia. The venue for the new track is Albert Park, which played host to non-championship Formula One races in the 1950s. So, it seems the history of the Australian Grand Prix has gone full circle.

Street setting *Riccardo Patrese passes the Stag Hotel in downtown Adelaide.*

THE BUSINESS OF FORMULA ONE

Make no mistake, Formula One is not only a high-adrenaline sport, but a high budget one, too. As speeds have escalated, so has the cost of competing, spawning a world of business that would shame the top financial corporations. Without big money, drivers would be left on the starting grid.

Forget about Grand Prix racing as a sport for a moment and think of it as part of a new global service industry. Motor racing, like all the world's major sports and entertainments, is now big business, with Formula One – the multinational monster that wants to eat money faster than it can be fed – at its pinnacle.

Yet, unlike industries that adhere to the normal economic laws of supply and demand, Formula One does not provide a tangible product or service – it supplies the rather abstract notion of several cars all trying to complete a set number of revolutions of a circuit before the rest do. Nevertheless, it still needs cash to operate, so where does this come from?

Some of Formula One's money comes from the vast numbers of spectators paying money to witness the spectacle in the flesh and some from the television companies wanting to televise this strange ritual for the benefit of millions of couch potatoes across the globe. But by far the greater part comes from sponsorship.

Sponsors' dream *Hill, Schumacher and Verstappen on the podium.*

THE ROLE OF SPONSORSHIP

It has been conservatively estimated that sponsorship, either from commercial companies or from trade sponsors supplying engines, tyres, and the like, is worth something like half a billion dollars a year to Formula One. The actual amount involved is not something about which the ever-cautious FIA will give a straight answer, but it is certainly almost incomprehensibly vast.

Gold Leaf tobacco was the first major commercial sponsor to enter Formula One. That was with Lotus back in 1968 and it signalled the end of the age of innocence for the sport of Grand Prix racing. Nowadays, the whole infrastructure of Formula One is based on sponsorship and without it the sport would not be able to exist in anything like its present form. For a top team, not including the monetary value of engine, fuel and tyre deals, a budget for a season can easily be as high as $50 million – to pay for research, salaries, testing, car construction and the thousands of other costs incurred in the business of Formula One.

Since Gold Leaf's arrival, sponsors have come and sponsors have gone, but even through some of the worst recessions the twentieth century could contrive to manufacture, Formula One has never looked back. It continues to attract new sponsors from inside and outside the automobile industry like ants to a picnic. But why would a firm like Marlboro or Canon or Renault or

Colours of Benetton *Michael Schumacher helped his team market Benetton clothing by winning the 1994 world title.*

Goodyear pour vast sums into this most esoteric of pursuits? The simple answer is that Formula One is an image that ultimately sells things, be they cars or cigarettes or soft drinks.

If an automobile manufacturer supplies the engine for the car that takes the World Championship, that sense of engineering excellence is reflected through the rest of its products, while if a cigarette manufacturer is on the side of the winning car, its products are imbued with an extra glamour that instantly enhances their desirability.

And as advertising campaigns go, Formula One is a remarkably cost-effective medium. Name sponsorship of a front-running Grand Prix team may cost $30 million, but compare that to the figures talked about for a conventional year-long TV campaign with a target audience approaching a billion people and it all makes extremely good sense.

However, a company sponsoring a Formula One team will not stop solely at putting its name on the flanks of a car. Additionally, a whole infrastructure of support activities will add to the public's awareness of its involvement – everything from saturation poster campaigns in the vicinity of a race itself to on-circuit hospitality, to success advertising on television and in the media. All reinforce the link between the prestige and technical excellence of Grand Prix racing and the product being advertised, and all add up to extra sales of a product in the long-term.

Moving billboards *It's not just the cars that carry livery.*

The problems of advertising

Of course, there are many critics of the overt advertising seen on Grand Prix cars. Some say the sport has been prostituted by its reliance on commercial cash. Many dream of a return to the simplicity of the 1950s and 1960s, but most criticism is directed at Formula One's willingness to be involved with health damaging products such as tobacco and alcohol.

The wider argument might also be that cars themselves are the ultimate health-damaging product, but on the vexed question of cigarettes and alcohol, Formula One's defenders point out that the name "Marlboro" on a car does not create new smokers, it merely alters the brand loyalty of existing smokers. True or not, with many governments clamping down hard on the advertising of tobacco products, Formula One will soon be forced to look elsewhere for a replacement for its biggest golden egg. And, despite the abundance of potential Formula One sponsors, teams do have to go out and look for the money. For most teams a commercial department with the task of wooing and enticing sponsors is just as important as a driver or a chief designer. Potential sponsors do need to be convinced of the wisdom of investing in Formula One and of its long-term benefits to their particular company.

Sponsor packages come in a bewildering number of shapes, sizes, permutations and prices, from the car-dominating Rothmans or Marlboro logos on the side of a Williams or a McLaren, to a discreet name on a wing mirror or an end plate. All have vast potential if exploited correctly, but for an organization not au fait with the global grip of Grand Prix racing, a sticker the size of an airmail envelope travelling at 200mph could need some careful explaining before the penny – or the million dollars – drops.

Ultimately, for commercial sponsors cost will depend on size and location as well as the team's reputation and history. In Ferrari's case, a huge financial investment by Marlboro was rewarded with just two discreet logos behind the driver, yet this was regarded as more than satisfactory by the tobacco giant, given the team's worldwide support and its prestige. For suppliers of engines, fuel and tyres, logos on the car will usually be part of an offset package. But again, size and location will depend on the value of a particular supply deal and the nature of the product being used.

Often, a sponsor's colour scheme becomes as famous as the team it supports – the ultimate return on an investment. Marlboro and John Player Special are prime examples. And, taking things one step further, the Benetton clothing company was not just content with title sponsorship, but actually bought and renamed the Toleman team in the mid-1980s.

Golden win *Millions of consumers watched Damon Hill's Silverstone win.*

HITACHI
Racing
BRITISH
GRAND PR
SILVERSTON
1994
Formula 1
CHAMPION

THE ORGANIZATION OF FORMULA ONE

Commercial sponsorship enters the coffers of Formula One teams by a direct route. However, the money that comes in from the races themselves and from television takes a slightly more complex path. To understand it, one must look first at how the sport is run.

There are four main areas that need to be covered by the organizing bodies of a sport like Grand Prix racing: the sporting side, which settles how race meetings are run, how points are scored, etc; the technical side, which determines the rules for the construction of cars and engines and also includes such matters as safety; the organizational side, which decides which races are held, where, when and which teams are allowed to compete, how teams get to races outside Europe, etc; and the commercial side, which deals with the finances of the sport, the television coverage, travel funds and other monetary aspects.

For Formula One the FIA (Fédération Internationale de l'Automobile) covers all the sporting and technical aspects, while the organizational and commercial side of the sport is taken care of almost single-handedly by one man – Bernie Ecclestone.

Ecclestone has a foot in two camps, being the vice-president of Promotional Affairs at the FIA and the president of the Formula One Constructors' Association (FOCA), the body formed by the teams themselves. Ironically, FOCA and FIA were during the early 1980s involved in bitter wrangles which threatened to tear the sport of Formula One apart, but eventually led to today's stability and apparent harmony.

Power brokers *Max Mosley (left) and Bernie Ecclestone.*

Ecclestone's importance in the scheme of Grand Prix racing has grown considerably from the 1970s onwards until he is now probably the most powerful man in Formula One – many would say even more powerful than the president of the FIA himself. It is Ecclestone who negotiates television and race deals and it is Ecclestone who distributes the financial proceeds.

Money from television and race promoters comes to the teams in two separate ways – prize money and travel money. Travel money is paid to the top ten teams in the Constructors' World Championship and covers such items as air-freighting the equipment to races outside Europe.

Prize money, however, is a more secretive affair. For a single Grand Prix prize money is set at several million dollars and is paid out to teams in a pre-determined manner, based on qualifying positions, finishing positions and positions at set times during the races.

The Concord Agreement, a confidential document covering the fundamental running and stability of Formula One, includes details of prize money and its distribution.

But even with the vast sums of money circulating within the sport, there are still the haves and the have-nots. As in most things, success tends to breed success and the money gravitates towards the more successful teams, leaving those at the back of the grid to struggle on with shoestring budgets.

The top three *Schumacher, Hill and Berger (top to bottom) finished one, two, three in the 1994 rankings, but Berger had the fattest salary cheque thanks to a multi-million pound deal with Marlboro and Ferrari. Hill was worst off, earning less in the year than occasional team mate Mansell did for one race.*

THE DRIVERS

In Formula One there are two types of drivers: those who are paid and those who pay. And as a rule of thumb, the lower down the grid a team is, the more likely it is to have one or more paying drivers on board.

Formula One – indeed, motor racing in general – is one of the few sports in which money can get its participant on to the field of play. In comparison with football or rugby or baseball, where the players taking part at the highest level have been carefully nurtured over many years and are assumed to be the best of the crop, it does seem odd that a Grand Prix grid may not contain the best 26 drivers in the world. But such are the harsh realities of life in certain areas of the world's most expensive sport that often cheques do speak louder than talent.

Not all paying drivers are unworthy of a place in Formula One, however. Since the early careers of most Formula One drivers are a desperate attempt to be noticed by teams higher up the grid, many are placed in a lower team by a personal sponsor as part of a longer-term gameplan. It was just such a situation that saw Elf and Marlboro pack out the Formula One grids of the late 1970s and early 1980s with several French and Italian drivers of genuine talent, including Alain Prost, René Arnoux and Michele Alboreto.

As a filter to ensure that Formula One "rent-a-drivers" are not completely without talent, the FIA requires all Grand Prix drivers to qualify for a Superlicence before being allowed to attempt to qualify for a Grand Prix. But, with numerous loopholes in the Superlicence procedure, many would claim that the situation is less than satisfactory and that the talent gap between the Formula One elite and some backmarkers is still dangerously wide.

At the front of the grid, thanks to commercial sponsorship, driver talent is the bottom line and the cream of the world's drivers are rewarded handsomely for their labours. But still the Faustian possibility of paying it back with the ultimate price remains, despite the many advances in driver safety in recent years.

The late 1980s saw driver salaries begin to rocket and in the early part of the 1990s the likes of Ayrton Senna, Alain Prost and Nigel Mansell were able to ask for – and for the most part receive – salaries nudging $10 million for a single season of racing. Now salaries appear to have stabilized, but still the sport's top earners, such as Michael Schumacher and Gerhard Berger, are successfully negotiating contracts with salaries of over $8 million.

However, a paid driver's income is not just a set salary. On top of that, he may negotiate a performance-related bonus based on World Championship points scored and his position in the final standings. When driving for Benetton in the early 1990s, three-times world champion Nelson Piquet based everything bar a small retainer on wins and championship points – and promptly won three Grands Prix in two seasons with the team as an extremely lucrative twilight to his career.

A driver will almost certainly have a series of personal sponsors who will be given helmet and overall space beside that earmarked by the team's sponsors. For a top driver it is a bonus on top of the salary, but for a lesser driver it is more money in the kitty to pay for his drive. Amazingly, a small patch on the arm of a top driver's overalls, can cost as much as $500,000.

At the back of the grid, the cost of a paid drive, just like the cost of sponsorship, is dependent on the team. In recent seasons the rear of the field has often resembled an expensive game of musical chairs as one driver is pushed or jumps ship.

Many will try to succeed in Formula One, but few actually do. And yet there seems to be a never-ending supply of the optimistc, the naive and the wealthy, clutching their dreams of Grand Prix stardom.

Man with the mike *Murray Walker's frenetic delivery entertains millions.*

THE MEDIA

As befits a sport with such global appeal, Formula One attracts massive media coverage around the world. Naturally, however, in an age when television is the god of communications, the visual media are cultivated with the most vigour by the FIA.

Recent figures have shown that at least part of every round of the Formula One World Championship is seen by almost a quarter of the Earth's population. In sport, only the Olympics or the soccer World Cup finals can compete. But these are events that take place for just a few days every four years. Formula One takes place 16 weekends a year, every year. Given such compelling statistics, it is little wonder that companies such as Marlboro or Elf wish to be so heavily involved.

In the past television coverage was a messy, incomplete business, with local companies broadcasting their home races and overseas coverage remaining a sporadic, hit-and-miss affair. But now, just like so many other aspects of Formula One, Bernie Ecclestone and the Formula One Constructors' Association have homogenized and streamlined the whole package. A local company will still provide on-track coverage – the BBC in Britain, for instance – but FOCA controls the distribution of coverage throughout the rest of the world. And, by making the product readily available, FOCA has pushed Formula One into more countries and more households than could ever have been dreamed of.

Even in the satellite age Europe remains the true heartland of Formula One, but many other places are catching on and catching up.

In most European countries, every moment that Formula One cars are on the track during a Grand Prix weekend is available live and direct, either through terrestrial or satellite coverage, and every year the number of other countries adopting that same level of coverage is growing.

It is strange to think that for 16 weekends a year Michael Schumacher and Gerhard Berger are projected on to probably more retinas than the President of the United States – except in the United States itself, where Formula One continues to come a poor third in the TV viewers' four-wheeled affections, just behind stock-car and Indycar racing.

Newspaper coverage

In addition to the torrents of television coverage of Formula One are the acres of printed words published on Formula One every year. From the tabloids, through the quality journals, to the specialist racing press, Formula One is manna from heaven, with its danger, glamour, wealth, "wars", political intrigue and sometimes bewildering plot lines making it both a cerebral challenge and a soap opera.

Grand Prix racing has often been described as a microcosm of the world and that is probably a pretty accurate analogy.

Three countries more than any others stand out as the bastions of Formula One in print – Britain, Italy and France. Of the three, Britain is the best example for showing the various levels of coverage that have evolved and which between them have all the bases covered.

For the tabloids, Formula One is definitely soap opera in the same way that the Royal Family is soap opera. Instead of a sport, Formula One almost becomes "who is doing what with whom", with the drivers developing larger-than-life personas and often sensationalist traits. In this way Michael Schumacher becomes a bully-boy, Nigel Mansell a British bulldog and Ayrton Senna the moody Latin with a secret death wish. It is often superficial, but it is just another aspect of the ultra-successful creed of titillation that the tabloids have now adopted across the board.

Going up a level in terms of coverage, we then reach the broadsheets and their world in which team owners are known as Mr Williams or Mr Dennis and drivers, like jockeys or footballers, are called by their surnames.

Broadsheet coverage of Formula One is less sensationalist and more sober. News is news and opinions and character assessments are left to the columns of the writers. The sport itself – the actual racing – is dealt with more thoroughly and the nationalistic stance of the tabloids is somewhat toned down.

But whether tabloid or broadsheet, Formula One will always take a backseat to football, or whatever the seasonal national sport is, and coverage will be seasonal and cyclical. This is where the specialist magazine comes into its own. Specialist magazines appeal to the Formula One enthusiast and to those involved directly in the sport. The coverage is of a comprehensive nature: every aspect of the sport is explored and to a far greater depth than the newspapers are able to give.

Specialist publications

Basically, the role of the specialist magazine is to provide the total picture. In Britain, *Autosport* and *Motoring News* are the two weekly publications successfully attempting that, with combined sales of over 120,000 copies a week.

As well as all the current Formula One news, a magazine like *Autosport* also includes interviews, race reports, features, previews, statistics and – very importantly – provides a visual record far superior to that of the newspapers and often of television itself. But, on the negative side, a weekly cannot be as instant as a newspaper and hence must be capable of providing much greater perspective and insight.

In Italy *Autosprint* and *Auto & Sport* fulfil the weekly specialist role, but the general coverage, too, is able to reach a greater level – albeit with a distinct Ferrari bias – thanks to the specialist sporting newspapers, such as *Gazetta dello Sport* available in the country. And this situation is repeated in France, where *L'Equipe* sports paper plays the daily role and *Autohebdo* fills the role of the weekly specialist.

Looking at television, newspaper and specialist magazine coverage as a whole, the factual side of Formula One is well served, with even the most anally retentive of its fans able to sate their thirst for knowledge. On the fictional side, however, Grand Prix racing has proved a tricky beast to tie down.

At the cinema films involving Formula One have tended to fall into one of two camps – the deadly dull and leaden-scripted or the ultra-sensationalist with casualty figures approaching those on a battlefield. And, with modern Grand Prix cars now bristling with on-board cameras and live television coverage an ever-improving art form, it is difficult to see how the genre can continue when its past is littered with turkeys that even Elvis would have refused to appear in, while the real thing is considerably more exciting, anyway.

In printed fiction Formula One gets more of the sensationalist treatment, with sex, blackmail and accidents the recurring strands. Bob Judd is the Raymond Chandler and Jackie Collins of Grand Prix fiction, with a style and a flair for plots that sometimes border on the bizarre – Semtex earplugs spring to mind – offbeat, but enjoyable, nonetheless. But whether a Bob Judd novel will ever make the leap to celluloid remains to be seen.

Britain's motor sporting weekly *Autosport has been bringing the best of Formula One to motor racing fans since 1950.*

THE CARS, THE EQUIPMENT AND THE RULES

It may look like a missile with a man attached, but the modern Formula One car is a complex solution to that most basic requirement – the ability to move around a twisting ribbon of tarmac faster than anything else.

A Formula One car is the ultimate performance statement, right? Wrong, actually, but it's very close. The cars can go like greased lightning, but their performance remains checked by hundreds of regulations. However, this simply encourages the designers and engineers to find ever more intelligent solutions to the equation. The smallest of performance advantages can be the difference between success and failure. And the spin-off from their ingenuity is often enjoyed by the man in the street in his family saloon. After all, the best brains in Formula One produced such driver aids as anti-locking brakes.

THE CARS

Your car may have a 3-litre engine, but it's unlikely to almost snap your neck under heavy acceleration. A Formula One car can. What it would do to your neck under high-speed cornering doesn't bear thinking about. Today's Grand Prix cars are fighter planes for the track. They're awesome!

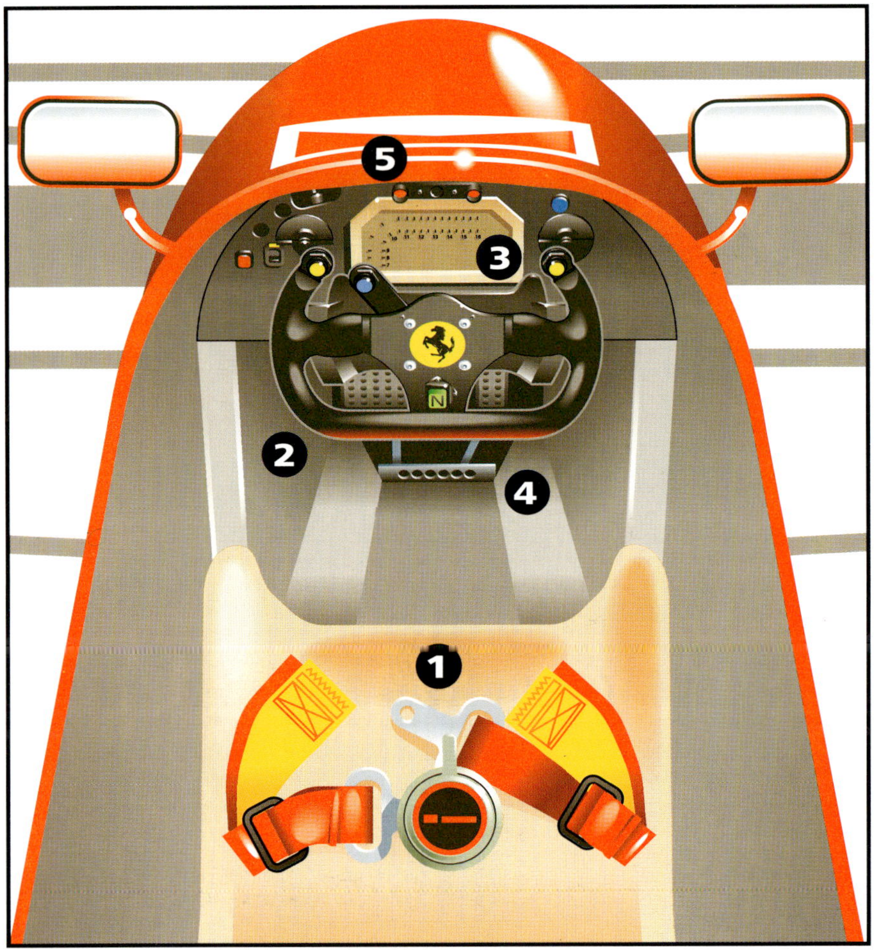

COCKPIT

The FIA has determined that every cockpit must be of certain minimum dimensions, so as to ensure that a driver 1.90 metres tall is able to fit comfortably within it. The cockpit opening must be at least the area of a standard template, and a driver has to be able to get out of it within seven seconds.

1 Seat *Each seat is moulded to the contours of its specific driver and bolted to the monocoque. The driver is held in place by a six-point safety harness.*

2 Steering Wheel *The steering of a Formula One car is designed to be optimized at high speed. Hence the small-diameter wheel is very heavy at low speeds, but gives an extremely direct and precise feel at high speed.*

3 Gear Shift *The driver can change up or down by flicking paddles attached behind the steering wheel. Such a system allows him to change with a single finger while keeping a full, two-handed control of the wheel.*

4 Pedals *Many teams are now moving to a two-pedal layout, where the driver accelerates with his right foot and brakes with his left. In such a case the clutch is operated by a further paddle located behind the steering wheel.*

5 Dash *The dash read-out is kept simple and is now presented as an LED (light-emitting diode) display. Revs and fuel consumption are supplemented by such things as oil and water temperature warnings and, in some cases, a reading of the gear selected, plus lap times.*

Chassis

The chassis, or "tub", or monocoque, owes more to the aerospace industry than to anything from the world of road cars. The chassis is made from carbon fibre, kevlar and other ultra-strong man-made fibres. It is formed from sheets and honeycomb, impregnated with special adhesive resins, which are then baked in autoclaves. The finished chassis is not only strong, but is also immensely stiff, which is important for the optimum use of a car's aerodynamics and suspension.

Fuel tank

The fuel tank is positioned behind the driver, within the monocoque, in an aircraft-specification bag tank that is designed not to rupture. Fuel lines are self-sealing, should the engine be ripped off in an accident, while the fuel filler is also of an aircraft specification, to minimize the chance of fuel blow-back or leakage. The FIA places strict regulations on the type of fuel that may be used.

Air box

Much time is spent on optimizing the flow of air to the engine.

Safety features

A modern Formula One car must have passed a number of severe, mandatory crash tests before it is allowed on to the track. The car must be fitted with front and side deformable structures, a forward and a rear roll-over bar, all of which must survive FIA-designated load and impact tests, and must conform to certain dimensions for the size of the cockpit. As well as the aircraft-style fuel tank, the car must carry on-board extinguishers for the engine compartment and the cockpit, and medical air for the driver. A rear light must be fitted for racing in poor visibility.

Engine

Formula One engines are limited to a maximum capacity of 3 litres – a limit introduced for 1995, and a reduction from the previous capacity of 3.5 litres. The engine must be normally aspirated and of a maximum 12 cylinders. Of late, V8 or V10s have been the norm and even that bastion of the 12-cylinder engine, Ferrari, will soon make the switch to a V10. Typically, a modern Formula One engine will rev to around 15,000rpm, producing roughly 650bhp.

Gearbox

Gearboxes are attached to the rear of the engine and can be either transverse, where the gear shafts run across the car, or longitudinal, where the gear shafts run fore and aft along the car. Most cars run six-speed gearboxes in which a shift is initiated by the driver using thumb-operated paddles behind the steering wheel.

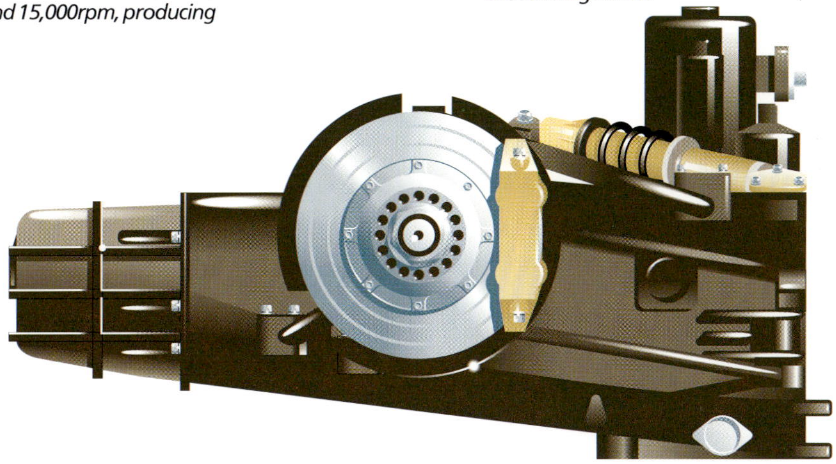

Aerodynamics

Despite the regulations allowing the aerodynamicist a very narrow range within which to work, the aerodynamic complexity of a Formula One car is amazing. The car must have as low a drag as possible for speed on the straights, but it must also produce as much aerodynamic downforce – lift in reverse – as possible to push the car on to the track and hence make its tyres work at maximum efficiency. Front and rear wings, together with a diffuser at the rear of the car under the gearbox, are the main areas where downforce is generated.

Tyres

In dry conditions Formula One cars use a slick tyre, i.e. one with no tread pattern. This maximizes the contact patch of the tyre, giving the greatest possible amount of grip, and also allows for better heating characteristics. In wet weather, treaded tyres are used to dissipate track water. The FIA limits the maximum width and diameter of a tyre. Tyres use different compounds according to the track condition and the temperature. A tyre will have maximum grip at a certain optimum temperature, but its performance will eventually tail off because of wear or changes in its adhesive qualities brought on by the build-up of heat.

Suspension

Formula One cars use a suspension known as double wishbone. The wheel is attached to the chassis at the front, or the gearbox at the rear, by two steel or carbon fibre "wishbones". The road forces are transmitted to the springs and damper by a separate pushrod. In Formula One, in order to optimize the aerodynamics, suspensions are set very stiff, giving quite a harsh ride to the driver.

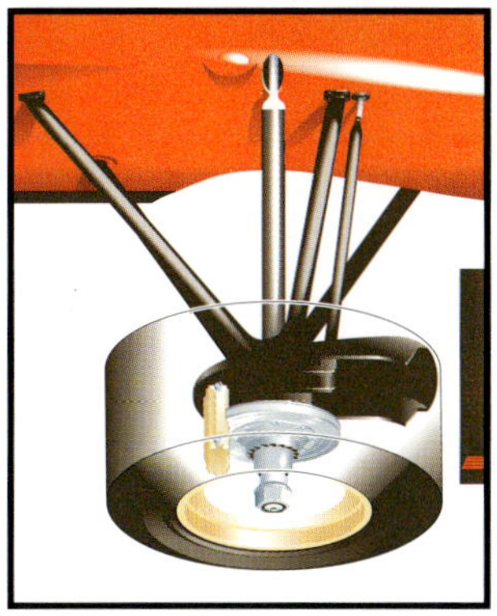

DRIVER EQUIPMENT

While rules have been changed to make a Formula One car as safe as possible, a driver "goes to the office" dressed for action. He's clad to be fire-proof, physically trained to be match-fit, but as yet, not mentally prepared to be infallible.

The helmet must comply with the FIA's strict regulations about impact testing. It must be full-face and its lining is made of materials which will absorb energy in the event of an accident. The aperture for the driver's eyes is made as small as possible and the perspex visor is covered with a number of tear-off strips to counter the build-up of oil and flies. Attachments for the medical air bottle and a drinks bottle, together with a radio mouth and earpiece, are built into the helmet.

The overalls, too, must meet with all the FIA's safety requirements on flame resistance. The one-piece overall is usually made from three-layer nomex, with elasticated cuffs at the wrists and ankles, and a high neck. Nomex underwear, including socks and a balaclava, is worn under the overalls.

In the past fitness was something that tended to be neglected. However, in recent times the realization that Formula One racing is not a sedentary occupation, but is in fact an extremely physical sport has led to an awareness of the advantages of fitness. It comes down to two key areas – stamina and strength. Improving stamina can lead to better mental concentration over a full Grand Prix distance and helps to lessen the effects of losing up to two pints of bodily fluid. Improving specific strength helps to counter the immense forces imposed on the driver, especially his head, during cornering and, again, aids mental concentration. Drivers will have their own fitness programmes and diets which are just as rigorous and specific as any found in sports such as athletics, football or tennis.

Like fitness, the benefits of psychological training have only recently been fully recognized. As long as there has been racing drivers have psyched themselves up, but now the appliance of science allows a driver to focus and to add an edge to his concentration and mental stamina. This results in more consistent lap times, faster lap times and the ability to handle race pressure and fatigue in a more positive manner. The result also seems to be a spooky ability to shrug off the sorts of accidents considered unsurvivable just a few years ago. The drivers of the 1950s and 1960s may have scoffed at such "affectations", but for the modern driver anything that gives him that little bit extra is vital.

You've watched the race and know what the green light and the chequered flag mean. You understand how drivers qualify for the race, but do you know what the black flag signifies? Back in 1994, it appears that the Benetton team didn't during the British Grand Prix… It pays to understand the rules.

Wired for sound *...and for oxygen. This is Gerhard Berger.*

Ready for the office *Damon Hill models his work clothes.*

THE RULES OF FORMULA ONE

All Grands Prix are held over a three-day period, with the first two days reserved for practice and qualifying and the third day for the race itself.

For every Grand Prix except Monaco, Sunday is the race day, with Friday and Saturday reserved for practice and qualifying. However, Monaco traditionally takes the Friday as a statutory rest day and instead uses Thursday and Saturday for qualifying.

Two one-hour sessions of qualifying, one on each afternoon of the two practice and qualifying days, determine the grid. The fastest time for each driver from the two sessions combined will determine the grid order. The fastest 26 cars in practice are allowed to start the race.

Tyres are limited to seven sets per car per Grand Prix meeting and laps are limited to 12 per official qualifying session.

The grid will form up in its qualifying order and will then carry out one parade lap. No overtaking is allowed on the parade lap.

The cars will then re-form on the grid and, when the starter is satisfied that all the cars are in their correct places, he will initiate the starting lights. A red light will be followed up to seven seconds later by the green light. Cars moving before the green light will be penalized for a jumped start.

A Grand Prix is run to a maximum length of 200 miles or a maximum duration of two hours. Points are awarded to the first six finishers in the descending order 10–6–4–3–2–1. The winner is the first person to complete the specified number of laps, or in the case of a stoppage, the person who has completed the greatest distance.

If the race has to be stopped, half points will be awarded if less than half distance has been run at the time of the stoppage and a restart is not possible. If a restart is possible, the grid will re-form in its order at the time of the stoppage and the winner is determined on aggregate times for the two portions of the race.

A chequered flag is shown to signal the end of the race. A yellow flag is shown to warn of a hazard ahead and to signify no overtaking.

A red flag means the race is being stopped and drivers must stop racing and return to the grid, but be prepared to stop at any point if necessary.

A black and white diagonalled flag

Marlboro
Marlboro
BIEFFE
G. BERGER

displayed with the number of a car warns a driver that he is committing an action, or has a problem with his car, which, if continued, will result in his being ordered to the pits.

A black flag and a car's number means that this car must come into the pits.

Refuelling during the race and the changing of tyres are both allowed in Formula One racing. To avoid pit-lane confusion, the FIA limits the number of persons allowed in the pitlane and also asks teams to pre-specify a time during the race when they will pit.

Pit stops for tyres allow cars to run softer and hence more gripping tyres, while stops for fuel allow the cars to run lighter. The strategy must be such that the total time spent decelerating into the pits, at stand-still, then accelerating again, must be less than the time gained from softer tyres and a reduced weight.

Stops for tyres may need as little as five seconds from stop to start but, since fuel flow rate is limited by the FIA's designated refuelling equipment, fuel and tyre stops may take over ten seconds, depending on the amount of fuel being taken on board.

For 1996 refuelling may be made illegal in Grand Prix racing, because of the safety problems that always appear to surround it.

Pit-stop action *A fuel and ytyre stop must be perfectly orchestrated and take less than 10 seconds.*

Race marshal *Standing to attention, ready to wave the relevant flag.*

Marlboro
PEUGEOT
Marlboro
PEUGEOT
PEUGEOT
Marlboro
PEUGEOT
Marlboro
PEUGEOT

THE CULTURE OF FORMULA ONE

The car is an icon: the racing car is its most glamorous incarnation, with Formula One its high profile pinnacle. And with its mixture of speed, glamour and danger Formula One has spawned a worldwide culture.

For a sport considered mechanical and cold by its detractors, Grand Prix racing can still bring out the extremes of human emotion among its participants and its followers – sadness, euphoria, excitement, the sheer primitive thrill of being on the edge. But, of course, it's also a sport that by its very nature is manna for the statistician, the analyst, the techno-buff. Simply, Grand Prix racing has the ingredients to appeal on every level.

No global sport is viable in the twentieth century unless it attracts fans. And no global sport, bar football, attracts as many fans as Formula One – both trackside and armchair. And just as football fans around the world display their allegiance and their emotions in different ways from country to country, so do Formula One's followers.

In Britain it's the cult of the ordinary bloke doing extraordinary things; in Brazil it's a man taking the dreams of his countrymen beyond the slums and the chaos and bestowing national pride; in Japan it's the escape valve from lives of order and regulation; in Italy it's Ferrari!

Ferrari fever *The ultra-passionate Tifosi worship at their shrine.*

ITALY: THE TIFOSI AND THEIR LOVE ... FERRARI

Sport's legends are usually built around human achievement – Pelé, Babe Ruth, Bradman, Nicklaus. The great names in motor racing, such as Fangio and Moss, are lodged in even the most uninterested minds. But in Italy the emphasis is shifted and it is the car, not the driver, which takes on the status of a legend and is adored by the public.

In Italy, that most splendidly anarchic of all countries, Ferrari is king. The Pope may be God's representative on Earth, but a Ferrari would undoubtedly be the supreme being's favoured mode of transport should he choose to mix with the mortals.

The Italian fans, with their lyrical title of "Tifosi", have elevated Ferrari and its blood-red Grand Prix cars into deities. The Bible may have a downer on worshipping false idols, but the Tifosi, dwellers in the very heart of Roman Catholicism, would undoubtedly take serious issue with Ferrari being labelled a false idol.

There are three shrines to which the Tifosi come to worship: the Autodromos of Imola and Monza, in which they gather in their thousands in the spring and early autumn respectively, and the place in which Ferraris undergo their sometimes less than miraculous conception – the factory at Maranello.

The Italian love affair with Ferrari began seriously in the early 1950s when the company formed by Enzo Ferrari began to make a serious mark on world motor racing. The team was a focus of national pride for a country still recovering from the ravages of the Second World War and it was now that the image of the car itself became a more powerful symbol of Italian achievement than

"Mansell mania" *Nigel Mansell is engulfed after winning the 1992 British Grand Prix, showing how the British public could react like the Tifosi.*

the exploits of even Alberto Ascari.

Through the late 1950s and into the 1960s world titles won by Britons Mike Hawthorn and John Surtees and the American Phil Hill in Ferraris all served to reinforce the Tifosi's love of the car and the drivers inside it, rather than of Italian drivers. The fact that Ferrari himself, who described the pleasure he derived from racing as his "terrible joys", was loathe to put Italians in his cars following the tragic death of Lorenzo Bandini in one at Monaco.

In the 1970s Austrian Niki Lauda gave Maranello two more world titles, with the South African Jody Scheckter adding another. But it was a man who never won a title, and indeed only won a handful of Grands Prix, who epitomized the ideal of a hero in a Ferrari. The Canadian Gilles Villeneuve became the darling of the Tifosi in the late 1970s and early 1980s as he took the cars to places they should not have been, but was killed driving for the Prancing Horse at Zolder in 1982.

Since then Ferrari's success has been sporadic or, more recently, almost non-existent. Nigel Mansell, "Il Leone" as he was dubbed by the Tifosi, and Alain Prost briefly rekindled the glory days at the turn of this decade. But since then, the team has struggled and the Tifosi, while still just as passionate about their beloved scarlet cars, have lived mainlyon their memories.

As the 1990s have progressed the stands at Monza and Imola have grown emptier and the banners of the Tifosi have flown in smaller numbers. Yet still the heart of Ferrari beats within the breast of Italy and, when the sleeping giant of Maranello awakes from its slumbers again, as it surely will, the Tifosi will once again celebrate as they did in the past. "Forza Ferrari."

BRITAIN: "HE WILL WALK AMONG US"

During the late 1950s, the whole of the 1960s and the early 1970s Britain utterly dominated Grand Prix racing. The likes of Jim Clark, Jackie Stewart and Graham Hill were each multiple world champions, while Peter Collins, Mike Hawthorn and, of course, Stirling Moss all grabbed their share of the headlines.

And yet there was never the passion among the British fans that the Italian Tifosi could generate. British reserve and its sense of fair play seemed to stunt ability to celebrate achievement, as did the feeling that these were rich playboys in a continental sport – a feeling never shared by the far poorer Italians, who had much more reason to think along those lines.

It was not until the emergence of James Hunt as a Grand Prix force in the mid-1970s that British fans and the British public began to relate to a driver and began to support him with any strong degree of devotion. The British love a working-class hero, a boy made good, but Hunt certainly wasn't that. Yet his dashing, irreverent, anti-establishment character struck a national chord that climaxed with a near-riot at the 1976 British Grand Prix at Brands Hatch, when "crowd power" saw Hunt reinstated for the restart after a start-line shunt.

With Hunt's withdrawal from the

limelight, Britain reverted to its previous attitude of subdued affection for Grand Prix racing, although in the late 1970s and early 1980s the British spectators had little to cheer about apart from the occasional exploit of Ulsterman John Watson. It was true that British-built cars dominated the racing scene, but these sponsor-bedecked machines could never excite an Anglo-Saxon in the same way that a Ferrari could an Italian.

It was not until 1985 that British Formula One fans again discovered their passion for the sport. And when they did, it was all down to one man, a former engineer from Birmingham called Nigel Mansell. In that 1985 season Mansell, driving for Williams, won for the first time on the home ground of Brands Hatch. His Formula One career had begun back in 1980 after he had battled through the lower formulae, seemingly against the odds. Before making the jump to Formula One, Mansell had recovered from a broken back, had worked as a window cleaner to help finance his racing and had put a second mortgage on his house.

Something clicked with the British public. He was one of them and the cult of "Mansell mania" gathered pace, fuelled by his victories in the 1986 and 1987 British Grands Prix. But just to further his case with the public, Mansell suffered two separate accidents – at Adelaide in 1986 and at Suzuka the following year – that destroyed his title chances at the end of both of those seasons. With the British always seemingly to favour a brave loser rather than a winner, Mansell could do no wrong in the eyes of the fans, despite his lack of popularity with the media as a whole.

In 1988 Mansell endured a season with Williams in which the team's supply of the dominant Honda engine had been transferred to McLaren. A battling second at Silverstone added to the legend, but it was a move to Ferrari in 1989 and 1990, then a triumphant return to Williams in 1991 that elevated Mansell to the ranks of Britain's sporting elite.

Then, in 1992 – the year that "Our Nige" finally landed the world title – "Mansell mania" reached its undoubted peak. Over 200,000 fans saw Mansell win the British Grand Prix and subsequently invaded the track with what could have been tragic consequences. The rarefied world of Formula One had seen crowds more suited to the football stadia and wondered where it would lead to next.

In fact, Mansell moved to the United States and Indy Cars for 1993. He won the title at his first attempt, but it was victory on distant shores. Meanwhile, Damon Hill tried to take on the mantle of Mansell, but never quite achieved it. "Hill mania" was tame compared to the tabloid-fuelled Mansell days and eventually the moustachioed messiah returned for four races in 1994.

A full-time return in 1995 confirmed his enduring appeal, with the mania and fervour taking up exactly where they left off as soon as Mansell's signature on the McLaren contract was confirmed.

Mansell's early comeback results were never awesome after the debacle of him being too big for the car, but a sold out British Grand Prix was testimony to his high standing.

BRAZIL: SENNA AND THE PRIDE OF A NATION

Brazil, despite its massive national resources, its huge population and its enormous size, is a country of extreme poverty. It is also a country where the glaring differences between the haves and the have-nots are in full view, wherever one goes.

It may come as a surprise, then, that the Brazilian people as a whole, the vast majority of them the have-nots, cast aside any bitterness or envy and took the son of a super-rich São Paulo businessman to their collective heart. Ayrton Senna became a positive symbol for Brazil on the international stage, and the people loved him for it.

It was not the same feeling of national pride invoked in Italy by Ferrari. Senna, like that other great symbol, the Brazilian national football team, provided a human face for Brazil's achievements abroad. For many he was something tangible that could always be aspired to, despite the yawning chasm between the fantasies and the harsh realities of the countless millions living in the barrios. In terms of popularity, Senna and the footballer Pelé are probably the country's two all-time sporting heroes.

Senna's standing in his home country was probably only fully understood by the rest of the world following his death in the 1994 San Marino Grand Prix. National mourning and the millions who lined the streets of São Paulo to watch his funeral procession pass were the visible side of grief. But beyond that, the sense of collective loss ran deeper and was in fact only partially lessened by the national football team's victory in the World Cup.

The loss of Senna has changed the attitude of Brazil to Formula One, and it has also changed the expectations about those who attempt to follow him. The climate he leaves behind in Brazil is one that still embraces Grand Prix racing, but one that will always judge future achievements against those of Senna.

A nation mourns *The whole of Brazil shut down for Ayrton Senna's funeral, making his symbolism clear for all to see.*

Japanese fanaticism *Race fans form polite queues for Grand Prix tickets.*

JAPAN: LOVE AFFAIR OR MERELY A FAD

Japan has the world's politest fans, but also, in their own way, some of the most fanatical. The country's love affair with Formula One was a late developer. Honda had dabbled in Formula One during the 1960s, but it was not until their return to the event in 1983 that the Japanese, with their insatiable thirst for all things western and an innate desire to be able to escape, if only temporarily, from the bonds of conformity, were really hooked.

As Honda built itself into the most successful engine supplier of the 1980s, so the first pukka Japanese drivers began to filter into Formula One. But on the whole, the Japanese fans reserved their affections for the likes of Prost, Mansell and, most notably, Ayrton Senna.

When the first Japanese Grand Prix since 1977 took place in 1987 at Suzuka, over two million people applied for the 100,000 tickets by means of a lottery. Since then demand has never waivered and Japan has now been able to secure a second Grand Prix. It remains to be seen whether a reputation for being notoriously fickle in matters of sport will also apply to Grand Prix racing.

GERMANY AND FRANCE: A LONG TIME COMING

France and Germany have one thing in common when it comes to Grand Prix racing: they both had to wait a very long time for their first world champion.

In France's case it took until 1985 and Alain Prost. For Germany it took a while longer, almost ten years in fact, until Michael Schumacher won the 1994 world championship. This long wait for success has helped shape the appetite of the French and German fans of Grand Prix racing, but in different ways.

France has always regarded itself as being the cradle of motor racing as we know it. It held the first recognized Grand Prix and Paris is the headquarters for the FIA but, until Prost's rise to prominence, French Grand Prix successes had been sporadic, with the likes of Trintignant, Behra, Depailler, Laffite and Pironi winning races, but not titles. Because of this, the French retained their interest in Formula One racing, but never scaled the heights of patriotic fervour that the Italians did, and never developed the almost blasé attitude of the British in the 1960s. They instead kept the middle ground of almost detached unconcern.

The problem when Prost finally did bring home the title for the "gloire de la France" was that this feeling of Gallic detachment appeared to have become the norm, and his victory did not provide the cue for French enthusiasm which might have been expected.

With Prost now retired, the French car giant and successful Formula One engine supplier, Renault, is left to supply the glory. However, since the French are by nature more interested in the human condition than the mechanical one, Renault's role seems chiefly to provide proof of its engineering competence for the notoriously patriotic French car market, rather than to inspire pride in French hearts.

Germany, too, retained a low-key interest in Formula One before it finally acquired a world champion. But, in contrast to France, its national clamour since then has rivalled "Mansell mania" in its intensity Like France Germany had a strong racing tradition, in which the pre-war Auto Union and Mercedes teams, the return of Mercedes briefly to dominate in the 1950s and the ever-daunting challenge of the Nurburgring until its removal from the Grand Prix scene in 1976, all played their part. However, for German drivers, successes were few and far between, and in the 1970s and 1980s it was Porsche's sports cars which hogged the headlines in the nation's press, but failed to capture the imagination of the German public in a way that only Grand Prix racing can.

The arrival of Michael Schumacher on the scene was the catalyst for an enormous change in attitude. His exploits with the Benetton team, together with his quite ordinary background, soon gave the Germans a new national hero. In 1993 and 1994 Hockenheim was completely sold out for his home Grand Prix. In that 1994 season, when Schumacher finally launched a concerted championship challenge, his popularity was aided enormously by the controversy he provoked as a result of certain technical and racing incidents. The German people saw it as a conspiracy against the whole country and gave their man Schumacher even greater support. But of course, just as with "Mansell mania", this cult of personality attracted extreme elements, including the new German political right wing, who were happy to see a German beating the world.

Now, with Schumacher the world champion, the fervour of his compatriots shows no signs of dying down. Two Grands Prix in Germany in 1995 were both sell-outs many months in advance and the country still appears unable to get enough of its new "Wunderkind".

THE UNITED STATES: THE LEGACY OF THE STREETS

With Indy Car racing and NASCAR stock cars to contend with, Formula One's grip on the American consciousness was never strong. Now, it is virtually non-existent. To see why, one has only to look at the path Formula One trod in the United States during the early 1980s. An established Grand Prix at Watkins Glen (a permanent circuit in upstate New York) was lost to Formula One after 1980. But in its place the FIA chose to give the American public exactly what it did not want – street race after tedious street race. California's Long Beach race around the streets, established in 1976, had been quite acceptable when it had the grandeur of Watkins Glen to complement it. But the shoddy tracks of Detroit, Dallas, Las Vegas and Phoenix, with their average speeds below 100mph just could not compete with the 200mph-plus spectacle of Indy 500. Grand Prix racing gradually lost its grip – a situation not helped by a lack of top-line American Formula One drivers – until finally, after the Phoenix Grand Prix of 1991, Montreal remained the sole venue for Formula One on the North American continent. If Formula One is to ever to return to the United States and re-establish itself in the minds of a sports-satiated American public, it has an uphill, many would say impossible, task ahead of it.

AMONG MY SOUVENIRS

Starting with the cars and working down to badges, stamps and coins, Grand Prix racing has spawned a huge market in collectibles. Along with the cars themselves – if they are not broken up by the teams at the end of each season – comes a whole range of what could be termed first-hand souvenirs: engines, bodywork, seats, wheels, overalls, helmets – in fact anything.

Often the items end their life as an offbeat coffee table or wine rack. But even the most unlikely or seemingly throw-away item, like a spark plug or a piston ring, can find itself the centrepiece of a desk ornament or paperweight. Just like a pig in China, where everything is consumed bar the "oink", Grand Prix fans will find a place for every last scrap of a redundant Formula One machine. It is all part of feeling close to the sport you enjoy and, since Formula One is the domain of an elite few, this is often the closest that a fan will get to the men and machines.

Next to the first-hand collectibles, T-shirts, banners and, of course, baseball caps, are the most widely collected ephemera. Just as in football, the display of allegiance to one's chosen team or driver is a widespread phenomenon. Not surprisingly, Ferrari is the most commonly seen image, but others do get a share, such as Williams and Mansell during their glory days together, or the fly-attracting yellow T-shirts that marked Camel's brief reign as a major Formula One sponsor.

Books and videos

The bread and butter of the Grand Prix ephemera industry are the books, videos and models produced in their thousands every year. Indeed, each of these is probably important enough to be regarded as an industry in itself, fuelling the armchair enthusiast's insatiable desire for all things Formula One.

Looking at the books that sell well, one could almost substitute cricket for Formula One as the subject matter. Biographies and autobiographies of drivers are sure-fire winners, especially if the subject matter is larger than life and/or dead, as can be seen by the sheer volume of books appearing after the death of Senna. After that, the next most popular is any volume covering the statistics of Formula One (see Anoraks), followed by books on marques and books dealing with specific events and races.

Like all sporting books, those dealing with Formula One vary wildly in their quality. Only a few manage to invoke the spirit and spectacle of Grand Prix racing on the printed page – a shortcoming of no concern to those of the statistical bent.

Videos tend to sell best in three distinct categories – seasonal reviews, driver and marque histories, and accident compilations. This last category is regarded with some distaste by many fans of Formula One, but it would be naive to deny that part of the sport's appeal, especially to its more peripheral followers, is the element of danger involved. Whatever the ethical shortcomings of videos showing the dark side of Formula One, those producing them are merely pandering to a market that undoubtedly exists.

Models

Like all mechanical sports, Grand Prix racing provides ample fuel for the model builder. Formula One

Idol worship *If you can't touch your idol, you can still buy the T-shirt. Grand Prix racing has spawned a massive souvenir industry. Get you hats, caps, books…*

models and the bewildering array of formats available are the subject of a whole library of books and magazines in themselves. The subject matter is colourful, plentiful and ever-changing, but still narrow enough to be appealing to the completist. The popularity of models comes not just from the pleasure derived in building and displaying them, but also from their being another link between the rarefied world of the real Formula One and those who can only look on from the outside.

The models come in a bewildering range of scales, materials and prices, unbuilt or built, and encourage further diversification with their sheer variety. For those who enjoy the technology of Formula One, the Japanese Tamiya company's plastic kits are regarded as the market leaders, while for those who prefer the cars as an aesthetic whole, a number of firms model complete Grand Prix grids in small-scale metal and plastic formats. Whatever the modeller's tastes, someone will cater for it.

Anoraks

Grand Prix racing, just like cricket, or seemingly any sport played in the United States, lends itself perfectly to that breed of fan known as the "anorak". Formula One produces acres and acres of statistics and hence provides manna from heaven for the sports bore.

Is knowing the chassis number and history of the Williams FW07 driven to victory by Clay Regazzoni in the 1979 British Grand Prix essential for your continued well-being? Does a race-by-race breakdown of the Grand Prix career of Hector Rebaque fill you with unbridled joy? If the answer is yes, you may well be an anorak.

The specialist press of course goes some way to sating the anorak's appetite for trivia, but it is left to an even more specialized breed of fanzine and statistical periodical to supply such people with their ultimate "fix". All over the world, like-minded individuals are gathered together, dissecting the most obscure facts and statistics relating to Formula One. Sigmund Freud would most probably have described it as "anal retention". Most reasonable people call it "not having a life". But nevertheless, the anorak is as important to the infrastructure and continuing health of the culture of Formula One as the Tifosi.

CONTROVERSIES AND DISASTERS

Formula One is not only fast and furious but dramatic too. Indeed it is often more of a soap opera than an episode of "Neighbours". If the racing isn't enough to entertain, the accidents and political undertones that are ever present mean that controversies and disasters are never far away.

High speeds huge budgets and massive egos – that's Formula One. But it's also about high risk and endless controversy. They seem to go hand in hand. So much is at stake that people don't seen to be able to stop themselves. Whether it's fuelled by greed and self interest or politics, Formula One is never dull. But self-interest aside, Formula One will never shake off one spectre: danger. Until Senna and Ratzenberger died in 1994, Formula One had had a golden spell of 12 years without a fatality. Thirty years ago, it was unusual to go 12 months without one …

FAMOUS DISPUTES

If anything out of the ordinary happens in Formula One, there's normally a reason for it. The car shooting off into the distance might be running with illegal fuel, or it may be underweight. That's always been the way as teams look for that "unfair advantage". Some have been caught, others have got away with it. Outrageous behaviour has not been confined to the track, as Formula One has always attracted some strange characters who have arrived with a bang and been led away with a whimper, sometimes by the police …

Hunt and Lauda, 1976

Austrian Niki Lauda went into the season as Ferrari's defending world champion. He dominated the early races and was odds-on for back-to-back titles. His great rival was James Hunt, who had leapt at a McLaren drive when Emerson Fittipaldi left to race his family's team. There were personal dramas for both men in the background as well. Hunt's marriage had broken down and his wife Suzy was involved with actor Richard Burton. Lauda had turned a tractor over on himself.

James beat Niki in Spain as the Austrian struggled with corseted broken ribs. But the McLaren was disqualified for being millimetres too wide. Later it was reinstated.

The Ferraris clashed on the first lap of the British Grand Prix and Hunt's car was damaged in the melee. The crowd rioted when they were told their golden boy would not be allowed to restart, giving McLaren time to fix it. Hunt went on to win but later the governing body overturned that decision and gave second-placed Lauda the win.

At the next race, Niki was terribly burned when he crashed at Nurburgring. Despite being administered the last rites, he was back driving less than six weeks later, at Monza. In the meantime, Hunt won in Holland and was closing in on the Austrian's championship lead.

They arrived at Monza with Ferrari's appeal over the British Grand Prix pending. Monza is Ferrari territory and when McLaren and Penske were made to start from the back of the grid, strong suspicions were aroused. The rule specified that commercial fuel of the highest octane on sale in France, Germany, Great Britain and Italy could be used, with a tolerance of +1. Texaco, suppliers of Hunt's fuel, stated that five-star petrol in Britain had an octane rating of 101.2, making McLaren's reading of 101.6 within the tolerance.

However, the Italians quoted the Octel company, suppliers of lead to the petrol industry, which said the highest octane to be found commercially in any of the four countries was 100. Penske's reading, incidentally, was 105.7! The McLarens of Hunt and Jochen Mass, together with Watson's Penske, were therefore put to the back, ensuring that Hunt would pose no threat.

In the race, James crashed trying to force past Tom Pryce and was spat on as he returned to the pits. "If I stopped and looked someone in the eye, they would smile and produce an autograph book," he said. "It was pathetic."

The governing body then ruled in favour of Ferrari in the matter of the British Grand Prix, robbing Hunt of his win and giving Lauda a further three points. It looked all over until Hunt won in the USA and Canada. The championship went down to the wire in Japan, where Lauda, unable to blink properly and clear water from his eye – a legacy of the burns from his accident – retired in streaming rain. The conditions, he said, were too dangerous. Hunt's third place gave him the title by a point.

False cheer *James Hunt thought he'd won the 1976 British Grand Prix*

John Player
Grand Prix

No smiling faces *Villeneuve is furious as Pironi uncorks at Imola in 1982.*

Villeneuve and Pironi, 1982

At Imola in 1982 the Ferraris finished one-two, with Didier Pironi ahead of Gilles Villeneuve. On the rostrum, they neither spoke nor shook hands. Villeneuve left immediately afterwards in his helicopter.

A couple of days later, *Autosport*'s Nigel Roebuck spoke to Villeneuve who said: "He (Pironi) was there, looking like the hero, and I looked like the spoiled bastard who sulked. I knew it would look like that but I still thought it was better to get away..."

Villeneuve was adamant that Pironi had stolen the race: "First of all, we knew we were marginal on fuel. In fact, the cars were topped up on the grid. For three-quarters of the race we were fighting with Arnoux, lapping at around 1min 35.5 sec. When René blew up I took the lead and we got a 'slow' sign from the pits. That means 'hold position' and it has done ever since I have been at Ferrari. Imola was going to be my race because I was in front of Pironi when Arnoux dropped out. If it had been the other way round, tough luck for me.

"As soon as the Renault was out, I slowed. The only thing in my head was making the fuel last. Pironi had dropped back and that let him catch up. I made a mistake coming out of a corner and he passed me. I wasn't worried; I figured he'd lead for a few laps and then give it back. Maybe he wanted to put on a show. But what worried me was that he was going so quickly, which meant I had to go quickly, too. How can you obey a 'slow' sign if your team-mate does not? So I got back in front on lap 49 (out of 60) and slowed things down.

"Can you imagine a scene where two Ferraris, leading in Italy, run out of fuel on the last lap? That was my only thought. So I lapped in 1-37, 1-38 for three laps and then he passes me again. I thought it was bloody stupid. On lap 59 I passed him on the approach to Tosa. I thought he lifted a little, but he says he had a small engine problem. Whatever it was, I got by, and even at that stage I thought he was being honest. He was obeying the pit signal. He'd left it late, but never mind. I led that lap, having slowed the pace yet again.

"I went into that last lap so easily you can't believe, still worried about the fuel. I changed up a thousand revs early. I was almost cruising down the straight, because I was not expecting him to pass me again. All of a sudden I saw him coming up on me. I didn't block him and he comes inside me with wheels almost locked, passes and wins the race. He let me by on lap 59 because he wanted to draft me on lap 60. And I was stupid enough to believe he was being honourable.

"After the race I thought that everyone would realize what had happened, but no. Pironi says we had engine problems and that there were no team orders. What really pissed me off was that Piccinini (the Ferrari team boss) confirmed that to the press. My engine was perfect, and there were team orders. People seemed to think that we had the battle of our lives! Jesus Christ! I'd been ahead of him most of the race, qualified a second and a half quicker than him. Where was my problem? I think I've proved that, in equal cars, if I want someone to stay behind me... well, I think he stays behind..."

Pironi's story was this: "The only person to ask is Marco Piccinini. He was in charge of the orders and he didn't have any for this race. When I passed Villeneuve for the first time, it was because he had made a mistake and gone off the circuit. The first 'slow' sign we got was a few laps after that, and I was leading.

"Gilles overtook me after that, and by then we knew we had a lot of fuel left because of the way we drove the first half of the race. You will remember that this was the race where the FOCA teams carried out their boycott. I didn't say this at the time, but we had a meeting before the race, Arnoux, Prost, Gilles and me, in my motor home. We agreed to make a spectacle for the first half of the race so long as our positions on the lap after half distance were the same as on the grid. We started the real race at half distance and so had plenty of fuel. The team didn't know that, only the mechanics knew. But Prost and Arnoux, they will tell you the same."

Just as the lap times supported Villeneuve's view that he was slowing the pace later in the race, so the lap chart bears out Pironi. Lap 31 was half distance. Arnoux was on pole from Prost, Villeneuve and Pironi. Prost retired early and after René had led the first 26 laps, Gilles led from laps 27 to 30. The next lap sees Arnoux back ahead, as agreed, and a video of the race shows Gilles offering little resistance.

Enzo Ferrari expressed sympathy for Pironi but came down firmly on Villeneuve's side. Before the next race, at Zolder, Villeneuve had not spoken to Pironi. "I haven't said a word to him and I'm not going to again. Ever. I'll do my own thing in future. It's war."

With seven minutes of final qualifying remaining for the Zolder race, Pironi was a tenth of a second quicker than Villeneuve. The French-Canadian went out for his final effort and came upon Jochen Mass, touring in his March. There was a misunderstanding, the Ferrari was launched into a somersault and Villeneuve was thrown out and killed.

A few weeks later Pironi took pole at the Circuit Gilles Villeneuve in Montreal, dedicating it to his former team-mate. Then he stalled on the line and Riccardo Paletti was killed when he ploughed into the back of the Ferrari. At Hockenheim, Pironi, now favourite for the title, collided with Prost's Renault in appalling conditions and suffered leg injuries which finished his career. He took to offshore powerboat racing and was killed off Cowes in 1987.

Chapman and the FIA, 1982

Colin Chapman was perhaps the greatest innovator the world of Formula One has ever seen. He proved many times over that you can have more than one world-beating idea in a lifetime. In the middle of 1982, he was sure that he had had another. It was just that the people in charge of the sport decided not to let him use it.

What was it? The ground-breaking Lotus 88. And how did this car differ from the others? It had two chassis, one piggy-backing on top of the other, with the aim of the top one being forced down on to the second through aerodynamic loads without affecting the lower chassis, which should have meant improved cornering capabilities. But the trouble was, it was just too confusing and was banned after it turned up for the first Grand Prix of the year.

Chapman refused to take this lying down and brought the car back out three months later at the British Grand Prix. Farce followed. Deemed legal on the Wednesday, the two 88Bs were allowed to practise on the Thursday, then the FIA, the sport's governing body overruled the race organizers – the RAC MSA – and decided the cars were illegal after all. This left Lotus with next to no time to convert the cars back to a previous (legal) specification, and the drivers even less time to qualify. Elio de Angelis managed to make the cut with a solitary flier, while Nigel Mansell failed to qualify for his home Grand Prix, a race he would go on to win four times.

Prost and Renault, 1983

It was Renault which bucked a trend and moved away from the 3-litre normally aspirated engine regulations of the 1970s towards a 1.5-litre turbocharged unit. The writing was on the wall when Jean-Pierre Jabouille won the 1979 French Grand Prix with a turbo.

Until 1983, however, largely because of the accidents to Villeneuve and Pironi the previous season, the normally aspirated brigade was able to retain its grasp on the world championship. By 1983, though, it was clear that either Renault, Ferrari, or Brabham, with its BMW turbos, would win the title. Possessing considerably more experience than its rivals, Renault was determined that it would be the company to claim the spoils.

Simultaneously, Alain Prost was emerging as France's greatest driver. He had left McLaren at the end of his debut season in 1980 in order to join Renault. There had been three wins in 1981, followed by another two in 1982. He was most people's championship favourite for 1983.

Closing in *Hill reels in Schumacher in Adelaide. We all know what happened…*

Alain started his challenge with his second win in the French Grand Prix, adding wins at Spa, Silverstone and the Osterreichring. He warned the Renault management about complacency, however, and the strength of Nelson Piquet's Brabham-BMW. Finally, the championship battle went down to the wire in South Africa, and Renault flew a number of French journalists there in the expectation of winning the championship. Prost, however, retired early on and Piquet went on to steal the title.

Prost had already had differences of opinion with the Renault management, and although he had re-signed with the French team after Monza, he was shown the door. Prost is understood to have demanded a number of changes within the team on the Monday following the Kyalami fiasco. After the meeting, he was told that, instead, Renault had decided to change its drivers. With Eddie Cheever also dropped, Renault signed Patrick Tambay and Derek Warwick.

From there, Renault's fortunes went in the opposite direction to Prost's, the team failing to win another race as a constructor. Prost joined Niki Lauda at McLaren and, after losing the 1983 championship to Piquet by a single point, Prost said that at least he couldn't have lost by less. He was wrong! In 1984 he lost by a half point to Lauda. He made amends with back-to-back titles in 1985–86. Renault did not have the benefit of Prost's services for another ten years, until Alain won the title in a Williams-Renault.

Schumacher and Hill, 1994

Formula One fans will remember 1994 as a year clouded with controversy and acrimony, with drama right to the end as Michael Schumacher headed for his first World Championship amid allegations of cheating, coupled with disqualifications and bans. At Silverstone he broke grid order, earning a two-race suspension, and at Spa he was disqualified. However, the worst moment of all came when he and Damon Hill collided in the final race at Adelaide. Hill's car was so badly damaged that he was unable to continue, thus losing his chance to gain the World Championship.

Brain box *Colin Chapman was always trying to outwit his rivals.*

TRAGEDIES OF THE TRACK

Jim's darkest day *Jim Clark had a nightmare at Monza in 1961 when he was involved in a crash that cost 15 lives.*

The urge to compete and the desire to win are among the most powerful human instincts and these instincts are surely the very essence of all sporting activities – and none more so than motor racing. The racing driver is a true twentieth-century hero, whose combination of ability and skill have given him mastery over what is undoubtedly a dangerous profession as he risks all to win. The celebration of speed provides an enthralling and thrilling spectacle on the race track but it should not be forgotten that death and disaster are never very far away.

Motor racing, by its very nature, is dangerous and danger is an element which it is impossible to remove altogether, no matter how much progress is made with high-technology materials. Two Grands Prix, however, stand out above the rest as black weekends in the sport's history: the Belgian Grand Prix of 1960 and the San Marino Grand Prix of 1994.

Tragedy at Spa, 1960

Spa has always been notorious for its changing weather conditions which themselves cause it to be a hazardous place. In separate incidents during the 1960 race, two young British drivers, Chris Bristow and Alan Stacey, both left the circuit and died. Fifth, two laps down that day, was Jim Clark the great Scot who would go on to be the World Champion in 1963 and 1965.

The first senior international race of Clark's career had been at Spa in 1958 and he had witnessed a fatality on that occasion too. But in the 1960 race he was next upon one of the accident scenes and finished the race with a blood-spattered car. The events of the day had a profound effect upon him and it was a measure of his greatness that, despite a deep-seated hatred of the place thereafter, Clark won the Belgian Grand Prix in 1962 and in the three following years.

Disaster at Monza, 1961

Just 15 months after that dark day at Spa, Jim Clark had another nightmare, this time in the 1961 Italian Grand Prix at Monza. On only the second lap of the race, when fighting with World Championship leader

Wolfgang von Trips, the two cars touched on the entry to the Parabolica. The German's Ferrari was launched up a bank and into the crowd, killing 14 spectators before being flung back on to the track. Von Trips was thrown from the car, dying instantly. Clark was also pitched from his car, but escaped without serious injury. This incident handed the World Championship to von Trips' American team-mate, Phil Hill.

One-way traffic, 1973

Any death in racing circumstances is a disaster, but one that could have been averted is doubly so. Sadly, this was the case in the 1973 Dutch Grand Prix, and a highly promising young British driver lost his life as a result.

Roger Williamson was in only his second Grand Prix with a privately-entered March. On the ninth lap, it is thought his car had a puncture, for it veered off the circuit, struck a barrier and was pitched back across the track, ending up inverted and on fire.

It was at this point that a bad crash turned into a disaster, for not one marshal proved to be of any use, those near the scene clearly not willing to get stuck in. Indeed, only British driver David Purley really did anything, grabbing an extinguisher from a marshal, then going into the flames time and time again in an attempt to free his friend. His efforts were to prove futile, and Williamson burned to death. Purley was awarded the George Medal for bravery.

To add to the marshalling inadequacies, there was a fire tender near by, but it was not allowed to go to the accident against the flow of traffic along the edge of the track. This awful incident led to calls for a professional band of marshals to follow the Grand Prix circus wherever it travelled. Two decades later, this still hasn't happened, although the standard of marshalling has improved markedly.

Blind brow, 1977

A marshalling error accounted for the life of another British driver less than four years after the death of Roger Williamson at the South African Grand Prix at Kyalami. Tom Pryce was running in the midfield in his Shadow when his team-mate, Renzo Zorzi, suffered engine failure and pulled off the track opposite the pits. As the Italian climbed out, the engine caught fire. He returned to the car, pressed the fire extinguisher button and smothered the blaze. But two marshals decided to go to help, running across the track just beyond a blind brow. And they did this just as Pryce and Hans Stuck crested the hill side by side. Pryce hit one of the marshals head-on, killing him instantly. Pryce, too, was dead, having been hit by the marshal's extinguisher, but his car hurtled on down to the first corner, Crowthorne, where it rammed Jacques Laffite's Ligier. The Frenchman was out of the race, but fortunate to have escaped with his life.

A weekend from hell, 1994

Imola 1994 was truly Formula One's worst weekend in living memory. In Friday practice Rubens Barichello had a fearsome accident at the Variante Bassa when he entered the fourth gear chicane too quickly in his Jordan. The car ran wide and took off over a kerb, flying straight into the catch netting. Mercifully, Rubens missed the heavy iron support posts and, although unconscious for a while, escaped with cuts and bruises. He was back at the circuit on Saturday, although he took no further part in the meeting.

In Saturday practice, Austrian Roland Ratzenberger, who had just one Grand Prix start to his name in the Pacific Grand Prix a couple of weeks earlier, suffered an enormous accident on the long flat-out approach to Tosa. He had made a front wing adjustment to his Simtek in qualifying and on the lap before his accident he had weakened the assembly in a minor off-track excursion. The wing flew off the car and, robbed of front down force, the vehicle hurtled into the concrete retaining wall. Ratzenberger died from a broken neck.

Ayrton Senna, always a man to show great concern at any accident, had visited Barichello the day before and now he went down to the scene of Ratzenberger's accident, something for which he was ticked off by the officials. It had been the first fatality at a Grand Prix meeting for 12 years, but the very next day Senna died in his dreadful crash at Tamburello, the flat-out left-hander preceding the spot where Ratenberger had crashed. Senna's Williams-Renault made no attempt to take the corner and, although the three times world champion managed to get on to the brakes for around one second, his impact speed with the concrete retaining wall was still 135mph.

Chilling omen *Roland Ratzenberger died at Imola the day before Senna.*

Drivers Gerhard Berger, Michele Alboreto, Nelson Piquet and Riccardo Patrese had all survived similar accidents at the same part of the track, probably at even higher speed, but luck was not with Senna. The right front wishbone came back and pierced his helmet, inflicting a fatal head wound. Possibly the greatest of them all was gone.

The results of the official investigation into Senna's accident have still not been published, as magistrate Maurizio Passarini examines charges against members of the Williams team. It seems almost certain, however, that a steering column failure was a contributory cause of the accident.

CHAMPIONSHIP RECORDS

Juan Manuel Fangio is the most successful Formula One driver of all time, correct? Well, with five world titles to his name, he's still out in front. But he hasn't won the most Grands Prix though. No, that's all-time record points scorer Alain Prost, leading the way with 51 wins to his name. Prost has also set more fastest laps than any other driver. The late Ayrton Senna was the master of the flying lap, with almost twice as many pole positions to his credit as the next most prolific qualifier. Riccardo Patrese started a record 256 Grands Prix over a spell of 16 years before he quit Formula One. While the fastest race, the 1971 Italian Grand Prix, also produced the closest-ever finish. For many these statistics are almost as gripping as the racing itself.

Note: Statistics given are correct as of the end of the 1994 season.

MOST WINS

51	Alain Prost	Fr
41	Ayrton Senna	Bra
31	Nigel Mansell	GB
27	Jackie Stewart	GB
25	Jim Clark	GB
	Niki Lauda	A
24	Juan Manuel Fangio	Arg
23	Nelson Piquet	Bra
16	Stirling Moss	GB
14	Jack Brabham	Aus
	Emerson Fittipaldi	Bra
	Graham Hill	GB
13	Alberto Ascari	It
12	Mario Andretti	USA
	Alan Jones	Aus
	Carlos Reutemann	Arg
10	James Hunt	GB
	Ronnie Peterson	Swe
	Jody Scheckter	SAf
	Michael Schumacher	Ger
9	Gerhard Berger	A
	Damon Hill	GB
8	Denny Hulme	NZ
	Jacky Ickx	Bel
7	René Arnoux	Fr

MOST POLES

65	Ayrton Senna	Bra
33	Jim Clark	GB
	Alain Prost	Fr
32	Nigel Mansell	GB
28	Juan Manuel Fangio	Arg
24	Niki Lauda	A
	Nelson Piquet	Bra
18	Mario Andretti	USA
	René Arnoux	Fr
17	Jackie Stewart	GB
16	Stirling Moss	GB
14	Alberto Ascari	It
	James Hunt	GB
	Ronnie Peterson	Swe
13	Jack Brabham	Aus
	Graham Hill	GB
	Jacky Ickx	Bel
10	Gerhard Berger	A
	Jochen Rindt	A
8	Riccardo Patrese	It
	John Surtees	GB
7	Jacques Laffite	Fr
6	Emerson Fittipaldi	Bra
	Phil Hill	USA
	Jean-Pierre Jabouille	Fr
	Alan Jones	Aus
	Carlos Reutemann	Arg

MOST POLES IN A SEASON

14	Nigel Mansell	GB	1992
13	Alain Prost	Fr	1993
	Ayrton Senna	Bra	1988
	Ayrton Senna	Bra	1989
10	Ayrton Senna	Bra	1990
9	Niki Lauda	A	1974
	Niki Lauda	A	1975
	Ronnie Peterson	Swe	1973
	Nelson Piquet	Bra	1984
8	Mario Andretti	USA	1978
	James Hunt	GB	1976
	Nigel Mansell	GB	1987
	Ayrton Senna	Bra	1986
	Ayrton Senna	Bra	1991
7	Mario Andretti	USA	1977
	Jim Clark	GB	1963
	Ayrton Senna	Bra	1985
6	Alberto Ascari	It	1953
	Jim Clark	GB	1962
	Jim Clark	GB	1965
	Jim Clark	GB	1967
	James Hunt	GB	1977
	Michael Schumacher	Ger	1994
	Jackie Stewart	GB	1971

MOST FASTEST LAPS

41	Alain Prost	Fr
30	Nigel Mansell	GB
28	Jim Clark	GB
25	Niki Lauda	A
23	Juan Manuel Fangio	Arg
	Nelson Piquet	Bra
20	Stirling Moss	GB
19	Ayrton Senna	Bra
16	Gerhard Berger	A
	Michael Schumacher	Ger
15	Clay Regazzoni	Swi
	Jackie Stewart	GB
14	Jacky Ickx	Bel
13	Alan Jones	Aus
	Riccardo Patrese	It
12	René Arnoux	Fr
11	Alberto Ascari	It
	John Surtees	GB
10	Mario Andretti	USA
	Jack Brabham	Aus
	Damon Hill	GB
	Graham Hill	GB
9	Denny Hulme	NZ
	Ronnie Peterson	Swe
8	James Hunt	GB

MOST POINTS SCORED

(drivers with more than 100 points)

768.5	Alain Prost	Fr
610	Ayrton Senna	Bra
482.5	Nelson Piquet	Bra
480	Nigel Mansell	GB
420.5	Niki Lauda	A
359	Jackie Stewart	GB
306	Gerhard Berger	A
298	Carlos Reutemann	Arg
281	Emerson Fittipaldi	Bra
	Riccardo Patrese	It
270	Graham Hill	GB
255	Jim Clark	GB
253	Jack Brabham	Aus
248	Denny Hulme	NZ
246	Jody Scheckter	SAf
245	Juan Manuel Fangio	Arg
228	Jacques Laffite	Fr
209	Clay Regazzoni	Swi
206	Ronnie Peterson	Swe
201	Michael Schumacher	Ger
188.5	Bruce McLaren	NZ
186.5	Michele Alboreto	It
185.5	Stirling Moss	GB
181	René Arnoux	Fr
	Jacky Ickx	Bel
180	Mario Andretti	USA
	John Surtees	GB
179	James Hunt	GB
169	John Watson	GB
160	Damon Hill	GB
159.5	Keke Rosberg	Fin
139	Alberto Ascari	It
	Patrick Depailler	Fr
133	Dan Gurney	USA
132	Thierry Boutsen	Bel
122	Elio de Angelis	It
116.3	Giuseppe Farina	It
112.5	Mike Hawthorn	GB
107	Richie Ginther	USA
	Jochen Rindt	A
103	Patrick Tambay	Fr
101	Didier Pironi	Fr
	Gilles Villeneuve	Can
100	Jean Alesi	Fr

Speed *Senna had 65 pole positions.*

The winner *Alain Prost celebrates.*

Racer *Patrese had more Grands Prix.*

Bubbly *Mansell's done a lot of this.*

MOST GRANDS PRIX CONTESTED

(drivers with more than 100 starts listed)

256	Riccardo Patrese	It
208	Andrea de Cesaris	It
204	Nelson Piquet	Bra
199	Alain Prost	Fr
194	Michele Alboreto	It
185	Nigel Mansell	GB
176	Graham Hill	GB
	Jacques Laffite	Fr
171	Niki Lauda	A
163	Gerhard Berger	A
	Thierry Boutsen	Bel
161	Ayrton Senna	Bra
152	John Watson	GB
149	René Arnoux	Fr
147	Derek Warwick	GB
146	Carlos Reutemann	Arg
144	Emerson Fittipaldi	Bra
135	Jean-Pierre Jarier	Fr
132	Eddie Cheever	USA
	Clay Regazzoni	Swi
131	Martin Brundle	GB
128	Mario Andretti	USA
126	Jack Brabham	Aus
123	Ronnie Peterson	Swe
116	Jacky Ickx	Bel
	Alan Jones	Aus
114	Keke Rosberg	Fin
	Patrick Tambay	Fr
112	Denny Hulme	NZ
	Jody Scheckter	SAf
111	John Surtees	GB
110	Pierluigi Martini	It
109	Philippe Alliot	Fr
108	Elio de Angelis	It
105	Jochen Mass	Ger
102	Joakim Bonnier	Swe
101	Bruce McLaren	NZ

NARROWEST WINNING MARGIN

0.010s	1971 Italian Grand Prix Gethin/Peterson
0.014s	1986 Spanish Grand Prix Senna/Mansell
0.050s	1982 Austrian Grand Prix deAngelis/Rosberg
0.080s	1969 Italian Grand Prix Stewart/Rindt
0.100s	1954 French Grand Prix Fangio/Kling
	1961 French Grand Prix Baghetti/Gurney
0.200s	1955 British Grand Prix Moss/Fangio
	1955 Dutch Grand Prix Fangio/Moss
	1967 Italian Grand Prix Surtees/Brabham
0.210s	1981 Spanish Grand Prix Villeneuve/Laffite
0.215s	1992 Monaco Grand Prix Senna/Mansell
0.232s	1985 Dutch Grand Prix Lauda/Prost
0.288s	1990 Hungarian Grand Prix Boutsen/Senna
0.300s	1950 Swiss Grand Prix Farina/Fagioli
	1956 French Grand Prix Collins/Castellotti

FASTEST EVER WIN

150.755mph	1971 Italian Grand Prix at Monza
149.492mph	1970 Belgian Grand Prix at Spa
148.597mph	1993 Italian Grand Prix at Monza
147.139mph	1968 Belgian Grand Prix at Spa
147.109mph	1991 Italian Grand Prix at Monza
147.076mph	1970 Italian Grand Prix at Monza
146.997mph	1990 Italian Grand Prix at Monza
146.968mph	1969 Italian Grand Prix at Monza
146.844mph	1994 Italian Grand Prix at Monza
146.450mph	1992 Italian Grand Prix at Monza

SLOWEST EVER WIN

61.330mph	1950 Monaco Grand Prix at Monaco
62.619mph	1984 Monaco Grand Prix at Monaco
63.849mph	1972 Monaco Grand Prix at Monaco
64.725mph	1957 Monaco Grand Prix at Monaco
64.943mph	1956 Monaco Grand Prix at Monaco
65.813mph	1955 Monaco Grand Prix at Monaco
66.676mph	1959 Monaco Grand Prix at Monaco
67.480mph	1960 Monaco Grand Prix at Monaco
67.986mph	1958 Monaco Grand Prix at Monaco
70.131mph	1954 South African Grand Prix at East London

MOST WINS IN A SEASON

9	Nigel Mansell	GB	1992
8	Michael Schumacher	Ger	1994
	Ayrton Senna	Bra	1988
7	Jim Clark	GB	1963
	Alain Prost	Fr	1984
	Alain Prost	Fr	1988
	Alain Prost	Fr	1993
	Ayrton Senna	Bra	1991
6	Mario Andretti	USA	1978
	Alberto Ascari	It	1952
	Jim Clark	GB	1965
	Juan Manuel Fangio	Arg	1954
	James Hunt	GB	1976
	Nigel Mansell	GB	1987
	Ayrton Senna	Bra	1989
	Ayrton Senna	Bra	1990
	Jackie Stewart	GB	1969
	Jackie Stewart	GB	1971
5	Alberto Ascari	It	1953
	Jack Brabham	Aus	1960
	Emerson Fittipaldi	Bra	1972
	Damon Hill	GB	1994
	Alan Jones	Aus	1980
	Niki Lauda	A	1975
	Niki Lauda	A	1976
	Niki Lauda	A	1984
	Nigel Mansell	GB	1986
	Nigel Mansell	GB	1991
	Alain Prost	Fr	1985
	Alain Prost	Fr	1990
	Jochen Rindt	A	1970
	Ayrton Senna	Bra	1993
	Jackie Stewart	GB	1973

MOST CONSECUTIVE WINS

9	Alberto Ascari	*It*	1952/53
5	Jack Brabham	*Aus*	1960
	Jim Clark	*GB*	1965
	Nigel Mansell	*GB*	1992
4	Jack Brabham	*Aus*	1966
	Jim Clark	*GB*	1963
	Juan Manuel Fangio	Arg	1953/54
	Alain Prost	*Fr*	1993
	Jochen Rindt	*A*	1970
	Michael Schumacher	*Ger*	1994
	Ayrton Senna	*Bra*	1988
	Ayrton Senna	*Bra*	1991
3	Jim Clark	*GB*	1967/68
	Juan Manuel Fangio	*Arg*	1954
	Juan Manuel Fangio	*Arg*	1957
	Damon Hill	*GB*	1993
	Damon Hill	*GB*	1994
	Alan Jones	*Aus*	1979
	Alan Jones	*Aus*	1980/81
	Niki Lauda	*A*	1975
	Niki Lauda	*A*	1975/76
	Nigel Mansell	*GB*	1991
	Nigel Mansell	*GB*	1992
	Stirling Moss	*GB*	1957/58
	Alain Prost	*Fr*	1984/85
	Alain Prost	*Fr*	1990
	Ayrton Senna	*Bra*	1989
	Jackie Stewart	*GB*	1969
	Jackie Stewart	*GB*	1971

MOST PERFECT SCORES

(wins from pole with fastest lap)

11	Jim Clark	*GB*
9	Juan Manuel Fangio	*Arg*
8	Alain Prost	*Fr*
7	Ayrton Senna	*Bra*
5	Alberto Ascari	*It*
	Nigel Mansell	*GB*
4	Jacky Ickx	*Bel*
	Stirling Moss	*GB*
	Michael Schumacher	*Ger*
	Jackie Stewart	*GB*
3	Jack Brabham	*Aus*
	Niki Lauda	*A*
	Nelson Piquet	*Bra*
	John Surtees	*GB*
2	Mario Andretti	*USA*
	Graham Hill	*GB*
	James Hunt	*GB*
	Alan Jones	*Aus*
	Jacques Laffite	*Fr*
1	Gerhard Berger	*A*
	Tony Brooks	*GB*
	Giuseppe Farina	*It*
	Mike Hawthorn	*GB*
	Damon Hill	*GB*
	Phil Hill	*USA*
	Ronnie Peterson	*Swe*
	Clay Regazzoni	*Swi*
	Carlos Reutemann	*Arg*
	Jochen Rindt	*A*
	Jo Siffert	*Swi*
	Gilles Villeneuve	*Can*

MOST CONSECUTIVE POINTS SCORES

21	Juan Manuel Fangio	*Arg*	1953/54/55/56
15	Carlos Reuteman	*Arg*	1980/81
13	Alberto Ascari	*It*	1952/53
12	Jim Clark	*GB*	1963/64
11	Graham Hill	*GB*	1961/62/63
	Niki Lauda	*A*	1975/76
	Nelson Piquet	*Br*	1987
9	Martin Brundle	*GB*	1992
	Graham Hill	*GB*	1963/64
	Graham Hill	*GB*	1965
	Alain Prost	*Fr*	1985
	Alain Prost	*Fr*	1986
	Alain Prost	*Fr*	1988/89
8	François Cevert	*Fr*	1973
	Elio de Angelis	*It*	1984
	Elio de Angelis	*It*	1984/85
	Denny Hulme	*NZ*	1972/73
	Bruce McLaren	*NZ*	1962/63
	Nigel Mansell	*GB*	1986
	Alain Prost	*Fr*	1989
	Alain Prost	*Fr*	1993
	Jody Scheckter	*SAf*	1974
	Ayrton Senna	*Bra*	1987
	Ayrton Senna	*Bra*	1988
	Ayrton Senna	*Bra*	1991/92

MOST DRIVERS' WORLD CHAMPIONSHIP TITLES

5	Juan Manuel Fangio	*Arg*	1951, 1954–57
4	Alain Prost	*Fr*	1985–86, 1989, 1993
3	Jack Brabham	*Aus*	1959–60, 1966
	Niki Lauda	*A*	1975–77, 1984
	Nelson Piquet	*Bra*	1981, 1983, 1987
	Ayrton Senna	*Bra*	1988, 1990–91
	Jackie Stewart	*GB*	1969, 1971, 1973
2	Alberto Ascari	*It*	1952–53
	Jim Clark	*GB*	1963, 1965
	Emerson Fittipaldi	*Bra*	1972, 1974
	Graham Hill	*GB*	1962, 1968
1	Mario Andretti	*USA*	1978
	Giuseppe Farina	*It*	1950
	Mike Hawthorn	*GB*	1958
	Phil Hill	*USA*	1961
	Denis Hulme	*NZ*	1967
	James Hunt	*GB*	1976
	Alan Jones	*Aus*	1980
	Nigel Mansell	*GB*	1992
	Jochen Rindt	*A*	1970
	Keke Rosberg	*Fin*	1982
	Jody Scheckter	*SAf*	1979
	Michael Schumacher	*Ger*	1994
	John Surtees	*GB*	1964

MOST CONSTRUCTORS' TITLES

8	Ferrari	1961, 1964, 1975–77, 1979, 1982–83
7	Lotus	1963, 1965, 1968, 1970, 1972–73, 1978
	McLaren	1974, 1984–85, 1988–91
	Williams	1980–81, 1986–87, 1992–94
2	Brabham	1966–67
	Cooper	1959–60
1	BRM	1962
	Matra	1969
	Tyrrell	1971
	Vanwall	1958

MOST WINS PER MAKE

104	Ferrari
	McLaren
79	Lotus
78	Williams
35	Brabham
23	Tyrrell
17	BRM
16	Cooper
15	Benetton
	Renault

NUMBER OF GRANDS PRIX CONTESTED PER MAKE

537	Ferrari
490	Lotus
410	McLaren
394	Brabham
350	Tyrrell
329	Williams
293	Ligier
255	Arrows
230	March
201	Benetton

NUMBER OF POLES PER MAKE

113	Ferrari
107	Lotus
79	McLaren
73	Williams
39	Brabham
31	Renault
14	Tyrrell
12	Alfa-Romeo
11	BRM Cooper

NUMBER OF FASTEST LAPS PER MAKE

119	Ferrari
83	Williams
71	Lotus
69	McLaren
40	Brabham
25	Benetton
20	Tyrrell
18	Renault
15	BRM
	Maserati

The Lotus beaters *Chapman and Clark.*

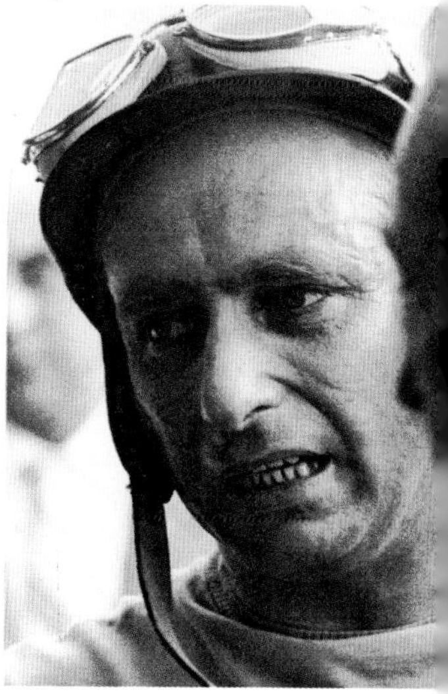

Icon *50's hero Fangio won five times.*

CHRONOLOGY OF FORMULA ONE

1894 First race held in France.

1904 First French Grand Prix.

1921 First Italian Grand Prix.

1922 Introduction of 2-litre limit is first international regulation.

1925 First Belgian Grand Prix.

1926 Engine capacity reduced to 1.5-litre. First British and German Grands Prix.

1928 Free capacity rule introduced.

1929 First Monaco Grand Prix

1934 Cars limited to maximum weight of 750 kg.

1934-39 Mercedes-Benz and Auto Union teams change face of motor racing.

1938 Dick Seaman wins German Grand Prix.

1945 Racing returns after war.

1946 International governing bodies take on collective name of the Fédération Internationale de l'Automobile.

1947 Alfa dominates year of revival.

1948 New Formula One is adopted for 1.5-litre supercharged and 4.5-litre normally aspirated cars. Maserati and new Ferrari marque appear. Achille Varzi dies at Swiss Grand Prix. Alfa, citing economics, withdraws despite a successful year.

1949 Juan Manuel Fangio makes European debut. Ill-fated BRM V16 unveiled.

1950 First FIA Drivers' World Championship – six European Grands Prix, plus Indy 500. Alfa returns with Fangio, Giuseppe Farina and Luigi Fagioli, and dominates championship. Farina pips Fangio for title.

1951 Alfa dominates, but Ferrari and Froilan Gonzales achieve a breakthrough at British Grand Prix. Alfa's Fangio clinches title – his first of five – from Ferrari's Alberto Ascari at last race. BRM and Girling introduce disc brakes.

1952 World Championship is run for 2-litre normally aspirated cars after Alfa withdrawal. Ferrari dominates, with Ascari an easy champion.

1953 Ascari and Ferrari do it again. Classic duel between Hawthorn's Ferrari and Fangio's Maserati in French Grand Prix sees first British win since 1923.

1954 2.5-litre normally aspirated Formula One is introduced, luring Mercedes back. Fangio takes second title after starting year with Maserati and ending it with Mercedes.

1955 Stirling Moss joins Fangio for a Mercedes steamroller and Fangio's third title. Ascari dies in sports car crash at Monza. Tony Brooks and Connaught take first all-British Grand Prix win since 1924 at non-championship Syracuse Grand Prix. Mercedes withdraws after Le Mans disaster.

1956 Fangio dominates in a Lancia-Ferrari for title number four. British challenge strengthens, with Moss and Peter Collins winning Grands Prix and Vanwall finding its feet.

1957 Fangio moves to Maserati for fifth title. His four wins include a classic battle with the Ferraris of Collins and Hawthorn at the Nurburgring race. Moss moves to Vanwall and wins British (with Brooks), Pescara and Italian Grands Prix.

1958 Ferrari's Mike Hawthorn becomes Britain's first world champion with single Grand Prix win in France. Peter Collins, Stuart Lewis-Evans and Luigi Musso killed in tragic year. Grieving Hawthorn dies in road accident. Fangio retires. Moss takes first rear-engined Grand Prix victory for Cooper. Vanwall wins inaugural Constructors' Cup.

1959 Rear-engined cars take over. Works Cooper driver Jack Brabham wins title as Moss's private Cooper falters. Cooper wins Constructors' Cup as Vanwall withdraws and Ferrari struggles. Lotus makes debut.

1960 Brabham and Cooper do the double again. Lotus scores its first win. Ferrari wins Italian Grand Prix when British teams boycott bumpy banked track. Last year for Indy 500 in World Championship.

1961 Formula One changes to 1.5-litre normally aspirated engines as sop to Ferrari. Ferrari dominates with V6 Dino. Phil Hill is first US champion, but team-mate Wolfgang von Trips is killed at Monza. Lotus picks up crumbs – Moss wins in Germany, Innes Ireland in USA.

1962 Britain back in control, with Coventry Climax and BRM V8s. World champion Graham Hill (BRM) and Jim Clark (Lotus) are new stars. Moss has career-ending accident at Goodwood. Monocoque Lotus 25 revolutionizes Formula One. Bruce McLaren wins in Monaco in car bearing own name.

1963 Clark and Lotus win seven out of ten Grands Prix. British whitewash as Hill wins twice for BRM and ex-motorcycle world champion John Surtees once for Ferrari.

1964 British domination continues. Three-way shoot-out at Mexican finale between Surtees' Ferrari, Hill's BRM and Clark's Lotus. Surtees takes title.

1965 Second titles for Lotus and Clark. Clark wins six of ten Grands Prix. Jackie Stewart scores first of 27 wins in Italy, while Honda and Goodyear score their first win with Richie Ginther in Mexico.

1966 Shaky debut season for 3-litre formula. Jack Brabham takes title with Brabham-Repco combination.

1967 Denny Hulme gives Brabham second consecutive title. Ferrari's Lorenzo Bandini dies at Monaco. Ford Cosworth DFV, the most successful Formula One engine ever, wins on debut at Zandvoort in Jim Clark's Lotus.

1968 Jim Clark, Lodovico Scarfiotti, Mike Spence and Jo Schlesser all die in a tragic season. Clark's accident, in a Formula Two race at Hockenheim, seems inexplicable. Hill restores Lotus morale with first DFV-powered title. Wings and aerodynamics take on new significance. Gold Leaf Lotus heralds in the age of sponsorship.

1969 Jackie Stewart, Tyrrell-run Matras and DFVs dominate, winning six Grands Prix plus Drivers' and Constructors' titles. Graham Hill scores fifth Monaco win.

1970 Rindt becomes first posthumous world champion after crashing in practice for Italian Grand Prix. Bruce McLaren dies testing his CanAm car. Piers Courage's death adds to another terrible year. Jack Brabham retires. First Formula One March and Tyrrell's self-built car make their debuts.

1971 Stewart takes a second title, giving Tyrrell its first as a constructor. Pedro Rodriguez and Jo Siffert are both killed.

1972 Fittipaldi and Lotus win title with five victories. Stewart is second after illness. Jo Bonnier dies at Le Mans.

1973 Stewart decides it's his last season – and wins third title. Five more wins give him record 27 victories, beating Fangio's 24. Stewart's team-mate Cevert dies in practice for US Grand Prix.

1974 Fittipaldi wins title after moving to McLaren. Peter Revson dies after crashing in practice for South African Grand Prix.

1975 Five-times winner Lauda takes first title as Ferrari revival gathers pace. DFV meets its match with Ferrari's potent flat-12. Mark Donohue dies after accident in Austrian Grand Prix warm-up. James Hunt and Hesketh win Dutch Grand Prix. Graham Hill and protégé Tony Brise killed in light aircraft accident.

1976 Hunt wins world title with McLaren at rain-soaked Japanese finale. Lauda takes it to wire despite near-fatal accident at the Nurburgring. Politics mar title battle.

1977 Lauda and Ferrari take title again, but the Austrian switches to Brabham for 1978. Renault's ungainly RS01 brings 1.5-litre turbocharged engines to Formula One. Lotus 78 introduces ground effect. Tom Pryce killed in freak South African Grand Prix tragedy.

1978 Mario Andretti becomes world champion as he and team-mate Ronnie Peterson dominate in Lotus's ground effect 79. Peterson dies from complications after starting line shunt in Italian Grand Prix. Brabham's "fan car" wins Swedish Grand Prix and is banned. Ferrari's Gilles Villeneuve becomes first Canadian to win a Grand Prix.

1979 Ground effect is de rigeur. Ferrari are back. Jody Scheckter takes title ahead of team-mate Villeneuve. Clay Regazzoni takes first win for Williams at Silverstone. Alan Jones follows it up with four more. Jean-Pierre Jabouille and Renault score first win for a turbocharged engine. Villeneuve and René Arnoux's dice at Dijon is seasonal highlight. Lauda and Hunt retire.

1980 Alan Jones and Williams win title after fighting off Nelson Piquet's Brabham. FISA/FOCA "war" blights season. Patrick Depailler is killed testing at Hockenheim. Regazzoni paralysed at Long Beach Grand Prix. Nigel Mansell makes debut with Lotus.

1981 Piquet and Brabham snatch title from Williams's Carlos Reutemann in Las Vegas finale. Ferrari turbo signals beginning of end for normally aspirated engines. Alain Prost scores first three of his 51 Grand Prix victories. McLaren's carbonfibre monocoque revolutionizes Formula One car construction.

1982 Turbulent season sees Williams's Keke Rosberg emerge champion with a single victory as Renault unreliability throws the title. Year supplies 11 different winners, including newly un-retired Niki Lauda. Villeneuve and Pironi feud at Imola. Villeneuve dies in practice in Belgium. Pironi suffers career-ending injuries at German Grand Prix. Riccardo Paletti dies in Canada.

1983 Renault lets another one go as Piquet wins title number two, courtesy of Brabham and BMW – the first turbocharged world champions. Ground effect is banned with introduction of flat bottoms. Michele Alboreto scores DFV's last win.

1984 Lauda takes third title by half a point from team-mate Prost. TAG-powered McLarens win 12 of the 16 Grands Prix. Ayrton Senna stars in rain-soaked Monaco Grand Prix in amazing debut year.

1985 Prost becomes France's first world champion. Ayrton Senna scores maiden win in Portugal for Lotus. Mansell breaks duck by winning European Grand Prix at Brands Hatch. Manfred Winkelhock and Stefan Bellof die in sports car accidents. Lauda retires again.

1986 High-speed blow-out for Mansell at Adelaide hands second title to McLaren's Prost – first back-to-back winner in 26 years. Elio de Angelis dies while testing.

1987 Nelson Piquet takes third title after diffident season with Williams-Honda. Mansell, with six wins, comes within a whisker but is thwarted by misfortune. Mansell's successful pursuit of Piquet at Silverstone is year's highlight. 3.5-litre normally aspirated engines are introduced alongside turbos.

1988 McLaren gets Senna and Honda's V6 and dominates year, winning 15 of 16 Grands Prix, with first-time champion Senna winning eight and Prost seven. Ferrari's Gerhard Berger is only other winner. Last season of turbo era.

1989 Title number three for Prost at McLaren. Third consecutive title for Honda, now with 3.5-litre V10. Feud between Prost and team-mate Senna culminates in collision at Japanese Grand Prix. Mansell leads Ferrari revival. Prost signs for 1990. Berger escapes fiery Imola crash. Renault re-enters Formula One.

1990 Senna's second title with McLaren and Honda. Licence wrangles put Senna's participation in doubt. Prost and Senna collide in Japan again. Prost and Mansell feud at Ferrari. Mansell announces retirement, then signs for Williams. Martin Donnelly seriously injured during Spanish Grand Prix qualifying.

1991 Senna fights off challenge of Mansell, Williams and Renault to take third title. McLaren's seventh Drivers' title in eight years; Honda's fifth in a row. Ferrari politics force Prost to quit after first winless season in 11 years. Michael Schumacher makes debut.

1992 Nigel Mansell finally wins world title with Williams after dominant year, but quits for Indycars. Renault's first ever title. Schumacher takes maiden win at Spa.

1993 Prost returns to take fourth title with Williams. Senna drives race of his career at wet/dry European Grand Prix at Donington. Prost retires. Mansell wins Indycar title at first attempt.

1994 Ayrton Senna dies in San Marino Grand Prix at Imola after Roland Ratzenberger's death in practice. Major rule changes brought in as a result. Benetton's Michael Schumacher emerges champion, beating Williams's Damon Hill at Adelaide finale. Mansell returns to the Williams team for four races, winning the closing round in Australia

INDEX

Page numbers in **bold** refer to pictures; WC is the abbreviation for World Championship

A

Adelaide, Australian Grand Prix 220
advertising 222
aerodynamics 229
Aida, Japanese Grand Prix 219
Aintree, British Grand Prix 208
Akira Akagi 88
Alboreto, Michele
achievements 126
WC 1983 51
WC 1984 52, 53
WC 1985 54, 55
WC 1986 57
WC 1987 58, 59
WC 1988 60, 61
WC 1989 62
alcohol advertising 222
Aldridge, Geoff 94
Alesi, Jean 101, **201**
achievements 126, 128, **128**
WC 1989 62, 84
WC 1990 64
WC 1991 66, 67
WC 1992 68
WC 1993 70
WC 1994 72, 73
Alfa Romeo 75
P1 11
P2 11, 75
P3 12
Tipo 158 75, **75**
Tipo 177 75
Tipo B 75
V12 75
WC 1950 15
WC 1951 16
Alliot, Philippe, achievements 128
Allison, Cliff, WC 1960 25
Ambrosio, Franco 76, 98
America, racing origins 10
American Automobile Association
Indianapolis 12
national championship 10
Amon, Chris 28, 88
achievements 128
WC 1967 32
WC 1968 33
WC 1969 34
WC 1970 35
WC 1971 36, 90
WC 1972 37
WC 1974 39
Anderson, Gary 84
Andretti, Mario
achievements 128–9, **128**
WC 1968 33
WC 1969 34
WC 1971 36
WC 1976 41, 188
WC 1977 42, 87
WC 1978 43, **43**, 87
WC 1979 44
WC 1981 46
WC 1982 48, 49
Andretti, Michael
achievements 129, **129**
WC 1993 70
anoraks 239
Argentinian Grand Prix 196
Arnoux, René 100
achievements 129, **129**
WC 1979 44
WC 1980 45
WC 1981 47
WC 1982 48, 49
WC 1983 50, 51
WC 1984 52, 53
WC 1985 54
WC 1986 56
Arrows 43, 76
AZ **76**
Arundell, Peter
achievements 129
WC 1964 29
Ascari, Alberto 75, **81**, 85, **127**
achievements 129–30
death 20, 75, 85
WC 1950 15
WC 1951 16
WC 1952 17, **17**
WC 1953 18, **18**, 182
WC 1954 19
WC 1955 20
Ascari, Antonio 11, **11**
"Atmo" drivers 58
Attwood, Richard
achievements 130
WC 1968 33
Australian Grand Prix 220
Austrian Grand Prix 212
WC 1964 29
Auto & Sport 226
Auto Union 13, 92
Auto Union Type A 13
Autodelta 75
Autohebdo 226
Automobile Club de France (ACF) 8
Autosport 226
Autosprint 226
Avus, German Grand Prix 210

B

"B Bira" 133
Baghetti, Giancarlo
achievements 130
WC 1961 26, 184, **184**
WC 1962 27
WC 1963 28
Bailey, Julian 130, **130**
Baldi, Mario, achievements 130
Balestre, Jean-Marie 64, 67
Bandini, Lorenzo
achievements 130–1
death 32
WC 1962 27
WC 1964 29
WC 1965 30
WC 1966 31
WC 1967 32
Baracca, Francesco 81
Barilla, Paolo 93
Barnard, John 46, 91
Barrichello, Rubens 84
accident 245
achievements 131, **131**
WC 1994 72
Behra, Jean
achievements 131
death 24
WC 1952 17
WC 1955 20
WC 1956 21
WC 1958 23
WC 1959 24
Belgian Grand Prix 214
Bell, Derek 100, 131, **131**
Bellof, Stefan
achievements 131–2
death 55
WC 1984 52
WC 1985 54
Belmondo, Paul 94
Beltoise, Jean-Pierre 90
achievements 132
WC 1968 33
WC 1969 34
WC 1972 37, **37**
WC 1974 39
Benetton 77, 222, **222**
Benetton, Luciano 77
Benz, Karl 9
Berger, Gerhard **224**, **231**
achievements 132, **132**
WC 1985 54
WC 1986 56, 57
WC 1987 58, 59
WC 1988 60, **60**, 61
WC 1989 62, 63
WC 1990 64, 65
WC 1991 66, 67
WC 1992 68, 69
WC 1993 71
WC 1994 72, 73
Berlin, German Grand Prix 210
Bernard, Eric 132–3, **133**
Berthon, Peter 79
Bhanuban, Prince Birabongse 133
Bianchi, Lucien 133
billboards **222**
black flag 232
black and white flag 230
Blundell, Mark
achievements 133
WC 1993 70, 71
WC 1994 73
Boesel, Raul 133, **133**
Boillot, Georges 11
Bonetto, Felice
achievements 133
WC 1951 16
Bonnet, René 90
Bonnier, Jo
achievements 133, 135
death 37
WC 1959 24, 79
WC 1960 25
WC 1961 26
WC 1962 27
WC 1965 30
bonuses 225
books 238
Bordino, Pietro **10**
Borgudd, Slim 135
Borzacchini, Baconin 12, 89
Boutsen, Thierry
achievements 135
WC 1984 52
WC 1985 54
WC 1987 58, 59
WC 1988 60, 61
WC 1989 62, 63
WC 1990 64, 65
Bowmaker/Lola, withdrawal 28
Brabham, David 99, **99**, 135
Brabham, Jack **24**, **31**, 78
achievements 106–7
own cars 28
retirement 36
V8 31
WC 1955 20, 80
WC 1957 22
WC 1958 23
WC 1959 24, 80
WC 1960 25
WC 1961 26
WC 1962 27
WC 1963 28
WC 1964 29
WC 1965 30
WC 1966 31, 78
WC 1967 32, **32**
WC 1970 35, 78
Brabham (team) 78
BT33 78
BT44 78
BT49 44
"fan car" 43
T46B 78, **78**
WC 1964 29
WC 1966 31
WC 1967 32
WC 1972 37
Brabham-Alfa 75
Brambilla, Vittorio 88
achievements 136
WC 1975 40
Brands Hatch, British Grand Prix 209
Brazil, racing culture 236
Brazilian Grand Prix 197
Briatore, Flavio 77, 86
Brise, Tony
achievements 136
death 113
Bristow, Chris
achievements 136
crash 109
death 25, 244
Britain, racing culture 235–6
British Grand Prix 208–9
1973 187
British Motor Racing Research Trust 79
British Racing Motors *see* BRM
British Racing Partnership 24
BRM 79
H16 31, 79
Marlboro 37
P261 79
rear-engined car 25
V8 engine 27
Broadley, Eric 83, 100
broadsheets 226
Brooklands
British Grand Prix 208
opening 10
Brooks, Tony
achievements 136
retirement 26
WC 1955 20
WC 1956 21
WC 1957 22, **22**
WC 1958 23
WC 1959 24
WC 1961 26
Brown, Paul 94
Brundle, Martin
achievements 136, 138
WC 1984 52, 53
WC 1985 54
WC 1989 62
WC 1992 68, 69
WC 1994 72, 73
Bucknum, Ronnie 83
achievements 138

WC 1965 30
Buenos Aires, Argentinian Grand Prix 196
Bugatti, Ettore 11

C

Caffi, Alex, achievements 138
Campari, Giuseppe, death 89
Canadian Grand Prix 204
1991 193
Capelli, Ivan 88
achievements 138
WC 1988 61
WC 1990 65
Caracciola, Rudolf 12, 13, 92
cars 228–9
Castellotti, Eugenio
achievements 139
death 22
WC 1955 20
WC 1956 21
WC 1957 22
Catalunya, Spanish Grand Prix 201
Cecotto, Johnny
achievements 139
broken legs 53
Ceirano brothers 85
Cevert, François 101
achievements 139
death 38
WC 1970 35
WC 1971 36
WC 1972 37
WC 1973 38, **38**
Chapman, Colin 25, 87, 109
death 50
FIA dispute 242–3
Charron, Fernand 10
chassis 13, 228
Cheever, Eddie
achievements 139
WC 1981 46
WC 1982 48
WC 1983 50, 51
WC 1984 52
WC 1988 61
chequered flag 230
Chiron, Louis 12, 13, 139
Chiti, Carlo 75
chronology 250–1
cigarettes 222
Circuit de Nevers, French Grand Prix 207
circuits 194–220
Clark, Jim 87, 244–5, **244**
achievements 108–9
death 33
WC 1960 25
WC 1961 26
WC 1962 27
WC 1963 28
WC 1964 29, **29**
WC 1965 30, **30**
WC 1966 31
WC 1967 32
Clermont-Ferrand, French Grand Prix 206
Climax V8 27
Coaker, Graham 88
cockpit 228
collectibles 238–9
Collins, Peter 77, 87, 102, **102**
achievements 140, **140**
death 23
WC 1956 21
WC 1957 22, 183
WC 1958 23
Columbo, Gioacchino 75
Comas, Erik, achievements 140
Concord Agreement 224
controversies 240–5
Cooper, Charles 80
Cooper, John 17, 23, 80, 102, 107
Cooper team 80
Cooper-Bristol 17
Cooper-Climax 24
Coppuck, Frank 94
Costin, Frank 102
Coulthard, David
achievements 140 **140**
WC 1994 73
Courage, Piers 103
achievements 141
death 35
WC 1969 34
culture 234–9
Czaikowski, Count, death 89

D

D50 85
Daimler, Gottlieb 9
Dallas, United States Grand Prix 198
Dalmas, Yannick 141, **141**
Daly, Derek
achievements 141
WC 1981 47
WC 1982 49
Danner, Christian
achievements 141, **141**, 143
WC 1986 56
dash read-out 228
de Angelis, Elio
achievements **142**, 143
death 56, 78
WC 1981 46, 47
WC 1982 49
WC 1983 50
WC 1984 52, 53
WC 1985 54
WC 1986 56
de Cesaris, Andrea 93
achievements 143, **143**
WC 1982 48, 49, 75
WC 1983 51
WC 1984 52
WC 1985 54, 55
WC 1987 58
WC 1991 67, 84
de Graffenried, Emmanuel 143
de Montaignac, Marquis 8, **9**
de Montariol, M 8, **9**
de Portago, Alfonso
achievements 143–4
death 22
WC 1956 21
de Rouvre, Cyril 86
Dennis, Ron 46, 91
Depailler, Patrick 101
achievements 144, **144**
death 45, 75
WC 1974 39
WC 1976 41
WC 1978 43, 189
WC 1979 44
WC 1980 45
Depression 11, 12
Dernie, Frank 82
Detroit, United States Grand Prix 198
DFVs 33, 50–1
Dijon-Prenois, French Grand Prix 207
disasters 240–5
disputes 240–3
Donnelly, Martin
achievements 144
WC 1990 65
Donnington Park, British Grand Prix 208
Donohue, Mark 95
achievements 144
death 40, 95
double wishbone 229
Dragoni, Eugenio 100
driver equipment 230
drivers 225
Ducarouge, Gérard 86
Dumfries, Johnny
achievements 144
WC 1986 56, 57
Dutch Grand Prix 215
tragedy 245
WC 1952 17

E

East London, South African Grand Prix 199
Ecclestone, Bernie 37, 75, 78, 213, 224, **224**, 225
Edwards, Guy, achievements 145
Elford, Vic, achievements 145
engines 229
petrol 9
twin-overhead cam 11
English Racing Automobiles (ERA) 79
equipment
cars 228–9
drivers 230
Ertl, Harald, achievements 145
Estoril, Portuguese Grand Prix 218
Etancelin, Philippe, achievements 145
European Drivers' Championship 13
European Grand Prix 200

F

Fabi, Teo
achievements 145, **145**
WC 1984 53
WC 1985 54, 55
WC 1986 56, 57
Fagioli, Luigi 13, 92
achievements 146
WC 1950 15
WC 1951 16
Fairman, Jack, achievements 146
"fan car" 43
Fangio, Juan Manuel 89
achievements 110–11, **110**
Pau Grand Prix 13
retirement 23
WC 1950 15, **15**
WC 1951 16, 75
WC 1952 17
WC 1953 18, 182
WC 1954 19
WC 1955 20, **20**, 85
WC 1956 21, **21**
WC 1957 22, **22**, 183, **183**
WC 1958 23
Farina, Giuseppe
achievements 146, **146**
WC 1950 15, **15**, **75**
WC 1951 16
WC 1952 17
WC 1953 18
WC 1954 19
Fascism 13
fatigue 230
Fédération Internationale de l'Automobile (FIA) 16, 224, 242–3
Ferrari 81, **81**, 234–5
246 Dino 23
312T3 43
312T4 44
"sharknose" 26, 81
Tipo 146 81
V6 turbo engine 46
V8 engine 29
WC 1951 16
WC 1952 17
WC 1953 18
WC 1974 39
Ferrari, Enzo 12, 81
Ferris, Geoff 95
FIA *see* Fédération Internationale de l'Automobile
Fiat
805.405 11
early cars 11
Fischer, Rudi, WC 1952 17
fitness 230
Fittipaldi, Christian 76, 93, **93**
achievements 146, **146**
WC 1993 71
Fittipaldi, Emerson 87, 197
achievements 147, **147**
WC 1970 35
WC 1972 37
WC 1973 38
WC 1974 39, 91
WC 1975 40
WC 1976 41
WC 1978 43
WC 1980 45
Fittipaldi team, Wolf merger 45
Fittipaldi, Wilson, achievements 147
flags 230
Flockhart, Ron
achievements 147
WC 1956 21
FOCA *see* Formula One Constructors' Association
Follmer, George 98
achievements 147
WC 1973 38
Footwork 76
Formula Libre races 12
Formula One Constructors' Association (FOCA) 224, 225
Formula Two rules 16–17
four-wheel drive 34
France, racing culture 237
French Grand Prix 206–7
1953 182
1961 184
Frentzen, Heinz-Harald 97, 147–8, **147**
Frère, Paul
achievements 148
WC 1956 21
fuel tank 228
Fuji Speedway, Japanese Grand Prix 219

G

Gachot, Bertrand 84, **84**, 94, **94**, 148, **148**
Ganley, Howden, achievements 148
"garagistes" 74
Gardner, Derek 101
Gartner, Jo, death 56
Gazetta dello Sport 226
gear shift 228
gearbox 229
Gendebien, Olivier, achievements 148
German Grand Prix 210
1957 183
1968 185
Germany, racing culture 237
Gethin, Peter
achievements 148–9
WC 1971 36, 186, **186**
Ghinzani, Piercarlo 149, **149**
Giacomelli, Bruno 75
achievements 149, **149**
WC 1980 45
WC 1981 47
WC 1983 50
Gifard, Pierre 8
Ginther, Richie 79
achievements 149
WC 1961 26
WC 1962 27
WC 1963 28, **28**
WC 1964 29
WC 1965 30, 83
WC 1966 31
Giunti, Ignazio 149
Gold Leaf tobacco 221
Gonzalez, Froilan
achievements 149–50, **149**
WC 1951 16, **16**
WC 1953 18
WC 1954 19
Goodwood, 1962 27
Goodyear, withdrawal 46
Gordon Bennett, John 10
Gounon, Jean-Marc 99
Goux, Jules 11
Great Depression 11, 12
Gregory, Masten **27**, 150
grid order 230
Grouillard, Olivier, achievements 150, **150**
ground effect cars 42, 44
Ligier 86
Lotus 87
Williams 103
Wolf 104
Guerrero, Roberto, achievements 150
Gugelmin, Mauricio
achievements 150
WC 1989 62
WC 1990 65
Gurney, Dan **27**, 107
achievements 150–1
All American Racers 31
WC 1960 25
WC 1961 26
WC 1962 27
WC 1963 28, 78
WC 1964 29
WC 1965 30
WC 1967 32, 83

H

Haas, Carl, WC 1985 54
Hailwood, Mike
achievements 151
WC 1963 28
WC 1973 38

WC 1974 39
Hakkinen, Mika
achievements 151, **151**
WC 1991 66
WC 1993 71
WC 1994 72, 73
Hawthorn, Mike 81
achievements 151–2, **151**
death 23
WC 1952 17
WC 1953 18, 182, **182**
WC 1954 19
WC 1955 20
WC 1956 21
WC 1957 22, 183
WC 1958 23, **23**
Head, Patrick 103, 104
helmets 230
Henry, Ernest 11
Henton, Brian
achievements 152
WC 1981 46
Herbert, Johnny 77, 84, 152, **152**
Herd, Robin 88, 91
Hermanos Rodriguez Circuit, Mexican Grand Prix 205
Herrmann, Hans
achievements 152–3
WC 1954 19
Hesketh, Lord Alexander 82, **82**
Hesketh (team) 41, 82
Hesnault, François, WC 1984 52
Hill, Damon **224**
achievements **152**, 153
Schumacher dispute 243
WC 1993 70, 71, **71**
WC 1994 72, **72**, 73
Hill, Graham 79, 87
achievements 112–13
death 40
own team 40
WC 1960 25
WC 1961 26
WC 1962 27, **27**
WC 1963 28, **28**
WC 1964 29
WC 1965 30
WC 1967 32
WC 1968 33, **33**
WC 1969 34
Hill, Phil
achievements 153
WC 1959 24
WC 1960 25
WC 1961 26, 81
WC 1962 27
WC 1963 28
Hitler, Adolf 13, 92
Hockenheim, German Grand Prix 210, 211
Honda 83, 237
RA271 83
RA273 83
RA300 83, **83**
RA301 83
RA302 83
return 50
WC 1965 30
Honda, Soichiro 83
Hondola 83
Horsley, Anthony "Bubbles" 82
Huhnlein, Adolf 13
Hulme, Denny 91
achievements 153, **153**
WC 1965 30
WC 1966 31
WC 1967 32, **32**
WC 1968 33
WC 1969 34
WC 1970 35
WC 1971 36
WC 1972 37
WC 1973 38
WC 1974 39
Hungarian Grand Prix 213
Hungaroring, Hungarian Grand Prix 213
Hunt, David 87
Hunt, James 82, 91, 104, 235, **241**
achievements 153–5, **154**
Lauda dispute 240
retirement 44
WC 1973 38
WC 1974 39
WC 1975 40, **40**
WC 1976 41, **41**, 188
WC 1977 42

I

Ickx, Jacky 104
achievements 155, **155**
WC 1968 33
WC 1969 34
WC 1970 35
WC 1971 36
WC 1972 37
WC 1973 38
WC 1974 39
WC 1976 41
Imola
San Marino Grand Prix 200
tragedy 245
Indianapolis 12
Indianapolis 500 14
Indianapolis Motor Speedway, opening 10
Interlagos, Brazilian Grand Prix 197
Ireland, Innes
achievements 155
WC 1960 25
WC 1961 26
Irvine, Eddie 84
achievements 155
Senna confrontation 71
Italian Grand Prix 216–17
1971 186
Italy, racing culture 234–5

J

Jabouille, Jean-Pierre 96, 100
achievements 156, **156**
Renault V6 engine 42
retirement 47
WC 1979 44
WC 1980 45
Jacarapagua 197
Jano, Vittorio 75, 85
Japan, racing culture 237
Japanese Footwear Corporation 76
Japanese Grand Prix 219
1976 188
Jarama, Spanish Grand Prix 201
Jarier, Jean-Pierre 98
achievements 156, **156**
WC 1974 39
WC 1975 40
WC 1976 41
WC 1978 43
Jenkins, Alan 76
Jerez, Spanish Grand Prix 201
Jim Clark Cup 58, 59
Johansson, Stefan
achievements 156–7, **156**
WC 1983 50
WC 1985 54, 55
WC 1986 56, 57
WC 1987 58, 59
WC 1989 63
John Player Special 37, 222
Jones, Alan 98, 103
achievements 157, **157**
WC 1977 42
WC 1978 43
WC 1979 44
WC 1980 45, **45**
WC 1981 46, 47
WC 1986 56
Jordan, Eddie 84
Jordan team 84
Junk Formula 12

K

Katayama, Ukyo 101, 157, **157**
Keegan, Rupert, achievements 157
Kling, Karl
achievements 157, 159
WC 1954 19
WC 1955 20
Koinigg, Helmuth, death 39, 100
Kyalami
South African Grand Prix 199
tragedy 245

L

Lafitte, Jacques 86, **86**
achievements **158**, 159
WC 1979 44
WC 1980 45
WC 1981 47
WC 1982 48
WC 1983 50
WC 1984 52
WC 1985 54, 55
WC 1986 56, 57
Lagardère, Jean-Luc 90
Lammers, Jan, achievements 159
Lamy, Pedro, achievements 159
Lancia 85
D50 19, 85
withdrawal 20
Lancia, Gianni 85
Lancia, Vincenzo 85
Lang, Hermann **13**
Larini, Nicola 159, **159**
Larrousse, Gerard 58
Las Vegas, United States Grand Prix 198
Lauda, Niki 91
accident 41
achievements 114–15, **115**
Hunt dispute 240
retirement 44
WC 1971 36
WC 1973 79
WC 1974 39, 81
WC 1975 40, **40**
WC 1976 41
WC 1977 42, **42**
WC 1978 43
WC 1982 48, 49
WC 1983 50, 51, 190
WC 1984 52, 53, **53**
WC 1985 54, 55
Le Castellet, French Grand Prix 206
Le Mans
French Grand Prix 206
tragedy 20
Lehto, JJ 94, 97, 159–60
Lenoir, Etienne 9
L'Equipe 226
Levegh, Pierre, Le Mans 20
Lewis-Evans, Stuart
achievements 160
WC 1958 23
Ligier 86
JS5 86
JS7 86
JS11 86
Ligier, Guy 86, 160
Lombardi, Lella 160, **160**
Long Beach 198
Lotus 87
Cosworth engine 32
Lotus 18 25, 87
Lotus 25 27, 87
Lotus 78 42, 87
Lotus 79 43
Lotus 88 46, 87
WC 1971 36
WC 1972 37
WC 1973 38
WC 1979 44
Love, John
achievements 160
WC 1967 32
Lunger, Brett, achievements 160

M

McBain, Jock 109
McLaren, Bruce 91
achievements 161, **161**
death 35
own team 31
WC 1959 24, 80
WC 1960 25, **25**, 80
WC 1961 26
WC 1962 27
WC 1963 28
WC 1964 29
WC 1966 31
WC 1968 33
WC 1969 34
McLaren (team) 91
M23 38, 91
MP4/10 **91**
Ron Dennis takeover 46
WC 1968 33
WC 1984 52
Maggs, Tony, achievements 161
Maglioli, Umberto, achievements 161
Magny-Cours, French Grand Prix 206, 207
Mairesse, Willy
achievements 161
WC 1963 28
Mansell, Nigel **2**, 103, 236
achievements 116–17
retirement announcement 65
WC 1980 45
WC 1981 46, 47
WC 1982 48
WC 1983 50, 51
WC 1984 52, 53
WC 1985 54, 55
WC 1986 56–7, **57**
WC 1987 58, **58**, 59
WC 1988 60, 61
WC 1989 62, 63, **63**
WC 1990 65
WC 1991 66, 67, 193
WC 1992 68, **68**, 69, **69**
WC 1993 70
WC 1994 73
Manzon, Robert
achievements 161
WC 1952 17
March 88
721G 88
721X 88
arrival 35
return 46
Marimon, Onofre
achievements 162
death 19
WC 1953 18
Marlboro 37, 222
Martini, Pierluigi 93
achievements 162, **162**
WC 1985 54
Maserati 89
250F 19, 89
4CLT 89
withdrawal 22, 23
Maserati, Alfieri 89
Mass, Jochen
achievements 162
WC 1975 40
WC 1977 42
WC 1982 49
Matra 90
MS80 90
V12 46, 90
withdrawal 34
Mayer, Teddy 91
Mayer, Timmy, death 101
Mays, Raymond 79
media 225–6
Mercedes 13, 92
W196 19, **19**, **92**
W25 13
WC 1954 19
Merzario, Arturo
achievements 162
WC 1973 38
Mexican Grand Prix 205
Mexico City, Mexican Grand Prix 205
Mieres, Roberto, achievements 162
Miles, John, achievements 162
Mille Miglia 12
Miller 122 11
Minardi 93
Minardi, Giancarlo 93
models 238–9
Modena, Stefano
achievements 162–3, **162**
WC 1989 62
WC 1991 66
Monaco Grand Prix 202–3
1984 191
monocoque 228
Montermini, Andrea 99
Montjuich Park, Spanish Grand Prix 201
Montreal, Canadian Grand Prix 204
Monza
disaster 244–5
Italian Grand Prix 216–17
Morbidelli, Gianni 76, 93, 163, **163**
Moreno, Roberto
achievements 163
WC 1990 65
Mosley, Max 88, **224**
Mosport Park, Canadian Grand Prix 204
Moss, Stirling 87, 89, **89**, 92, 102
achievements 118–19, **119**
Goodwood 1962 27
WC 1951 16
WC 1952 17
WC 1954 19
WC 1955 20, 85
WC 1956 21

WC 1957 22
WC 1958 23, 80
WC 1959 24
WC 1960 25, **25**
WC 1961 26
Motor Racing Developments (MRD) 78
Motoring News 226
Murray, Gordon 78
Musso, Luigi
achievements 163
death 23
WC 1958 23
WC 1954 19
WC 1955 20
WC 1956 21
WC 1957 22

N

Nakajima, Satoru
achievements 163, **163**, 165
WC 1987 58, 59
WC 1990 64
Nakamura, Yoshio 83
Nannini, Alessandro 93
achievements **164**, 165
WC 1988 60, 61
WC 1989 63, 77
WC 1990 64, 65
Nazzaro, Carlo **10**
Nazzaro, Felice 11
Neubauer, Alfred 92
WC 1954 19
WC 1955 20
Newey, Adrian 88
newspaper coverage 226
Nichols, Don 98
Nichols, Steve 97
Nilsson, Gunnar
achievements 165, **165**
death 43, 75
WC 1977 42
WC 1978 43
Nivelles, Belgian Grand Prix 214
Nomex 230
Nurburgring, German Grand Prix 210
Nuvolari, Tazio 12, **12**, 13, 75, 89

O

Ohashi, Wataru 76
Oliver, Jackie 76, 98
achievements 165
WC 1968 33
WC 1973 38
Oporto, Portuguese Grand Prix 218
organization 224
origins 8–13
Orsi, Cavallieri Adolfo 89
Osterreichring, Austrian Grand Prix 212
Otto, Nikolaus 9
oval racing tracks 10
overalls 230
Owen Organization 79
Owen, Sir Alfred 79

P

Pace, Carlos 100
achievements 165
death 42
WC 1975 40
WC 1977 42
Pacific 94
Paletti, Ricardo, death 49
Palmer, Jonathan
achievements 166, **166**
WC 1984 53
WC 1985 54
WC 1987 58, 59
Panhard, racing origins 8
Panis, Olivier 86, 166, **166**
parade lap 230
Parkes, Mike, achievements 166
Parnell, Reg 28
achievements 166
WC 1950 15
WC 1951 16
Parnelli 39
Patrese, Ricardo
achievements 166–7, **166**
WC 1978 43, 75
WC 1980 45
WC 1981 46, 47
WC 1982 48, 49
WC 1983 50, 51
WC 1984 52, 53
WC 1986 56
WC 1987 59
WC 1989 62, 63
WC 1990 64
WC 1991 66, 67, **67**
WC 1992 68, 69
WC 1993 71
Paul Ricard, French Grand Prix 206–7
pedals 228
Pedralbes, Spanish Grand Prix 201
Penske 39, 95
Penske, Roger 95
Pescara Grand Prix, WC 1957 22
Pescarolo, Henri 90
achievements 167
WC 1968 33
Peterson, Ronnie 88
achievements 167, **167**
death 43, 75, 87
WC 1971 36
WC 1972 37
WC 1973 38
WC 1974 39
WC 1976 41
WC 1977 42
WC 1978 43, 87, 189
petrol engine 9
Peugot
racing origins 8
twin-overhead cam engine 11
Phoenix, United States Grand Prix 198
Piquet, Nelson 78, 103
achievements 167–8, **167**
WC 1980 45
WC 1981 46, **46**, 47
WC 1982 48, 49
WC 1983 50, 51, **51**
WC 1984 52, 53
WC 1985 54, 55
WC 1986 56, 57
WC 1987 58, **58**, 59
WC 1988 60
WC 1990 65, 77
WC 1991 66
Pironi, Didier
achievements 168, **168**
retirement 49
Villeneuve dispute 242, **242**
WC 1978 43
WC 1980 45, 86
WC 1981 47
WC 1982 48, **48**, 49
Pirro, Emanuele 77
achievements 168, **168**
WC 1989 62
pit stops 232
points 230
Pook, Chris 198
Poore, Dennis, WC 1952 17
Porsche 84
arrival 26
withdrawal 28
Portuguese Grand Prix 218
1985 192
Postlewaite, Harvey 81, 82, 97, 104
prize money 224
Prost, Alain 96, 103, 237
achievements 120–1, **121**
Renault dispute 243
WC 1981 46, **46**, 47
WC 1982 48, 49
WC 1983 50, **50**, 51
WC 1984 52, 53, 91, 191
WC 1985 54, 55, **55**
WC 1986 56, 57
WC 1987 58, 59
WC 1988 60, 61
WC 1989 62, 63, **63**
WC 1990 64, 65, 81
WC 1991 66
WC 1993 70, 71
Pryce, Tom 98
achievements 168–9
death 42, 245
WC 1975 40
psychological training 230
Purley, David 169, 245

Q

qualifying sessions 230

R

Ratzenberger, Roland **245**
death 72, 99, 245
Rebaque, Hector
achievements 169
WC 1981 46, 47
records 246–9
red flag 230
Redman, Brian, achievements 169
Rees, Alan 76, 88
refuelling 232
Regazzoni, Clay 103
achievements 169, **169**
paralysis 45
WC 1970 35
WC 1971 36
WC 1972 37
WC 1973 38
WC 1974 39
WC 1975 40
WC 1976 41
WC 1977 42
WC 1979 44
Reims
French Grand Prix 206
WC 1963 28
Renault 96, 237
Prost dispute 243
RS10 44
"rent-a-drivers" 225
Ress, Leo 97
restarts 230
Reutemann, Carlos 103, 196
achievements 169, **169**, 171
retirement 48
WC 1972 37
WC 1974 39
WC 1975 40
WC 1977 42
WC 1978 43
WC 1979 44
WC 1980 45
WC 1981 46, 47, **47**
WC 1982 48
Revson, Peter 98
achievements 171
death 39
WC 1972 37
WC 1973 38, 187, **187**
WC 1974 39
Rindt, Jochen
achievements **170**, 171
death 35, 87
WC 1964 29
WC 1965 30
WC 1966 31
WC 1968 78
WC 1969 34
WC 1970 35, **35**, 87
Rodriguez, Pedro
achievements 171
death 36
WC 1963 28
WC 1967 32
WC 1970 35, 79
WC 1971 36
Rodriguez, Ricardo
achievements 171–2, **171**
death 27
WC 1962 27
Rosberg, Keke 103, 104
achievements 172, **172**
WC 1979 44
WC 1980 45
WC 1982 48, 49, **49**
WC 1983 50, 51
WC 1984 52, 53
WC 1985 54, 55, **56**
WC 1986 56, 57
Rosemeyer, Bernd 13
Rosier, Louis, achievements 172
Rouen-Les-Essarts, French Grand Prix 206
Rudd, Tony 79
rules 230–2

S

safety 14, 229
Sala, Luís Pérez 93, 172
salaries 225
Salazar, Eliseo
achievements 172
WC 1982 49
Salvadori, Roy
achievements 172–3, **173**
WC 1956 21
WC 1958 23
WC 1962 27
San Marino Grand Prix 200
Sanesi, Consalvo, achievements 173
Sauber, Peter 97
Sauber (team) 97
Scarfiotti, Ludovico
achievements 173
death 33
Scheckter, Ian, achievements 173
Scheckter, Jody 101, 104, **104**
achievements 173, **173**
WC 1973 38
WC 1974 39
WC 1975 40
WC 1976 41
WC 1977 42
WC 1978 43
WC 1979 44, **44**, 81
WC 1980 45
Schell, Harry 102
achievements 173
WC 1956 21
WC 1958 23
Schenken, Tim, achievements 173
Schlesser, Jean-Louis, WC 1988 61
Schlesser, Jo, death 33, 83, 86
Schumacher, Michael 84, **224**, 237
achievements 174, **174**
Hill dispute 243
WC 1991 67, 77
WC 1992 68, 69
WC 1993 70, 71, 77
WC 1994 72, **72**, 73, 77, **77**
scoring system 14
Scott-Watson, Ian 109
seats 228
Sebring, United States Grand Prix 198
Second World War 13
Segrave, Henry 11
Senna, Ayrton 91, 103, 236
achievements 122–3
death 72, 245
WC 1984 52, 53, 191
WC 1985 54, 55, 192, **192**
WC 1986 56, 57
WC 1987 58, 59, **59**
WC 1988 60, 61, **61**
WC 1989 62, 63
WC 1990 64, **64**, 65
WC 1991 66, **66**, 67
WC 1992 68, 69
WC 1993 70, 71
WC 1994 72
Serafini, Dorino 15
Serra, Chico
achievements 174
WC 1981 46
Servoz-Gavin, Johnny
achievements 174
retirement 35
WC 1969 34
Shadow 38, 76, 98
shared drives 14
"shark nose" 81
Siffert, Jo 88
achievements 174
death 36
WC 1964 29
WC 1965 30
WC 1966 31
WC 1968 33
WC 1970 35
WC 1971 36
Silverstone, British Grand Prix 208–9
Simca 90
Simtek 99
skirts controversy 46–7
slick tyres 229
Sommer, Raymond
achievements 175
WC 1950 15
South African Grand Prix 199
1978 189
tragedy 245
Southgate, Tony 79, 98
souvenirs 238–9
Spa
Belgian Grand Prix 214
tragedy 244
Spanish Grand Prix 201
specialists publications 226
Spence, Mike

achievements 175
death 33
WC 1965 30
WC 1967 32
sponsorship 221–2, 225
Stacey, Alan 109
death 25, 244
stamina 230
Stanley, Louis 79
starting lights 230
statistics 246–9
steering wheels 228
Stewart, Jackie 101
achievements 124–5
WC 1965 30, **30**
WC 1966 31
WC 1967 32
WC 1968 33, 185, **185**
WC 1969 34, **34**, 90
WC 1970 35
WC 1971 36
WC 1972 37
WC 1973 38, **38**
Stommelen, Rolf 100
achievements 175
WC 1975 40
stoppages 230
Street, Robert 9
Streiff, Philippe
achievements 175, **175**
broken neck 62
WC 1985 55
WC 1987 58
strength 230
strikes, WC 1982 48
Stuck, Hans-Joachim 13, 175
Sunbeam V12 **11**
Superlicence 48, 225
Surer, Marc
achievements 175
injury 56
WC 1981 47
WC 1984 52
Surtees, John 83, **83**, 100
achievements 175–6, **176**
WC 1960 25
WC 1962 27
WC 1963 28
WC 1964 29, 81
WC 1965 30
WC 1966 31
WC 1967 32
WC 1969 34
Surtees (team) 100
TS19 100
suspension 229
Susuki, Aguri, achievements 176
Suzuka, Japanese Grand Prix 219

T

tabloids 226
Tambay, Patrick
achievements 176, **176**
WC 1978 43
WC 1982 49
WC 1983 50, 51
WC 1984 52, 53, 96
WC 1985 54
WC 1986 56
Targ Florio race 12
Tarquini, Gabriele, achievements 176–7
Taruffi, Piero
achievements 177
WC 1952 17
WC 1955 20
Tauranac, Ron 78, 107
Taylor, Trevor
achievements 177
WC 1962 27
teams 74–104
television 225
Tetu, Michel 86
Thackwell, Mike, achievements 177
Ti Circuit, Japanese Grand Prix 219
tifosi 234–5
Tipo 146 81
Tipo 156 81
Tipo 158 75, **75**
Tipo 177 75
Tipo B 75
tobacco advertising 222
Toleman team 77
tragedies 244–5
travel money 224
treaded tyres 229
Trintignant, Maurice 80
achievements 177
WC 1954 19
WC 1955 20
WC 1956 21
WC 1957 22
WC 1958 23
turbo cars 58
twin-overhead cam engine 11
tyres 229, 230, 232
Tyrrell, Ken 33, 35, 90, 101, **101**
Tyrrell (team) 101

U

Uhlenhaut, Rudi 92
United States, racing culture 238
United States Grand Prix 198
United States Grand Prix (West) 198
1983 190
Universal Oil Products (UOP) 98

V

V16 BRM 15
Vandervell, Tony 22, 102
Vanwall 24, 102
Varzi, Achille 12, 13
Verstappen, Jos
achievements 177
fire 73
WC 1994 72
videos 238
Villeneuve, Gilles
achievements 177, **177**
death 49
Pironi dispute 242, **242**
WC 1977 42
WC 1978 43
WC 1979 44, **44**, 81
WC 1981 47
WC 1982 48, **48**
Villoresi, Luigi 85
achievements 178
WC 1951 16
WC 1952 17
WC 1953 18
von Brauchitsch, Manfred 13, 92
von Trips, Wolfgang
achievements 178
death 26, 109, 245
WC 1957 22
WC 1960 25
WC 1961 26

W

Walker, Murray **225**
Walker, Rob 80
WC 1958 23
WC 1965 30
WC 1966 31
Walkinshaw, Tom 77
Walter Wolf Racing 42
war 13
Warr, Peter 104
Warsteiner beer company 76
Warwick, Derek 96
achievements 178, **178**
WC 1981 46
WC 1982 49
WC 1983 50, 51
WC 1984 52, **52**, 53
WC 1986 56
WC 1987 59
WC 1988 61
WC 1990 65
Wass, Dave 76
Watkins Glen, United States Grand Prix 198
WC 1963 28
Watson, John 95, **95**, 100
achievements 178, **178**
WC 1977 42
WC 1981 47
WC 1982 48, 49
WC 1983 50, 51, 190, **190**
WC 1985 55
WC *see* World Championships
Wendlinger, Karl 97, **97**
achievements 179, **179**
WC 1994 73
Wharton, Ken, achievements 179
Whitehead, Peter, achievements 179
Wiggins, Keith 94
Williams, Frank 82, 103, 104
Williams (team) 103
FW07 44
Williamson, Roger
achievements 179
death 38, 245
Winkelhock, Manfred
achievements 179
death 55
Wirth, Nick 99
Wisell, Reine, achievements 179
wishbones 229
Wolf (team) 45, 104
Wolf, Walter 82, 103, 104
Wolf-Williams 82
World Championships 14–173
1950-1959 15–24
1960-1969 25–34
1970-1979 35–44
1980-1989 45–63
1990-1994 64–73

Y

yellow flag 230

Z

Zanardi, Alessandro
achievements 179
WC 1993 71
Zandvoort, Dutch Grand Prix 215
Zeltweg airfield, Austrian Grand Prix 212
Zolder, Belgian Grand Prix 214
Zorzi, Renzo 98, 245
Zuccarelli, Paul 11

ACKNOWLEDGEMENTS

The publishers would like to thank the following sources for their kind permission to reproduce the photographs in this book:

Allsport Simon Bruty, Tony Duffy, John Gichigi, Mike Hewitt, Darrell Ingham, Steve Munday, Pascal Rondeau, Steve Swope, Anton Want; **Allsport Historical/Hulton Deutsch Collection**; **Allsport Historical/MSI**; **Autosport**; **Colorsport**; **Mary Evans Picture Library**; **Formula One Pictures**; **LAT Photographic**; **Marlboro McLaren Mercedes Team**; **Mercedes-Benz**; **Thomas Mitchell**; **Popperfoto**; **Rex Features**; **Sport & General**.

Special thanks are also due to Daffyd Bynon at Allsport and Jed Leicester at Autosport.

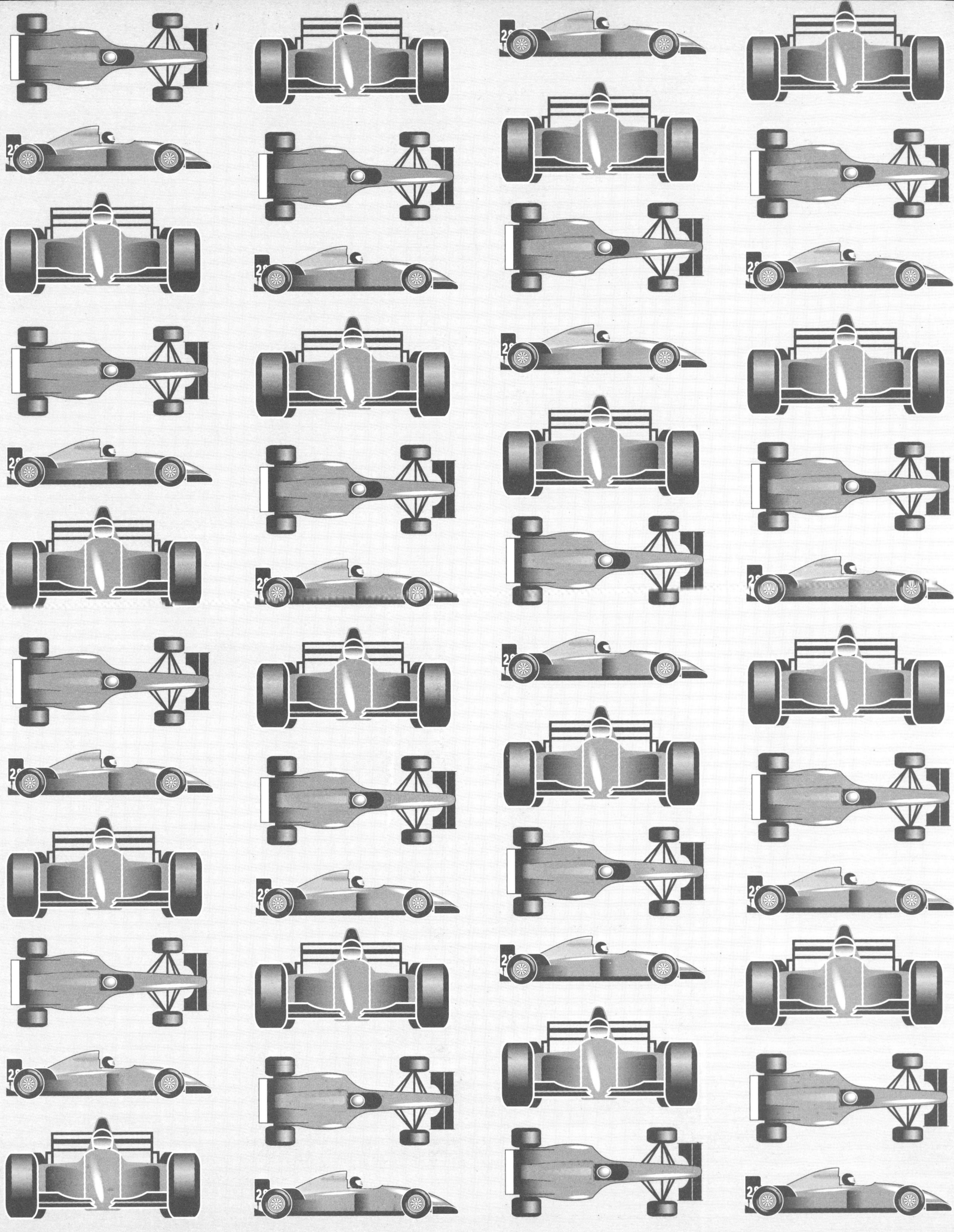